THE PALE KING

Also by David Foster Wallace

The Broom of the System

Girl with Curious Hair

Infinite Jest

A Supposedly Fun Thing I'll Never Do Again

Brief Interviews with Hideous Men

Everything and More

Oblivion

Consider the Lobster

McCain's Promise

This Is Water

THE PALE KING

An Unfinished Novel

DAVID FOSTER WALLACE

HAMISH HAMILTON
an imprint of
PENGUIN BOOKS

HAMISH HAMILTON

Published by the Penguin Group
Penguin Books Ltd, 80 Strand, London WC2R 0RL, England
Penguin Group (USA) Inc., 375 Hudson Street, New York, New York 10014, USA
Penguin Group (Canada), 90 Eglinton Avenue East, Suite 700, Toronto, Ontario, Canada M4P 2Y3 (a division of Pearson Penguin Canada Inc.)
Penguin Ireland, 25 St Stephen's Green, Dublin 2, Ireland (a division of Penguin Books Ltd)
Penguin Group (Australia), 250 Camberwell Road, Camberwell, Victoria 3124, Australia (a division of Pearson Australia Group Pty Ltd)
Penguin Books India Pvt Ltd, 11 Community Centre, Panchsheel Park, New Delhi – 110 017, India
Penguin Group (NZ), 67 Apollo Drive, Rosedale, Auckland 0632, New Zealand (a division of Pearson New Zealand Ltd)
Penguin Books (South Africa) (Pty) Ltd, 24 Sturdee Avenue, Rosebank, Johannesburg 2196, South Africa

Penguin Books Ltd, Registered Offices: 80 Strand, London WC2R 0RL, England

www.penguin.com

First published in the USA by Little, Brown and Company 2011
First published in Great Britain by Hamish Hamilton 2011

2

The following chapters have appeared previously, in slightly different form, in the following publications:

Chapter 6, published as 'Good People' in the *New Yorker*
Chapter 16, published as 'A New Examiner' in *The Lifted Brow* and *Harper's*
Chapter 33, published as 'Wiggle Room' in the *New Yorker*
Chapter 35, published as 'The Compliance Branch' in *Harper's*

Printed in Great Britain by Clays Ltd, St Ives plc

A CIP catalogue record for this book is available from the British Library

HARDBACK ISBN: 978-0-241-14480-0

TRADE PAPERBACK ISBN: 978-0-241-14514-2

www.greenpenguin.co.uk

Editor's Note

In 2006, ten years after the publication of David Foster Wallace's *Infinite Jest,* Little, Brown made plans to release an anniversary edition of that glorious novel. Celebrations were set up at bookstores in New York and Los Angeles, but as the events neared, David demurred about attending. I telephoned to try to persuade him. "You know I'll come if you insist," he said. "But please don't. I'm deep into something long, and it's hard for me to get back into it when I'm pulled away."

"Something long" and "a long thing" were the terms David used to talk about the novel he'd been writing in the years since *Infinite Jest.* He published many books in those years—story collections in 1999 and 2004 and gatherings of essays in 1997 and 2005. But the question of a new novel loomed, and David was uncomfortable speaking about it. Once when I pressed him, he described working on the new novel as like wrestling sheets of balsa wood in a high wind. From his literary agent, Bonnie Nadell, I heard occasional reports: David was taking accounting classes as research for the novel. It was set at an IRS tax return processing center. I had had the enormous honor of working with David as his editor on *Infinite Jest,* and had seen the worlds he'd conjured out of a tennis academy and a rehab center. If anyone could make taxes interesting, I figured, it was him.

At the time of David's death, in September 2008, I had not seen a word of this novel except for a couple stories he had published in magazines, stories with no apparent connection to accountancy or taxation. In November, Bonnie Nadell joined Karen Green, David's widow, to go through his office, a garage with one small window at their home in Claremont, California. On David's desk Bonnie found a neat stack of manuscript, twelve chapters totaling nearly 250 pages. On the label of a disk containing those chapters he had written "For LB advance?" Bonnie had talked with David about pulling together a few chapters of his novel to send to Little, Brown in order to commence negotiations for a new contract and advance against royalties. Here was that partial manuscript, unsent.

Exploring David's office, Bonnie and Karen found hundreds and hundreds of pages of his novel in progress, designated with the title "The Pale King." Hard drives, file folders, three-ring binders, spiral-bound notebooks, and floppy disks contained printed chapters, sheaves of handwritten pages, notes, and more. I flew to California at their invitation and two days later returned home with a green duffel bag and two Trader Joe's sacks heavy with manuscripts. A box full of books that David had used in his research followed by mail.

Reading this material in the months after returning, I found an astonishingly full novel, created with the superabundant originality and humor that were uniquely David's. As I read these chapters I felt unexpected joy, because while inside this world that David had made I felt as if I were in his presence, and was able to forget awhile the awful fact of his death. Some pieces were neatly typed and revised through numerous versions. Others were drafts in David's minuscule handwriting. Some—those chapters from the desk among them—had been recently polished. Others were much older and contained abandoned or superseded plotlines. There were notes and false starts, lists of names, plot ideas, instructions to himself. All these materials were gorgeously alive and charged with observations; reading them was the closest thing to seeing his amazing mind at play upon the world. One leather-bound workbook was still closed around a green felt marker with which David had recently written.

Nowhere in all these pages was there an outline or other indication of what order David intended for these chapters. There were a few broad notes about the novel's trajectory, and draft chapters were often preceded or followed by David's directions to himself about where a character came from or where he or she might be headed. But there was no list of scenes, no designated opening or closing point, nothing that could be called a set of directions or instructions for *The Pale King*. As I read and reread this mass of material, it nevertheless became clear that David had written deep into the novel, creating a vividly complex place—the IRS Regional Examination Center in Peoria, Illinois, in 1985—and a remarkable set of characters doing battle there against the hulking, terrorizing demons of ordinary life.

Karen Green and Bonnie Nadell asked me to assemble from these pages the best version of *The Pale King* that I could find. Doing so has been a challenge like none I've ever encountered. But having read these draft pages and notes, I wanted those who appreciate David's work to be able to see what he had created—to be allowed to look once more inside that extraordinary mind. Although not by any measure a finished work, *The Pale King* seemed to me as deep and brave as anything David had written. Working on it was the best act of loving remembrance I was capable of.

In putting this book together I have followed internal clues from the chapters themselves and from David's notes. It was not an easy task: even a chapter that appeared to be the novel's obvious starting point is revealed in a footnote, and even more directly in an earlier version of that chapter, to be intended to arrive well after the novel begins. Another note in the same chapter refers to the novel as being full of "shifting POVs, structural fragmentation, willed incongruities." But many of the chapters revealed a central narrative that follows a fairly clear chronology. In this story line, several characters arrive at the Peoria Regional Examination Center on the same day in 1985. They go through orientation and begin working in and learning about the vast world of IRS tax returns processing. These chapters and these recurring characters have an evident sequence that forms the novel's spine.

Other chapters are self-contained and not part of any chronology.

Arranging these freestanding sections has been the most difficult part of editing *The Pale King*. It became apparent as I read that David planned for the novel to have a structure akin to that of *Infinite Jest*, with large portions of apparently unconnected information presented to the reader before a main story line begins to make sense. In several notes to himself, David referred to the novel as "tornadic" or having a "tornado feeling"—suggesting pieces of story coming at the reader in a high-speed swirl. Most of the non-chronological chapters have to do with daily life at the Regional Examination Center, with IRS practice and lore, and with ideas about boredom, repetition, and familiarity. Some are stories from various unusual and difficult childhoods, whose significance gradually becomes clear. My aim in sequencing these sections was to place them so that the information they contain arrives in time to support the chronological story line. In some cases placement is essential to the unfolding story; in others it is a matter of pace and mood, as in siting short comic chapters between long serious ones.

The novel's central story does not have a clear ending, and the question inevitably arises: How unfinished is this novel? How much more might there have been? This is unknowable in the absence of a detailed outline projecting scenes and stories yet to be written. Some notes among David's manuscript pages suggest that he did not intend for the novel to have a plot substantially beyond the chapters here. One note says the novel is "a series of setups for things to happen but nothing ever happens." Another points out that there are three "high-end players... but we never see them, only their aides and advance men." Still another suggests that throughout the novel "something big *threatens* to happen but doesn't actually happen." These lines could support a contention that the novel's apparent incompleteness is in fact intentional. David ended his first novel in the middle of a line of dialogue and his second with large plot questions addressed only glancingly. One character in *The Pale King* describes a play he's written in which a man sits at a desk, working silently, until the audience leaves, at which point the play's action begins. But, he continues, "I could never decide on the action, if there was any." In the section titled "Notes and Asides" at the end of the book I have extracted some of David's notes about characters and story. These

notes and lines from the text suggest ideas about the novel's direction and shape, but none strikes me as definitive. I believe that David was still exploring the world he had made and had not yet given it a final form.

The pages of the manuscript were edited only lightly. One goal was to make characters' names consistent (David invented new names constantly) and to make place names, job titles, and other factual matters match up throughout the book. Another was to correct obvious grammatical errors and word repetitions. Some chapters of the manuscript were designated "Zero drafts" or "freewriting," David's terms for first tries, and included notes such as "Cut by 50% in next draft." I made occasional cuts for sense or pace, or to find an end point for a chapter that trailed off unfinished. My overall intent in sequencing and editing was to eliminate unintentional distractions and confusions so as to allow readers to focus on the enormous issues David intended to raise, and to make the story and characters as comprehensible as possible. The complete original drafts of these chapters, and the entire mass of material from which this novel was culled, will ultimately be made available to the public at the University of Texas's Harry Ransom Center, which houses all of David Foster Wallace's papers.

David was a perfectionist of the highest order, and there is no question that *The Pale King* would be vastly different had he survived to finish it. Words and images recur throughout these chapters that I am sure he would have revised: the terms "titty-pinching" and "squeezing his shoes," for example, would probably not be repeated as often as they are. At least two characters have Doberman hand puppets. These and dozens of other repetitions and draft sloppinesses would have been corrected and honed had David continued writing *The Pale King*. But he did not. Given the choice between working to make this less-than-final text available as a book and placing it in a library where only scholars would read and comment on it, I didn't have a second's hesitation. Even unfinished, it is a brilliant work, an exploration of some of life's deepest challenges, and an enterprise of extraordinary artistic daring. David set out to write a novel about some of the hardest subjects in the world—sadness and boredom—and to make that exploration nothing less than dramatic, funny, and deeply moving. Everyone who worked with David knows well how he resisted letting the world see work that was not refined to his exacting standard. But an unfinished novel is what we have, and how can we not look? David, alas, isn't here to stop us from reading, or to forgive us for wanting to.

—Michael Pietsch

THE PALE KING

We fill pre-existing forms and when we
fill them we change them and are changed.

—Frank Bidart, "Borges and I"

§1

Past the flannel plains and blacktop graphs and skylines of canted rust, and past the tobacco-brown river overhung with weeping trees and coins of sunlight through them on the water downriver, to the place beyond the windbreak, where untilled fields simmer shrilly in the A.M. heat: shattercane, lamb's-quarter, cutgrass, sawbrier, nutgrass, jimsonweed, wild mint, dandelion, foxtail, muscadine, spine-cabbage, goldenrod, creeping charlie, butter-print, nightshade, ragweed, wild oat, vetch, butcher grass, invaginate volunteer beans, all heads gently nodding in a morning breeze like a mother's soft hand on your cheek. An arrow of starlings fired from the windbreak's thatch. The glitter of dew that stays where it is and steams all day. A sunflower, four more, one bowed, and horses in the distance standing rigid and still as toys. All nodding. Electric sounds of insects at their business. Ale-colored sunshine and pale sky and whorls of cirrus so high they cast no shadow. Insects all business all the time. Quartz and chert and schist and chondrite iron scabs in granite. Very old land. Look around you. The horizon trembling, shapeless. We are all of us brothers.

Some crows come overhead then, three or four, not a murder, on the wing, silent with intent, corn-bound for the pasture's wire beyond which one horse smells at the other's behind, the lead horse's tail obligingly lifted. Your shoes' brand incised in the dew. An alfalfa breeze. Socks' burrs. Dry scratching inside a culvert. Rusted wire and tilted posts more a symbol of restraint than a fence per se. NO HUNTING. The shush of the interstate off past the windbreak. The pasture's crows standing at angles, turning up patties to get at the worms underneath, the shapes of the worms incised in the overturned dung and baked by the sun all day until hardened, there to stay, tiny vacant lines in rows and inset curls that do not close because head never quite touches tail. Read these.

§2

From Midway Claude Sylvanshine then flew on something called Consolidated Thrust Regional Lines down to Peoria, a terrifying thirty-seater whose pilot had pimples at the back of his neck and reached back to pull a dingy fabric curtain over the cockpit and the beverage service consisted of a staggering girl underhanding you nuts while you chugged a Pepsi. Sylvanshine's window seat was in 8-something, an emergency row, beside an older lady with a sacklike chin who could not seem despite strenuous efforts to open her nuts. The core accounting equation A = L + E can be dissolved and reshuffled into everything from E = A – L to beyond. The craft rode the updrafts and downdrafts like a dinghy in a gale. The only service into Peoria was regional out of either St. Louis or the two Chicagos. Sylvanshine had an inner ear thing and couldn't read on planes but did read the emergency laminated card, twice. It was mostly illustrations; for legal reasons, the airline had to presume illiteracy. Without being aware that he was doing so, Sylvanshine mentally repeated the word *illiterate* several dozen times until the word ceased to mean anything and became just a rhythmic sound, not unlovely but out of sync with the propellers' flux's pulse. It was something he did when he was under stress and did not want an incursion. His point of departure was Dulles after a Service shuttle from Shepherdstown/Martinsburg. The three major codifications of US tax law being of course '16, '39, and '54, with '81 and '82's indexing and anti-abuse provisions also relevant. The fact that another major recodification was on the horizon would not, obviously, be on the CPA exam. Sylvanshine's private goal was to pass the CPA exam, thereby immediately advancing two paygrades. The extent of the recodification would, of course, depend in part on the Service's success in carrying out the Initiative's directives. The job and the exam had to occupy two separate parts of his mind; it was crucial that he maintain separation of powers. Separation of the two areas. Calculating depreciation recapture for §1231 assets is a five-step process. The flight took fifty minutes and seemed much longer. There was nothing to do and nothing would hold still in his head in all the confined noise and after the nuts were gone there was nothing else for Sylvanshine to do to occupy his mind but try to look at the ground which appeared close enough that he could make out house colors and the types of different vehicles on the pale interstate the plane seemed to tack back and forth across. The card's figures opening emergency doors and pulling cords and crossing their arms funereally with their seat cushions on their chests seemed amateurishly drawn and their features little more than bumps; you couldn't see fear or relief or really anything on their faces as they slid down the emergency chutes in the drawing. Emergency doors' handles opened in one way and emergency hatches over the wings opened in a totally different way. Components of equity include common stock, retained earnings, and how many different types of SE transaction. Distinguish between perpetual and periodic inventory and explain the relation(s) between a physical inventory and the cost of goods sold. The darkly gray head ahead of him gave off a scent of Brylcreem that was even now surely soaking and staining the little paper towel on the seat top. Sylvanshine wished again that Reynolds was with him on the flight. Sylvanshine and Reynolds were both aides to Systems icon Merrill Errol ('Mel') Lehrl although Reynolds was a GS-11 and Sylvanshine only a miserable and pathetic GS-9. Sylvanshine and Reynolds had lived together and gone everywhere together since the Rome REC debacle in '82. They weren't homosexual; they just lived together and both worked closely with Dr. Lehrl at Systems. Reynolds had both his CPA and a degree in Information Systems Management although he was only slightly more than two years Claude Sylvanshine's senior. This asymmetry was just one more thing that compromised Sylvanshine's self-regard since Rome and made him doubly loyal and grateful to Systems Director Lehrl for having salvaged him from the debris of the catastrophe in Rome and believing in his potential once his niche as a cog in the system was found. The double-entry method invented by Italian Pacioli during the same period as C. Columbus et alia. The card indicated that this was the type of aircraft whose emergency oxygen was a fire-extinguisherish thing beneath the seats rather than dropping from overhead. The primitive opacity of the figures' faces was actually scarier than fear or some kind of visible expression would have been. It was unclear whether the card's primary function was legal or PR or both. He briefly tried to remember the definition of *yaw*. Every so often while studying for the exam this winter Sylvanshine would burp and it would seem like more than a burp; it would taste like he'd almost thrown up a little. A light rain made a moving lace on the window and distended the crosshatched land they went over. At root, Sylvanshine saw himself as a dithering ninny with at most one marginal talent whose connection to him was itself marginal.

Here is what occurred at the Service's Rome NY Northeast Regional Examination Center on or about the date in question: Two departments had fallen behind and reacted in a regrettably unprofessional fashion, an atmosphere of extreme stress was allowed to cloud judgment and overrule set procedures, the department attempting to hide the growing pile of returns and cross-audit receipts and W-2/1099 copies rather than duly reporting the backlog and requesting that some of the excess be rerouted to other centers. There failed to be full disclosure and prompt remedial action. Just where the failure and breakdown had occurred was still a matter of controversy despite blamestorming sessions at the very highest levels of Compliance, though ultimately the responsibility lay with the Rome REC Director despite the fact that it was never quite established whether the department heads had made her fully aware of the extent of the backlog. The dark Service joke about this Director now had been that her desk had had a Trumanesque wooden plaque on it which read: WHAT BUCK? It had taken three weeks for District Audit sections to start howling over the shortfall of examined returns for audit and/or Automated Collections Systems and the complaints had slowly worked their way up and over into Inspections as anyone should have been able to figure was only a matter of time. The Rome Director had taken early retirement and one Group Manager had been fired outright, which was exceedingly rare for GS-13s. It was obviously important that remedial action be quiet and that undue publicity not compromise the public's full faith and confidence in the Service. No one threw forms away. Hid, yes, but not destroyed or discarded. Even in the midst of disastrous departmental psychosis no one could bring himself to burn, shred, or pack in Hefties and discard. That would have been a real disaster—that would have become public. The emergency hatch's window was nothing more than several layers of plastic, it appeared, the inside of which gave ominously under digital pressure. Over the window was a stern injunction against opening the emergency hatch accompanied by an iconic triptych explaining how to open just this hatch. As a system, in other words, it was poorly thought through. What was now called *stress* used to be called *tension* or *pressure.* Pressure was now more like something you put on someone else, as in high-pressure salesmen. Reynolds said one of Dr. Lehrl's interbranch liaisons had described the Peoria REC as a 'real pressure cooker,' although that was in terms of Exams, not Personnel, to which latter Sylvanshine was posted as advance and ground-laying for *a possible Systems full-out.* The truth, which Reynolds had stopped just short of expressing as such, was that the assignment couldn't be that sensitive if they trusted it to Sylvanshine. There were, according to his researches, registration slots for the CPA examination at Peoria College of Business on November 7 and 8, and at Joliet Community College November 14–15. Duration of this posting unknown. One of the most effective isometric exercises for the deskbound is to sit up quite straight and tighten the large muscles of the buttocks, holding for a count of eight, then release. It tones, aids blood flow and alertness, and can, unlike other isometric exercises, be performed even in public, being largely obscured by the desk's material mass. Avoid grimacing or loud exhalations upon release. Preferential transfers, liquidation provisions, unsecured creditors, claims against bankruptcy estate as per Ch. 7. He had his hat in his lap, over the belt. Systems Director Lehrl had started as a GS-9 auditor in Danville VA before the éclat and rapid rise. He had the strength of ten men. When Sylvanshine studied for the exam now the worst thing was that studying any one thing would set off a storm in his head about all the other things he hadn't studied and felt he was still weak on, making it almost impossible to concentrate, causing him to fall ever further behind. He'd been studying for the CPA exam for three and a half years. It was like trying to build a model in a high wind. 'The most important component in organizing a structure for effective study is:' something. What killed him were the story problems. Reynolds had passed the exam on his first sit. Yaw was rotating slightly from side to side. The word for pitching forward and back was something else. Axes were involved. There was something called gimble or 'gimbal' that came into his mind whenever he saw the Donagan kid at Lombard High who then later ended up at Mission Control for the last two *Apollo*s and had his picture in a glass case by the Office at Lombard. The worst then was that he knew what teachers were the last people suited for their jobs, and they then smelled some part of this knowledge on him and were at their worst when he was watching. It was a loop. Sylvanshine's senior yearbook in his trunk in storage in Philly was almost wholly unsigned. The older party next door was still trying to open her package of nuts with her teeth but had been clear on not wanting help or needing help. The projected benefit obligation (PBO) equals the present value of all benefits attributed by the pension benefit formula to employee services rendered prior to that date. If you spell it fast with stress on the *h* and the *a* and then the second *a* and the *h* again then *headache* becomes a lilting children's rhymed refrain, something to jump rope to. Look down your shirt and spell *attic.* One of the teenagers outside the video arcade next to the facilities at Midway had worn a black tee shirt with the words SYMPATHY FOR NIXON TOUR and then a long list of cities in tiny appliqué letters. The teen, who was not on the flight, had then sat briefly across from Sylvanshine in the gate area and had picked at his face with a concentration that wasn't at all like the absent face-picking and feeling at parts of the face that accompanied concentrated work in the Service. Sylvanshine still dreamed of desk drawers and air ducts stuffed with forms and forms' edges protruding from grilles over the ducts and the utility closet stacked to the top with Hollerith cards and the Inspections Division lady forcing the door and the cards all falling out on her like McGee's closet as the whole debacle caught up to them after they fell behind on cross-audit receipts at the Rome REC. He dreamed still of Grecula and Harris disabling the Fornix mainframe with something poured from a thermos into the rear vent as hisses and bits of blue-tinged smoke issued. The teen had had no vocational aura at all; this happened with some people. Ethical standards comprising the exam's whole first unit, about which there were also many Service jokes. A violation of the profession's ethical standards most likely would have occurred when: Such was the propellers' otherworldly sound that Sylvanshine now could hear nothing more than drifting syllables of the exchanges around him. The woman's claw on the steel armrest between them was a horrible sight that he declined to attend to. Old people's hands frightened and repelled him. He'd had grandparents whose hands he could remember in their laps looking alien and clawlike. Upon incorporation, Jones, Inc. issues common stock at a price in excess of its par value. It was difficult not to imagine the faces of those whose jobs were writing these questions. What they thought about, what their professional hopes and dreams were. Many of the questions were like little stories with all the human meat left out. On December 1, 1982, Clark Co. leases office space for three years at a monthly rental of $20,000. For a count of one hundred, Sylvanshine tried flexing first one buttock and then the other instead of both buttocks at once, which required concentration and a strange type of noncontrol, like trying to wiggle your ears in the mirror. He tried the inclined-to-the-side thing of stretching out his neck's muscles on each side very gently and gradually but still got a look from the older lady, who with her dark dress and staved-in face appeared more and more skull-like and frightening and like some type of omen of death or crushing failure on the CPA exam, which two things had collapsed in Sylvanshine's psyche to a single image of his silently, expressionlessly pushing a wide industrial mop down a corridor lined with frosted-glass doors bearing other men's names. Even the sight of a mop, rollable bucket, or custodian with his name woven in red Palmer script on the breast pocket of his gray jumpsuit (as at Midway, outside the men's room whose little yellow sign warned bilingually of wet floors, the cursive name something beginning with *M,* Morris or Maurice, the man fitted to his job like a man to the exact pocket of space he displaces) now rattled Sylvanshine to the point where precious time was lost before he could even think about how to set up a workable schedule for maximally efficient reviewing for the exam, even mentally, which he did every day. His great weakness was strategic organization and apportionment of time, as Reynolds pointed out at every opportunity, enjoining Claude to for Christ's sake just take a book off the stack and study instead of sitting there noodling impotently about how best to study. Stuffing returns behind cabinets and into air ducts. Locking desk drawers so filled with cross-reference forms that they could not open anyhow. Hiding things beneath other things in Tingles' baskets. Reynolds had simply appeared at the Director's office before the hearing and the whole personal disaster seemingly vanished in some bureaucratic puff of violet smoke and a week later Sylvanshine was unpacking his boxes at Systems in Martinsburg under Dr. Lehrl. The whole thing felt like being in a near traffic fatality avoided by inches and later not being able even to think of the whole thing lest you begin shaking and be unable to function, it had been such a near-disaster. The entire Fats Pod had melted down. The small sound of a simulated bell accompanied the overhead glyph of seat belts and cigarettes lighting up or disappearing; Sylvanshine looked up every time without consciously intending to. In obtaining evidential matter in support of financial statement assertions, the auditor develops specific audit objectives in light of those assertions. An infant keened in some aisle behind him; Sylvanshine imagined the mother simply unbuckling and withdrawing to some other aisle and leaving it there. In Philly, after the frenzy surrounding the introduction of inflation indexes that new templates had to be configured for in '81, he had been diagnosed with a stress-related pinched nerve in his neck and upper back which the enforced unnatural posture of the tiny narrow 8-B and the deathlike claw on the armrest beside him aggravated if he gave it his attention. It was true: The entire ball game, in terms of both the exam and life, was what you gave attention to vs. what you willed yourself to not. Sylvanshine viewed himself as weak or defective in the area of will. Most of what others esteemed or valued in him was unwilled, simply given, like a person's height or facial symmetry. Reynolds called him weak-minded and it was true. He had a serial memory of their neighbor Mr. Satterthwaite filling in scuffs on his postal uniform's shoes with a black pen which then before he was aware of it expanded into a whole narrative memory of Mr. and Mrs. Satterthwaite, who were childless and did not if you first met them appear all that friendly or interested in children, nevertheless allowing their backyard to become the de facto HQ for all the children in the neighborhood and even the slapdash and unsound tree house they had allowed Sylvanshine and the Roman Catholic boy with the tic like a chronic wince to try to construct in one of their trees, and Sylvanshine could not recall whether it was because the boy's family had moved away that the tree house was not completed or whether the move had taken place later and the tree house had simply been too slapdash and sap-soaked to continue with. Mrs. Satterthwaite had had lupus and was often indisposed. Deviation rates, precision limits, stratified sampling. As Dr. Lehrl had explained it, entropy was a measure of a certain type of information that there was no point in knowing. Lehrl's axiom was that the definitive test of the efficiency of any organization structure was information and the filtering and dissemination of information. Real entropy had zippo to do with temperature. Another effective concentration device was to summon into one's mind a soothing and low-pressure outdoor scene, either imagined or from memory, which was even more effective if the scene comprised or included a pond lake brook or stream, as water had been proven to have a calming and centering effect on the involuntary nervous system, but try as he might after the buttock exercises Sylvanshine could summon only a jagged primary-color array that looked like a psychedelic poster or something resembling what you see if you're poked in the eye and then close your eye in pain. The oddness of the word *indisposed.* Prove that the relation of long-term bond prices to long-term capital gains tax rates is not inverse. He knew who on the plane was in love, who would say they were in love because it was what you were supposed to say, and who would say they were not in love. Reynolds's own professed take on marriage/family was that from boyhood on he had never liked fathers and had no wish to be one. In three separate venues in today's various airports Sylvanshine had found himself locking eyes with thirty-year-old men who had infants in high-tech papooselike packs on their backs, their wives with quilted infant-supply bags at their sides, the wives in charge, the men appearing essentially soft or softened in some way, desperate in a resigned way, their stride not quite a trudge, their eyes empty and overmild with the weary stoicism of young fathers. Reynolds would call it not stoicism but acquiescence to some large and terrible truth. The term *dependent* includes any person who qualifies as a dependency exemption, or would otherwise qualify as a dependency exemption except that the gross income and joint return tests are not met. Name two standard devices by which fiduciaries may legally shift tax liability to beneficiaries. The term *passive losses* was not even on the CPA exam. It was vital to divide Service priorities and Exam priorities into two exclusive modules or networks. One of four stated projects was to enhance Peoria 047's ability to distinguish legitimate investment partnerships from tax shelters whose entire purpose was to avoid taxes. The key was identifying passive vs. active losses. The actual project was to create both a case and a control structure for the automation of crucial Examination functions at the Peoria Center. The goal was to have automation in place by the time Revenue Rulings against certain passive-loss provisions were codified in next year's tax law. The older lady's rouge very red and a paperback with a bookmark's tongue unopened in her lap; the veinous and piebald claw. Sylvanshine's seat number was right there stamped onto the brushed steel of the armrest, next to the claw. Its nails were deeply, perfectly red. The smell of his mother's polish remover, of her makeup compact, the way wisps of her hair escaped the bun and curled down the back of her neck in the steam of the kitchen when he and O'Dowd had returned from the Satterthwaites' backyard with hammered thumbs and sap in their lashes. Wisps and flashes of uncolored cloud flashed past the window. Above and below were a different story, but there was always something disappointing about clouds when you were inside them; they ceased to be clouds at all. It just got really foggy. *Yaw* was *way* in a mirror, it occurred for no reason. Sylvanshine then spent some time trying to feel the fact that his personal body was traveling at the same speed as the craft he was inside. On a large jet it felt like merely sitting in a loud narrow room; here at least the changes in the seat's and belt's pressures against him allowed him to be aware of movement, and there seemed to be some security in the physical candor of this, which partly offset the fragility and spatter-potential of the sound of the propellers, which Sylvanshine tried to think of what the props sounded like but could not except as a gnawingly hypnotic rotary hum so total that it might have been silence itself. A lobotomy involved some kind of rod or probe inserted through the eyesocket, the term was always 'frontal' lobotomy; but was there any other kind? Knowing that internal stress could cause failure on the exam merely set up internal stress about the prospect of internal stress. There must be some other way to deal with the knowledge of the disastrous consequences fear and stress could bring about. Some answer or trick of the will: the ability not to think about it. What if everyone knew this trick but Claude Sylvanshine? He tended to conceptualize some ultimate, platonic-level Terror as a bird of prey in whose mere aloft shadow the prey was stricken and paralyzed, trembling as the shadow enlarged and became inevitability. He frequently had this feeling: What if there was something essentially wrong with Claude Sylvanshine that wasn't wrong with other people? What if he was simply ill-suited, the way some people are born without limbs or certain organs? The neurology of failure. What if he was simply born and destined to live in the shadow of Total Fear and Despair, and all his so-called activities were pathetic attempts to distract him from the inevitable? Discuss important differences between reserve accounting and charge-off accounting in the tax treatment of bad debts. Surely fear is a type of stress. Tedium is like stress but its own Category of Woe. Sylvanshine's father, whenever something professionally bad happened—which was a lot—had a habit of saying 'Woe to Sylvanshine.' There is an anti-stress technique called Thought Stopping. The excess present value index is the ratio of the present value of future cash inflows to the initial investment. Segment, significant segment, combined segment revenue, absolute combined segment revenue, operating profit. Material price variance. Direct material price variance. He thought of the removable grate over the air duct above his and Ray Harris's desk in the Rome REC and the sound of the grate being removed and then jammed back into place and driven home with the heel of Harris's hand, and then recoiled from the thought in a way that made it feel as if the craft were accelerating. The interstate highway below disappeared and then sometimes reappeared at a spot Sylvanshine had to squash his cheek right up against the plastic inner window to see, then as the rain recommenced and he could tell they were beginning descent it reappeared in the window's center, light traffic crawling with a futile pointless pathos you could never sense on the ground. What if it felt as slow to actually drive as it looked from this perspective? It would be like trying to run under water. The whole ball game was perspective, filtering, the choice of perception's objects. Sylvanshine tried to envision the small plane as seen from the ground, a cruciform shape against the old-bathwater color of the cloud cover, its lights blinking complexly in the rain. He imagined rain on his face. It was light, a West Virginia rain; he hadn't heard one unit of thunder. Sylvanshine had once been on a first date with a Xerox rep who had complex and slightly repulsive patterns of callus on her fingers from playing the banjo semi-professionally as her off-time passion; and he remembered, as the overhead bell again rang and the sign lit, the no-cigarette glyph legally redundant, the pads' calluses deep yellow in the low dinnerlight as he'd spoken to the musician about forensic accounting's intricacies and the hivelike organization of the Northeast REC, which was only one small part of the Service, and the Service's history and little-understood ideals and sense of mission and the old joke (to him) about how Service employees in social situations would go to such absurd lengths to avoid telling people that they worked for the IRS because it often cast such a social pall because of popular perceptions of the Service and its employees, all the while watching the calluses as the woman worked her knife and fork, and that he'd been so nervous and tense that he'd yammered on and on about himself and never asked her sufficiently about herself, her history with the banjo and what it meant to her, which was why she hadn't liked him enough and they hadn't connected. He'd never given the woman with the banjo a chance, he saw now. That what appears to be egoism so often isn't. In some ways, Sylvanshine was a whole different person now in Systems. Their descent was mainly a heightening of the specificity of what lay below—fields revealed as plowed and perpendicularly furrowed and silos as adjoined by canted chutes and belts and an industrial park as individual buildings with reflective windows and complicated clumps of cars in the parking lots. Each car not only parked by a different human individual but conceived, designed, assembled from parts each one of which was designed and made, transported, sold, financed, purchased, and insured by human individuals, each with life stories and self-concepts that all fit together into a larger pattern of facts. Reynolds's dictum was that reality was a fact-pattern the bulk of which was entropic and random. The trick was homing in on which facts were important—Reynolds was a rifle to Sylvanshine's shotgun. The feeling of a slight trickle of blood from his right nostril was a hallucination and to be ignored absolutely; the feeling simply did not exist. Sinus trouble ran in Sylvanshine's family in the worst way. Aurelius of ancient Rome. First principles. Exemptions vs. deductions, for AGI vs. from AGI. A loss sustained from a nonbusiness bad debt is always classified as a short-term capital loss and may therefore be deducted on Schedule D as per the following IRC §: One building's roof had what was either a marked helipad or a complicated visual signal to the planes descending overhead, and the pitch of the propellers' doubled hum was different and his right sinus was even now ballooning redly in his skull and they really were descending, the term was controlled descent, the interstate now rococo with exits and half-cloverleafs and the traffic denser and with something insistent about it, and the claw rose from the steel armrest as there appeared a body of water below, a lake or delta, and Sylvanshine felt one of his feet was asleep as he tried to recall the peculiar crossed-arm configuration with which the figures on the card held their seat cushions to their chests in the unlikely event of a water landing, and now they did really and truly yaw and their speed became more evident in the rate of passage of things below in what had to be an older district of Peoria *qua* human city, close-packed blocks of sooty brick and angled roofs and a television antenna with a flag attached, and a flash of a bourbon-colored river that was not the previous body of water but might have been connected to it, nothing like the stately and befrothed stretch of Potomac that obtruded through Systems' windows on Antietam's hallowed site, noting that the stewardess in her fold-down seat had her head down and arms about her own legs where at year's end the aggregate fair value of Brown's salable securities exceeds the aggregate carrying amount at the beginning of the year as out of nowhere appeared an expanse of pale cement rising to meet them with no warning bell or announcement and his soda can wedged in the seat pocket as the gray death's-head beside whipped right and left and the propellers' shimmering sound shifted either pitch or timbre, and the older lady stiffening in her seat and raising her pleated chin in fear and repeating what sounded to Sylvanshine like the word *chump* as veins stood bluely in the fist before her, in which was enclosed the crushed and bulbous but still unopened foil pack of off-brand nuts.

'The fifth effect has more to do with you, how you're perceived. It's powerful although its use is more restricted. Pay attention, boy. The next suitable person you're in light conversation with, you stop suddenly in the middle of the conversation and look at the person closely and say, "What's wrong?" You say it in a concerned way. He'll say, "What do you mean?" You say, "Something's wrong. I can tell. What is it?" And he'll look stunned and say, "How did you know?" He doesn't realize something's *always* wrong, with everybody. Often more than one thing. He doesn't know everybody's always going around all the time with something wrong and believing they're exerting great willpower and control to keep other people, for whom they think nothing's ever wrong, from seeing it. This is the way of people. Suddenly ask what's wrong, and whether they open up and spill their guts or deny it and pretend you're off, they'll think you're perceptive and understanding. They'll either be grateful, or they'll be frightened and avoid you from then on. Both reactions have their uses, as we'll get to. You can play it either way. This works over 90 percent of the time.'

And stood—having squeezed by the powdery older lady, she being the type that waits in her seat until all others have deplaned and then exits alone, with a counterfeit dignity—holding his effects in an aisle whose crammed front portion was all regional business travelers, men of business, willfully homely midwestern men on downstate sales calls or returning from the Chicago HQs of companies whose names end with '-co,' men for whom landings like this yaw-wobbled horror just past are business as usual. Paunched and blotchy men in double-knit brown suits and tan suits with attaché cases ordered from in-flight catalogues. Men whose soft faces fit their jobs like sausage in its meaty casing. Men who instruct pocket recorders to take a memo, men who look at their watches out of reflex, men with red foreheads all mashed standing in a metal chute as the props' hum descends the tonal scale and ventilation ceases, this the type of commuter airplane whose stairs must be rolled up alongside before the door opens, for legal reasons. The glazed impatience of businessmen standing closer to strangers than they would ever choose to, chests and backs nearly touching, suit bags slung over shoulders, briefcases knocking together, more scalp than hair, breathing one another's smells. Men who cannot bear to wait or stand still forced to stand still all together and wait, men with calfskin Day-Timers and Franklin Quest Time Management certificates and the classic look of unwilled tight confinement, the look of a local merchant on the verge of an SSI-withholding lapse, undercapitalized, illiquid, trying to cover the monthly nut, fish thrashing in the nets of their own obligations. Two eventual suicides on this plane, one forever classed as an accident. In Philly there had been a whole subgroup of implacable metal-minded GS-9s tasked to nothing but going after small businesses who'd fallen behind on SSI withholding, although in Rome for almost a year the only Compliance staff taking SSI alerts from Martinsburg had been Eloise Prout, a.k.a. Dr. Yes, a fortyish GS-9 in a macramé hat who ate lunch at her desk out of a complex system of Tupperware containers and was a dinner whore of the most pathetic sort, the boys in Examinations christening her Dr. Yes after she'd reportedly slept with Sherman Garnett on nothing but the promise—not honored—of a walk around the town commons with the snow stopped and everything crisp and white. The Eloise Prout who came in so low every month on referral and recovery quotas that any other GS-9 would have worn the brown helmet but dim kindly REC Mr. Orkney had kept her on, Prout apparently a car-crash widow with a GS-9 salary that barely bought cat food, Sylvanshine was well aware, his foot pulsing with new blood and excusing himself each time someone bumped his carry-on, his third post in four years and still a GS-9 with a promise of 11 if he passed the CPA exam this spring and acquitted himself well in this post as Systems' eyes on the ground through the March 15 corporate and then April 15 storms of 1040s and ESTs for Peoria 047 to examine, having sat for the exam twice so far and so far passing only Managerial with a Low Pass, Sylvanshine's rep in Philly following him to Rome and locking him firmly into Level 1 Returns, not even Fats or Review, which had made him little more than a professional letter-opener, which Soane, Madrid, et al. had not been shy about observing.

Sylvanshine tended to do his deskwork in a kind of frenzy as opposed to the slow, austere, methodical disposition of truly great accountants, his first group supervisor in Rome had told him, a lifetime third-shifter who wore an eccentric coat and always left the REC carrying a little rhomboid carton of delivered Chinese for his wife, who was said to be some kind of shut-in. This GS-11 had early in his career been posted at the St. Louis Service Center, literally in the shadow of the strange scary giant metal arch thing, to which mail came daily in great wheezing eighteen-wheel trailer rigs backing up to the dock's long conveyor, and on breaks in the break room the group leader had liked to lean back holding his umbrella and blow silvery clouds of cigar smoke up at the fluorescent lights and reminisce about summer in the Midwest, of which region Sylvanshine and the other young eastern GS-9s were ignorant and in whom the group leader somehow planted visions of fishing barefoot on the banks of motionless rivers and a moon you could read the paper by and everyone always saying Hi to everyone else every time they saw them and moving in a kind of cheery slo-mo. Named Bussy, Mr. Vince or Vincent Bussy, who wore a Kmart parka with a hood with a fake fur fringe, and could walk chopsticks over his knuckles like a magician with a shiny coin, and disappeared following Sylvanshine's second REC Christmas party, when his wife (i.e., Mrs. Bussy) had suddenly appeared in the midst of the revel in an off-white nightie and identical unzipped Kmart parka and approached the Assistant Regional Commissioner for Examinations and, speaking slowly and atonally and with total conviction, told him that her husband Mr. Bussy had said that he (the ARCE) had the potential to be a really truly evil person if he grew a somewhat larger set of balls, Bussy one week thereafter gone so abruptly that his umbrella remained hanging from the Pod's communal coatrack for almost a quarter until someone finally took it down.

They deplaned and descended and collected the carry-on bags that had been confiscated and tagged at Midway and now rested in a motley row on the wet tarmac beside the airplane, and stood then briefly en masse on a complexly painted cement expanse while someone with orange earmuffs and clipboard counted them and then crosschecked the count with a previous count undertaken at Midway. The whole operation seemed somewhat ad hoc and slapdash. On the steep and portable staircase, Sylvanshine had derived the usual satisfaction from putting his hat on his head and adjusting its angle all with one hand. His right ear popped and crackled slightly with each swallow. The wind was warm and steamy. A large hose extended from a small truck to the commuter plane's stomach and appeared to be refueling the craft for its turnaround to Chicago. Up and back again and again all day. There was a strong scent of fuel and wet cement. The older lady, evidently uncounted, now descended the frightening stairs and went to some type of long automobile that Sylvanshine had not noticed parked off the airplane's starboard side. A wing obtruded, but Sylvanshine could see that she did not open her own door. A distant tree line's tops bent left in the wind and came straight again. Because of previous problems with accidents traceable to poor snap decisions in Philly, Sylvanshine no longer drove. He was over 75 percent certain that the packet of nuts was now inside the older lady's handbag. There was some type of consultation between the employee with the clipboard and another person with orange earmuffs. Several of the other passengers were making pointed gestures of looking at their watches. The air was warm and close and well beyond humid or muggy. They were all becoming damp on the sides of themselves that faced the wind. Sylvanshine now noticed that the dark topcoats many of the businessmen wore were quite similar, as were the flares of the upturned collars. No one else wore any type of hat. He was trying to pay close attention to his surroundings as a way to avert thought and anxiety. The administrative or logistical delay was occurring under a baggy sky and a rain so fine it seemed to come sideways with the wind instead of fall. There was no sound of rain on Sylvanshine's hat. The fur of Mr. Bussy's hood's fringe had been dirty in a sort of queasy way that got worse over the two years he served as Sylvanshine's group supervisor in Returns Processing. Some of the more assertive passengers were walking unguided down the red-lined path that led through the fence's gate and toward the terminal. Sylvanshine, who had checked bags, was concerned about sanctions for unauthorized departure from the tarmac. On the other hand, he had an assigned schedule to keep. Part of what kept him standing in the restive group of men awaiting authorization to enter the airport was a kind of paralysis that resulted from Sylvanshine's reflecting on the logistics of getting to the Peoria 047 REC—the issue of whether the REC sent a van for transfers or whether Sylvanshine would have to take a cab from the little airport had not been conclusively resolved—and then how to arrive and check in and where to store his three bags while he checked in and filled out his arrival and Post-code payroll and withholding forms and orientational materials then somehow get directions and proceed to the apartment that Systems had rented for him at government rates and get there in time to find someplace to eat that was either in walking distance or would require getting another cab—except the telephone in the alleged apartment wasn't connected yet and he considered the prospects of being able to hail a cab from outside an apartment complex were at best iffy, and if he told the original cab he'd taken to the apartment to wait for him, there would be difficulties because how exactly would he reassure the cabbie that he really was coming right back out after dropping his bags and doing a quick spot check of the apartment's condition and suitability instead of it being a ruse designed to defraud the driver of his fare, Sylvanshine ducking out the back of the Angler's Cove apartment complex or even conceivably barricading himself in the apartment and not responding to the driver's knock, or his ring if the apartment had a doorbell, which his and Reynolds's current apartment in Martinsburg most assuredly did not, or the driver's queries/threats through the apartment door, a scam that resided in Claude Sylvanshine's awareness only because a number of independent Philadelphia commercial carriage operators had proposed heavy Schedule C losses under the proviso 'Losses Through Theft of Service' and detailed this type of scam as prevalent on the poorly typed or sometimes even handwritten attachments required to explain unusual or specific C-deductions like this, whereas were Sylvanshine to pay the fare and the tip and perhaps even a certain amount in advance on account so as to help assure the driver of his honorable intentions re the second leg of the sojourn there was no tangible guarantee that the average taxi driver—a cynical and ethically marginal species, hustlers, as even their smudged returns' very low tip-income-vs.-number-of-fares-in-an-average-shift ratios in Philly had indicated—wouldn't simply speed away with Sylvanshine's money, creating enormous hassles in terms of filling out the internal forms for getting a percentage of his travel per diem reimbursed and also leaving Sylvanshine alone, famished (he was unable to eat before travel), phoneless, devoid of Reynolds's counsel and logistical savvy in the sterile new unfurnished apartment, his stomach roiling in on itself in such a way that it would be all Sylvanshine could do to unpack in any kind of half-organized fashion and get to sleep on the nylon travel pallet on the unfinished floor in the possible presence of exotic

Midwest bugs, to say nothing of putting in the hour of CPA exam review he'd promised himself this morning when he'd overslept slightly and then encountered last-minute packing problems that had canceled out the firmly scheduled hour of morning CPA review before one of the unmarked Systems vans arrived to take him and his bags out through Harpers Ferry and Ball's Bluff to the airport, to say even less about any kind of systematic organization and mastery of the voluminous Post, Duty, Personnel, and Systems Protocols materials he should be receiving promptly after check-in and forms processing at the Post, which any reasonable Personnel Director would expect a new examiner to have thoroughly internalized before reporting for the first actual day interacting with REC examiners, and which there was no way in any real world that Sylvanshine could expect himself to try to review and internalize on either a sixteen-hour fast or after a night on the pallet with his damp raincoat as a pillow—he had been unable to pack the special contoured orthotic pillow for his neck's chronic pinched or inflamed nerve; it would have required its own suitcase and thereby exceeded the baggage limit and incurred an exorbitant surcharge which Reynolds refused to let Sylvanshine pay out of simple principle—with the additional problem of securing any sort of substantive breakfast or return ride to the REC in the morning without a phone, or how without a phone one was supposed even to verify whether and when the apartment phone was going to be activated, plus of course the ominous probability of oversleeping the next morning due to both travel fatigue and his not having packed his traveler's alarm clock—or at any rate not having been certain that he'd packed it instead of allowing it to go into one of the three large cartons that he had packed and labeled but done a hasty, slipshod job of writing out Contents Lists for the boxes to refer to when unpacking them in Peoria, and which Reynolds had pledged to insert into the Service's Support Branch shipping mechanism at roughly the same time Sylvanshine's flight was scheduled to depart from Dulles, which meant two or possibly even three days before the cartons with all the essentials Sylvanshine had not been able to fit in his bags arrived, and even then they would arrive at the REC and it was as yet unclear how Claude would then get them home to the apartment—the realization about the traveler's alarm having been the chief cause of Sylvanshine's having to unlock and open all the carefully packed luggage that morning on arising already half an hour late, to try to locate or verify the inclusion of the portable alarm, which he had failed to do—the whole thing presenting such a cyclone of logistical problems and complexities that Sylvanshine was forced to do some Thought Stopping right there on the wet tarmac surrounded by restive breathers, turning 360° several times and trying to merge his own awareness with the panoramic vista, which except for airport-related items was uniformly featureless and old-coin gray and so remarkably flat that it was as if the earth here had been stamped on with some cosmic boot, visibility in all directions limited only by the horizon, which was the same general color and texture as the sky and created the specular impression of being in the center of some huge and stagnant body of water, an oceanic impression so literally obliterating that Sylvanshine was cast or propelled back in on himself and felt again the edge of the shadow of the wing of Total Terror and Disqualification pass over him, the knowledge of his being surely and direly ill-suited for whatever lay ahead, and of its being only a matter of time before this fact emerged and was made manifest to all those present in the moment that Sylvanshine finally, and forever, lost it.

§3

'Speaking of which, what do you think of when you masturbate?'

'...'

'...'

'What?'

Neither had said a word for the first half hour. They were doing the mindless monochrome drive up to Region HQ in Joliet again. In one of the fleet's Gremlins, seized as part of a jeopardy assessment against an AMC dealership five quarters past.

'Look, I think we can presume you masturbate. Something like 98 percent of all men masturbate. It's documented. Most of the other 2 percent are impaired in some way. We can forgo the denials. I masturbate; you masturbate. It happens. We all do it and we all know we all do it and yet no one ever discusses it. It's an incredibly boring drive, there's nothing to do, we're stuck in this embarrassing car—let's push the envelope. Let's discuss it.'

'What envelope?'

'Just what do you think of? Think about it. It's a very interior time. It's one of life's only occasions of real self-sufficiency. It requires nothing outside you. It's bringing yourself pleasure with nothing but your own mind's thoughts. Those thoughts reveal a lot about you:

what you dream of when you yourself choose and control what you dream.'

'. . .'

'. . .'

'Tits.'

'Tits?'

'You asked me. I'm telling you.'

'That's it? Tits?'

'What do you want me to say?'

'Just tits? In isolation from anybody? Just abstract tits?'

'All right. Fuck off.'

'You mean just floating there, two tits, in empty space? Or nestled in your hands, or what? Is it always the same tits?'

'This is me learning a lesson. You ask a question like that and I go what the hell and I answer it and you run a DIF-3 on the answer.'

'Tits.'

'. . .'

'. . .'

'So what do *you* think about, then, Mr. Envelope Guy?'

§4

From the *Peoria Journal Star,*
Monday, November 17, 1980, p. C-2:

IRS WORKER DEAD FOR FOUR DAYS

Supervisors at the IRS's regional complex in Lake James township are trying to determine why no one noticed that one of their employees had been sitting dead at his desk for four days before anyone asked if he was feeling all right.

Frederick Blumquist, 53, who had been employed as a tax return examiner with the agency for over thirty years, suffered a heart attack in the open-plan office he shared with twenty-five coworkers at the agency's Regional Examination Center on Self-Storage Parkway. He quietly passed away last Tuesday at his desk, but nobody noticed until late Saturday evening when an office cleaner asked how the examiner could still be working in an office with all the lights off.

Mr. Blumquist's supervisor, Scott Thomas, said, 'Frederick was always the first guy in each morning and the last to leave at night. He was very focused and diligent, so no one found it unusual that he was in the same position all that time and didn't say anything. He was always absorbed in his work, and kept to himself.'

A postmortem examination by the Tazewell County Coroner's Office yesterday revealed that Blumquist had been dead for four days after suffering from a coronary. Ironically, according to Thomas, Blumquist was part of a special task force of IRS agents examining the tax affairs of medical partnerships in the area when he died.

§5

It is this boy who dons the bright-orange bandolier and shepherds the lower grades' kids through the crosswalk outside school. This is after finishing his Meals on Wheels breakfast tour of the charity home for the aged downtown, whose administrator lunges to bolt her office door when she hears his cart's wheels in the hall. He has paid out of pocket for the steel whistle and the white gloves held palm-out at cars while children who did not dress themselves cross behind him, some trying to run despite WALK, DON'T RUN!!, the happy-face sandwich board he also made himself. The autos whose drivers he knows he waves at and gives an extra-big smile and tosses some words of good cheer as the crosswalk clears and the cars peel out and barrel through, some joshing around a little by swerving to miss him only by inches as he laughs and dances aside and makes faces of pretended terror at the flanks and rear bumpers. (The time that one station wagon didn't miss him really *was* an accident, and he sent the lady several notes to make absolutely sure she knew he understood that, and asked a whole lot of people he hadn't yet gotten the opportunity to make friends with to sign his cast, and decorated the crutches very carefully with bits of colored ribbon and tinsel and adhesive sparkles, and even before the minimum six weeks the doctor sternly prescribed he'd donated the crutches to Calvin Memorial's pediatrics wing in order to brighten up some other less lucky and happy kid's convalescence, and by the end of the whole thing he'd been inspired to write a very long theme to enter in the annual Social Studies Theme Competition about how even a painful and debilitating accidental injury can yield new opportunities for making friends and reaching out to others, and while the theme didn't win or even get honorable mention he honestly didn't care, because he felt like writing the theme had been its own reward and that he'd gotten a lot out of the whole nine-draft process, and was honestly happy for the kids whose themes did win prizes, and told them he was 100-plus percent sure they deserved it and that if they wanted to preserve their prize themes and maybe even make display items out of them for their parents he'd be happy to type them up and laminate them and even fix any spelling errors he found if they'd like him to, and at home his father puts his hand on little Leonard's shoulder and says he's proud that his son's such a good sport, and offers to take him to Dairy Queen as a kind of reward, and Leonard tells his father he's grateful and that the gesture means a lot to him but that in all honesty he'd like it even more if they took the money his father would have spent on the ice cream and instead donated it either to Easter Seals or, better yet, to UNICEF, to go toward the needs of famine-ravaged Biafran kids who he knows for a fact have probably never even *heard* of ice cream, and says that he bets it'll end up giving both of them a better feeling even than the DQ would, and as the father slips the coins in the coin slot of the special bright-orange UNICEF volunteer cardboard pumpkin-bank, Leonard takes a moment to express concern about the father's facial tic again and to gently rib him about his reluctance to go in and have the family's MD look at it, noting again that according to the chart on the back of his bedroom door the father is three months overdue for his annual physical and that it's almost eight months past the date of his recommended tetanus booster.)

He serves as hall monitor for Periods 1 and 2 (he's half a grade ahead on credits) but gives far more official warnings than actual citations—he's there to serve, he feels, not run people down. Usually with the warnings he dispenses a smile and tells them you're young exactly once so enjoy it, and to go get out of here and make this day count why don't they. He does UNICEF and Easter Seals and starts a recycling program in three straight grades. He is healthy and scrubbed and always groomed just well enough to project basic courtesy and respect for the community of which he is a part, and he politely raises his hand in class for every question, but only if he's sure he knows not only the correct answer but the formulation of that answer that the teacher's looking for that will help advance the discussion of the overall topic they're covering that day, often staying after class to double-check with the teacher that his take on her general objectives is sound and to ask whether there was any way his in-class answers could have been better or more helpful.

The boy's mom has a terrible accident while cleaning the oven and is rushed to the hospital, and even though he's beside himself with concern and says constant prayers for her stabilization and recovery he volunteers to stay home and field calls and relay information to an alphabetized list of relatives and concerned family friends, and to make sure the mail and newspaper are brought in, and to keep the home's lights turned on and off in a random sequence at night as Officer Chuck of the Michigan State Police's Crime Stoppers public-school outreach program sensibly advises when grown-ups are suddenly called away from home, and also to call the gas company's emergency number (which he has memorized) to have them come check on what may well be a defective valve or circuit in the oven before anyone else in the family is exposed to risk of accidental harm, and also (secretly) to work on an immense display of bunting and pennants and WELCOME HOME and WORLD'S GREATEST MOM signs which he plans to use the garage's extendable ladder (with a responsible neighborhood adult holding it and supervising) to very carefully affix to the front of the home with water-soluble glue so that it'll be there to greet and cheer the mom when she's released from Critical Care with a totally clean bill of health, which Leonard calls his father repeatedly at the Critical Care ward pay phone to assure him that he has absolutely no doubt of, the totally clean bill of health, calling hourly right on the dot until there's some kind of mechanical problem with the pay phone and when he dials it he just gets a high tone, which he duly reports to the telephone company's special 1-616-TROUBLE line, remembering to include the specific pay phone's eight-digit Field Product Code (which he'd written down all of just in case) as the small-print technical material on the 1-616-TROUBLE line at the very back of the phone book recommends for most rapid and efficient service.

He can produce several different kinds of calligraphy and has been to origami camp (twice) and can do extraordinary freehand sketches of local flora and can whistle all six of Telemann's *Nouveaux Quatuors* as well as imitate just about any birdcall that Audubon could ever have thought of. He sometimes writes academic publishers about possible errors of category and/or syntax in their textbooks. Let's not even mention spelling bees. He can make over twenty different kinds of admiral, cowboy, clerical, and multiethnic hats out of ordinary newspaper, and he volunteers to visit the school's K–2 classrooms teaching the little kids how, an offer the Carl P. Robinson Elementary principal says he appreciates and has considered very carefully before declining. The principal loathes the mere sight of the boy but does not quite know why. He sees the boy in his sleep, at nightmares' ragged edges—the pressed checked shirt and hair's hard little part, the freckles and ready generous smile: anything he can do. The principal fantasizes about sinking a meat hook into Leonard Stecyk's bright-eyed little face and dragging the boy face-down behind his Volkswagen Beetle over the rough new streets of suburban Grand Rapids. The fantasies come out of nowhere and horrify the principal, who is a devout Mennonite.

Everyone hates the boy. It is a complex hatred, one that often causes the haters to feel mean and guilty and to hate themselves for feeling this way about such an accomplished and well-meaning boy, which then tends to make them involuntarily hate the boy even more for arousing such self-hatred. The whole thing is totally confusing and upsetting. People take a lot of aspirin when he's around. The boy's only real friends among kids are the damaged, the handicapped, the fat, the last-picked, the *non grata*—he seeks them out. All 316 invitations to his eleventh-birthday *BLOWOUT BASH*—322 invitations if you count the ones made on audiotape for the blind—are offset-printed on quality vellum with matching high-rag envelopes addressed in ornate Phillippian II calligraphy he's spent three weekends on, and each invitation details in Roman-numeraled outline form the itinerary's half-day at Six Flags, private PhD-guided tour of the Blanford Nature Center, and Reserved Banquet Area w/ Free Play at Shakee's Pizza and Indoor Arcade on Remembrance Drive (the whole day gratis and paid for out of the Paper and Aluminum Drives the boy got up at 4:00 A.M. all summer to organize and spearhead, the balance of the Drives' receipts going to the Red Cross and the parents of a Kentwood third-grader with terminal spina bifida who dreams above all else of seeing the Lions' Night Train Lane play live from his motorized wheelchair), and the invitations explicitly call the party this—a *BLOWOUT BASH*—in balloon-shaped font as the caption to an illustrated explosion of good cheer and -will and no-holds-barred-let-out-all-the-stops *FUN,* with the bold-faced proviso **PLEASE—NO PRESENTS REQUIRED** in each of each card's four corners; and the 316 invitations, sent via First-Class Mail to every student, instructor, substitute instructor, aide, administrator, and custodian at C. P. Robinson Elementary, yield a total attendance of nine celebrants (not counting parents or LPNs of the incapacitated), and yet an undauntedly fine time is had by all, and such is the consensus on the Honest Appraisal and Suggestion Cards (also vellum) circulated at party's end, the massive remainders of chocolate cake, Neapolitan ice cream, pizza, chips, caramel corn, Hershey's Kisses, Red Cross and Officer Chuck pamphlets on organ/tissue donation and the correct procedures to follow if approached by a stranger respectively, kosher pizza for the Orthodox, designer napkins, and dietetic soda in souvenir *I Survived Leonard Stecyk's 11th Birthday Blowout Bash 1964* plastic glasses w/ built-in lemniscate Krazy Straws the guests were to keep as mementos all donated to the Kent County Children's Home via procedures and transport that the birthday boy has initiated even while the big Twister free-for-all is under way, out of concerns about melted ice cream and staleness and flatness and the waste of a chance to help the less fortunate; and his father, driving the wood-panel station wagon and steadying his cheek with one hand, avows again that the boy beside him has a large, good heart, and that he is proud, and that if the boy's mother ever regains consciousness as they so very much hope, he knows she'll be just awful proud as well.

The boy makes As and enough occasional Bs to keep himself from getting a swelled head about marks, and his teachers shudder at the sound of even just his name. In the fifth grade he undertakes a district collection to provide a Special Fund of nickels for anyone at lunch who's already spent their milk money but still might for whatever reason want or feel they need more milk. The Jolly Holly Milk Company gets wind of it and puts a squib about the Fund and an automated line drawing of the boy on the side of some of their half-pint cartons. Two-thirds of the school ceases to drink milk, while the Special Fund itself grows so large that the principal has to requisition a small safe for his office. The principal is now taking Seconal to sleep and experiencing fine tremors, and on two separate occasions is cited for Failure to Yield at marked crosswalks.

A teacher in whose homeroom the boy suggests a charted reorganization of the coat hooks and boot boxes lining one wall so that the coat and galoshes of the student whose desk is nearest the door would themselves be nearest the door, and the second-nearest's second-nearest, and so on, speeding the pupils' egress to recess and reducing delays and possible quarrels and clots of half-bundled kids at the classroom door (which delays and clots the boy had taken the trouble this quarter to chart by statistical incidence, with relevant graphics and arrows but all names withheld), this tenured and highly respected veteran teacher ends up brandishing blunt scissors and threatening to kill first the boy and then herself, and is put on Medical Leave, during which she receives thrice-weekly Get Well cards, with neatly typed summaries of the class's activities and progress in her absence sprinkled with glitter and folded in perfect diamond shapes that open with just a squeeze of the two long facets inside (i.e., inside the cards), until the teacher's doctors order her mail to be withheld until improvement or at least stabilization in her condition warrants.

Right before 1965's big Halloween UNICEF collection three

sixth-graders accost the boy in the southeast restroom after fourth period and do unspeakable things to him, leaving him hanging from a stall's hook by his underpants' elastic; and after being treated and released from the hospital (a different one than his mother is a patient in the long-term convalescent ward of), the boy refuses to identify his assailants and later circumspectly delivers to them individualized notes detailing his renunciation of any and all hard feelings about the incident, apologizing for whatever unwitting offense he might have given to provoke it, exhorting his attackers to please put the whole thing behind them and not in any way self-recriminate over it—especially down the line, because the boy's understanding was that these were the sorts of things that could sometimes really haunt you later on down the line in adulthood, citing one or two journal articles the attackers might have a look at if they wanted documentation on the long-term psychological effects of self-recrimination—and, in the notes, professing his personal hope that an actual friendship might conceivably result from the whole regrettable incident, along which lines he was also enclosing an invitation to attend a short no-questions-asked Conflict Resolution Roundtable the boy has persuaded a local community services outreach organization to sponsor after school the following Tuesday *'(Light Refreshments Served!),'* after which the boy's PE locker along with the four on either side are destroyed in an act of pyrotechnic vandalism that everyone on both sides in the subsequent court trial agrees got totally out of hand and was not a premeditated attempt to injure the night custodian or to do anything like the amount of structural damage to the Boys' locker room it ended up doing, and at which trial Leonard Stecyk appeals repeatedly to both sides' counsel for the opportunity to testify for the defense, if only as a character witness. A large percentage of the boy's classmates hide—take actual evasive action—when they see him coming. Eventually even the marginal and infirm stop returning his calls. His mother has to be turned and her limbs manipulated twice a day.

§6

They were up on a picnic table at that one park by the lake, by the edge of the lake with part of a downed tree in the shallows half hidden by the bank. Lane A. Dean Jr. and his girlfriend, both in blue jeans and button-up shirts. They sat up on the table's top portion and had their shoes on the bench part that people sat on and picnicked in carefree times. They had gone to different high schools but the same junior college, where they had met in campus ministries. It was springtime, the park's grass was very green and the air suffused with honeysuckle and lilacs both, which was almost too much. There were bees, and the angle of the sun made the water of the shallows look dark. There had been more storms that week, with some downed trees and the sound of chainsaws all up and down his parents' street. Their postures on the picnic table were both the same forward kind with their shoulders rounded and elbows on their knees. In this position the girl rocked slightly and once put her face in her hands but she was not crying. Lane was very still and immobile and looking past the bank at the downed tree in the shallows and its ball of exposed roots going all directions and the tree's cloud of branches all half in the water. The only other individual nearby was a dozen spaced tables away by himself, standing upright. Looking at the torn-up hole in the ground there where the tree had gone over. It was still early yet and all the shadows wheeling right and shortening. The girl wore a thin old checked cotton shirt with pearl-colored snaps with the long sleeves down and she always smelled very good and clean, like someone you could trust and deeply care about even if you weren't in love. Lane Dean had liked the smell of her right away. His mother called her *down to earth* and liked her, thought she was good people, you could tell—she made this evident in little ways. The shallows lapped from different directions at the tree as if almost teething on it. Sometimes when alone and thinking or struggling to turn a matter over to Jesus Christ in prayer, he would find himself putting his fist in his palm and turning it slightly as if still playing and pounding his glove to stay sharp and alert in center. He did not do this now, it would be cruel and indecent to do this now. The older individual stood beside his picnic table, he was at it but not sitting, and looked also out of place in a suit coat or jacket and the kind of older men's hat Lane's grandfather wore in photos as a young insurance man. He appeared to be looking across the lake. If he moved, Lane didn't see it. He looked more like a picture than a man. There were not any ducks in view.

One thing Lane Dean did was reassure her again that he'd go with her and be there with her. It was one of the few safe or decent things he could really say. The second time he said it again now she shook her head and laughed in an unhappy way that was more just air out her nose. Her real laugh was different. Where he'd be was the waiting room, she said. That he'd be thinking about her and feeling bad for her, she knew, but he couldn't be in there with her. This was so obviously true that he felt like a ninny that he'd kept on about it and now knew what she had thought every time he went and said it; it hadn't brought her comfort or eased the burden at all. The worse he felt, the stiller he sat. The whole thing felt balanced on a knife or wire; if he moved to put his arm up or touch her the whole thing could tip over. He hated himself for sitting so frozen. He could almost visualize himself tiptoeing through something explosive. A big stupid-looking tiptoe like in a cartoon. The whole last black week had been this way and it was wrong. He knew it was wrong, he knew something was required of him and knew it was not this terrible frozen care and caution, but he pretended to himself he did not know what it was that was required. He pretended it had no name. He pretended that not saying aloud what he knew to be right and true was for her sake, was for the sake of her needs and feelings. He also worked dock and routing at UPS, besides school, but traded to get the day off after they'd decided together. Two days before, he had awakened very early and tried to pray but could not. He was freezing more and more solid, he felt like, but he hadn't thought of his father or the blank frozenness of his father, even in church, that once had filled him with such pity. This was the truth. Lane Dean Jr. felt sun on one arm as he pictured in his mind an image of himself on a train, waving mechanically to something that got smaller and smaller as the train pulled away. His father and his mother's father had the same birthday, a Cancer. Sheri's hair was colored an almost corn blond, very clean, the skin through the central part pink in the light. They'd sat up here long enough that only their right side was shaded now. He could look at her head, but not at her. Different parts of him felt unconnected to each other. She was smarter than him and they both knew it. It wasn't just school—Lane Dean was in accounting and business and did all right, he was hanging in there. She was a year older, she was twenty, but it was also more—she had always seemed to Lane to be on good terms with her life in a way age could not account for. His mother had put it that she *knew what it was she wanted,* which was nursing and not an easy program at Peoria Junior College, and plus she worked hostessing at the Embers and had bought her own car. She was serious in a way Lane liked. She had a cousin that died when she was thirteen, fourteen, that she'd loved and been close with. She only talked about it that once. He liked her smell and the downy hair on her arms and the way she exclaimed when something made her laugh. He had liked just being with her and talking to her. She was serious in her faith and values in a way that Lane had liked and now, sitting here with her on the table, found himself afraid of. This was an awful thing. He was starting to believe he might not be serious in his faith. He might be somewhat of a hypocrite, like the Assyrians in Isaiah, which would be a far graver sin than the appointment—he had decided he believed this. He was desperate to be good people, to still be able to feel he was good. He rarely before had thought of damnation and hell, that part of it didn't speak to his spirit, and in worship services he more just tuned himself out and tolerated hell when it came up, the same way you tolerate the job you have got to have to save up for what it is you want. Her tennis shoes had little things and items doodled on them from sitting in her class lectures. She stayed looking down like that. Little notes or reading assignments in Bic in her neat round hand on the rubber elements around the sneaker's rim. Lane A. Dean looking at her inclined head's side's barrettes in the shape of blue ladybugs. The appointment was for afternoon, but when the doorbell rang so early and his mother'd called to him up the stairs, he had known, and a terrible kind of blankness had commenced falling through him.

He told her that he did not know what to do. That he knew if he was the salesman of it and forced it upon her that was awful and wrong. But he was trying to understand, they'd prayed on it and talked it through from every different angle. Lane said how sorry she knew he was, and that if he was wrong in believing they'd truly decided together when they decided to make the appointment she should please tell him, because he thought he knew how she must have felt as it got closer and closer and how she must be so scared, but that what he couldn't tell was if it was more than that. He was totally still except for moving his mouth, it felt like. She did not reply. That if they needed to pray on it more and talk it through, why then he was here, he was ready, he said. He said the appointment could get moved back; if she just said the word they could call and push it back to take more time to be sure in the decision. It was still so early in it, they both knew that, he said. This was true, he felt this way, and yet he also knew he was also trying to say things that would get her to open up and say enough back that he could see her and read her heart and know what to say to get her to go through with it. He knew this without admitting to himself that this is what he wanted, for it would make him a hypocrite and a liar. He knew, in some locked-up little part of him, why it was that he'd gone to no one to open up and seek their life counsel, not Pastor Steve or the prayer partners at campus ministries, not his UPS friends or the spiritual counseling available through his parents' old church. But he did not know why Sheri herself had not gone to Pastor Steve—he could not read her heart. She was blank and hidden. He so fervently wished it never happened. He felt like he knew now why it was a true sin and not just a leftover rule from past society. He felt like he had been brought low by it and humbled and now did understand and believe that the rules were there for a reason. That the rules were concerned with him personally, as an individual. He'd promised God he had learned his lesson. But what if that, too, was a hollow promise, from a hypocrite who repented only after, who promised submission but really only wanted a reprieve? He might not even know his own heart or be able to read and know himself. He kept thinking also of 1 Timothy 6 and the hypocrite therein who *disputeth over words.* He felt a terrible inner resistance but could not feel what it was it so resisted. This was the truth. All the different angles and ways they had come at the decision together did not ever include it, the word—for had he once said it, avowed that he did love her, loved Sheri Fisher, then it would have all been transformed, it would be a different stance or angle but a difference in the very thing they were praying and deciding on together. Sometimes they had prayed together over the phone in a kind of half code in case anybody accidentally picked up another extension. She continued to sit as if thinking, in the pose of thinking like almost that one statue. They were on that one table. He was the one looking past her at the tree in the water. But he could not say he did, it was not true.

But nor did he ever open up and tell her straight out he did not love her. This may be his *lie by omission.* This may be the frozen resistance—were he to look straight at her and tell her he didn't, she would keep the appointment and go. He knew this. Something in him, though, some terrible weakness or lack of values, would not tell her. It felt like a muscle he just did not have. He didn't know why, he could not do it or even pray to do it. She believed he was good, serious in his values. Part of him seemed willing to more or less just about lie to someone with that kind of faith and trust and what did that make him? How could such a type of individual even pray? What it really felt like was a taste of the reality of what might be meant by hell. Lane Dean had never believed in hell as a lake of fire or a loving God consigning folks to a burning lake of fire—he knew in his heart this was not true. What he believed in was a living God of compassion and love and the possibility of a personal relationship with Jesus Christ through whom this love was enacted in human time. But sitting here beside this girl as unknown to him now as outer space, waiting for whatever she might say to unfreeze him, now he felt like he could see the edge or outline of what a real vision of hell might be. It was of two great and terrible armies within himself, opposed and facing each other, silent. There would be battle but no victor. Or never a battle—the armies would stay like that, motionless, looking across at each other and seeing therein something so different and alien from themselves that they could not understand, they could not hear each other's speech as even words or read anything from what their faces looked like, frozen like that, opposed and uncomprehending, for all human time. Two hearted, a hypocrite to yourself either way.

When he moved his head, the part of the lake farther out flashed with sun; the water up close wasn't black now and you could see into the shallows and see that all the water was moving but gently, this way and that, and in this same way he besought to return to himself as Sheri moved her leg and started to turn beside him. He could see the man in the suit and gray hat standing motionless now at the lake's rim, holding something under one arm and looking across at the opposite side where little forms on camp chairs sat there in a row in a way that meant they had lines in the water for crappie, which mostly only your blacks from the East Side ever did, and the little white shape at the row's end a Styrofoam creel. In his moment or time at the lake now just to come, Lane Dean first felt he could take this all in whole; everything seemed distinctly lit, for the circle of the pin oak's shade had rotated off all the way and they sat now in sun with their shadow a two-headed thing in the grass to the left before them. He was looking or gazing again at where the downed tree's branches seemed to bend so sharply just under the shallows' surface when he was given then to know that through all this frozen silence he'd despised he had, in truth, been praying all the while, or some little part of his heart he could not know or hear had, for he was answered now with a type of vision, what he later would call within his own mind a vision or *moment of grace.* He was not a hypocrite, just broken and split off like all men. Later on, he believed that what happened was he had a moment of almost seeing them both as Jesus might see them—as blind but groping, wanting to please God despite their inborn fallen nature. For in that same given moment he saw, quick as light, into Sheri's heart, and was made therein to know what would occur here as she finished turning to him and the man in the hat watched the fishing and the downed elm shed cells in the water. This down-to-earth girl who smelled good and wanted to be a nurse would take and hold one of his hands in both of hers to unfreeze him and make him look at her, and she would say that she cannot do it. That she is sorry she did not know this sooner, she hadn't meant to lie, she'd agreed because she wanted to believe she could, but she cannot. That she will carry this and have it, she has to. With her gaze clear and steady. That all night last night she prayed and searched herself and decided this is what love commands of her. That Lane should please please sweetie let her finish. That listen—this is her own decision and obliges him to nothing. That she knows he does not love her, not that way, has known it all this time, and that it's all right. That it is as it is and it's all right. She will carry this, and have it, and love it and make no claim on Lane except his good wishes and respecting what she has to do. That she releases him, all claim, and hopes he finishes up PJC and does so good in his life and has all joy and good things. Her voice will be clear and steady, and she will be lying, for Lane has been given to read her heart. To see her. One of the opposite side's blacks raises his arm in what might be greeting, or waving off a bee. There is a mower cutting grass someplace off behind them. It will be a terrible, make-or-break gamble born out of the desperation in Sheri Fisher's soul, the knowledge that she can neither do this thing today nor carry a child alone and shame her family. Her values block the way either way, Lane can see, and she has no other options or choice, this lie is not a sin. Galatians 4:16, *Have I then become your enemy?* She is gambling that he is good. There on the table, neither frozen nor yet moving, Lane Dean Jr. sees all this, and is moved with pity and with also something more, something without any name he knows, that is given to him to feel in the form of a question that never once in all the long week's thinking and division had even so much as occurred—why is he so sure he doesn't love her? Why is one kind of love any different? What if he has no earthly idea what love is? What would even Jesus do? For it was just now he felt her two small strong soft hands on his, to turn him. What if he is just afraid, if the truth is no more than this, and if what to pray for is not even love but simple courage, to meet both her eyes as she says it and trust his heart?

§7

'New?' There were agents on each side of him and Sylvanshine thought it a bit odd that it was the one with the pink little timorous face of a hamster who turned as if to address him but the one on the other side looking away who had said it. 'New?' They were four rows back from the driver, about whose posture in his seat there was something odd.

'As opposed to what?' Sylvanshine's neck down through his shoulder blade was on fire, and he could feel the start of a jumping muscle in one of his eyelids. Explain the tax treatment of somebody giving appreciated stock to a charity vs. that same person selling the stock and giving the proceeds to the charity. The sides of the rural road looked chewed. The light outside was the sort of light that makes you turn on your headlights but then keeps them from doing any good because technically it's still light out. It was unclear if this was a van or a max. capacity 24 bus. The one who'd asked had a sideburn and the invulnerable smile of someone who's had two airport cocktails and nothing but nuts. The driver of the last van, to which Sylvanshine as a GS-9 had been assigned, rode the wheel as if his shoulders were too heavy for his back. As if clinging to the wheel to support himself. What kind of driver wore a white paper cap? A strap was all that held the vertiginous pile of bags in place. 'I'm the Special Assistant to the new Human Resources Systems Deputy, whose name is Merrill Lehrl, who is coming soon.'

'New to the Post. Freshly assigned I meant.' The man's voice was clear even though he seemed to address the window, which was unclean. Sylvanshine felt hemmed in; the seats were more a cushioned bench and there were no armrests to provide even the illusion or impression of personal space. Plus the van swayed alarmingly on the road, which was either a road or a sort of rural highway, and you could hear the chassis's springs. The rodential man, whose aura was timid but kind, a sad kind man who lived in a cube of fear, had his hat in his lap. Capacity 24 and full. There was the yeasty smell of wet men. The energy level was low; they were all coming back from something that had consumed a lot of energy. Sylvanshine could almost literally see the small pink man drinking Pepto-Bismol straight out of the bottle and going home to a woman who treated him like an uninteresting stranger. The two men either worked together or knew each other very well; they were talking in tandem without even being quite aware of it. An alpha-beta tandem, which meant either Audit or CID. It occurred to Sylvanshine that the window held a faint oblique reflection of him and that the alpha of the two men was amusing himself slightly by addressing Sylvanshine's reflection as if it were him, while the hamster affected the facial expression of address but said nothing. Stock donations are disguised capital-gains treatments—there was also a sound, gassy and tinkly like half a bar of calliope, when the driver downshifted or the boxy van swayed hard on a reverse-S next to a billboard that read DOWNSIZE <u>THIS</u> and then a picture Sylvanshine didn't catch, and while the urbane man was offhandedly introducing them (Sylvanshine didn't catch the names, which he knew would cause trouble because it was insulting to have forgotten people's names, especially if you were attached to an alleged wunderkind in Personnel and Personnel was your business, and he would have to go through all sorts of conversational gymnastics in the future to avoid using their names, and God help him if they were climbers and expected one day to come up and have him make introductions to Merrill, although if they were CID this would be less likely because Investigations and Fraud usually had their own infrastructure and office space, often in a separate building, at least in Rome and Philly, because forensic accountants like to think of themselves more as law enforcement than Service, and didn't as a rule much mix, and in fact the taller man, Bondurant, did identify both himself and Britton as CID GS-9s, which Sylvanshine was too occupied with mortification at missing their names to internalize until much later that evening, when he would recollect the substance of the conversation and experience a moment of relief). The timorous man rarely lied; the more urbane CID agent lied rather a lot, Sylvanshine could feel. The window clicked with a fine rain, the sort of rain that stabs you but doesn't get you wet. Little drops—tiny drops—peened on the glass, in which the less strictly dependable of the two cupped his chin and let out a sigh that was at least partly for effect. Somewhere behind was the sound of a handheld video game, and the small sounds of other agents watching the game's progress over the shoulder of the man who was playing the game, who was silent. The van or bus's wipers made a small shrieking sound on every second pass—it occurred to Sylvanshine that the driver looked as if he was almost resting his chin on top of the wheel because he was leaning way forward to try to get closer to the windshield the way anxious people or people with poor eyesight will do when they're having trouble seeing. The slicker of the two CIDs in the window had an almost kite-shaped face, both square and pointy at the cheekbones and chin; Bondurant could feel the sharp pressure of his chin in his palm and the way the edge of the window's casement dug in a straight line between the bones of his elbow. Everyone but Sylvanshine knew where they'd all been and what they'd been doing in Joliet, but none of them were thinking about it in any kind of informative way because that's not how people think about what they've just done. From outside the vehicle it was clear what it was—both the shape and the sway of it, as well as the fact that the top layer of tan paint had been shoddily applied and in places the headlights of the cars behind it picked up flashes of the bright colors beneath, the ballooned letters and icons on sticks at angles that suggested yumminess in some mysterious way only children get. Inside was the sound of the engine and the fluctuant murmur of small conversations melted by anticipation of the end of something—a conference or retreat, perhaps, or maybe an in-service training; Rome personnel had always been going to Buffalo or Manhattan for In-Service Trainings—and the handheld game, and a slight rustle or twitter in the breathing of the pale pink fellow, who Sylvanshine could feel was looking at the right side of his face, and the sound of Bondurant asking Sylvanshine about the Rome post's CID division, and from one spot ahead and one behind and to the right the tinny whisper of people listening to things on possible headphones—a sure sign of a younger agent, and it occurred to Sylvanshine that the last time he'd seen any sort of black or Latin person had been at the Chicago airport that wasn't O'Hare but he couldn't quite seem to lasso the name and felt odd getting his ticket receipt out of his case—while the smaller appeared to be watching him, waiting for him to do something that would betray some sort of inadequacy or deficit in retention. Describe the advantages of Octal Machine Language over Binary Machine Language in designing a Level-2 program for tracking regularities in the cash-flow sheets of related corporations, name two essential advantages for a franchise to filing Schedule 20-50 returns as a subsidiary of its parent company rather than filing as an autonomous corporate entity—and there it was again, the snatch of forced-air music that Sylvanshine couldn't place but made him want to leave his seat and go chase something on foot in the company of all the children in the neighborhood, all of whom come boiling out of their respective front doors and hotfooting it up the street holding currency aloft, and before he could think, Sylvanshine said, 'Bizarre as this sounds, can either of you every so often hear—?'

'Mister Squishee,' now said the agent to his right in a baritone that didn't go with his body at all. 'Fourteen Mister Squishee iterant-route frozen-confection S corp out of East Peoria trucks seized together with office facilities, receivables, and equity holdings of four out of the seven members of the family who owned what the Region's counsel convinced the Seventh Circuit was de facto a privately held S corp,' Bondurant said. 'Disgruntled employee, falsified depreciation schedules for everything from freezers to trucks like this here—'

'Jeopardy assessment,' Sylvanshine said, mostly to show he knew the lingo. The seat directly ahead of Sylvanshine was unoccupied, yielding a view of the crossed and meaty neck of whoever sat ahead of that, his head covered by a Busch hat pushed back to communicate relaxation and informality.

'This is an ice-cream truck?'

'Wonderful for morale, isn't it? Like the paint job fools anybody that you've got the Post's cream riding back in something that used to sell Nutty Buddies and was driven by a guy in a big lumpy white outfit and rubber face so he looked like a blancmange.'

'Driver used to drive this for Mister Squishee.'

'That's why we're going so slowly.'

'Limit's fifty-five; take a look at what-all's stacked up behind us flashing their brights if you want.'

The smaller, pinker man, Britton, had a round, downy face. He was in his thirties and it wasn't clear if he shaved. The odd thing was that Sylvanshine's neighborhood in King of Prussia had been a planned community, with speed bumps, whose neighborhood association had prohibited solicitation of any kind, especially with a calliope—Sylvanshine had never in his life chased an ice-cream truck.

'Driver still bonded—the seizure just went through last quarter, the DD decides that the margin on keeping the trucks and drivers in service through the length of the bond so outweighs what's realized auctioning them that everybody below G-11 now rides in Mister Squishee trucks,' Bondurant said. His hand moved with his chin when he spoke, which struck Sylvanshine as awkward-looking and false.

'Mrs. Short-Run Thinking.'

'Terrible for morale. Not to mention the PR debacle of kids and their parents seeing trucks they associate with innocence and delicious Caramel Crunch Pushups now seized and as it were shanghaied by the Service. Including surveillance.'

'We conduct surveillance in these trucks, if you can believe it.'

'They practically throw stones.'

'Mister Squishee.'

'Some of the music's worse; some of the trucks there's a snatch of it every time they shift.'

They passed another sign, this out the right side but Sylvanshine could see it: IT'S SPRING, THINK FARM SAFETY.

Bondurant, ass tired from two days in a folding chair, was looking without really looking at a twelve-acre expanse of cornfield—they plowed the cornstalks under just as they were harrowing the fields for seed in April instead of plowing them under in the fall so they'd have all winter to rot and fertilize the ground, which with organophosphate fertilizers and such Bondurant supposed it wasn't worth the two days in the fall to plow them under, plus for some reason Higgs's daddy had told him but he'd forgot they liked to have the ground all clodded up in the winter, it protected something about the ground—and without being aware of it found himself thinking about the nubbly field reminiscent of the armpit of a girl who didn't shave her armpits very often, and without being conscious of any of the connections between the field that now passed and was replaced in the window by a stand of wild oak and the armpit and the girl was thinking in a misdirected way of Cheryl Ann Higgs, now Cheryl Ann Standish and now a data-entry girl at American Twine and a divorced mother of two in a double-wide trailer her ex had apparently been arrested for trying to burn up shortly after Bondurant got GS-9'd over to CID, who'd been his date at Peoria Central Catholic prom in '71 when they'd both made Prom Court and Bondurant was second-runner-up to king and wore a powder-blue tux and rented shoes too skinny for his feet and she didn't fuck him that night even at post-Prom when all the other fellows took turns getting fucked by their dates in the black and gold Chrysler New Yorker they'd gone in and rented for the night from the shortstop's daddy at Hertz and got stains in so the shortstop had to spend the summer out at the airport at the Hertz desk working off the detailing of the New Yorker. Danny something, his daddy died not much later, but he couldn't play Legion ball that summer because of it and couldn't stay sharp and barely made the team in college ball at NIU and lost his scholarship and God knows what-all became of him but none of the stains were Bondurant and Cheryl Ann Higgs's despite all his entreaties. He hadn't used the bottle of schnapps because if he'd brought her home drunk her daddy'd have either killed him or grounded her.

Bondurant's life's greatest moment so far was on 5-18-73 as a sophomore and the pinch-hit triple in the last home game at Bradley that drove in Oznowiez the future triple-A catcher to beat SIU-Edwardsville and get Bradley into the Missouri Valley playoffs, which they lost but still hardly a day at the desk with his feet up and clipboards stacked in his lap goes by that he doesn't see the balloon of the SIU slider hanging and feel the vibrationless thip of the meat of the bat connecting and hear the two-bell clatter of the aluminum bat fall as he sees the ball kind of pinball off the l.f. fence post by the foul line and twang off the other fence of the foul line and see and he could swear hear both fences jingle from the force of the ball, which he'd hit so hard he'll feel it forever but can't summon anywhere near that kind of recall of what Cheryl Ann Higgs felt like when he slipped inside her on a blanket by the pond out back past the stand past the edge of the pasture of the small dairy spread Mr. Higgs and one of his uncountable brothers operated, though he does well remember what each of them had been wearing and the smell of the pond's new algae near the runoff pipe whose gurgle was nearly brooklike, and the look on Cheryl Ann Higgs's face as her posture and supine position became acquiescent and Bondurant had known he was home free as they say but had avoided her eyes because the expression in Cheryl Ann's eyes, which without ever once again thinking about it Tom Bondurant has never forgotten, was one of blank terminal sadness, not so much that of a pheasant in a dog's jaws as of a person who's about to transfer something he knows in advance he can never get sufficient return on. The next year had seen them drop into the crazy-obsessive love spiral in which they'd break up and then not be able to stay away from each other, until one time she was able to stay away, and that was all she wrote.

The small light-pink CID agent Britton had, without any sort of throat-clearing or segue, asked Sylvanshine what he was thinking, which seemed to Sylvanshine grotesquely and almost obscenely inappropriate and invasive, rather like asking what your wife looked like naked or what your private restroom functions smelled like, but of course it would be impossible to say any of this aloud, particularly for someone whose job here involved cultivating good relations and uncluttered lines of communication for Merrill Lehrl to exploit when he arrived—to mediate for Merrill Lehrl and to at once gather information on as many aspects and issues involved in the examination of returns as possible, since there were some difficult, delicate decisions to make, decisions whose import extended far beyond this provincial post and any way it went it was going to be painful. Sylvanshine, turning slightly but not all the way (a flare of orange in his left shoulder blade) to meet at least Gary Britton's left eye, realized that he had very little emotional or ethical 'read' on Britton or anyone on the bus but Bondurant, who was having some kind of wistful memory and was cultivating the wistfulness, reclining a bit in it as one would in a warm bath. When something large and oncoming passed, the windshield's big rectangle was for a moment incandesced and opaque with water, which the wipers heaved mightily to displace. Britton's gaze—seemed to Sylvanshine more like looking *at* his right eye than *into* it. (At this time it moved through Thomas Bondurant's mind, which lended to be tornadic, as he looked out the window but more back and in at his own memory, that one could look out a window, look in a window as there was the gold ponytail and a flash of creamy shoulder *in* the window, through a window [close to 'out'], or even *at* a window, as in examining the pane's clarity and whether it was clean.) The gaze nevertheless seemed to be one of expectancy, and Sylvanshine felt again past the emptiness of his stomach and the pinched nerve in his clavicle how opaque the bus's overall mood was and different from the horror-fraught tension of the Philadelphia 0104's hundred and seventy agents or the manic torpor of tiny 408's dozen in Rome. His own mood, the complex hybrid of destination-fatigue and anticipatory fear one feels at the end not of a journey but a move, did not in any way complement the mood of the former Squishee truck nor of the urbane wistful older agent to his left nor of the human blank-spot who'd asked an invasive question whose honest answer would entail acknowledging the invasion, putting Sylvanshine in a personnel-relations bind before he'd even arrived at the Post, which seemed for a moment terribly unfair and flushed Sylvanshine with self-pity, a feeling not as dark as the wing of despair but tinged carmine with a resentment that was both better and worse than ordinary anger because it had no specific object. There seemed no one in particular to blame; something in Gary or Gerry Britton's aspect made it obvious that his question was some inevitable extension of his character and that he was no more to be blamed for it than an ant was to be blamed for crawling on your potato salad at a picnic—creatures just did what they did.

§8

Under the sign erected every May above the outer highway reading IT'S SPRING, THINK FARM SAFETY and through the north ingress with its own defaced name and signs addressed to soliciting and speed and universal glyph for children at play and down the blacktop's gauntlet of double-wide showpieces past the rottweiler humping nothing in crazed spasms at chain's end and the sound of frying through the kitchenette window of the trailer at the hairpin right and then hard left along the length of a speed bump into the dense copse as yet uncleared for new single-wides and the sound of dry things snapping and stridulation of bugs in the duff of the copse and the two bottles and bright plastic packet impaled on the mulberry twig, seeing through shifting parallax of saplings' branches sections then of trailers along the north park's anfractuous roads and lanes skirting the corrugate trailer where it was said the man left his family and returned sometime later with a gun and killed them all as they watched *Dragnet* and the torn abandoned sixteen-wide half overgrown by the edge of the copse where boys and their girls made strange agnate forms on pallets and left bright torn packs until a mishap with a stove blew the gas lead and ruptured the trailer's south wall in a great labial tear that exposes the trailer's gutted insides to view from the edge of the copse and the plurality of eyes as the needles and stems of a long winter noisomely crunch beneath a plurality of shoes where the copse leaves off at a tangent past the end of the undeveloped cul-de-sac where they come now at dusk to watch the parked car heave on its springs. The windows steamed nearly opaque and so alive in the chassis that it seems to move without running, the boat-sized car, squeak of struts and absorbers and a jiggle just short of true rhythm. The birds at dusk and the smell of snapped pine and a younger one's cinnamon gum. The shimmying motions resemble those of a car traveling at high speeds along a bad road, making the Buick's static aspect dreamy and freighted with something like romance or death in the gaze of the girls who squat at the copse's risen edge, appearing dyadic and eyes half again as wide and solemn, watching for the sometime passage of a limb's pale shape past a window (once a bare foot flat against it and itself atremble), moving incrementally forward and down each night in the week before true spring, soundlessly daring one another to go get up close to the heaving car and see in, which the only one who finally does so then sees naught but her own wide eyes reflected as from inside the glass comes a cry she knows too well, which wakes her again each time across the trailer's cardboard wall.

There were fires in the gypsum hills to the north, the smoke of which hung and stank of salt; then the pewter earrings vanished without complaint or even mention. Then a whole night's absence, two. The child as mother to the woman. These were auguries and signs: Toni Ware and her mother abroad again in endless night. Routes on maps that yield no sensible shape or figure when traced.

At night from the trailer's park the hills possessed of a dirty orange glow and the sounds of living trees exploding in the fires' heat did carry, and the noise of planes plowing the undulant air above and dropping thick tongues of talc. Some nights it rained fine ash which upon contacting turned to soot and kept all souls indoors such that throughout the park every trailer's window possessed of the underwater glow of televisions and when many were identically tuned the sounds of the programs came clear to the girl through the ash as if their own television were still with them. It had vanished without comment prior to their last move. That last time's sign.

The park's boys wore wide rumpled hats and cravats of thong and some displayed turquoise about their person, and of these one helped her empty the trailer's sanitary tank and then pressed her to fellate him in recompense, whereupon she promised that anything emerging from his trousers would not return there. No boy near her size had successfully pressed her since Houston and the two who put something in her pop that made them turn sideways in the air and she could not then fight and lay watching the sky while they did their distant business.

At sunset then the north and west were the same color. On clear nights she could read by the night sky's emberlight seated on the plastic box that served as stoop. The screen door had no screen but was still a screen door, which fact she thought upon. She could fingerpaint in the soot on the kitchenette's rangetop. In incendiary orange to the deepening twilight in the smell of creosote burning in the sharp hills upwind.

Her inner life rich and multivalent. In fantasies of romance it was she who fought and overcame thereon to rescue some object or figure that never in the reverie resolved or took to itself any shape or name.

After Houston her favorite doll had been the mere head of a doll, its hair prolixly done and the head's hole threaded to meet a neck's own thread; she had been eight when the body was lost and it lay now forever supine and unknowing in weeds while its head lived on.

The mother's relational skills were indifferent and did not include truthful or consistent speech. The daughter had learned to trust actions and to read sign in details of which the run of children are innocent. The battered road atlas had then appeared and lay athwart the counter's medial crack opened to the mother's home state over whose representation of her place of origin lay a spore of dried mucus spindled through with a red thread of blood. The atlas stayed open that way nigh on one week unreferred to; they ate around it. It gathered wind-drift ash through the torn screen. Ants vexed all the park's trailers, there being something in the fire's ash they craved. Their point of formication the high place where the kitchenette's woodgrain paneling had detached in prior heat and bowed outward and from which two vascular parallel columns of black ants descended. Standing eating out of cans at the anodized sink. Two flashlights and a drawer with different bits of candles which the mother eschewed for her cigarettes were her light unto the world. A little box of borax in each of the kitchenette's corners. The water in buckets from the coinwash tap, the trailer a standalone with sides' wires hanging and its owner's whereabouts unreckoned by the park's elders, whose lawn chairs sat unmolested by ash in the smoke tree's central shade. One of these, Mother Tia, told fortunes, leathery and tremorous and her face like a shucked pecan fully cowled in black and two isolate teeth like a spare at the Show Me Lanes, and owned her own cards and tray on which what ash collected showed white, calling her *chulla* and charging her no tariff on terms of the Evil Eye she claimed to fear when the girl looked at her through the screen's hole with the telescope of a rolled magazine. Two ribby and yellow-eyed dogs lay throbbing in the smoke tree's shade and rose only sometimes to bay at the planes as they harried the fires.

The sun overhead like a peephole into hell's own self-consuming heart.

Yet one more sign being when Mother Tia refused then to augur and doing so in terms of pleading for clemency instead of bare refusal to the reedy laughter of the shade's other elders and widows; no one understood why she feared the girl and she would not say, lower lip caught behind one tooth as she traced the special letter over and over on nothing in the air before her. Whom she would miss, and whose memory in trust therefore the doll's head also would carry.

The mother's relational skills being indifferent to this degree since the period of clinical confinement in University City MO wherein the mother had been denied visits for eighteen business days and the girl had evaded Family Services during this period and slept in an abandoned Dodge vehicle whose doors could be secured with coat hangers twisted just so.

The girl looked often at the open atlas and the city thereon marked with a sneeze. She had herself been born there, just outside, in the town that bore her own name. Her second experience of the kind her books made seem sweet through indifferent speech had occurred in the abandoned car in University City MO at the hands of a man who knew how to dislodge one coat hanger with the straightened hook of another and told her face beneath his fingerless mitten there were two different ways this right here could go.

The longest time she had ever subsisted wholly on shoplifted food was eight days. Not more than a competent shoplifter. Their time at Moab UT an associate once said that her pockets had no imagination and was soon thereafter pinched and made to spear litter by the highway as she and the mother had passed in the converted camper driven by 'Kick,' the seller of pyrite and self-made arrowheads around whom the mother said not ever one word but sat before the radio painting each nail a different color and who had once punched her stomach so hard she saw colors and smelled up close the carpet's grit base and could hear what her mother then did to distract 'Kick' from further attentions to this girl with the mouth on her. This being also how she learned to cut a brake line so the failure would be delayed until such time as the depth of the cut determined.

At night on the pallet in the ruddled glow she dreamt also of a bench by a pond and the somnolent mutter of ducks while the girl held the string of something that floated above with a painted face, a kite or balloon. Of another girl she would never see or know of.

Once on the nation's interstate highway system the mother had spoken of a headless doll she herself had kept and clung to through the hell on earth years of her Peoria girlhood and her own mother's *nervous illness* (her profile bunched up as she pronounced it) during which the mother's mother had refused to let her outside the house over which she had engaged itinerant men to nail found and abandoned hubcaps to every inch of the exterior in order to deflect the transmissions of one Jack Benny, a rich man whom the grandmother had come to believe was insane and sought *global thought control* by radio wave of a special pitch and hue. ('"Nobody that mean's going to let the world go"' was an indirect quotation or hearsay when driving, which the mother could do while simultaneously smoking and using an emery board.) The girl made it her business to read signs and know the facts of her own history past and present. To beat broken glass into powder requires an hour with a portion of brick on a durable surface. She had shoplifted ground chuck and buns and kneaded powdered glass into the meat and cooked it on a windowscreen brazier at the rear of the abandoned Dodge and had left such painstaking meals of sandwich on the front seat for days running before the man who had pressed her used his coat hanger tool to jimmy the vehicle and steal them whereupon he returned no more; the mother then released into the girl's care soon. Imbrication by disk is impossible, but the grandmother's specifications were that each hubcap touch those on every possible side. Thus the electrification of one became the charge of all, to counter the waves' bombardment. The creation of a lethal field which jammed radios all down the block. Twice cited for diverting the home's amperage, the old woman had found a generator someplace that would run if noisily on kerosene and bounced and shook beside the bomb-shaped propane tank outside the kitchen. The young mother was sometimes permitted outside to bury the sparrows that alit on the home and sent up their souls in a single flash and bird-shaped ball of smoke.

The girl read stories about horses, bios, science, psychiatry, and *Popular Mechanics* when obtainable. She read history in a determined way. She read *My Struggle* and could not understand all the fuss. She read Wells, Steinbeck, Keene, Laura Wilder (twice), and Lovecraft. She read halves of many torn and castoff things. She read a coverless *Red Badge* and knew by sheer feel that its author had never seen war nor knew that past some extremity one floated just above the fear and could blinklessly watch it while doing what had to be done or allowed to stay alive.

The trailer park's boy who had pressed her there in the hanging smell of their own sewage now assembled his friends outside the trailer at night there to lurk and make inhuman sounds in the ashfall as the daughter's daughter drew circles within circles about her own given name on the map and the arteries leading thereto. The gypsum fires and the park's lit sign were the poles of the desert night. The boys burped and howled at the moon and the howls were nothing like the real thing and their laughter was strained and words indifferent to the love they said swelled them and would visit upon her past counting.

In these the mother's absences with men the girl sent for catalogues and Free Offers which daily did arrive by mail with samples of products that people with homes would buy to enjoy at their leisure like the girl, who considered herself home tutored and did not ride the bus with the park's children. These all possessed the stunned smeared look of those who are poor in one place; the trailers, sign, and passing trucks were the furniture of their world, which orbited but did not turn. The girl often imagined them in a rearview, receding, both arms raised in farewell.

Asbestos cloth cut carefully into strips one of which placed in the pay dryer when the mother of the would-be assailant had deposited her load and returned to the Circle K for more beer caused neither the boy nor mother to be seen anymore outside their double-wide, which rested on blocks. The boys' serenades ceased as well.

A soup can of sewage or roadkill carcass when placed beneath the blocks or plasticized lattice of a store-bought porch attachment would fill and afflict that trailer with a plague's worth of soft-bodied flies. A shade tree could be killed by driving a short length of copper tubing into its base a handsbreadth from ground; the leaves would commence to embrown straightaway. The trick with a brake or fuel line was to use strippers to whet it to almost nothing instead of cutting it clean through. It took a certain feel. Half an ounce of packets' aggregate sugar in the gas tank disabled all vehicles but required no art. Likewise a penny in the fuse box or red dye in a trailer's water tank accessible through the sanitation panel on all but late-year models of which the Vista Verde park had none.

Begat in one car and born in another. Creeping up in dreams to see her own conceiving.

The desert possessed of no echo and in this was like the sea from which it came. Sometimes at night the sounds of the fire carried, or the circling planes, or those of long-haul trucks on 54 for Santa Fe whose tires' plaint had the quality of distant surf's lalation; she lay listening on the pallet and imagined not the sea or the moving trucks themselves but whatever she right then chose. Unlike the mother or bodiless doll, she was free inside her head. An unbound genius, larger than any sun.

The girl read a biography of Hetty Green, the matricide and accused forger who had dominated the Stock Market while saving scraps of soap in a dented tin box she carried on her person, and who feared no living soul. She read *Macbeth* as a color comic with dialogue in boxes.

The performer Jack Benny had cupped his own face with a hand in a manner the mother, when lucid, had told her she'd seen as tender and pined for, dreamt of, inside the home and its carapace of electric shields while her own mother wrote letters to the FBI in code.

Near sunrise the red plains to the east undimmed and the terrible imperious heat of the day bestirred in its underground den; the girl placed the doll's head on the sill to watch the red eye open and small rocks and bits of litter cast shadows as long as a man.

Never once in five states worn a dress or leather shoes.

At dawn of the fires' eighth day her mother appeared in a vehicle made large by its corrugated shell behind whose wheel sat an unknown male. The side of the shell said LEER.

Thought blocking, overinclusion. Vagueness, overspeculation, woolly thinking, confabulation, word salad, stonewalling, aphasia. Delusions of persecution. Catatonic immobility, automatic obedience, affective flattening, dilute I/Thou, disordered cognition, loosened or obscure associations. Depersonalization. Delusions of centrality or grandeur. Compulsivity, ritualism. Hysterical blindness. Promiscuity. Solipsismus or ecstatic states (rare).

> This Girl's D./P.O.B.: 11-4-60, Anthony IL.
>
> Girl's Mother's D./P.O.B.: 4-8-43, Peoria IL.
>
> Most Recent Address: 17 Dosewallips Unit E, Vista Verde Estates Mobile Home Park, Organ NM 88052.
>
> Girl's H.W.E./H.: 5' 3", 95 lbs., Brown/Brown.
>
> Mother's Stated Occupations, 1966–1972 (from IRS Form 669-D [Certificate of Subordination of Federal Tax

Lien, District 063(a)], 1972): Cafeteria Dish and Food Area Cleaning Assistant, Rayburn-Thrapp Agronomics, Anthony IL; Skilled Operator of Silkscreen Press Until Injury to Wrist, All City Uniform Company, Alton IL; Cashier, Convenient Food Mart Corporation, Norman OK and Jacinto City TX; Server, Stuckey's Restaurants Corp., Limon CO; Assistant Adhesive Product Mixing Scheduling Clerk, National Starch and Chemical Company, University City MO; Hostess and Beverage Server, Double Deuce Live Stage Night Club, Lordsburg NM; Contract Vendor, Cavalry Temporary Services, Moab UT; Canine Confinement Area Organization and Cleaning, Best Friends Kennel and Groom, Green Valley AZ; Ticket Agent and Substitute Night Manager, Riské's Live XX Adult Entertainment, Las Cruces NM.

They drove then once more at night. Below a moon that rose round before them. What was termed the truck's backseat was a narrow shelf on which the girl could sleep if she arranged her legs in the gap behind the real seats whose headrests possessed the dull shine of unwashed hair. The clutter and yeast smell bespoke a truck that was or had been lived in; the truck and its man smelled the same. The girl in cotton bodice and her jeans gone fugitive at the knees. The mother's conception of men was that she used them as a sorceress will dumb animals, as sign and object of her unnatural powers. Her spoken word aloud for these at which the girl gave no reproof, *familiar.* Swart and sideburned men who sucked wooden matches and crushed cans with their hands. Whose hats' brims had sweatlines like the rings of trees. Whose eyes crawled over you in the rearview. Men inconceivable as ever themselves being children or looking up naked at someone they trust, with a toy. To whom the mother talked like babies and let them treat her like a headless doll, *manhandle.*

At an Amarillo motel the girl had her own locked room out of earshot. The hangers were affixed to the closet's rod. The doll's head wore lipstick of pink crayon and looked at TV. The girl often wished she had a cat or some small pet to feed and reassure as she stroked its head. The mother feared winged insects and carried cans of spray.

Mace on a chain and melted cosmetics and her faux-leather snap case for cigarettes and lighter at once in a handbag of imbricate red sequins the girl had produced for Christmas in Green Valley with only a very small tear near the base where the electronic tag had been forced with a file and then used to carry out the same bodice the girl now wore, on which stitched pink hearts formed a fenceline at breast level.

The truck smelled also of spoilt provision and had a window with vanished crank he rolled up and down with pliers. A card taped to one visor proclaimed that hairdressers teased it till it did stand up. His teeth were missing at one side; the glovebox was locked. The mother at thirty with face commencing to display the faint seams of the plan for the second face life had in store for her and which she feared would be her own mother's and in University City's confined time sat with knees bunched up rocking and scratched at herself essaying to ruin the face's plan. The sepia photo of the mother's mother at the girl's own age in a pinafore on horsehair seat rolled into the doll's head and carried with soapscraps and three library cards in her given name. Her diary in the round case's second lining. And the lone photo of her mother as a child outdoors in winter dazzle in so many coats and hats that she and the propane tank might be kin. The electrified house out of view and the circle of snowmelt around its base and the mother behind the little mother holding her upright; the child had had croup and such a fever she was feared not to live and her mother had realized she had no pictures of her baby to keep if she died and had bundled her up and sent her out into the snow to wait while she begged a snapshot with a neighbor's Land Camera so her baby might not be forgotten when she died. The photo distorted from long folding and no footprints in view anywhere in the picture's snow that the girl could see, the child's mouth wide open and eyes looking up at the man with the camera in trust that this made sense, this was how right life occurred. The girl's plans for the grandmother, much refined with age and accrued art, occupied much of the latest diary's first third.

Her mother and not the male was at the wheel when she woke to the clatter of gravel in Kansas. A truck stop receded as something upright ran in the road behind them and waved its hat. She asked where they were but did not ask after the man who through three states had driven with the same offending hand on the mother's thigh that had touched her, a hand studied through the seats' gap by the doll's head held just so and its detachment and airborne flight seen in the same dream the lurch and sounds first seemed part of. The daughter thirteen now and starting to look it. Her mother's eyes were distant and low-lidded in the company of men; now in Kansas she made faces at the rearview and chewed gum. 'Ride up front up out of there up here why don't you.' The gum smelt cinnamon and its folded foil could make a glovebox pick by wrapping round to smooth a file's emery at the point.

Outside a Portales rest stop, under a sun of beaten gold, the girl supine and half asleep in a porous nap on the little back shelf had suffered the man to hoist himself about behind the truck's wheel and form his hand into an unsensual claw and send it out over the seatback to squeeze her personal titty, to throttle the titty, eyes pale and unprurient, she playing dead and staring unblinking past him, the man's breathing audible and khaki cap pungent, manhandling the titty with what seemed an absent dispassion, leaving off only at the high heels' sound in the lot outside. Still a stark advance over the previous year's Cesar, who worked at painting highway signs and had green grains forever in the pores of his face and hands and required both mother and girl to keep the washroom door open no matter what their business inside, himself then in turn improved over Houston's district of warehouses and gutted lofts whereat had fallen in with them for two months 'Murray Blade,' the semiprofessional welder whose knife in its forearm's spring clip covered a tattoo of just that knife between two ownerless blue breasts the squeeze of a fist made swell at the sides which amused him. Men with leather vests and tempers who were tender when drunk in ways that made your back's skin pebble up.

The 54 highway east was not federal and the winds of oncoming rigs struck the truck and its shell and caused yaw the mother steered against. All windows down against the man's stored smell. An unmentionable thing in the glovebox the mother said to shut she couldn't look. The card with its entendre made French curls in their backwash and disappeared against the past road's shimmer.

West of Pratt KS they purchased and ate Convenient Mart burritos heated in the device provided for that purpose. A great huge unfinishable Slushee.

Behind her carapace of disks and foil the mother's mother held when madman Jack Benny or his spiral-eyed slaves came for them the best defense at hand was to play dead, to lie with blank eyes open and not blink or breathe while the men holstered their ray guns and walked about the house and looked at them, shrugging and telling one another they were too late because look here the woman and her nubile daughter were already deceased and best left be. Forced to practice together in the twin beds with open bottles of pills on the table betwixt and hands composed on their chests and eyes wide and breathing in such a slight way that the chest never rose. The older woman could hold her open eyes unblinking a very long time; the mother as child could not and they soon enough closed of their own, for a living child is no doll and does need to blink and breathe. The older woman said one could self-lubricate at will with the proper application of discipline and time. She said her decade on a carnival necklace and had a small nickel lock on the mailbox. Windows covered with foil in the crescents between the caps' black circles. The mother carried drops and always claimed her eyes were dry.

Riding up front was good. She did not ask about the truck's man. It was his truck they were in but he was not in the truck; it was hard to locate something to complain about in this. The mother's relatings were least indifferent when the two faced the same; she made small jokes and sang and sent small looks the daughter's way. All the world beyond the reach of the headlamps' beams was much obscured. Hers was her grandmother's maiden name, Ware. She could put her soles against the truck's black dash and look out between her knees, the whole of the headlights' tongue of road between them. The broken centerline shot Morse at them and the bone-white moon was round and clouds moved across it and took shape as they did so. First fingers then whole hands and trees of lightning fluttered on the west horizon; nothing came behind them. She kept looking for following lights or signs. The mother's lipstick was too bright for the shape of her mouth. The girl did not ask. The odds were high. The man was either the species of man who would file a report or else would essay to follow like a second 'Kick' and find them for leaving him waving his hat in the road. If she asked, the mother's face would go saggy as she thought of what to say when the truth was she hadn't thought at all. The girl's blessing and lot to know their two minds both as one, to hold the wheel as Murine was again applied.

They had a sit-down breakfast in Plepler MO in a rain that foamed the gutters and beat against the café's glass. The waitress in nurse-white had a craggy face and called them both honey and wore a button which said I have got but one nerve left and you are upon that nerve and flirted with the workingmen whose names she knew while steam came out of the kitchen over the counter above which she clipped sheets from her pad, and the girl used their toothbrush in a restroom whose lock had no hasp. The front door's hung bell sounded on use to signal custom. The mother wanted biscuits and hashbrowns and mush with syrup and they ordered and the mother sought a dry match and soon the girl heard her laughing at something the men at the counter said. Rain rolled through the street and cars passed slowly and their truck with its shell faced the table and still had its parking lights on, which she saw, and saw also within her mind the truck's legal owner still there in the road outside Kismet holding his hands extended into claws at the space where the truck had receded from view while the mother beat the wheel and blew hair from her eyes. The girl dragged toast through her yolk. Of the two men who entered and filled the next booth one had similar whiskers and eyes beneath a red cap gone black with rain. The waitress with her little stub pencil and pad said unto these:

'What are you settin' in a dirty booth for?'

'So as I can be closer to you, darling.'

'Why you could have set over right there and been closer yet.'

'Shoot.'

§9

AUTHOR'S FOREWORD

Author here. Meaning the real author, the living human holding the pencil, not some abstract narrative persona. Granted, there sometimes is such a persona in *The Pale King*, but that's mainly a pro forma statutory construct, an entity that exists just for legal and commercial purposes, rather like a corporation; it has no direct, provable connection to me as a person. But this right here is me as a real person, David Wallace, age forty, SS no. 975-04-2012,[1] addressing you

1 Little-known fact: The only US citizens anywhere whose Social Security numbers start with the numeral 9 are those who are, or at some time were, contract employees of the Internal Revenue Service. Through its special relationship with the Social Security Administration, the IRS issues you a new SS number on the day your contract starts. It's like you're born again, ID-wise, when you enter the Service. Very few ordinary citizens know about this. There's no reason they should. But consider your own Social Security number, or those of the people close enough to you that you're entrusted with their SS. There's only one digit that these SS numbers never start with. That number is 9. 9's reserved for the Service. And if you're issued one, it stays with you for the rest of your life, even if you happen to have left the IRS long ago. It sort of marks you, numerically. Every April—and quarterly, of course, for those who are self-employed and pay quarterly ESTs—those tax returns and ESTs whose filers' SS numbers start with 9 are automatically pulled and routed through a special processing and exam program in the Martinsburg Computer Center. Your status in the system is forever altered. The Service knows its own, always.

from my Form 8829–deductible home office at 725 Indian Hill Blvd., Claremont 91711 CA, on this fifth day of spring, 2005, to inform you of the following:

All of this is true. This book is really true.

I obviously need to explain. First, please flip back and look at the book's legal disclaimer, which is on the copyright page, verso side, four leaves in from the rather unfortunate and misleading front cover. The disclaimer is the unindented chunk that starts: 'The characters and events in this book are fictitious.' I'm aware that ordinary citizens almost never read disclaimers like this, the same way we don't bother to look at copyright claims or Library of Congress specs or any of the dull pro forma boilerplate on sales contracts and ads that everyone knows is there just for legal reasons. But now I need you to read it, the disclaimer, and to understand that its initial 'The characters and events in this book...' includes this very Author's Foreword. In other words, this Foreword is defined by the disclaimer as itself fictional, meaning that it lies within the area of special legal protection established by that disclaimer. I need this legal protection in order to inform you that what follows[2] is, in reality, not fiction at all, but substantially true and accurate. That *The Pale King* is, in point of fact, more like a memoir than any kind of made-up story.

This might appear to set up an irksome paradox. The book's legal disclaimer defines everything that follows it as fiction, including this Foreword, but now here in this Foreword I'm saying that the whole thing is really nonfiction; so if you believe one you can't believe the other, & c., & c. Please know that I find these sorts of cute, self-referential paradoxes irksome, too—at least now that I'm over thirty I do—and that the very last thing this book is is some kind of clever metafictional titty-pincher. That's why I'm making it a point to violate protocol and address you here directly, as my real self; that's why all the specific identifying data about me as a real person got laid out at the start of this Foreword. So that I could inform you of the truth:

2 This is a term of art; what I really mean is that everything that surrounds this Foreword is essentially true. The Foreword's having now been moved seventy-nine pages into the text is due to yet another spasm of last-minute caution on the part of the publisher, re which please see just below.

The only bona fide 'fiction' here is the copyright page's disclaimer—which, again, is a legal device: The disclaimer's whole and only purpose is to protect me, the book's publisher, and the publisher's assigned distributors from legal liability. The reason why such protections are especially required here—why, in fact, the publisher[3]

3 At the advice of its corporate counsel, the publishing company has declined to be identified by name in this Author's Foreword, despite the fact that anyone who looks at the book's spine or title page will know immediately who the company is. Meaning it's an irrational constraint; but so be it. As my own counsel has observed, corporate attorneys are not paid to be totally rational, but they are paid to be totally cautious. And it is not hard to see why a registered US corporation like this book's publisher is going to be cautious about even the possibility of appearing to thumb its nose at the Internal Revenue Service or (this from some of the corporate counsel's hysterical early memos) to be 'abetting' an author's violation of the Nondisclosure Covenant that all Treasury employees are required to sign. Nevertheless—as my lawyer and I had to point out to them about 105 times before the company's counsel seemed to get it—the version of the Nondisclosure Covenant that's binding on *all* Treasury employees, not just on agents of the Bureau of Alcohol, Tobacco and Firearms and of the Secret Service, as formerly, was instituted in 1987, which happens to be the year that computers and a high-powered statistical formula known as the ANADA (for 'Audit–No Audit Discriminant Algorithm') were first used in the examination of nearly all individual US tax returns. I know that's a pretty involved and confusing data-dump to inflict on you in a mere Foreword, but the crux here is that it is the ANADA,[a] and the constituents of its formula for determining which tax returns are most apt to yield additional revenue under audit, that the Service is concerned to protect, and that that was why the Nondisclosure Covenant was suddenly extended to IRS employees in 1987. But I had already left the Service in 1987. The worst of a certain personal unpleasantness had blown over, and I'd been accepted for transfer at another college, and by autumn of 1986 I was back on the East Coast and again up and running in the private sector, albeit of course still with my new SS number. My entire IRS career lasted from May 1985 through June 1986. Hence my exemption from the Covenant. Not to mention that I was hardly in a position to know anything compromising or specific about the ANADA. My Service post was totally low-level and regional. For the bulk of my time, I was a rote examiner, a.k.a. a 'wiggler' in the Service nomenclature. My contracted civil service rank was a GS-9, which at that time was the lowest full-time grade; there were secretaries and custodians who outranked me. And I was posted to Peoria IL, which is about as far from Triple-Six and the Martinsburg Center as anyone could imagine. Admittedly, at the same time—and this is what especially concerned the publishing company's counsel—Peoria was a REC, one of seven hubs of the IRS's Examination Division, which was precisely the division that got eliminated or, more accurately (though this is arguable), transferred from the Compliance Branch to the newly expanded Technical Branch, by the advent of the ANADA and a digital Fornix network. This is

(a) By the way, no kidding about the formula's name. Were the Technical Branch statisticians aware that they were giving the algorithm such a heavy, almost thanatoid-sounding acronym? It's actually doubtful. As all too many Americans now know, computerized programs are totally, maddeningly literal and nonconnotative; and so were the people in Technical Branch.

has insisted upon them as a precondition for acceptance of the manuscript and payment of the advance—is the same reason the disclaimer is, when you come right down to it, a lie.[4]

Here is the real truth: What follows is substantially true and accurate. At least, it's a mainly true and accurate partial record of what I saw and heard and did, of whom I knew and worked alongside and under, and of what-all eventuated at IRS Post 047, the Midwest Regional Examination Center, Peoria IL, in 1985–86. Much of the book is actually based on several different notebooks and journals I

rather more esoteric, contextless Service information than I'd anticipated having to ask you to swallow right at the beginning, and I can assure you that all this gets explained and/or unfolded in much more graceful, dramatically apposite terms in the memoir itself, once it gets under way. For now, just so you're not totally flummoxed and bored, suffice it to say that Examinations is the IRS division tasked with combing and culling various kinds of tax returns and classifying some as '20s,' which is Service shorthand for tax returns that are to be forwarded to the relevant District office for audit. Audits themselves are conducted by revenue agents, who are usually GS-9s or -11s, and employed by the Audit Division. It's hard to put all this very smoothly or gracefully—and please know that none of this abstract information is all that vital to the mission of this Foreword. So feel free to skip or skim the following if you wish. And don't think the whole book will be like this, because it won't be. If you're burningly interested, though, each tax return pulled, for whatever reason(s) (some of which were smart and discerning and others, frankly, wacko and occult, depending on the wiggler), by a line examiner and forwarded for audit is supposed to be accompanied by an IRS Series 20 Internal Memo, which is where the term '20' comes from. Like most insular and (let's be frank) despised government agencies, the Service is rife with special jargon and code that seems overwhelming at first but then gets internalized so quickly and used so often that it becomes almost habitual. I still, sometimes, dream in Servicespeak. To return to the point, though, Examinations and Audits were two of the main divisions of the IRS's Compliance Branch, and the publishing company's house counsel's concern was that the IRS's own counsel could, if they were sufficiently aggrieved and wanted to make trouble over the Nondisclosure Covenant thing, argue that I and several of the Post 047 REC coworkers and administrators who feature in this story should be grandfathered in under the constraints of the Nondisclosure Covenant, because we were not only employed by the Compliance Branch but posted at the REC that ended up figuring so prominently in the run-up to what came to be known variously as 'the New IRS,' 'the Spackman Initiative,' or just 'the Initiative,' which was ostensibly created by the Tax Reform Act of 1986 but was actually the result of a long, very complicated bureaucratic catfight between the Compliance Branch and the Technical Branch over Examinations and the Exam function in IRS operations. End of data-dump. If you're still reading, I hope enough of all that made sense for you to at least understand why the issue of whether or not I explicitly say the name of the publishing company was not one that I chose to spend a lot of time and editorial goodwill arguing about. You sort of have to pick your battles, as far as nonfiction goes.

4 (excepting the 'All rights reserved' part, of course)

kept during my thirteen months as a rote examiner at the Midwest REC. ('Based' means more or less lifted right out of, for reasons that will doubtless become clear.) *The Pale King* is, in other words, a kind of vocational memoir. It is also supposed to function as a portrait of a bureaucracy—arguably the most important federal bureaucracy in American life—at a time of enormous internal struggle and soul-searching, the birth pains of what's come to be known among tax professionals as the New IRS.

In the interests of full disclosure, though, I should be explicit and say that the modifier in 'substantially true and accurate' refers not just to the inevitable subjectivity and bias of any memoir. The truth is that there are, in this nonfiction account, some slight changes and strategic rearrangements, most of these evolving through successive drafts in response to feedback from the book's editor, who was sometimes put in a very delicate position with respect to balancing literary and journalistic priorities, on the one hand, against legal and corporate concerns on the other. That's probably all I should say on that score. There is, of course, a whole tortuous backstory here involving the legal vetting of the manuscript's final three drafts. But you will be spared having to hear much about all this, if for no other reason than that relating that inside story would defeat the very purpose of the repetitive, microscopically cautious vetting process and of all the myriad little changes and rearrangements to accommodate those changes that became necessary when, e.g., certain people declined to sign legal releases, or when one mid-sized company threatened legal action if its real name or identifying details of its actual past tax situation were used, disclaimer or no.[5]

5 This latter is a good example of the sort of thing that threw the publisher's legal people into a swivet of anality and caution. People often don't understand how seriously large US corporations take even a threat of litigation. As I eventually realized, it's not even so much a question of whether or not the publisher would lose a lawsuit; what really concerns them is the cost of defending against it, and the effect of those costs on the company's liability insurance premiums, which are already a major operating expense. Legal trouble is, in other words, a bottom-line issue; and the editor or in-house counsel who exposes a publishing company to possible legal liability had better be able to demonstrate to his CFO that every last reasonable bit of caution and due diligence was exercised on the manuscript, lest he wear what we in Exams used to call 'the brown helmet.' At the same time, it

In the final analysis, though, there are a lot fewer of these small, identity-obscuring changes and temporal rearrangements than one might have expected. For there are advantages to limiting a memoir's range to one single interval (plus relevant backstories) in what seems to us all now like the distant past. People don't much care anymore, for one thing. By which I mean people in this book. The publishing company's paralegals had far less trouble getting signed legal releases than counsel had predicted. The reasons for this are varied but (as my own lawyer and I had argued ahead of time) obvious. Of the persons named, described, and even sometimes projected into the consciousness of as so-called 'characters' in *The Pale King*, a majority have now left the Service. Of those remaining, several have reached levels of GS rank where they are more or less invulnerable.[6] Also, because of the time of year when drafts of the book were presented for their perusal, I am confident that certain other Service personnel were so busy and distracted that they did not really even read the manuscript and, after waiting a decent interval to give the impression of close study and deliberation, signed the legal release so that they could feel they had one less thing they were supposed to do. A few also seemed flattered at the prospect of someone's having paid them enough notice to be able, years later, to remember their contributions. A handful signed because they have remained, through the years, my personal friends; one of these is probably the most valuable, profound friend I've ever made. Some are dead. Two turned out to be incarcerated, of which one of these was someone you never would have thought or suspected.

isn't fair to attribute every last tactical change and deviation here to the publisher. I (meaning, again, the actual human David Wallace) also fear litigation. Like many Americans, I've been sued—twice, in fact, though both suits were meritless, and one was dismissed as frivolous before I was even deposed—and I know what so many of us know: Litigation is no fun, and it's worth one's time and trouble to try to head it off in advance whenever possible. Plus, of course, looming over the whole vetting-and-due-diligence process on *The Pale King* was the shadow of the Service, which no one in his right mind would ever even dream of wanting to piss off unnecessarily, or actually even to come to the full institutional attention of, since the Service, like civil litigation, can make your life miserable without ever getting one extra dime from you.

6 E.g., one is now an Assistant Regional Commissioner for Taxpayer Assistance in the Western Regional Commissioner's Office at Oxnard CA.

Not everyone signed legal releases; I don't mean to suggest that. Only that most did. Several also consented to be interviewed on-record. Where appropriate, parts of their tape-recorded responses have been transcribed directly into the text. Others have graciously signed additional releases authorizing the use of certain audio-visual recordings of them that were made in 1984 as part of an abortive IRS Personnel Division motivational and recruitment effort.[7] As an aggregate, they have provided reminiscences and concrete details that, when combined with the techniques of reconstructive journalism,[8] have yielded scenes of immense authority and realism, regardless of whether this author was actually corporeally right there on the scene at the time or not.

The point I'm trying to drive home here is that it's still all substantially true—i.e., the book this Foreword is part of—regardless of the various ways some of the forthcoming §s have had to be distorted, depersonalized, polyphonized, or otherwise jazzed up in order to conform to the specs of the legal disclaimer. This is not to say that this jazzing up is all just gratuitous titty-pinching; given the aforementioned legal-slash-commercial constraints, it's ended up being integral to the book's whole project. The idea, as both sides' counsel worked it out, is that you will regard features like shifting p.o.v.s, structural fragmentation, willed incongruities, & c. as simply the modern literary analogs of 'Once upon a time...' or 'Far, far away, there once dwelt...' or any of the other traditional devices that signaled the reader that what was under way was fiction and should be processed accordingly. For as everyone knows, whether con-

7 A signed, notarized 2002 FOIA request for copies of these videotapes is on file at the Internal Revenue Service's Office of Public Information, 666 Independence Avenue, Washington DC.... And yes: The Service's national HQ's street number really is '666.' So far as I know, it's nothing more than an unfortunate accident in the Treasury Department's assignment of office space after the Sixteenth Amendment was ratified in 1913. On the Regional levels, Service personnel tend to refer to the national office as 'Triple-Six'—the meaning of the term is obvious, though no one I was able to talk to seemed to know just when it came into use.

8 This loose term is meant to connote the dramatized reconstruction of an empirically real occurrence. It is a common and wholly respectable modern device used in both film (q.v. *The Thin Blue Line, Forrest Gump, JFK*) and literature (q.v. Capote's *In Cold Blood,* Wouk's *The Caine Mutiny,* Oates's *Zombie,* Crane's *The Red Badge of Courage,* Wolfe's *The Right Stuff,* & c., & c.).

sciously or not, there's always a kind of unspoken contract between a book's author and its reader; and the terms of this contract always depend on certain codes and gestures that the author deploys in order to signal the reader what kind of book it is, i.e., whether it's made up vs. true. And these codes are important, because the subliminal contract for nonfiction is very different from the one for fiction.[9] What I'm trying to do right here, within the protective range of the copyright page's disclaimer, is to override the unspoken codes and to be 100 percent overt and forthright about the present contract's terms. *The Pale King* is basically a nonfiction memoir, with additional elements of reconstructive journalism, organizational psychology, elementary civics and tax theory, & c. Our mutual contract here is based on the presumptions of (a) my veracity, and (b) your understanding that any features or semions that might appear to undercut that veracity are in fact protective legal devices, not unlike the boilerplate that accompanies sweepstakes and civil contracts, and thus are not meant to be decoded or 'read' so much as merely acquiesced to as part of the cost of our doing business together, so to speak, in today's commercial climate.[10]

Plus there's the autobiographical fact that, like so many other nerdy, disaffected young people of that time, I dreamed of becoming an 'artist,' i.e., somebody whose adult job was original and creative instead of tedious and dronelike. My specific dream was of becoming an immortally great fiction writer à la Gaddis or Anderson, Balzac or Perec, & c.; and many of the notebook entries on which parts of this memoir are based were themselves literarily jazzed up and fractured;

9 The main way you can tell that the contracts are different is from our reactions to their breach. The feeling of betrayal or infidelity that the reader suffers if it turns out that a piece of ostensible nonfiction has made-up stuff in it (as has been revealed in some recent literary scandals, e.g. Kosinski's *Painted Bird* or that infamous Carcaterra book) is because the terms of the nonfiction contract have been violated. There are, of course, ways to quote-unquote cheat the reader in fiction, too, but these tend to be more technical, meaning internal to the story's own formal rules (see, e.g., the mystery novel's first-person narrator who doesn't reveal that he's actually the murderer until the last page, even though he obviously knew it all along and suppressed it just to jerk us around), and the reader tends to feel more aesthetically disappointed than personally dicked over.

10 Apologies for the preceding sentence, which is the product of much haggling and compromise with the publisher's legal team.

it's just the way I saw myself at the time. In some ways, you could say that my literary ambitions were the chief reason I was on hiatus from college and working at the Midwest REC at all, though most of that whole backstory is tangential and will be addressed only here in the Foreword, and very briefly, to wit:

In a nutshell, the truth is that the first pieces of fiction I was ever actually paid for involved certain other students at the initial college I went to, which was extremely expensive and highbrow and attended mainly by graduates of elite private schools in New York and New England. Without going into a whole lot of detail, let's just say that there were certain pieces of prose I produced for certain students on certain academic subjects, and that these pieces were fictional in the sense of having styles, theses, scholarly personas, and authorial names that were not my own. I think you get the idea. The chief motivation behind this little enterprise was, as it so often is in the real world, financial. It's not like I was desperately poor in college, but my family was far from wealthy, and part of my financial aid package involved taking out large student loans; and I was aware that student-loan debt tended to be very bad news for someone who wanted to pursue any sort of artistic career after college, since it's well known that most artists toil in ascetic obscurity for years before making any real money at their profession.

On the other hand, there were many students at that college whose families were in a position not only to pay their whole tuition but apparently also to give their kids money for whatever personal expenses came up, with no questions asked. 'Personal expenses' here refers to things like weekend ski trips, ridiculously expensive stereo systems, fraternity parties with fully stocked wet bars, & c. Not to mention that the entire campus was less than two acres, and yet most of the students had their own cars, which it also cost $400 per semester to park in one of the college lots. It was all pretty incredible. In many respects, this college was my introduction to the stark realities of class, economic stratification, and the very different financial realities that different sorts of Americans inhabited.

Some of these upper-class students were indeed spoiled, cretinous, and/or untroubled by questions of ethics. Others were under great family pressure and failing, for whatever reasons, to work up to what their parents considered their true grade potential. Some just didn't manage their time and responsibilities well, and found themselves up against the wall on an assignment. I'm sure you get the basic picture. Let's just say that, as a way of positioning myself to pay off some of my loans at an accelerated rate, I provided a certain service. This service was not cheap, but I was quite good at it, and careful. E.g., I always demanded a large enough sample of a client's prior writing to determine how he tended to think and sound, and I never made the mistake of delivering something that was unrealistically superior to someone's own previous work. You can probably also see why these sorts of exercises would be good apprentice training for someone interested in so-called 'creative writing.'[11] The enterprise's proceeds were invested in a high-yield money market account; and interest rates at that time were high, whereas student loans don't even start accruing interest until one leaves school. The overall strategy was conservative, both financially and academically. It's not as if I was doing several of these commissioned fictional pieces a week or anything. I had plenty of my own work to do too, after all.

To anticipate a likely question, let me concede that the ethics here were gray at best. This is why I chose to be honest, just above, about not being impoverished or needing the extra income in order to eat or anything. I was not desperate. I was, though, trying to accumulate some savings against what I anticipated[12] to be debilitating post-grad debt. I am aware that this is not an excuse in the strict sense, but I do believe it serves as at least an explanation; and there were also other, more general factors and contexts that might be seen as mitigating. For one, the college itself turned out to have a lot of moral hypocrisy about it, e.g., congratulating itself on its diversity and the leftist piety of its politics while in reality going about the business of preparing elite kids to enter elite professions and make a great deal of money, thus increasing the pool of prosperous alumni donors. Without anyone ever discussing it or even allowing

11 (which, FYI, there were few or no formal classes in at that time)

12 (correctly, it turned out)

themselves to be aware of it, the college was a veritable temple of Mammon. I'm not kidding. For instance, the most popular major was economics, and the best and brightest of my class all seemed obsessed with a career on Wall Street, whose own public ethos at the time was 'Greed is good.' Not to mention that there were retail cocaine dealers on campus who made a lot more than I ever did. Those were just a few of what I might, if I chose, offer as extenuating factors. My own attitude about it was detached and professional, not unlike a lawyer's. The basic view I held was that, whereas there may have been elements of my enterprise that might technically qualify as aiding or abetting a client's decision to violate the college's Code of Academic Honesty, that decision, as well as the practical and moral responsibility for it, rested with the client. I was undertaking certain freelance writing assignments for pay; why certain students wanted certain papers of a certain length on certain topics, and what they chose to do with them after delivery, were not my business.

Suffice it to say that this view was not shared by the college's Judicial Board in late 1984. Here the story gets complex and a bit lurid, and an SOP memoir would probably linger on the details and the rank unfairnesses and hypocrisies involved. I'm not going to do that. I am, after all, mentioning all this only to provide some context for the ostensibly 'fictional'-looking formal elements of the non-SOP memoir that you have (I hope) bought and are now enjoying. Plus, of course, also to help explain what I was even doing in one of the most tedious and dronelike white-collar jobs in America during what should have been my junior year at an elite college,[13] so that this obvious question isn't left to hang distractingly all through the book (a type of distraction I personally despise, as a reader). Given these limited objectives, then, the whole Code-of-AH debacle is probably best sketched in broad schematic strokes, to wit:

13 Junior year, by the way, was when many of the college's other, more privileged students, including several who'd been my freelance clients, were enjoying their traditional 'semester abroad' at places like Cambridge and the Sorbonne. I'm just mentioning this. There's no expectation that you're going to wring your hands over whatever hypocrisy and unfairness you may discern in this state of affairs. In no sense is this Foreword a bid for sympathy. Plus it's all water long under the bridge now, obviously.

(1a) Naive people are, more or less by definition, unaware that they're naive. (1b) I was, in retrospect, naive. (2) For various personal reasons, I was not a member of any campus fraternity, and so was ignorant of many of the bizarre tribal customs and practices in the college's so-called 'Greek' community. (3a) One of the college's fraternities had instituted the phenomenally stupid and shortsighted practice of placing behind their billiard room's wet bar a two-drawer file cabinet containing copies of certain recent exams, problem sets, lab reports, and term papers that had earned high grades, which were available for plagiarism. (3b) Speaking of phenomenally stupid, it turned out that not just one but *three* different members of this fraternity had, without bothering to consult the party from whom they'd commissioned and received them, tossed papers that were not technically their own into this communal file cabinet. (4) The paradox of plagiarism is that it actually requires a lot of care and hard work to pull off successfully, since the original text's style, substance, and logical sequences have to be modified enough so that the plagiarism isn't totally, insultingly obvious to the professor who's grading it. (5a) The type of spoiled, cretinous frat boy who goes into a communal file cabinet for a term paper on the use of implicit GNP price deflators in macroeconomic theory is also the type who will not know or care about the paradoxical extra work that good plagiarism requires. He will, however incredible it sounds, just plunk down and retype the thing, word for word. (5b) Nor, even more incredibly, will he take the trouble to verify that none of his fraternity brothers is planning to plagiarize the same term paper for the same course. (6) The moral system of a college fraternity turns out to be classically tribal, i.e., characterized by a deeply felt sense of honor, discretion, and loyalty to one's so-called 'brothers,' coupled with a complete, sociopathic lack of regard for the interests or even humanity of anyone outside that fraternal set.

Let's just end the sketch there. I doubt you need a whole diagram to anticipate what came down, nor much of a primer in US class dynamics to understand, of the eventual five students placed on academic probation or forced to retake certain courses vs. the one student formally suspended pending consideration of expulsion and possible[14] referral of the case to the Hampshire County District Attorney, which one of these was yours truly, the living author, Mr. David Wallace of Philo IL, to which tiny lifeless nothing town neither I nor my family were at all psyched about the prospect of having me return and sit around watching TV for the at least one and possibly two semesters that the college's administration was going to take its sweet time considering my fate.[15] Meanwhile, by the terms of the 1966 Federal Claims Collection Act's §106(c-d), the repayment clock on my Guaranteed Student Loans started running, as of 1 January 1985, at 6¼ percent interest.

Again, if any of that seems vague or ablated, it's because I am giving you a very stripped down, mission-specific version of just who and where I was, life-situation-wise, for the thirteen months I spent as an IRS examiner. Moreover, I'm afraid that just how I landed in this government post at all is a background item that I can explain only obliquely, i.e., by ostensibly explaining why I can't discuss it.[16] First, I'd ask you to bear in mind the above-cited disinclination to have me return and serve out my limbo at home in Philo, which mutual reluctance in turn involves a whole lot of issues and history between my family and me that I couldn't get into even if I wanted to (see below). Second, I would inform you that the city of Peoria IL is roughly ninety miles from Philo, which is a distance that permits general familial monitoring without any of the sort of detailed, close-quarters knowledge that might confer feelings of concern or responsibility. Third, I

14 (but highly unlikely, given the college's concern with its reputation and PR)

15 Sorry about that text sentence. The truth is that the whole frat-cabinet-and-cascading-scandal's-need-for-a-scapegoat situation still sometimes gets me jacked up, emotionally speaking. Two facts might make the durability of these emotions easier to understand: (a) of the five other students found by the J-Board to have either bought term papers or plagiarized from those who had, two ended up graduating *magna cum laude,* and (b) a third now serves on the college's Board of Trustees. I'll just leave those as stark facts and let you draw your own conclusions about the whole shabby affair. *Mendacem memorem esse oportet.*

16 And please forgive the contrivance here. Given the familio-legal strictures detailed just below, this kind of anti-explanation is the only permissible way for me to avoid having my whole presence at IRS Post 047 be some enormous, unexplained, and unmotivated blank, which in certain types of fiction might be (technically) OK, but in a memoir would constitute a deep and essential breach of contract.

could direct your attention to Congress's 1977 Fair Debt Collection Practices Act §1101, which turns out to override the Federal Claims Collection Act's §106(c-d) and to authorize deferment of Guaranteed Student Loan repayments for documented employees of certain government agencies, including guess which one. Fourth, I am allowed, after exhaustive negotiations with the publisher's counsel, to say that my thirteen-month contract, posting, and GS-9 civil service paygrade were the result of certain *sub-rosa* actions on the part of a certain unnamed relative[17] with unspecified connections to the Midwest Regional Commissioner's Office of a certain unnamed government agency. Last and most important, I am also permitted to say, albeit in language not wholly my own, that members of my family were almost unanimous in declining to sign the legal releases required for any further or more specific use, mention, or representation of the aforesaid relatives or any likeness thereof in any capacity, setting, form, or guise, inclusive of references *sine damno,* within the written work heretofore entitled *The Pale King,* and that this is why I can't get into anything more specific about the overall hows and whys. End of explanation of absence of real explanation, which, however irksome or opaque it may come off, is (again) still preferable to having the question of why/how I was working at the Midwest Regional Examination Center just hang there huge and unaddressed through the whole text to follow,[18] like the proverbial elephant in the room.

Here I should also probably address one other core-motivation-type question that bears on the matter of veracity and trust raised several ¶s above, viz., why a nonfiction memoir at all, since I'm primarily a fiction writer? Not to mention the question of why a memoir restricted to a single, long-past year I spent in exile from anything I even remotely cared about or was interested in, serving out time as little more than one tiny ephemeral dronelike cog in an immense federal bureaucracy?[19] There are two different kinds of valid answer

17 (*not* a parent)

18 Q.v. FN 2, *supra.*

19 The word *bureaucracy* is notwithstanding that part of the run-up to the whole 'New IRS' thing was an increasing anti- or post-bureaucratic mentality on the part of both Triple-Six and Region. See,

here, one being personal and the other more literary/humanistic. The personal stuff it's initially tempting to say is just none of your business...except that one disadvantage of addressing you here directly and in person in the cultural present of 2005 is the fact that, as both you and I know, there is no longer any kind of clear line between personal and public, or rather between private vs. performative. Among obvious examples are web logs, reality television, cellphone cameras, chat rooms...not to mention the dramatically increased popularity of the memoir as a literary genre. Of course *popularity* is, in this context, a synonym for profitability; and actually

for one quick example, this snippet from an interview with Mr. Donald Jones, a GS-13 Team Leader in the Midwest REC's Fats group from 1984 through 1990:

> Perhaps it would help to define *bureaucracy*. The term. What we're talking about. All they said you had to do was refer to the dictionary. Administration characterized by diffusion of authority and adherence to inflexible rules of operation, unquote. Inflexible rules of operation. An administrative system in which the need or desire to follow complex procedures impedes effective action, unquote. They had transparencies of the definition projected up on the wall during meetings. They said he had them all recite them as nearly some type of catechism.

Meaning, in discursive terms, that the couple of years in question here saw one of the largest bureaucracies anywhere undergo a convulsion in which it tried to reconceive itself as a non- or even anti-bureaucracy, which at first might sound like nothing more than an amusing bit of bureaucratic folly. In fact, it was frightening; it was a little like watching an enormous machine come to consciousness and start trying to think and feel like a real human. The terror of concurrent films like *Terminator* and *Blade Runner* was based around just this premise... but of course in the case of the Service the convulsions, and fallout, although more diffuse and undramatic, had an actual impact on Americans' lives.

N.B. Mr. Jones's 'they' is referring to certain high-level figures who were exponents of the so-called 'Initiative,' which it is totally impractical here to try to explain abstractly (although q.v. Item 951458221 of §14, Interview Documentary, which consists of a long and probably not ideally focused version of such an explanation from Mr. Kenneth ['Type of Thing Ken'] Hindle, one of the oldest wigglers in the Rotes group to which I ended up [after a great deal of initial confusion and misassignment] being tasked), except to say that the only such figure anyone at our low level ever even laid eyes on was the Technical Branch's M. E. Lehrl and his strange team of intuitives and occult ephebes, who were (it emerged) tasked to help implement the Initiative as it pertained to Examinations. If that doesn't make any sense at this point, please don't worry about it. I went back and forth on the issue of what to explain here vs. what to let unfold in a more natural, dramatic way in the memoir itself. I finally decided to offer certain quick, potentially confusing explanations, betting that if they're too obscure or baroque right now you just won't pay much attention to them, which, again, I hasten to assure you is totally OK.

that fact alone should suffice, personal-motivation-wise. Consider that in 2003, the average author's advance[20] for a memoir was almost 2.5 times that paid for a work of fiction. The simple truth is that I, like so many other Americans, have suffered reverses in the volatile economy of the last few years, and these reverses have occurred at the same time that my financial obligations have increased along with my age and responsibilities[21]; and meanwhile all sorts of US writers—some of whom I know personally, including one I actually had to lend money to for basic living expenses as late as spring 2001—have recently hit it big with memoirs,[22] and I would be a rank hypocrite if I pretended that I was less attuned and receptive to market forces than anyone else.

As all mature people know, though, it's possible for very different kinds of motives and emotions to coexist in the human soul. There is no way that a memoir like *The Pale King* could be written solely for financial gain. One paradox of professional writing is that books written solely for money and/or acclaim will almost never be good

20 If you're interested, this term is shorthand for an unrefundable advance payment against the author's projected royalties (through a 7½%–15% set of progressive margins) on sales of a book. Since actual sales are difficult to predict, it is in the writer's financial interest to receive the largest possible advance, even though the lump-sum payment can create tax problems for the year of receipt (thanks largely to the 1986 Tax Reform Act's elimination of income averaging). And given, again, that predicting actual sales is an inexact science, the size of the up-front author advance that a publishing company is willing to pay for the rights to a book is the best tangible indication of the publisher's willingness to 'support' that book, w/ the latter term meaning everything from the number of copies printed to the size of the marketing budget. And this support is practically the only way for a book to gain the attention of a mass audience and to garner significant sales—like it or not, that's just the commercial reality today.

21 By age forty, artist or no, the reality is that only an imprudent chump would neglect to start saving and investing for eventual retirement, especially in this era of tax-deferred IRA and SEP-IRA plans with such generous annual tax-exempt caps—and extra-especially if you can S-corp yourself and let the corporation make an additional annual pension contribution, over and above your IRA, as a contractual 'employee benefit,' thereby exempting that extra amount from your taxable income, too. The tax laws right now are practically down on one knee, begging upper-income Americans to take advantage of this provision. The trick, of course, is earning enough to qualify as an upper-income American—*Deos fortioribus adesse.*

22 (Despite his sudden celebrity and windfall I am still, almost four years later, awaiting repayment of the loan's principal from this unnamed writer, which I mention not to whinge or be vindictive, but merely as one more small part of my financial condition *qua* motivation.)

enough to garner either. The truth is that the larger narrative encompassing this Foreword has significant social and artistic value. That might sound conceited, but rest assured that I wouldn't and couldn't have put three years' hard labor (plus an additional fifteen months of legal and editorial futzing) into *The Pale King* if I were not convinced it was true. Have, e.g., a look at the following, which was transcribed verbatim from remarks by Mr. DeWitt Glendenning Jr., the Director of the Midwest Regional Examination Center during most of my tenure there:

> If you know the position a person takes on taxes, you can determine [his] whole philosophy. The tax code, once you get to know it, embodies all the essence of [human] life: greed, politics, power, goodness, charity.

To these qualities that Mr. Glendenning ascribed to the code I would respectfully add one more: boredom. Opacity. User-unfriendliness.

This all can be put another way. It might sound a bit dry and wonkish, but that's because I'm boiling it down to the abstract skeleton:

1985 was a critical year for American taxation and for the Internal Revenue Service's enforcement of the US tax code. In brief, that year saw not only fundamental changes in the Service's operational mandate, but also the climax of an involved intra-Service battle between advocates and opponents of an increasingly automated, computerized tax system. For complex administrative reasons, the Midwest Regional Examination Center became one of the venues in which this battle's crucial phase played out.

But that's only part of it. As alluded to in an FN way above, subtending this operational battle over human vs. digital enforcement of the tax code was a deeper conflict over the very mission and *raison* of the Service, a conflict whose fallout extended from the corridors of power at Treasury and Triple-Six all the way down to the most staid and backwater District office. At the highest levels, the struggle here was between traditional or 'conservative'[23] officials who saw tax and

23 (meaning, somewhat confusingly, classically liberal)

its administration as an arena of social justice and civic virtue, on the one hand, and those more progressive, 'pragmatic' policymakers who prized the market model, efficiency, and a maximum return on the investment of the Service's annual budget. Distilled to its essence, the question was whether and to what extent the IRS should be operated like a for-profit business.

Probably that's all I should say right here in terms of summary. If you know how to search and parse government archives, you can find voluminous history and theory on just about every side of the debate. It's all in the public record.

But here's the thing. Both then and now, very few ordinary Americans know anything about all this. Nor much about the deep changes the Service underwent in the mid-1980s, changes that today directly affect the way citizens' tax obligations are determined and enforced. And the reason for this public ignorance is not secrecy. Despite the IRS's well-documented paranoia and aversion to publicity,[24] secrecy here had nothing to do with it. The real reason why US citizens were/are not aware of these conflicts, changes, and stakes is that the whole subject of tax policy and administration is dull. Massively, spectacularly dull.

It is impossible to overstate the importance of this feature. Consider, from the Service's perspective, the advantages of the dull, the arcane, the mind-numbingly complex. The IRS was one of the very first government agencies to learn that such qualities help insulate them against public protest and political opposition, and that abstruse dullness is actually a much more effective shield than is secrecy. For the great disadvantage of secrecy is that it's interesting. People are drawn to secrets; they can't help it. Keep in mind that the period we're talking was only a decade after Watergate. Had the Service tried to hide or cover up its conflicts and convulsions, some enterprising journalist(s) could have done an exposé that drew a lot of attention and interest and scandalous fuss. But this is not at all what happened. What happened was that much of the high-level

24 (attitudes that are not wholly unjustified, given TPs' hostility to the Service, politicians' habit of bashing the agency to score populist points, & c.)

policy debate played out for two years in full public view, e.g., in open hearings of the Joint Committee on Taxation, the Senate Treasury Procedures and Statutes Subcommittee, and the IRS's Deputy and Assistant Commissioners' Council. These hearings were collections of anaerobic men in drab suits who spoke a verbless bureaucratese—terms like 'strategic utilization template' and 'revenue vector' in place of 'plan' and 'tax'—and took days just to reach consensus on the order of items for discussion. Even in the financial press, there was hardly any coverage; can you guess why? If not, consider the fact that just about every last transcript, record, study, white paper, code amendment, revenue-ruling, and procedural memo has been available for public perusal since date of issue. No FOIA filing even required. But not one journalist seems ever to have checked them out, and with good reason: This stuff is solid rock. The eyes roll up white by the third or fourth ¶. You just have no idea.[25]

Fact: The birth agonies of the New IRS led to one of the great and terrible PR discoveries in modern democracy, which is that if sensitive issues of governance can be made sufficiently dull and arcane, there will be no need for officials to hide or dissemble, because no one not directly involved will pay enough attention to cause trouble. No one will pay attention because no one will be interested, because, more or less *a priori,* of these issues' monumental dullness. Whether this PR discovery is to be regretted for its corrosive effect on the democratic ideal or celebrated for its enhancement of government efficiency depends, it seems, on which side one takes in the deeper debate over ideals vs. efficacy referenced on p. 82, resulting in yet another involuted loop that I won't tax your patience by trying to trace out or make hay of.

25 I'm reasonably sure that I am the only living American who's actually read all these archives all the way through. I'm not sure I can explain how I did it. Mr. Chris Acquistipace, one of the GS-11 Chalk Leaders in our Rote Exams group, and a man of no small intuition and sensitivity, proposed an analogy between the public records surrounding the Initiative and the giant solid-gold Buddhas that flanked certain temples in ancient Khmer. These priceless statues, never guarded or secured, were safe from theft not despite but because of their value—they were too huge and heavy to move. Something about this sustained me.

To me, at least in retrospect,[26] the really interesting question is why dullness proves to be such a powerful impediment to attention. Why we recoil from the dull. Maybe it's because dullness is intrinsically painful; maybe that's where phrases like 'deadly dull' or 'excruciatingly dull' come from. But there might be more to it. Maybe dullness is associated with psychic pain because something that's dull or opaque fails to provide enough stimulation to distract people from some other, deeper type of pain that is always there, if only in an ambient low-level way, and which most of us[27] spend nearly all our time and energy trying to distract ourselves from feeling, or at least from feeling directly or with our full attention. Admittedly, the whole thing's pretty confusing, and hard to talk about abstractly...but surely something must lie behind not just Muzak in dull or tedious places anymore but now also actual TV in waiting rooms, supermarkets' checkouts, airports' gates, SUVs' backseats. Walkmen, iPods, BlackBerries, cell phones that attach to your head. This terror of silence with nothing diverting to do. I can't think anyone really believes that today's so-called 'information society' is just about information. Everyone knows[28] it's about something else, way down.

The memoir-relevant point here is that I learned, in my time with the Service, something about dullness, information, and irrelevant complexity. About negotiating boredom as one would a terrain, its levels and forests and endless wastes. Learned about it extensively, exquisitely, in my interrupted year. And now ever since that time have noticed, at work and in recreation and time with friends and even the intimacies of family life, that living people do not speak much of the dull. Of those parts of life that are and must be dull. Why this silence? Maybe it's because the subject is, in and of itself, dull...only then we're again right back where we started, which is tedious and irksome. There may, though, I opine, be more to it...as in vastly more, right here before us all, hidden by virtue of its size.

26 (which is, after all, memoirs' specialty)

27 (whether or not we're consciously aware of it)

28 (again, whether consciously or not)

§10

Notwithstanding Justice H. Harold Mealer's famous characterization, included in the Fourth Appellate Circuit's majority opinion on *Atkinson et al. v. The United States,* of a government bureaucracy as 'the only known parasite larger than the organism on which it subsists,' the truth is that such a bureaucracy is really much more a parallel world, both connected to and independent of this one, operating under its own physics and imperatives of cause. One might envision a large and intricately branching system of jointed rods, pulleys, gears, and levers radiating out from a central operator such that tiny movements of that operator's finger are transmitted through that system to become the gross kinetic changes in the rods at the periphery. It is at this periphery that the bureaucracy's world acts upon this one.

The crucial part of the analogy is that the elaborate system's operator is not himself uncaused. The bureaucracy is not a closed system; it is this that makes it a world instead of a thing.

§11

From Assistant Commissioner of Internal Revenue for Human Resources, Management & Support's Office of Employee Assistance & Personnel Overview Internal Memorandum 4123-78(b)

Conclusion of ACIRHRMSOEAPO Survey/Study 1-76—11-77: AMA/DSM(II)-authorized syndromes/symptoms associated with Examinations postings in excess of 36 months (average term of posting on report: 41.4 months), in reverse order of incidence (per medical/EAP service claim per IRSM §743/12.2(f-r)):

Chronic paraplegia
Temporary paraplegia
Temporary paralysis agitans
Paracatatonic fugues
Formication
Intracranial edema
Spasmodic dyskinesia
Paramnesia
Paresis

Phobic anxiety (numerical)
Lordosis
Renal neuralgia
Tinnitus
Peripheral hallucinations
Torticollis
Cantor's sign (dextral)
Lumbago
Dihedral lordosis
Dissociative fugues
Kern-Børglundt syndrome (radial)
Hypomania
Sciatica
Spasmodic torticollis
Low startle threshold
Krendler's syndrome
Hemorrhoids
Ruminative fugues
Ulcerative colitis
Hypertension
Hypotension
Cantor's sign (sinistral)
Diplopia
Hemeralopia
Vascular headache
Cyclothymia
Blurred vision
Fine tremors
Facial/digital ticcing
Localized anxiety
Generalized anxiety
Kinesthetic deficits
Unexplained bleeding

§12

Stecyk started at the end of the block and came up the first flagstone walkway with his briefcase and rang the bell. 'Good morning,' he said to the older lady who answered the door in what was either a robe or very casual housedress (it was 7:20, so bathrobes were not only probable but downright appropriate) whose collar she was holding tightly closed with one hand and was looking through the door's crack at different points over Stecyk's shoulders as if certain there must be someone else behind him. Stecyk said, 'My name is Leonard Stecyk, I go by Leonard but Len is also perfectly fine as far as I'm concerned, and I've recently had the opportunity to move in and set up housekeeping in 6F in the Angler's Cove complex just up the street there, I'm sure you've seen it either leaving home or returning, it's just right up the street there at 121, and I'd like to say Hello and introduce myself and say I'm pleased to be part of the neighborhood and to offer you as a token of greetings and thanks this free copy of the US Post Office's 1979 National Zip Code Directory, listing the zip codes for every community and postal zone in each state of the United States in alphabetical order, and also'—shifting the briefcase under his arm to open the directory and hold it out open to the woman's view—something seemed wrong with one of the lady's eyes, as if she were having trouble with a contact lens or perhaps had some foreign matter under the upper lid, which could be uncomfortable—'additionally listing here on the back of the last page and inside the rear cover, the cover's the continuation, the addresses and toll-free numbers of over forty-five government agencies and and services from which you can receive free informational material, some of which is almost shockingly valuable, see I've put small asterisks next to those, which I know for a fact are helpful and an extraordinary bargain, and which are of course after all when you come right down to it paid for with your tax dollars, so why not extract value from the contributions if you know what I mean, though of course the choice is entirely up to you'—the lady was also turning her head slightly in the way of someone whose hearing wasn't quite what it used to be, noting which Stecyk put the briefcase down to ink one or two extra asterisks by numbers that in this case might be of special help. Then making a large motion of handing it over and letting the postal directory hang there in midair just outside the door while the lady had her face screwed up and seemed to be deciding whether to disengage the door's chain in order to accept it. 'Maybe I'll just be leaning it up here against the milkbox'—pointing down at the milkbox—'and you can peruse it at leisure at your own convenience later in the day or really whatever you might choose to do,' Stecyk said. He liked to make a small jest or sally of employing a motion as if he were tipping his hat even though his hand never made contact with the hat; he felt it was both courtly and amusing. 'Hidey ho, then,' he said. He proceeded back down the walkway, missing all the cracks and hearing the door behind him close only as he reached the sidewalk and made a sharp right and took eighteen strides to the next walkway and a sharp right to the door, which had a wrought-iron security door installed before it and at which there was no answer after three rings and shave-and-haircut knock. He left his card with his new address and the gist of his greeting and offer and another 1979 zip code directory (the 1980 directory would not be out until August; he had an order in) and proceeded down the walkway, a spring to his step, his smile so wide it almost looked like it hurt.

§13

It was in public high school that this boy learned the terrible power of attention and what you pay attention to. He learned it in a way whose very ridiculousness was part of what made it so terrible. And terrible it was.

At age sixteen and a half, he started to have attacks of shattering public sweats.

As a child, he'd always been a heavy sweater. He had sweated a lot when playing sports or when it was hot, but it didn't especially bother him. He just wiped himself off more often. He couldn't remember anyone ever saying anything about it. Also, it didn't seem to smell bad; it's not like he stank. The sweating was just something particular about him. Some kids were fat, some were unusually short or tall or had crazy teeth, or stuttered, or smelled like mildew no matter what clothes they wore—he just happened to be someone who sweated heavily, especially in the humidity of summertime, when just riding his bike in dungarees around Beloit made him sweat like crazy. It all barely even registered on him, so far as he could remember.

In his seventeenth year, though, it started to bother him; he became self-conscious about the sweating thing. This was surely related to puberty, the stage where you suddenly get much more concerned about how you appear to other people. About whether there might be something visibly creepy or gross about you. Within weeks of the start of the school year, he became both more and differently aware that he seemed to sweat more than the other kids did. The first couple months of school were always hot, and many of the old high school's classrooms didn't even have fans. Without trying to or wanting to, he started to imagine what his sweating might look like in class: his face gleaming with a mixture of sebum and sweat, his shirt sodden at the collar and pits, his hair separated into wet little creepy spikes from his head's running sweat. It was the worst if he was in a position where he thought girls could maybe see it. The classrooms' desks were all crammed together. Just the presence of a pretty or popular girl in his sight line would make his internal temperature rise—he could feel it happening unwilled, even against his will—and start the heavy sweating.[1]

Except at first, as autumn of that seventeenth year deepened and the weather cooled and dried and the leaves turned and fell and could be raked for pay, he had reason to feel that the sweating problem was receding, that the real problem had been the heat, or that without the muggy summer heat there would now no longer be as much occasion for the problem. (He thought of it in the most general and abstract terms possible. He tried never to let himself think of the actual word *sweat*. The idea, after all, was to try and be as unself-conscious about it as possible.) Mornings now were chilly, and the high school's classrooms weren't hot anymore, except near the rears' clanking radiators. Without letting himself be wholly aware of it, he had started hurrying a little bit between periods to get to the

1 Psychodynamically, he was, as a subject, coming to a late and therefore traumatic understanding of himself as also an object, a body among other bodies, something that could see and yet also be seen. It was the sort of binary self-concept that many children attain as early as age five, often thanks to some chance encounter with a mirror, puddle, window, or photograph seen in just the right way. Despite the boy's having the average ration of reflectors available to him in childhood, though, this developmental stage was retarded in his case somehow. The understanding of himself as also an object-for-others was in his case deferred to the very cusp of adulthood—and, like most repressed truths, when it finally burst through, it came as something overwhelming and terrible, a winged thing breathing fire.

next class early enough that he wouldn't get stuck in a desk by a radiator, which was hot enough to jump-start a sweat. But it involved a delicate balance, because if he hurried too fast through the halls between periods, this exertion could also cause him to break a light sweat, which increased his preoccupation and made it easier for the sweating to get more severe in the event that he thought people might be noticing it. Certain other examples of balancing and preoccupation like this existed, most of which he tried to keep from conscious thought as much as possible without being wholly aware of why he was doing this.[2]

For there were, by this time, degrees and gradations of public sweating, from a light varnish all the way up to a shattering, uncontrollable, and totally visible and creepy sweat. The worst thing was that one degree could lead to the next if he worried about it too much, if he was too afraid that a slight sweat would get worse and tried too hard to control or avoid it. The fear of it could bring it on. He did not truly begin to suffer until he understood this fact, an understanding he came to slowly at first and then all of an awful sudden.

What he thought of as easily the worst day of his life so far followed an unseasonably cold week in early November where the problem had started to seem so manageable and under control that he felt he might actually be starting to almost forget about it altogether. Wearing dungarees and a rust-colored velour shirt, he sat far from the radiator in the middle of a middle row of student desks in World Cultures and was listening and taking notes on whatever module of the textbook they were covering, when a terrible thought rose as if from nowhere inside him: *What if I all of a sudden start sweating?* And on that one day this thought, which presented mostly as a terrible sudden fear that washed through him like a hot tide, made him break instantly into a heavy, unstoppable sweat, which the secondary thought that it must look even creepier to be sweating when it wasn't

2 In clinical terms, he was fighting to re-repress a truth that had been too long repressed in the first place, a confinement from which it had taken on far too much psychic energy ever, once it had burst through the mirror (so to speak), to be willed back out of conscious awareness. Consciousness just doesn't work this way.

even hot in here to anyone else made worse and worse as he sat very still with his head down and face soon running with palpable rivulets of sweat, not moving at all, torn between the desire to wipe the sweat from his face before it actually began to drip and someone saw it dripping and the fear that any kind of wiping movement would draw people's attention and cause those in the desks on either side of him to see what was happening, that he was sweating like crazy for no reason. It was by far the worst feeling he had ever had in his life, and the whole attack lasted almost forty minutes, and for the rest of the day he went around in a kind of trance of shock and spent adrenaline, and that day was the actual start of the syndrome in which he understood that the worse his fear of breaking into a shattering public sweat was, the better the chances that he'd have something like what happened in World Cultures happen again, maybe every day, maybe more than once a day—and this understanding caused him more terror and frustration and inner suffering than he had ever before even dreamed that somebody could ever experience, and the total stupidity and weirdness of the whole problem just made it that much worse.

Dating from that day in World Cultures, his dread of it happening again, and his attempts to avert or avoid or control this fear, began to inform almost every moment of his day. The fear and preoccupation only happened in class or lunch at school—not in last-period PE, since sweating in PE wouldn't be seen as all that weird and so didn't inspire the special kind of fear that primed him for an attack. Or it also happened at any crowded function like Scout meetings or Christmas dinner in the stuffy, overheated dining room of his grandparents' home in Rockton, where he could literally feel the table's candles' extra little dots of heat and the body heat of all the relatives crowded around the table, with his head down trying to look like he was studying his plate's china pattern as the heat of the fear of the heat spread through him like adrenaline or brandy, that physical spread of internal heat that he tried so hard not to dread. It didn't happen in private, at home in his room, reading—in his room with the door closed it often didn't even occur to him—or in the library in one of the little private carrels like an open cube, where no one could see him or it would be easy to just get up anytime and leave.[3] It happened only in public with people around him and crowded in rows or around a well-lit table where you had to wear your new red Christmas sweater and your shoulders and elbows were almost actually touching the cousins crammed in on both sides and everyone all trying to talk at the same time over the steaming food and all looking at each other so there was every chance that people could see even the first flushed little pinpricks of it on his forehead and upper face that then, if the fear of it getting out of control grew too great, would swell to shining beads and soon start to visibly run, and it was impossible to wipe his face off with a napkin because he feared that the weird sight of wiping his face in wintertime would draw all his relatives' attention to what was going on, which is what he would have traded his very soul not to have happen. It could basically happen anyplace where it was hard to leave without drawing attention to himself. To raise your hand in class and ask for a bathroom pass as heads turned to look—just the thought of it filled him with total dread.

He could not understand why he was so afraid of people possibly seeing him sweat or thinking it was weird or gross. Who cared what people thought? He said this over and over to himself; he knew it was true. He also repeated—often in a stall in one of the boys' restrooms at school between periods after a medium or severe attack, sitting on the toilet with his pants up and trying to use the stall's toilet paper to dry himself without the toilet paper disintegrating into little greebles and blobs all over his forehead, squeezing thick pads of toilet paper onto the front of his hair to help dry it—Franklin Roosevelt's speech from US History II in sophomore year: *The only thing we have to fear is fear itself.* He would mentally repeat this to himself over and over. Franklin Roosevelt was right, but it didn't help—knowing it was the

3 It especially didn't happen when he was alone in the upstairs bathroom in front of the mirror, trying to make an attack happen so he could study it in the mirror and see for himself, objectively, how bad and obvious it looked from various angles and how far away it was visible from. He hoped, and on some level believed, that it maybe wasn't as obvious or bizarre-looking as he was always afraid it was during an actual attack, but he could never verify this because he could never get a real attack to happen when he wanted it to, only when he totally, totally did not.

fear that was the problem was just a fact; it didn't make the fear go away. In fact, he started to think that thinking of the speech's line so much just made him all the more afraid of the fear itself. That what he really had to fear was fear of the fear, like an endless funhouse hall of mirrors of fear, all of which were ridiculous and weird. He started to sometimes catch himself talking to himself about the sweating thing and fear in a kind of very fast faint whisper that he'd been doing without being aware of it, and now he began to really consider that he might be going crazy. Most of the craziness he'd seen on TV involved people laughing maniacally, which now seemed totally bizarre to him, like a joke that wasn't only not funny but made no sense at all. Imagining laughing about the attacks or the fear was like imagining trying to come up to somebody and start trying to explain what was going on, like his Scoutmaster or the guidance counselor—it was unimaginable; there was no way.

High school became a daily torment, even as his grades improved even more, due to the increased reading and studying he did because it was only when he was in private and totally absorbed and concentrating on something else that he was OK. He also got into word search and number puzzles, which he found absorbing. In class or the lunchroom, it was a constant preoccupation to not think about it and not let the fear reach the point where his temperature went up and his attention telescoped to where all he could feel was the uncontrolled heat and sweat starting to pop out on his face and back, which, the minute he felt the sweat popping out and beading, his fear went through the roof and all he could think of was how he could get out of there to the restroom without drawing attention. It only happened sometimes, but he dreaded it all the time, even though he knew all too well that the constant dread and preoccupation were what primed him to have these attacks. He thought of them as *attacks,* though not from anything outside him but rather from some inner part of himself that was hurting or almost betraying him, as in *heart attack.* Similarly, *primed* became his inner code word for the state of hair-trigger fear and dread that could cause him to have an attack at almost any time in public.

His main way of dealing with being constantly primed and preoccupied with the fear of it all the time at school was that he developed various tricks and tactics for what to do if an attack of public sweating started and threatened to go totally out of control. Knowing where all the exits were to any room he entered wasn't a trick, it became just something he now automatically did, like knowing just how far the nearest exit was and if it could be got to without drawing much attention. The school's lunchroom was an example of someplace that was easy to get out of with no one really noticing, for instance. Leaving the classroom during an attack in a class was out of the question, however. If he just got up and ran out of the room, as he always yearned to do during an attack, there would be all kinds of disciplinary problems, and everyone would want an explanation, including his parents—plus when he came back to that class the next day, everyone would know he'd run out and would want to know what had made him freak out, and the net result would be a lot of attention on him in the class, and the fear that everyone would be noticing him and looking at him, which would prime him all over again. Or if he ever actually raised his hand and asked the teacher for a restroom pass, it would draw all the bored students in the rows' attention to who'd spoken up, and their heads would all turn to look and there he would be, sweating and dripping and looking bizarre. His only hope then would be that he'd look sick, people would think he was sick or about to maybe throw up. This was one of the tricks—to cough or sniff and feel uncomfortably at his glands if he feared an attack, so if it got out of control he could hope people would maybe just think he was sick and shouldn't have come to school that day. That he wasn't weird, he was just sick. It was the same with pretending he didn't feel well enough to eat his lunch at lunch period—sometimes he wouldn't eat and would bus the full tray and then leave and go eat a sandwich he brought from home in a baggie in a restroom stall. That way, people might be more apt to think he was sick.

Other tactics included sitting in a row as far back in the classroom as he could, so most people would be in front of him and he didn't have to worry about them seeing him if he had an attack, which only worked in classes without a seating chart,[4] and could also backfire in the nightmare scenario he tried so hard not to think about. And also avoiding the hot radiators, naturally, and desks between girls, or trying to secure the desk at the very end of a row so that in case of emergency he could avert his head from the rest of the row, but in a subtle way that didn't look weird—he'd just swing his legs out from the row into the aisle and cross his ankles and lean out that way. He stopped riding his bike to the high school because the exercise of riding could warm him up and prime him with anxiety before first period had even started. Another trick, by the start of third quarter, was walking to school without a winter coat in order to get cold and sort of freeze his nervous system, which he could only do when he was the last one to leave the house, because his mother would have a spasm if he tried to leave without a coat. There was also wearing multiple layers that he could remove if he felt it coming on in a class, although removing layers could look weird if he was also coughing and feeling his glands—in his experience, sick people didn't normally remove layers. He was somewhat aware he was losing weight but didn't know how much. He also began to cultivate a habitual gesture of brushing his hair back from his forehead, which he practiced in the bathroom mirror in order to make it look like just an unconscious habit but was really all designed to help brush sweat from his forehead out of sight into his hair in the event of an attack—but this too was a delicate balance, because past a certain point the gesture was no longer helpful, since if the front part of his hair got wet enough to separate into those creepy little wet spikes and strands, then the fact that he was sweating became even more obvious, if people were to look over. And the nightmare scenario that he dreaded more than anything was for him to be in the back and to start having such a shattering, uncontrollable attack that the teacher, all the way up at the front of the room, noticed he was soaked and running with visible sweat and interrupted class to ask if he was all right, causing everyone to turn way around in their chairs to look. In the nightmares

4 This boy's surname, which was *Cusk,* placed him near the front of those classes with assigned seating.

there was a literal spotlight on him as they all turned in their seats to see who the teacher was so worried and/or grossed out by.[5]

In February his mother made a breezy, half-joking comment about his love life and if there were any girls he especially liked this year, and he almost had to leave the room, he almost burst into tears. The idea now of ever asking a girl out, of taking a girl out and having her looking at him from right there close up, expecting him to be thinking about her instead of how primed he was and whether he was going to start sweating—this filled him with dread, but at the same time it made him sad. He was bright enough to know there was something sad about it. Even as he gladly quit Scouts just four badges short of Eagle, and turned down a shy, kind of socially anonymous girl from College Algebra and Trigonometry's invitation to the Sadie Hawkins dance, and faked being sick at Easter so he could stay home by himself reading ahead in *Dorian Gray* and trying to jump-start an attack in the mirror of his parents' bathroom instead of driving down with them to Easter dinner at his grandparents', he felt a bit sad about it, as well as relieved, plus guilty about the various lies of the excuses he gave, and also lonely and a bit tragic, like someone in the rain outside a window looking in, but also creepy and disgusting, as though his secret inner self was creepy and the attacks were just a symptom, his true self trying to literally leak out—though none of all this was visible to him in the bathroom's glass, whose reflection seemed oblivious[6] to all that he felt as he searched it.

5 Under any reputable Depth-based interpretation, a search- or spotlight serves as a manifest dream-symbol of human attention. On the level of latent content, however, the recurring nightmare could be interpreted as signifying anything from, e.g., a repressed narcissistic desire for others' notice to an unconscious recognition of the boy's own excessive preoccupation with himself as the suffering's proximate cause. At clinical issue would be such questions as the dream-spotlight's source, the teacher-figure's status as either imago or archetype (or, perhaps, as projected self-image, since it is in this figure that distress is externalized as affect), and the subject's own associations concerning such terms as *gross, attack,* and *shattering.*

6 There are secrets within secrets, though—always.

§14

It's an IRS examiner in a chair, in a room. There is little else to see. Facing the tripod's camera, addressing the camera, one examiner after another. It's a cleared card-storage room off the radial hall of the Regional Examination Center's data processing pod, so the air-conditioning is good and there's none of summer's facial shine. Two at a time are brought in from the wiggle rooms; the examiner on deck is behind a vinyl partition, for prebriefing. The prebriefing is mostly just watching the intro. The documentary's intro is represented as coming from Triple-Six via the Regional Commissioner's HQ up in Joliet; the tape's case has the Service seal and a legal disclaimer. The putative working title is *Your IRS Today*. Possibly for public TV. Some of them are told it's for schools, civics classes. This is in the prebriefing. The interviews are represented as PR, with a serious purpose. To humanize, demystify the Service, help citizens understand how hard and important their job is. How much at stake. That they're not hostile or machines. The prebriefer reads from a series of printed cards; there's a mirror in the near corner for the on-deck subject to straighten his tie, smooth out her skirt. There's a release to sign, specially crafted—each examiner reads it closely, a reflex; they're still on the clock. Some are psyched. Excited. There's something about the prospect of attention, the project's real purpose. It's DP Tate's baby, conceptually, though Stecyk did all the work.

There's also the VCR monitor for letting them see the provisional intro, whose crudeness is acknowledged up front in the prebriefing, the need for tweaking. It's all set pieces and shots from photo archives whose stylized warmth does not fit the voiceover's tone. It's disorienting, and no one is sure what is up with the intro; the prebriefers stress it's just for orientation.

'The Internal Revenue Service is the branch of the United States Treasury Department charged with the timely collection of all federal taxes due under current statute. With over one hundred thousand employees in more than one thousand national, regional, district, and local offices, your IRS is the largest law enforcement agency in the nation. But it is more. In the body politic of the United States of America, many have likened your IRS to the nation's beating heart, receiving and distributing the resources which allow your federal government to operate effectively in the service and defense of all Americans.' Shots of highway crews, Congress as seen from the Capitol's gallery, a porch's mailman laughing about something with a homeowner, a contextless helicopter with the archive code still in the lower right corner, a Welfare clerk smiling as she hands a check to a black woman in a wheelchair, a highway crew with their hardhats raised in greeting, a VA rehab center, & c. 'The heart, too, of these United States as a team, each income earner chipping in to share resources and embody the principles that make our nation great.' One of the prebriefers' cards directs her here to lean in and insert that the voiceover script is a working draft and that the final product's voiceover will have real human inflections—to use their imagination. 'The lifeblood of this heart: the men and women of today's IRS.' Now a number of shots of what may be real but unusually attractive Service employees, mainly GS-9s and -11s in ties and shirtsleeves, shaking hands with taxpayers, bent smiling over the books of an auditee, beaming in front of a Honeywell 4C3000 that is in fact an empty chassis. 'Far from faceless bureaucrats, these [inaudible] men and women of today's IRS are citizens, taxpayers, parents, neighbors, and members of their community, all charged with a sacred task: to keep the lifeblood of government healthy and circulating.' A group still of what's either an Exams or Audit team arranged not by grade but by height, all waving. A shot of the same incised seal and motto that flank the REC's north facade. 'Just like the nation's *E pluribus unum*, our Service's founding motto, *Alicui tamen faciendum est*, says it all—this difficult, complex task must be performed, and it is your IRS who roll up their sleeves and do it.' It's laughably bad, hence its intrinsic plausibility to the wigglers, including of course the failure to translate the motto for an audience of TPs who all too often actually misspell their names on returns, which the Service Center systems catch and kick over to Exams, wasting everyone's time. But are presumed to know classical Latin, it seems. Perhaps really testing whether the prebriefed examiners catch this error—it's often hard to know what Tate's up to.

The chair is unpadded. It's all very spartan. The light is the REC's fluorescence; there are no lamps or bounces. No makeup, though in the prebriefing examiners' hair is carefully combed, sleeves rolled up exactly three flat turns, blouses opened at the top button, ID cards unclipped from the breast pocket. No director per se in the room; no one to say to act natural or tell them about the loopholes of editing. A technician at the tripod's camera, a boom man with headphones for levels, and the documentarian. The Celotex drop ceiling's been removed for acoustical reasons. Exposed piping and four-color bundles of wire running above the former ceiling's struts, out of the frame. The shot is just the examiner in the folding chair before a cream-colored screen that blocks off a wall of blank Hollerith cards in cardboard flats. The room could be anywhere, nowhere. Some of this is explained, theorized in advance; the prebriefing is precisely orchestrated. A tight shot, they explain, from the torso up, extraneous movements discouraged. Examiners are used to keeping still. There's a monitor room, a former closet, attached, with Toni Ware and an off-clock tech inside, watching. It's a video monitor. They are miked for the earplug that the documentarian/interlocutor stops wearing when it turns out to emit a piercing feedback sound whenever the Fornix card reader across the wall runs a particular subroutine. The monitor is video, like the camera, with no lighting or makeup. Pale and stunned, faces' planes queerly shadowed—this is not a problem, though on video some of the faces are a drained gray-white. Eyes are a problem. If the examiner looks at the documentarian instead of the camera, it can appear evasive or coerced. It's not optimal, and the prebriefer's advice is to look into the camera as one would a trusted friend's eyes, or a mirror, depending.

The prebriefers, both GS-13s on loan from some Post where Tate has unspecified suction, were themselves prebriefed in Stecyk's office. Both are credible, in coordinated navy and brown, the woman with something hard beneath the charm that suggests an ascent through Collections. The man is a blank to Ware, though; he could be from anywhere.

As is to be expected, some examiners are better than others. At this. Some can actuate, forget the setting, the stilted artifice, and speak as from the heart. So that with these, briefly, the recording techs can forget the job's sheer tedium, the contrivance, the stiffness of standing still at machines that could run on their own. The techs are, in other words, engaged by the better ones; attention requires no effort. But only some are better...and the question at the monitor is why, and what it means, and whether what it means will matter, in terms of results, when the whole thing is given to Stecyk to track down the line.

Videotape File 047804(r)
© 1984, Internal Revenue Service
Used by Permission
945645233

'It's a tough job. People think deskwork, pushing papers, how hard can it be. Government work, the job security, pushing papers along. They don't get it why it's hard. I've been here now three years. That's twelve quarters. All my reviews have been good. I won't be doing rotes forever, trust me. Some of the fellows in our group are fifty, sixty. They've been doing rote exams over thirty years. Thirty years of looking at forms, crosschecking forms, filling out the same memos on the same forms. There's something in some of their eyes. I don't know how to explain it. My grandparents' apartment building had a boiler man, a janitor. This was up near Milwaukee. Coal heat, this old fellow fed the coal furnace every couple hours. He'd been there forever; he was almost blind from looking into the mouth of that furnace. His eyes were... The older ones here are like that; their eyes are almost like that.'

968223861

'Three or four years ago, the new president, the current one, got elected into office on the promise of big defense spending and a massive tax cut. This is known. The idea was that the tax cut would stimulate economic growth. I'm not certain how this was supposed to work—a lot of the, like, upper policy ideas didn't reach us directly, they just trickled down to us through administrative changes in the Service. The way you know the sun's moved because now the shadows in your room are different. You know what I'm saying.'

Q.

'All of a sudden there were all these reorganizations, sometimes one right after the other, and repostings. Some of us stopped even unpacking. This is where I've been the longest now. I had no background in exams. I came out of Service Centers. I got reposted here from 029, the Northeast Service Center, Utica. New York, but upstate, in the third quarter, '82. Upstate New York is beautiful, but the Utica Center had a lot of problems. At Utica I was in general data processing; I was more like a troubleshooter. Before that I was at Service Center substation 0127, Hanover NH—I was in payment processing, then refund processing. The Northeast districts were all in octal code and the forms with sprocket holes that they hired Vietnamese girls to sit there and tear off. Hanover had a lot of refugees. It was eight, nine years ago, but a whole different era. This here is a much more complex organization.'

Q.

'I'm single, and single men are the ones in the Service that get reposted the most. Any repost is a hassle for Personnel; reposting a family is worse. Plus you have to offer incentives for people with families to move, it's a Treasury reg. Regulation. If you're single, though, you stop even unpacking.

'It's hard to meet women in the Service. It's not the most popular. There's a joke; can I tell it?'

Q.

'You meet a woman you like at, like, a party. She goes, what do you do. You go, I'm in finance. She goes, what kind. You go, sort of a type of accounting, it's a long story. She says, oh, who for. You go, the government. She goes, city, state? You go, federal. She goes, oh, what branch. You go, US Treasury. On it goes, narrowing down. At some point she figures it out, what you're dancing around, and she's gone.'

928874551

'Sugar in a cake has several different functions. One, for instance, is to absorb moisture from the butter, or perhaps shortening, and release it slowly over time, keeping the cake moist. Using less sugar than the recipe calls for produces what's known as a dry cake. Don't do that.'

973876118

'Suppose you think along the lines of power, authority. Inevitability. You've got your two kinds of people now, when you get down to it. On one hand you've got your rebel mentality whose whole bag or groove or what have you is going against power, rebelling. Your spit-in-the-wind type that feels powerful going against the power and the Establishment and what have you. Then, type two, you've got your other type, which is the soldier personality, the type that believes in order and power and respects authority and aligns themselves with power and authority and the side of order and the way the whole thing has got to work if the system's going to run smoothly. So imagine you're a type two type. There's more than they think. The age of the rebel is over. It's the eighties now. If You're a Type Two, We Want You—that should be their slogan. In the Service. Check out the blowing wind, man. Join up with the side that *always* gets paid. We shit you not. The side of the law and the force of the law, the side of the tide and gravity and that one law where everything always gradually gets a little hotter until the sun up and blows. Because you got your two unavoidables in life, just like they say. Unavoidability—now that's power, man. Either be a mortician or join the Service, if you want to line yourself up with the real power. Have the wind at your back. Tell them listen: Spit *with* the wind, it goes a whole lot further. You can trust me on that, my man.'

917229047

'I had an idea I'd try and write a play. Our stepmother always went to plays; she'd drag us all down to the civic center all the time on weekends for matinees. So I got to know all about the theater and plays. So this play, because they'd ask me—family, fellows at the driving range—to give an idea what it was like. It would be a totally real, true-to-life play. It would be unperformable, that was part of the point. This is to give you an idea. The idea's that a wiggler, a rote examiner, is sitting poring over 1040s and attachments and cross-filed W-2s and 1099s and like that. The setting is very bare and minimalistic—there's nothing to look at except this wiggler, who doesn't move except for every so often turning a page or making a note on his pad. It's not a Tingle—it's just a regular desk, so you can see him. But that's it. At first there was a clock behind him, but I cut the clock. He sits there longer and longer until the audience gets more and more bored and restless, and finally they start leaving, first just a few and then the whole audience, whispering to each other how boring and terrible the play is. Then, once the audience have all left, the real action of the play can start. This was the idea—I told my stepmom all about it, it was going to be a realistic play. Except I could never decide on the action, if there was any, if it's a realistic play. That's what I tell them. It's the only way to explain it.'

965882433

'There have been frequent studies. Two-thirds of taxpayers think an exemption and a deduction are the same thing. Don't know what a capital gain is. Four percent every year don't sign their returns. Shit, two-thirds of people don't know how many senators a state has. Something like three-quarters can't name the branches of government. This is not rocket science we're doing here. The truth is, most of our time is wasted. The system kicks us mostly shit. You spend ten minutes filling out a 20-C on an unsigned return, it goes back to the SC, a bullshit letter audit requesting a signature, nothing at stake.

And then now in Rotes we're reviewed on the basis of increased revenue from audits down the line. It's a joke. Most of the stuff we're looking at isn't auditable, it's just rank stupidity. Carelessness. You should see people's handwriting—average people, educated people. The truth is, they waste our time. They need a better system.'

981472509

'Tate is a moth at the arc lights of power. Pass it on.'

951458221

'It's a fascinating question. The background is interesting, if you delve into it. Type of thing. One of the tenets of the incoming administration was the belief that marginal tax rates could be lowered, especially in the top brackets, without causing a catastrophic loss of revenue. This had been an explicit part of the campaign. Platform type of thing. I'm no economist. I know the theory was that lower marginal rates would spur investment and increased productivity, type of thing, and there would be a rising tide that would cause an increase in the tax base that would more than offset the decrease in marginal rates. There is a whole technical theory behind this, though some dismissed this as voodoo science. Type of thing. By late in the first year, sure enough, the regs are different, the top brackets are lowered. It goes on that way. By, say, two years in, though, it's fair to say the results contradicted the theory. Revenues were down, and these were hard numbers that could not be fudged or massaged. There were also, I believe, very large increases in defense spending, and the federal budget deficit was the greatest in history. In adjusted dollars type of thing. You have to understand that this was all playing out at a far higher level of government than the level we're working at here. But anyone could understand the budget problems were a real rock-and-hard-place type of thing, since backpedaling and raising marginal rates again was politically unacceptable, ideologically you could say, as was compromising on the military, and gutting social spending any further would make relations with Congress unworkable. Type of thing. All of this one could almost know just from reading the newspaper, if you knew what to look for.'

Q.

'Yes, but in terms of what we knew here, at our level here in the Service. Some of it was not in the papers. I know the executive branch had several different plans and proposals they were considering, to address this problem. The deficits, the hard place. My sense is that most of these were not appealing. Type of thing. Understand, all this is filtering down from a great height, administratively. The version we got here on the regional level is that someone very high up in the Service's structure, someone close to what's known around here as the Three-Personed God, resurrected a policy paper originally written in either 1969 or 1970 by a macroeconomist or systems consultant on the staff of the former Assistant Commissioner for Planning and Research at Triple-Six. The one that resurrected it was, under this account, an Assistant Deputy Commissioner for Systems, which by that time had absorbed the Planning and Research Branch as now a division of Systems in a reorganization, Systems had, type of thing, although that previous Planning and Research AC was also now the DCS.'

Q.

'Now meaning in terms of when the Spackman Memo was resurrected, which was in or around the fourth quarter of 1981.'

Q.

'The DCS is part of what's known as the Three-Personed God, the [inaudible] term for the top triad of Commissioner, Deputy Commissioner for Systems, and Chief Counsel. The three top spots in the Service organization. The national office of the Service is known as Triple-Six because of the address. Type of thing.'

Q.

'These types of high-level proposals and white papers are generated all the time. Planning and Research has what amounts to think tanks type of thing. This is common knowledge. Full-time teams exclusively tasked to generating long-range studies and proposals. There's a famous policy paper from a P&R group in the 1960s, type of thing, on the implementation of tax protocols following a nuclear exchange. Called "Fiscal Planning for Chaos," which became rather a famous term around here, a kind of joke when things became hectic, chaos type of thing. Overall, few of them are made public. From the mid-sixties. Your tax dollar at work type of thing. This one that was resurrected in this context, though, was far less grand or explosive. I don't know its precise title. Sometimes it's known as the Spackman Memo or the Spackman Initiative, but I know of no one that knows who the eponymous Spackman was, type of thing, whether he was the author of the policy paper or the P&R official for whom the thing was written. It was generated, after all, in 1969, which was lifetimes ago in the institutional life of the Service. Most of them get filed away, type of thing. Understand, this is a compartmented agency. Many of the procedures and priorities of Triple-Six are simply out of our area. Type of thing. The Initiative's reorganizations, though, affect us directly, as I'm sure someone has explained. The original paper was said to be several hundred pages in length and very technical, as economics tends to be. Type of thing. But on a general level, the effective principle of the part or parts that came to later light was said to be quite simple, and it—[inaudible]—through routes unknown, it came to the attention of parties at the very highest levels of either the Service or the Treasury Department, and created interest because, in the budgetary impasse of the current executive branch, it appeared to describe a politically more appealing way to ameliorate the rock-and-hard-place of unexpectedly low tax revenues, high defense outlays, and an uncuttable base floor in social spending. At root, type of thing, the paper's proposal was said to be very simple, and of course the current executive approves of simplicity, arguably because this administration is somewhat of a reaction type of thing, or backlash, against the complex social engineering of the Great Society, which was a very different era for tax policy and administration. But its preference for simple, instinctive arguments is common knowledge. Type of thing. By the way, I can't help noticing you're wincing.'

Q.

'By all means.'

Q.

'As we understood it, the Spackman paper's root observation was that increasing the efficiency with which the Service enforced the extant tax code could provably increase net revenues to the US Treasury without any corresponding change in the code or a raising in marginal rates. Type of thing. Meaning it directed attention to Compliance and the tax gap. Should I define the gap, type of thing? Is this already defined by someone else? Are you asking everyone the same type of thing for this? Would the Service prefer that I not go into this?'

Q.

'I suppose it's self-evident, type of thing. It's the difference between total tax revenues lawfully due the US Treasury in a given year and total taxes actually collected by the Service in that year. It is rarely spoken of openly, largely [inaudible]. It is now the *bête noir* type of thing of the Service's focus. Though not at the time. It had been estimated, in the Spackman paper, that between six and seven billion dollars lawfully due the US Treasury in 1968 had not been remitted. Spackman's econometric projections placed the tax-gap figure for 1980 at close to twenty-seven billion, which appeared, by the time of the paper's resurrection, to be overly optimistic. Excluding appeals and litigation, the measured tax gap for 1980 was actually in excess of thirty-one and a half billion dollars. What was remarkable was that the tax gap's size had not been much remarked on or made the object of serious attention. I believe this is why it's rarely spoken of openly, the institutional stupidity of this, type of thing. Or that this is why the Spackman paper never received serious attention, although as I said, policy papers like this are generated by Systems all the time. Institutions can be much less intelligent than the individuals that make them up. Type of thing. There's also the fact that the Service is concerned to have the taxpaying public see it as nothing but a completely efficient, all-knowing instrument of tax collection—there are complex psychodynamics involved in taxation and the public's willingness to comply with tax law. For one thing, too much efficiency can be misconstrued as hostility, excessive aggression type of thing, which increases TP hostility and can actually negatively affect the public's compliance and the Service's mandate and budget, type of thing. Meaning the whole matter is complex, type of thing, and the psychodynamics are outside our area, and my understanding of it all is quite vague and general, type of thing, though we know that it is a matter of considerable interest and study at Triple-Six. Spackman's report, the subsection of interest, was resurrected by some person or persons close to the Three-Personed God. There are conflicting versions as to just whom. Type of thing. I'm speaking of a period roughly two and a half years ago.'

Q.

'At root, according to the policy paper, the gap was a matter of compliance. Type of thing. Obviously—since the gap represented a given percentage of noncompliance. But the subsection of the memo of interest concerned the parts of the tax gap that could be profitably addressed by the Service. Reduced, ameliorated. Type of thing. Meaning heightened revenue. A certain portion of the annual tax gap was due to an underground cash economy, barter mechanisms and in-kind exchanges, illicit income, and certain very sophisticated tax-avoidance mechanisms for the wealthy that could not be addressed in the short term. But Spackman's paper's analysis argued that a significant portion of the gap was the result of remediable misreporting, including Individual Forms 1040, which he argued could be addressed and ameliorated in the short term. The short term, for understandable reasons, the current administration was particularly keen on. Hence the intersection of technical policy and politics, which is how change occurs at the national level, then trickles down to us in the trenches, type of thing, through reorganizations and changes in Performance Review criteria, since 1040s are the purview of Rote Exams. Should I explain the different areas and types of examinations done here?'

Q.

'Not at all. On a root level, Spackman's memo broke the remediable, 1040-related portions of the tax gap down into three broad areas, categories, type of thing—nonfiling, underreporting, and underpayment. Nonfiling, in most cases, is the purview of CID. Criminal Investigations. Underpayment is handled through the Collections Division, a very different outfit, both philosophically and operationally, from what we do here in Exams, type of thing, although our two divisions, Exams and Collections, along, of course, with Audits, form the brunt of the Initiative. Which is also, organizationally, the Compliance Branch. At root, as examiners, we here deal with underreporting. Type of thing. Understated income, invalid deductions, overstated expenses, improperly claimed credits. Discrepancies, type—'

Q.

'At the root level, the argument of the Spackman Initiative, as it's come to be called here, both philosophically and organizationally, was that these three elements of the tax gap could be ameliorated by increasing the efficiency of the IRS respecting compliance. It's not difficult to see why this notion caught the political administration's eye as a potential third option, a way to help address the increasingly untenable revenue shortfall without raising rates or cutting outlays. Type of thing. Needless to say, this is all very simplified. I am attempting to explain the extraordinary developments that have taken place in the structure and operations of the Service as we here at the regional level experience it. It has been, to say the least, an unusually exciting year. And the root cause of the excitement, and also a certain amount of controversy, is the Spackman Initiative. This is what it came to be called. A sweeping, far-reaching reorientation in the Service's institutional sense of itself and its role in policy. Type of thing. Listen—are you all right?'

Q. [Pause, interval of static.]

'—of thing, which Triple-Six also found advantageous, argued that, under certain technical conditions, each dollar added to the Service's annual budget could be made to yield over sixteen dollars in additional revenue to Treasury. A good deal of this argument's body was devoted to considering the IRS's peculiar status and function as a federal agency. A federal agency is, by definition, an institution. A bureaucracy. But the Service was also the only agency in the federal apparatus whose function was revenue. Income. Meaning whose mandate was to maximize the legal return on each dollar invested in its annual budget. Type of thing. More than any other, then, according to the resurrected Spackman, there was compelling reason to conceive, constitute, and operate the IRS as a business—a going, for-profit concern type of thing—rather than as an institutional bureaucracy. At root, the Spackman report was intensely antibureaucratic. Its model was more classically free-market. The attractiveness of this to the free-market conservatives of the current administration should be understandable. This, after all, is an era of business deregulation. How best, and how much, to in a sense deregulate the IRS—which, of course, as a federal agency, was set up and operates as a set of legal regulations and mechanisms for enforcement—this was a thorny and still-evolving type of question type of thing. Some saw Spackman as an ideologue. Not every proposal in the original paper was resurrected—not everything became part of the Initiative. But the time was right, politically speaking, type of thing, for at least the root essence of Spackman's proposal. It would be difficult to overemphasize the consequences of this shift in philosophy and mandate for those of us on the ground of the effort. The Initiative. For example, an intensive new recruitment and hiring effort and an almost 20 percent increase in Service personnel, the first such increase since TRA '78. I refer also to a massive and seemingly endless restructuring of the Service's Compliance Branch, the most relevant [inaudible] of which to us here was the fact that the seven Regional Commissioners have assumed more autonomy and authority under the more de-decentralized operational philosophy of the Spackman Initiative.'

Q.

'This is another complicated subject, one that involves an extensive knowledge of US tax law and the history of the Service as part of the executive branch and yet also overseen by Congress. A critical part of what's now known as the Spackman Initiative involved finding an efficient middle way between two opposing tendencies that had hampered the Service's operations for decades, one being the decentralization mandated by the 1952 King Commission in Congress, the other being the extreme bureaucratic and political centrism of the national administration at Triple-Six. One could say that the 1960s was an era, speaking within the institutional history of the Service, in which the District office predominated. The 1980s is shaping itself to be the era of the Region. Type of thing. As an organizational middle ground between the many Districts and unitary

Triple-Six administration. Administrative, structural, logistical, and procedural decisions are now far more in the hands of the Regional Commissioner and his deputies, that, in turn, delegate responsibilities according to flexible but coherent operational guidelines, type of thing, which results in more root autonomy for the centers.'

Q.

'Each Region including one Service Center and, with one current exception, one Examination Center. Shall I explain the exception?'

Q.

'At root, under the Initiative, Regional Service and Examination Centers are allowed considerably more latitude in structure, personnel, systems, and operations protocols, resulting in increased authority and responsibility on the part of these facilities' Directors. The guiding idea is to free these large central processing facilities from oppressive or hidebound regulations which impede effective action. Type of thing. At the same time, extreme pressure is applied with respect to one and only one primary, overarching goal: results. Increased revenue. Reduced noncompliance. Reduction of the gap. Not quite quotas, of course—never that, of course, for reasons involving fairness and public perception—but close. We've all watched the news, you and I, and yes, more aggressive auditing is part of the picture. Type of thing. But the shifts and emphases in the Audits Divisions are largely changes of degree, a quantitative type of thing—including the advent of automated letter audits, which again is outside our area of working knowledge here. For us, however, in Examinations, there has been a dramatic, qualitative shift in operational philosophy and protocols. It can be felt by the lowliest GS-9 at her keypunch console. If Audits are the Initiative's weapon, type of thing, we in Exams are the telemetrists, tasked with determining where best to point that weapon. As deregulated, there is now only one overriding operational question: Which returns are most profitable to audit, and how are those returns most efficiently to be found?'

947676541

'I have an unusually high tolerance for pain.'

928514387

'Well, my dad used to like to mow the lawn in little patches and strips. He'd do the east corner of the front yard, come in the house for a while, then do the southwest strip of the back lawn and a little square at the south fence, come back in, and like that. He had a lot of little rituals like that, it's how he was. You know? It took a while to realize he did this with the lawn because he liked the feeling of being done. Of having a job and feeling like he did it and it was done. It's a solid little feeling, it's like you're a machine that knows it's running well and doing what it was made to do. You know? By dividing the lawn into like seventeen small little sections, which our mom thought was nuts as usual, he could feel the feeling of finishing a job seventeen times instead of just once. Like, "I'm done. I'm done again. Again, hey look, I'm done."

'Well, some of the same thing is at work here. In Rotes. I like it. An average 1040 takes around twenty-two minutes to go through and examine and fill out the memo on. Maybe a little longer depending on your criteria, some teams tweak the criteria. You know. But never more than half an hour. Each completed one gives you that solid little feeling.

'The thing here is that the returns never stop. There's always a next one to do. You never really finish. But on the other hand, it was the same with the lawn, you know? At least when it rained enough. By the time he got around to the last little section he'd marked off, the first patch would be ready to mow again. He liked a short, groomed-looking lawn. He spent a lot of time out there, come to think of it. A lot of his time.'

951876833

'It was on either *Twilight Zone* or *Outer Limits*—one of those. A claustrophobic guy who gets worse and worse until he's so claustrophobic that he starts screaming and carrying on, and they trundle him off to a mental asylum, and in the asylum they put him in isolation in a straitjacket in a tiny little room with a drain in the floor, a room the size of a closet, which you can see would be the worst thing possible for a claustrophobic, but they explain to him through a slit in the door that it's the rules and procedures, that if somebody's screaming they have to be put in isolation. Hence, the guy's damned, he's in there for life—because as long as he's screaming and trying to beat himself unconscious against the wall of the room, they're going to keep him in that little room, and as long as he's in that little room, he's going to be screaming, because the whole problem is that he's a claustrophobic. He's a living example of how there has to be some slack or play in the rules and procedures for certain cases, or else sometimes there's going to be some ridiculous foul-up and someone's going to be in a living hell. The episode was even called "Rules and Procedures," and none of us ever forgot it.'

987613397

'I don't believe I have anything to say that isn't in the code or Manual.'

943756788

'Mother called it being in a stare. She referred to my father in this, a habit he had in the midst of almost whatever. He was a kindly individual, a bookkeeper for the school district. Being in a stare referred to staring fixedly and without expression at something for extensive periods of time. It can happen when you haven't had enough sleep, or too much sleep, or if you've overeaten, or are distracted, or merely daydreaming. It is not daydreaming, however, because it involves gazing at something. Staring at it. Usually something straight ahead—a shelf on a bookcase, or the centerpiece on the dining room table, or your daughter or child. But in a stare, you are not really looking at this thing you are seeming to stare at, you are not even really noticing it—however, neither are you thinking of something else. You in truth are not doing anything, mentally, but you are doing it fixedly, with what appears to be intent concentration. It is as if one's concentration becomes stuck the way an auto's wheels can be stuck in the snow, turning rapidly without going forward, although it looks like intent concentration. And now I too do this. I find myself doing it. It's not unpleasant, but it is strange. Something goes out of you—you can feel your face merely hanging loose, with no muscles or expression. It frightens my children, I know. As if your face, like your attention, belongs to someone else. Sometimes now in the mirror, in the bathroom, I'll come to myself and catch myself in a stare, without any recognition. The man has been dead for twelve years now.

'This is the new challenge of it here. From outside the examiner, there was no guarantee that anyone could distinguish the difference between doing the job well and being in what she called the stare, staring at the returns files but not engaged by them, not truly paying attention. So long as you processed your given number of returns each day for throughput, they could not be sure. Not that I did this, my being in stares occurs after the day here, or before, when preparing. But I know they would worry: Who is the good examiner, and who is fooling them, spending their day in a stare, or thinking of other things. This can happen. But now, this year, they can know, they know who is doing the job. It becomes true later, the difference. Because they now log your eventuated revenue instead of your throughput. This is the change for us. Now it is easier, we are looking for something, what will cause ER, not just how many returns can one put through. This helps us pay attention.'

984057863

'Our house was outside of the city, off one of the blacktop roads. We had us a big dog that my daddy would keep on a chain in the front yard. A big part German shepherd. I hated the chain but we didn't have a fence, we were right off the road there. The dog hated that chain. But he had dignity. What he'd do, he'd never go out to the length of the chain. He'd never even get out to where the chain got tight. Even if the mailman pulled up, or a salesman. Out of dignity, this dog pretended like he chose this one area to stay in that just happened to be inside the length of the chain. Nothing outside of that area right there interested him. He just had zero interest. So he never noticed the chain. He didn't hate it. The chain. He just up and made it not relevant. Maybe he wasn't pretending—maybe he really up and chose that little circle for his own world. He had a power to him. All of his life on that chain. I loved that damn dog.'

§15

An obscure but true piece of paranormal trivia: There is such a thing as a *fact psychic*. Sometimes in the literature also known as a *data mystic*, and the syndrome itself as *RFI* (= *Random-Fact Intuition*). These subjects' sudden flashes of insight or awareness are structurally similar to but usually far more tedious and quotidian than the dramatically relevant foreknowledge we normally conceive as ESP or precognition. This, in turn, is why the phenomenon is so little studied or publicized, and why those possessed of RFI almost universally refer to it as an affliction or disability. In what few reputable studies and monographs exist, examples nevertheless abound; indeed, abundance, together with irrelevance and the interruption of normal thought and attention, composes the essence of the RFI phenomenon. The middle name of the childhood friend of a stranger they pass in a hallway. The fact that someone they sit near in a movie was once sixteen cars behind them on I-5 near McKittrick CA on a warm, rainy October day in 1971. They come out of nowhere, are inconvenient and discomfiting like all psychic irruptions. It's just that they're ephemeral, useless, undramatic, distracting. What Cointreau tasted like to someone with a mild head cold on the esplanade of Vienna's state opera house on 2 October 1874. How many people faced southeast to witness Guy Fawkes's hanging in 1606. The number of frames in *Breathless.* That someone named Fangi or Fangio won the 1959 Grand Prix. The percentage of Egyptian deities that have animal faces instead of human faces. The length and average circumference of Defense Secretary Caspar Weinberger's small intestine. The exact (not estimated) height of Mount Erebus, though not what or where Mount Erebus is.

In the case of GS-9 fact psychic Claude Sylvanshine on, say, 12 July 1981, the precise metric weight and speed of a train moving southwest through Prešov, Czechoslovakia, at the precise moment he's supposed to be crosschecking 1099-INT receipts with the tax return of Edmund and Willa Kosice, whose home's shutters were replaced in 1978 by someone whose wife once won three rounds of bingo in a row at St. Bridget's Church in Troy MI, even though the Kosices' residential address is Urbandale IA—reason for RFI incongruity unknown to Sylvanshine, for whom the factoids are just one more distraction he has to shake off in the noise and overall frenzied low morale of the Philadelphia REC. Then the Toltec god of corn, except in Toltec glyphs, so that to Sylvanshine it looks like an abstract drawing of origin unknown. The winner of the 1950 Nobel Prize in physiology slash medicine.

Datum: At least one-third of ancient rulers' seers and magicians were in fact fired or killed early in their tenure because it emerged that the bulk of what they foresaw or intuited was irrelevant. Not incorrect, just irrelevant, pointless. The human appendix's real reason. Norbert Wiener's name for the little leather ball that was his only friend as a sickly child. The number of blades of grass in the front lawn of one's mailman's home. They intrude, crash, rattle around. One reason Sylvanshine's gaze is always so intent and discomfiting is that he's trying to filter out all sorts of psychically intuited and intrusive facts. The amount of parenchyma in a certain fern in the waiting room of an orthodontist in Athens GA, though not and never what parenchyma might be. That the 1938 featherweight WBA champ had mild scoliosis in the region T10-12. Nor does he look it up—you don't chase these facts down; they're like lures that lead you nowhere. He's learned this from hard experience. The rate in astronomical units with which System ML435 is moving away from the Milky Way. He tells no one of the intrusions. Some are connected, but rarely in any way that yields what someone with true ESP would call meaning. The metric weight of all the lint in all the pockets of everyone at the observatory in Fort Davis TX on the 1974 day when a scheduled eclipse was obscured by clouds. Perhaps one in every four thousand such facts is relevant or helpful. Most are like having someone sing 'The Star-Spangled Banner' in your ear while you're trying to recite a poem for a prize. Claude Sylvanshine can't help it. That someone he passes in the street's great-great-great-grandmother's baby sister who died of whooping cough in 1844's name was Hesper. The cost, in adjusted dollars, of that obscured eclipse; the FCC broadcasting license of the Christian station the observatory's director listened to as he drove home, where he'd find his wife frazzled and the milkman's hat on the kitchen counter. The shape of the clouds on the afternoon two people he's never met conceived their child, who was miscarried six weeks in. That the pioneer of pullable consumer luggage was the ex-husband of a People Express stew who'd spent over eighteen months driving himself almost insane trying to research luggage manufacturing specs and pending patent applications because he couldn't believe no one had thought of mass-marketing this feature already. The USPTO registration number of the machine that attached the paper housing to the milkman's hat. The average molecular weight of peat. The affliction kept a secret from everyone everywhere since fourth grade when Sylvanshine knew the name of his homeroom teacher's husband's first love's childhood cat who'd lost one side's whiskers in a mishap near the coal stove in Ashtabula OH, verified only when he wrote a little illustrated booklet and the husband saw the name and whiskerless crayon drawing of Scrapper, turned ivory white, and dreamed intensely for three nights, unknown to anyone.

The fact psychic lives part-time in the world of fractious, boiling minutiae that no one knows or could be bothered to know even if they had the chance to know. The population of Brunei. The difference between mucus and sputum. How long a piece of gum has resided on the underside of the third-row fourth-from-left seat of the

Virginia Theater, Cranston RI, but not who put it there or why. Impossible to predict what facts will intrude. Constant headaches. The data sometimes visual and queerly backlit, as by an infinitely bright light an infinite distance away. The amount of undigested red meat in the colon of the average forty-three-year-old adult male resident of Ghent, Belgium, in grams. The relation between the Turkish lira and the Yugoslavian dinar. The year of death for undersea explorer William Beebe.

Tastes a Hostess cupcake. Knows where it was made; knows who ran the machine that sprayed a light coating of chocolate frosting on top; knows that person's weight, shoe size, bowling average, American Legion career batting average; he knows the dimensions of the room that person is in right now. Overwhelming.

§16

Lane Dean Jr. and two older examiners from a different Pod are outside one of the unalarmed door exits between Pods, on a hexagram of cement surrounded by maintained grass, watching the sun on the fallow fields just south of the REC. None of them are smoking; they're just being outside for a bit. Lane Dean hasn't come outside with the other two; he just happened to step out for air on the break at the same time. He's still looking for a really desirable, diverting place to go during breaks; they're too important. The other two guys know each other or work on the same team; they've come out together; one senses it's a routine of long standing.

One of the men gives a sort of artificial-looking gap and stretch. 'Jeez,' he says. 'Well, Midge and I went over to the Bodnars' on Saturday. You know Hank Bodnar, from over in K-team at Capital Exams, with the glasses with the lenses that turn dark by themselves outside, what are they called.' The man has his hands behind his back and goes up and down on his toes rapidly, like someone waiting for a bus.

'Uh-huh.' The other man, who's perhaps five years younger than the man who went to the Bodnars', is contemplating some kind of benign cyst or growth on the inside of his wrist. The heat is accumulating at mid-morning, and the electric sound of the locusts in the wild grasses rises and falls in the parts of the fields the sun is striking. Neither man has introduced himself to Lane Dean, who's standing farther from them than they are from each other, though not so far away that he could be seen as wholly disconnected from the conversation. Maybe they're giving him privacy because they can see he's new and still adjusting to the unbelievable tedium of the exam job. Maybe they're shy and awkward and not sure how to introduce themselves. Lane Dean, whose slacks have ridden up so far he'd have to go into a stall in a men's room to extract them, feels like running out into the fields in the heat and running in circles and flapping his arms.

'We were supposed to go over the weekend before, the what, the seventh that would be,' the first man says, looking out at a vista with nothing really particular to hold the eye, 'but our youngest had a temperature and a little bit of a sore throat, and Midge didn't want to leave her with the sitter if she had a temperature. So she called to cancel, and Midge and Alice Bodnar worked it out so we all just moved it up a week, seven days to the day, that way it was easy to remember. You know how mama bears get when their little cubs run a temperature.'

'Don't have to tell me,' Lane Dean inserts from several feet away, laughing a little too heartily. One shoe is in the shadow of the pod's overhang and one is in the morning sun. Lane Dean is starting now to feel desperate about the fact that the break's fifteen minutes are ticking inexorably away and he is going to have to go back in and examine returns for another two hours before the next break. There's an empty Styrofoam cup on its side in the ashtray unit of a small waste can in the alcove. Being in a conversation makes the time pass differently; it's not clear whether it's better or worse. The other man is still examining his wrist's thing, holding the forearm up like a surgeon after scrubbing. If you think of the locusts as actually screaming, the whole thing becomes much more unsettling. The normal protocol is not to hear them; they cease to register on you after a while.

'So anyhow,' the first examiner says. 'We go over, have a drink. Midge and Alice Bodnar get to talking about some new drapes they're looking at for the living room, on and on. Pretty dry stuff, wife stuff. So Hank and me end up in the den, because Hank he collects coins—seriously, he's a serious coin collector from what I could see, not just those cardboard albums with circular holes, he really knows his business. And he wanted to show me a picture of a coin he was thinking about acquiring, for his collection.' The other man had looked up for the first real time when the guy telling the story mentioned coin collecting, which is a hobby that to Lane Dean, as a Christian, has always seemed debased and distorted in a number of ways.

'A nickel, I think,' the first fellow is saying. He keeps lapsing into what seems like almost talking to himself, while the second man starts and stops examining the growth thing. You get the idea that this is the sort of interchange the two men have had on breaks for many, many years—it's such a habit it's not even conscious anymore. 'Not a buffalo nickel, but some kind of five-cent piece with an alternate backing that's well-known; I don't know much about coins but even I'd heard of it, which means it must be pretty well-known. But I can't think of the correct term for it.' He laughs in a way that sounds almost pained. 'Right out of my head. I can't remember it now.'

'Alice Bodnar's a pretty good little cook,' the other fellow says. The plastic tabs of a light-brown clip-on tie show slightly around his shirt's collar. The knot of the tie itself is tight as a knuckle; there'd be no way to loosen it. From where he stands, Lane Dean has a better, more circumspect view of this second examiner. The growth on the inside of his wrist is the size of a child's nose and composed of what looks almost like horn or hard, outgrowthy material, and appears reddened and slightly inflamed, though this may be because the second fellow picks at it so much. How could one not? Lane Dean knows that he might well become sickeningly fixated on the man's wrist's thing if they worked at adjoining Tingles in the same Pod—trying to look at it without being observed, making resolutions not to look at it, etc. It slightly appalls him that he almost envies whoever is at that table, imagines the reddened cyst and its career as an object of distraction and attention, something to hoard the way a crow hoards shiny useless things it happens to find, even strips of aluminum foil or little bits of a locket's broken chain. He feels an odd desire to ask the man about the growth, what is its deal, how long, etc. It's happened, just as the man said: Lane Dean no longer needs to look at his watch on breaks. There are now six minutes left.

'Jeez, well, there was a whole plan to poach some salmon fillets and eat out on the porch with the salmon with this special little sage glaze Midge and Alice wanted to make up and scalloped potatoes—I think scalloped; maybe you call them au gratin. And a big salad, so big you couldn't pass the bowl around, even; it had to be on a little separate table.'

The second man is now carefully rolling his shirtsleeve down and buttoning it back over the wrist with the thing, though when he sits over returns and the sleeve pulls back slightly Dean bets that the rim of the cyst's red penumbra will still show slightly over the cuff, and that the cuff's movement back and forth over the growth throughout the examination day might be part of what makes it look red and sore—it might hurt in a tiny, sickening way each time the man's cuff pulls forward or back over the little growth of horn.

'But it was such a nice day. Hank and I were in the den, that has a set of those large types of windows that look out over part of the front lawn and the street; there were some neighborhood kids riding bicycles up and down the street and yelling and just having a hell of a time. We decided, Hank did, what the hell, it's such a hell of a nice day, let's see if the girls want to barbecue. So we got out Hank's grill, a big Weber model with wheels that you could roll it out if you leaned it backwards; there were three legs but only two with wheels—you know what I'm talking about.'

The second man leans out and spits neatly through his teeth into the grass at the edge of the hexagram. He's maybe forty, silver hairs in the hair on the side of his head in the sun, Lane Dean can see. Lane Dean imagines running out into the field in an enormous circle, flapping his arms like Roddy McDowall.

'So we did, wheeled it out,' the first man says. 'And barbecued the salmon instead of poaching it, though everything else was the same, and Midge and Alice talked about where they got the salad bowl, that had all these little carvings around up near the rim, the thing had to weigh five pounds. Hank grilled them on the patio, and we ate there on the porch because of the bugs.'

'What do you mean?' Lane Dean asks, aware of the slight edge of hysteria in his voice.

'Why,' says the first, heavier guy, 'the sun was going down. The skeeters come down off the golf course out by Fairhaven. No way we're going to sit out on the patio, get eaten alive. Nobody even had to say anything about it.' The man sees Lane Dean still looking at him, his head cocked exaggeratedly in a curiosity he didn't one bit feel.

'Well, it's a screen porch.' The second man is looking at Lane Dean like, who is this guy?

The man who'd eaten supper at the other people's house laughs. 'Best of both worlds. A screen porch.'

'Unless it rains,' the second man says. Both of them laugh ruefully.

§17

'I'd always from early on as a child I think somehow imagined Revenue men as like those certain kinds of other institutional heroes, bureaucratic, small-*h* heroes—like police, firemen, Social Service workers, Red Cross and VISTA people, the people who keep the records at SSI, even certain kinds of clergy and religious volunteers—trying to stitch or bandage the holes that all the more selfish, glitzy, uncaring, "Me-First" people are always making in the community. I mean more like police and fire department office and clerical personnel rather than the ones who everyone knows about and get in the newspaper for what they do. I don't mean the kind of heroes that "put their lives on the line." I suppose what I'm saying is that there are other kinds. I wanted to be one. The kind that seemed even more heroic because nobody applauded or even thought about them, or if they did it was usually as some enemy. The sort of person who's on the Clean Up Committee instead of playing in the band at the dance or being there with the prom queen, if you know what I mean. The quiet kind who cleans up and does the dirty job. You know.'

§18

'And Desk Names are back. This is another plus under Glendenning. Nothing against the Pale King, but the consensus is that Mr. Glendenning is more agent-morale-oriented, and Desk Names are one example.'

[Off-camera prompt.]

'Well, they're just what it says. Instead of your name. There's a plate on your desk with your Desk Name. Your Name de Gear as they say. No more worrying some burger whose shoes you maybe have to squeeze a little bit knows your name, maybe they find out where you and your family live—don't think this isn't on an agent's mind.'

[Off-camera prompt.]

'Though it's not exactly like before the Pale King. It got out of hand, there's no denying. There's no obvious joke Desk Names now. Which to be honest got old fast and nobody misses; nobody wants a taxpayer thinking he's silly. We are far from silly around here. No more Phil Mypockets or Mike Hunt or Seymour Booty. Although nobody least of all Mr. Glendenning says you can't still use the Desk Name as a tool. In the great battle for the hearts and minds. If you're smart, you'll use it as a tool. We rotate; seniority chooses the plate. This quarter, my Desk Name is Eugene Fusz—you can see it right on the nameplate here. They look pretty good now. One type of tool is you use a Desk Name where the subject isn't sure how to pronounce it. Is it like *fuse,* is it like *fuss,* is it like *fuzz?* The burger sure doesn't want to offend you. Other good ones are Fuchs, Traut, Wiener, Ojerkis, Büger, Tünivich, Schoewder, Wënkopf. There's over forty-three plates extant. La Bialle, Bouhel. Umlauts are always good; umlauts seem to drive them especially nuts. It's just one more little off-balance tactic. Plus a small little smile on a gray day and so forth and so on. Hanratty applied for a Peanys plate for third quarter—it's under review, Mr. Rosebury said. There's a line, after all, under Glendenning. This is about revenue. It ain't exactly the Chuckle Hut we're running here.'

§19

'There's something very interesting about civics and selfishness, and we get to ride the crest of it. Here in the US, we expect government and law to be our conscience. Our superego, you could say. It has something to do with liberal individualism, and something to do with capitalism, but I don't understand much of the theoretical aspect—what I see is what I live in. Americans are in a way crazy. We infantilize ourselves. We don't think of ourselves as citizens—parts of something larger to which we have profound responsibilities. We think of ourselves as citizens when it comes to our rights and privileges, but not our responsibilities. We abdicate our civic responsibilities to the government and expect the government, in effect, to legislate morality. I'm talking mostly about economics and business, because that's my area.'

'What do we do to stop the decline?'

'I have no idea what we do. As citizens we cede more and more of our autonomy, but if we the government take away the citizens' freedom to cede their autonomy we're now taking away their autonomy. It's a paradox. Citizens are constitutionally empowered to choose to default and leave the decisions to corporations and to a government we expect to control them. Corporations are getting better and better at seducing us into thinking the way they think—of profits as the *telos* and responsibility as something to be enshrined in symbol and evaded in reality. Cleverness as opposed to wisdom. Wanting and having instead of thinking and making. We cannot stop it. I suspect what'll happen is that there will be some sort of disaster—depression, hyperinflation—and then it'll be showtime: We'll either wake up and retake our freedom or we'll fall apart utterly. Like Rome—conqueror of its own people.'

'I can see taxpayers not wanting to part with money. It's a natural human thing. I didn't like getting audited either. But shit, you've got basic facts to counterbalance that—we voted these guys in, we choose to live here, we want good roads and a good army to protect us. So you ante up.'

'That's a little simplistic.'

'It seems like, suppose you're in a lifeboat with other people and there's only so much food, and you have to share it. You've only got so much and it's got to go around, and everybody's really hungry. Of course you want all the food; you're starving. But so is everybody else. If you ate all the food you couldn't live with yourself afterward.'

'The others'd kill you, too.'

'But the point is psychological. Of course you want it all, of course you want to keep every dime you make. But you don't, you ante up, because it's how things have to be for the whole lifeboat. You sort of have a duty to the others in the boat. A duty to yourself not to be the sort of person who waits till everybody is asleep and then eats all the food.'

'You're talking like a civics class.'

'Which you never had, I'm betting. What are you, twenty-eight? Did your school have civics when you were a boy? Do you even know what civics is?'

'It was a cold war thing they started in the schools. The Bill of Rights, the Constitution, the Pledge of Alliance, the importance of voting.'

'Civics is the branch of political science that quote concerns itself with citizenship and the rights and duties of US citizens.'

'*Duty*'s kind of a harsh word. I'm not saying it's their duty to pay their taxes. I'm just saying it doesn't make any sense not to. Plus we catch you.'

'I don't think this will be the conversation you want to have, but if you really want my opinion I'll tell you.'

'Fire away.'

'I think it's no accident that civics isn't taught anymore or that a young man like yourself bridles at the word *duty*.'

'We've gotten soft, you're saying.'

'I'm saying that the sixties—which God love them did a lot for raising people's consciousness in a whole lot of areas, such as race and feminism—'

'Not to mention Vietnam.'

'No, mention it, because here was a whole generation where most of them now for the first time questioned authority and said that their individual moral beliefs about the war outweighed their duty to go fight if their duly elected representatives told them to.'

'In other words that their highest actual duty was to *themselves*.'

'Well, but to themselves as *what*?'

'This all seems pretty simplistic, you guys. It's not like everybody that was protesting was doing it out of duty. It became fashionable to protest the war.'

'Neither the ultimate-duty-is-to-self element nor the fashionable element is irrelevant.'

'You're saying that protesting Vietnam led to tax cheating?'

'No, he's saying it led to the sort of selfishness that has us all trying to eat all the boat's food.'

'No, but I think whatever led to it becoming actually fashionable to protest a war opened the door to what's going to bring us down as a country. The end of the democratic experiment.'

'Did I tell you he was a conservative?'

'But that's just a put-down. There are all kinds of conservatives depending on what it is they want to conserve.'

'The sixties were America's starting to decline into decadence and selfish individualism—the Me generation.'

'There was more decadence in the twenties than there was in the sixties, though.'

'You know what I think? I think the Constitution and *Federalist Papers* of this country were an incredible moral and imaginative achievement. For really the first time in a modern nation, those in power set up a system where the citizens' power over their own government was to be a matter of substance and not mere symbolism. It was utterly priceless, and it will go down in history with Athens and the Magna Carta. The fact that it was a utopia which for two hundred years actually *worked* makes it beyond priceless—it's literally a miracle. And—and now I'm speaking of Jefferson, Madison, Adams, Franklin, the real church Fathers—what raised the American experiment beyond great imagination and made it very nearly work was not just these men's intelligence but their profound moral enlightenment—their sense of civics. The fact is that they cared more about the nation and the citizens than about themselves. They could have just set America up as an oligarchy where powerful eastern industrialists and southern landowners controlled all the power and ruled with an iron hand in a glove of liberal rhetoric. Need I say Robespierre, or the Bolsheviks, or the Ayatollah? These Founding Fathers were geniuses of civic virtue. They were heroes. Most of their effort went into restraining the power of government.'

'Checks and balances.'

'Power to the People.'

'They knew the tendency of power to corrupt—'

'Jefferson supposedly boinking his own slaves and having whole litters of mulatto children.'

'They believed that centralizing power in its dispersal among a concerned, educated, civic-minded electorate would ensure against America devolving into one more instance of nobles and peasants, rulers and serfs.'

'An educated landowning *white male* electorate, we should keep in mind.'

'And this is one of the paradoxes of the twentieth century with its apex in the sixties. Is it good to make things fairer and to allow the whole citizenry to vote? Yes, plainly so, in theory. And yet it's very easy to judge ancestors through the lens of the present instead of trying to see the world as they might have seen it. The Founding Fathers' enfranchisement of only wealthy landed educated males was designed to place power in the hands of the people most like themselves—'

'Doesn't sound all that new or experimental to me, Mr. Glendenning.'

'They believed in rationality—they believed that persons of privilege, literacy, education, and moral sophistication would be able to emulate them, to make judicious and self-disciplined decisions for the good of the nation and not just to advance their own interests.'

'It's certainly an imaginative and ingenious rationalization of racism and male chauvinism, that's for sure.'

'They were heroes, and like all true heroes they were modest and didn't regard themselves as all that exceptional. They assumed their descendants would be like them—rational, honorable, civic-minded. Men with at least as much concern for the common good as for personal advantage.'

'How did we get from the sixties to this?'

'And instead we get the dickless or crooked leaders we've got today.'

'We elect what we deserve.'

'But it's something very odd. That they could have been so prescient and farsighted about erecting checks against the accumulation of power in any one branch of government, their healthy fear of government, and yet their naive belief in the civic virtue of the common people.'

'Our leaders, our government is us, all of us, so if they're venal and weak it's because we are.'

'I hate it when you synopsize what I'm trying to say and get it wrong, but I don't quite know what to say. Because it's stronger than that. I don't think the problem is our leaders. I voted for Ford and I'll likely vote for Bush or maybe Reagan and I'll feel solid about my vote. But we see it here, with TPs. We're the government, its worst face—the rapacious creditor, the stern parent.'

'They hate us.'

'They hate the government—we're just the most convenient incarnation of what they hate. There's something very curious, though, about the hatred. The government *is* the people, leaving aside various complications, but we split it off and pretend it's not us; we pretend it's some threatening Other bent on taking our freedoms, taking our money and redistributing it, legislating our morality in drugs, driving, abortion, the environment—Big Brother, the Establishment—'

'The Man.'

'With the curious thing being that we hate it for appearing to usurp the very civic functions we've ceded to it.'

'Inverting the Founding Fathers' device of ceding political power to the people instead of the government.'

'Consent of the governed.'

'But it's gone farther than that, and the sixties idea of personal freedom and appetite and moral license has something to do with it, though I'm damned if I can quite figure it out. Only that something queer is going on in terms of civics and selfishness in this country, and we here in the Service get to see it in some of its most extreme manifestations. We now, as citizens and businessmen and consumers and whatall, we expect government and law to function as our conscience.'

'Isn't that what laws are for?'

'You mean our superego? In loco parentis?'

'It has something to do with liberal individualism, and something to do with the Constitution's overestimate of individual character, and it has something to do with consumer capitalism—'

'That's pretty vague.'

'It is vague. I'm not a political scientist. But it's not vague in its consequences; the concrete reality of its consequences is what our jobs are about.'

'But the Service has been around since long before the decadent sixties.'

'Let him finish.'

'I think Americans in 1980 are crazy. Have gone crazy. Regressed somehow.'

'The quote lack of discipline and respect for authority of the decadent seventies.'

'If you don't shut up I'm going to put you up on the roof of the elevator and you can stay there.'

'It may sound reactionary, I know. But we can all feel it. We've changed the way we think of ourselves as citizens. We don't think of ourselves as citizens in the old sense of being small parts of something larger and infinitely more important to which we have serious responsibilities. We do still think of ourselves as citizens in the sense of being beneficiaries—we're actually conscious of our rights as American citizens and the nation's responsibilities to us and ensuring we get our share of the American pie. We think of ourselves now as eaters of the pie instead of makers of the pie. So who makes the pie?'

'Ask not what your country can do for you...'

'Corporations make the pie. They make it and we eat it.'

'It's probably part of my naïveté that I don't want to put the issue in political terms when it's probably irreducibly political. Something has happened where we've decided on a personal level that it's all right to abdicate our individual responsibility to the common good and let government worry about the common good while we all go about our individual self-interested business and struggle to gratify our various appetites.'

'You can blame some of it on corporations and advertising surely.'

'I don't think of corporations as citizens, though. Corporations are machines for producing profit; that's what they're ingeniously designed to do. It's ridiculous to ascribe civic obligations or moral responsibilities to corporations.'

'But the whole dark genius of corporations is that they allow for individual reward without individual obligation. The workers' obligations are to the executives, and the executives' obligations are to the CEO, and the CEO's obligation is to the Board of Directors, and the Board's obligation is to the stockholders, who are also the same customers the corporation will screw over at the very earliest opportunity in the name of profit, which profits are distributed as dividends to the very stockholders-slash-customers they've been fucking over in their own name. It's like a fugue of evaded responsibility.'

'You're leaving out Labor Unions advocating for labor and mutual funds and the SEC's effects on share-price over basis.'

'You are a complete genius of irrelevancy, X. This isn't a seminar. DeWitt's trying to get at the heart of something here.'

'Corporations aren't citizens or neighbors or parents. They can't vote or serve in combat. They don't learn the Pledge of Allegiance. They don't have souls. They're revenue machines. I don't have any problem with that. I think it's absurd to lay moral or civic obligations on them. Their only obligations are strategic, and while they can get very complex, at root they're not civic entities. With corporations, I have no problem with government enforcement of statutes and regulatory policy serving a conscience function. What my problem is is the way it seems that we as individual citizens have adopted a corporate attitude. That our ultimate obligation is to ourselves. That unless it's illegal or there are direct practical consequences for ourselves, any activity is OK.'

'I'm regretting this conversation more and more. It—you like movies?'

'You bet.'

'Are you kidding?'

'Nothing like cozying up on a rainy evening with a Betamax and a good film.'

'Suppose it was determined that the increasing violence of US films correlated with a rise in violent-crime statistics. I mean, suppose the statistics weren't merely *suggestive* but actually demonstrated *conclusively* that the increasing number of graphically violent films like *Clockwork Orange* or *The Godfather* or *The Exorcist* had a causal correlation with the real-world rates of mayhem.'

'Let's not forget *The Wild Bunch*. Plus *Clockwork Orange* is British.'

'Shut up.'

'Define *violent,* though. Can't it mean vastly different things to different people?'

'I'll throw you off this elevator, X, I swear to God I will.'

'What would we expect the Hollywood corporations that make the movies to do? Would we really expect them to care about their films' effect on violence in the culture? We might posture and send nasty letters. But the corporations, underneath all the PR bullshit, reply that they're in business to make money for their stockholders, and that they'd give one fart in a stiff wind about what some statistics say about their products only if the government forced them to regulate the violence.'

'Which would run into some First-Amendment trouble, big-time.'

'I don't think Hollywood studios are owned by stockholders; I think the vast bulk of them are owned by parent companies.'

'*Or* if what? If ordinary moviegoing people stopped going in droves to see ultraviolent movies. The movie people can say they're only doing what corporations were designed to do—meet a demand and make as much money as is legally possible.'

'This whole conversation is dull.'

'Sometimes what's important is dull. Sometimes it's work. Sometimes the important things aren't works of art for your entertainment, X.'

'My point is this. And I'm sorry, X, because if I knew more about what I was talking about I could make the point faster, but I'm not used to talking about it and have never been much able even to put it into words in any sort of order—the whole thing is usually more a tornado in my head as I'm driving in in the morning thinking about what's on the docket for the day. My only point on the movies is this: Would these statistics cause much of a decline in the crowds that go to see these ultraviolent movies in such droves? They wouldn't. And that's the craziness; that's what I mean. What would we do? We'd bitch at the water cooler about these damn soulless corporations who don't give a shit about the state of the nation but only care about making a buck. A few of them might write the *Journal Star*'s op-ed page or even their Congressman. There ought to be a law. Regulate it, we'd say. But come Saturday night, they'd still go see whatever damn violent movie they and the Mrs. want to see.'

'It's like they expect the government to be the parent that takes away the dangerous toy, and until it does they'll go right on playing with it. A toy dangerous to *others*.'

'They don't think of themselves as responsible.'

'I think what's changed somehow is they don't think of themselves as *personally* responsible. They don't think of it like that their personal, individual going and buying a ticket for *The Exorcist* is what adds to the demand that keeps the corporate machines coming out with more and more violent movies to satisfy the demand.'

'They expect the government to do something about it.'

'Or corporations to grow souls.'

'That example makes it a lot easier to see your point, Mr. Glendenning,' I said.

'I'm not sure *The Exorcist* is the best example. *The Exorcist* isn't all that violent so much as sick. Now *The Godfather*—that's violent.'

'Never did see *The Exorcist,* because Mrs. G. said she'd rather have all her fingers and toes cut off with dull scissors than sit through a piece of trash like that. But from what I heard and read it was damn violent.'

'I think the syndrome is more the not-voting one, the I'm-so-small-and-the-mass-of-everyone-else-is-so-big-what-possible-difference-does-what-I-do-make, so they stay home and watch *Charlie's Angels* instead of going to vote.'

'And then they bitch and moan about their elected leaders.'

'So maybe it's not a sense of the individual citizen not being responsible so much as they're so tiny and the government and rest of the country is so big they've got no chance of having any kind of real impact, so they just have to look out for themselves as best they can.'

'Not to mention how big corporations are; like how is one guy not having a *Godfather* ticket going to influence Paramount Pictures one way or the other? Which is all still bullshit; it's a way to rationalize not being responsible for your tiny part of which way the country goes.'

'All this is part of it, I think. And it's hard to peg just what the difference is. And I'm wary about doing the old-fart move of saying people aren't civic-minded like they were in the good old days and the country's going to shit. But it seems like citizens—whether on taxes or littering, you name it—did feel like they were part of Everything, that the huge Everybody Else that determined policy and taste and the common good was in fact made up of a whole lot of individuals just like them, that they were in fact *part* of Everything, and that they had to hold up their end and pull their weight and assume what they did made some difference the same way Everybody Else did, if the country was going to stay a nice place to live.'

'Citizens feel alienated now. It's like me-against-everyone-else.'

'*Alienated*'s one of those big sixties words.'

'But how did this alienated small selfish make-no-difference thing result from the sixties, since if the sixties showed anything good it showed that like-minded citizens can think for themselves and not just swallow what the Establishment says and they can band together and march and agitate for change and there can be real change; we pull out of 'Nam, we get Welfare and the Civil Rights Act and women's lib.'

'Because corporations got in the game and turned all the genuine principles and aspirations and ideology into a set of fashions and attitudes—they made Rebellion a fashion pose instead of a real impetus.'

'It's awful easy to vilify corporations, X.'

'Doesn't the term *corporation* itself come from *body,* like "made into a body"? These were artificial people being created. What was it, the Fourteenth Amendment that gave corporations all the rights and responsibilities of citizens?'

'No, the Fourteenth Amendment was part of Reconstruction and was intended to give full citizenship to freed slaves, and it was some corporation's sharpy counsel that persuaded the Court that corporations fit the Fourteenth's criteria.'

'We're talking C corps here, right?'

'Because it's true—it's not even clear now when you say *corporation* whether we're talking about Cs or Ss, LLCs, corporate associations, plus you've got closely-helds and public, plus those sham corporations that are really just limited partnerships loaded up with nonrecourse debt to generate paper losses, which are basically just parasites on the tax system.'

'Plus C corps contribute by double taxation, so it's hard to say they're nothing but a negative in the revenue sphere.'

'I'm giving you a look of complete scorn and derision, X; what do you imagine it is we *do* here?'

'Not to mention fiduciary instruments that function almost identically to corporations. Plus franchise-spreads, flowthrough trusts, NFP foundations established as corporate instruments.'

'None of this matters. And I'm not even really talking about what we do here except in the sense that it puts us in a position to see civic attitudes close up, since there's nothing more concrete than a tax payment, which after all is your money, whereas the obligations and projected returns on the payments are abstract, at the abstract level the whole nation and its government and the commonweal, so attitudes about paying taxes seem like one of the places where a man's civic sense gets revealed in the starkest sorts of terms.'

'Wasn't it the Thirteenth Amendment that blacks and corporations exploited?'

'Let me throw him off, Mr. G., I'm pleading with you.'

'Here's something worth throwing out there. It was in the 1830s and '40s that states started granting charters of incorporation to larger and regulated companies. And it was 1840 or '41 that de Tocqueville published his book about Americans, and he says somewhere that one thing about democracies and their individualism is that they by their very nature corrode the citizen's sense of true community, of having real true fellow citizens whose interests and concerns were the same as his. This is a kind of ghastly irony, if you think about it, since a form of government engineered to produce equality makes its citizens so individualistic and self-absorbed they end up as solipsists, navel-gazers.'

'De Tocqueville is also talking about capitalism and markets, which pretty much go hand in hand with democracy.'

'I just don't think this is what I was trying to talk about. It's easy to blame corporations. DeWitt's saying if you think the corporations are evil and it's the government's job to make them moral, you're deflecting your own responsibility to civics. You're making the government your big brother and the corporation the evil bully your big brother's supposed to keep off you at recess.'

'De Tocqueville's thrust is that it's in the democratic citizen's nature to be like a leaf that doesn't believe in the tree it's part of.'

'What's interesting in a depressing way is that tacit hypocrisy—I, the citizen, will keep buying big gas-guzzlers that kill trees and tickets for *The Exorcist* until the government passes a law, but then when the government *does* pass a law I'll bitch about Big Brother and getting the government off our back.'

'See for instance the cheat-rate and the appeals percentage after audit.'

'It's more like I want a law to keep *you* from gas-guzzling and seeing *The Wild Bunch,* but not me.'

'Not in my backyard is the hue and cry.'

'Lady gets stabbed over off the river, houses up and down the block hear her screaming, nobody even sets foot outside.'

'Not get involved.'

'Something's happened to people.'

'People saying those damned tobacco companies while they smoke.'

'It's not fair to put down any critique of the corporate role in this kind of civic decline as just a simple knee-jerk demonization of corporations, though. The corporate agenda of maximizing profit by creating demand and trying to make demand inelastic can play a catalyst role in this syndrome Mr. Glendenning's trying to limn without being the devil or bent on world domination or something.'

'I believe Nichols has another two cents here.'

'I think he's trying to say something.'

'Because I think it goes beyond politics, civics.'

'I'm listening at least, Stuart.'

'Not even on a tree but more like leaves on the ground in the wind, blown this way and that way by the wind, and each time a gust blows it the citizen says, "Now I choose to blow this way; this is my decision." '

'With the wind being Nichols's corporate menace.'

'It's almost more a matter of metaphysics.'

'Yee ha.'

'Hoo doggy.'

'Say what we're in now is some transition in the economy and society between the age of industrial democracy and the stage that comes after, where what industrial democracy was about was production and the economy depended on constantly increasing production and the democracy's big tension was between industry's needs for policies that abetted production and citizens' needs to both benefit from all the production and still have their basic rights and interests protected from industry's simpleminded emphasis on production and profits.'

'I'm not sure where the metaphysics comes in here, Nichols.'

'Maybe it's not metaphysics. Maybe it's existential. I'm talking about the individual US citizen's deep fear, the same basic fear that you and I have and that everybody has except nobody ever talks about it except existentialists in convoluted French prose. Or Pascal. Our smallness, our insignificance and mortality, yours and mine, the thing that we all spend all our time not thinking about directly, that we are tiny and at the mercy of large forces and that time is always passing and that every day we've lost one more day that will never come back and our childhoods are over and our adolescence and the vigor of youth and soon our adulthood, that everything we see around us all the time is decaying and passing, it's all passing away, and so are we, so am I, and given how fast the first forty-two years have shot by it's not going to be long before I too pass away, whoever imagined that there was a more truthful way to put it than "die," "pass away," the very sound of it makes me feel the way I feel at dusk on a wintry Sunday—'

'Anybody got the time? How long we been in here, three hours?'

'And not only that, but everybody who knows me or even knows I exist will die, and then everybody who knows those people and might even conceivably have even heard of me will die, and so on, and the gravestones and monuments we spend money to have put in to make sure we're remembered, these'll last what—a hundred years? two hundred?—and they'll crumble, and the grass and insects my decomposition will go to feed will die, and their offspring, or if I'm cremated the trees that are nourished by my windblown ash will die or get cut down and decay, and my urn will decay, and before maybe three or four generations it will be like I never existed, not only will I have passed away but it will be like I was never here, and people in 2104 or whatever will no more think of Stuart A. Nichols Jr. than you or I think of John T. Smith, 1790 to 1864, of Livingston, Virginia, or some such. That everything is on fire, slow fire, and we're all less than a million breaths away from an oblivion more total than we can even bring ourselves to even try to imagine, in fact, probably that's why the manic US obsession with production, produce, produce, impact the world, contribute, shape things, to help distract us from how little and totally insignificant and temporary we are.'

'This is supposed to be news to us. News flash: We're going to die.'

'Why do you think people buy insurance?'

'Let him finish.'

'Now this is depressing instead of just boring.'

'The post-production capitalist has something to do with the death of civics. But so does fear of smallness and death and everything being on fire.'

'I smell Rousseau at the root here, the same way you were talking about de Tocqueville before.'

'As usual DeWitt's way ahead of me. It probably does start with Rousseau and the Magna Carta and the French Revolution. This emphasis on man as the individual and on the rights and entitlements of the individual instead of the responsibilities of the individual. But corporations and marketing and PR and the creation of desire and need to feed all the manic production, the way modern advertising and marketing seduce the individual by flattering all the little psychic delusions with which we deflect the horror of personal smallness and transience, enabling the delusion that the individual is the center of the universe, the most important thing—I mean the individual individual, the little guy watching TV or listening to the radio or leafing through a shiny magazine or looking at a billboard or any of the million different daily ways this guy comes into contact with Burson-Marsteller's or Saachi & Saachi's big lie, that *he* is the tree, that his first responsibility is to his own happiness, that everyone else is the great gray abstract mass which his life depends on standing apart from, being an individual, being *happy*.'

'Doing your own thing.'

'That's your bag.'

'Shaking off the shackles of authority and conformity, of authoritarian conformity.'

'I'm going to need to use the head very soon, I'm afraid.'

'That's more the sixties than the French Revolution, man, then.'

'But if I'm getting DeWitt's thrust, the fulcrum was the moment in the sixties when rebellion against conformity became fashionable, a pose, a way to look cool to the others in your generation you wanted to impress and get accepted by.'

'Not to mention laid.'

'Because the minute it became not just an attitude but a fashionable one, that's when the corporations and their advertisers can step in and start reinforcing it and seducing people with it into buying the things the corporations are producing.'

'The first time was 7 Up with its *Sgt. Pepper* psychedelia and kids in sideburns and saying "the Uncola." '

'But wait. The sixties rebellion in lots of ways opposed the corporation and the military-industrial complex.'

'The man in the gray flannel.'

'What *is* gray flannel anyway? Has anybody ever seen anybody ever in gray flannel?'

'The only flannel I've got is PJs, man.'

'Is Mr. Glendenning even awake?'

'He looks awful pale.'

'Everybody looks pale in the dark, man.'

'I mean is there any more total symbol of conformity and marching in lockstep than the corporation? Assembly lines and punching the clock and climbing the ladder to the corner office? You've done field audits at Rayburn-Thrapp, Gaines. Those guys can't wipe their ass without a policy memo.'

'But we're not talking about the interior reality of the corporation. We're talking about the face and voice the corporate advertisers start using in the late sixties to talk the customer into thinking he needs all this stuff. It starts talking about the customer's psyche being in bondage to conformity and the way to break out of the conformity is not to *do* certain things but to *buy* certain things. You make *buying* a certain brand of clothes or pop or car or necktie into a gesture of the same level of ideological significance as wearing a beard or protesting the war.'

'Virginia Slims and women's libbers.'

'Alka-Seltzer.'

'I think the I'm-going-to-die connection slipped by me at some point here.'

'I think Stuart's tracing the move from the production-model of American democracy to something more like a consumption-model, where corporate production depends on a team approach whereas being a customer is a solo venture. That we're turning into consuming citizens instead of producing citizens.'

'Just wait sixteen quarters till '84. Just wait for the tidal wave of ads and PR that promote this or that corporate product as the way to escape the gray 1984 totalitarianisms of the Orwellian present.'

'How does buying one kind of typewriter instead of another help subvert government control?'

'It won't be government in a couple years, don't you see?'

'There won't be typewriters, either. Everyone'll have keyboards cabled into some sort of central VAX, and things won't even have to be on paper anymore.'

'The paperless office.'

'Rendering Stu here obsolete.'

'No, you're missing the genius of it. It'll all be played out in the world of images. There'll be this incredible political consensus that we need to escape the confinement and rigidity of conforming, of the dead fluorescent world of the office and the balance sheet, of having to wear a tie and listen to Muzak, but the corporations will be able to represent consumption-patterns as the way to break out—use this type of calculator, listen to this type of music, wear this type of shoe because everyone else is wearing conformist shoes. It'll be this era of incredible prosperity and conformity and mass-demographics in which all the symbols and rhetoric will involve revolution and crisis and bold forward-looking individuals who dare to march to their own drummer by allying themselves with brands that invest heavily in the image of rebellion. This mass PR campaign extolling the individual will solidify enormous markets of people whose innate conviction that they are solitary, peerless, non-communal, will be massaged at every turn.'

'But what role will government play in this 1984 scenario?'

'Just as DeWitt said—the government will be the parent, with all the ambivalent love-hate-need-defy charges that surround the parent-figure in the mind of the adolescent, which in this case I'm respectfully disagreeing with DeWitt in the sense that I don't think the American nation today is infantile so much as adolescent—that is, ambivalent in its twin desire for both authoritarian structure and the end of parental hegemony.'

'We'll be the cops they call when the party gets out of hand.'

'You can see where it's going. The extraordinary political apathy that followed Watergate and Vietnam and the institutionalization of grass-roots rebellion among minorities will only deepen. Politics is about consensus, and the advertising legacy of the sixties is that consensus is repression. Voting'll be unhip: Americans now vote with their wallets. Government's only cultural role will be as the tyrannical parent we both hate and need. Look for us to elect someone who can cast himself as a Rebel, maybe even a cowboy, but who deep down we'll know is a bureaucratic creature who'll operate inside the government mechanism instead of naively bang his head against it the way we've watched poor Jimmy do for four years.'

'Carter represents the last gasp of true New Frontier sixties idealism, then. His obvious decency and his political impotence have been conjoined in the voter's psyche.'

'Look for a candidate who can do to the electorate what corporations are learning to do, so Government—or, better, Big Government, Big Brother, Intrusive Government—becomes the image against which this candidate defines himself. Though paradoxically for this persona, to have weight the candidate'll also have to be a creature of government, an Insider, with a flinty-eyed entourage of bureaucrats and implementers who we'll be able to see can actually run the machine. Plus of course a massive campaign budget courtesy of guess who.'

'We're now very very very far afield from what I started out trying to describe as my thinking about taxpayers' relation to government.'

'This describes Reagan even better than Bush.'

'The Reagan symbolism's just too bold. This is just my opinion. Of course the marvelous thing for the Service about a possible Reagan presidency is that he's already anti-tax on the record. Flat-out, no hedging. No rise in the tax rates—in fact in New Hampshire he went on record as wanting to lower marginal rates.'

'This is good for the Service? Another politician trying to score points by trashing the tax system?'

'My own view: I see a Bush-Reagan ticket. Reagan for symbolism, the Cowboy, Bush the quiet insider, doing the unsexy work of actual management.'

'Not to mention his hike-defense-spending rhetoric. How are you going to lower marginal rates and increase defense spending?'

'Even a child could see the contradiction in that.'

'Stuart's saying it's good for the Service because lowering marginal rates but increasing spending can happen only if collection of tax is made more efficient.'

'Meaning the reins are off. Meaning the Service's quotas go up.'

'But also meaning a quiet reduction in the constraints on our auditing and collection mechanisms. Reagan'll set us up as the black-hatted rapacious Big Brother he secretly needs. We—the stitch-mouthed accountants in dull suits and thick specs, punching the keys on our adding machines—*become* the Government: the authority everyone gets to hate. Meanwhile Reagan triples the Service budget and makes technology and efficiency serious objectives. It'll be the best era the Service has had since '45.'

'But meanwhile increasing taxpayers' hatred of the Service.'

'Which paradoxically, a Reagan would need. The Service's more aggressive treatment of TPs, especially if it's high-profile, would seem to keep in the electorate's mind a fresh and eminently disposable image of Big Government that the Rebel Outsider President could continue to define himself against and decry as just the sort of government intrusion into the private lives and wallets of hardworking Americans he ran for the office to fight against.'

'You're saying the next president will be able to *continue* to define himself as an Outsider and Renegade when he's actually *in* the White House?'

'You're still underestimating the taxpayers' need for the lie, for the surface rhetoric they can keep telling themselves while deep down they can rest assured that Daddy's in control and everyone's still safe. The way adolescents make a big deal of rebelling against parental authority while they borrow the keys to Daddy's car and use

Daddy's credit card to fill it with gas. The new leader won't lie to the people; he'll do what corporate pioneers have discovered works far better: He'll adopt the persona and rhetoric that let the people lie to *themselves*.'

'Let's get back to how a Bush or Reagan would triple the Service budget for a second? Is this good for us on a District level? What are the implications for a Peoria or a Creve Coeur?'

'Of course the marvelous double irony of the Reduce Government candidate is that he's financed by the corporations that are the backs government tends to be the most oppressively on the back of. Corporations, as DeWitt pointed out, whose beady little brains are lit by nothing but net profit and expansion, and who we deep-down expect government to keep in check because we're not equipped to resist their consumerist seductions by the strength of our own character, and whose appeal to the faux rebel is the modern rhetoric that's going to get Bush-Reagan elected in the first place, and who are going to benefit enormously from the laissez-faire deregulation Bush-Reagan will enable the electorate to believe will be undertaken in their own populist interests—in other words we'll have for a president a symbolic Rebel against his own power whose election was underwritten by inhuman soulless profit-machines whose takeover of American civic and spiritual life will convince Americans that rebellion against the soulless inhumanity of corporate life will consist in buying products from corporations that do the best job of representing corporate life as empty and soulless. We'll have a tyranny of conformist nonconformity presided over by a symbolic outsider whose very *election* depended on our deep conviction that his persona is utter bullshit. A rule of image, which because it's so empty makes everyone terrified—they're small and going to die, after all—'

'Christ, the death thing again.'

'—and whose terror of not really ever even existing makes them that much more susceptible to the ontological siren song of the corporate buy-to-stand-out-and-so-exist gestalt.'

§20

The quiet, pleasant family two houses down from Lotwis (who was retired after thirty years of service in the County Recorder of Deeds) and his wife were then replaced by a single female of unknown background and occupation who had two large dogs that tended to make a lot of noise. That was all right. Lotwis had a dog of his own that barked a lot sometimes, and so did some of the other people in the neighborhood. The neighborhood was one where people's dogs were going to bark behind their fences and people were sometimes going to burn their trash or keep junked cars in their yards. The neighborhood was now classed Semirural in the Recorder's office, but in the Eisenhower and Kennedy and Johnson years it had been classed Subd. Class 2, a development class, in fact the city's first recorded subdivision. It hadn't taken off and gone upscale and spread like Hawthorne 1 and 2 or Yankee Ridge, built out in the seventies on repossessed farmland out east of town. It was twenty-eight houses on two perpendicular blacktop roads and had stayed that way, and the part of the city that spread out south to approach it was not upscale, it was light industry and some warehouses and seed concerns, and the only developments in terms of your basic housing out anywhere near were one large trailer park and one smaller one that hemmed the old subdivision in on the north and west; to the south was the interstate and serious farmland all the way to the pleasant little grain-town of Funk's Grove thirteen miles south on 51. But so. Within sight if Lotwis was up on his roof tending to gutters or the screen on his chimney was an auto wrecker's yard and Southtown Wholesale and Custom Meats, which was, when you cut through all the fancy language, a butcher's. But so the folks that lived out here that the Lotwises had watched slowly move in and settle the neighborhood were folks with an independent streak that were willing to live out near trailer parks and a slaughterhouse and have a rural mailman who brought the mail in his own private car and leaned way over to get it in the boxes out by the street, all in return for the benefits of living in a Class 2 zone without hemmed-in houses and subheaded ordinances on burning your trash or having your washer's outflow pipe empty into the gulley by the road or dogs with some spirit that were protective and barked up a storm at night.

'I'm glad you said this,' she said. Her name was Toni; she'd introduced herself when he came to her door. 'Now I'll know. If anything happens to these dogs. If they run off, or limp, or anything—I'll kill you, your family, burn your house down, and sow salt. I have nothing to live for but these dogs. If they want to run they're going to run. If you don't like it you can take it up with me. But if anything gets done to these dogs I'll decide it was you and I'll sacrifice my life and freedom to destroy you and everyone you love.'

So Lotwis just let her alone.

§21

Rubbing his eyes wearily. 'So let me get this straight. On $218,000 of gross billing on your Schedule C you realize $37,000 net.'

'It's all documented. I've supplied all receipts and W-2s.'

'Yes, the W-2s. We've got $175,471 in W-2s on sixteen employees—investigators, support personnel, research aides.'

'It's all right there. You've got copies of their returns.'

'Except what I found striking is they're all in terribly low marginal brackets. Terribly low-paid. Why not four or five employees highly paid?'

'The logistics of my business are complex. Much of the work is low-paid but time-consuming.'

'Except I dropped in on one of your researchers—a Mrs. Thelma Purler.'

'Ulp.'

'At the Oakhaven Assisted Living Center, where she resides.'

'Ulp.'

'In a wheelchair, with one of those old-fashioned ear horns even to hear your questions, and to which she replied—let me see'—checking his notes—'Roodle, roodle roodle roodle.'

'I um er.'

Turning off his recorder, which has no tape in it.

'So we're looking at potential criminal fraud, which is CID and not my department. We could go talk to—or dig up—these other employees. You'll go to jail. So here's what we can do. You have a one-hour opportunity to fill out an amended 1040 for last year. On which you omit the employee salary deductions. You pay real tax due, plus penalties for underpayment and late filing. You proceed with an employee of this department to your bank, where you cut a cashier's check for the total. At which time I destroy your original return, and the CID receives no referral.'

§22

I'm not sure I even know what to say. To be honest, a good bit of it I don't remember. I don't think my memory works in quite the way it used to. It may be that this kind of work changes you. Even just rote exams. It might actually change your brain. For the most part, it's now almost as if I'm trapped in the present. If I drank, for instance, some Tang, it wouldn't remind me of anything—I'd just taste the Tang.

From what I understand, I'm supposed to explain how I arrived at this career. Where I came from, so to speak, and what the Service means to me.

I think the truth is that I was the worst kind of nihilist—the kind who isn't even aware he's a nihilist. I was like a piece of paper on the street in the wind, thinking, 'Now I think I'll blow this way, now I think I'll blow that way.' My essential response to everything was 'Whatever.'

This was especially after high school, when I drifted for several years, in and out of three different colleges, one of them two different times, and four or five different majors. One of these might have been a minor. I was pretty much of a wastoid. Essentially, I had no motivation, which my father referred to as 'initiative.' Also, I remember that everything at that time was very fuzzy and abstract. I took a lot of psychology and political science, literature. Classes where everything was fuzzy and abstract and open to interpretation and then those interpretations were open to still more interpretations. I used to write my class papers on the typewriter the day they were due, and usually I got some type of B with 'Interesting in places' or 'Not too bad!' written underneath the grade as an instructional comment. The whole thing was just going through the motions; it didn't mean anything—even the whole point of the classes themselves was that nothing meant anything, that everything was abstract and endlessly interpretable. Except, of course, there was no argument about the fact that you had to turn in the papers, you had to go through the motions themselves, although nobody ever explained just why, what your ultimate motivation was supposed to be. I'm 99 percent sure that I took just one Intro Accounting class during all this time, and did all right in it until we hit depreciation schedules, as in the straight-line method vs. accelerated depreciation, and the combination of difficulty and sheer boredom of the depreciation schedules broke my initiative, especially after I'd missed a couple of the classes and fallen behind, which with depreciation is fatal—and I ended up dropping that class and taking an incomplete. This was at Lindenhurst College—the later Intro class at DePaul had the same title but a somewhat different emphasis. I also remember that incompletes peeved my father quite a bit more than a low grade, understandably.

I know three separate times during this unmotivated period I withdrew from college and tried working so-called real jobs. One was that I was a security guard for a parking garage on North Michigan, or taking tickets for events at the Liberty Arena, or briefly on the production line at a Cheese Nabs plant working the cheese product injector, or working for a company which made and installed gymnasium floors. Then, after a while, I couldn't handle the boredom of the jobs, which were all unbelievably boring and meaningless, and I'd quit and enroll someplace else and essentially try to start college over again. My transcript looked like collage art. Understandably, this routine wore thin with my father, who was a cost systems supervisor for the City of Chicago—although during this time he lived in

Libertyville, which is describable as an upper-bourgeois northern suburb. He used to say, dryly and with a perfectly straight face, that I was shaping up to be an outstanding twenty-yard-dash man. This was his way of squeezing my shoes. He read a great deal and was into dry, sardonic expressions. Although on one other occasion, after taking an incomplete or withdrawing somewhere and coming back home, I remember I was in the kitchen getting something to eat and heard him arguing with my mother and Joyce, telling them I couldn't find my ass with both hands. That was the angriest I think I ever saw him get during this unfocused period. I don't remember the exact context, but knowing how dignified and essentially reserved my father usually was, I'm sure I must have just done something especially feckless or pathetic to provoke him. I don't remember my mother's response or exactly how I came to overhear the remark, as eavesdropping on your parents seems like something that only a much smaller child would do.

My mother was more sympathetic, and whenever my father started squeezing my shoes about the lack-of-direction thing, my mother would stick up for me to some extent and say I was trying to find my path in life, and that not every path is outlined in neon lights like an airport runway, and that I owed it to myself to find my path and let things unfold in their own way. From what I understand of basic psychology, this is a fairly typical dynamic—son is feckless and lacks direction, mother is sympathetic and believes in son's potential and sticks up for him, father is peeved and endlessly criticizes and squeezes son's shoes but still, when push comes to shove, always ponies up the check for the next college. I can remember my father referring to money as 'that universal solvent of ambivalence' in connection with these tuition checks. I should mention that my mother and father were amicably divorced by this time, which was also somewhat typical of that era, so there were all those typical divorce dynamics in play as well, psychologically. The same sort of dynamics were probably being played out in homes all over America—the child trying to sort of passively rebel while still financially tied to the parent, and all the typical psychological business that goes along with that.

Anyhow, all this was in the Chicagoland area in the 1970s, a period that now seems as abstract and unfocused as I was myself. Maybe the Service and I have this in common—that the past decade seems much longer ago than it really was, because of what's happened in the intervening time. As for myself, I had trouble just paying attention, and the things I can remember now seem mostly pointless. I mean really remember, not just have a general impression of. I remember having fairly long hair, meaning long on all four sides, but nevertheless it was also always parted on the left side and held in place with spray from a dark red can. I remember the color of this can. I can't think of this period's hair without almost wincing. I can remember things I wore—a lot of burnt orange and brown, red-intensive paisley, bell-bottom cords, acetate and nylon, flared collars, dungaree vests. I had a metal peace-sign pendant that weighed half a pound. Docksiders and yellow Timberlands and a pair of shiny low brown leather dress boots which zipped up the sides and only the sharp toes showed under bell-bottoms. The little sensitive leather thong around the neck. The commercial psychedelia. The obligatory buckskin jacket. The dungarees whose cuffs dragged on the ground and dissolved into white thread. Wide belts, tube socks, track shoes from Japan. The standard getup. I remember the round, puffy winter coats of nylon and down that made us all look like parade balloons. The scratchy white painter's pants with loops for supposed tools down the side of the thigh. I remember everyone despising Gerald Ford, not so much for pardoning Nixon but for constantly falling down. Everyone had contempt for him. Very blue designer jeans. I remember the feminist tennis player Billie Jean King beating what seemed like an old and feeble man player on television and my mother and her friends all being very excited by this. 'Male chauvinist pig,' 'women's lib,' and 'stagflation' all seemed vague and indistinct to me during this time, like listening to background noise with half an ear. I don't remember what I did with all my real attention, what-all it was going towards. I never did anything, but at the same time I could normally never sit still and become aware of what was really going on. It's hard to explain. I somewhat remember a younger Cronkite, Barbara Walters, and Harry Reasoner—I don't think I watched much news. Again, I suspect this was more typical than I thought at the time. One thing you learn in Rote Exams is how disorganized and inattentive most people are and how little they pay attention to what's going on outside of their sphere. Somebody named Howard K. Smith was also big in news, I remember. You almost never hear the word *ghetto* anymore, now. I remember Acapulco Gold versus Colombia Gold, Ritalin versus Ritadex, Cylert and Obetrol, Laverne and Shirley, Carnation Instant Breakfast, John Travolta, disco fever, and children's tee shirts with the 'Fonz' on them. And 'Keep On Truckin' ' shirts, which my mother loved, where walking people's shoes and soles looked abnormally large. Actually preferring, like most children my age, Tang to real orange juice. Mark Spitz and Johnny Carson, the celebration in 1976 with fleets of antique ships coming into a harbor on TV. Smoking pot after school in high school and then watching TV and eating Tang out of the jar with a finger, wetting my finger and sticking it in, over and over, until I'd look down and couldn't believe how much of the jar was gone. Sitting there with my wastoid friends, and so on and so forth—and none of it meant anything. It's like I was dead or asleep without even being aware of it, as in the Wisconsin expression 'didn't know enough to lay down.'

I remember in high school getting Dexedrine from a kid whose mother had them prescribed for her for pep, and the weird way they tasted, and the remarkable way they made the thing of counting while reading or speaking disappear—they were called black beauties—but the way after a while they made your lower back ache and gave you terrible, terrible breath. Your mouth tasted like a long-dead frog in a cloudy jar in Biology when you first opened the jar. It's still sickening just to think about. There was also the period when my mother was so upset when Richard Nixon got reelected so easily, which I remember because it was around then that I tried Ritalin, which I bought from a guy in World Cultures class whose little brother in primary school was supposedly on Ritalin from a doctor who didn't keep track of his prescriptions very well, and which some people didn't think were anything special compared to black beauties, Ritalin, but I liked them very much, at first because it made sitting and studying for long periods of time possible and even interesting, and which I really, really liked, but it was hard to get much of—Ritalin was—especially after evidently the little brother wigged out one day at primary school from not taking his Ritalin and the parents and doctor discovered the irregularities with the prescriptions and suddenly there was no pimply guy in pink sunglasses selling four-dollar Ritalin pills out of his locker in junior hall.

I seem to remember in 1976 my father openly predicting a Ronald Reagan presidency and even sending their campaign a donation—although in retrospect I don't think Reagan even really ran in '76. This was my life before the sudden change in direction and eventually entering the Service. Girls wore caps or dungaree hats, but most guys were essentially uncool if they wore a hat. Hats were things to make fun of. Baseball caps were for the rednecks downstate. Older men of any seriousness still sometimes wore business-type hats outside, though. I can remember my father's hat now almost better than his face under it. I used to spend time imagining what my father's face looked like when he was alone—I mean his facial expression and eyes—when he was by himself in his office at work at the City Hall annex downtown and there was no one to shape a certain expression for. I remember my father wearing madras shorts on weekends, and black socks, and mowing the lawn like that, and sometimes looking out of the window at what he looked like in that getup and feeling actual pain at being related to him. I remember everyone pretending to be a samurai or saying, 'Excuse *me!*' in all sorts of different contexts—this was cool. To show approval or excitement, we said, 'Excellent.' In college, you could hear the word *excellent* five thousand times a day. I remember some of my attempts to grow sideburns at DePaul and always ending up shaving them off, because at a certain point they got to where they looked just like pubic hair. The smell of Brylcreem in my father's hatband, Deep Throat, Howard Cosell, my mother's throat showing ligaments on either side when she and Joyce laughed. Throwing her hands around or bending over. Mom was always a very physical laugher—her whole body gets involved.

There was also the word *mellow* that was used constantly, although even early on in its use this word bugged me; I just didn't like it. I still probably used it sometimes, though, without being aware I was doing it.

My mother's the sort of somewhat lanky type of older woman who seems to become almost skinny and tough with age instead of ballooning out, becoming ropy and sharp-jointed and her cheekbones even more pronounced. I remember sometimes thinking of beef jerky when I would first see her, and then feeling terrible that I had that association. She was quite good-looking in her day, though, and some of the later weight-loss was also nerve-related, because after the thing with my father her nerves got worse and worse. Admittedly, too, one other factor in her sticking up for me with my father as to drifting in and out of school was the past trouble I'd had with reading in primary school when we'd lived in Rockford and my father had worked for the City of Rockford. This was in the mid-1960s, at Machesney Elementary. I went through a sudden period where I couldn't read. I mean that I actually could read—my mother knew I could read from when we'd read children's books together. But for almost two years at Machesney, instead of reading something I'd count the words in it, as though reading was the same as just counting the words. For example, 'Here came Old Yeller, to save me from the hogs' would equate to ten words which I would count off from one to ten instead of its being a sentence that made you love Old Yeller in the book even more. It was a strange problem in my developmental wiring at the time which caused a lot of trouble and embarrassment and was one reason why we ended up moving to the Chicagoland area, because for a while it looked as though I would have to attend a special school in Lake Forest. I have very little memory of this time except for the feeling of not especially wanting to count words or intending to but just not being able to help it—it was frustrating and strange. It got worse under pressure or nervousness, which is typical of things like that. Anyhow, part of my mother's fierce defense of letting me experience and learn things in my own way dates from that time, when the Rockford School District reacted to the reading problem in all sorts of ways that she didn't think were helpful or fair. Some of her consciousness-raising and entry into the women's lib movement of the 1970s probably also dates from that time of fighting the bureaucracy of the school district. I still sometimes lapse into counting words, or rather usually the counting goes on when I'm reading or talking, as a sort of background noise or unconscious process, a little like breathing.

For instance, I've said 2,752 words right now since I started. Meaning 2,752 words as of just before I said, 'I've said,' versus 2,754 if you count 'I've said'—which I do, still. I count numbers as one word no matter how large a given number is. Not that it actually means anything—it's more like a mental tic. I don't remember exactly when it started. I know I had no trouble learning to read or reading the Sam and Ann books they teach you to read with, so it must have been after second grade. I know that my mother, as a child in Beloit WI, where she grew up, had an aunt who had a thing of washing her hands over and over without being able to stop, which eventually got so bad she had to go to a rest home. I seem to remember thinking of my mother as in some way associating the counting thing more with that aunt at the sink and not seeing it as a form of retardation or inability to just sit there and read as instructed, which is how Rockford school authorities seemed to see it. Anyhow, hence her hatred of traditional institutions and authority, which was another thing that helped gradually alienate her from my father and imperil their marriage, and so on and so forth.

I remember once, in I think 1975 or '76, shaving off just one sideburn and going around like that for a period of time, believing the one sideburn made me a nonconformist—I'm not kidding—and getting into long, serious conversations with girls at parties who would ask me what the lone sideburn 'meant.' A lot of the things I remember saying and believing during this period make me literally wince now, to think of it. I remember KISS, REO Speedwagon, Cheap Trick, Styx, Jethro Tull, Rush, Deep Purple, and, of course, good old Pink Floyd. I remember BASIC and COBOL. COBOL was what my father's cost systems hardware ran at his office. He was incredibly knowledgeable about the era's computers. I remember Sony's wide pocket transistors and the way that many of the city's blacks held their radios up to their ear whereas white kids from the suburbs used the optional little earplug, like a CID earbud, which had to be cleaned almost daily or else it got really foul. There was the energy crisis and recession and stagflation, though I cannot remember the order in which these occurred—although I do know the main energy crisis must have happened when I was living back at home after the Lindenhurst College thing, because I got my mother's tank siphoned out while out partying late at night with old high school friends, which my father was not thrilled about, understandably. I think New York City actually went bankrupt for a while during this period. There was also the 1977 disaster of the State of Illinois's experiment with making the state sales tax a progressive tax, which I know upset my father a lot but which I neither understood nor cared about at the time. Later, of course, I would understand why making a sales tax progressive is such a terrible idea, and why the resulting chaos more or less cost the governor at the time his job. At the time, though, I don't remember noticing anything except the unusually terrible crowds and hassle of shopping for the holidays in late '77. I don't know if that's relevant. I doubt anyone outside the state cares very much about this, though there are still some jokes about it among the older wigglers at the REC.

I remember feeling the actual physical feeling of hatred of most commercial rock—such as for disco, which if you were cool you pretty much had to hate, and all rock groups with one-word place names. Boston, Kansas, Chicago, America—I can still feel an almost bodily hatred. And believing that I and maybe one or two friends were among the very, very few people who truly understood what Pink Floyd was trying to say. It's embarrassing. Most of these almost feel like some other person's memories. I remember almost none of early childhood, mostly just weird little isolated strobes. The more fragmented the memory is, though, the more it seems to feel authentically mine, which is strange. I wonder if anyone feels as though they're the same person they seem to remember. It would probably make them have a nervous breakdown. It probably wouldn't even make any sense.

I don't know if this is enough. I don't know what anybody else has told you.

Our common word for this kind of nihilist at the time was *wastoid.*

I remember rooming in a high-rise UIC dorm with a very mod, with-it sophomore from Naperville who also wore sideburns and a leather thong and played the guitar. He saw himself as a nonconformist, and also very unfocused and nihilistic, and deeply into the school's wastoid drug scene, and drove what I have to admit was a very cool-looking 1972 Firebird that it eventually turned out his parents paid the insurance on. I cannot remember his name, try as I might. UIC stood for the University of Illinois, Chicago Campus, a gigantic urban university. The dorm we roomed in was right on Roosevelt, and our main windows faced a large downtown podiatric clinic—I can't remember its name, either—which had a huge raised electrified neon sign that rotated on its pole every weekday from 8:00 to 8:00 with the name and mnemonic phone number ending in 3668 on one side and on the other a huge colored outline of a human foot—our best guess was a female foot, from the proportions—and I remember that this roommate and I formulated a kind of ritual in which we'd make sure to try to be at the right spot at our windows at 8:00 each night to watch the foot sign go dark and stop rotating when the clinic closed. It always went dark at the same time the clinic's windows did and we theorized that everything was on one main breaker. The sign's rotation didn't stop all at once. It more like slowly wound down, with almost a wheel-of-fortune quality about where it would finally stop. The ritual was that if the sign stopped with the foot facing away, we would go to the UIC library and study, but if it stopped with the foot or any significant part of it facing our windows, we would take it as a 'sign' (with the incredibly obvious double entendre) and immediately blow off any homework or supposed responsibility we had and go instead to the Hat, which at that time was the currently hip UIC pub and place to hear bands, and would drink beers and play quarters and tell all the other kids whose parents were paying their tuition about the ritual of the rotating foot in a way that we all appeared nihilistically wastoid and hip. I'm seriously embarrassed to remember things like this. I can remember the podiatrist's sign and the Hat and what the Hat looked and even smelled like, but I cannot remember this roommate's name, even though we probably hung out together three or four nights a week that year. The Hat had no relation to Meibeyer's, which is the main sort of pub for rote examiners here at the REC, and also has a hat motif and an elaborate display-rack of hats, but these are meant to be historical IRS and CPA hats, the hats of serious adults. Meaning the similarity is just a coincidence. There were actually two Hats, as in a franchise—there was the UIC one on Cermak and Western, and another one down in Hyde Park for the more motivated, focused kids at U of Chicago. Everybody at our Hat called the Hyde Park Hat 'the Yarmulke.' This roommate was not a bad or evil guy, although he turned out to be able to play only three or four real songs on the guitar, which he played over and over and over, and blatantly rationalized his selling of drugs as a form of social rebellion instead of just pure capitalism, and even at the time I knew he was a total conformist to the late-seventies standards of so-called nonconformity, and sometimes I felt contemptuous of him. I might have despised him a little. As if I was exempt, of course—but this kind of blatant projection and displacement was part of the nihilist hypocrisy of the whole period.

I can remember the 'Uncola,' and the way Noxzema commercials always played a big bump-and-grind theme. I seem to remember a lot of wood-pattern designs on things that were not wood, and station wagons with side panels engineered to look like wood. I remember Jimmy Carter addressing the nation in a cardigan, and something about Carter's brother turning out to be a wastoid and public boob embarrassing the president just by being related to him.

I don't think I voted. The truth is that I don't remember if I voted or not. I probably planned to and said I was going to and then got distracted somehow and didn't get around to it. That would be about par for the period.

Obviously, it probably goes without saying that I partied heavily during this whole period. I don't know how much I should say about this. But I didn't party any more or less than everyone else I knew did—in fact, very precisely neither more nor less. Everyone I knew and hung out with was a wastoid, and we knew it. It was hip to be ashamed of it, in a strange way. A weird kind of narcissistic despair. Or just to feel directionless and lost—we romanticized it. I did like Ritalin and certain types of speed like Cylert, which was a little unusual, but everyone had their idiosyncratic favorites when it came to partying. I didn't do incredible amounts of speed, as the kinds I liked were hard to get—you more had to stumble across it. The roommate with the blue Firebird was obsessed with hashish, which he always described as *mellow*.

Looking back, I doubt if it ever occurred to me that the way I felt towards this roommate was probably the way my father felt about me—that I was just as much a conformist as he was, plus a hypocrite, a 'rebel' who really just sponged off of society in the form of his parents. I wish I could say I was aware enough for this contradiction to sink in at the time, although I probably would have just turned it into some kind of hip, nihilistic joke. At the same time, sometimes I know I worried about my directionlessness and lack of initiative, how abstract and open to different interpretations everything seemed at the time, even about how fuzzy and pointless my memories were starting to seem. My father, on the other hand, I know, remembered everything—in particular, physical details, the precise day and time of appointments, and past statements which were now inconsistent with present statements. But then, I would learn that this sort of close attention and total recall was part of his job.

What I really was was naive. For instance, I knew I lied, but I hardly ever assumed that anybody else around me might be lying. I realize now how conceited that is, and how unfocused that lets actual reality be. I was a child, really. The truth is that most of what I really know about myself I learned in the Service. That may sound too much like sucking up, but it's the truth. I've been here five years, and I've learned an incredible amount.

Anyhow, I can also recall smoking pot with my mother and her partner, Joyce. They grew their own, and it wasn't exactly potent, but that wasn't really the point, because with them it was more of a sort of liberated political statement than a matter of getting high, and my mother almost seemed to make it a point to smoke pot whenever I was over there visiting them, and while it made me a little uncomfortable, I don't ever remember refusing to 'fire up' with them, even though it embarrassed me somewhat when they used college terms like this. At that time, my mother and Joyce co-owned a small feminist bookstore, which I knew my father resented having helped finance through the divorce settlement. And I can remember once sitting around on their Wrigleyville apartment's beanbag chairs, passing around one of their large, amateurishly rolled doobersteins—which was the hip, wastoid term for a joint at that time, at least around the Chicagoland area—and listening to my mother and Joyce recount very vivid, detailed memories from their early childhoods, and both of them laughing and crying and stroking one another's hair in emotional support, which didn't really bother me—their touching or even kissing one another in front of me—or at least by then I'd had plenty of time to get used to it, but I can remember becoming more and more paranoid and nervous at the time, because, when I tried hard to think of some of my own childhood memories, the only really vivid memory I could remember involved me pounding Glovolium into my Rawlings catcher's mitt, which my father had gotten me, and that day of getting the Johnny Bench Autograph mitt I remembered very well, although Mom and Joyce's was not the place to wax all sentimental about my father getting me something, obviously. The worst part was then starting to hear my mother recount all these memories and anecdotes of my own childhood, and realizing that she actually remembered much more of my early childhood than I did, as though somehow she'd seized or confiscated memories and experiences that were technically mine. Obviously, I didn't think of the term *seize* at the time. That's more a Service term. But smoking pot with my mother and Joyce was usually just not a pleasant experience at all, and often totally weirded me out, now that I think about it—and yet I did it with them almost every time. I doubt my mother enjoyed it much, either. The whole thing had an air of pretense of fun and liberation about it. In retrospect, I get the feeling that my mom was trying to get me to see her as changing and growing up right there with me, both on my side of the generation gap, as though we were still as close as we were when I was a child. As both being nonconformists and giving my father the finger, symbolically. Anyhow, smoking pot with her and Joyce always felt a bit hypocritical. My parents split up in February 1972, in the same week that Edmund Muskie cried in public on the campaign trail, and the TV had clips of him crying over and over. I can't remember what he was crying about, but it definitely sunk his chances in the campaign. It was the sixth week of theater class in high school where I first learned the term *nihilist*. I know I didn't feel any real hostility towards Joyce, by the way, although I do remember always feeling sort of edgy when it was just her and me, and being relieved when my mother got home and I could sort of relate to both of them as a couple instead of trying to make conversation with Joyce, which was always complicated because there always felt like a great deal more subjects and things to remember not to bring up than there were to actually talk about, so that trying to make chitchat with her was like trying to slalom at Devil's Head if the slalom's gates were only inches apart.

In hindsight, I realized later that my father was actually kind of witty and sophisticated. At the time, I think I thought of him as barely alive, as like a robot or slave to conformity. It's true that he was uptight, anal, and quick with the put-downs. He was a hundred percent conventional establishment, and totally on the other side of the generation gap—he was forty-nine when he died, which was in December 1977, which obviously means he grew up during the Depression. But I don't think I ever appreciated his sense of humor about all of it—there was a way he sort of wove his pro-establishment views into a dry, witty style that I don't remember ever getting or understanding his jokes in at the time. I didn't have much of a sense of humor then, it seems, or else I did the standard child's thing of taking everything he said as a personal comment or judgment. There was stuff I knew about him, which I'd picked up through the years of childhood, mostly from my mother. Like that he'd been really, really shy when they'd first met. How he had wanted to go to more than just technical college but he had bills to pay—he was in logistics and supply in Korea but had already gotten married to my mother before he was posted overseas, and so upon discharge he immediately had to find a job. This is what people her age did then, she explained—if you met the right person and were at least out of high school, you got married, without even ever really thinking about it or questioning yourself. The point is that he was very smart and somewhat unfulfilled, like many of his generation. He worked hard because he had to, and his own dreams were put on the back burner. This is all indirectly, from my mother, but it fit with certain bits and pieces that even I couldn't help being aware of. For instance, my father read all the time. He was constantly reading. It was his whole recreation, especially after the divorce—he was always coming home from the library with a stack of books with that clear library plastic wrap on the covers. I never paid any attention to what the books were or why he read so much—he never talked about what he was reading. I don't even know what his favorite kinds were, as in history, mysteries, or what. Looking back now, I think he was lonely, especially after the divorce, as the only people you could call his friends were colleagues from his job, and I think he essentially found his job boring—I don't think he felt much personal investment in the City of Chicago's budget and expenditure protocols, especially as it wasn't his idea to move here—and I think books and intellectual issues were one of his escapes from boredom. He was actually a very smart person. I wish I could remember more examples of the sort of things he'd say—at the time, I think they seemed more hostile or judgmental than like he was making fun of both of us at the same time. I do remember he sometimes referred to the so-called younger generation (meaning mine) as 'This thing America hath wrought.' That's not a very good example. It's almost like he thought the blame went both ways, that there was something wrong with the whole country's adults if they could produce kids like this in the 1970s. I remember once in October or November 1976, at twenty-one, during another period of time off, after being enrolled at DePaul—which actually didn't go well at all, the first time I was at DePaul. It was basically a disaster. They kind of invited me to leave, actually, which was the only time that had happened. The other times, at Lindenhurst College and then later at UIC, I'd withdrawn on my own. Anyhow, during this time off, I was working the second shift at a Cheese Nabs factory in Buffalo Grove and living there at my father's house in Libertyville. There was no way I was crashing at my mother and Joyce's apartment in the Wrigleyville section of Chicago, where the rooms all had bead curtains instead of doors. But I didn't have to punch in at this mindless job until six, so I'd mostly just hang around the house all afternoon until it was time to leave. And sometimes during this period my father would be away for a couple of days—like the Service, the City of Chicago's financial departments were always sending their more technical people to conferences and in-services, which I would come to learn later here in the Service are not like the big drunken conventions of private industry but are usually highly intensive and work-centered. My father said the city in-services were mostly just tedious, which was a word he used a fair amount, *tedious*. And on these trips it was just me living in the house, and you can imagine what used to happen when I'd be there on my own, especially on weekends, even though I was supposed to be in charge of looking after the house while he was gone. But the memory is of him coming home early one afternoon in '76 from one of these work trips, like a day or two before I'd thought he told me he was going to be home, and coming in the front door and finding me and two of my old so-called friends from Libertyville South high school in the living room—which, due to the slightly raised design of the front porch and front door, was in effect a sunken living room that more or less started right inside the front door, with one small set of stairs leading down into the living room and another set leading up to the house's second floor. Architecturally, the house's style is known as a raised ranch, like most of the other older homes on the street, and it had another set of stairs leading from the second-floor hallway down into the garage, which actually supports part of the second story—that is, the garage is, structurally, a necessary part of the house, which is what's distinctive about a raised ranch. At the moment he entered, two of us were slumped on the davenport with our dirty feet up on his special coffee table, and the carpeting was all littered with beer cans and Taco Bell wrappers—the cans were my father's beer, which he bought in bulk twice a year and stored in the utility room closet and normally drank maybe a total of two per week of—with us sitting there totally wasted and watching *The Searchers* on WGN, and one of the guys listening to Deep Purple on my father's special stereo headphones for listening to classical music on, and the coffee table's special oak or maple top with big rings of condensation from the beer cans all over it because we'd turned the house's heat way up past where he normally allowed it to be, in terms of energy conservation and expense, and the other guy next to me on the davenport leaning over in the middle of taking a huge bong hit—this guy was famous for being able to take massive hits. Plus, the whole living room reeked. When then, suddenly, in the memory, I heard the distinctive sound of his footsteps on the broad wooden porch and the sound of his key in the front door, and only a second later my father suddenly comes in on a wave of very cold, clear air through the doorway with his hat and overnight bag—I was in the paralyzed shock of the totally busted kid, and I sat there paralyzed, unable to do anything and yet seeing each frame of him coming in with horrible focus and clarity—and him standing there at the edge of the few stairs down to the living room, taking his hat off with the trademark gesture that involved both his head and his hand as he stood there taking in the scene and the three of us—he'd made no secret of not much liking these old high school friends, who were the same guys I'd been out partying with when my mom's gas cap was stolen and the tank siphoned out, and none of us had any money left by the time we found the car, and I had to call my father and he had to take the train down after work to pay for gas so I could get the Le Car back to my mom and Joyce, who co-owned it and used it for bookstore business—with the three of us now slumped there all totally wasted and paralyzed, one of the guys wearing a ratty old tee shirt that actually said FUCK YOU across the chest, the other coughing out his mammoth hit in shock, so that a plume of pot smoke went rolling out across the living room towards my father—in short, my memory is of the scene being the worst confirmation of the worst kind of generation-gap stereotype and parental disgust for their decadent, wastoid kids, and of my father slowly putting down his bag and case and just standing there, with no expression and not saying anything for what felt like such a long time, and then he slowly made a gesture of putting one arm up in the air a little and looking up and said, *'Look on my works, ye mighty, and despair!,'* and then picked up his overnight bag again and without a word walked up the upstairs stairs and went into their old bedroom and closed the door. He didn't slam it, but you could hear the door close quite firmly. The memory, strangely, which is horribly sharp and detailed up to there, then totally stops, like a tape that's just run out, and I don't know what happened after that, like getting the guys out of there and hurriedly trying to clean everything up and turn the thermostat back down to sixty-eight, though I do remember feeling like complete shit, not so much like I'd been 'busted' or was in trouble as just childish, like a spoiled little selfish child, and imagining what I must have looked like to him, sitting there in litter in his house, wasted, with my dirty feet on the marked-up coffee table he and my mother had saved up for and gotten at an antique store in Rockford when they were still young and didn't have much money, and which he prized, and rubbed lemon oil in all the time, and said all he asked was that I should please keep my feet off of it and use a coaster—like, for a second or two seeing what I actually must have looked like to him as he stood there looking at us treating his living room like that. It wasn't a pretty picture, and it felt even worse as he hadn't yelled or squeezed my shoes about it—he just looked weary, and sort of embarrassed for both of us—and I remember for a second or two I could actually feel what he must have been feeling, and for an instant saw myself through his eyes, which made the whole thing much, much worse than if he'd been furious, or yelled, which he never did, not even the next time he and I were alone in the same room—which I don't remember when this was, like whether I skulked out of the house after cleaning everything up or whether I stayed there to face him. I don't know which one I did. I didn't even understand what he said, although obviously I understood he was being sarcastic, and in some way blaming himself or making fun of himself for having produced the 'work' that had just thrown the Taco Bell wrappers and bags on the floor instead of bothering to get up and take like eight steps to throw them away. Although later on, I just stumbled on the poem it turned out he was quoting from, in some kind of weird context at the Indianapolis TAC, and my eyes just about bulged out of my head, because I hadn't even known it was a poem—and a famous one, by the same British poet who evidently wrote the original *Frankenstein*. And I didn't even know my father read British poetry, much less that he could quote from it when he was upset. In short, there was probably much more to him than I was aware of, and I don't remember even realizing how little I knew about him, really, until after he was gone and it was too late. I expect that this sort of regret is typical, as well.

Anyhow, this one terrible memory of looking up from the davenport and seeing myself through his eyes, and of his sad, sophisticated way of expressing how sad and disgusted he was—this kind of sums up the whole period for me now, when I think of it. I also remember both of those former friends' names, too, from that fucked-up day, but obviously that's not relevant.

Things began to get much more vivid, focused, and concrete in 1978, and in retrospect I suppose I agree with Mom and Joyce that this was the year I 'found myself' or 'put away childish things' and began the process of developing some initiative and direction in my life, which obviously led to my joining the Service.

Though it's not directly connected to my choice of the IRS as a career, it's true that my father being killed in a public-transit accident in late 1977 was a sudden, horrible, and life-changing kind of event, which I obviously hope never to have to repeat in any way again. My mother took it especially hard, and had to go on tranquilizers, and she ended up being psychologically unable to sell my father's house, and left Joyce and the bookstore and moved back into the house in Libertyville, where she still lives today, with certain pictures of my father and of them as a young couple still in the house. It's a sad situation, and an armchair psychologist would probably say that she blamed herself somehow for the accident, even though I, more than anyone, would be in a position to know that that wasn't true, and that, in the final analysis, the accident was no one's fault. I was there when it happened—the accident—and there is no denying that it was one hundred percent terrible. Even today, I can remember the whole thing in such vivid, concrete detail that it almost seems more like a recording than a memory, which I'm told is not unusual for traumatic events—and yet there was also no way to recount for my mother exactly what happened from start to finish without almost destroying her, as she was already so grief-stricken, although just about anyone could have seen that a lot of her grief was unresolved conflicts and hang-ups over their marriage and the identity crisis she'd had in 1972 at age forty or forty-one and the divorce, none of which she got to really deal with at the time because she'd thrown herself so deeply into the women's lib movement and consciousness-raising and her new circle of strange, mostly overweight women who were all in their forties, plus her new sexual identity with Joyce almost right away, which I know must have just about killed my father, given how straitlaced and conventional he tended to be, although he and I never talked about it directly, and he and my mother somehow managed to stay reasonably good friends, and I never heard him say anything about the matter except some occasional bitching about how much of his agreed-upon support payments to her were going into the bookstore, which he sometimes referred to as 'that financial vortex' or just 'the vortex'—all of which is a whole long story in itself. So we never really talked about it, which I doubt is all that unusual in these sorts of cases.

If I had to describe my father, I would first say that my mother and father's marriage was one of the only ones I've seen in which the wife was noticeably taller than the man. My father was 5' 6" or 5' 6½", and not fat but stocky, the way many shorter men in their late forties are stocky. He might have weighed 170. He looked good in a suit—like so many men of his generation, his body almost seemed designed to fill out and support a suit. And he owned some good ones, most single-button and single-vent, understated and conservative, in mainly three-season worsteds and one or two seersucker for hot weather, in which he also eschewed his usual business hat. To his credit—at least in retrospect—he rejected the so-called modern style's wide ties, brighter colors, and flared lapels, and found the phenomenon of leisure suits or corduroy sport coats nauseating. His suits were not tailored, but they were nearly all from Jack Fagman, a very old and respected men's store in Winnetka which he had patronized ever since our family relocated to the Chicagoland area in 1964, and some of them were really nice. At home, in what he called his 'mufti,' he wore more casual slacks and double-knit dress shirts, sometimes under a sweater vest—his favorite of these was argyle. Sometimes he wore a cardigan, though I think that he knew that cardigans made him look a little too broad across the beam. In the summer, there was sometimes the terrible thing of the Bermuda shorts with black dress socks, which it turned out were the only kind of socks my father even owned. One sport coat, a 36R in midnight-blue slubbed silk, had dated from his youth and early courtship of my mother, she had explained—it was hard for her to even hear about this jacket after the accident, much less help tell me what to do with it. The clothes closet contained his best and third-best topcoats, also from Jack Fagman, with the empty wooden hanger still between them. He used shoe trees for his dress and office footwear; some of these were inherited from his own father. ('These' obviously referring to the shoe trees, not the shoes.) There was also a pair of leather sandals which he'd received as a Christmas gift, and not only had never worn but hadn't even removed the catalogue tag from when it fell to me to go through his clothes closet and empty out the contents. The idea of lifts in his shoes would just never have occurred to my father. At that time, I had never to my knowledge seen a shoe tree, and didn't know what they were for, since I never took care of any of my shoes, or valued them.

My father's hair, which had evidently been almost light brown or blond when he was younger, had first darkened and then become suffused with gray, its texture stiffer than my own and tending to curl in the back during humid weather. The back of his neck was always red; his overall complexion was florid in the way that certain stocky older men's faces are florid or ruddy. Some of the redness was congenital, probably, and some psychological—like most men of his generation, he was both high-strung and tightly controlled, a type A personality but with a dominant superego, his inhibitions so extreme that it came out mainly as exaggerated dignity and precision in his movements. He almost never permitted himself any kind of open or prominent facial expression. But he was not a calm person. He did not speak or act in a nervous way, but there was a vibe of intense tension about him—I can remember him seeming to give off a slight hum when at rest. In hindsight, I suspect he was probably only a year or two from needing blood pressure medication when the accident occurred.

I remember being aware that my father's overall posture or bearing seemed unusual for a shorter man—many short men tend to stand ramrod straight, for understandable reasons—in terms of his seeming not slumped but more like slightly bent forward at the waist, at a slight angle, which added to the sense of tension or always walking into some kind of wind. I know that I wouldn't understand this prior to entering the Service and seeing the bearing of some of the older examiners who spend all day for years at a desk or Tingle table, leaning forward to examine tax returns, primarily to identify those that should be audited. In other words, it's the posture of someone whose daily work means sitting very still at a desk and working on something in a concentrated way for years on end.

I really know very little about the reality of my father's job and what-all it entailed, though I certainly now know what cost systems are.

On the face of it, my entering a career in the IRS might appear connected to my father's accident—in more humanistic terms, connected to my 'loss' of a father who was himself an accountant. My father's technical area was accounting systems and processes, which is actually closer to data processing than real accountancy, as I would later understand. For myself, however, I am convinced that I would now be in the Service regardless, given the dramatic event that I remember totally changing my focus and attitude which occurred the following fall, during the third semester of my returning to DePaul and when I was retaking Intro Accounting, along with American Political Theory, which was another class I'd gotten an incomplete in at Lindenhurst through basically not knuckling down and putting in the work. It's true, though, that I may have done this—retaking Intro Accounting—at least partly to please or try to pay back my father, or to at least lessen the self-disgust I had felt after his walking into the nihilistic scene in the living room which I just mentioned. It was probably only a couple days after that scene and my father's reaction that I took the CTA commuter line down to Lincoln Park and started trying to reenroll for my last two years—in terms of credits, four terms—at DePaul, although due to certain technicalities I couldn't officially reenter until the fall of '77—another long story—and, thanks to knuckling down and also swallowing my pride and getting some extra help to deal with depreciation and amortization schedules, finally did pass, along with DePaul's version of American Political Theory—which they called American Political Thought, although it and the Lindenhurst version of the course were nearly identical—in the Fall 1978 semester, though not exactly with final grades to write home about, because I largely neglected serious studying for these two classes' final exams due to (somewhat ironically) the dramatic event, which occurred accidentally during an entirely different DePaul class, one I was not even really taking but sort of bumbled into through an inattentive screw-up during the final review period just before Christmas break, and was so dramatically moved and affected by that I barely even studied for my regular courses' final exams, though this time not out of carelessness or sloth but because I decided I had some very important, sustained, concentrated thinking to do after the dramatic encounter with the substitute Jesuit in Advanced Tax, which was the class I've mentioned sitting in on by mistake.

The fact is that there are probably just certain kinds of people who are drawn to a career in the IRS. People who are, as the substitute father said that final day in Advanced Tax, 'called to account.' Meaning we are talking about almost a special kind of psychological type, probably. It's not a very common type—perhaps one in 10,000—but the thing is that the sort of person of this type who decides that he wants to enter the Service really, really wants to, and becomes very determined, and will be hard to put off course once he's focused in on his real vocation and begun to be actively drawn to it. And even one in 10,000, in a country as large as America, will add up to a fair number of people—roughly 20,000—for whom the IRS fulfills all the professional and psychological criteria for a real vocation. These twenty or so thousand comprise the Service's core, or heart, and not all of them are high-ranked in the IRS administration, although some of them are. These are 20,000 out of the Service's total of over 105,000 employees. And there are no doubt core characteristics that these people have in common, predictive factors which at some point or other kick in and cause a genuine calling to pursue tax accounting and systems administration and organizational behavior and to devote themselves to helping administer and enforce the tax laws of this country as spelled out in Title 26 of the Code of Federal Regulations and the Revised Internal Revenue Code of 1954, plus all the statutes and regulations entailed by the Tax Reform Act of 1969, the Tax Reform Act of 1976, the Revenue Act of 1978, and so on and so forth. What these reasons and factors are, and to what extent they coexist with the particular talents and dispositions the Service is in need of—these are interesting questions, which today's IRS takes an active interest in understanding and quantifying. In terms of myself and how I got here, the important thing is that I discovered I had them—the factors and characteristics—and discovered this suddenly, by what seemed at the time like nothing more than a feckless mistake.

I've left out the matter of recreational drug abuse during this period, and the relation of certain drugs to how I got here, which in no way represents an endorsement of drug abuse but is just part of the story of the factors that eventually drew me to the Service. But it's complicated, and somewhat indirect. It's obvious that drugs were a big part of the whole scene in this era—this is well-known. I remember in the later seventies, the supposedly coolest recreational drug around Chicagoland college campuses was cocaine, and given how anxious I was at that time to conform, I'm sure I would have used more cocaine, or 'coke,' if I'd liked the effects. But I didn't—like it, I mean. It didn't cause euphoric excitement for me, it more just made me feel as though I'd had a dozen cups of coffee on an empty stomach. It was a terrible feeling, even though people around me like Steve Edwards talked about cocaine as if it was the greatest feeling of all time. I didn't get it. I also didn't like the way it made the people who had just done cocaine's eyes bulge out and their lips move around on their face in strange, uncontrollable ways, and the way even shallow or obvious ideas suddenly seemed incredibly profound to them. My overall memory of this cocaine period was of being at some kind of party with someone on cocaine who kept talking to me in this very rapid, intense way, and of me trying to subtly back away, and of every time I take a step backwards they take a step forwards, and so on and so forth, until they've backed me against a wall of the party and my back is literally up against the wall and they're talking very fast only inches from my face, which was something I didn't like at all. This actually happened at parties during this period. I think I have some of my father's inhibition. Close bodily proximity to someone who's very excited or upset is something I've always had a difficult time with, which is one reason why the Audits Division was out of the question for me during the selection and posting phase at the TAC—which I should explain stands for 'Training and Assessment Center,' which roughly one quarter of today's Service's contract personnel above the grade of GS-9 have started out by attending, especially those who—like me—entered through a recruitment program. As of now, there are two such centers, one in Indianapolis and a slightly larger one in Columbus OH. Both TACs are divisions of what is commonly known as Treasury School, as the Service is technically a branch of the US Treasury Department. But Treasury also includes everything from the Bureau of Alcohol, Tobacco, and Firearms to the US Secret Service, so 'Treasury School' now stands for over a dozen different training programs and facilities, including the Federal Law Enforcement Academy in Athens GA, to which those posted to Criminal Investigations from the TAC are sent for specialized training which they share with ATF agents, the DEA, federal marshals, and so on and so forth.

Anyhow, downers like Seconal and Valium simply made me go to sleep and sleep through whatever noise, including alarm clocks, happened to occur for the next fourteen hours, so these were not high on my list of favorites, either. You have to understand that most of these drugs were both plentiful and easy to get during this period. This was especially true at UIC, where the roommate I watched the foot and hung out so frequently at the Hat with was something of a human vending machine of recreational drugs, having established connections with mid-level dealers in the western suburbs, whom he always got extremely paranoid and suspicious if you asked him anything about, as if these were mafiosi instead of usually just young couples in apartment complexes. I know one thing he liked about me, though, as a roommate, was that there were so many different types of drugs that I didn't like or that didn't agree with me that he didn't have to be constantly worried about my discovering his stash—which he usually kept in two guitar cases in the back of his half of the closet, which any idiot could have figured out from his behavior with the closet or the number of cases he had back there versus the one guitar he actually brought out and played his two songs over and over with—or ripping him off. Like most student dealers, he did not deal cocaine, as there was too much money involved, not to mention coked-out people pounding on your door at 3:00 in the morning, so that cocaine was handled more by slightly older guys in leather hats and tiny little rat-like mustaches who operated out of bars like the Hat and King Philip's, which was another fashionable pub of the period, near the Mercantile Exchange on Monroe, where they also serviced younger commodity traders.

The UIC roommate was usually generously stocked in psychedelics, which by that time had definitely passed into the mainstream, but personally psychedelics frightened me, mostly because of what I remembered happening to Art Linkletter's daughter—my parents had been very into watching Art Linkletter in my childhood.

Like any normal college student, I liked alcohol, especially beer in bars, though I didn't like drinking so much that I got sick—being nauseated is something I essentially can't stand. I'd much rather be in pain than sick to my stomach. But I also, like almost everyone else who wasn't an evangelical Christian or part of Campus Crusade, liked marijuana, which in the Chicagoland area during that period was called pot or 'blow.' (Cocaine was not called blow by anyone I ever knew, and only hippie posers ever called pot 'grass,' which had been the hip sixties term but was now out of fashion.) This pot usage had peaked during high school, but I still sometimes smoked pot in college, although I suspect this was largely a matter of just doing what everyone else did—at Lindenhurst, for instance, almost everyone smoked marijuana constantly, including openly on the south quad on Wednesdays, which everyone called 'hash Wednesday.' I should add that now that I am with the IRS, of course, my pot-smoking days are long behind me. For one thing, the Service is technically a law enforcement agency, and it would be hypocritical and wrong. Relatedly, the whole culture of the Examinations Division is inimical to smoking pot, as even rote exams requires a very sharp, organized, and methodical type of mental state, with the ability to concentrate for long periods of time, and, even more important, the ability to choose what one concentrates on versus ignoring, an ability which smoking marijuana would all but destroy.

There was, however, sporadically throughout this whole period, the matter of Obetrol, which is chemically related to Dexedrine but did not have the horrible breath and taste-in-the-mouth thing of Dexedrine. It was also related to Ritalin, but much easier to get, as Obetrol was the prescription appetite suppressant of choice for overweight women for several years in the mid-seventies, and which I liked very much, somewhat for the same reasons I'd liked Ritalin so much that one time, though also partly—in this later period, with me five years older than high school—for other reasons which are harder to explain. My affinity for Obetrol had to do with self-awareness, which I used to privately call 'doubling.' It's hard to explain. Take pot, for instance—some people report that smoking it makes them paranoid. For me, though, although I liked pot in some situations, the problem was more specific—smoking pot made me self-conscious, sometimes so much so that it made it difficult to be around people. This was another reason why smoking pot with my mother and Joyce was so awkward and tense—the truth is that I actually preferred to smoke pot by myself, and was much more comfortable with pot if I could be high by myself and just sort of space out. I'm mentioning this as a contrast with Obetrol, which you could either take as a regular capsule or untwist the halves of and crush the tiny little beads into powder and snort it up with a straw or rolled bill, rather like cocaine. Snorting Obetrols burns the inside of the nose something terrible, though, so I tended to prefer the old-fashioned way, when I took them, which I used to privately refer to as Obetrolling. It's not like I went around constantly Obetrolling, by the way—they were more recreational, and not always easy to get, depending on whether the overweight girls you knew at a given college or dorm were serious about dieting or not, which some were and some weren't, as with anything. One coed that I got them from for almost a whole year at DePaul wasn't even very overweight—her mother sent them to her, along with cookies she'd baked, weirdly—evidently the mother had some serious psychological conflicts about food and weight that she tried to project onto the daughter, who was not exactly a fox but was definitely cool and blasé about her mother's neurosis about her weight, and more or less said, 'Whatever,' and was content to offload the Obetrols for two dollars apiece and to share the cookies with her roommate. There was also one guy in the high-rise dorm on Roosevelt who took them by prescription, for narcolepsy—sometimes he would just fall asleep in the middle of whatever he was doing, and he took Obetrol out of medical necessity, since they were evidently very good for narcolepsy—and he would every once in a while give a couple away if he was in an expansive mood, but he never actually sold or dealt them—he believed it was bad karma. But for the most part, they were not hard to get, although the roommate from UIC never carried Obetrols for sale and squeezed my shoes about liking them, referring to the stimulants as 'Mother's little helper' and saying that anyone who wanted them could just ring the doorbell of any overweight housewife in the Chicagoland area, which was obviously an exaggeration. But they were not all that popular. There weren't even any street names or euphemisms for them—if you were looking for them, you had to just say the brand name, which for some reason seemed terribly uncool, and not enough people I knew were into them to make *Obetrolling* any kind of candidate for a hip term.

The reason I bring up pot is for contrast. Obetrolling didn't make me self-conscious. But it did make me much more self-aware. If I was in a room, and had taken an Obetrol or two with a glass of water and they'd taken effect, I was now not only in the room, but I was aware that I was in the room. In fact, I remember I would often think, or say to myself, quietly but very clearly, *'I am in this room.'* It's difficult to explain this. At the time, I called it 'doubling,' but I'm still not entirely sure what I meant by this, nor why it seemed so profound and cool to not only be in a room but be totally aware that I was in the room, seated in a certain easy chair in a certain position listening to a certain specific track of an album whose cover was a certain specific combination of colors and designs—being in a state of heightened enough awareness to be able to consciously say to myself, *'I am in this room right now. The shadow of the foot is rotating on the east wall. The shadow is not recognizable as a foot because of the deformation of the angle of the light of the sun's position behind the sign. I am seated upright in a dark-green easy chair with a cigarette burn on the right armrest. The cigarette burn is black and imperfectly round. The track I am listening to is "The Big Ship" off of Brian Eno's* Another Green World, *whose cover has colorful cutout figures inside a white frame.'* Stated so openly, this amount of detail might seem tedious, but it wasn't. What it felt like was a sort of emergence, however briefly, from the fuzziness and drift of my life in that period. As though I was a machine that suddenly realized it was a human being and didn't have to just go through the motions it was programmed to perform over and over. It also had to do with paying attention. It wasn't like the normal thing with recreational drugs which made colors brighter or music more intense. What became more intense was my awareness of my own part in it, that I could pay real attention to it. It was that I could look at, for instance, a dorm room's walls of institutional tan or beige and not only see them but be aware that I was seeing them—this was the dorm at UIC—and that I normally lived within these walls and was probably affected in all kinds of subtle ways by their institutional color but was usually unaware of how they made me feel, unaware of what it felt like to look at them, unaware usually of even their color and texture, because I never really looked at anything in a precise, attentive way. It was kind of striking. Their texture was mostly smooth, but if you really focused your attention there were also a lot of the little embedded strings and clots which painters tend to leave when they're paid by the job and not the hour and thus have motivation to hurry. If you really look at something, you can almost always tell what type of wage structure the person who made it was on. Or of the shadow of the sign and the way that the placement and height of the sun at the time affected the shape of the shadow, which mainly appeared to contract and expand as the real sign rotated across the street, or of the way that turning the little desk lamp next to the chair on and off changed the room's interplay of light and the different objects in the room's shadows and even the specific shade of the walls and ceiling and affected everything, and—through the 'doubling'—also being aware that I was turning the lamp off and on and noticing the changes and being affected by them, and by the fact that I knew I was noticing them. That I was aware of the awareness. It maybe sounds abstract or stoned, but it isn't. To me, it felt alive. There was something about it I preferred. I could listen to Floyd, say, or even one of the roommate's constant records from his bedroom like *Sgt. Pepper*, and not only hear the music and each note and bar and key change and resolution of each track, but know, with the same kind of awareness and discrimination, that I was doing this, meaning really listening—*'Right now I am listening to the second chorus of the Beatles' "Fixing a Hole"'*—but also being aware of the exact feelings and sensations the music produced in me. That may sound all drippy-hippie, getting in touch with inner feelings and all that business. But based on my experience during that time, most people are always feeling something or adopting some attitude or choosing to pay attention to one thing or one part of something without even knowing we're doing it. We do it automatically, like a heartbeat. Sometimes I'd be sitting there in a room and become aware of how much effort it was to pay attention to just your own heartbeat for more than a minute or so—it's almost as though your heartbeat wants to stay out of awareness, like a rock star avoiding the limelight. But it's there if you can double up and make yourself pay attention. Same with music, too, the doubling was being able to both listen very closely and also to feel whatever emotions the music evoked—because obviously that's why we're into music, that it makes us feel certain things, otherwise it would just be noise—and not only have them, listening, but be aware of them, to be able to say to yourself, *'This song is making me feel both warm and safe, as though cocooned like a little boy that's just been taken out of the bath and wrapped in towels that have been washed so many times they're incredibly soft, and also at the same time feeling sad; there's an emptiness at the center of the warmth like the way an empty church or classroom with a lot of windows through which you can only see rain on the street is sad, as though right at the center of this safe, enclosed feeling is the seed of emptiness.'* Not that you'd necessarily say it that way, just that it was distinct and palpable enough to be said that specifically, if you wanted to. And being aware of that distinctness, as well. Anyhow, this was why I was into Obetrol. The point wasn't just to zone out on pretty music or back somebody up against a party wall.

And nor was it just good or pleasurable things you were aware of, on Obetrol or Cylert. Some of the stuff it brought into awareness wasn't pleasant, it was just reality. Like sitting in the UIC dorm room's little living room and listening to the roommate-slash-social-rebel from Naperville in his bedroom talking on his phone—this so-called nonconformist had his own phone line, paid for by guess who—talking to some coed, which if there was no music or TV on, you couldn't help overhearing through the walls, which were notoriously easy to put your fist through if you were the type that punched walls, and listening to his rap of ingratiating patter to this coed, and not only sort of disliking him and feeling embarrassed for him at the affected way he talked to girls—as if anybody who was paying any attention could miss seeing how hard he was trying to project this idea of himself as hip and radical without being the slightest bit aware of how it really looked, which was spoiled, insecure, and vain—and listening and feeling all this, but also being uncomfortably aware that I was, meaning having to consciously feel and be aware of these inner reactions instead of just having them operate in me without quite admitting them to myself. I don't think I'm explaining it very well. Like having to be able to say to yourself, *'I am pretending to sit here reading Albert Camus's* The Fall *for the Literature of Alienation midterm, but actually I'm really concentrating on listening to Steve try to impress this girl over the phone, and I am feeling embarrassment and contempt for him, and am thinking he's a poser, and at the same time I am also uncomfortably aware of times that I've also tried to project the idea of myself as hip and cynical so as to impress someone, meaning that not only do I sort of dislike Steve, which in all honesty I do, but part of the reason I dislike him is that when I listen to him on the phone it makes me see similarities and realize things about myself that embarrass me, but I don't know how to quit doing them—like, if I quit trying to seem nihilistic, even just to myself, then what would happen, what would I be like? And will I even remember this when I'm not Obetrolling, or will I just go back to being irritated by Steve Edwards without quite letting myself be aware of it, or why?'* Does this make sense? It could be frightening, because I would see all this with uncomfortable clarity, although I would not have used a word like *nihilism* during that period without trying to make it sound cool or like an allusion, which to myself, in the clarity of doubling, I wouldn't have been tempted to do, as I did things like this only when I wasn't really aware of what I was doing or what my real agenda was, but rather on some kind of strange, robotic autopilot. Which, when I did Obetrol—or once, at DePaul, a variant called Cylert, which only came in 10 mg. tablets, and was only available one time in a very special situation that never repeated—I tended to realize again that I wasn't even really aware of what was going on, most of the time. Like taking the train instead of actually driving yourself somewhere and having to know where you were and make decisions about where to turn. On the train, one can simply space out and ride along, which is what it felt as though I was doing most of the time. And I'd be aware of this too, on these stimulants, and aware of the fact that I was aware. The awarenesses were fleeting, though, and after I came off of the Obetrol—which usually involved a bad headache—afterward, it felt as though I barely remembered any of the things I'd become aware of. The memory of the feeling of suddenly coming awake and being aware felt vague and diffuse, like something you think you see at the outer periphery of your vision but then can't see when you try to look directly at it. Or like a fragment of memory which you're not sure whether it was real or part of a dream. Just as I'd predicted and been afraid of when I'd been doubled, of course. So it wasn't all fun and games, which was one reason why Obetrolling felt true and important instead of just goofy and pleasurable like pot. Some of it was uncomfortably vivid. As in not merely waking up to an awareness of my dislike of the roommate and his denim workshirts and guitar and all of the so-called friends who came around and had to pretend to like him and find him cool in order to get their gram of hash from him or whatever, and not just disliking the whole rooming situation and even the nihilistic ritual of the foot and the Hat, which we pretended was a lot cooler and funnier than it was—as it wasn't as though we did it just once or twice but basically all the time, it was really just an excuse not to study or do our work and instead be wastoids while our parents paid our tuition, room, and board—but also being aware, when I really looked at it, that part of me had chosen to room with Steve Edwards because part of me actually sort of enjoyed disliking him and cataloguing things about him that were hypocritical and made me feel a sort of embarrassed distaste, and that there must be certain psychological reasons why I lived, ate, partied, and hung around with a person I didn't even really like or respect very much...which probably meant that I didn't respect myself very much, either, and that was why I was such a conformist. And the point is that, sitting there overhearing Steve tell the girl on the phone that he'd always felt today's women had to be seen as more than just sex objects if there was going to be any hope for the human race, I would be articulating all this to myself, very clearly and consciously, instead of just drifting around having all these sensations and reactions about him without ever being quite aware of them. So it basically meant waking up to how unaware I normally was, and knowing that I'd be going back to sleep like that when the artificial effect of the speed wore off. Meaning it wasn't all fun and games. But it did feel *alive,* and that's probably why I liked it. It felt like I actually *owned* myself. Instead of renting or whatever—I don't know. But that analogy sounds too cheap, like a cheap witticism. It's hard to explain, and this is probably more time than I should take to explain it. Nor am I obviously trying to give any pro-drug-abuse message here. But it was important. I like now to think of the Obetrol and other subtypes of speed as more of a kind of signpost or directional sign, pointing to what might be possible if I could become more aware and alive in daily life. In this sense, I think that abusing these drugs was a valuable experience for me, as I was basically so feckless and unfocused during this period that I needed a very clear, blunt type of hint that there was much more to being an alive, responsible, autonomous adult than I had any idea of at the time.

On the other hand, it goes without saying the key is moderation. You couldn't spend all your time taking Obetrols and sitting there doubled and aware and still expect to take care of business effectively. I remember not getting Camus's *The Fall* read in time, for instance, and having to totally bullshit my way through the Literature of Alienation midterm—in other words, I was cheating, at least by implication—but not feeling much about it one way or the other, that I can recall, except a sort of cynical, disgusted relief when the prof's grader wrote something like 'Interesting in places!' under the B. Meaning a meaningless bullshit response to meaningless bullshit. But there was no denying it was powerful—the feeling that everything important was right there and I could sometimes wake up almost in mid-stride, in the middle of all the meaningless bullshit, and suddenly be aware of it. It's hard to explain. The truth is that I think the Obetrol and doubling was my first glimmer of the sort of impetus that I believe helped lead me into the Service and the special problems and priorities here at the Regional Examination Center. It had something to do with paying attention and the ability to choose what I paid attention to, and to be aware of that choice, the fact that it's a choice. I'm not the smartest person, but even during that whole pathetic, directionless period, I think that deep down I knew that there was more to my life and to myself than just the ordinary psychological impulses for pleasure and vanity that I let drive me. That there were depths to me that were not bullshit or childish but profound, and were not abstract but actually much realer than my clothes or self-image, and that blazed in an almost sacred way—I'm being serious; I'm not just trying to make it sound more dramatic than it was—and that these realest, most profound parts of me involved not drives or appetites but simple attention, awareness, if only I could stay awake off speed.

But I couldn't. As mentioned, usually afterwards I couldn't even recall what had seemed so clear and profound about what I'd come to be aware of in that cheap green previous tenant's easy chair, which somebody had just left there in the room when he'd moved out of the dorm, and which had something broken or bent in its frame under the cushions and kind of tilted to one side when you tried to lean back, so you had to sit up very straight and erect in it, which was an odd feeling. The whole doubling incident would be covered with a sort of mental fuzz the next morning, especially if I woke up late—which I usually did, given what was essentially a kind of amphetamine's effects on getting to sleep—and had to more or less hit the floor running and hurry to class without even noticing anyone or anything I was running past. In essence, I was one of those types that have a terror of being late but still always seem to be running late. If I came into something late I'd often be too tense and wound up at first even to be able to follow what was going on. I know I inherited the fear of lateness from my father. Plus, it's true that sometimes the heightened awareness and self-articulation of doubling on Obetrols could go too far—*'Now I am aware that I am aware that I'm sitting up oddly straight, now I'm aware that I feel an itch on the left side of my neck, now I'm aware that I'm deliberating whether to scratch or not, now I'm aware of paying attention to that deliberation and what the ambivalence about scratching feels like and what those feelings and my awareness of them do to my awareness of the intensity of the itch.'* Meaning that past a certain point, the element of choice of attention in doubling could get lost, and the awareness could sort of explode into a hall of mirrors of consciously felt sensations and thoughts and awareness of awareness of awareness of these. This was attention without choice, meaning the loss of the ability to focus in and concentrate on just one thing, and was another big incentive for moderation in the use of Obetrols, especially late at night—I have to admit that I know that once or twice I got so lost in the halls or stacked layers of awareness of awareness that I went to the bathroom right there on the sofa—this was up at Lindenhurst College, where there were three roommates per suite and a semi-furnished 'social room' in the suite's center, where the sofa was—which, even at the time, seemed like a clear sign of loss of basic priorities and failure to take care of business. For some reason now, I sometimes have a mental picture of me trying to explain to my father how I somehow became so totally focused and aware that I sat there and wet my pants, but the picture cuts off just as his mouth opens for a response, and I'm 99 percent sure this is not a real memory—how could he know anything about a davenport all the way up in Lindenhurst?

For the record, it is true that I miss my father and was very upset about what happened, and sometimes I feel quite sad at the thought that he is not here to see the career path I've chosen, and the changes in me as a person as a result, and some of my PP-47 performance evaluations, and to talk about cost systems and forensic accounting with from a vastly more adult perspective.

And yet these flickers of deeper awareness, whether drug-induced or not—for it is arguable how much that ultimately matters—probably had more of a direct effect on my life and direction's change and my entering the Service in 1979 than did my father's accident, or possibly even more than the dramatic experience I underwent in the Advanced Tax review class that I had sat in on by mistake during my second, ultimately much more focused and successful enrollment at DePaul. I've mentioned this mistaken final review already. In a nutshell, the story of this experience is that DePaul's Lincoln Park campus had two newer buildings that looked very alike, were literally almost mirror images of one another, by architectural design, and were connected at both the first floor and—by an overhead transom not unlike our own at the Midwest REC—at the third floor, and DePaul's accounting and political science departments were in the two different buildings of this identical set, whose names I don't recall at this moment. Meaning the buildings' names. It was the last regular class day for Tuesday-Thursday classes of the Fall '78 term, and we were to be reviewing for the final exam in American Political Thought, which was to be all essay questions, and on my way to the final review I know I was trying to mentally review the areas that I wanted to make sure at least someone in the class asked about—it didn't have to be me—in terms of how extensively they would be covered on the final. Except for Intro Accounting, I was still taking mostly psychology and political science classes—the latter ones mostly due to the requirements for declaring a major, which you had to satisfy in order to graduate—but now that I wasn't merely trying to squeak by on last-minute bullshit, these classes were obviously much harder and more time-consuming. I remember that most of DePaul's version of American Political Thought was on *The Federalist Papers,* by Madison et al., which I had had before at Lindenhurst but remembered almost none of. In essence, I was so intent on thinking about the review and the final exam that what happened is that I took the wrong building entrance without noticing it, and ended up in the correct third-floor room but the wrong building, with this room being such an identical mirror image of the adjoining building's correct room, directly across the transom, that I didn't immediately notice the error. And this classroom turned out to contain the final review day of Advanced Tax, a famously difficult course at DePaul that was known as the accounting department's equivalent of what organic chemistry was for science majors—the final hurdle, the weed-out class, requiring several prerequisites and open to senior accounting majors and postgrads only, and said to be taught by one of DePaul's few remaining Jesuit professors, meaning with the official black-and-white clothing ensemble and absolutely zero sense of humor or desire to be liked or 'connecting' with the students. At DePaul, the Jesuits were notoriously unmellow. My father, by the way, was raised as a Roman Catholic but had little or nothing to do with the church as an adult. My mom's family was originally Lutheran. Like many of my generation, I wasn't raised as anything. But this day in the identical classroom also turned out to be one of the most unexpectedly powerful, galvanizing events of my life at that time, and made such an impression that I even remember what I was wearing as I sat there—a red-and-brown-striped acrylic sweater, white painter's pants, and Timberland boots whose color my roommate—who was a serious chemistry major, no more Steve Edwardses and rotating feet—called 'dogshit yellow,' with the laces untied and dragging, which was the way everyone I knew or hung out with wore their Timberlands that year.

By the way, I do think that awareness is different from thinking. I am similar to most other people, I believe, in that I do not really do my most important thinking in large, intentional blocks where I sit down uninterrupted in a chair and know in advance what it is I'm going to think about—as in, for instance, *'I am going to think about life and my place in it and what's truly important to me, so that I can start forming concrete, focused goals and plans for my adult career'*—and then sit there and think about it until I reach a conclusion. It doesn't work like that. For myself, I tend to do my most important thinking in incidental, accidental, almost daydreamy ways. Making a sandwich, taking a shower, sitting in a wrought-iron chair in the Lakehurst mall food court waiting for someone who's late, riding the CTA train and staring at both the passing scene and my own faint reflection superimposed on it in the window—and suddenly you find you're thinking about things that end up being important. It's almost the opposite of awareness, if you think about it. I think this experience of accidental thinking is common, if perhaps not universal, although it's not something that you can ever really talk to anyone else about because it ends up being so abstract and hard to explain. Whereas in an intentional bout of concentrated major thinking, where you sit down with the conscious intention of confronting major questions like *'Am I currently happy?'* or *'What, ultimately, do I really care about and believe in?'* or—particularly if some kind of authority figure has just squeezed your shoes—*'Am I essentially a worthwhile, contributing type of person or a drifting, indifferent, nihilistic person?,'* then the questions often end up not answered but more like beaten to death, so attacked from every angle and each angle's different objections and complications that they end up even more abstract and ultimately meaningless than when you started. Nothing is achieved this way, at least that I've ever heard of. Certainly, from all evidence, St. Paul, or Martin Luther, or the authors of *The Federalist Papers,* or even President Reagan never changed the direction of their lives this way—it happened more by accident.

As for my father, I have to admit that I don't know how he did any of the major thinking that led him in the directions he followed all his life. I don't even know whether there *was* any major, conscious thinking in his case. Like many men of his generation, he may well have been one of those people who can just proceed on autopilot. His attitude towards life was that there are certain things that have to be done and you simply have to do them—such as, for instance, going to work every day. Again, it may be that this is another element of the generation gap. I don't think my father loved his job with the city, but on the other hand, I'm not sure he ever asked himself major questions like *'Do I like my job? Is this really what I want to spend my life doing? Is it as fulfilling as some of the dreams I had for myself when I was a young man serving in Korea and reading British poetry in my bunk in the barracks at night?'* He had a family to support, this was his job, he got up every day and did it, end of story, everything else is just self-indulgent nonsense. That may actually have been the lifetime sum-total of his thinking on the matter. He essentially said 'Whatever' to his lot in life, but obviously in a very different way from the way in which the directionless wastoids of my generation said 'Whatever.'

My mother, on the other hand, changed her life's direction very dramatically—but again, I don't know whether this was as a result of concentrated thinking. In fact, I doubt it. That is just not how things like this work. The truth is that most of my mother's choices were emotionally driven. This was another common dynamic for her generation. I think that she liked to believe that the feminist consciousness-raising and Joyce and the whole thing of her and Joyce and the divorce were the result of thinking, like a conscious change of life-philosophy. But it was really emotional. She had a sort of nervous breakdown in 1971, even though nobody ever used that term. And maybe she would eschew 'nervous breakdown' and say instead that it was a sudden, conscious change in beliefs and direction. And who can really argue with something like that? I wish I had understood this at the time, because there were ways in which I know I was kind of nasty and condescending to my mother about the whole Joyce and divorce thing. Almost as though I unconsciously sided with my father, and took it upon myself to say all the nasty, condescending things that he was too self-disciplined and dignified to allow himself to say. Even speculating about it is probably pointless—as my father said, people are going to do what they're going to do, and all you can really do is play the hand that life deals you to the best of your ability. I never knew with any certainty whether he even really missed her, or was sad. When I think of him now, I realize he was lonely, that it was very hard for him divorced and alone in that house in Libertyville. After the divorce, in some ways he probably felt free, which of course has its good sides—he could come and go as he pleased, and when he squeezed my shoes about something he didn't have to worry about choosing his words carefully or arguing with someone who was going to stick up for me no matter what. But freedom of this kind is also very close, on the psychological continuum, to loneliness. The only people you're really ultimately 'free' with in this way are strangers, and in this sense my father was right about money and capitalism being equal to freedom, as buying or selling something doesn't obligate you to anything except what's written in the contract—although there's also the social contract, which is where the obligation to pay one's fair share of taxes comes in, and I think my father would have agreed with Mr. Glendenning's statement that 'Real freedom is freedom to obey the law.' That all probably doesn't make much sense. Anyhow, it's all just abstract speculation at this point, because I never really talked to either of my parents about how they felt about their adult lives. It's just not the sort of thing that parents sit down and openly discuss with their children, at least not in that era.

Anyhow, it would probably help to provide some background info. The easiest way to define a tax is to say that the amount of the tax, symbolized as T, is equal to the product of the tax base and tax rate. This is usually symbolized as $T = B \times R$, so you can then get $R = T/B$, which is the formula for determining whether a tax rate is progressive, regressive, or proportional. This is very basic tax accounting. It is so familiar to most IRS personnel that we don't even have to think about it. But anyhow, the critical variable is T's relationship to B. If the ratio of T to B stays the same regardless of whether B, the tax base, goes up or down, then the tax is proportional. This is also known as a flat-rate tax. A progressive tax is where the ratio T/B increases as B increases and decreases as B decreases—which is essentially the way today's marginal income tax works, in which you pay 0 percent on your first 2,300 dollars, 14 percent on your next 1,100 dollars, 16 percent on your next 1,000, and so on and so forth, up to 70 percent of everything over $108,300, which is all part of the US Treasury's current policy that, in theory, the more annual income you have, the greater the proportion of your income your income tax obligation should represent—although obviously it does not always work this way in practice, given all of the various legal deductions and credits which are part of the modern tax code. Anyhow, progressive tax schedules can be symbolized by a simple ascending bar graph, each bar of which represents a given tax bracket. Sometimes a progressive tax is also called a graduated tax, but this is not the Service's term for it. A regressive tax, on the other hand, is where the ratio T/B increases as B decreases, meaning you pay the highest tax rates on the smallest amounts, which arguably doesn't make much sense in terms of fairness and the social contract. However, regressive taxes can often appear in disguise—for instance, opponents of state lotteries and cigarette taxes often claim that what these things amount to is a disguised regressive tax. The Service has no opinion on this issue either way. Anyhow, income taxes are almost always progressive, given our country's democratic ideals. Here, on the other hand, are some of the types of taxes which are usually proportional or flat: real property, personal property, customs, excise, and especially sales tax.

As many people here remember, in 1977, during high inflation, high deficits, and my second enrollment at DePaul, there was a state fiscal experiment in Illinois in which the state sales tax was to be made progressive instead of proportional. This was probably my first experience of seeing how the implementation of tax policy can actually affect people's lives. As mentioned, sales taxes are normally almost universally proportional. As I now understand it, the idea behind trying a progressive sales tax was to raise state tax revenues while not inflicting hardship on the state's poor or discouraging investors, plus also to help combat inflation by taxing consumption. The idea was that the more you bought, the more tax you paid, which would help discourage demand and ease inflation. The progressive sales tax was the brainchild of someone high up in the State Treasurer's Office in 1977. Just who this person was, or whether he wore the brown helmet in some way after the resulting disaster, I do not know, but both the state treasurer and the governor of Illinois definitely lost their jobs over the fiasco. Whoever's fault it ultimately was, though, it was a major tax-policy boner, which actually could have been easily prevented if anyone in the State Treasurer's Office had bothered to consult with the Service about the advisability of the scheme. Despite the existence of both the Midwest Regional Commissioner's Office and a Regional Examination Center within Illinois's borders, however, it's an established fact that this never occurred. Despite state revenue agencies' reliance on federal tax returns and the Service's computer system's master files in the enforcement of state tax law, there is a tradition of autonomy and distrust among state revenue offices for federal agencies like the IRS, which sometimes results in key communication lapses, of which the 1977 Illinois sales tax disaster is, within the Service, a classic case, and the subject of numerous professional jokes and stories. As almost anyone here at Post 047 could have told them, a fundamental rule of effective tax enforcement is remembering that the average taxpayer is always going to act out of his own monetary self-interest. This is basic economic law. In taxation, the result is that the taxpayer will always do whatever the law allows him to do in order to minimize his taxes. This is simple human nature, which the Illinois officials either failed to understand or neglected to see the implications of for sales tax transactions. It may be a case of the State Treasurer's Office allowing the whole matter to get so complex and theoretical that they failed to see what was right in front of their nose—the base, B, of a progressive tax cannot be something which can be easily subdivided. If it can be easily subdivided, then the average taxpayer, acting out of his own economic interest, will do whatever he can legally do to subdivide the B into two or more smaller Bs in order to avoid the effective progression. And this, in late 1977, was precisely what happened. The result was retail chaos. At, for instance, the supermarket, shoppers would no longer purchase three large bags of groceries for $78 total and submit to paying 6, 6.8, and 8.5 percent on those parts of their purchases over $5.00, $20.00, and $42.01, respectively—they were now motivated to structure their grocery purchase as numerous separate small purchases of $4.99 or less in order to take advantage of the much more attractive 3.75 percent sales tax on purchases under $5.00. The difference between 8 percent and 3.75 percent is more than enough to establish incentive and make citizens' economic self-interest kick in. So, at the store, you suddenly had everyone buying under $5.00 worth of groceries and running out to their car and putting the little bag in the car and running back in and buying another amount under $5.00 and running out to their car, and so on and so forth. Supermarkets' checkout lines started going all the way to the back of the store. Department stores were just as bad, and I know gas stations were even worse—only a few months after the supply shock of OPEC and fights in gas lines over rationing, now, in

Illinois that autumn, fights also broke out at gas stations from drivers being forced to wait as people ahead of them at the pump tried putting $4.99 worth in and running in and paying and running back out and resetting the pump and putting in another $4.99, and so on. It was the exact opposite of mellow, to say the least. And the administrative burden of calculating sales tax over four separate margins of purchases just about broke retail stores. Those with automated registers and bookkeeping systems saw the systems crash under the new load. From what I understand, the high administrative costs of the new bookkeeping burden got passed along and caused an inflationary spike in Illinois, which then further aggrieved consumers who were already peeved because the progressive sales tax was economically forcing them to go through checkout lines half a dozen times or more, in many cases. There were some riots, especially in the southern part of the state, which abuts Kentucky and tends not to be what you'd call understanding or sympathetic about government's need to collect revenue in the first place. The truth is that northern, central, and southern Illinois are practically different countries, culturally speaking. But the chaos was statewide. The state treasurer was burnt in effigy. Banks saw a run on ones and change. From the perspective of administrative costs, the worst part came when enterprising businesses saw a new opportunity and started using 'Subdividable!' as a sales inducement. Including, for instance, used-car dealers that were willing to sell you a car as an agglomeration of separate little transactions for front bumper, right rear wheel well, alternator coil, spark plug, and so on, the purchase structured as thousands of different $4.99 transactions. It was technically legal, of course, and other big-ticket retailers soon followed—but I think it was when Realtors also got into the practice of subdividing that things really fell apart. Banks, mortgage brokers, dealers in commodities and bonds, and the Illinois Department of Revenue all saw their data processing systems buckle—the progressive sales tax produced a veritable tidal wave of subdivided-sales information that drowned the existing technology. The whole thing was repealed after less than four months. Actually, the state legislators came back to Springfield from their Christmas recess in order to convene and repeal it, as that period had been the most disastrous for retail commerce—holiday-season shopping in 1977 was a nightmare that people still sometimes chat ruefully about with strangers when they become stuck in checkout lines here in the state even now, years later. Rather the same way extreme heat or mugginess will make people reminisce together about other terrible summers they both remember. Springfield is the state capital, by the way, as well as the site of an incredible amount of Lincoln memorabilia.

Anyhow, it was also at this time that my father was killed unexpectedly in a CTA subway accident in Chicago, during the almost indescribably horrible and chaotic holiday shopping rush of December 1977, and the accident actually occurred while he was in the process of weekend Christmas shopping, which probably helped contribute to making the whole thing even more tragic. The accident was not on the famous 'El' part of the CTA—he and I were in the Washington Square station, to which we'd ridden in from Libertyville on the commuter line in order to transfer to a subway line going further downtown. I think we were ultimately headed to the Art Institute gift shop. I was back at my father's house for the weekend, I remember, at least partly because I had intensive studying to do for my first round of final exams since reenrolling at DePaul, where I was living in a dorm on the Loop campus. In retrospect, part of the reason for coming home to Libertyville to cram may also have been to give my father an opportunity to watch me apply myself to serious studying on a weekend, though I don't remember being aware of this motivation at the time. Also, for those who do not know, the Chicago Transit Authority's train system is a mishmash of elevated, conventional underground, and high-speed commuter rails. By prior agreement, I came into the city with him on Saturday in order to help him find some kind of Christmas gift for my mother and Joyce—a task I imagine he must have found difficult every year—and also, I think, for his sister, who lives with her husband and children in Fair Oaks OK.

Essentially, what happened in the Washington Square station, where we were transferring downtown, is that we descended the cement steps of the subway level into the dense crowds and heat of the platform—even in December, Chicago's subway tunnels tend to be hot, although not nearly as unbearable as during the summer months, but, on the other hand, the platforms' winter heat is undergone while wearing a winter coat and scarf, and it was also extremely crowded, it being the holiday shopping rush, with the additional frenzy and chaos of the progressive sales tax being under way this year as well. Anyhow, I remember that we reached the bottom of the stairs and the platform's crowds just as the train slid in—it was stainless steel and tan plastic, with both full and partially pulled-off holly decals around some of the cars' windows—and the automatic doors opened with a pneumatic sound, and the train stood idling for the moment as large masses of impatient, numerous-small-purchase-laden holiday shoppers pushed on and off. In terms of crowdedness, it was also the peak shopping hours of Saturday afternoon. My father had wanted to do the shopping in the morning before the downtown crowds got completely out of control, but I had overslept, and he had waited for me, although he was not pleased about it and did not disguise this. We finally left after lunch—meaning, in my case, breakfast—and even on the commuter line into the city, the crowds had been intense. Now we arrived on the even more crowded platform at a moment that most subway riders will acknowledge as awkward and somewhat stressful, with the train idling and the doors open but one never knowing for sure how much longer they'll stay that way as you move through the platform's crowds, trying to get to the train before the doors close. You don't quite want to break into a run or start shoving people out of the way, as the more rational part of you knows it's hardly a matter of life and death, that another train will be along soon, and that the worst that can happen is that you'll barely miss it, that the doors will slide shut just as you get to the train, and you will have barely missed getting on and will have to wait on the hot, crowded platform for a few minutes. And yet there's always another part of you—or of me, anyhow, and I'm quite sure, in hindsight, of my father—which almost panics. The idea of the doors closing and the train with its crowds of people who did make it inside pulling away just as you get up to the doors provokes some kind of strange, involuntary feeling of anxiety or urgency—I don't think there's even a specific word for it, psychologically, though possibly it's related to primal, prehistoric fears that you would somehow miss getting to eat your fair share of the tribe's kill or would be caught out alone in the veldt's tall grass as night falls—and, though he and I had certainly never talked about it, I now suspect that this deep, involuntary sense of anxiety about getting to idling trains just in time was especially bad for my father, who was a man of extreme organization and personal discipline and precise schedules who was always precisely on time for everything, and for whom the primal anxiety of just barely missing something was especially intense—although on the other hand he was also a man of enormous personal dignity and composure, and would normally never allow himself to be seen shouldering people aside or running on a public platform with his topcoat billowing and one hand holding his dark-gray hat down on his head and his keys and assorted pocket change audibly jingling, not unless he felt some kind of intense, irrational pressure to make the train, the way it is often the most disciplined, organized, dignified people who, it turns out, are under the most intense internal pressure from their repressions or superego, and can sometimes suddenly kind of snap in various small ways and, under enough pressure, behave in ways which might at first seem totally out of sync with your view of them. I was not able to see his eyes or facial expression; I was behind him on the platform, partly because he walked more quickly in general than I did—when I was a child, the term he used for this was 'dawdle'—although, on that day, it was partly also because he and I were in the midst of yet another petty psychological struggle over the fact that I had overslept and made him, according to his perspective, 'late,' there being therefore something pointedly impatient about his rapid stride and hurry through the CTA station, to which I was responding by deliberately not increasing my own normal pace very much or making much of an effort to keep up with him, staying just far enough behind him to annoy him but not far enough back quite to warrant his turning and actually squeezing my shoes over it, as well as assuming a kind of spacey, apathetic demeanor—much like a dawdling child, in fact, though of course I would never have acknowledged this at the time. In other words, the basic situation was that he was peeved and I was sulking, but neither of us was consciously aware of this, nor of how habitual, for us, this sort of petty psychological struggle was—in retrospect, it seems to me that we did this sort of thing to one another constantly, out of possibly nothing more than unconscious habit. It's a typical sort of dynamic between fathers and sons. It may even have been part of the unconscious motivation behind my indifferent drifting and lump-like sloth at all of the various colleges he had to get up on time every day and go to work to pay for. Of course, none of this entered into my awareness at the time, much less ever got acknowledged or discussed by either of us. In some sense, you could say that my father died before either of us could become aware of how invested we actually were in these petty little rituals of conflict, or of how much it had affected their marriage that my mother had so often been put in the role of mediator between us, all of us acting out typical roles which none of us were conscious of, like machines going through their programmed motions.

I remember, hurrying through the platform's crowds, that I saw him turn sideways to shoulder his way between two large, slow-moving Hispanic women who were heading towards the train's open doors with twine-handled shopping bags, one of which my father's leg jostled and caused to swing slightly back and forth. I don't know whether these women were actually together or were just forced by their size and the surrounding crowds' pressure to walk so closely side by side. They were not among those interviewed after the accident, which means they were probably on the train by the time it happened. I was only eight to ten feet behind him by this time, and openly hurrying to catch up, as there was the idling downtown train just ahead, and the idea of my father just making it onto the train but of me lagging too far behind him and getting to the doors just as they closed, and of watching his face's expression framed by holly decals as we looked at one another through the doors' glass portions as he pulled away in the train—I think anyone could imagine how peeved and disgusted he would be, and also vindicated and triumphant in our little psychological struggle over hurry and 'lateness,' and I could now feel my own rising anxiety at the thought of him making the train and me just barely missing it, so at this point I was trying to close the gap between us. I still, to this day, do not know whether my father was aware then that I was almost right behind him, or that I was nearly butting and shoving people out of the way myself in my hurry to catch up, because, as far as I know, he did not look back over his shoulder or signal to me in any way as he made for the train's doors. During all of the litigation that followed, none of the respondents or their counsel ever once disputed the fact that CTA trains are not supposed to be able to begin moving unless all of the doors are completely closed. Nor did anyone seek to challenge my account of the exact order of what happened, as at this point I was a few feet at most behind him, and witnessed the whole thing with what everyone conceded was terrible clarity. The two halves of the car's door had begun to slide shut with their familiar pneumatic sound just as my father reached the doors and shot out one arm in between the halves to keep them from closing so that he could squeeze his way in, and the doors closed on his arm—too firmly, evidently, to allow either the rest of my father to squeeze through the doors' gap or to allow the doors to be forced back open enough to let him withdraw his arm, which it turned out was caused by a possible malfunction involving the machinery that controlled the force with which the doors closed—by which time the subway train had begun moving, which was another blatant malfunction—special circuit breakers between the doors' sensors and the train operator's console are supposed to disengage the throttle if any of the doors on any car are open (as one can imagine, we all learned a great deal about CTA trains' design and safety specifications during the litigation following the accident)—and my father was being forced to trot with gradually increasing speed alongside it, the train, releasing his hold on his head's hat to pound with his fist against the doors as two or possibly three men inside the subway car were now at the slight gap in the doors, trying to pull or pry them open further enough to at least allow my father to extract his arm. My father's hat, which he prized and owned a special hat block for, flew off and was lost in the platform's dense crowds, in which a visibly widening gap or tear appeared—by which I mean it appeared in the crowd further down the platform, which I could see from my own place, trapped in the crowd at the platform's edge at a point further and further behind the widening gap or fissure that opened in the platform's crowds as my father was forced to run faster and faster at the accelerating train's side and people moved or leapt back to avoid being knocked onto the track. Given that many of these people were also holding numerous small, subdivided packages and individually purchased bags, many of these could be seen flying up in the air and rotating or spilling their contents in various ways above the widening gap as shoppers jettisoned their purchases in an attempt to leap clear of my father's path, so that part of the appearance of the gap was the illusion that it was somehow spurting or raining consumer goods. Also, the causal issues related to legal liability for the incident turned out to be incredibly complex. The manufacturer's specifications for the doors' pneumatic systems did not adequately explain how the doors could close with such force that a healthy adult male could not withdraw his arm, which meant that the manufacturer's claim that my father—perhaps out of panic, or because of injury to his arm—failed to take reasonable action to extricate his arm was difficult to refute. The male subway riders who appeared to be attempting so forcefully to pry the doors open from within subsequently vanished down the track with the departing train and were not successfully identified, this due partly to the fact that the subsequent transit and police investigators did not pursue these identifications very aggressively, possibly as it was clear, even at the scene, that the incident was a civil and not criminal matter. My mother's first lawyer did place personal ads in the *Tribune* and *Sun-Times* requesting that these two or three passengers come forward and be deposed for legal purposes, but for what they claimed were reasons of expense and practicability, these ads were quite small, and were buried in the Classified section towards the rear of the paper, and ran for what my mother would later claim was an unreasonably brief and unaggressive period of time during which all too many Chicagoland residents left the city for the holidays anyhow—so that this eventually became one more protracted, complex element of the litigation's second phase.

At the Washington Square station, the official 'scene of the accident'—which, in a fatality, is legally deemed to be '[the] location at which death or injuries causing death are sustained'—was listed at 65 yards off of the subway platform, in the southbound tunnel itself, at which point the CTA train was determined to have been traveling at between 51 and 54 miles per hour and portions of my father's upper body impacted the iron bars of a built-in ladder protruding from the tunnel's west wall—this ladder had been installed to allow CTA maintenance personnel to access a box of multi-bus circuitry in the tunnel's ceiling—and the trauma, confusion, shock, noise, screaming, rain of small individual purchases, and nearly stampede-like evacuation of the platform as my father cut an increasingly forceful and high-velocity swath through the dense crowds of shoppers all disqualified even those few people who still remained there on the scene—most of them injured, or claiming injury—as 'reliable' witnesses for authorities to interview. Shock is evidently common in situations of graphic death. Less than an hour after the accident, all that any bystanders could seem to remember were screams, loss of holiday purchases, concern for personal safety, and vivid but fragmentary details as to my father's affect and actions, various rippling things the onrushing air did to his topcoat and scarf, and the successive injuries he appeared to receive as he was borne at increasing speed towards the platform's end and fully or partly collided with a wire mesh trash receptacle, several airborne packages and shopping bags, a pillar's steel rivets, and an older male commuter's steel or aluminum luggage cart—this last item was somehow knocked by the impact across the tunnel and onto the northbound tracks, causing sparks from that track's third rail and adding to the stampeding crowds' chaos. I remember that a young Hispanic or Puerto Rican man wearing what looked to be a type of tight black hairnet was interviewed while holding my father's right shoe, a tasseled Florsheim loafer, of which the toe portion and welt were so abraded by the platform's cement that the sole's front portion had detached and was hanging loose, and that the man could not recall how he'd come to be holding it. He, too, was later determined to be in shock, and I can clearly remember seeing the Hispanic man afterward again in the triage area of the emergency room—which was at Loyola

Marymount Hospital, only one or two blocks away from the Washington Square CTA station—seated in a plastic chair and trying to fill out forms on a clipboard with a ballpoint pen attached by a piece of white string to the clipboard, still holding the shoe.

And the wrongful-death litigation was, as mentioned, incredibly complex, even though it all technically never even proceeded past the initial legal stages of determining whether the City of Chicago, the CTA, the CTA's Maintenance Division (the emergency brake's cord in the car to which my father was forcibly appended was discovered to have been vandalized and cut, although expert opinion was divided on whether the forensic evidence represented a very recent cut or one of weeks' duration. Evidently, the microscopic evaluation of severed plastic fibers can be interpreted in just about any way one's interests lead one to interpret it), the train's manufacturer of record, the train's engineer, his immediate supervisor, AFSCME, and the over two dozen different subcontractors and vendors of various components of the various systems adjudged by the forensic engineers retained by our legal team to have played a part in the accident should, as respondents, be classified in the action as strictly liable, liable, negligent, or FEDD, the latter abbreviation standing for 'failure to exercise due diligence.' According to my mother, our legal team's client liaison had confided to her that the multiplicity of named respondents was just an initial strategic gambit, and that we would ultimately be primarily suing the City of Chicago—which was, of course, my father's employer, in an ironic twist—citing 'common carrier tort law' and a precedent case entitled *Ybarra v. Coca-Cola* to justify collapsing liability onto the shoulders of the respondent that could be shown to have been most cheaply and efficiently able to take reasonable steps to prevent the accident—presumably by having required more stringent quality-assurance of the doors' pneumatics and sensors in the CTA's contract with the train's manufacturer of record, a responsibility which fell, in a further irony, at least partly to the City of Chicago's bursar's office's cost systems division, in which one of my father's own responsibilities had involved weighted evaluations of up-front cost versus liability exposure in certain classes of city agencies' contracts—although fortunately, it turned out that

CTA capital equipment expenditures were vetted by a different detail or team in cost systems. Anyhow, to my mother's, Joyce's, and my dismay, it became evident to us that our legal team's major criterion for arguing for different companies', agencies', and municipal entities' different liability designations involved those different possible respondents' cash resources and their respective insurance carriers' record of settlement in similar cases—that is, that the entire process was about numbers and money rather than anything like justice, responsibility, and the prevention of further wrongful, public, and totally undignified and pointless deaths. To be honest, I'm not sure that I'm explaining all this very well. As mentioned, the whole legal process was so complicated as to almost defy description, and the junior associate that the legal team had assigned to keep us apprised of developments and evolving strategies for the first sixteen months was not exactly the clearest or most empathetic counsel one could have hoped for. Plus it goes without saying that we were also all really upset, understandably, and my mother—whose emotional health had always been pretty delicate since the breakdown or abrupt changes of 1971–72 and subsequent divorce—was going in and out of what could probably be classified as disassociative shock or conversion reaction, and had actually moved back into the house in Libertyville that she'd shared with my father prior to their separation, supposedly 'just temporarily' and for reasons that changed each time Joyce or I pressed her on whether this moving back there was a very good idea for her, and she was generally not in good shape at all, psychologically speaking. In fact, after only the first round of depositions in an ancillary lawsuit between one of the respondents and its insurance company over just what percentage of the legal costs for the respondent's defense against our ongoing suit were covered in the respondent's liability policy with the insurance company—plus, to further complicate matters, a former partner in the lead law firm that was representing my mother and Joyce was now representing the insurance company, whose national headquarters turned out to be in Glenview, and there was a subsidiary set of briefs and depositions in that case concerning whether this fact could in any way constitute a conflict of interest—and procedurally, this ancillary suit had to be resolved or settled before preliminary depositions in our own suit—which by that point had evolved into the twin classifications of civil liability and wrongful death, and was so complex that it took almost a year for the team's litigators even to agree on how to file it correctly—such that, by this point, my mother's emotional state reached the point where she elected to discontinue all litigation, a decision which privately upset Joyce very much but which she, Joyce, was legally powerless to enjoin or influence, and there was then a very complicated domestic struggle in which Joyce kept trying, without my mother's knowledge, to get me to reinitiate the suit with myself, who was over twenty-one and the decedent's dependent and son, as sole plaintiff. But for complicated reasons—chief among them that I had been listed as a dependent on both my parents' 1977 federal tax returns, which, in my mother's case, would have been promptly disallowed in even a routine office audit, but which escaped notice in the more primitive Examinations environment of the Service in that era—it emerged that in order to do this, I would have had to have my mother declared legally 'non compos mentis,' which would have required a mandatory two-week psychiatric hospitalization for observation before we could obtain a legal declaration from a court-authorized psychiatrist, which was something no one in the family was even close to having the stomach for. So after sixteen months, the whole litigation process ended, with the exception of our former legal team's subsequent suit against my mother for recovery of fees and expenses that, to all appearances, the contract that Joyce and my mother signed had explicitly waived in lieu of a 40 percent contingency fee. The recondite arguments by which our former team was attempting to have this contract declared null and void because of some ambiguity in the legal language of one of their own contract's subclauses were never explained or made clear enough to me to be able to tell if they were anything more than frivolous or not, as at this juncture I was in my final semester at DePaul and also in the process of recruitment by the Service, and my mother and Joyce had to hire yet another lawyer to defend my mother against the former lawyers' suit, which still, if you can believe it, still drags on to this day, and is one of the main reasons my mother will give as a rationale for having become a virtual shut-in in the Libertyville house, where she still now resides, and for letting the home's telephone service lapse, although evidence of some kind of major psychological deterioration had already appeared much earlier, actually probably even in the midst of the original litigation and her moving back home to my father's house following the accident, with the first psychological symptom I can remember involving her growing preoccupation with the welfare of the birds in a nest of finches or starlings that for years had been up over one of the joists on the large, open wooden porch, which had been one of the chief attractions of the Libertyville house when my parents had made the original decision to move there, the obsession then progressing from that one nest to the neighborhood's birds in general, and she began having more and more standing and tube-style feeders installed on the porch and the front lawn and buying and leaving out more and more seed and then eventually also all different kinds of human food and various 'bird supplies' for them on the steps of the porch, at one low point including tiny pieces of furniture from a dollhouse from her girlhood in Beloit, which I knew she had treasured as memorabilia as I'd heard her recount all sorts of childhood anecdotes to Joyce about how much she'd treasured the thing and had collected miniature furniture for it, and which she'd kept for many years in the storage room of the Libertyville house, along with a lot of memorabilia from my own early childhood in Rockford, and Joyce, who has remained my mother's loyal friend and sometimes virtual nurse—even though she did, in 1979, fall head over heels in love with the attorney who helped them close Speculum Books under Chapter 13 provisions, and is now married to him and lives with him and his two children in Wilmette—Joyce agrees that the tedious, complex, cynical endlessness of the accident's legal fallout was a large part of what kept my mother from processing the trauma of my father's passing and working through some of the prior, 1971-era unresolved emotions and conflicts which the accident had now brought rushing back up to the surface. Although at a certain point you have to just suck it up and play the hand you're dealt and get on with your life, in my own opinion.

But I remember once, during an afternoon on which he'd paid

me to help him with some light yard work, asking my father why he never seemed to dispense direct advice about life the way my friends' fathers did. At the time, his failure to give advice seemed to me to be evidence that he was either unusually taciturn and repressed, or else that he just didn't care enough. In hindsight, I now realize that the reason was not the former and never the second, but rather that my father was, in his own particular way, somewhat wise, at least about certain things. In this instance, he was wise enough to be suspicious of his own desire to seem wise, and to refuse to indulge it—this could make him seem aloof and uncaring, but what he really was was disciplined. He was an adult; he had himself firmly in hand. This remains largely theory, but my best guess as to his never dispensing wisdom like other dads is that my father understood that advice—even wise advice—actually does nothing for the advisee, changes nothing inside, and can actually cause confusion when the advisee is made to feel the wide gap between the comparative simplicity of the advice and the totally muddled complication of his own situation and path. I'm not putting this very well. If you begin to get the idea that other people can actually *live* by the clear, simple principles of good advice, it can make you feel even worse about your own inabilities. It can cause self-pity, which I think my father recognized as the great enemy of life and contributor to nihilism. Although it's not as though he and I talked about it in any depth—that would have been too much like advice. I can't remember how he specifically answered that day's question. I remember asking it, including where we stood and how the rake felt in my hands as I asked it, but then there's a blank after that. My best guess, derived from my knowledge of our dynamics, would be that he would say trying to advise me about what to do or not do would be like the childhood fable's rabbit 'begging' not to be thrown in the briar patch. Whose name escapes me, though. But obviously meaning he felt it would have the reverse effect. He might have even laughed in a dry way, as though the question was comical in its lack of awareness of our dynamics and the obvious answer. It would probably be the same if I had asked him if he believed I didn't respect him or his advice. He might act as if he was amused that I was so unaware of myself, that I was incapable of respect but didn't even know it. It is, as mentioned, possible that he simply didn't like me very much, and that he used a dry, sophisticated wittiness to sort of try to deal with that fact within himself. It would, I imagine, be hard on someone not to be able to like your own offspring. There would obviously be some guilt involved. I know that even the slumped, boneless way I sat when watching TV or listening to music peeved him—not directly, but it was another thing I used to overhear him speaking about in arguments with my mother. For what it's worth, I accept the basic idea that parents instinctively do 'love' their offspring no matter what—the evolutionary reasoning behind this premise is too obvious to ignore. But actually 'liking' them, or enjoying them as people, seems like a totally different thing. It may be that psychologists are off-base in their preoccupation with children's need to feel that their father or some other parent loves them. It also seems valid to consider the child's desire to feel that a parent actually likes them, as love itself is so automatic and preprogrammed in a parent that it isn't a very good test of whatever it is that the typical child feels so anxious to pass the test of. It's not unlike the religious confidence that one is 'loved unconditionally' by God—as the God in question is defined as something that loves this way automatically and universally, it doesn't seem to really have anything to do with you, so it's hard to see why religious people claim to feel such reassurance in being loved this way by God. The point here is not that every last feeling and emotion must be taken personally as about you, but only that, for basic psychological reasons, it's difficult not to feel this way when it comes to one's father—it's simply human nature.

Anyhow, all this is part of the question of how I came to be posted here in Examinations—the unexpected coincidences, changes in priorities and direction. Obviously, these sorts of unexpected things can happen in all sorts of different ways, and it's dangerous to make too much of them. I remember having one roommate—this was at Lindenhurst College—who was a self-professed Christian. I actually had two roommates in the Lindenhurst dorm suite, with a shared communal 'social room' in the center and three small single bedrooms leading off of it, which was an excellent rooming setup—but one of these roommates in particular was a Christian, as was his girlfriend. Lindenhurst, which was the first college I attended, was a peculiar place in that it was primarily a school full of Chicagoland-area hippies and wastoids, but also had a fervent Christian minority who were totally separate from the overall life of the school. *Christian* in this case meaning evangelical, just like Jimmy Carter's sister, who, if I remember it correctly, was reported as going around performing freelance exorcisms. The fact that members of this evangelical branch of Protestantism refer to themselves as just 'Christians,' as though there were only one real kind, is usually enough to characterize them, at least as far as I was concerned. This one had come in via the suite's third roommate, whom I knew and liked, and who arranged the whole three-way rooming situation without me or the Christian ever meeting one another until it was too late. The Christian was definitely not anyone I would have gone out and recruited to room with on my own, although in fairness, he didn't much care for my lifestyle or what rooming with me involved, either. The arrangement ended up being highly temporary, anyhow. I remember that he was from upstate Indiana, was fervently involved in a college organization called Campus Crusade, and had numerous pairs of dress chinos and blue blazers and Topsiders, and a smile that looked as though someone had plugged him in. He also had an equally evangelical Christian girlfriend or platonic female friend who would come over a great deal—she practically lived there, from what I could see—and I have a clear, detailed memory of one incident when the three of us were all in the communal area, which in these dormitories' nomenclature was called the 'social room,' but in which I often liked to sit on the third roommate's soft old vinyl sofa alone instead of in my tiny bedroom, to read, double on Obetrol, or sometimes smoke my little brass one-hitter and watch TV, prompting all sorts of predictable arguments with the Christian, who often liked to treat the social room as a Christian clubhouse and have his girlfriend and all his other high-wattage Christian friends in to drink Fresca and fellowship about Campus Crusade matters or the fulfillment of apocalyptic prophecy, and so on and so forth, and liked to squeeze my shoes and remind me that it was called 'the social room' when I asked them all whether they didn't have some frightening pamphlets to get out of there and go distribute somewhere or something. In hindsight, it seems obvious that I actually liked despising the Christian because I could pretend that the evangelicals' smugness and self-righteousness were the only real antithesis or alternative to the cynical, nihilistically wastoid attitude I was starting to cultivate in myself. As if there was nothing in between these two extremes—which, ironically, was exactly what the evangelical Christians also believed. Meaning I was much more like the Christian than either of us would ever be willing to admit. Of course, at barely nineteen, I was totally unaware of all this. At the time, all I knew is that I despised the Christian and enjoyed calling him 'Pepsodent Boy' and complaining about him to the third roommate, who was in a rock band besides his classes and was usually not around the suite very much, leaving the Christian and me to mock and bait and judge and use one another to confirm our respective smug prejudices.

Anyhow, at one juncture, I, the Christian roommate, and his girlfriend—who might technically have been his fiancée—were all sitting around in the suite's social room, and for some reason—quite possibly unprompted—the girlfriend was seeing fit to tell me the story of how she was 'saved' or 'born again' and became a Christian. I remember almost nothing about her except for the fact that she wore pointy-toed leather cowboy boots decorated with flowers—that is, not cartoons of flowers or isolated floral designs but a rich, detailed, photorealist scene of some kind of meadow or garden in full bloom, so that the boots looked more like a calendar or greeting card. Her testimony, as best as I can now recall, was set on a certain day an unspecified amount of time before, a day when she said she was feeling totally desolate and lost and nearly at the end of her rope, sort of wandering aimlessly in the psychological desert of our younger generation's decadence and materialism and so on and so forth. Fervent Christians are always remembering themselves as—and thus, by extension, judging everyone else outside their sect to be—lost and hopeless and just barely clinging to any kind of interior sense of value or reason to even go on living, before they were 'saved.' And that she happened, on this one day, to be driving along a county road outside her hometown, just wandering, driving aimlessly around in one of her parents' AMC Pacer, until, for no particular reason she was aware of inside herself, she turned suddenly into the parking lot of what turned out to be an evangelical Christian church, which by coincidence happened to be right in the middle of holding an evangelical service, and—for what she again claimed was no discernible reason or motive she could have named—she wandered aimlessly in and sat down in the rear of the church in one of the plushly cushioned theater-type seats their churches tend to use instead of wooden pews, and just as she sat down, the preacher or father or whatever they called them there evidently said, 'There is someone out there with us in the congregation today that is feeling lost and hopeless and at the end of their rope and needs to know that Jesus loves them very, very much,' and then—in the social room, recounting her story—the girlfriend testified as to how she had been stunned and deeply moved, and said she had instantly felt a huge, dramatic spiritual change deep inside of her in which she said she felt completely reassured and unconditionally known and loved, and as though now suddenly her life had meaning and direction to it after all, and so on and so forth, and that furthermore she had not had a down or empty moment since, not since the pastor or father or whatever picked just that moment to reach out past all the other evangelical Christians sitting there fanning themselves with complimentary fans with slick full-color ads for the church on them and to just kind of verbally nudge them aside out of the way and somehow address himself directly to the girlfriend and her circumstances at just that moment of deep spiritual need. She talked about herself as though she were a car whose pistons had been pulled and valves ground. In hindsight, of course, there turned out to be certain parallels with my own case, but the only real response I had at the time was that I felt annoyed—they both always annoyed the hell out of me, and I can't remember what I could have been doing that day sitting there in conversation with them, the circumstances—and I can remember making a show of having my tongue pressing against the inside of my cheek in such a way as to produce a visible bulge in my cheek and giving the girlfriend in the boots a dry, sardonic look, and asking her just what exactly had made her think the evangelical pastor was talking to her directly, meaning her in particular, as probably everyone else sitting there in the church audience probably felt the same way she did, as pretty much every red-blooded American in today's (then) late-Vietnam and Watergate era felt desolate and disillusioned and unmotivated and directionless and lost, and that what if the preacher or father's saying 'Someone here's lost and hopeless' was tantamount to those *Sun-Times* horoscopes that are specially designed to be so universally obvious that they always give their horoscope readers (like Joyce every morning, over vegetable juice she made herself in a special machine) that special eerie feeling of particularity and insight, exploiting the psychological fact that most people are narcissistic and prone to the illusion that they and their problems are uniquely special and that if they're feeling a certain way then surely they're the only person who is feeling like that. In other words, I was only pretending to ask her a question—I was actually giving the girlfriend a condescending little lecture on people's narcissism and illusion of uniqueness, like the fat industrialist in Dickens or *Ragged Dick* who leans back from a giant dinner with his fingers laced over his huge stomach and cannot imagine how anyone in that moment could be hungry anywhere in the whole world. I also remember that the Christian's girlfriend was a large, copper-haired girl with something slightly wrong with one of the teeth on either side of her front teeth, which overlapped one of the front teeth in a distracting way, because during that day's conversation she gave me a big smug smile and said that, why, she didn't think that my cynical comparison was any kind of refutation or nullification of her vital Christ experience that day or its effect on her inner rebirth at all, not one little bit. She may have looked over at the Christian for reassurance or an 'Amen' or something at this juncture—I can't remember what the Christian was doing all through this exchange. I do, though, remember giving her a big, exaggerated smile right back and saying, 'Whatever,' and thinking inwardly she wasn't worth wasting time arguing with, and what was I even doing here talking to them, and that she and Pepsodent Boy deserved one another—and I know sometime soon after that I left them together in the social room and went off while thinking about the whole conversation and feeling somewhat lost and desolate inside, but also consoled that I was at least superior to narcissistic rubes like these two so-called Christians. And then I have a slightly later memory of me standing at a party with a red plastic cup of beer and telling somebody the story of the interchange in such a way that I appeared smart and funny and the girlfriend was a total fool. I know I was nearly always the hero of any story or incident I ever told people about during this period—which, like the thing with the lone sideburn, is a memory that makes me almost wince now.

Anyhow, it seems like a very long time ago. But the point of even remembering the conversation, I think, is that there was an important fact behind the Christian girl's 'salvation' story which I simply hadn't understood at the time—and, to be honest, I don't think she or the Christian did, either. It's true that her story was stupid and dishonest, but that doesn't mean the experience she had in the church that day didn't happen, or that its effects on her weren't real. I'm not putting it very well, but I was both right and wrong about her little story. I think the truth is probably that enormous, sudden, dramatic, unexpected, life-changing experiences are not translatable or explainable to anyone else, and this is because they really *are* unique and particular—though not unique in the way the Christian girl believed. This is because their power isn't just a result of the experience itself, but also of the circumstances in which it hits you, of everything in your previous life-experience which has led up to it and made you exactly who and what you are when the experience hits you. Does that make any sense? It's hard to explain. What the girl with the meadow on her boots had left out of the story was why she was feeling so especially desolate and lost right then, and thus why she was so psychologically 'primed' to hear the pastor's general, anonymous comment in that personal way. To be fair, maybe she couldn't remember why. But still, all she really told was her little story's dramatic climax, which was the preacher's comment and the sudden inward changes she felt as a result, which is a little like telling just the punch line of a joke and expecting the person to laugh. As Chris Acquistipace would put it, her story was just data; there was no fact-pattern. On the other hand, it's always possible that the 25,834 words so far of my own life-experience won't seem relevant or make sense to anyone but me—which would make this not unlike the Christian girl's own attempt to explain how she got to where she was, assuming she was even sincere about the dramatic changes inside. It's easy to delude yourself, obviously.

Anyhow, as mentioned, a crucial element in my entering the Service was ending up in the wrong but identical classroom at DePaul in December 1978, which I was so immersed in staying focused for the *Federalist Papers* review that I didn't even notice my error until the prof walked in. I couldn't tell whether he was the real fearful Jesuit or not. I only later found out that he wasn't the Advanced Tax instructor of record—there had evidently been some sort of personal emergency for the course's regular Jesuit prof, and this one had taken over as a sub for the last two weeks. Hence the initial confusion. I remember thinking that, for a Jesuit, the prof was in definite 'mufti.' He wore an archaically conservative dark-gray suit whose boxy look might have been actual flannel, and his dress shoes' shine was dazzling when the classroom's overhead fluorescents hit them at the proper angle. He seemed lithe and precise; his movements had the brisk economy of a man who knows time is a valuable asset. In terms of realizing my mistake, this was also when I stopped mentally reviewing the *Federalist* and became aware of a markedly different vibe among the students in this classroom. Several wore neckties under sweater vests, a couple of these vests being actual argyle. Every last shoe I could see was a black or brown leather business shoe, their laces neatly tied. To this day, I do not know precisely how I took the wrong building's door. I am not the sort of person who gets lost easily, and I knew Garnier Hall, as it's where the Intro Accounting class also met. Anyhow, to reiterate, on this day I had somehow gone to 311 Garnier Hall, instead of my own political science class's identical 311 Daniel Hall directly across the transom, and had sat down along the side wall near the room's extreme rear, a spot from which, once I came out of my preoccupation and realized my error, I would have had to cause a lot of disruption and moving of book bags and down jackets in order to get out—the room was completely filled by the time the substitute came in. Later, I learned that a few of the room's most obviously serious and adult-looking students, with actual briefcases and accordion files instead of backpacks, were graduate students in DePaul's advanced-degree business program—the Advanced Tax course was that advanced. Actually, DePaul's whole accounting department was very serious and strong—accounting and business administration were institutional strengths that DePaul was known for and spent a good deal of time extolling in its brochures and promotional materials. Obviously, this isn't why I had reenrolled at DePaul—I had next to no interest in accounting except, as mentioned, to prove something or compensate my father by finally passing Intro. The school's accounting program turned out to be so high-powered and respected, though, that nearly half of that classroom's Advanced Tax students were already signed up to take the February 1979 CPA exam, although at that time I barely knew what this licensing exam even was, or that it took several months of study and practice to prepare for. For instance, I learned later that the final exam in Advanced Tax was actually designed to be a microcosm of some of the taxation sections of the CPA exam. My father, by the way, also held a CPA license, though he rarely used it in his job with the city. In hindsight, though, and in the light of all that eventuated from that day, I'm not even sure I would have walked out even if the logistics of leaving hadn't been so awkward—not once the substitute came in. Even though I really did need that final-exam review in American Political Thought, I still may have stayed. I'm not sure I can explain it. I remember he came briskly in and hung his topcoat and hat on a hook on the corner's flag-stand. To this day, I can never be totally sure whether bumbling into the wrong building's 311 right before final exams might not just have been one more bit of unconscious irresponsibility on my part. You cannot analyze sudden, dramatic experiences like this this way, though—especially in hindsight, which is notoriously tricky (though I obviously did not understand this during the exchange with the Christian girl in the boots).

At the time, I did not know how old the substitute was—as mentioned, I only learned later that he was filling in for the class's real Jesuit father, whose absence seemed unmourned—or even his name. My main experience with substitutes had been in high school. In terms of age, all I knew was that he was in that amorphous (to me) area between forty and sixty. I don't know how to describe him, though he made an immediate impression. He was slender, and in the room's bright lighting he looked pale in a way that seemed luminous instead of sickly, and had a steel-colored crew cut and a sort of pronounced facial bone structure. Overall, he looked to me like someone in an archaic photo or daguerreotype. His business suit's trousers were double pleated, which added to the impression of box-like solidity. Also, he had good posture, which my father always referred to as a person's 'carriage'—upright and square-shouldered without seeming stiff—and as he came briskly in with his accordion file filled with neatly organized and labeled course materials, all of the room's accounting students seemed unconsciously to shift and sit up a little straighter at their little desks. He pulled down the A/V screen before the board much as one would pull down a window's shade, using his pocket handkerchief to touch the screen's handle. To the best of my recollection, nearly everyone in the room was male. A handful were also oriental. He was getting his materials out and arranging them, looking down at his desktop with a little formal smile. What he was actually doing was the teacherly thing of acknowledging the roomful of students without looking at them. They in turn were totally focused, to a man. The whole room was different from political science or psychology classes, or even Intro Accounting, where there was always litter on the floor and people slouched back on their tailbones in their seats and looked openly up at the clock or yawned, and there was always a constant restless, whispery undertone which the Intro Accounting professor pretended wasn't there—maybe the normal profs no longer even heard the sound, or were immune to students' open displays of tedium and inattention. When the substitute accounting professor entered, however, this room's whole voltage changed. I don't know how to describe it. Nor can I totally rationally explain why I stayed—which, as mentioned, meant missing the final review in American Political Thought. At the time, continuing to sit there in the wrong class seemed like just one more feckless, undisciplined impulse. Maybe I was embarrassed to have the sub see me leave. Unlike the Christian girlfriend, I never seem to recognize important moments at the time they're going on—they always seem like distractions from what I'm really supposed to be doing. One way to explain it is that there was just something about him—the substitute. His expression had the same burnt, hollow concentration of photos of military veterans who'd been in some kind of real war, meaning combat. His eyes held us whole, as a group. I know I suddenly felt uncomfortable about my painter's pants and untied Timberlands, but if the substitute reacted to them one way or the other, he gave no sign. When he signified the official start of class by looking at his watch, it was with a crisp gesture of bringing his wrist sharply out and around, like a boxer's left cross, the force pulling up the sleeve of his suit jacket slightly to disclose a stainless steel Piaget, which I remember at the time struck me as a surprisingly racy watch for a Jesuit.

He used the white A/V screen for transparencies—unlike the Intro prof, he didn't write things in chalk on the blackboard—and when he put the first transparency on the overhead projector and the room's lights dimmed, his face was lit from below like a cabaret performer's, which made its hollow intensity and facial structure even more pronounced. I remember there was a sort of electric coolness in my head. The diagram projected behind him was an upward curve with bar graphs extending below its various sections, the curve steep near the origin and flattening somewhat at the apex. It looked a bit like a wave preparing to break. The diagram was unlabeled, and only later would I recognize it as representing the progressive marginal rate schedules for the 1976 federal income tax. I felt unusually aware and alert, but in a different way from doubling or Cylert. There were also several curves and equations and glossed citations from USTC §62, many of whose subsections had to do with complex regulations about the distinction between deductions 'for' adjusted gross income versus deductions 'from' AGI, which the substitute said formed the basis of practically every truly effective modern individual tax-planning strategy. Here—though I realized this only later, after recruitment—he was referring to structuring one's affairs so that as many deductions as possible were deductions 'for' adjusted gross income, as everything from the Standard Deduction to medical-expense deductions are designed with AGI-based floors (*floor* meaning, for example, that as only those medical expenses in excess of 3 percent of AGI were deductible, it was obviously to the advantage of the average taxpayer to render his AGI—known also sometimes as his '31,' as it was then on Line 31 of the Individual 1040 that one entered AGI—just as low as possible).

Admittedly, though, however alert and aware I felt, I was probably more aware of the effects the lecture seemed to be having on me than of the lecture itself, much of which was over my head—understandably, as I hadn't even finished Intro Accounting yet—and yet was almost impossible to look away from or not feel stirred by. This was partly due to the substitute's presentation, which was rapid, organized, undramatic, and dry in the way of people who know that what they are saying is too valuable in its own right to cheapen with concern about delivery or 'connecting' with the students. In other words, the presentation had a kind of zealous integrity that manifested not as style but as the lack of it. I felt that I suddenly, for the first time, understood the meaning of my father's term 'no-nonsense,' and why it was a term of approval.

I remember I did notice that the class's students all took notes, which in accounting classes means that one has to internalize and write down one fact or point from the professor while at the same time still listening intently enough to the next point to be able to write it down next, as well, which requires a kind of intensively split concentration that I did not get the hang of until well into T&A in Indianapolis the following year. It was a totally different type of note-taking from the kind in humanities classes, which involved mainly doodles and broad, abstract themes and ideas. Also, the Advanced Tax students had multiple pencils lined up on their desks, all of which were extremely sharp. I realized that I almost never had a sharp pencil at hand when I really wanted one; I had never taken the trouble to keep them organized and sharpened. The only touch of what might have been dry wit in the lecture was occasional statements and quotes that the substitute interpolated into the graphs by sometimes writing them on the current transparency, projecting them onto the A/V screen without comment and then pausing while everyone copied them all down as quickly as possible before he changed to the next transparency. I still remember one such example—'What we now need to discover in the social realm is the moral equivalent of war,' with the only written attribution at the end being 'James,' which, at the time, I believed referred to the biblical apostle James, for obvious reasons—although he said nothing to explain or reinforce the quote while the six straight rows of students—some of whose glasses reflected the projection's light in ways that gave them an openly robotic, conformist aspect, with twin squares of white light where their eyes should have been, I remember being struck by—dutifully transcribed it. Or one other example, which was preprinted on its own transparency and credited to Karl Marx, the well-known father of Marxism—

> 'In Communist society it will be possible for me to do one thing today and another tomorrow, to hunt in the morning, fish in the afternoon, rear cattle in the evening, criticize after dinner, just as I please'—

about which the substitute's only gloss was the dry statement 'Emphasis added.'

What I'm trying to say is that it was ultimately much more like the evangelist girlfriend with the boots' own experience than I could have ever admitted at the time. Obviously, through just the 2,235-word story of a memory, I could never convince anybody else that the innate, objective quality of the substitute's lecture would also have glued anybody else to their seat and made them forget about their final review in American Political Thought, or of the way that much of what the Catholic father (I thought) said or projected seemed somehow aimed directly at me. I can, though, at least help explain why I was so 'primed' for experiencing it this way, as I'd already had a kind of foretaste or temblor of just this experience shortly before the mistake in final-review classes' rooms occurred, though it was only later, in retrospect, that I understood it—meaning the experience—as such.

I can clearly remember that a few days earlier—meaning on the

Monday of the last week of regular classes for the Fall '78 term—I was sitting there all slumped and unmotivated on the old yellow corduroy couch in our DePaul dorm room in the middle of the afternoon. I was by myself, wearing nylon warm-up pants and a black Pink Floyd tee shirt, trying to spin a soccer ball on my finger, and watching the CBS soap opera *As the World Turns* on the room's little black-and-white Zenith—not Obetrolling or blowing off anything in particular but essentially still just being an unmotivated lump. There was certainly always reading and studying for finals I could do, but I was being a wastoid. I was slouched way down on my tailbone on the couch, so that everything on the little TV was framed by my knees, and watching *As the World Turns* while spinning the soccer ball in an idle, undirected way. It was technically the roommate's television, but he was a serious pre-med student and always at the science library, though he had taken the trouble to rig a specially folded wire coat hanger to take the place of the Zenith's missing antenna, which was the only reason it got any reception at all. *As the World Turns* ran on CBS from 1:00 to 2:00 in the afternoon. This was something I still did too much during that final year, sitting there wasting time in front of the little Zenith, and several times I'd gotten passively sucked into CBS afternoon soap operas, where the shows' characters all spoke and emoted broadly and talked to one another without any hitch or pause in intensity whatsoever, it seemed, so that there was something almost hypnotic about the whole thing, especially as I had no classes on Monday or Friday and it was all too easy to sit there and get sucked in. I can remember that many of the other DePaul students that year were hooked on the ABC soap opera *General Hospital,* gathering in great avid, hooting packs to watch it—with their hip alibi being that they were actually making fun of the show—but, for reasons that probably had to do with the Zenith's spotty reception, I was more of a CBS habitué that year, particularly *As the World Turns* and *Guiding Light,* which followed *As the World Turns* at 2:00 P.M. on weekdays and was actually in some ways an even more hypnotic show.

Anyhow, I was sitting there trying to spin the ball on my finger and watching the soap opera, which was also heavily loaded with commercials—especially in the second half, which soap operas tend to load with more commercials, as they figure that you're already sucked in and mesmerized and will sit still for more ads—and at the end of every commercial break, the show's trademark shot of planet earth as seen from space, turning, would appear, and the CBS daytime network announcer's voice would say, *'You're watching* As the World Turns,*'* which he seemed, on this particular day, to say more and more pointedly each time—*'You're watching* As the World Turns,' until the tone began to seem almost incredulous— *'You're watching* As the World Turns'—until I was suddenly struck by the bare reality of the statement. I don't mean any sort of humanities-type ironic metaphor, but the literal thing he was saying, the simple surface level. I don't know how many times I'd heard this that year while sitting around watching *As the World Turns,* but I suddenly realized that the announcer was actually saying over and over what I was literally doing. Not only this, but I also realized that I had been told this fact countless times—as I said, the announcer's statement followed every commercial break after each segment of the show—without ever being even slightly aware of the literal reality of what I was doing. I was not Obetrolling at this moment of awareness, I should add. This was different. It was as if the CBS announcer were speaking directly to me, shaking my shoulder or leg as though trying to arouse someone from sleep— *'You're watching* As the World Turns.' It's hard to explain. It was not even the obvious double entendre that struck me. This was more literal, which somehow had made it harder to see. All of this hit me, sitting there. It could not have felt more concrete if the announcer had actually said, *'You are sitting on an old yellow dorm couch, spinning a black-and-white soccer ball, and watching* As the World Turns, *without ever even acknowledging to yourself this is what you are doing.'* This is what struck me. It was beyond being feckless or a wastoid—it's like I wasn't even there. The truth is I was not even aware of the obvious double entendre of *'You're watching* As the World Turns' until three days later—the show's almost terrifying pun about the passive waste of time of sitting there watching something whose reception through the hanger didn't even come in very well, while all the while real things in the world were going on and people with direction and initiative were taking care of business in a brisk, no-nonsense way—

meaning not until Thursday morning, when this secondary meaning suddenly struck me in the middle of taking a shower before getting dressed and hurrying to what I intended—consciously, at any rate—to be the final-exam review in American Political Thought. Which may have been one reason why I was so preoccupied and took the wrong building's entrance, I suppose. At the time, though, on Monday afternoon, all that hit home with me was the reiteration of the simple fact of what I was doing, which was, of course, nothing, just slumped there like something without any bones, uninvolved even in the surface reality of watching Victor deny his paternity to Jeanette (even though Jeanette's son has the same extremely rare genetic blood disorder that's kept putting Victor in the hospital throughout much of the semester. Victor may in some sense have actually 'believed' his own denials, I remember thinking, as he essentially seemed like that kind of person) between my knees.

But nor is it as though I consciously reflected on all of this at the time. At the time, I was aware only of the concrete impact of the announcer's statement, and the dawning realization that all of the directionless drifting and laziness and being a 'wastoid' which so many of us in that era pretended to have raised to a nihilistic art form, and believed was cool and funny (I too had thought it was cool, or at least I believed I thought so—there had seemed to be something almost romantic about flagrant waste and drifting, which Jimmy Carter was ridiculed for calling 'malaise' and telling the nation to snap out of it) was, in reality, not funny, not one bit funny, but rather frightening, in fact, or sad, or something else—something I could not name because it has no name. I knew, sitting there, that I might be a real nihilist, that it wasn't always just a hip pose. That I drifted and quit because nothing meant anything, no one choice was really better. That I was, in a way, too free, or that this kind of freedom wasn't actually real—I was free to choose 'whatever' because it didn't really matter. But that this, too, was because of something I chose—I had somehow chosen to have nothing matter. It all felt much less abstract than it sounds to try to explain it. All this was happening while I was just sitting there, spinning the ball. The point was that, through making this choice, I didn't matter, either. I didn't stand for anything. If I wanted to matter—even just to myself—I would have to be less free, by deciding to choose in some kind of definite way. Even if it was nothing more than an act of will. All of these awarenesses were very rapid and indistinct, and the realizations about choosing and mattering were as far as I got—I was also still trying to watch *As the World Turns,* which tended to get steadily more dramatic and compelling as it progressed towards the hour's end, as they always wanted to make you remember to tune in again the next day. But the point was that I realized, on some level, that whatever a potentially 'lost soul' was, I was one—and it wasn't cool or funny. And, as mentioned, it was only a few days later that I mistakenly ended up across the transom in the final-class session of Advanced Tax—which was, I should stress, a subject which at that time I had zero interest in, I believed. Like most people outside the industry, I imagined tax accountancy to be the province of fussy little men with thick glasses and elaborate stamp collections, more or less the opposite of hip or cool—and the experience of hearing the CBS announcer spell out surface reality over and over, of suddenly really being aware of hearing him, and of seeing the little screen between my knees, beneath the spinning ball on my finger's point was part of what put me in a position, I think, whether mistakenly or not, to hear something that changed my direction.

I remember that the third-floor's hallway's bell had rung at the end of the scheduled time for Advanced Tax that day without any of the students doing that end-of-class thing in humanities classes of fidgeting around to gather their materials together or leaning over their desks to retrieve their bags and briefcases from the floor, even as the substitute turned off the overhead projector and raised the A/V screen with a smart snap of his left hand, replacing the handkerchief in his suit coat's pocket. They all remained quiet and attentive. As the room's overhead lights came back on, I remember glancing and seeing that the older, mustachioed student beside me's class notes were almost unbelievably neat and well-organized, with Roman numerals for the lecture's main points and lowercase letters, inset numbers, and double indents for subheadings and corollaries. His handwriting itself looked almost automated, it was that good. This was despite the fact that they were essentially written in the dark. Several digital watches beeped the hour in sync. Just like its mirror opposite across the transom, Garnier 311's floor was tiled in an institutional tan-and-brown pattern that was either checkerboard or interlocking diamonds, depending on one's angle or perspective. All of this I remember very clearly.

Though it would be over a year before I understood them, here are just a few of the substitute's review lecture's main areas, as denumerated in the older business student's notes:

Imputed Income → Haig-Simons Formula
Constructive Receipt
Limited Partnerships, Passive Losses
Amortization and Capitalization → 1976 TRA §266
Depreciation → Class Life System
Cash Method v. Accrual Method → Implications for AGI
Inter vivos Gifts and 76 TRA
Straddle Techniques
4 Criteria for Nontaxable Exchange
Client Tax Planning Strategy ('Tailoring the Transaction')
    v. IRS Exams Strategy ('Collapsing the Transaction')

It was, as mentioned, the final regular class day of the term. The end of the final regular class, in the humanities courses I was used to taking, was usually the moment for the younger professor to try to make some kind of hip, self-mocking summation— *'Mr. Gorton, would you briefly summarize what we've learned over the past sixteen weeks, please?'*—as well as instructions about the logistics of the final exam or paper, and final grades, and perhaps wishes for a good holiday recess (it was two weeks before Christmas 1978). In Advanced Tax, though, when the substitute turned from raising the screen, he gave none of the bodily signals of completion or transition to final instructions or summary. He stood very still—noticeably stiller than most people stand when they stand still. Thus far, he had spoken 8,206 words, counting numeric terms and operators. The older males and Asians all still sat there, and it seemed that this instructor was able to make eye contact with all forty-eight of us at once. I was aware that part of this substitute's vibe of dry, aloof, effortless authority was due to the way the class's upperclassmen all paid such attention to his every word and gesture. It was obvious that they respected this substitute, and that it was a respect that he didn't have to return, or feign returning, in order to accept. He was not anxious to 'connect' or be liked. But nor was he hostile or patronizing. What he seemed to be was 'indifferent'—not in a meaningless, drifting, nihilistic way, but rather in a secure, self-confident way. It's hard to describe, although I remember the awareness of it very clearly. The word that kept arising in my mind as he looked at us and we all watched and waited—although all of this took place very quickly—was *credibility,* as in the phrase 'credibility gap' from the Watergate scandal, which had essentially been going on while I was at Lindenhurst. The sounds of other accounting, economics, and business administration classes emptying into the hallway were ignored. Instead of gathering together his materials, the substitute—who, as mentioned, I thought at the time was a Jesuit father in 'mufti'—had put his hands behind his back and paused, looking at us. The whites of his eyes were extremely white, the way usually only a dark complexion can make eyes' whites look. I've forgotten the irises' color. His complexion, though, was that of someone who had rarely been out in the sun. He seemed at home in thrifty, institutional fluorescent light. His bow tie was perfectly straight and flush even though it was the hand-tied kind, not a clip-on.

He said, 'You will want something of a summation, then. An hortation.' (It is not impossible that I misheard him and what he actually said was 'exhortation.') He looked quickly at his watch, making the same right-angled movement. 'All right,' he said. A small smile played around his mouth as he said 'All right,' but it was clear that he wasn't joking or trying to slightly undercut what he was about to say, the way so many humanities profs of that era tended to mock themselves or their hortations in order to avoid seeming uncool. It only struck me later, after I'd entered the Service's TAC, that this substitute was actually the first instructor I'd seen at any of the schools I'd drifted in and out of who seemed a hundred percent indifferent about being liked or seen as cool or likable by the students, and realized—I did, once I'd entered the Service—what a powerful quality this sort of indifference could be in an authority figure. Actually, in hindsight, the substitute may have been the first genuine authority figure I ever met, meaning a figure with genuine 'authority' instead of just the power to judge you or squeeze your shoes from their side of the generation gap, and I became aware for the first time that 'authority' was actually something real and authentic, that a real authority was not the same as a friend or someone who cared about you, but nevertheless could be good for you, and that the authority relation was not a 'democratic' or equal one and yet could have value for both sides, both people in the relation. I don't think I'm explaining this very well—but it's true that I did feel singled out, spindled on those eyes in a way I neither liked nor didn't, but was certainly aware of. It was a certain kind of power that he exerted and that I was granting him, voluntarily. That respect was not the same as coercion, although it was a kind of power. It was all very strange. I also noticed that now he had his hands behind his back, in something like the 'parade rest' military position.

He said to the accounting students, 'All right, then. Before you leave here to resume that crude approximation of a human life you have heretofore called a life, I will undertake to inform you of certain truths. I will then offer an opinion as to how you might most profitably view and respond to those truths.' (I was immediately aware that he didn't seem to be talking about the Advanced Tax final exam.) He said, 'You will return to your homes and families for the holiday vacation and, in that festive interval before the last push of CPA examination study—trust me—you will hesitate, you will feel dread and doubt. This will be natural. You will, for what seems the first time, feel dread at your hometown chums' sallies about accountancy as the career before you, you will read the approval in your parents' smiles as an approval of your surrender—oh, I have been there, gentlemen; I know every cobble in the road you are walking. For the hour approaches. To begin, in that literally dreadful interval of looking down before the leap outward, to hear dolorous forecasts as to the sheer drudgery of the profession you are choosing, the lack of excitement or chance to shine on the athletic fields or ballroom floors of life heretofore.' True, some of it I didn't quite get—I don't think too many of us in the classroom had spent a lot of time 'shining on ballroom floors,' but that might have been just a generational thing—he obviously meant it as a metaphor. I certainly got what he meant about accounting not seeming like a very exciting profession.

The substitute continued, 'To experience commitment as the loss of options, a type of death, the death of childhood's limitless possibility, of the flattery of choice without duress—this will happen, mark me. Childhood's end. The first of many deaths. Hesitation is natural. Doubt is natural.' He smiled slightly. 'You might wish to recall, then, in three weeks' time, should you be so disposed, this room, this moment, and the information I shall now relay to you.' He was obviously not a very modest or diffident person. On the other hand, his form of address didn't sound nearly as formal or fussy at the time in Advanced Tax as it now sounds when I repeat it—or rather his summation was formal and a bit poetic but not artificially so, like a natural extension of who and what he was. It was not a pose. I remember thinking that maybe the sub had mastered that trick in Uncle Sam posters and certain paintings of seeming to look right at you no matter what angle you faced him from. That perhaps all the hushed and solemn older other students (you could hear a pin) felt picked out and specifically addressed as well—though, of course, that would make no difference as to its special effect on me, which was the real issue, just as the Christian girlfriend's story would have already demonstrated if I'd been aware and attentive enough to hear what the actual point she was trying to make was. As mentioned, the version of me that listened to that story in 1973 or '74 was a nihilistic child.

After one or two other comments, with his hands still clasped behind his back, the substitute continued, 'I wish to inform you that the accounting profession to which you aspire is, in fact, heroic. Please note that I have said "inform" and not "opine" or "allege" or "posit." The truth is that what you soon go home to your carols and toddies and books and CPA examination preparation guides to stand on the cusp of is—heroism.' Obviously, this was dramatic and held everyone's attention. I remember thinking again, as he said this, of the A/V screen's quote I had thought was biblical: 'the moral equivalent of war.' It seemed strange, but not ridiculous. I realized that my thinking about this quote was probably the first time I'd ever considered the word *moral* in any context other than a term paper—this was part of what I had initially started to become aware of a few days prior, in the experience while watching *As the World Turns.* The substitute was only of about average height. His eyes did not cut or wander. Some of the students' glasses reflected light, still. One or two were still taking notes, but other than that, nobody except the substitute spoke or moved.

Continuing on without pause, he said, 'Exacting? Prosaic? Banausic to the point of drudgery? Sometimes. Often tedious? Perhaps. But brave? Worthy? Fitting, sweet? Romantic? Chivalric? Heroic?' When he paused, it wasn't just for effect—at least not totally. 'Gentlemen,' he said, '—by which I mean, of course, latter adolescents who aspire to manhood—gentlemen, here is a truth: Enduring tedium over real time in a confined space is what real courage is. Such endurance is, as it happens, the distillate of what is, today, in this world neither I nor you have made, heroism. Heroism.' He made a point of looking around, gauging people's reaction. Nobody laughed; a few looked puzzled. I remember I was starting to have to go to the bathroom. In the classroom's fluorescent lights, he cast no shadow on any side. 'By which,' he said, 'I mean true heroism, not heroism as you might know it from films or the tales of childhood. You are now nearly at childhood's end; you are ready for the truth's weight, to bear it. The truth is that the heroism of your childhood entertainments was not true valor. It was theater. The grand gesture, the moment of choice, the mortal danger, the external foe, the climactic battle whose outcome resolves all—all designed to appear heroic, to excite and gratify an audience. An audience.' He made a gesture I can't describe: 'Gentlemen, welcome to the world of reality—there is no audience. No one to applaud, to admire. No one to see you. Do you understand? Here is the truth—actual heroism receives no ovation, entertains no one. No one queues up to see it. No one is interested.'

He paused again and smiled in a way that was not one bit self-mocking. 'True heroism is you, alone, in a designated work space. True heroism is minutes, hours, weeks, year upon year of the quiet, precise, judicious exercise of probity and care—with no one there to see or cheer. This is the world. Just you and the job, at your desk. You and the return, you and the cash-flow data, you and the inventory protocol, you and the depreciation schedules, you and the numbers.' His tone was wholly matter-of-fact. It suddenly occurred to me that I had no idea how many words he'd spoken since that 8,206th one at the conclusion of the review. I was aware of how every detail in the classroom appeared very vivid and distinct, as though painstakingly drawn and shaded, and yet also of being completely focused on the substitute Jesuit, who was saying all this very dramatic or even romantic stuff without any of the usual trappings or flourishes of drama, standing now quite still with his hands again behind his back (I knew the hands weren't clasped—I could somehow tell that he was more like holding the right wrist with the left hand) and his face's planes unshadowed in the white light. It felt as though he and I were at opposite ends of some kind of tube or pipe, and that he really was addressing me in particular—although obviously in reality he couldn't have been. The literal reality was that he was addressing me least of all, since obviously I wasn't enrolled in Advanced Tax or getting ready to take the final and then go home and sit at my childhood desk in my old bedroom in my parents' house cramming for the dreaded CPA exam the way it sounded as if many of these others in the room were. Nevertheless—as I wish I'd been able to understand earlier, since it would have saved me a lot of time and cynical drifting—a feeling is a feeling, nor can you argue with results.

Anyhow, meanwhile, in what essentially seemed to be a recapitulation of his main points so far, the substitute said, 'True heroism is *a priori* incompatible with audience or applause or even the bare notice of the common run of man. In fact,' he said, 'the less conventionally heroic or exciting or adverting or even interesting or engaging a labor appears to be, the greater its potential as an arena for actual heroism, and therefore as a denomination of joy unequaled by any you men can yet imagine.' It seemed then that a sudden kind of shudder went through the room, or maybe an ecstatic spasm, communicating itself from senior accounting major or graduate business student to senior accounting major or grad business student so rapidly that the whole collective seemed for an instant to heave—although, again, I am not a hundred percent sure this was real, that it took place outside of me, in the actual classroom, and the (possible) collective spasm's moment was too brief to be more than sort of fleetingly aware of it. I also remember having a strong urge to lean over and tie my boots' laces, which never translated itself into real action.

At the same time, it might be fair to say that I remembered the substitute Jesuit as using pauses and bits of silence rather the way more conventional inspirational speakers use physical gestures and expressions. He said, 'To retain care and scrupulosity about each detail from within the teeming wormball of data and rule and exception and contingency which constitutes real-world accounting—this is heroism. To attend fully to the interests of the client and to balance those interests against the high ethical standards of FASB and extant law—yea, to serve those who care not for service but only for results—this is heroism. This may be the first time you've heard the truth put plainly, starkly. Effacement. Sacrifice. Service. To give oneself to the care of others' money—this is effacement, perdurance, sacrifice, honor, doughtiness, valor. Hear this or not, as you will. Learn it now, or later—the world has time. Routine, repetition, tedium, monotony, ephemeracy, inconsequence, abstraction, disorder, boredom, angst, ennui—these are the true hero's enemies, and make no mistake, they are fearsome indeed. For they are real.'

One of the accounting students now raised his hand, and the substitute paused to answer a question about adjusted cost basis in the tax classification of gifts. It was at some point in his answer to this that I heard the substitute use the phrase 'IRS wiggler.' Since that day, I have never once heard the term anywhere outside of the Examination Center at which I'm posted—it is a piece of Service insider shorthand for a certain class of examiner. In retrospect, then, this definitely should have raised a red flag in terms of the substitute's experience and background. (By the way, the term 'FASB' stood for

Financial Accounting Standards Board, though obviously I would not learn this until entering the Service the following year.) Also, I should probably acknowledge an obvious paradox in the memory—despite how attentive and affected by his remarks about courage and the real world I was, I was not aware that the drama and scintillance I was investing the substitute's words with actually ran counter to those words' whole thrust. That is to say, I was deeply affected and changed by the hortation without, as it now appears, really understanding what he was talking about. In retrospect, this seems like further evidence that I was even more 'lost' and unaware than I knew.

'Too much, you say?' he said. 'Cowboy, paladin, hero? Gentlemen, read your history. Yesterday's hero pushed back at bounds and frontiers—he penetrated, tamed, hewed, shaped, made, brought things into being. Yesterday's society's heroes generated facts. For this is what society is—an agglomeration of facts.' (Obviously, the more real Advanced Tax students who gingerly got up and left, the more my feelings of being particularly, uniquely addressed increased. The older business student with two lush, perfectly trimmed sideburns and incredible notes beside me was able to close his briefcase's metal clasps without any sound at all. On the wire rack beneath his desk was a *Wall Street Journal* that he'd either not read or had perhaps been able to read and refold so perfectly it looked untouched.) 'But it is now today's era, the modern era,' the substitute was saying (which was difficult to argue with, obviously). 'In today's world, boundaries are fixed, and most significant facts have been generated. Gentlemen, the heroic frontier now lies in the ordering and deployment of those facts. Classification, organization, presentation. To put it another way, the pie has been made—the contest is now in the slicing. Gentlemen, you aspire to hold the knife. Wield it. To admeasure. To shape each given slice, the knife's angle and depth of cut.' However transfixed I still was, I was also aware, by this point, that the substitute's metaphors seemed to be getting a bit jumbled—it was hard to imagine the remaining orientals making much sense of cowboys and pies, since they were such specifically American images. He went to the flag-stand in the corner of the room and retrieved his hat, a dark-gray business fedora, old but very well cared for. Instead of putting the hat on, he held it up aloft.

'A baker wears a hat,' he said, 'but it is not our hat. Gentlemen, prepare to wear the hat. You have wondered, perhaps, why all real accountants wear hats? They are today's cowboys. As will you be. Riding the American range. Riding herd on the unending torrent of financial data. The eddies, cataracts, arranged variations, fractious minutiae. You order the data, shepherd it, direct its flow, lead it where it's needed, in the codified form in which it's apposite. You deal in facts, gentlemen, for which there has been a market since man first crept from the primeval slurry. It is you—tell them that. Who ride, man the walls, define the pie, serve.' There was no way not to notice how different he looked now from the way he'd appeared at the beginning. Ultimately, it wasn't clear whether he'd planned or prepared his final hortation or exhortation or not, or whether he was just speaking passionately from the heart. His hat was noticeably more stylish and European-looking than my father's had been, its welt sharper and band's feather pegged—it had to be at least twenty years old. When he raised his arms in conclusion, one hand still held the hat—

'Gentlemen, you are called to account.'

One or two of the remaining students clapped, a somehow terrible sound when it's only a few scattered hands—like a spanking or series of ill-tempered slaps. I remember having a visual flash of something lying in its crib and waving its limbs uselessly in the air, its mouth open and wet. And then of walking back across the transom and down and out of Daniel and over to the library in a strange kind of hyperaware daze, both disoriented and very clear, and then the memory of that incident essentially ends.

After that, the first thing I can remember doing over the holiday recess in Libertyville was getting a haircut. I also then went to Carson Pirie Scott's in Mundelein and bought a dark-gray ventless wool suit with a tight vertical weave and double-pleat trousers, as well as a bulky box-plaid jacket with wide notched lapels, which I ended up almost never wearing, as it had a tendency to roll at the third button and produce what almost looked like a peplum when it was buttoned all the way. I also bought a pair of Nunn Bush leather wing tips and three dress shirts—two white oxfords and one light-blue sea island weave. All three collars were of the button-down type.

Except for practically dragging my mother to Wrigleyville for Christmas dinner at Joyce's, I spent nearly the whole holidays in the house, researching options and requirements. I remember I was also deliberately trying to do some sustained, concentrated thinking. My inner feelings about school and graduating had totally changed. I now felt suddenly and totally behind. It was a bit like the feeling of suddenly looking at your watch and realizing you're late for an appointment, but on a much larger scale. I had only one term left now before I was supposed to graduate, and I was exactly nine required courses short of a major in accounting, to say nothing of trying to sit for the CPA exam. I bought a Barron's guide to the CPA exam at a Waldenbooks in the Galaxy Mall off of Milwaukee Road. It was given three times a year, and it lasted two days, and you were strongly advised to have had both intro and intermediate financial accounting, managerial accounting, two semesters of auditing, business statistics—which, at DePaul, was another famously brutal class—intro data processing, one or preferably two semesters of tax, plus either fiduciary accounting or accounting for nonprofits, and one or more semesters of economics. A fine-print insert also recommended proficiency in at least one 'high-level' computer language like COBOL. The only computer class I'd ever finished was Intro Computer World at UI-Chicago, where we'd mostly played homemade Pong and helped the prof try to recollate 51,000 Hollerith punch cards he'd stored data for a project on and then accidentally dropped on a slick stairway. And so on and so forth. Plus, I looked at a business-stats textbook and discovered that you needed calculus, and I hadn't even had trigonometry—in my senior year of high school, I'd taken Perspectives on Modern Theater instead of trig, which I well remembered my father squeezing my shoes about. Actually, my hatred of Algebra II and refusal to take any more math after that was the occasion for one of the really major arguments that I heard my parents have in the years before they separated, which is all kind of a long story, but I remember overhearing my father saying that there were only two kinds of people in the world—namely, people who actually understood the technical realities of how the real world worked (via, his obvious point was, math and science), and people who didn't—and overhearing my mother being very upset and depressed at what she saw as my father's rigidity and small-mindedness, and her responding that the two basic human types were actually the people so rigid and intolerant that they believed there were only two basic human types, on one side, versus people who believed that there were all different types and varieties of people with their own unique gifts and destinies and paths through life that they had to find, on the other, and so forth. Anyone eavesdropping on the argument, which had started as a typical exchange but escalated into an especially heated one, could quickly tell that the real conflict was between what my mother saw as two extremely different, incompatible ways of seeing the world and treating the people you were supposed to love and support. For instance, it was during this argument that I overheard my father say the thing about my being unable to find my ass even if it had a large bell attached to it, which my mother heard mainly as him passing cold, rigid judgment on somebody he was supposed to love and support, but which, in retrospect, I think might have been the only way my father could find to say that he was worried about me, that I had no initiative or direction, and that he didn't know what to do as a father. As is well-known, parents can have vastly different ways of expressing love and concern. Of course, much of my interpretation is just speculative—there's obviously no way to know what he really meant.

Anyhow, the upshot of all my concentrated thinking and research over the holiday recess was that it looked as though I would basically have to start college all over again, and I was then almost twenty-four. And the financial situation at home was in total flux due to the complex legalities of the wrongful death suit that was under way at the time.

As a side note, there was no amount of alteration that could have made my father's suits fit me. At that time, I was a 40L/30 with a 34 inseam, whereas the bulk of my father's suits were 36R/36/30. The suits and archaic silk blazer ended up being given to Goodwill after Joyce and I cleaned out most of his things from his closet and study and workshop, which was a very sad experience. My mother, as mentioned, was spending more and more time watching the neighborhood birds at the tube feeders which she'd hung around the front porch and the standing feeders in the yard—my father's house's living room had a large picture window with an excellent view of the porch, yard, and street—and often wearing a red chenille robe and large fuzzy slippers all day, and neglecting both her normal interests and personal grooming, which increasingly worried everyone.

After the holidays, just as it was beginning to snow, I made an appointment to speak with DePaul's Associate Dean for Academic Affairs (who was definitely a real Jesuit, and wore the official black-and-white uniform, and also had a yellow ribbon tied to the knob of his office door) about the experience in Advanced Tax and the turnaround in my direction and focus, and about now being so behind in terms of that focus, and to broach the possibility of maybe continuing my enrollment an extra year with deferred tuition in order to help make up some of my deficits in terms of an accounting major. But it was awkward, because I had actually been in this father's office before, two or three years prior, under, to put it mildly, very different circumstances—namely, getting my shoes squeezed and being threatened with academic probation, in response to which I think I may actually have said, aloud, 'Whatever,' which is the sort of thing that Jesuits do not take kindly to. Thus, in this appointment the Associate Dean's demeanor was patronizing and skeptical, and amused—he seemed to find the change in my appearance and stated attitude more comical than anything else, as if he regarded it as a prank or joke, or some kind of ploy to try to buy myself one more year before having to go out and fend for myself in what he termed 'the world of men,' and there was no way to adequately describe for him the awarenesses and conclusions I'd come to while watching daytime television and then later bumbling into the wrong final class without sounding childish or insane, and essentially I was shown the door.

This was in early January 1979, on the day it was just beginning to snow—I can remember watching large, tentative, individual flakes of snow falling and blowing around aimlessly in the wind generated by the train through the window of the CTA commuter line from Lincoln Park back up to Libertyville, and thinking, *'This is my crude approximation of a human life.'* As far as I recall, the yellow ribbons all over the city were because of the hostage trouble in the Mideast and the assault on US embassies. I knew very little about what was going on, partly because I had not watched any TV since that experience in mid-December with the soccer ball and *As the World Turns*. It is not as though I made any conscious decision to renounce television after that time. I just cannot remember watching any after that day. Also, after the pre-holiday experiences, I now felt far too far behind to be able to afford to waste time watching TV. Part of me was frightened that I'd actually become galvanized and motivated too late and was somehow going to just at the last minute 'miss' some crucial chance to renounce nihilism and make a meaningful, real-world choice. This was also all taking place during what emerged as the worst blizzard in the modern history of Chicago, and at the start of the Spring '79 term, everything was in chaos because DePaul's administration kept having to cancel classes because no one who lived off-campus could guarantee they could get in to school, and half of the dorms couldn't reopen yet because of frozen pipes, and part of my father's house's roof cracked because of the weight of accumulated snow and there was a big structural crisis that I got stuck dealing with because my mother was too obsessed with the logistical problems of keeping the snow from covering up all the birdseed she left out. Also, most of the CTA trains were out of service, and buses were abruptly canceled if it was determined that the plows couldn't keep certain roads clear, and every morning of that first week I had to get up very early and listen to the radio to see if DePaul was even having classes that day, and if they were, I'd have to try to slog in. I should mention that my father didn't drive—he'd been a devotee of public transportation—and my mother had given Joyce the Le Car as part of the arrangement they made regarding the dissolution of the bookstore, so there was no car, although occasionally I could get rides from Joyce, although I hated to impose—she was over there mostly to look in on my mother, who was obviously in a decline, and about whom we were all increasingly worried, and it later turned out Joyce had spent a great deal of time doing research into north-county psychological services and programs and trying to determine what kind of special care my mother might need and where it could be found. Despite the snow and temperatures, for instance, my mother now abandoned her practice of watching the birds from inside through the window and progressed to standing on or near the steps to the porch and holding up tube feeders herself in her upraised hands, and appeared prepared to stay in this position long enough to actually develop frostbite if someone didn't intervene and remonstrate with her to come inside. The numbers and noise-level of birds involved were also problematic by this time, as some in the neighborhood had already pointed out even before the blizzard had struck.

On one level, I'm fairly sure that it was on WBBM-AM—a very dry, conservative, all-news station which my father had favored, but whose weather-related cancellations reports were the most comprehensive in the area—that I first heard mention of the Service's aggressive new recruiting-incentive program. 'The Service' obviously being shorthand for the Internal Revenue Service, better known to taxpayers as the IRS. But I also have a partial memory of actually first seeing an advertisement for this recruitment program in a sudden, dramatic way that now, in retrospect, seems so heavily fateful and dramatic that perhaps it is more the memory of a dream or fantasy I had at the time, which essentially consisted of me waiting in the Galaxy Mall food court area while Joyce was helping my mother negotiate another large delivery order from Fish 'n Fowl Pet Plaza. Certain elements of this memory are certainly credible. It is true that I had trouble seeing animals for sale in cages—I have always had difficulty with cages and seeing things caged—and I often did wait for my mother outside in the food court while they were in Fish 'n Fowl. I was there to help carry bags of seed in the event that delivery orders were refused or delayed on account of the severe weather, which, as many Chicagoans still recall, remained intense for quite some time, all but paralyzing the whole area. Anyhow, according to this memory, I was sitting at one of the many stylized plastic tables in the Galaxy Mall's food court, looking absently down at the table's pattern of star- and moon-shaped perforations, and saw, through one such perforation, a portion of the *Sun-Times* that someone had evidently discarded on the floor beneath the table, which was open to the Business Classified section, and the memory involves seeing this from above the table in such a way that a beam of light from the food court's overhead lighting far above fell through one of the star-shaped perforations in the tabletop and illuminated—as if by a symbolically star-shaped spotlight or ray of light—one particular advertisement among all the page's other ads and notices of business and career opportunities, this being a notice about the IRS's new recruitment-incentive program under way in some sections of the country, of which the Chicagoland area was one. I'm simply mentioning this memory, whether it's actually as credible as the more pedestrian WBBM memory or not, as another illustration of how motivationally 'primed' I seemed to be, in retrospect, for a career in the Service.

The IRS recruiting station for the Chicagoland area was in a kind of temporary storefront-type office space on West Taylor Street, right near to the UIC campus where I'd spent a joyless and hypocritical 1975–76 school year, and almost across the street from the Chicago Fire Department Academy, whose apprentice firemen actually used to show up sometimes in full slicker-and-boot regalia at the Hat, where they were banned from drinks involving seltzer or carbonation of any kind—which involves a long explanation which I won't go into here. Nor, luckily, was the podiatrist's sign with the rotating foot visible from this side of the Kennedy Expressway. That huge, rotating foot represented one of the childish things I was anxious to put away.

I remember the sun had finally emerged—although this later turned out to be only a temporary break or 'eye' in the storm system, and there was more severe winter weather on the way two days hence. There were now four or more feet of new snow on the ground, and much more in places where high-speed plows had cleared the streets and formed mammoth drifts along the sides, and you had to pass through almost a kind of tunnel or nave to get to the sidewalk itself, where you then floundered whenever you passed a property whose owner wasn't civic-minded enough to shovel the sidewalk. I was wearing flared green corduroys whose cuffs were soon almost up around my knees, and my heavy Timberlands—which were not great on actual traction, I had discovered—were packed with snow. It was so bright that it was difficult to see. It felt almost like a polar expedition. When the sidewalks were simply too piled up, you had to try to clamber back over the drifts and walk in the street. Understandably, traffic was light. The streets were now more like canyons with sheer white sides, and the high drifts and business-district buildings beyond cast complex, flat-topped shadows that sometimes formed bar graphs you walked right across. I had been able to catch a bus transfer as far as Grant Park, but no closer. The river was frozen and piled high with snow which the plows had tried to dump there. By the way, I know that it's doubtful that anyone outside the Chicagoland area is very interested in the great 1979 winter storm anymore, but for me it was a vivid, critical time whose memory is unusually clear and focused. To me, this remembered clarity is a further sign of the clear demarcation in my own awareness and sense of direction before and after the substitute in Advanced Tax. It wasn't so much the rhetoric about heroism and wrangling, much of which seemed a bit over-the-top to me even then (there are limits). I think part of what was so galvanizing was the substitute's diagnosis of the world and reality as already essentially penetrated and formed, the real world's constituent info generated, and that now a meaningful choice lay in herding, corralling, and organizing that torrential flow of info. This rang true to me, though on a level that I don't think I even was fully aware existed within me.

Anyhow, it took a while even to find it. I can remember that a few corners' stop signs had only the polygonal sign portion visible above the drifts, and several storefronts' doors had their mail slots frozen open and long tongues of windblown snow on their carpet. Many of the city's maintenance and garbage trucks also had blades affixed to their grilles and were serving as extra plows as Chicago's mayor tried to respond to the public outcry over the inefficient disposal of snow. On Balbo, there were some remains of snowmen in front yards, whose heights indicated the ages of whoever had made them. The storm had blown some of their eyes and pipes away or rearranged their features—from a distance, they looked sinister or deranged. It was very quiet, and so bright that when you closed your eyes there was only a lit-up blood-red in there. There were a few harsh sounds of snow shovels, and a high distant snarling sound that I only later remembered as being one or more snowmobiles on Roosevelt Road. Some of the yards' snowmen wore a father's old or cast-off business hat. One very high, clotted drift had an open umbrella visible at its top, and I recall a frightening few minutes of digging and shouting downward into the hole, because it almost looked as if a person carrying an umbrella might have gotten abruptly buried in mid-stride. But it turned out to be just an umbrella which someone had abandoned by opening it and shoving it handle-down into the snowbank, perhaps as some kind of prank or gesture to play with people's minds.

Anyhow, it emerged that the Service had recently instituted a program of recruiting new contract employees in much the same way as the new volunteer armed forces—with heavy advertising and inducements. There turned out to be good institutional reasons for the aggressive recruiting, only some of which had to do with competition from the private accounting sector.

By the way, only lay and popular media refer to all IRS contract employees as 'agents.' Within the Service, where personnel are more often identified by the branch or division in which they're posted, 'agent' usually refers to those in the Criminal Investigation Division, which is comparatively small and handles cases of tax evasion so egregious that criminal penalties more or less have to be sought in order to make an example of the TP, which is essentially designed to motivate overall compliance. (By the way, given that the federal tax system still proceeds largely on voluntary compliance, the psychology of the Service's relation to taxpayers is complex, requiring a public impression of extreme efficiency and thoroughness, together with an aggressive system of penalties, interest, and, in extreme cases, criminal prosecution. In reality, though, Criminal Investigations is somewhat of a last resort, since criminal penalties rarely tend to yield additional revenue—a TP in prison has no income and is thus obviously not in a position to pay down his delinquency—whereas the credible threat of prosecution can function as a spur to repayment and future compliance, as well as having a motivating effect on other taxpayers considering criminal evasions. For the Service, in other words, 'public relations' is actually a vital, complex part of both mission and efficacy.) Similarly, while 'examiner' is often the popular term—even among some private tax professionals—for the IRS employee who conducts an audit, whether in the field or the appropriate District office, the Service's own internal term for such a post is 'auditor'—the term 'examiner' refers to an employee tasked with the actual selection of certain tax returns for audit, although he never deals with the TP directly. Examinations is, as mentioned, the responsibility of Regional Examination Centers such as Peoria's Midwest REC. Organizationally, Examinations, Audits, and Criminal Investigation are all divisions of the IRS's Compliance Branch. At the same time, though, it is true that certain mid-level auditors are known technically within the Service's personnel hierarchy as 'revenue agents.' It's also true that members of the Internal Inspections Division are sometimes classified as 'agents,' with the Inspections Division being rather like the Service's version of law enforcement agencies' Internal Affairs. In essence, they are tasked with investigating charges of malfeasance or criminal behavior on the part of Service employees or administration. Administratively, IID is part of the Internal Control Branch of the IRS, which also includes both the Personnel and Systems Divisions. The point, I suppose, is that, as with most large federal agencies, the structure and organization of the Service is highly complex—in fact, there are departments within the Internal Control branch tasked exclusively to studying the Service's own organizational structure and determining ways to help maximize efficiency in terms of the Service's mission.

Set amid the dazzling paralysis of the Chicago Loop, the IRS recruiting station was not, at first blush, a very dramatic or compelling-looking place. There was also a US Air Force recruiting office in the same storefront, separated from the IRS's space only by a large polyvinyl screen or shield, and the fact that the USAF office played an orchestral version of the familiar 'Off we go into the wild blue yonder' musical theme over and over again on a repeating track in its reception area may well have had something to do with the IRS recruiter's problem with his head and face, which were prone to small spastic jerks and grimaces at various times, and was, at first, difficult not to stare at and to act casual in the presence of. This Service recruiter, who appeared unshaven and had a cowlick that seemed to comprise almost the whole right side of his head, also wore his sunglasses indoors, and had an involved stain on one lapel of his suit jacket, and his necktie—unless my eyes had not yet adjusted from the brilliant dazzle of floundering southwest through fallen snow all the way from the Buckingham Fountain bus stop in Grant Park—might have been an actual clip-on. On the other hand, I had melted snow up to my groin, and frozen birdseed on my down coat, as well as two different winter-weight turtlenecks on beneath that, and probably did not look very promising either. (There was obviously no way that I was going to wear any of my new Carson's business apparel to clamber through chest-high snowdrifts.) Besides the distracting martial music from across the screen, the IRS recruiting station itself was overheated, and smelled of sour coffee and a brand of stick-style deodorant which I couldn't place. Several empty Nesbitt's soda cans were arranged atop an overfull wastebasket, around which a litter of balled-up papers suggested idle hours of trying to throw balled-up papers into it—a pastime I knew well from 'studying' at the UIC library on the evenings when the podiatrist's sign's foot had so ruled. I also remember an open box of doughnuts whose glaze had gone unappetizingly dull.

Nevertheless, I wasn't here to judge anything, nor to make hasty commitments. I was here to try to verify the seemingly almost incredible incentives for entering the Service that had been detailed by the advertisement I'd either heard or perhaps seen two days prior. It eventually emerged that the recruiter had been on duty without relief for several days because of the storm, which was probably the reason for his condition—the Service's standards for personal appearance on-post are normally fairly stringent. When one of the city's large, makeshift plows came by, the noise shook the storefront's window, which faced south and was untinted—forming another possible explanation for the recruiter's sunglasses, which I still found disconcerting. The recruiter's desk was flanked by flags and a large easel with institutional charts and advertisements on large pieces of posterboard, and hanging slightly askew on the wall above and behind the desk was a framed print of the Internal Revenue Service seal, which, the recruiter explained, depicted the mythic hero Bellerophon slaying the Chimera, as well as the Latin motto on a long furling banner along the bottom, *'Alicui tamen faciendum est,'* which essentially means *'He is the one doing a difficult, unpopular job.'* It turned out that, for reasons dating all the way back to the permanent institution of a federal income tax in 1913, Bellerophon was the Service's official symbol or figure, rather the way the bald eagle is the United States as a whole's.

In return for a commitment of two to four years, depending on the specific incentive scheme, the Internal Revenue Service was offering up to a total of $14,450 for college or continuing technical education. That was, of course, $14,450 before applicable taxes, I remember the IRS recruiter stipulating with a smile I did not, at that point, know how to interpret. Also, by an elaborate arrangement which the recruiter highlighted for me on a fold-out document that outlined all the Service's various incentive schedules in complex diagrams with dotted lines and extremely small type, if the continuing education led to either a CPA license or a master's degree in the accounting or tax fields from an accredited institution, there were several grades of further inducements to extend one's employee contract with the IRS, including an option to attend classes while posted at either a Regional Service Center or Regional Examination Center, to which the recruiter explained that newer Service personnel were commonly posted for their first several quarters after what the recruiter called 'T and A.' In order to qualify for the incentive package, one had to complete the twelve-week course at an IRS Training and Assessment Center, or TAC, which is what the recruiter's rather cynical 'T and A' also stood for. Also, employees nearly always refer to the IRS as 'the Service,' and the site at which one works as their IRS 'Post,' and they measure time of employment not in years or months but in terms of the Service calendar's four fiscal quarters, which correspond to the legal deadlines for mailing quarterly estimated tax, or 1040-EST, payments, the only unusual thing about which is that the second quarter runs from 15 April to 15 June, or only two months, and the fourth extends from 15 September to 15 January of the successive year—this is mainly so that the final quarter can comprise the entire taxable year through 31 December. The recruiter explained none of this in so many words at the time—much of it is just the sort of special institutional info one absorbs over time in an adult career.

Anyhow, by this time there were also two other would-be recruits in the office, one of whom I only remember as having a brightly colored one-piece snowsuit and a somewhat low, bulging forehead. The other, older man, though, had masking or duct tape holding his battered sneakers' soles on, and was shivering in a way that seemed to have nothing to do with temperature, and impressed me as quite probably an indigent or street person rather than a bona fide candidate for recruitment. I was trying to concentrate and study the incentive-schedule handout in my hand throughout the recruiter's more formal introductory presentation, and as a result, I know I failed to catch certain key details. Also, though, those details were sometimes actually drowned out by the cymbals and timpanis of the Air Force theme's crescendo portion on the screen's other side. We three, the recruiting presentation's audience, were in folding metal chairs arranged before his desk, which the recruiter initially stood to the side of, beside his display easel—I remember that the man with the low forehead had reversed his chair and was seated leaning forward with his hands on the chair's back and his chin atop his knuckles, whereas the third member of our audience was eating a doughnut after placing several others in side pockets of his khaki army coat. I remember the Service recruiter continually referred to an elaborate color chart or diagram that depicted the administrative structure and organization of the IRS. The depiction covered more than one chart, actually, and the recruiter—who sneezed several times without covering his nose or even averting his head, and also had more of the tiny neurological tic- or spasm-events at certain points in the unavoidably overheard 'Off we go . . .'—had to keep pulling different sections of posterboard to the front of the easel, and the whole thing was so complicated, and consisted of so many branches, sub-branches, divisions, and coordinating offices and sub-offices, as well as parallel or bilateral sub-offices and technology support divisions, that it appeared impossible to comprehend even the general sense of well enough to take a real interest in, though I obviously made it a conscious point to look as attentive and engaged as possible, if only to show that I was someone who could be trained to herd and process large amounts of info. At that juncture, I was obviously unaware that initial diagnostic screening of possible recruits was already under way, and that the excessive complexity and minutiae of the recruiter's presentation represented part of a psychological 'dispositional assessment' mechanism in use by the IRS's Personnel Division since 1967. Nor did I understand, when the other potential recruit (meaning the one who wasn't obviously just looking for a warm place off the street) began nodding off over his chair's back at the abstruseness of the presentation, that he had effectively eliminated himself as a candidate for all but the lowest-level IRS postings. Also, there were upwards of twenty different forms to fill out, many of which were redundant—it wasn't clear to me why one couldn't simply fill out one copy and then xerox a number of duplicates, but I again chose to keep my own counsel and simply fill out the same essential info over and over again.

Overall, despite comprising scarcely more than 5,750 total words, the initial recruiting presentation and processing lasted almost three hours, during which there were also several intervals when the recruiter trailed off and sat in a heavy, incongruous silence during which he may or may not have been asleep—the sunglasses made it impossible to verify. (I would later be informed that these unexplained pauses, too, were part of initial recruit screening and 'dispositional assessment,' that the shabby recruiting office was, in fact, under sophisticated videotape surveillance—one of the required forms had contained an 'Authorization to Record' buried in one of the subclause's boilerplate, which I obviously did not notice at the time—and that our fidget- and yawn-rates and certain characteristics of posture, position, and facial expression in certain contexts would be reviewed and compared to various psychological templates and predictive formulas which the Service's Internal Control Branch's Personnel Division's Recruitment and Training subdivision had developed several years prior, which is, in turn, a very long and complicated story involving the Service's emphasis, throughout the 1960s and '70s, on maximizing 'throughput,' meaning the highest possible efficiency in terms of the volume of tax returns and documents that could be processed, examined, audited, and adjusted in a given fiscal quarter. Though the Service's concept of efficiency would undergo changes in the 1980s, as new government priorities trickled down through the Treasury and Triple-Six, with an institutional emphasis on maximizing revenue rather than throughput of returns, the emphasis at the time—meaning January 1979—required screening recruits for a set of characteristics that boiled down to an ability to maintain concentration under conditions of extreme tedium, complication, confusion, and absence of comprehensive info. The Service was, in the words of one of the Examinations instructors at the Indianapolis TAC, looking for 'cogs, not spark plugs.'

Eventually, it was beginning to get dark and to snow again by the time the recruiter announced that the process was over, and we—by this time there were perhaps five or six of us in the audience, some having drifted in during the formal presentation—were then each given a ream-sized stack of stapled packets of materials in a large blue IRS binder. The recruiter's final instructions were that those of us who felt we were still potentially interested should go home and read these materials closely, and return the next day—which would, if I remember right, have been a Friday—for the next stage of the recruitment process.

To be honest, I had expected to be interviewed and asked all sorts of questions about my background, experience, and direction in terms of career and commitment. I expected that they would want to verify I was serious and not just there to scam the IRS out of free tuition funding. Not surprisingly, I had expected that the Internal Revenue Service—which my father, whose job with the city had understandably involved dealings with the IRS on a variety of levels, feared and respected—would be acutely sensitive to the possibility of being scammed or conned in any way, and I remember, on the long trek in from the bus stop, that I had been apprehensive about what to say in response to tough questioning about the origin of my interest and goals. I'd been concerned about how to tell the truth without the Service's recruiters reacting the way the Associate Dean for Academic Affairs had just recently reacted, or thinking of me in anything like the way I had thought about the Christian girl with the multifloral boots in the Lindenhurst memory already mentioned. To the best of my recollection, though, I was required to say almost nothing that first day of recruiting after the initial hello and one or two innocuous questions—as well as my name, of course. Nearly all my input was, as I've mentioned, in the form of forms, many of which had bar codes in the lower left corners—this detail I remember because these were the first bar codes I can remember ever being aware of in my life up to then.

Anyhow, the recruiting office's binder full of homework was so unbelievably dry and obscure that you essentially had to read each line several times to derive any sense of what it was trying to say. I almost couldn't believe it. I had already gotten a taste of real accounting language from the assigned textbooks for Managerial Accounting and Auditing I, which were both just under way—when weather permitted—at DePaul, but the Service material made those textbooks look like child's play by comparison. The largest single packet in the binder was something on low-toner Xerox called *Statement of Procedural Rules,* which is actually from Title 26, §601 of the *Code of Federal Regulations.* A ninety-five-word section of a page that I remember that I flipped to at first at random and read, just to get an idea of what I would be having to try to read and process, was ¶1910, §601.201a(1)(g), subpart xi:

> For ruling requests concerning the classification of an organization as a limited partnership where a corporation is the sole general partner, see Rev. Proc. 72–13, 1972–1 CB 735. See also Rev. Proc. 74–17, 1974–1 CB 438, and Rev. Proc. 75–16, 1975–1 CB 676. Revenue Procedure 74–17 announces certain operating rules of the Service relating to the issuance of advance ruling letters

> concerning the classification of organizations formed as limited partnerships. Revenue Procedure 75–16 sets forth a checklist outlining required information frequently omitted from requests for rulings relating to classification of organizations for Federal tax purposes.

Essentially, the whole thing was like that. Nor, at the time, did I know we would have to try to practically memorize the entire 82,617-word *Procedural Rules* manual at the Training and Assessment Center, less for informational purposes—since every IRS examiner's Tingle table would have the *Procedural Rules* included in the *Internal Revenue Manual* right there in the bottom-right drawer, attached with a little chain so no one could take or borrow it, as we were all supposed to have it at our Tingle at all times—but more as a type of diagnostic tool for seeing who could sit there hour after hour and apply themselves to it versus who couldn't, which obviously bore on who could cut it at various levels of complexity and dryness (which, in turn, is why the Examinations component of the TAC's training course was known at the TAC as 'Camp Concentration'). My best guess at the time, sitting there in my childhood room in my father's house in Libertyville (the dorm at DePaul still wasn't open, as some frozen pipes had ruptured—the storm and its fallout still had much of the city paralyzed), was that requiring us to read this material was some kind of test or hurdle to help determine who was truly motivated and serious and who was just drifting around attempting to scam some easy tuition money from the government. I kept picturing the indigent character who ate all the doughnuts from that afternoon's presentation lying in a cardboard appliance box in an alley, reading a page of the packet and then setting it afire to provide light for reading the next page. In a certain way, I think that that was essentially what I was doing, too—I had to blow off nearly all my next day's accounting class assignments in order to stay up nearly all night getting through the Service material. It didn't feel feckless, though it also didn't feel especially romantic or heroic. It was more as if I simply had to make a choice of what was more important.

I read more or less the whole thing. I won't even say how many words in toto. It took until almost 5:00 A.M. At the very back—not all the way, but tucked between two pages of the transcript of a 1966 USTC case called *Uinta Livestock Corporation v. U.S.* near the back of the binder—were a couple of more forms to fill out, which reinforced my assumption that it really had been a kind of test to see if we were committed and interested enough to nut up and plow all the way through. I can't say I read everything carefully, of course. One of the few packets that wasn't totally eye-glazing was a rundown on the IRS Training and Assessment Centers and on the various types of entry-level posts available to recruits who came out of the TAC course with various levels of education and incentive packages. There were two IRS Training and Assessment Centers, in Indianapolis and Columbus OH, about which the packet had photos and regulations but nothing specific on what the training was actually like. As usually happens with photocopied photos, the images were mostly black masses with some indistinct white blobs; you couldn't really make out what was going on. Unlike the present day, the protocol in that era was that if you wanted a serious career in the Service, with a contract and civil service rank above GS-9, you had to go through a TAC course, which lasted twelve weeks. You also had to join the Treasury Employees union, although info on that criterion was not included in the packet. Otherwise you were, in essence, a temporary or seasonal worker, which the Service uses a lot of, especially in the lower levels of Returns Processing and Exams. I remember that the Post List's representation of the Service's structure was much simpler and less comprehensive than the recruiter's presentation's diagram, although this one also had a lot of asterisks and single and double lines connecting various parts of the page's grid, and the legend for these marks had been half cut off due to someone having xeroxed the thing at an angle. In that era, the six main nodes or Service branches consisted of Administration, Returns Processing, Compliance, Collections, Internal Control, Support Services, and something called Technical Branch, which was the only branch with the actual word *Branch* in its name on the diagram, which at the time I found curious. Each branch then branched into several subordinate divisions—thirty-six divisions in all, though in today's Service there are now forty-eight separate divisions, some with cross-coordinated and overlapping functions which have to be streamlined and overseen by the Divisional Liaison Division, which is itself—somewhat confusingly—a division of both the Administration and Internal Control Branches. Each division then also comprised numerous subdivisions, some of whose typeface got extremely small and hard to read. The Compliance Branch's Examinations Division, for example, comprised positions—though only those postings marked in italic font (which was practically impossible to make out on the Xerox) required a federal contract or TAC course—in clerical, cart, data entry, data processing, classification, correspondence, district office interface, regional office interface, duplicating services, procurement, research audit interface, secretarial, personnel, service center interface, computer center interface, and so forth, as well as formal 'rote examiner' posts grouped (in that era, though here at the Midwest REC now the group characterizations are quite a bit different) by the types of returns one specialized in, encoded on the diagram as 1040, 1040A, 1041, EST, and 'Fats,' which refers to a complex 1040 with more than four schedules or attachments. Also, corporate 1120 and 1120S tax returns are examined by special examiners known in Exams as 'immersives,' which the recruiting page did not include information on, as immersive exams are conducted by special elite, highly trained examiners who have their own special section of the REC facility.

Anyhow, as I still can recall, the obvious idea was that anyone who was truly serious would make their best attempt to read the whole contents of the binder, would see and complete the relevant portions of the forms at the back, and then would make the effort to somehow commute back in, weather permitting, to the West Taylor recruiting station the next day by 9:00 A.M. for something which the final sheet termed 'advanced processing.' It also snowed all night again, though not as heavily, and by 4:00 A.M. you could hear the terrible sound of the City of Libertyville's plows scraping the street's concrete raw outside my childhood room's window—also, the birdsounds at sunrise were incredible, causing lights in some of the other houses along our street to come on in irritation—and the CTA was still only running a staggered schedule. Still, even given the rush of commuters at that time of day and the rigors of the trek in from Grant Park, I arrived back at the storefront recruiting station no later than 9:20 A.M. (albeit covered with snow again), to find no one else there from the prior day except the same Service recruiter, looking even more exhausted and disheveled, who, when I came in and said I was ready for advanced processing, and gave him the forms from the homework I'd plowed through, looked from me to the forms and back again, giving me the exact kind of smile of someone who, on Christmas morning, has just unwrapped an expensive present he already owns.

§23

Dream: I saw rows of foreshortened faces over which faint emotions played like the light of distant fire. The placid hopelessness of adulthood. The complex regret. One or two, the most alive, looked better in an objectless way. Many others looked blank as the faces on coins. At the edges were office workers bustling at the endless small tasks involved in mailing, filing, sorting, their faces blankly avid, filled with the mindless energy you see in bugs, weeds, birds. The dream seemed to take hours, but when I'd come awake Superman's arms (the clock was a gift) would be in the same position as the last time I looked.

This dream was my psyche teaching me about boredom. I think I was very often bored as a child, but boredom is not what I knew it as—what I knew was that I *worried* a lot. I was a fretful, nervous, anxious, worried boy. These were my parents' words, and they became mine. Wet distended Sunday afternoons, while my mother and brother were at a recital and my father lay asleep on the couch in front of a Bengals game, with the libretto to *Norma* open on his chest, I felt the sort of soaring, ceilingless tedium that transcends tedium and becomes worry. I do not recall the things I worried about, but I remember the feeling, and it was an anxiety whose lack of a proper object is what made it horrible, free-floating. I'd look out the window and see the glass instead of anything past it. I'd think of the sorts of small games and toys and developmental projects my mother always suggested and within the boredom not only find them unappealing but be unable to imagine how anyone anywhere could possibly have the mindless energy to undertake any sort of child's amusements, or sit still in the silence long enough to read a picture book—the whole world was torpid, enervated, worry-logged. My parents' words and feelings became my own, as I took on the responsibilities of my role in the family drama, the nervous delicate son, object of my mother's concern, as my brother was the gifted, driven son whose piano filled the house after school and kept the twilight outside the windows where it belonged. In psychotherapy after the incident with my own son, I free-associated my way into recalling a Great Books presentation on Achilles and Hector in the eleventh grade, and I remembered realizing vividly that my family was Achilles, that my brother was Achilles' shield and I the family's heel, the part of the family my mother held tight to and made undivine, and that the recognition had come in the middle of my speech and left again so fast I'd not had time to grab it, though I did for much of my adolescence and early adulthood conceive of myself in terms of a heel or foot—my internal remonstrances often took the form of calling myself a 'heel,' for example, and it was true that people's feet, shoes, socks, and ankles were often the first things about them I noticed. Just as my father was the beaten but obdurate warrior—ground down every day in a campaign whose pointlessness was part of its corrosive power. My mother's role in the Achilles corpus remains unclear. I'm not sure, either, whether as a child my brother was conscious of the fact that his afternoon practice always coincided with my father's return home; in some respects I think my brother's whole piano career was designed around this requirement that there be light and music at 5:42 for my father's reentry, that in a way his life depended on it—every evening he made the opposite transition from that of the sun, death to life.

It is not surprising that I had trouble in grammar school, with its rows of empty faces and shadowless lights and wire mesh in the windows and a regimentation to primary education that still held on in the Midwest—memorization and regurgitation, tables, prescriptive grammar and diagrams of sentences, the only decorations the alphabet in construction paper on a cork guilloche that ran above the blackboard. Each classroom contained thirty student desks in five rows of six; each had flooring of white tile with insubstantial cloud-shapes of brown and gray that were discontinuous because whoever laid the tile didn't bother to match the patterns. Each room had a wall clock, manufactured by Benrus, with no second hand and a minute hand whose movements were discrete clicks instead of silent continuous clicks; the system of clocks was wired to the school's bell, which sounded at 55 past the hour, again at 00, and in a somehow more dire way at 02, signaling tardiness and interrupting each instructor's opening remarks. The school smelled of adhesive paste, rubber boots, sour cafeteria food, and a warm biotic odor of many bodies and the fixative of the tile floor as three hundred mammals slowly warmed the rooms throughout the day. Most of the teachers were sexless females, old (meaning older than my mother) and severe but not unkind, with a small dilution of younger males—one, in fourth-grade Mathematics, with the actual name Mr. Goodnature—drawn to teach children by the vague political idealism then just beginning to build (unknown to me) on college campuses far beyond my world. The young men were the worst, some actual martinets, depressed and bitter, because the idealism that had brought them to us was no match for the petrified bureaucracy of the Columbus School System or the listless passivity of children they'd dreamed of inspiring (read, indoctrinating) to a soft liberalism (*peace* was a big word with these men) that would replicate and flatter their own, children who were instead locked tight inside themselves and an institutional tedium they couldn't name but had already lost their hearts to.

§24

Author here.[1] I arrived for intake processing at Lake James IL's[2] IRS Post 047 sometime in mid-May of 1985. It was quite probably on or very

1 I won't keep saying this each time that I, the living author, am actively narrating. For now, I'm including it just as an innocuous cue to help you keep the book's various sections and agonists straight, since (as explained in the Author's Foreword) the legal situation here entails a certain degree of polyphony and flux.

2 At that time, Lake James was something between a suburb and an independent township of metropolitan Peoria. The same is true of other little outlying communities like Peoria Heights, Bartonville, Sicklied Ore, Eunice, & c., the latter two of which adjoined Lake James along certain unincorporated zones to the east and west. The whole separate-but-attached-district thing had to do with the city's inexorable expansion and encroachment into the rich agricultural land around it, which over time brought certain small, formerly isolated farming communities into Peoria's orbit. I know that these little satellite towns each had their own property-tax structure and zoning authority, but in many other respects (e.g., police protection) they functioned as outlying districts of Peoria proper. The whole thing could be extremely involved and confusing. For instance, the Regional Examination Center's street address was listed as 10047 Self-Storage Parkway, Lake James, IL, whereas the REC's official postal address was 'Internal Revenue Service Examination Center, Peoria IL 67452.' This may be because Peoria's USPS center on G Street downtown had a whole separate three-bin area for the REC, however, plus a pair of special tandem trucks that came out the restricted back road three times a day to the REC's loading docks behind the Annex. I.e., the mailing address may have been Peoria simply because that's where the REC's daily mountain of mail actually came to. That is, it may have been more a function of the relationship between the US Postal Service and the IRS than anything else. Like so many other features of the REC and Service, the

near Wednesday, May 15.[3] In any event, the point is that I journeyed to Peoria on whatever particular day in May from my family's home in Philo, to which my brief return had been shall we say untriumphant, and where certain members of my family had more or less been looking at their watches impatiently the whole brief time I was home. Without mentioning or identifying anyone in particular, let's just say that the prevailing attitude in my family tended to be 'What have you done for me lately?' or, maybe better, 'What have you achieved/earned/attained lately that may in some way (imaginary or not) reflect well on us and let us bask in some kind of reflected (real or not) accomplishment?' It was a bit like a for-profit company, my family, in that you were pretty much only as good as your last sales quarter. Although, you know,

answer to the physical-vs.-postal-location-incongruity question is doubtless incredibly complicated and idiosyncratic and would require far more time and energy to ferret out and truly understand than any sane person would want to expend. Another example: The really relevant, representative thing about Lake James as a township is that it has no lake. There is, in fact, a body of water called Lake James, but as a practical matter it's more of a large fetid pond, choked with algae from ag-runoff, a good dozen miles northwest of Lake James proper, closer to Anthony IL, which latter really is a separate township of Peoria and has its own zip code, & c., & c.... In other words, incongruities like these are complex and puzzling but not really all that important unless you're invested in the geographical minutiae of Peoria (the possibility of which I have decided I can safely presume is remote).

3 N.B.: I'm not going to be one of those memoirists who pretends to remember every last fact and thing in photorealist detail. The human mind doesn't work that way, and everyone knows it; it's an insulting bit of artifice in a genre that purports to be 100 percent 'realistic.' To be honest, I think you deserve better, and that you're intelligent enough to understand and maybe even applaud it when a memoirist has the integrity to admit that he's not some kind of eidetic freak. At the same time, I'm not going to waste time noodling about every last gap and imprecision in my own memory, a prime cautionary example of which is 'Irrelevant' Chris Fogle's vocational soliloquy (q.v. §22 above, which is actually heavily edited and excerpted) as part of the abortive 1984 Personnel Division motivational/recruitment faux documentary debacle, which ended up as a debacle in part because Fogle and two or three other maundering grandstanders took up so much film and time, and because Mr. Tate had failed to have his deputy, Mr. Stecyk, assign anyone on-site the responsibility of keeping someone's answer to the 'documentary question' under a certain sane ceiling, which meant that the supposed 'documentarian' and his crew had every incentive to let Fogle et al. go on and on while they stared into space and calculated the running amount of tiered overtime pay they were accruing. The whole thing, while obviously of archival value, was evidently an immense cluster-fuck, one of many that Tate authored when he indulged his administrative brainstorms instead of simply letting Stecyk do all the work of the Personnel office as usual.

whatever. I most definitely was not offered any kind of family ride to Peoria, though I may have gotten a quick lift to the bus station, which in Philo comprised one corner of the local IGA parking lot, which was not all that far but would have been ghastly to walk to wearing my three-piece corduroy suit in the gluey humidity of pre-dawn (which, in the lower Midwest, is also one of the two prime times of day for mosquito activity, the other being dusk, and mosquitoes there are not just a nuisance but serious business indeed) while carrying two heavy suitcases (this was a couple years before the sudden advance of someone in the luggage industry realizing that suitcases could be fitted with little wheels and telescoping handles so they could be pulled, which was just the sort of abrupt ingenious advance that makes entrepreneurial capitalism such an exciting system—it gives people incentive to make things more efficient). Plus I also had my beloved dispatch case, which was inherited from an older, non-immediate relative who'd been a staff officer in Hawaii during the latter part of World War II, and was a bit like a briefcase (i.e., the dispatch case was) except that it had no handle, and was therefore carried tucked under one's arm, and which contained the sorts of intimate or irreplaceable personal effects, toiletries, customized earplug case, dermatological salves and ointments, and important papers that any thinking person carries with him instead of trusting to the vagaries of baggage handling. These papers included my recent correspondence with both the Guaranteed Student Loan people and the IRS's Midwest Region's Office of the Deputy Regional Commissioner for Personnel, as well as my copy of the signed IRS contract and the Form 141-PO constituting my so-called 'Posting Orders' to the Midwest REC, both of which (i.e., both latter documents) I would evidently need in order to acquire my Service ID badge, which I'd been directed to do straightaway upon my arrival at the 'GS-9 Intake Station' at a certain particular time that was filled in by hand on a smeary, indifferently stamped line near the bottom of the Posting Orders.[4]

4 I no longer have this original two-page Form 141-PO, which vanished into the maw of the REC's Personnel and Internal Control Systems Problem Resolution filing systems during the whole eventual swivet and comedy of errors surrounding my initial misassignment to an Immersive Exams Pod, the story of which unfolds in full pathetic, ur-bureaucratic detail below.

(Quick aside here. *Pace* his overall self-indulgence and penchant for hand-wringing, §22's 'Irrelevant' Chris Fogle was actually on the money about one thing. Given the way the human mind works, it does tend to be small, sensuously specific details that get remembered over time—and unlike some so-called memoirists, I refuse to pretend that the mind works any other way than it really does. At the same time, rest assured that I am not Chris Fogle, and that I have no intention of inflicting on you a regurgitation of every last sensation and passing thought I happen to recall. I am about art here, not simple reproduction. What logorrheic colleagues like Fogle failed to understand is that there are vastly different kinds of truth, some of which are incompatible with one another. Example: A 100 percent accurate, comprehensive list of the exact size and shape of every blade of grass in my front lawn is 'true,' but it is not a truth that anyone will have any interest in. What renders a truth meaningful, worthwhile, & c. is its relevance, which in turn requires extraordinary discernment and sensitivity to context, questions of value, and overall point—otherwise we might as well all just be computers downloading raw data to one another.)

There was also, in one of the leather dispatch case's myriad ingenious little inner sleeves and snap pockets, a certain piece of supporting documentation in the form of personal intrafamily correspondence from a certain unnamed and non-immediate relative who enjoyed what today would be called significant 'juice' with the IRS's Midwest Regional Commissioner's Office in Joliet upstate,[5] which technically I was not supposed to even have (and which was somewhat

5 N.B.: With possible competition only from East St. Louis, Peoria and Joliet are well-known as the two grimmest, most blighted and depressed old factory cities in Illinois*, which fact turns out not to be a coincidence, since it affords statistically verifiable savings to the Service in terms of both facilities and labor. The location of most Regional HQs, RECs, and Service Centers in blighted and/or devitalized cities, which is traceable all the way back to the Service's big reorganization and decentralization after the King Commission's report to Congress in 1952, is just one sign of the deep pro-business and -bottom-line philosophies beginning to gather force in the Service as early as the Nixon administration.

* As part of the overall relevant context, be advised that Illinois's five largest cities and metro areas by population (excluding Chicago, which is more like its own galaxy) c. 1985 were, in descending order, Rockford, Peoria, Springfield, Joliet, and Decatur.

rumpled after its retrieval from the wastebasket of an unnamed and more immediate relative), but which it seemed prudent to have with me in case of some kind of bureaucratic emergency or last-resort need.[6] In general, my attitude toward bureaucracies was the same as that of most ordinary Americans: I hated and feared them (i.e., bureaucracies) and basically regarded them as large, grinding, impersonal machines—that is, they seemed rigidly literal and rule-bound the same way machines are, and just about as dumb.[7] Dating at least from a 1979 tangle with the state's DMV and our insurance provider over the terms and coverage of my Learner's Permit after an incident so laughably minor it could barely even be called a collision, my primary association with the word *bureaucracy* was an image of someone expressionless behind a counter, not listening to any of my questions or explanations of circumstance or misunderstanding but merely referring to some manual of impersonal regulations as he stamped my form with a number that meant I was in for some further kind of tedious, frustrating hassle or expense. I doubt that you need much prompting to understand why my recent experience with the college's Judicial Board and Dean of Students's office (q.v. §9 above) had done nothing to mitigate this view. Shameful or not, I figured that any possible bit of evidence of extra connective juice might serve to lift me out of some long gray line of faceless supplicants in the event of trouble or confusion[8] at the Regional Exam Center, which I

6 I do, by the way, still possess this letter, which for legal reasons I am told I cannot reproduce more than one single fair-use sentence of, for 'general flavor,' the sentence I've chosen being from the second immaculately copperplate-handwritten paragraph; to wit: 'He will be given only a small job to begin with, and it will be his business to work his way up by diligence and attentiveness,' in the margin next to which the unnamed addressee of this letter had absently jotted either 'HA!' or 'HAH!,' depending on how one tried to parse the spiky and almost indecipherable hand of someone for whom a 'quick cocktail before supper' involved a sixteen-ounce tumbler and no ice.

7 This was, keep in mind, the tail end of the era of mainframe computers, tape- and card-based data storage, & c., which now seems almost Flintstonianly remote.

8 However puerile it seems now, I know that I sometimes felt an irrational anxiety about the possibility that the recent unpleasantness at school might have found its way into some shadowily comprehensive data retrieval system to which the IRS was somehow linked, and that some kind of bell or siren would suddenly sound when I presented at the counter for my ID and badge, and so on...an irrational fear that I knew was irrational and so did not admit fully into my consciousness,

had conceived ahead of time as some kind of ur-bureaucratic version of Kafka's castle, an enormous DMV or Judicial Board.

By way of foreshadowing and advance explanation, I'll also admit up front here that there are portions of that arrival and intake day that I do not remember very well, due at least in part to the tsunami of sensuous input, technical data, and bureaucratic complication that awaited me when I arrived and was personally taken in hand and escorted—with a degree of solicitude that, however unexpected and confusing, would have been gratifying to just about anyone—to the REC's Personnel office, bypassing the GS-9 Intake Station (whose location was anyone's guess) that I'd been directed to find and stand in line at by the smeared and typo-ridden Posting Orders inside my dispatch case. As nearly always happens with human minds inundated by excessive input, I've retained only flashes and incomplete clips from that day, which I'll now go ahead and recount some specially selected relevant portions of, not only as a way to introduce the atmospherics of the REC and the Service, but also to help explain what might initially look like my passivity (it was more simple confusion[9]) in the face of what may seem, in the clarity of hindsight, like an obvious case of misassignment or mistaken identity. It was not obvious at the time, though; and expecting a person to have immediately seen it, understood it as an error, and taken immediate steps to

though at the same time I know that I spent at least some of the interminable time aboard the bus to Peoria idly constructing emergency plans and scenarios for how, if and when the bell or siren sounded, I might avoid returning home to Philo the same day I'd left and facing whoever it was who opened the door to my knock and saw me there on the home's filthy screen porch with my bags and dispatch case—at some moments I know that the unconscious anxiety consisted only of envisioning the expression on the face of whatever immediate relative opened the door, saw me, and opened his mouth to say something, at which time I became aware of the fact that I was having anxious fantasies and waved them away on the bus ride, returning to the unbelievably insipid book I'd been presented with as a 'gift' by my family, their idea of useful wisdom and support, this 'gift' presented to me at supper on the evening before my departure (which special farewell supper, by the way, had consisted of [a] leftovers and [b] steamed ears of corn that I had just had my braces tightened and couldn't even have hoped to try to eat), after first being told to open the gift very carefully so that the wrapping paper could be reused.

9 (plus, I'll admit, a certain amount of slack relief at what seemed to be the opposite of bells/sirens and possible rejection for ethical unfitness or whatever my unconscious had conjured; I think I'd been more afraid than I'd acknowledged to myself)

correct it is a bit like expecting someone to have noticed and fixed some incongruity in his surroundings at the very moment that a hundred flashbulbs suddenly went off in his eyes. There's only so much complex input the human nervous system can take, in other words.

I do remember standing there at the edge of the IGA supermarket lot in my suit with my bags and case as dawn officially broke. For those who've never experienced a sunrise in the rural Midwest, it's roughly as soft and romantic as someone's abruptly hitting the lights in a dark room. This is because the land is so flat that there is nothing to impede or gradualize the sun's appearance. It's just all of a sudden there. The temperature immediately goes up ten degrees; the mosquitoes vanish to wherever exactly it is that mosquitoes go to regroup. Just to the west, the roofline of St. Dymphna's church sprayed complex shadows over half the downtown. I was drinking a can of Nesbitt's, which is sort of my version of morning coffee. The IGA's lot abuts the downtown's main drag, which is the in-town extension of SR 130 and ingeniously named. Directly across this Main Street from the IGA were the bubbletop pumps and saurian logo of Clete's Sinclair, outside of which the best and brightest of Philo High used to gather on Friday nights to drink Pabst Blue Ribbon and search the adjacent lot's weeds for frogs and mice to throw at Clete's bug zapper, which he'd modified to hold 225 volts of charge.

This was, so far as I know, the only time I'd ridden a commercial bus line, and it was not an experience I'm eager to repeat. The bus was unclean, and some of the passengers appeared to have been aboard for several days running, with all that that entails in terms of hygiene and inhibition. I remember that the seatbacks seemed unnaturally high, and there was some kind of aluminum-alloy bar for your feet, and a button on the seat's arm for causing the back to recline, which in the case of my seat failed to work correctly. The arm's little flip-top ashtray was a nightmare of gum-wads and butts too numerous for the little lid even to close all the way. I remember seeing two or more nuns in full habit in one of the forward sections, and thinking that requiring nuns to travel by filthy commercial bus must have been in line with their sect's vow of poverty; but it still seemed incongruous and wrong. One of the nuns was doing a crossword puzzle. The trip took over four hours in toto, since the bus stopped at an endless number of sour little towns just like my own. The sun began shortly to broil the bus's rear and port side. The air-conditioning was more like a vague gesture toward the abstract idea of air-conditioning. There was a horrific piece of graffiti incised with knife or leather punch in the plastic of the seatback in front of me, which I looked at twice and then made a point of never looking directly at again. The bus had a lavatory in the wayback rear, which no one ever made any attempt to use, and I remember consciously deciding to trust that the passengers had good reason for not using it instead of venturing in and discovering that reason for myself. Empiricism has its limits. There is also, in memory, a contextless flash of some female's feet in clear polyurethane thongs, a tattoo of what was either ivy or barbed wire around one of her ankles. And a round-faced little boy[10] in shorts in the seat directly across the aisle, with red sprays of impetigo on his knees and a presumable guardian asleep in the adjoining seat (her seatback did recline), watching me as I ate the small box of raisins from the bag lunch I'd had to pack myself in the dark kitchen, the boy moving his whole head to follow the path of each raisin I brought to my mouth, and I peripherally trying to decide whether to offer to share some of the raisins or not (ultimately not: I was reading and didn't want to converse, not to mention that God only knew what this child's situation or story was; plus impetigo is notoriously contagious).

I will spare all of us much sensuous reminiscence about Peoria's main bus terminal—which was ghastly in the special way of bus stations in depressed downtowns everywhere—or of my over-two-hour wait there, except to say that its air was not conditioned or even circulated, and it was extremely crowded, and that there were a certain number of lone men and groups of two or three men, nearly all wearing suit coats and hats, or else holding their hats or slowly fan-

10 This boy had also spent the first several minutes after I'd boarded and gotten settled staring wide-eyed at the condition of the side of my face, making no effort to hide or disguise the clinical interest with which little children stare, all of which I'd of course seen (and in some ways almost appreciated) out of the corner of my eye.

ning themselves with them as they sat (none of them ever seemed to think to remove their coats or even loosen their ties); and I remember remarking even then that it was strange to see men in their adult prime wearing the business-type hats that normally one saw only on much older men of a certain background and station. A few of the hats were eccentric or unusual.

I know that I saw, during my survey of the pay-phone and vending-machine area near the entrance to the restrooms, what may have been an actual prostitute.

I well remember the subsequent roil of these same hatted men in the humidity and diesel fumes outside the terminal; and I well remember the two baked-bean-brown IRS transport sedans' arriving, finally, and pulling up at the terminal curb, and there turning out to be far too many other newly arrived or transferred IRS personnel,[11] all with abundant luggage, to fit everyone in the sedans, and the order of departure being determined not by the mandatory reporting times stamped on people's respective Forms 141-PO (as would appear to have been fair and rational) but by GS grade as evidenced by Service ID—which I didn't have, and my argument that it was precisely in order to *acquire* Service ID that I had been specifically ordered to be at the GS-9 Intake Station by 1340h. made no impression whatever, perhaps since several other, pushier personnel were also at that same time exclaiming to the driver while holding up their extant IRS IDs; and, slightly later, quite a few of us standing there watching the overfilled sedans recede from the curb into downtown traffic, and many of the other new personnel simply shrugging and going passively back inside the terminal, and my personal feeling that the whole thing was not only unfair and disorganized but a grim little foretaste indeed of what bureaucratic life was going to be like.

11 I.e., all these men with hats, which hats I would soon suspect and then outright learn were an Exam Division trademark (just as flat square shoulder-holsters for one's pocket calculator were the signature accessory of Audits, earbuds and stylized tie clips were Systems, and so on) such that the REC's group rooms, whether for rotes or immersives, all featured at least one wall with a peg-board of hooks for examiners' hats, since individual hat racks or hooks screwed into the edge of one's Tingle table created impediments for cart boys' carts...

Here, by the way, as a brief interpolation, is some preliminary general background that I have opted not to massage or smuggle in through the sort of graceless dramatic contrivance[12] so many stock memoirs resort to; to wit:

The IRS's Midwest Regional Examination Center is a roughly L shaped physical structure located off Self-Storage Parkway in the Lake James district of Peoria IL. What makes the facility's L shape only rough is that the REC's two perpendicular buildings are closely proximate but not continuous; they are, however, connected at the second and third floors by elevated transoms that are enclosed in olive-green fiberglass carbonate as a shield against inclement weather, since important documents and data storage cards are often conveyed across them. Neither heating nor air-conditioning service was ever reliably achieved in these elevated tunnels, and in summer months the Post's personnel refer to them as bataans, an apparent reference to the Bataan Death March of World War II's Pacific theater.

The larger of the site's two buildings, originally constructed in 1962, basically comprises Post 047's administrative offices, data processing, document storage, and Support Service facilities. The other, which is where the bulk of actual examinations of US tax returns takes place, is not owned by the IRS but instead back-leased through a proprietary holding company established by the shareholder trustees of one Mid West Mirror Works (*sic*), a glass-and-amalgam manufacturer that vanished into the protections of UCC Ch. 7 in the mid-1970s.

Incorporated in 1845 and perhaps best known as the birthplace of barbed wire in 1873, Peoria plays a vital role in the IRS's Midwest Regional structure. Located medially between East St. Louis, Illinois's Regional Service Center, and Joliet, Illinois's Regional Commissioner's Office, and serving the region's nine states and fourteen

12 (e.g., having one character inform another of stuff they both actually already know, in order to get this information across to the reader—which I've always found irksome in the extreme, not to mention highly suspicious in a 'nonfiction' memoir, although it is true [if mysterious] that mass-market readers seem not to mind being jerked around this way)

IRS districts, the Midwest REC's staff of more than 3,000 employees examines the math and veracity of some 4.5 million tax returns per year.[13] Though the Service's nationwide structure comprises seven regions in toto, there are (following the Rome NY REC's spectacular administrative meltdown in 1982)[14] only six currently operating Regional Examination Centers, these being located at Philadelphia PA, Peoria IL, Rotting Flesh LA, St. George UT, La Junta CA, and Federal Way WA, to which tax returns are forwarded by either the relevant region's Service Center or the IRS's central computer facility in Martinsburg WV.

Among the notable businesses and industries based in metropolitan Peoria as of 1985 are included Rayburn-Thrapp Agronomics; American Twine, the nation's second-largest manufacturer of string, wire, and low-diameter rope; Consolidated Self Storage, one of the first corporations in middle America to utilize the franchise financing model; the Farm & Home Insurance Group; the Japanese-owned remains of Nortex Heavy Equipment; and the national HQ of Fornix Industries, a privately held maker of keypunch and card-reading equipment, one of whose largest remaining customers of that time was the US Treasury. Of Peoria's employers, however, the Internal Revenue Service has ranked first ever since American Twine lost exclusive patent rights to Type 3 barbed wire in 1971.

End of interpolation; return to mnemonic real time.

After who knows how many attempts, back in the fetid terminal, to find a working pay phone and to prevail on someone at the Form 141-PO's 'employee assistance number' (which turned out to be incorrect or out of order), it was eventually in either the fourth or fifth Service vehicle to appear at the terminal that I finally secured

13 N.B.: Some of this is more or less lifted from the packet of IRS orientation materials that new hires and transfers received at Intake & Processing; hence the somewhat dead, bureaucratic flavor, which I have elected not to jazz up or prettify.

14 I have, however, worked in relevant details that were obviously not in the official materials. The Rome debacle was not something the Service had any interest in publicizing, even internally; but it also figured prominently in the whole high-level struggle over the so-called 'Initiative' and its implementation. None of which I had any idea of or interest in on this first day, it goes without saying.

transport to the REC, now direly late for my appointed check-in time, which tardiness I could imagine being blamed for by some expressionless person whose finger also controlled the Intake system's moral bell/siren.

The next salient fact of that day is that traffic along the city's circumambient Self-Storage Parkway was totally horrible. The section of SSP around Peoria's east side was lined with franchise restaurants and things like Kmarts, and auto dealerships with gaudy tethered parade balloons and blinking neon signs. There was an entire separate four-lane access road leading to something called Carousel Mall, which one shuddered even to think about.[15] Behind all this commerce (i.e., behind as seen from the east side, heading south around the city's perimeter, with the slow and silty Illinois River coming in and out of view on the Gremlin's left side) was the ruined-looking skyline of downtown Peoria, a bar graph of sooty brick and missing windows and a sense of hard pollution even though no smoke issued from any of the smokestacks. (This was several years before attempted gentrification of the old downtown.)

The Service vehicle in question was a two-door orange or yellow AMC Gremlin, albeit fitted with a high-powered whip antenna and a Service-seal decal on the driver's-side door. Interior signs prohibited smoking and/or food. The vehicle's rigid plastic interior was clean, but it was also extremely hot and stuffy. I could feel myself beginning to perspire, which is obviously not a pleasant sensation at all inside a three-piece corduroy suit. No one spoke to me or even acknowledged my existence—although I had, as I may or may not have mentioned, a severe dermatological condition during this period, and was more or less used to not being looked at or acknowledged after an initial involuntary gasp and expression of sympathy or distaste (depending), which is to say that I no longer took it all that personally. There

15 One of the pieces of freelance work I'd completed just before the fraternity-file idiocy blew up in everyone's face had been the first two chapters of a rather likable but disorganized sociology major's senior thesis on shopping malls as the modern functional analog of medieval cathedrals (with some of the parallels being downright striking), and I had no stomach left for shopping malls, even though they were often the only places anymore that had movie theaters, the grand old downtown palaces being now either shuttered or converted to Adult.

were no general offers to adjust the air-conditioning, or even standardly polite questions about whether any of the AC's trickle was reaching us in the cramped backseat, where between myself and an older GS-11 whose homburg was mashed down almost around his eyes by the roof's pressure on its crown sat a long-jawed younger man in a gray polyester sport coat and tie, maybe roughly my age, his feet on the medial hump and knees thus up almost to his chest, who was already sweating prodigiously, and who kept surreptitiously wiping rivulets of sweat off his forehead and then wiping his fingers off on his shirt with a motion that looked strangely as if he were pretending to scratch himself under his sport coat rather than wipe off his wet fingers. He did this over and over in my peripheral vision. The whole thing was very strange. His smile was an anxious and totally false rictus, his profile a branching mass of running droplets, some of which were actually falling onto his sport coat and dappling the lapels. He gave off a palpable aura of tension or fear, or perhaps claustrophobia—there was the unexplainable feeling that I'd hurt him terribly if I spoke to him or asked if he was feeling OK. Another older IRS employee sat up front beside the driver, both men also hatless (the driver with a monastic-looking *coupe de zéro* haircut) and staring straight ahead, neither of them speaking or moving, even when the vehicle was completely stopped in traffic. From the side, the skin of the older employee's chin's underside and upper throat had the scrotal or lizardy cast of some men's advanced middle age (not unlike the then-current US president's, whose face, on television, often looked as though it was melting down into his throat, which I remember making his jet-black pompadour and harlequin ovals of rouge look all the more incongruous). We alternated between sitting stopped in traffic and moving at roughly cortege speed. The sun beat palpably on the Gremlin's metal roof; a franchise bank's digital Time & Temp sign, which we sat idling in view of for several minutes, kept flashing first the time and then YOU DONT WANT TO KNOW, presumably for temperature, which seemed to me an ominous preview of Peorian wit and culture. You can imagine for yourself the air quality and overall smells involved.

I had never before been in a crowded vehicle for so long a time with no radio playing and no one in the car saying anything, even once, ever, feeling utterly isolated at the same time that I was crammed in so closely with other people that we were all breathing one another's air the whole time.[16] Every so often, the IRS driver would knead the back of his neck, which had obviously become stiff from the strange position he was forced to hold his head in in order to see through the dashboard's set of protrusive signs. The early part of the ride's chief excitement: A period of furious itching along the left side of my ribcage gave rise to fears (understandable, but luckily unfounded) that the former boy on the bus's impetigo had somehow been pneumatic or contagious without direct contact, which fears I had to quell because there was obviously no way to untuck my shirt and check the area's appearance. Meanwhile, the older Serviceman in the antiquated hat had opened an accordion file and spread two or three dark-brown manila folders in his lap and was perusing various forms and printouts, moving them from one folder to another according to some scheme or system I had no way of understanding, since I was watching the whole thing in my leftward peripheral vision past the steady cascade of droplets of sweat off the tip of the nose of the man on the hump, who was now sweating in a way I had previously seen only on the squash courts of college and in the case of a mild infarction suffered by an unnamed older relative on Thanksgiving Day 1978. I spent much of my own time drumming my fingers impatiently on the dispatch case—which was now especially soft and moist from the heat of the Gremlin's interior, and made a satisfying series of splattish noises when drummed on—which, though drumming absently on something in an otherwise silent space is usually one of the fastest ways to drive those around you crazy and get them to speak to you, if only to ask you to knock it off, no one in the Gremlin commented on or even seemed to notice.

Self-Storage Parkway more or less circles Peoria and composes the boundary between the city proper and its outlying suburbs. It is

16 True, there had been silent rides aplenty with my own family, though the AM radio then was always playing Easy Listening music at high volume, which helped explain-slash-cover the absence of conversation.

what now, in 2005, would be just a typical multilane exurban highway, complete with the paradoxical combination of high speed limit and traffic lights every quarter-mile, which lights were obviously placed to help give consumers and commuters access to all the retail commerce packed along SSP's length down at least the entire east side we were trying to traverse. As of the mid-1980s, Self-Storage Parkway was elevated over interstate junctions, and crossed the tobacco-colored Illinois River at two points via WPA-era iron bridges whose rivets wept orange rust and inspired, shall we say, less than total confidence.

Moreover, the closer we came to metro Peoria's southeast side and the special access road to the Examination Center, the worse the traffic became. The reason for this was apparent from that first day: It was institutional stupidity in all its manifold forms and names. Item one. The highway people were broadening this section of Self-Storage Parkway into three lanes, but the construction served to reduce the extant two lanes to just one; the right lane was closed off with orange cones, even in sections where no construction was ongoing and the lane looked clear and navigable. And, of course, single-lane traffic always moves exactly as fast as the very slowest vehicle in line. Item two. There were, as mentioned, traffic lights every eighth- to quarter-mile, and yet the single southbound lane's line of traffic was substantially longer than the distance between any two such traffic lights, so that our progress was dependent not just on the color of the next traffic light ahead but also on the colors of the two or three lights beyond that. It was the obverse of gridlock. It seemed like very bad urban planning or traffic-management or whatever exactly the discipline involved here was, and I could feel the corduroy of my suit getting sodden along the entire area of contact with the Gremlin's patterned plastic seat, as well as along the hip and upper thigh that were mashed up against the human sprinkler next to me, who was by now radiating both heat and an acrid, panicky smell that made me turn my head and pretend to be concentrating hard on something in view beyond the window (which rolled down only halfway, due to some design flaw or obscure safety feature). There is no point in describing the gauntlet of franchise retail and shopping centers and auto and tire and motorcycle / Jet Ski outlets and self-serve gas plazas with built-in convenience stores and national fast food brands we crawled through, since it's now the same basic gauntlet around every US city—I believe the economic term is 'monoculture.' Item three. It emerged, finally, that the turnoff from the parkway to the Examination Center was *not* serviced with a traffic light, even though it also became visually obvious, when we got within view, that a good percentage of the cars currently in the single lane ahead of us on SSP were also bound for and hence turning in to the REC and its blacktop access road. (Though it would be a maddeningly long time before even this simple fact was explained to me, the REC's two main eight-hour shifts in that period were 7:10 A.M. to 3:00 P.M. and 3:10 P.M. to 11:00 P.M., which meant that there was a tremendous amount of Service- and employee-owned vehicle traffic between the hours of 2:00 and 4:00.) Meaning that it was actually the Exam Center itself, together with the absence of a traffic light and the abortive SSP construction,[17] that had helped cause the hellacious backup, because

17 GS-9 Chris Fogle would later explain (probably as I and whoever else was around rotated our hand in the air in the please-get-on-with-it way that almost everyone started involuntarily rotating their hand to convey whenever 'Irrelevant' Chris was on a roll) that the widening of Self-Storage Parkway had been stalled for over a year, first because a supplementary bond issue was being challenged in district court by a conservative Illinois citizens' taxation watchdog group, and second because the extremely harsh regional winters and abrupt spring thaws that then so often refroze again a day later (all of which is true) caused whatever part of the new, freshly built SSP third lane that had not been treated with a special type of industrial sealant to heave and crack, and the courts had halted the previous year's construction at just the point when this sealant was going to be applied with some kind of rare and very expensive piece of heavy machinery that had to be rented far in advance from a single specialty-distributor in either Wisconsin or Minnesota (I still have an actual sense-memory of the way my hand would begin rotating in the air, almost involuntarily, when Fogle started foundering in extraneous detail—he was unpopular out of all proportion to his character, which was actually decent and well-meaning to a fault; he was one of the low-level True Believers on whom the Service depended so heavily for so much of the inglorious gruntwork and heavy lifting of day-to-day operations, and what eventually happened to him was a great injustice, I've always thought, since in his case he really did need the drugs and took them entirely for professional reasons; it wasn't recreational by any means), with, of course, the legal injunction and failure to apply the sealant then causing heavy damage the following winter and spring, and roughly doubling the cost of the construction over the civil engineering firm's initial bid. Meaning that it was all a horrific mess of litigation and engineering mishaps that, as usual, placed a chronic, annoying, tedious burden on the ordinary commuters of the city. By the way, it emerged that another reason traffic on the circumambient SSP was so chronically bad even before the

there were also a large number of vehicles in the oncoming, north-eastbound lanes trying to turn left, i.e. across our single lane, to enter the REC's access road as well, which required that the vehicle at the front of our lane's line for the right turn wait and wave the oncoming car through its left turn, which only a very few did, since traffic jams often bring out the most aggressive, me-first elements of the human makeup and cause behavior that itself, perversely, exacerbates the traffic jam—this right here perhaps being the place to mention a behavior that we began seeing more and more of as we inched closer to the REC turnoff. Certain private vehicles[18] in our lane veered rightward into the narrow gravel 'breakdown lane,' in which they sped up and were able to pass dozens of other vehicles, illegally, which in and of itself would not have been a big deal except for the fact that as the REC turnoff approached and the breakdown lane began to narrow and disappear they then sought to merge left

construction nightmare was that, understood not as an agglomeration of human beings but as a going economic concern, Peoria had come in the 1980s to assume the same basic doughnut shape as so many other formerly industrial cities: The downtown center was empty and denuded, all but dead, while at the same time a robust collection of malls, plazas, franchises, business and light-industrial parks, town house developments, and apartment complexes had pulled most of the city's life out into an exurban ring. The mid-1990s would see a partial renaissance and gentrification of the riverside downtown—some of the factory and warehouse sites were converted to condos and high-concept restaurants; artists and younger professionals took some others for division into lofts, & c.—though much of this optimistic development was spurred by the establishment of riverboat casinos just off what had been the main industrial set of offload docks, casinos that were not locally owned and whose base revenues Peoria never even got a plausible cut of, the entire downtown rejuvenation spurred by incidental, small-potato tourist spending...viz., on the part of people who came for the casinos, which, since casinos are in the business of separating people from the cash they would otherwise use to shop and dine out, meant that the actual relationship between casino revenues and tourist spending was inverse, which, given casinos' deserved reputation for extreme profitability, meant that any levelheaded person could have predicted the steeply declining revenue curve that within just a few years caused most of the 'New Downtown' renaissance to sputter, especially when the casinos (after prudently waiting a decent interval) all opened their own restaurants and retail shops. And so on... the same basic thing played out in cities all over the Midwest.

18 (identifiable as such in memory because they were not Gremlins, Mercury Montegos, or Ford Econoline vans. It emerged that the REC's Support Service fleet of government vehicles were nearly all derived from a jeopardy-assessment seizure against a conjoint auto dealership in downstate Effingham, an explanation of which would be way too long and digressive to inflict on you here.)

back into the legal single lane, which required someone in that lane to stop to let them in again, which further clotted traffic in the regular lane...meaning that the selfish, me-first vehicles were significantly worsening the very jam that they'd sought to bypass; they gained an extra couple of minutes by making the jam and delay slightly worse for everyone else in the shimmering line of cars in our lane. Within a couple weeks of daily commutes down SSP from the special low-cost Service housing[19] to the REC each day, this selfish, me-first behavior with the breakdown lane began to fill me with such disgust and malice that I can still, to this day, remember some of the vehicles that chronically did it, i.e., the same kind of idiotic, solipsistic behavior that causes stampedes in public places in the event of a fire and results in the authorities finding huge numbers of blackened, trampled bodies at the front doors of places after the fires or riots have been quelled, people prevented from getting out precisely by the panic and selfishness with which they all rushed and clotted the exit and got in each other's way, causing everyone to die horribly, which I have to admit is what I began wishing for the various Vegas, Chevettes, and a particular light-blue AMC Pacer with one of those

19 Brief, unavoidable aside: For the first six quarters of a contracted posting, examiners without dependents could avail themselves of special Service housing in a set of apartment complexes and converted motels along the eastern edge of SSP's circumambient ring, government-owned through either seizures or tax sales during the recession of the early 1980s. There is, of course, a whole other long and tediously involved story here, including the fact that the housing situation had been vastly complicated by the large number of transfers and personnel reshufflings all RECs had undergone as (a) a result of the mid-Atlantic REC's foundering and dissolution in 1981 and (b) the early phases of the so-called 'Intiative' which it turned out bore directly on the Midwest REC. The point, though, was that this housing was offered both to facilitate ease of transfers and to offer a financial inducement, since the monthly rent at (for instance) the Angler's Cove complex was at least $150 a month less than the going rents for comparable housing in the private sector. My own motives for accepting this housing option should be clear...although it is also true that the IRS in 1986 began treating the difference between the subsidized and free-market rents as 'implied income' and taxing it, which as you can imagine caused no end of ill will among Service employees, who are also of course US citizens and taxpayers, and whose annual tax returns receive special scrutiny every year because of the distinctive '9's at the head of our ID/SS numbers, & c., & c. In retrospect, the whole Service housing thing was probably not worth it, given all the bureaucratic hassles and idiocies involved (q.v. below), although the monthly savings in rent were substantial.

fish-shaped Christian decals on the bubble of a back window[20] that made this maneuver almost every morning.

An additional bit of bureaucratic idiocy: As mentioned, plastic signs within the car interdicted smoking, eating, & c., as turned out to be the case in all Service vehicles used for employee transport, by internal regs cited in the lower-right portion of the signs themselves[21]—except that AMC Gremlins' interiors were so cramped, and the plastic used therein so cheap and thin, that there was nowhere to mount the eight-inch signs except on the dashboard's top, where they blocked sections of the lower windshield and forced our driver to assume a contorted position with his tonsured head almost over on his right shoulder in order to see the road just ahead between the edges of the mandatory signs. This, so far as I could see, was beyond the pale in terms of both safety and anything like sense.

Set within a large expanse of very green close-clipped grass bordered on both sides by cornfields' windbreaks of trees and tangled shrubbery, the Midwest Regional Examination Center lay a good five hundred yards back from the parkway, these five hundred yards filled with nothing except verdant and weirdly dandelionless grass mowed to the consistency of baize. The contrast between the baronial splendor of the lawn and the squat, institutional ugliness of the

20 We observed that it was almost always the private cars and pickups that clotted things by selfishly trying to shortcut through the breakdown lane and then merging back in. Service vehicles, including the Support Services vans that ran back and forth between the wiggler housing at north Peoria's Angler's Cove and the Oaks, never deviated from the legal lane, the Service drivers being non-contract hourly workers who had no incentive to hurry or try to cut corners, which presented a different set of problems for us who were required to be at our Tingle tables by a certain very definite time at the start of the shift; but from the point of view of orderly traffic it was still probably a good administrative move on Support Services' part, although it meant that the Support Services drivers, whose jobs were chiropractically sadistic as well as boring and repetitive beyond belief, couldn't join the Treasury union, didn't qualify for health insurance, & c.

21 These cited regulations, when the Internal Revenue Manual's whole code of regulations was perused in a period of examination downtime with literally nothing else to do to occupy one's time, exposed a strange kind of error: The cars' and vans' interior signs' citations actually referred to the regulation that required the signs to be 'displayed in a prominent, unobscured location' within each vehicle; it was really a regulation two regs above that cited reg that interdicted eating, tobacco, & c. within Service-owned transport. That is, the signs' cited reg referred to the sign itself, not to the regulation the sign was supposed to signify.

REC itself was stark and incongruous, and there was plenty of time to ponder it as the Gremlin crawled along and the guy next to me dripped steadily onto both of us. The older man at the other end of the backseat had what looked at first to be a green thimble on one finger, which turned out to be the green traction-rubber that most wigglers wore and all called PCs for 'pinkie cheaters.' A large 4-H billboard some distance past the REC's one-way entrance read IT'S SPRING, THINK FARM SAFETY, which I knew to be a 4-H sign because every March–May there was an identical one just out past the instant-coffee factory on SR 130 west of Philo.[22] The state 4-H held bake sales and car washes all year to provide for these billboards (w/ comma splice *sic*), which by 1985 were so ubiquitous that no one paid any attention to them.[23]

I also remember that I had to move and twist my own neck awkwardly in order to make out the Exam Center's various features through the impediments of the car's required signs. From this distance and set of perspectives, the REC appeared at first to be a single huge right-angled structure, with its facing[24] tan or beige cement side mammoth and sheer, and just a bit of foreshortened side-building's roof visible past the access road, which road extended in a broad

22 At 158 employees, the vacuum-sublimation-and-caffeine-supplementation works for Bright Eyes Instant Coffee represented Philo's last remaining claim to industry. A subsidiary of Rayburn-Thrapp Agronomics, Bright Eyes was a regional high-caf brand, recognizable in Midwest stores by the jar's crude graphic of an electrified-looking squirrel with bulging blazing suns for eyes and what looked like tiny bolts of cartoon lightning shooting out from its splayed extremities. When Archer Daniels Midland Co. absorbed Rayburn-Thrapp Agronomics in 1991, Bright Eyes was (mercifully*) discontinued. More than this I am legally enjoined from telling you by the refusal of certain members of my family to sign the appropriate legal releases. Suffice it to say that I know a lot more about the chemistry, manufacture, and ambient odors of instant coffee than anyone would voluntarily want to, and that the smells were not at all the cozy comforting breakfastish aromas that one might naively imagine (they were closer to burning hair, actually, when the wind was right).

> * As early as the 1970s, there had been evidence linking artificially enhanced caffeine to everything from arrhythmias to Bell's palsy, though the first class-action suit was not filed until 1989.

23 A further irony: During an April 1987 tornado outside De Kalb, a detached portion of one of these FARM SAFETY billboards whirled in and for all practical purposes decapitated a soybean farmer—that was pretty much it for the 4-H sign.

24 (i.e., facing south and SSP, on which we were moving west at literally the rate of a toddler's crawl)

one-way curve around the main building's rear, which rear itself turned out to actually be the REC's front, with its enormous self-regarding facade. In a similar distortion, what looked, from a distance, like a bona fide circumambient 'road' from the parkway in to and around the REC turned out to be more like a crude rural mew or driveway, narrow and high, banked with deep runoff ditches, and with freakish speed bumps set at such close intervals that travel over about five mph on the access road was impossible; one could see the occupants of any vehicle traveling faster than that being thrown about their cars' interior like rag dolls by the impact with the speed bumps, which were each over eight inches high. Beginning a couple hundred yards in from SSP, parking lots of various modest sizes extended outward from the access road, rather like square-cut jewels encrusting a bracelet or tiara.[25]

There was, from our vantage, no visible sign identifying the site as an IRS or even government facility (which, again, was semi-explained by the fact that what appeared from Self-Storage to be the REC's front was in fact the rear, and of only one of the two distinct buildings). All there were were two small wooden directional signs—ENTRANCE ONLY; EXIT ONLY—at the semicircular access road's two junctions with SSP. The former sign also included what turned out to be the REC's street (though not postal) address. Given the access road's circular shape, the exit was some thousand or more yards farther west down the parkway, almost within the shadow of the FARM SAFETY billboard. I could hear the man up next to me breathing rapidly, as if almost beginning to hyperventilate; neither of us had even once looked directly at the other. I noticed that only the ENTRANCE side of the access road had parking lots appended; the distant EXIT side, which curved out from behind the rear (i.e., it later emerged, the two separate buildings' fronts) of the REC was a one-way vector back out to Self-Storage Parkway, with the exit's intersection also

25 Again, much of this is from the actual notebook in which these impressions were recorded. I'm aware that I'm describing the access road from a distance but attributing to it qualities that became evident only as we got very slowly closer and closer and then were actually on it. Part of this is artful compression; part is that it's next to impossible to take coherent notes in a moving auto.

minus any kind of traffic light or directional signal, which absence caused further snarls and delays for commuters trying to reach the REC's entrance from the west.

As I may or may not have mentioned, it was already well past the mandated 1340h. reporting time stamped on my 141-PO. Certain obvious and understandable emotions attended this fact, especially since (a) 0.0 percent of this lateness was my fault, and (b) the closer we got to the REC, the slower our progress in traffic became. In order to distract myself from these facts and emotions, I began to compile a list of the logistical absurdities that became evident once the Service vehicle got close enough to the entrance for the REC's access road to become visible through my unoccluded side window. The following are condensed from an unusually long, intense, unpunctuated notebook entry[26] composed at least in part within the Gremlin itself. To wit:

Besides the oncoming left turns and the loathsome me-firsters trying to remerge from the breakdown lane, the main cause of the excruciating slowness with which our line of cars on the westbound Self-Storage south of the city inched forward to make the right turn into the Examination Center's access road was what emerged as the even worse, more costive and paralyzed jam of vehicles on the access road itself. This was chiefly caused by the fact that the access road's appended parking lots were already quite full, and that the farther along the access road the lots were, the fuller they were, and full also of IRS employee vehicles trolling for available parking places. Given the extreme heat and humidity, the most desirable parking lots were clearly the ones directly behind[27] the main building, less than a hundred yards from the central REC entrance. Employees in the more peripheral lots were required to walk along the narrow, ditch-flanked access road all the way around behind[28] to that central

26 (inscribed with a pencil that had long since gone blunt and dull, which is something I detest; there would have had to be considerable psychic pressure/incentive for me to be willing to write with a dull pencil)

27 Again, the 'behind' is from the perspective of the parkway. Given that what we were approaching was the main building's rear, the premium lots were actually 'in front' of the REC, though that front faced away from Self-Storage.

28 Ibid.

entrance, which resulted in a great deal of teetering along the access road's unpaved edge, plus some staggering and windmilling of arms; and we saw at least one employee slip and cartwheel into the drainage ditch by the road's side and have to be pulled manually back up by two or three others, all of whom held their hats to their heads with one hand, such that the rescued employee then had an enormous smeary grass stain all the way up one side of his slacks and sport coat, and dragged one seemingly injured leg behind him as he and his companions passed from view along the road's curve.[29] The whole problem was as obvious as it was stupid. Given the heat, hassle, and actual danger of pedestrian travel along the access road, it was totally understandable that most employee vehicles seemed to eschew the nearer (that is, nearer to us, hence farther from the REC itself) lots and to proceed to the far more desirable lots around back, lots that turned out to be closest to the main REC entrance and to be separated from it only by a wide, paved, and easily traversed plaza. But if those best, closest lots were full (as of course, given human nature and the above incentives, they were likely to be; the most desirable lots will obviously also be the most crowded lots), the incoming vehicles could not backtrack out the way they came in order to settle for spots in the progressively more distant and less desirable lots they had passed on their way in quest of the best lots—for, of course, the access road was one-way[30] all the way around its curve, so vehicles that couldn't find a spot in the best lots had now to proceed forward all the way back out away from the REC to the EXIT ONLY sign, turn left without any kind of light onto Self-Storage, drive the several hundred yards east back to the REC entrance with its ENTRANCE ONLY sign, and then try to turn left (against oncoming traffic, which obvi-

29 Let's mainly skip the issue of the additional crowding and dysfunction caused by outer lots' pedestrians trying to negotiate the access road's narrow edge past the solid line of cars that filled that road, much of which problem could have been solved simply by installing a sidewalk across the immaculate lawn and some kind of entrance in the front (i.e., what appeared to be the front; it was actually the building's rear). In essence, the baronial splendor of the REC's grass was a testament to the idiocy and hassle of the whole thing's planning.

30 It had to be: It wasn't nearly wide enough to sustain two-way traffic, not to mention the additional space taken up by pedestrians trying to walk to/from their vehicles along the road's edge.

ously further slowed our own, westbound lane's tortured progress) into the access road again in order to park in some of the less desirable lots out nearer the parkway, from which they then had to join the line of pedestrians tightrope-walking along the road's edge back toward the main entrance around back.

In short, it all seemed like just phenomenally bad planning, resulting in gross inefficiency, waste, and frustration for everyone involved.[31] Three obvious remedies presented themselves, which were sketched in outline form in my notebook, although whether I jotted them down right there *in situ* during the maddening Sisyphean so-near-and-yet-far stasis or entered them later that day—during which there were plenty of additional stretches of downtime with nothing to do except read the vapid book I'd already begun mordantly annotating on the bus ride—I will not pretend to recall. One remedy would be to institute some form of reserved parking, which would eliminate a good deal of the backup and clot resulting from people trolling for available spaces in the lots, as well as the 'incentive' problem of employee vehicles all beelining for the most desirable two or three lots near the REC's central entrance (which of course we hadn't yet seen from Self-Storage Parkway; the entrance's location was deduced from the apparent desirability of the parking lots behind [from our perspective] the building, given the number of cars heading for it, which was clearly linked to some form of tangible incentive. The employee beside me now looked, peripherally, as though he'd been mechanically raised out of a body of water, which made the pretense of my not noticing the incredible sweating even

31 What I did not at that time know was that, as the result of certain complex Compliance Branch reorganizations related to the implementation of the 'Initiative,' the Midwest REC had had a net gain of more than three hundred new employees over the previous two fiscal quarters. One theory among the rote examiners at Angler's Cove was that this had helped tip some delicate balance in the REC's parking situation, exacerbated by the construction on Self-Storage and the elimination, for what were represented as morale reasons, of reserved parking for those with civil service grades above GS-11. The latter had been the idea of Mr. Tate, the REC's Director of Personnel, who'd regarded reserved parking as elitist and corrosive to REC morale. The syndrome of DP Richard Tate's instituting a policy that resulted in far more problems than it resolved was so familiar that wigglers referred to it as 'dicktation.'

more creepy and farcical). Another anodyne would obviously be to widen the access road and make it two-way. Admittedly, this could expose the REC to some additional short-term inconvenience and snarl along the same general lines as the widening of Self-Storage Parkway, although it was difficult to envision the widening of the access road taking anywhere near as long, since it wouldn't be subject to the delays and conflicting agendas of the democratic process. The third remedy would be to sacrifice, for the greater good and convenience of everyone except perhaps the REC's landscaping contractor, the virid expanse of the empty front (i.e., what turned out to be the rear) lawn, and to place on it not only a paved walkway but maybe an actual transverse spur that would allow vehicles on the EXIT portion of the road to cross back over to the ENTRANCE portion without having to make lightless left turns both onto and off the jammed parkway. Not to mention of course simply placing some goddamn traffic lights at the two intersections, which it was next to impossible to imagine the Internal Revenue Service not having enough suction with the municipal and state authorities to be able to demand just about any time it pleased.[32] Not to mention the sheer strangeness of having it be (it emerged) the REC's mammoth *rear* facing Peoria's main orbital road. It seemed, on slow approach, both craven and arrogant, like pre-modern priests who faced away from the communicants during Catholic mass. Everything from logistics to elementary civics would seem to dictate that a major government facility's front should face the public it serves. (Recall that I had not yet seen the REC's stylized front facade, which was identical to those of the nation's other six RECs, and had been installed after an uncaught typo in the enlarged construction and technology budget after the King Commission IRS reforms had been permitted to pass into law, that typo mandating that Regional Service and Examination Cen-

32 At the time, I knew nothing of the bureaucratic hostilities between the IRS and the state of Illinois, these dating all the way back to the state's brief introduction of a progressive sales tax, which top officials at Triple-Six under the Carter administration had joined others in the editorial pages of major financial dailies in ridiculing and in abusing the 'brain trust' behind the state's revenue scheme, causing bad blood which continued, in the form of many small types of petty hassles and inaccommodation, through the 1980s.

ters' facades' 'form specifications' rather than 'form*al* specifications' be '...matched as closely as possible to the specific services the centers perform.'[33])

As to our actual physical arrival at the center's main entrance on that first day, all I can say by way of summary is that there is an indescribable thrill about seeing one's own printed name on a sign held up at a crowded place of disembarkation. I suppose part of it is that one feels especially picked out and—to use the bureaucratic term—validated. The special sign with my name on it held aloft by an attractive, official-looking woman in a bright-blue blazer was also, obviously, after all the ignominies and demeaning hassles, and consequent lateness, surprising, though not so surprising that any person could be reasonably expected to have seen it as immediate evidence of some error or confusion—there was, after all, the aforementioned matter of nepotistic juice and the letter in my dispatch case.

This was also when it emerged that the REC's ostensible rear was really the front, and that the two orthogonal parts of the center were not continuous, and that the main building's facade was stylized in a strange and kind of intimidating way that one would concede it was maybe prudent to keep from facing, or looming over, the crowded public road just south. Even without the crowding and chaos, the whole huge main-entrance area was complex and disorienting. There were flags, coded signs, directional arrows, and a kind of broad concrete plaza with what looked to have been a fountain but had no water spurting.[34] The main building's square shadow extended almost all the way across the plaza to the two highly desirable parking lots opposite, neither of which was all that large. And there was the REC's elaborate and obviously expensive facade, which extended from just above the main entrance to the middle of what appeared to be the fifth floor; it was some kind of tile or mosaic representation of a blank IRS 1978 Form 1040, both pages of it, complete in all detail down to verso Line 31's slot for the computation of **'Adjusted Gross Income'** and recto Line 66's terminal **'BALANCE DUE'** box, which

33 Factoid courtesy of GS-9 Robert Atkins (knows all, tells all).

34 (It turned out that the fountain was broken and an obscure hydraulic part was on order.)

box served, along with the form's myriad other slots and boxes and inset squares, as what looked to be windows. The detail was striking and the cream, salmon, and celadon of the offset colors realistic, if slightly dated.[35] Also, to make the whole thing even more overwhelming/disorienting when seen all at once from the circular spur off the access road whence Service vehicles could pull right up and offload their passengers without having to park (which would have necessitated going all the way back out and around again, since the parking lots just opposite the entrance, across the plaza, were completely full and even had some extra vehicles parked in prohibited corner spaces that would keep other vehicles from being able to back out of their spaces and exit), the giant 1040, which was realistically proportioned to scale and so was slightly longer than it was wide, was flanked at either distant end by a large, round inset intaglio or glyph of some kind of chimerical combat and a Latin phrase, indecipherable in the right-hand side's deep shadow, which turned out to be the Service's official seal and motto (none of which I had been told in my contractual materials [which, as mentioned, tended to be both cryptic and tonally stern or urgent, really little more than engines of apprehension as far as I'd been concerned, sitting in my family's unused parlor and trying to parse them]). By way of one more detail, the whole elaborate facade assembly was reflected—though in an angled and laterally foreshortened way that made the edge's glyph and motto look closer together than they actually were—by the garishly mirrored exterior side of the REC's other structure, a.k.a. the 'REC Annex,' which lay at almost a perfect right angle to the main facade and was connected at two floors to the main building's west edge by what then appeared to be large green tubes supported by blinding (since not in the main building's shadow) forests of slender anodized or stainless steel poles, which metal supports looked strange and millipedic from this angle and were further reflected in blinding little angled slices by the edges of the Annex's mirrored exterior.

35 There had been certain changes and modifications in the 1040 since 1978, the details of which I would come to know all too well over the coming months.

One or two of the mirrored panels were broken or cracked, however, I remember noting.[36]

(Also, please keep in mind that I knew none of the REC structures' actual history or logistics on that initial day; I'm trying to stay faithful to the memory of that experience itself, although there is no avoiding a successive description of various elements that were, at the time, obviously simultaneous—certain distortions are just part and parcel of linear English.)

Re the human element: The broad cement area around the main entrance, as first seen by us from over the mass of other brown and orange/yellow Service vehicles disgorging passengers, was an enormous teeming roil of Service employees all milling around, holding 141-POs in their distinctive dark-yellow Service envelopes, with luggage and briefcases and accordion files, many of them hatted, and various REC or perhaps Regional HQ support personnel in gas-blue blazers with clipboards and sheaves of printout paper that they had rolled into ad hoc megaphones that they spoke through while they held their clipboards up in the air to get people's attention, evidently trying to collect those arrivals with similar 141-PO job designations and/or GS-grades into cohesive groups for 'targeted check-in' at various 'Intake Stations' set up around the REC's main lobby, which lobby, as seen through the entrance's glass doors, was surprisingly small and cheesy-looking, and had various battered-looking folding tables set up with crude signs made of tented manila folders—the whole thing looked haphazardly jerry-rigged and chaotic, and one figured that there couldn't possibly be this many newly arrived and/or reassigned transfers to the REC as a typical daily thing, or else the disembarkation and check-in system would be much more permanent-looking and streamlined and less like some small-scale reenactment of the fall of Saigon. Again, though, all this was being perceived and processed in nothing more than a distracted flash—which occurred

36 N.B. that a detailed illustrative photo of the REC's mirrored Annex's west side's junction with the main building's facade circa 1985, which I made a point of including as Plate 1 in the original memoir, has been here deleted by the publisher for 'legal' reasons that (I opine) make no sense whatsoever. *Hiatus valde deflendus.*

as the Gremlin finally broke out of the access road's snarl and pulled up in the almost chilly air of the building's shade to double-park in the semicircular spur just outside the entrance[37]—because, as mentioned, a person's attention is more or less automatically drawn to a sign with one's name on it, especially if it seems to be one of only two named signs being held up in the whole madding bureaucratic roil outside the main entrance, and so I had almost immediately seen the ethnic-looking woman in the loud blazer standing a few paces to the right of the rightmost group of new arrivals clumped around a man with a raised clipboard and paper horn,[38] the female slightly off to the side and maybe ten feet directly beneath the facade's slot for reporting AGI on line 31, against the wall, holding either a piece of white cardboard or a small erasable whiteboard with the name DAVID WALLACE in neat block capitals. She was standing in a way that managed to connote weariness and boredom without any actual slumping, her legs well out and back supported by the wall, from bottom to crown, and staring straight ahead, holding the sign at chest level and staring into space with neither interest nor resignation. Of course I was now, as mentioned, through no fault of my own, terribly late, the anxiety of which mixed with the inevitable thrill of seeing one's name on a sign, not to mention a sign held by an exotic-looking female, plus a whole separate set of Ozymandian awe-and-folly reactions to the conjunction of the monumental 1040 mosaic combined with the self-appending chaos of the entrance area's crowds, to form a sort of sensory and emotional power-surge that I remember now much more vividly than any of the myriad details and impressions

37 Which we had to do because several other vehicles had double- and even triple-parked just ahead, and it was impossible to go any farther, and the driver simply put the car in park and sat rotating his neck stiffly, with both hands still on the steering wheel, as the more experienced Service employees began piling out.

38 Some of the entrance area's milling crowd's men were in shirtsleeves, and a swirling wind caused by the contrast in temperatures in and out of the building's shadow blew some of their neckties either back over their shoulders or (for a second or two) out straight from their chests in an arrowy way, as if they were impaled on their own neckties, which is what accounts for the strange memorability of this fragment as we pulled up.

(of which there were thousands or even millions, all obviously incoming at the same moment) of arrival. For she was visibly ethnic, even as seen in the deep pool of shade at the facade's base with various bits of blinding glare from the Annex's mirrored exterior, parts of which were catching bits of sun as it moved slightly west of due south. My initial guess was upper-caste Indian or Pakistani—one of my freshman roommates at college had been a wealthy Pakistani, with a marvelously burbly singsong accent, though he'd revealed himself over the year to be an unbelievable narcissist and general prick.[39] She was, at the distance from which the Gremlin disgorged us, more striking than pretty, or maybe you might say that she was pretty in a somewhat mannish, hard-faced way, with very dark hair and wide-set eyes in which was, as mentioned, the look of someone who was 'on duty' in the sort of way that involves having really nothing to do but stand there. It was the same expression one sees on security guards, college research-librarians on a Friday night, parking-lot attendants, grain silo operators, & c.—she stood there gazing into the middle distance as though at the end of a pier.

It was only outside the cramped Gremlin, when the cool air of the facade-shadowed front area first hit and chilled it, that I became aware that the whole left side of my suit was now wet from the ambient perspiration of the young man I'd been mashed up next to through the whole ride, though when I looked around for him in order to make a gesture at the darkened corduroy and give him an appropriate look of distaste, he was now nowhere to be seen.

Ms. F. Chahla Neti-Neti (according to her ID badge)'s expression changed, actually several different times, as I approached her with bags and a degree of direct eye contact that would have been inappropriate if she hadn't been holding a sign with my name on it. Here, if I haven't already done so, I should explain that in this period of what was basically late adolescence I had very bad skin—very, very

39 The Personnel representative, Ms. Neti-Neti, turned out to be what she called Persian. It was she whom 2K Bob McKenzie and some of the others in Hindle's Rotes group had christened 'the Iranian Crisis.'

bad, as in the dermatological category 'severe/disfiguring.'[40] On meeting or encountering me for the first time, most people either (a) looked only briefly at my face and then looked away, or (b) looked involuntarily stricken or pitying, or repelled, then could be seen struggling with themselves to superimpose on that expression another one that signified they either didn't see the bad skin or weren't especially bothered by it. The whole skin thing is a long story and for the most part not worth mentioning, except to emphasize again that by that time I was more or less reconciled to the skin thing and it didn't much bother me anymore, although it did make it difficult to shave with any precision, and I did tend to be very aware of whether I was standing in direct light and, if so, from just what angle that light originated—because in certain kinds of light the problem was very, very bad indeed, I knew. On this first encounter, I don't remember whether Ms. Neti-Neti was an (a) or a (b),[41] perhaps because my attention/memory was occupied by the way the Service ID badge clipped to her Personnel jacket's breast pocket had a head-shot photo that looked taken in very bright, almost magnesium-looking light, and I remember instantly calculating what this sort of photo's hideous light was going to do in terms of my face's blebular cysts and scabs, just as it had made this creamily dark Persian woman's complexion look dark gray, and had exaggerated the wide-setness of her eyes so

40 It had been the Pakistani roommate, in fact, who as early as Freshman Orientation Week had christened me with the unkind name that followed me throughout the next three semesters, 'the young man carbuncular.'

41 There is actually a third general class of reactive person, whose eyes would linger on my face in a kind of nakedly horrified fascination. These were usually people with a personal history of various kinds of moderate skin problems and a consequent interest in worst-case-type examples of bad skin that overrides (i.e., the interest does) their natural tact or inhibition. I had actually had strangers come up to me and start expounding on their own past or present skin problems, assuming that I couldn't fail to care or be interested, which I will admit I found irksome. Children, by the way, are not members of this (c) category—their interested stare is very different, and in general they (= children) are exempt from the whole taxonomy of reactors, since their social instincts and inhibitions are not yet fully evolved and it's impossible to take their reactions or lack of tact personally—see e.g. the kid on the bus, although obviously he also had a repellent problem of his own.

that in the ID photo she looked almost like a puma or some other strange kind of feline predator, along with the badge's displaying her first initial and surname, GS grade, Personnel affiliation, and a series of nine digits that I would only later understand to be her internally generated SS, which also functions as one's Service ID number.

The reason for even taking the time to mention the (a) or (b) reaction thing is that it is the only way to make sense of the fact that Ms. Neti-Neti's greeting was so verbally effusive and deferential—'Your reputation precedes you'; 'On behalf of Mr. Glendenning and Mr. Tate, we're just so extremely pleased to have you on board'; 'We're extremely pleased you were willing to take this posting'—without her face and eyes registering any such enthusiasm or even displaying any affect or interest in me or in why I was so late in arriving and had forced her to stand there holding up a sign for God only knew how long, which I personally would very much have wanted some kind of explanation of. Not to mention that the whole left side of my suit was wet, which I would have at least commented on in some concerned way, e.g. had the person fallen into a puddle or what. In short, not only was it surprising to be greeted in person with such enthusiastic words, but it was doubly surprising when the person reciting these words displayed the same kind of disengagement as, say, the checkout clerk who utters the words 'Have a nice day' while her expression indicates that it's really a matter of total indifference to her whether you drop dead in the parking lot outside ten seconds from now. And this whole doubly disorienting affectless monologue occurred as the woman led me away beneath the **'Paid Preparer's Information'** slots at the base of the great 1040's recto side toward a smaller, much less ostentatious set of doors some hundred yards west along the REC's tile facade.[42] At this close range, it was possible to

42 Nor did she offer to help me with any of my bags, despite the fact that the one I held with the same arm with which I had to sort of clamp my dispatch case against my side clunked painfully against the same knee it had been clunking against all day whenever I had to carry my bags from one spot to another, while my left side's wet clothes caused the spot on my ribs to start itching like mad again.

see that some of the facade's tiles were chipped and/or stained. We could also see various distorted parts of our reflections in the facade of the Annex building directly ahead (i.e., east), though it was several hundred yards distant and the partial reflections were very tiny and indistinct.

Ms. Neti-Neti chattered along almost the whole length of the facade. It goes without saying that it was hard to comprehend all this personal attention and (verbal) deference being directed at a GS-9 who was probably going to get assigned to opening envelopes or carrying stacks of obscure files from one place to another or something. My initial theory was that the unnamed relative who'd helped get me in the door here as a way to defer the mechanisms of Guaranteed Student Loan collection had a lot more administrative juice than I'd originally thought. Although, of course, as I tried to clunk my way along behind the ethnic lady in the shadow of the building's rear/front, that business about my 'reputation preced[ing]' me was worrisome, given some of the irrational anxieties I've already given more attention than they deserved just above.

Now it's becoming clear that I could spend an enormous amount of both our time just on describing this initial arrival and the compounding stack of confusions, miscommunications, and overall fuck-ups (at least one of which was mine—viz., leaving one of my suitcases in the outer waiting area of the REC's Personnel office, which I didn't even realize I'd done until I was on the shuttle back from the REC to the Angler's Cove apartment complex where my assigned IRS housing was located[43]) that attended that first day of posting, some of which took weeks to iron out. But only a few of these are relevant

43 Given the large number of both new employees and transfers who arrived with luggage that day (for reasons I wouldn't understand for some time), though, it's only fair to observe that the REC Personnel office might have done well to have set up some system whereby people got taken to housing first, dropped off their bags, and were only then conducted to the REC for intake and orientation. However difficult the logistics of that scheme might have been, the alternative was an enormous number of IRS employees having to carry their bags with them everywhere they went on that first day at the REC, including in cramped elevators and stairways, as well as piles of unattended bags in the corner of whatever rooms the various orientations and ID productions were going on in.

overall. One of the quirks of real human memory is that the most vivid, detailed recall doesn't usually concern the things that are most germane. The as it were forest. It's not just that real memory is fragmentary; I think it's also that overall relevance and meaning are conceptual, while the experiential bits that get locked down and are easiest, years later, to retrieve tend to be sensory. We live inside bodies, after all. Random examples of recalled snippets: Long and windowless interior halls, the burning in my forearms just before I had to set down the bags for a moment. The particular sound and cadence of Ms. Neti-Neti's heels on the hallways' flooring, which was of light-brown linoleum whose wax smelled strong in the unmoving air and reflected an endless series of shining parenthetical arcs where a custodian had swung his autowaxer from side to side in the empty hall at night. The place was a labyrinth of hallways, staircases, and fire doors with coded signs. Many of the halls seemed curved as opposed to straight, which I remember thinking was an illusion of perspective; the REC's exterior had nothing rounded or podular about it. In sum, the place was too overwhelmingly complex and repetitive to describe one's first experience of in any detail. Not to mention confusing: For instance, I know that our initial destination on arrival was one level below the main entrance and lobby. I know this in retrospect, because it's where the REC's Personnel office was, which I know was where Ms. Neti-Neti had been instructed to route me around the lobby check-ins and bring me directly... but I also have what feels like a clear sensuous memory of *climbing* at least one short set of stairs at some point, since it was climbing stairs with the luggage that caused the severest clunking of that one suitcase against the outside of my knee, which I could almost visualize the swelling and flamboyant bruising of. On the other hand, I don't suppose it's impossible that I'm confusing the order in which various parts of the REC were traversed.

I do know that at one point Ms. Neti-Neti herself apparently got confused or distracted, and opened the wrong door, and in the wedge of light before she could push the heavy door closed again I caught a glimpse of a long room filled with IRS examiners in long rows and columns of strange-looking tables or desks, each of which (desks) had a raised array of trays or baskets clamped to its top,[44] with flexible-necked desk lamps in turn clamped at angles to these fanned-out arrays, so that each of the IRS examiners worked in a small tight circle of light at what appeared to be the bottom of a one-sided hole. Row after row, stretching to a kind of vanishing point near the room's rear wall, in which there was incised another door. This, although I didn't know it at the time, was my first glimpse of an Immersives Room, of which the main REC structure contained a handful. The most striking thing about it was the quiet. There were at least 150 men and/or women in that room, all intently occupied and busy, and yet the room was so silent that you could hear an imperfection in the door's hinge as Ms. Neti-Neti pushed it closed against the force of its pneumatic strut. This silence I remember best of all, because it was both sensuous and incongruous: For obvious reasons, we tend to associate total quiet with emptiness, not with large groups of people. The whole thing lasted only a moment, though, after which we continued on our complex way, with Ms. Neti-Neti occasionally greeting or nodding at other Personnel officers in distinctive bright-blue jackets conducting small groups the other way—which in hindsight should have been additionally confusing, though I have no memory of feeling one way or another about it; I was still as it were reverberating from the sight of all those intent, totally silent examiners.

Here is probably an apt place for some exposition on my background re: silence and concentrated deskwork. In hindsight, I know that there was something about the silent, motionless intensity with which everyone in that opened door's instant was studying the tax-related documents before them that frightened and thrilled me. The scene was such that you just knew that if you were to open the door for another brief instant ten, twenty, or forty minutes later, it would look and sound just the same. I had never seen anything like it. Or

44 These were Tingle tables, an Examinations convention with which I became all too familiar—although no one I ever talked to knew the origin of 'Tingle,' as in whether it was eponymous, or sardonic, or what.

rather I had, in a way, for of course television and books often portray concentrated study or deskwork just this way, at least by implication. As in e.g. 'Irving knuckled down and spent the entire morning plowing through the paperwork on his desk'; 'Only when she had finished the report did the executive glance at her watch and see that it was nearly midnight. She had been completely absorbed in her task, and was only now aware that she had worked through supper, and was famished. Gracious, wherever did all the time go? she thought to herself.' Or even just as in 'He spent the day reading.' In real life, of course, concentrated deskwork doesn't go this way. I had spent massive amounts of time in libraries; I knew quite well how deskwork really was. Especially if the task at hand was dry or repetitive, or dense, or if it involved reading something that had no direct relevance to your own life and priorities, or was work that you were doing only because you had to—like for a grade, or part of a freelance assignment for pay from some lout who was off skiing. The way hard deskwork really goes is in jagged little fits and starts, brief intervals of concentration alternated with frequent trips to the men's room, the drinking fountain, the vending machine, constant visits to the pencil sharpener, phone calls you suddenly feel are imperative to make, rapt intervals of seeing what kinds of shapes you can bend a paperclip into, & c.[45] This is because sitting still and concentrating on just one task for an extended length of time is, as a practical matter, impossible. If you said, 'I spent the whole night in the library, working on some client's sociology paper,' you really meant that you'd spent between two and three hours working on it and the rest of the time fidgeting and sharpening and organizing pencils and doing skin-checks in the men's room mirror and wandering around the stacks opening volumes at random and reading about, say, Durkheim's theories of suicide.

45 For me, the pencil sharpener is a big one. I like a very particular sort of very sharp pencil, and some pencil sharpeners are a great deal better than others for achieving this special shape, which then is blunted and ruined after only a sentence or two, requiring a large number of sharpened pencils all lined up in a special order of age, remaining height, & c. The upshot is that nearly everyone I knew had distracting little rituals like this, of which rituals the whole point, deep down, was that they were distracting.

There was none of this diffraction in that split-second view of the room, though. One sensed that these were people who did not fidget, who did not read a page of, say, dull taxpayer explanation about the deduction of some item and then realize that they'd actually been thinking about the apple in their lunchbag and whether or not to maybe eat the apple right here and now until they realized that their eyes had passed over all the words (or, given the venue here, perhaps columns of figures) on the page without actually having read them at all—with *read* here meaning internalized, comprehended, or whatever we mean by really reading vs. simply having one's eyes pass over symbols in a certain order. Seeing this was kind of traumatic. I'd always felt frustrated and embarrassed about how much reading and writing time I actually wasted, about how much I sort of blinked in and out while trying to absorb or convey large amounts of information. To put it bluntly, I had felt ashamed about how easily I got bored when trying to concentrate. As a child, I think I'd understood the word *concentrate* literally and viewed my problems with sustained concentration as evidence that I was an unusually dilute or disorganized form of human being,[46] and had laid much of the blame for this on my family, who tended to need a lot of loud noise and distraction going on at all times and undertook almost every kind of activity with every available radio, stereo, and television set on, such that I'd taken to wearing special high-filter customized earplugs at home from the age of fourteen on. It took me all the way up to the age of finally getting away from Philo and entering a highly selective college to understand that the problem with stillness and concentration was more or less universal and not some unique shortcoming that was going to prevent me from ever really rising above my preterite background and achieving something. Seeing the enormous lengths that those elite, well-educated undergrads from all over the nation went to to

46 This sense of personal disorganization, which of course is very common, was for me heightened by the fact that I had very little trouble analyzing other people's basic character and motivations, strengths and weaknesses, & c., while all attempts at self-analysis resulted in a tangle of contradictory and hopelessly complex facts and tendencies, impossible to sort out or draw general conclusions from.

avoid, delay, or mitigate concentrated work was an eye-opening experience for me. In fact, the school's social structure was set up to prize and esteem students who could pass their classes and assemble a good transcript without ever working hard. People who skated by, doing the absolute minimum required for institutional/parental approval, were regarded as cool, while people who actually applied themselves to their assignments and to the work of their own education and achievement were relegated to the status of 'grinds' or 'tools,' the lowest caste in the college's merciless social hierarchy.[47]

The upshot, though, was that up until entering college, where everyone often lived and did homework together in plain mutual view, I'd had no opportunity to realize that fidgeting, distraction, and frequent contrived breaks were more or less universal traits. In high school, for example, homework is literally that—it's done at home, in private, with earplugs and KEEP OUT signs and a chair jammed up underneath the knob. Same with reading, working on journal entries, tabulating one's accounts from a paper route, & c. You're with your peers only in social or recreational settings, including classes, which at my own public high school were academic jokes. In Philo, educating yourself was something you had to do in spite of school, not because of it—which is basically why so many of my high school peers are still there in Philo even now, selling one another

47 I am reminded of an observation made during one of the wigglers' evening bull sessions in the room of Chris Acquistipace, who was a Chalk Leader and one of the only REC wigglers housed on the second floor of the Angler's Cove complex to display any friendliness or even an open mind toward me, despite the administrative foul-up that at first had me promoted even above the floor's other GS-9s. It was either Acquistipace or Ed Shackleford, whose ex-wife had taught high school, who observed that what was then starting to be codified as 'test anxiety' may well really have been an anxiety about *timed* tests, meaning exams or standardized tests, where there is no way to do the endless fidgeting and self-distraction that is part of 99.9 percent of real people's concentrated deskwork. I cannot honestly say that I remember whose observation it was; it was part of a larger discussion about younger examiners and television and the theory that America had some vested economic interest in keeping people over-stimulated and unused to silence and single-point concentration. For the sake of convenience, let's assume it was Shackleford. Shackleford's observation was that the real object of the crippling anxiety in 'test anxiety' might well be a fear of the tests' associated stillness, quiet, and lack of time for distraction. Without distraction, or even the possibility of distraction, certain types of people feel dread—and it's this dread, not so much the test itself, that people feel anxious about.

insurance, drinking supermarket liquor, watching television, awaiting the formality of their first cardiac.

Ms. Neti-Neti of Personnel, by the way, continued talking during much of the circuitous trip to Personnel. The truth is that most of what she said is no longer available to memory. Her tone was pleasant, professional; but she chattered so nonstop that one more or less involuntarily stopped listening to her after a little while, rather as with a six-year-old. Some of what she was saying was probably helpful and apposite REC information, though, and it's a bit of a shame that I can't resummon it now, since it would probably be useful and concise, memoir-wise, in ways that my own impressions and memories were not. I know that I kept stopping and switching various suitcases from one hand to the other to attenuate the burning sensation that comes from carrying the heavier bag on just, say, the right side for any length of time, and that it took a few such moments for Ms. Neti-Neti to understand what was happening and pause instead of continuing and ending up twenty or more yards ahead of me, at which time the fact that she was still talking became absurd, since there was literally no one there to hear her. The complete absence of any offers to help with any of the luggage was OK; that was attributable to gender codes, which I knew were especially rigid in the Middle East. But nothing drives home the awareness that someone's volubility and chatter are her own trip and have nothing to do with you quite like your falling behind and being literally absent and the chatter still proceeding, reaching you only as an indistinct stream of echoes off the hallways' surfaces. It would be disingenuous to say much more about the Iranian Crisis in the context of the first day, since what more I learned about her off-duty eccentricities and their origins in the Iranian upheavals of the late 1970s came only later when she seemed to emerge from a different wiggler's housing unit almost every morning during the month of August 1985. Her accent was mild and sounded more British than Mideastern or foreign, and her hair was a very dark black, with an almost liquid aspect to the perfect straightness with which it hung—from the rear, its contrast with the ghastly bright blue of the Personnel office's jacket was the only interesting or comely thing about that jacket. Also, because I spent so much time in various parts of her wake, I remember that she smelled faintly—as if the scent belonged not to her but to the Personnel jacket—of a certain mall-bought perfume that some unnamed member of my own family used to practically drench herself with eye-watering quantities of every morning.

Unlike the upper floors, the REC building's lower level is sectioned into roughly hexagonal pods, with corridors radiating from a central hub like spokes in a misshapen wheel. As you can imagine, this radial floor plan, so popular in the 1970s, made no immediate sense, given that the REC building itself was starkly rectangular, which added to the overall disorientation of that first day's descent toward the Intake mechanism.[48] The array of directional signs at each hub was so detailed and complex that it seemed designed only to increase the confusion of anyone not already sure where they were going and why.

48 Once again, I would only later learn that most wigglers and Support Services workers at the REC referred to the whole Intake/Orientation process as '*dis*orientation,' which was another bit of clumsy inside humor. On the other hand, no one in authority expected me to be as completely confused and overwhelmed as in fact I was on arrival, since it emerged that the Personnel office had mistaken me for a completely different David Wallace, viz. an elite and experienced Immersives examiner from Philadelphia's Northeast REC who had been lured to 047 through a complex system of shell-transfers and bureaucratic finagling. I.e., that there were not one but two David Wallaces whose contracted postings to 047 were to begin in this mid-May week. The computer-system problem behind this error is detailed in §38. It goes without saying that all these facts emerged only after a great deal of time, misunderstanding, and convolved hassle. They were the real explanation for Ms. Neti-Neti's scripted effusion and deference: It was actually that other, GS-13's name, ontologically speaking, that had been on her special whiteboard sign, though it's not as if 'David Wallace' is so common a US name that anyone could have reasonably expected me to posit right away that there'd been some freakish confusion about names and identities, especially during all the other confusion and ineptitude of 'disorientation.'

(N.B. Purely as an autobiographical aside, I'll insert that my use of my full middle name in published writing has its origins in this early confusion and trauma, i.e., trauma at being threatened at first with blame for the whole snafu, which, though egregious bullshit, was still understandably traumatic for a twenty-year-old green recruit with a fear of bureaucracies and one so-called 'honor code' violation, however specious and hypocritical, in his background already. For years afterward, I had morbid anxieties about there being God only knew how many other David Wallaces running around out there, doing God knows what; and I never again wanted to be professionally mistaken for or conflated with some other David Wallace. And then once you've fixed on a certain *nom de plume*, you're more or less stuck with it, no matter how alien or pretentious it sounds to you in your everyday life.)

This level had white flooring and walls with battleship-gray trim, and very bright inset fluorescents—it might as well have been a galaxy away from the main floor just above. At this point, it's probably best to keep the explanations as terse and compressed as possible, for realism's sake. The longer-term truth is that since I eventually came to be employed here—or, rather, it's better to say that I came to rest here, like a racquetball or caroming projectile, after the series of administrative mix-ups that almost resulted in disciplinary charges and/or Termination For Cause in the following weeks had been cleared up—it would be easy to impose on the Level 1 layout[49] and Personnel office a whole welter of detail, explanation, and background that was actually gleaned only later and not part of my arrival and dazed scurrying around with the Iranian Crisis at all. Which is a quirk of temporal memory—one tends to fill in gaps with data acquired only later, sort of the same way the brain automatically works to fill in the visual gap caused by the optical cord's exit through the back of the retina. As in, for example, the fact that the madhouse at the Exam Center's main entrance and lobby area upstairs, and the extremely long line of travel-weary employees in hats with baggage and brown Service expandable files of documentation and posting orders that now extended (i.e., this line did) all the way out through

49 The subterranean level, which had been excavated and added (at staggering expense) to the main building in 1974–75, was designated Level 1, and the ground floor was therefore technically Level 2, which was additionally confusing because not all of the REC's older, pre-excavation-and-addition signs had been changed out, and these signs and directories still identified the main, ground level as 1, the level above that 2, and so on, so that one could get any orientational help from these older directories and 'You Are Here' maps only if one knew in advance to recalibrate every level number upward by one, which was another piece of easily correctable institutional idiocy that Mr. Stecyk was grateful to have brought to his attention but embarrassed that he hadn't seen and fixed before, and in essence took full responsibility for, even though technically it was the responsibility of Mr. Lynn Hornbaker and the Physical Plant office to have seen and amended the signs many years before, which is one reason why the process of getting the new design and makeup of the signs contracted and requisitioned then turned out to be so fraught and pointlessly complex—by making the sign thing as difficult and complex as possible, Hornbaker's staff helped allay and diffuse responsibility for the signs' not having been caught and amended years before, such that by the time the REC Director's office heard about the issue, it was through a cloud of internal memos and cc's so involved and opaque that no one not directly involved would have paid anything more than vague attention to the very general details of the snafu.

one of the heavy hermetic fire doors[50] out into the fluorescent rotary at what later turned out to be the center of the central pod of Level 1, which line consisted of newly posted and/or transferred personnel waiting to have their passport-sized photo taken and their new Post 047 ID printed and run through the laminator, after which it would be almost too hot to hold for several minutes, such that you could see personnel holding their new IDs by one corner and fanning them rapidly back and forth through the air in order to cool them before attaching the gator clips to their breast pockets (as was required at all times on-post)... that all this mid-May roil and crowding was in fact due to a major restructuring of the IRS's Compliance Branch that was ongoing at all six operational RECs and over half of all Districts' Audit facilities (whose sizes varied widely) nationwide, scheduled to begin (i.e., the restructuring had been) exactly one month after the national individual income tax filing deadline of April 15, in order to allow the annual massive inflow of returns to have gone through its initial sorting and processing at the Regional Service Centers[51] and the attached checks to have been processed and deposited in the US Treasury via the six Regional Depository mechanisms... all of this uncovered later, informally, through confabs at Angler's Cove with Acquistipace, Atkins, Redgate, Shackleford, & c. Such that it would be misleading to go into any substantive detail or explanation at this point, since none of these truths yet existed, realistically speaking. Or the fact that it turned out one needed a valid IRS ID to access any of the shuttles from the complex to any of the special low-cost Post housing at two former commercial apartment complexes farther up Self-Storage Parkway, which was a Systems regulation nationwide and therefore the reason it was not Mr. Tate's or Stecyk's fault per se that new arrivals were required to schlep their luggage all over and stand in line with it as they waited to have their ID photo taken and fresh internal Social Security number generated, & c., though it was still irksome and idiotic not to have some

50 These double doors were gray steel, and this was the overall color scheme of Level 1—searing white and matte gray.

51 (the Midwest of which RSCs was in that era located in East St. Louis, two hours southwest)

mechanism in place for dealing with the luggage of new employees who didn't yet have an ID—all these facts are postdated, as it were.

What can validly be included among the experiences of the first day is that I was naturally surprised—a little thrilled, even—when I was exempted from the long and excruciatingly slow line that stretched from the central Level 1 rotary in to the makeshift ID station and instead got taken up to the front of the ID line and posed and shot and given my hot and redolently laminated ID card and gator clip right there on the spot. (I didn't yet know what the nine-digit sequence of numbers below the bar code signified, or that my old Social Security number, which as an American over age eighteen I knew pretty much by heart, would never again be used by anyone; it simply disappeared, from an identification standpoint.) Like being met by someone in authority with your name on a sign, it's almost inevitably gratifying to be specially escorted to the front of a line, no matter what looks of resentment or (in my case[52]) revulsion you receive from the preterite people in line who watch you being conducted up front and exempted from all the ordinary hassle and crowded wait. Plus some of the new personnel in line were clearly high-ranking transfers, and I was again both gratified and curious or even apprehensive about what kind of suction the distant relative who'd helped me arrange for the posting might turn out to have, and about what-all personal or biographical information had been relayed about me ahead of time, and to just whom. This bit of special treatment is legitimately part of the real memory-chain only if it's made clear that it (i.e., my being specially conducted to the front of the line) happened somewhat later on arrival day, after Ms. Neti-Neti had already taken me on a slightly different route along this central pod's rotary to the REC Personnel office itself, which was in a large suite of connected offices and reception areas in Level 1's southwest corner or vertex.[53] It had been her impression that I was supposed to

52 (FYI, late spring was always an exceptionally bad time, skin-wise, during this era; and the harsh fluorescents of Level 1 threw every blister, scab, and lesion into merciless relief.)

53 The logistical information, too, is postdated, strictly speaking. On the day itself, I couldn't have told you where in the building we even were by this time; no one could have.

have some kind of personal introductory audience with the DDP,[54] but either the Iranian Crisis was wrong about this, or the travel and traffic delays had caused me to forfeit the interview slot, or else some type of Personnel crisis had obtruded on the DDP's attention. For when we had descended to this level and negotiated the central rotary and skirted various parts of the line for ID, and had taken a number of labyrinthine turns and opened various fire doors, pausing ever more often so that I could redistribute the weight of my luggage, and had finally arrived at the Personnel office, we found the waiting area, outer offices, copier corridor, and special bisected room with a UNIVAC 1100 and remote terminal (connected, I learned later, by half-duplex Dataphone line to Region in upstate Joliet) across the hall already completely filled with IRS personnel sitting, standing, reading, staring into space, holding and twidgeling their various hats, and (I assumed—wrongly, as it turned out, although it's also true that Ms. Neti-Neti did nothing to disabuse me, instead disappearing into a side office and entering into a line of blue-jacketed people waiting to speak with a Personnel superior[55] in order to report my [i.e., the ostensible elite transfer's] arrival and to receive instructions about how to proceed in the absence of the special interview. It was this Assistant DDP who signed the internal Form 706-IC authorizing my being taken right up to the front of the line for Service ID processing, although it took Ms. Neti-Neti over twenty minutes[56] to reach the front of Mrs. van Hool's office's line and present

54 = Deputy Director of Personnel, which was Mr. Stecyk's official job title. My IRS contract, by the way, was signed not by Mr. Stecyk or by DP Richard Tate, but by Mr. DeWitt Glendenning Jr., whose bivalent titles were DREC (Director—Regional Examinations Center) and ARCE (Asst. Regional Commissioner for Examinations), but who was referred to by almost everyone as 'Dwitt.'

55 (This turned out to be Mrs. Marge van Hool, Mr. Stecyk's adjutant and right arm, who had the lashless, protuberant, unblinking eyes of a reptile or squid, something that could kill and eat you without its bulging alien stare ever changing, although Mrs. van Hool turned out to be the veritable salt of the earth, a classic instance of the truth that what most people look like has very little to do with their intrinsic human qualities... a truth I held quite dear at this time of my life.)

56 (during which interval, through momentary sight lines, I witnessed the Iranian Crisis first reading a paperback book and then at a later point attending to one sleeve of her gas-blue jacket with some kind of small portable sewing implement—she was clearly someone well-suited by temperament and/or experience to standing in long lines)

with her questions) doing nothing but sitting around on the taxpayer's dime in some kind of classic 'hurry up and wait' scenario.

Meanwhile, I was understandably tired and disoriented, and also frazzled (what today would be called 'stressed'), and hungry, and more than a little irritated, and was seated in a recently vacated[57] vinyl chair in the main waiting area, with my suitcases at my feet and dispatch case held against me in such a way as to hopefully obscure the dampness of my suit's left side, in direct view of the desk of the DDP's horrific secretary/receptionist, Mrs. Sloper, who on this first day gave me the exact same look of incurious distaste I would receive from her for the next thirteen months, and wore (this I sure remember) a lavenderish pantsuit against which the abundant rouge and kohl were even more ghastly. She was maybe fifty, and very thin and tendony, and had the same asymmetrical beehive coiffure as two different older females in my own family, and was made up like an embalmed clown, the stuff of nightmares. (Her face looked somehow held in place with pins.) Several times, at moments when there was enough of a gap in the mass of personnel to constitute a real line of sight, this secretary and I glanced at each other with mutual hatred and revulsion. She might actually have bared her teeth at me for an instant.[58] A few of the personnel seated or standing all around the room and connected hallways were reading files or filling out forms that might conceivably have had something to do with their assigned work, but most of them were staring vacantly into space or engaged together in wandering, desultory workplace conversations, the sort (as I learned) that neither start nor ever end. I could feel my pulse in two or three pemphigoid cysts along the line of my jaw, which meant that they were going to be really nasty ones. The nightmarish secretary had a small framed workplace cartoon on her desk's edge which featured a crude caricature of an angry face and below it the caption

57 (i.e., nauseously warmed by the heat of some stranger's back and bottom)

58 I would learn only much later that Mrs. Sloper's son had been badly burned in some kind of vehicle accident while in the service, and that the state of my skin hit her harder than the average mom. At the time, all I knew was that we despised each other on sight, as of course can happen with some people.

'I have got one nerve left...AND YOU'RE GETTING ON IT!,' which some of the administrative workers at Philo High had also displayed and expected people to applaud the wittiness of.

The fact that I was being paid for sitting here reading an insipid self-help book—my Service contract's period of employ had legally commenced at noon—while someone else who was being paid stood in a long line of similarly paid people simply in order to find out what to do with me: It all seemed massively wasteful and inept, a prime illustration of the view held among certain members of my family that government, government bureaucracy, and government regulation constituted the most wasteful, stupid, and un-American way to do anything, from regulating the instant-coffee industry to fluoridating the water.[59] At the same time, there were also flashes of anxiety that the delay and confusion might signify that the Service was considering whether to maybe disqualify and eject me based on some distorted record of allegedly unsavory behavior at the elite college I was on leave from, either with or without sirens. As every American knows, it is totally possible for contempt and anxiety to coexist in the human heart. The idea that people feel just one basic emotion at a time is a further contrivance of memoirs.

In short, I was there in the main waiting area for what felt like a very long time, and had all sorts of rapid, fragmentary impressions and reactions, of which I will include here only a few examples. I can remember hearing one middle-aged man who sat nearby saying 'Simmer down, boyo' to another older man seated kitty-corner to me across the doorway to one of the hallways extending out from the waiting area, except when I looked up from the book both these men were staring straight ahead, expressionless, with no sign of anyone needing to 'simmer down' in any conceivable way. Emerging from one radial hallway to traverse the edge of the waiting area and down another hallway was at least one good-looking girl, whose creamy pallor and

59 In the usual way of twenty-year-olds, when home in Philo, I made a point of arguing with members of my family about their political attitudes, and yet then outside the home I often found myself reflexively holding, or at least sympathizing with, those same parental attitudes. I suppose all this meant was that I hadn't yet formed a stable identity of my own.

cherrywood hair drawn to a knot with a store-bought bow I saw peripherally but then when I looked directly could see only the back of (i.e., the woman) as she went down the hall. I have to confess that I'm not sure just how much detail to actually indulge in, or how to keep myself from imposing on the waiting area and various personnel a familiarity earned only later. Telling the truth is, of course, a great deal trickier than most regular people understand. One of the waiting room's wastebaskets, I remember, contained an empty Nesbitt's can, which I interpreted as evidence that the REC's vending facilities might well include a Nesbitt's machine. Like all crowded rooms in summertime, the place was hot and stuffy. The smell of the sweat from my suit was not wholly my own; my flared collar was curling up slightly at the tips.

By this time, I had removed the mass-market paperback from my dispatch case and was reading it with partial attention—which was all that it deserved—while holding a ballpoint pen in my teeth. As I may have already mentioned in passing, the book had been given to me the day prior by an immediate relative (the same one whose wastebasket had contained the rumpled letter concerning my IRS posting from that other, less immediate relative) and was titled *How to Make People Like You: An Instant Recipe for Career Success,* and in essence I was 'reading' the book only to place certain tart, mordant margin-comments next to each bromide, cliché, or cloying bit of inauthentic pap, which meant just about every ¶. The idea was that I would mail the book back to this immediate relative a week or two hence, along with a voluble thank-you note filled with the gestures and tactics the book recommended—such as e.g. using the person's first name over and over again, emphasizing areas of agreement and shared enthusiasm, & c.—the overwhelming sarcasm of which this relative[60] would not detect until he then opened the book and saw the acerbic marginalia on every page. At school, I had once done certain freelance work for someone enrolled in an interdisciplinary course on Renaissance 'courtesy books' and the semiotics of etiquette, and the idea here was to allude to texts like *Peacham's Compleat*

60 (whose personal strengths did not include perceptiveness—and I am far from the only member of the family to observe this; trust me)

Gentleman and Chesterfield's *Letters to His Son* in the marginalia so as to make the implicit scorn all the more withering. It was just a fantasy, though. The truth was that I would never mail the book and note; it was a total waste of time.[61]

Crowded offices' waiting areas have their own special choreography, and I do know that at a certain further point the configuration of

61 There was, though, an oral exchange that I overheard involving two or possibly three unseen voices in the narrow hallway my chair was near the ingress of, from two REC personnel presumably standing waiting in some sort of line in that hallway, which I remember (the exchange) in detail because the waiting area's fluorescent lighting was gray-white and blinding and shadowless, the kind of light that makes people want to kill themselves, and I couldn't imagine spending nine hours a day in light like this, and so I was emotionally primed to pick this exchange out of the overall ambient noise of the room's exchanges, even though I could see neither party who was speaking; and I actually transcribed parts of the conversation in real time in a kind of personal shorthand on the inside of the pop psychology book's front cover, in order to transfer it later to the notebook (which is why I am able now to recount it in such potentially suspicious-looking detail); to wit:

'That's the short version?'

'Well, the point is just that Systems is not uncreative. You can't paint them all with the same brush.'

'Not uncreative? What kind of word is that?'

'The up-front cost-savings of fluorescent lights were obvious. All you had to do was compare power bills. Fluorescent lighting in Exam Centers was doctrine. But Lehrl found, at least in La Junta, that replacing the inset fluorescents with banked incandescents and desk lamps increased efficiency.'

'No, all the Systems boys found is that throughput of returns increased after fluorescents were changed out for lamps.'

'Again, no. What Lehrl's team found was that the net audit receipts of the Western REC's monthly throughput increased, for each of the three quarters following the installation of incandescents, by an amount next to which the combined installation cost and increased monthly power cost of incandescents was almost negligible, assuming you amortized the one-time expense of taking out all the fluorescents and fixing the ceiling.'

'But they never did prove that the incandescents had a direct causal link to the increased audit receipts.'

'But how do you prove that? A Region's balance sheet is thousands of separate pages. The increased receipts flowed from district offices spread all over the West. There's too many variables to account for—a single connection is unprovable. That's why it requires creativity. Lehrl's boys knew there was a correlation. They could just never get anyone at Triple-Six to accept it.'

'That's your interpretation.'

'They want everything quantified. But how do you quantify morale?'

...which transcription ended up making the book somewhat valuable, in terms of reproduction, decades later. So it was both a waste and not, depending on one's perspective and context.

personnel sitting and standing around altered enough that I enjoyed a sustained line of sight, over the book, into a select bit of the inner office of the Deputy Director of Personnel,[62] which office was basically a large wood-framed cubicle inset against the rear wall of the waiting area, the entrance to which was just behind and to the side of the nightmarish secretary/receptionist's desk, from which position she easily could and (one got the sense) often did shoot out a bony lavender arm into the space of the DDP's doorway to prevent someone from going in or even standing there knocking without her special *nihil obstat.* (Here being a veritable law of bureaucratic administration, it turned out: The more compassionate and effective the high-level official, the more unpleasant and Cerberusian the secretary who barred one's access to him.) Mrs. Sloper's desk's multiline telephone's handset had an attachment that let her rest it (i.e., the attachment) on her shoulder and be able still to use both hands for her secretarial tasks, without the violinish contortion of the neck required to hold a regular phone against one's shoulder. The little curved device or attachment, which was tan plastic, turned out to have been mandated by OSHA for certain classes of federal office workers. Personally, I'd never seen such a thing before. The office door behind her, which was partly ajar, featured frosted glass on which was inscribed the name and very long, complex title of the DDP (whom most of the Angler's Cove wigglers referred to by the facetious sobriquet of 'Sir John Feelgood,' which it took me several weeks to understand the Hollywood context and reference of [I detest commercial films, for the most part]). My sight line's particular angle was through the partly open door into a wedge-shaped section of the room inside. Within this section was a view of an empty desk with a name-and-title-plate so long that it actually extended beyond the width of the desk at both sides (i.e., of the desk), and a small bowler or rounded business hat hung at a slight angle from one

62 The Personnel Director's own large office was down at the end of one of the waiting area's radial corridors. As I would learn later, Mr. Tate, like many senior administrators, preferred to work out of view; he rarely interacted with anyone below the rank of GS-15.

of these protrusive sides, its brim occluding the last several letters on the plate so that what the desk's sign averred became:

L. M. STECYK DEPUTY ASSISTANT REGIONAL COMMISSIONER FOR EXAMINATIONS—PERSON which in a very different sort of mood might have been amusing.

To explain the context of this sight line into the office: Closest to me in terms of the personnel also sitting there waiting for something were two young unhatted males in two of a series of slightly different vinyl chairs at a slight angle to my left, both holding stacks of folders with color-coded tabs. Both seemed roughly college-age and wore short-sleeve shirts, poorly knotted ties, and tennis shoes, in contrast to the much more conventionally adult business-style dress of most of the rest of the room.[63] These boys, too, were engaged in some kind of long, aimless exchange. Neither crossed his legs as he sat; both their breast pockets had arrays of identical pens. From my angle of sight, their badges reflected the overhead lights and were impossible to parse. Mine was the only luggage in our area, some of which luggage was technically encroaching on the nearer kid's part of the room's floor, near his off-brand sneaker; and yet neither of them seemed aware of or curious about the luggage, or me. One might normally expect a kind of instant unspoken camaraderie between younger people in a workplace crowded mostly with older adults—rather the way two unconnected black people will often go out of their way to nod at or otherwise specially acknowledge each other if everyone

63 These, I learned, were 'turdnagels,' which term referred to low-grade or seasonal IRS support staff tasked mainly to inputting or extracting data on the REC's computer systems. Many of them were students at either the local junior college or Peoria College of Business, which was not an elite school. Like many low-caste or marginal groups, turdnagels turned out to be very tight-knit and exclusive, even when some of them were assigned to 'cart boy' duty and as a result tended to know and exchange pleasantries with many of the wigglers and higher-ranked immersives whose exam materials and supplies they (i.e., the turdnagels) had to courier back and forth in large carts filled with individual levels and boxes and trays that could be expanded like some enormous tackle box's tiers of compartments, so that the carts became enormous, complicated Rube Goldberg–like versions of a regular grocery or mail-room cart, and of which some (meaning the carts) clattered badly when they were pushed, because of all the moving parts and jerry-rigged tiers and compartments.

else around them is white—but these two acted as if someone their approximate age were not even there, even after I raised my head from *How . . . Success* twice and looked pointedly their way. It had nothing to do with the skin thing; I had a good antenna for the various ways of and motives for not being looked at. These two seemed practiced at screening out input in general, rather like commuters on subways in the larger cities of the East Coast. Their tone was very earnest. E.g.:

'How can you constantly be this obtuse?'

'Me, obtuse?'

'Jesus.'

'I'm not aware of being the least bit obtuse.'

'. . .'[64]

'I don't even know what you're talking about.'

'Good God.'

. . . but I couldn't determine whether it was a serious argument or just cynical collegiate titty-pinching to pass the time. At first, it seemed impossible to believe that the second kid was unaware that his protests of being unaware that he was obtuse played right into the hands of the colleague who was accusing him of obtuseness, i.e., being unaware. I was unsure whether or not to laugh, in other words. I had come to a ¶ in the book that explicitly recommended loud laughter at someone in a group's joke as being more or less an automatic way to signal or invite inclusion in that group, at least for purposes of conversation; the crude illustration was a line drawing of someone standing just outside a group of laughing people at a cocktail party or reception (they were all holding what were either shallow snifters or badly drawn martini glasses). The turdnagels, though, never turned their heads or even acknowledged my laughter, which was definitely loud enough to be audible even against the background noise. The point here being that it was at an extension of the angle over the shoulder of the 'nagel who denied having been obtuse, more or less pretending to be looking past them at something else in the way of someone whose attempt at eye contact or some moment of

64 (signifying that the first kid said nothing)

camaraderie has been rebuffed, that I enjoyed a momentary view into the actual office of the DDP, in which view the desk was empty but the office was not, for before the desk one man was squatting on his haunches before a chair in which another man[65] hunched forward with his[66] face in his hands. The posture, together with the movement of the suit coat's shoulders, made it pretty clear the second man was weeping. No one else among the crowds of personnel in the waiting area or standing in the lines that now extended out beyond the three narrow hallways[67] into the waiting room seemed aware at

65 More accurately, it was someone I presumed to be a man. . . . From my perspective, which was primarily behind the hunched person, he/she appeared to be wearing a suit jacket whose padded shoulders, in that era, were unisex.

66 (again, my assumption)

67 In effect, these people were standing in a kind of preliminary line just to enter the three hallways' lines in order to see various mid-level Personnel officers like Mrs. van Hool, who was just at that minute (extrapolating backward from Ms. Neti-Neti's imminent reappearance with the signed Form 706-IC) issuing her a crisp, decisive set of instructions as to what was to be done with and for the valued, veteran, high-ranking immersive exams specialist they believed me to be. (N.B. That examiner, transferred from Philadelphia's Northeast REC, being not only named David Wallace but having also been scheduled to arrive the following day, and whom the Iranian Crisis had actually been dispatched to wait for and personally escort, the Personnel computer systems having made a conflation error that will be explained in §38, and in effect collapsing that second, later-arriving David Wallace into me, explaining both the mistaken identity and the mistaken day . . . all of which it goes without saying is *post facto* knowledge that I had no way of either knowing or guessing at the time, since 'David Wallace,' though hardly the rarest name in the United States, is also not all that common. Nor did I or anyone else know, obviously, on May 15—on which date the other, older, more 'valuable' David Wallace was clearing out his Tingle table's trays and helping a senior cart boy collate and organize the files and supporting documents for distribution to other members of his Immersives Team in preparation for his transfer and flight the following day—that when, the following day, this senior transfer arrived at the appointed time and tried to check in at the GS-13 Intake Station in the Midwest REC lobby, he would be unable to do so—to check in and be permitted to proceed to the line for his new REC badge—because the GS-13 Intake Station would of course have him already listed as checked in and issued a new ID, that badge and GS-13 ID number (which was that other David Wallace's; he'd received it twelve years prior) having been already issued in Peoria to me, the author and 'real' (to me) David Wallace, who was obviously in no position to understand or explain (later) that the whole thing was an administrative fuck-up and not an intentional attempt to supplant or impersonate an IRS GS-13 with over twelve years of devoted service at a job whose difficulty and arcane complication I would shortly start discovering; but in any event, this snafu would end up explaining not just the effusive welcome and mistakenly high civil service grade and salary (which I won't pretend I wasn't pleasantly surprised by, albeit of course puzzled) but also, partly, the strange and—for me—pretty much unprecedented interlude in the

that moment of this little tableau, or of the fact that the DDP's office door was partly open. The weeper was facing away from me, for the most part,[68] but the man hunkered down before him with a hand on his padded shoulder and saying something in what you could tell was a not ungentle tone had a wide soft flushed or pinkish face with lush and (I thought) incongruous sideburns, a face slightly out of date, which, when his eye caught mine (I having forgotten, in my interest, that sight lines are by definition two-way) in the same moment when the loathsome secretary, still speaking on the phone, now saw me staring past her and reached out without even having to look at the door or its knob's position in order to pull it closed with an emphatic sound, spread (the administrator's face did, i.e., Mr. Stecyk's) in an involuntary expression of compassion and sympathy, an expression that seemed almost moving in its spontaneity and unself-conscious

dark electrical closet off one of the radial hallways extending from the Level 1 central corridor with Ms. Neti-Neti shortly after I was conducted to the head of the ID line and issued the new badge, in which (i.e., incident in the electrical closet) she backed me up against a warm series of inset circuit-boxes and administered what would, according to former president W. J. Clinton, not properly be considered 'sex,' but which to me was far and away the most sexual thing that had happened or would happen to me until almost 1989, all of which eventuated because of both the Personnel computer's failure to distinguish between two different internal David Wallaces and Mrs. van Hool's apparent instruction to Ms. Neti-Neti to extend to 'me' (i.e., to the GS-13 they'd so heavily recruited and gotten to transfer from the Northeast REC's elite Immersive Pod) 'every courtesy,' which it emerged was a very loaded and psychologically charged term for Chahla Neti-Neti, who'd come of economic age in the sybaritic but highly etiquette- and euphemism-intensive culture of pre-Revolutionary Iran (I learned this only later, obviously), and had, like many other nubile younger Iranian women with familial connections to the existing government, had to basically 'trade' or 'barter' sexual activities with high-level functionaries in order to get herself and two or three other members of her family out of Iran during the tense period when the displacement of the shah's regime was becoming more and more certain, and to whom 'extend[ing] every courtesy' therefore translated into a rapid, almost woodpeckerishly intensive round of fellatio, this apparently being the preferred method of pleasuring government functionaries from whom one sought favor but upon whose face one did not wish or could not bear to look. But it was still really exciting, albeit—for obvious reasons—extremely brief, and also helps explain why it was such a long time before I even realized that I'd left one of my pieces of luggage on the floor of the Personnel office's waiting area.... All of which background also would later explain the sobriquet 'Iranian Crisis' for Ms. Chahla Neti-Neti, whose breasts' shapes against the damp corduroy of my upper legs remain one of the most vivid sensuous memories of that whole cluster-fuck of my first several days as an IRS immersive.

68 (again helping to account for the gender confusion...)

candor, which, as explained above, I was not at all used to, and which I have no idea how my own face registered my reaction to in that moment of what felt like highly charged eye contact before his stricken face was replaced with the door's frosted glass and my own eyes dropped quickly to the book once more. I had not had my facial skin provoke such an expression before, not ever once, and it was that soft, bureaucratically mod face's expression that kept obtruding on my mind's eye in the darkness of the electrical closet as the Iranian Crisis's forehead impacted my abdomen twelve times in rapid succession and then withdrew to a receptive distance that seemed, in that charged instant, much farther away than it really could have been, realistically speaking.

§25

'Irrelevant' Chris Fogle turns a page. Howard Cardwell turns a page. Ken Wax turns a page. Matt Redgate turns a page. 'Groovy' Bruce Channing attaches a form to a file. Ann Williams turns a page. Anand Singh turns two pages at once by mistake and turns one back which makes a slightly different sound. David Cusk turns a page. Sandra Pounder turns a page. Robert Atkins turns two separate pages of two separate files at the same time. Ken Wax turns a page. Lane Dean Jr. turns a page. Olive Borden turns a page. Chris Acquistipace turns a page. David Cusk turns a page. Rosellen Brown turns a page. Matt Redgate turns a page. R. Jarvis Brown turns a page. Ann Williams sniffs slightly and turns a page. Meredith Rand does something to a cuticle. 'Irrelevant' Chris Fogle turns a page. Ken Wax turns a page. Howard Cardwell turns a page. Kenneth 'Type of Thing' Hindle detaches a Memo 402-C(1) from a file. 'Second-Knuckle' Bob McKenzie looks up briefly while turning a page. David Cusk turns a page. A yawn proceeds across one Chalk's row by unconscious influence. Ryne Hobratschk turns a page. Latrice Theakston turns a page. Rotes Group Room 2 hushed and brightly lit, half a football field in length. Howard

Cardwell shifts slightly in his chair and turns a page. Lane Dean Jr. traces his jaw's outline with his ring finger. Ed Shackleford turns a page. Elpidia Carter turns a page. Ken Wax attaches a Memo 20 to a file. Anand Singh turns a page. Jay Landauer and Ann Williams turn a page almost precisely in sync although they are in different rows and cannot see each other. Boris Kratz bobs with a slight Hassidic motion as he crosschecks a page with a column of figures. Ken Wax turns a page. Harriet Candelaria turns a page. Matt Redgate turns a page. Ambient room temperature 80° F. Sandra Pounder makes a minute adjustment to a file so that the page she is looking at is at a slightly different angle to her. 'Irrelevant' Chris Fogle turns a page. David Cusk turns a page. Each Tingle's two-tiered hemisphere of boxes. 'Groovy' Bruce Channing turns a page. Ken Wax turns a page. Six wigglers per Chalk, four Chalks per Team, six Teams per group. Latrice Theakston turns a page. Olive Borden turns a page. Plus administration and support. Bob McKenzie turns a page. Anand Singh turns a page and then almost instantly turns another page. Ken Wax turns a page. Chris 'The Maestro' Acquistipace turns a page. David Cusk turns a page. Harriet Candelaria turns a page. Boris Kratz turns a page. Robert Atkins turns two separate pages. Anand Singh turns a page. R. Jarvis Brown uncrosses his legs and turns a page. Latrice Theakston turns a page. The slow squeak of the cart boy's cart at the back of the room. Ken Wax places a file on top of the stack in the Cart-Out box to his upper right. Jay Landauer turns a page. Ryne Hobratschk turns a page and then folds over the page of a computer printout that's lined up next to the original file he just turned a page of. Ken Wax turns a page. Bob McKenzie turns a page. Ellis Ross turns a page. Joe 'The Bastard' Biron-Maint turns a page. Ed Shackleford opens a drawer and takes a moment to select just the right paperclip. Olive Borden turns a page. Sandra Pounder turns a page. Matt Redgate turns a page and then almost instantly turns another page. Latrice Theakston turns a page. Paul Howe turns a page and then sniffs circumspectly at the green rubber sock on his pinkie's tip. Olive Borden turns a page.

Rosellen Brown turns a page. Ken Wax turns a page. Devils are actually angels. Elpidia Carter and Harriet Candelaria reach up to their Cart-In boxes at exactly the same time. R. Jarvis Brown turns a page. Ryne Hobratschk turns a page. 'Type of Thing' Ken Hindle looks up a routing code. Some with their chin in their hand. Robert Atkins turns a page even as he's crosschecking something on that page. Ann Williams turns a page. Ed Shackleford searches a file for a supporting document. Joe Biron-Maint turns a page. Ken Wax turns a page. David Cusk turns a page. Lane Dean Jr. rounds his lips and breathes deeply in and out like that and bends to a new file. Ken Wax turns a page. Anand Singh closes and opens his dominant hand several times while studying a muscle in his wrist. Sandra Pounder straightens slightly and swings her head in a neck-stretching arc and leans forward again to examine a page. Howard Cardwell turns a page. Most sit up straight but lean forward at the waist, which reduces neck fatigue. Boris Kratz turns a page. Olive Borden raises the little hinged flag on her empty 402-C box. Ellis Ross starts to turn a page and then stops to recheck something higher up on the page. Bob McKenzie hawks mucus without looking up. 'Groovy' Bruce Channing worries his lower lip with a pen's pocket clip. Ann Williams sniffs and turns a page. Matt Redgate turns a page. Paul Howe opens a drawer and looks inside and closes the drawer without taking anything out. Howard Cardwell turns a page. Two walls' paneling painted over in Baker-Miller pink. R. Jarvis Brown turns a page. One Chalk per row, four rows per column, six columns. Elpidia Carter turns a page. Robert Atkins's lips are soundlessly moving. 'Groovy' Bruce Channing turns a page. Latrice Theakston turns a page with a long purple nail. Ken Wax turns a page. Chris Fogle turns a page. Rosellen Brown turns a page. Chris Acquistipace signs a Memo 20. Harriet Candelaria turns a page. Anand Singh turns a page. Ed Shackleford turns a page. Two clocks, two ghosts, one square acre of hidden mirror. Ken Wax turns a page. Jay Landauer feels absently at his face. Every love story is a ghost story. Ryne Hobratschk turns a page. Matt Redgate turns a page. Olive Borden stands and raises her hand with three fingers out for the cart boy. David Cusk turns a page. Elpidia Carter turns a page. Exterior temperature/humidity 96°/74%. Howard Cardwell turns a page. Bob McKenzie still hasn't spit. Lane Dean Jr. turns a page. Chris Acquistipace turns a page. Ryne Hobratschk turns a page. The cart comes up the group room's right side with its squeaky wheel. Two others in the third Chalk's row also stand. Harriet Candelaria turns a page. R. Jarvis Brown turns a page. Paul Howe turns a page. Ken Wax turns a page. Joe Biron-Maint turns a page. Ann Williams turns a page.

§26

A word or two on the 'phantom' phenomenon that's so much a part of Exams lore. Examiners' phantoms are not the same as real ghosts. *Phantom* refers to a particular kind of hallucination that can afflict rote examiners at a certain threshold of concentrated boredom. Or rather say the strain of trying to remain alert and punctilious in the face of extreme boredom can reach levels at which certain types of hallucination routinely occur.

One such hallucination is what's known in Exams as a visit from the phantom. Sometimes just as a visit, as in 'You'll have to forgive Blackwelder. He had a bit of a visit this afternoon, hence the tic.' Though most rote examiners suffer from hallucinations at one time or another, not every examiner gets visited. Only certain psychological types. One way you know they're not real ghosts: Every visitee's phantom is different, but their commonality is that the phantoms are always deeply, diametrically different from the examiners they visit. This is why they're so frightening. They tend to present as irruptions from a very rigid, disciplined type of personality's repressed side, what analysts would maybe call a person's shadow. Hypermasculine wigglers get visits from simpering queens in lingerie and clotted vaudevillian rouge and mascara, nancing about. Devout wigglers see demons; prudish ones see splayed harlots or priapistic gauchos. The immaculately hygienic get visits from filthy figures whose clothing jumps with fleas; the incredibly fussy and organized see whimpering wild-haired figures with strings around their fingers rummaging frantically through the Tingle's baskets for something crucial they've misplaced.

It's not like it happens every day. Phantoms afflict mainly certain sorts. Not so true ghosts.

Ghosts are different. Most examiners of any experience believe in the phantom; few know or believe in actual ghosts. This is understandable. Ghosts can be taken for phantoms, after all. In certain ways, phantoms serve as distracting background or camouflage from which it can be difficult to pick up the fact-pattern of actual ghosts. It's like the old cinematic gag of someone on Halloween being visited by a real ghost and complimenting what he thinks is a kid in a really great costume.

The truth is that there are two actual, non-hallucinatory ghosts haunting Post 047's wiggle room. No one knows whether there are any in the Immersive Pods; those Pods are worlds unto themselves.

The ghosts' names are Garrity and Blumquist. Much of the following info comes after the fact from Claude Sylvanshine. Blumquist is a very bland, dull, efficient rote examiner who died at his desk unnoticed in 1980. Some of the older examiners actually worked with him in rotes in the 1970s. The other ghost is older. Meaning dating from an earlier historical period. Garrity had evidently been a line inspector for Mid West Mirror Works in the mid-twentieth century. His job was to examine each one of a certain model of decorative mirror that came off the final production line, for flaws. A flaw was usually a bubble or unevenness in the mirror's aluminum backing that caused the reflected image to distend or distort in some way. Garrity had twenty seconds to check each mirror. Industrial psychology was a primitive discipline then, and there was little understanding of non-physical types of stress. In essence, Garrity sat on a stool next to a slow-moving belt and moved his upper body in a complex system of squares and butterfly shapes, examining his face's reflection at very close range. He did this three times a minute, 1,440 times per day, 356 days a year, for eighteen years. Toward the end he evidently moved his body in the complex inspectorial system of squares and butterfly shapes even when he was off-duty and there were no mirrors around. In 1964 or 1965 he had apparently hanged himself from a steam pipe in what is now the north hallway off the REC Annex's wiggle room. Among the staff at 047, only Claude Sylvanshine knows anything detailed about Garrity, whom he's never actually seen—and then most of what Sylvanshine gets is repetitive data on Garrity's weight, belt size, the topology of optical flaws, and the number of strokes it takes to shave with your eyes closed. Garrity is the easier of the wiggle room's two ghosts to mistake for a phantom because he's extremely chatty and distracting and thus is often taken by wigglers straining to maintain concentration as the yammering mind-monkey of their own personality's dark, self-destructive side.

Blumquist is different. When Blumquist manifests in the air near an examiner, he just basically sits with you. Silently, without moving. Only a slight translucence about Blumquist and his chair betrays anything untoward. He's no bother. It's not like he stares at you in an uncomfortable way. You get the sense that he just likes to be there. The sense is ever so slightly sad. He has a high forehead and mild eyes made large by his glasses. Sometimes he's hatted; sometimes he holds the hat by the brim as he sits. Except for those examiners who spasm out at any sort of visitation—and these are the rigid, fragile ones who are ripe for phantom-visits anyhow, so it's something of a vicious circle—except for these, most examiners accept or even like a visit from Blumquist. He has a few he seems to favor, but he is quite democratic. The wigglers find him companionable. But no one ever speaks of him.

§27

The Rotes orientation room was on the top floor of the REC building. You could hear the needly sounds of printers—next door was Systems. David Cusk had chosen a seat near the back below an air-conditioning vent that did not riffle the pages of his training packet and Internal Revenue Code. It was either a large room or a small auditorium. The room was brightly fluorescent-lit, and ominously warm. Industrial roller shade things were pulled over two broad sets of south windows, but you could feel the sun's heat radiating from the shades and from the Celotex ceiling. There were fourteen new examiners in a room that sat 108, not counting the raised stage thing with the podium and rotary slide projector, which Cusk's parents had one almost the like of.

The Compliance Training Officer was a woman with flat hair in a tan pantsuit and flats with two separate badges on either side of the jacket. She held a clipboard to her chest and had a pointer in one hand. The room had a whiteboard instead of a chalkboard. In the room's light her face was the color of suet. She was assisted by one of the Post's Personnel men whose bright-blue jacket was too short and showed the bones of his wrists. There was no one within six little bolted desks of Cusk on any side, and he'd also taken off his suit coat the way three other people in the desks had. The examiners who'd just come today had their luggage stacked neatly at the back on the opposite side of the room. Cusk had two pencils in his bag, both eraserless and so deeply chewed you couldn't tell what color they had been. He was teetering on the edge of an attack like the one in the car with the man with the horrible boiled-looking face watching him as his temperature spiked and it was all he could do not to clamber over the man and claw at the window for air. Like almost the other one only an hour later in the line for the badge, where once he had been in the line for a few minutes he was invested and couldn't leave the line without the man in the blue jacket asking a lot of questions that other people in the line would hear and look over, and by the time he got to stand there under the two hot lights he'd done the thing of pushing the hair back off his forehead so often that the hair stood up almost straight, which he didn't know until the ID came out all hot from the laminator and he saw the photo.

As Cusk discovered the year his grades had jumped in high school, his chances of an attack could be minimized if he paid very close and sustained attention to whatever was going on outside him. He had an associate's in Accounting from Elkhorn-Brodhead Community College. The problem was that at a certain level of arousal it was hard to pay attention to anything but the threat of an attack. Paying attention to anything but the fear was like hoisting something heavy with a pulley and rope—you could do it, but it took effort, and you got tired, and the minute you slipped you were back paying attention to the last thing you wanted to.

On the whiteboard was the acronym SHEAM, which had not yet been defined. Some examiners were transferring from other posts or had been through the twelve-week IRS training courses in Indianapolis or Rotting Flesh LA. Their orientation was somewhere else, and shorter.

The little desktops were bolted to the chairs' sides and forced people to sit in a very particular way. Little flexible lamps on stalks were bolted to the side of the desktop in the place where a right-handed person needed to place his elbow in order to take notes.

The whiteboard was rather small, and the new GS-9s had to refer to a small printed booklet for some of the diagrams that illustrated the procedures the Training Officer was explaining. Many of the diagrams were so complicated that they took more than one two-page spread and had to be continued on later pages.

First there were several forms to fill out. An oriental man collected them. The orientation people obviously believed that training sessions worked better and were easier to attend to if the presentation wasn't solo. This was not Cusk's experience. His experience was that the man with the prominent wrists and Adam's apple kept interrupting or providing unnecessary and distracting commentary. It was much easier and safer for David Cusk to pay attention to just one exterior thing at a time.

'One of the things you're going to hear a lot about is quotas. In the break rooms, the water cooler.'

'The Center has no illusions about gossip and scuttlebutt.'

'The older examiners like to tell tall tales about how things were in the bad old days.'

'On the public level, the Service has always denied quotas as gauges of work performance.'

'Because one of the things you'll be thinking, because it's natural, is: How will my work be evaluated? On what will my quarterly and annual performance reviews be based?'

The gangly man wrote a question mark on the whiteboard. Cusk's feet were hot in his dress chukkas, on one of which a scuff mark had been carefully colored in with a black pen.

The Training Officer said, 'Let's say, as a hypothetical, that at one point there were quotas.'

'But for what?'

'In 1984, the Service processed a total of over sixty million individual 1040s. There are six Regional Service Centers and six Regional Exam Centers. Do the math.'

'Well, in 1984, this Post had annual throughput of seven hundred sixty-eight thousand four hundred returns.'

'That math may not appear to add up.'

'That's because it's not sixty million divided by twelve.'

'It leaves out the factor of Martinsburg.'

Their employee handbooks contained a full-color photo of the Service's National Computer Center in Martinsburg WV, one of whose three layers of perimeter fencing was electrified and had to have its base swept up every morning during equinoctial bird migrations.

The problem was that the screen for the slide projector came down over the whiteboard, so that anything written on the whiteboard was obscured when a diagram or schema had to be projected. Also, the screen appeared to have something wrong with the lock on its roller mechanism and wouldn't stay down, so that the Personnel aide had to hunch down and grasp the pull ring to keep the screen in position while keeping his shadow off the screen, which required him to practically get on his knees. The image on the slide projector's screen was a crude map of the United States with six dots in various locales whose names were too blurred by the projector's diffracted beam to make out. Each dot had an arrowed line that terminated at a dot just slightly in and below the middle of the Atlantic Coast. Some of the room's new examiners were taking notes on the image, though Cusk couldn't have guessed what the notes contained.

'Let's say a 1040 return with a claim for a refund comes into the Western Region Service Center in Ogden, Utah.' The lady pointed to the leftmost block. The man held up a Hollerith card, whose shadow on the screen was like the most complicated domino of all time.

One of the window shades was canted slightly in its own roller, and through the resultant gap a plane of light from the southern exposure empaled the screen's right side. A series of black-and-white photographs began to cycle through the automated slide projector, both too quickly and too irresolute in the sun to quite parse. There appeared to be two incongruous photos of some kind of beach or lake scene, but they went past too quickly to be seen.

'Of course, your own RSC is in East St. Louis,' the man said from his place hunched down at the screen's bottom. He had some kind of regional accent that Cusk did not recognize.

'During the intensive processing season—'

'Which this is the tail end of—'

'The procedure is basically this. Seasonal employees remove the pre-bundled bundles of envelopes from special trucks, remove the bundling restraints, and feed the envelopes into an automated mail processor, known also as AMP, which is one of the Systems Division's latest improvements in the speed and efficiency of returns processing, with a peak of almost thirty thousand envelopes an hour.' A Fornix Industries advertising photo of a room-sized machine with numerous belts, blades, and lamps had already cycled past on the screen several images ago. 'Automated AMP processes include sorting, opening with ultra-fast milling knives, coding the edges of the different returns, sorting them onto different belts on which further temporary employees open them by hand—'

'The empty envelopes are then run through a special AMP candling scanner to ensure that they're empty, a feature that has ameliorated a great many administrative problems of the past.'

(Most of the shots just looked like a lot of people milling around a large room with a lot of bins and tables. The slides were so out of sync with the data being presented that it was impossible to pay attention to both—most of the wigglers averted their eyes from the screen.)

'When the envelopes are opened, the first task is to remove all checks and money orders enclosed. These are batched, recorded, and rushed by special courier to the nearest federal depository, which in the Western Region is in Los Angeles. The returns themselves are batched according to five basic types and status.' The man let go of the screen, which ascended with a pop that made people in the first few rows jump. The projector was still on, and a photo of several black women in horn-rim glasses keypunching data was superimposed on the Training Officer as she pointed at the codes for corporate returns, 1120; trusts and estates, 1041; partnerships, 1065; and the well-known Individual 1040 and 1040A; plus S corporations, which also filed 1120s.

'Of these, you're going to be concerned only with individual returns.'

'Corporates and fiduciaries—fiduciaries are, as you know, estates and trusts—are done at the District level.'

The Personnel man, who was trying to turn the slide projector off, said, 'And 1040s divide into simples and Fats—Fats including schedules beyond A, B, and C, or an excess of supporting schedules or attachments or more than three total pages of Martinsburg printout.'

'We haven't yet covered the Martinsburg part of the process yet, though,' the TO said.

'The point for you is that 1040 exams are divided into rotes and Fats, and you're tasked to rotes, which are relatively simple 1040 and 1040As, hence Rote Exams. Fats are done in Immersive Exams, which are staffed by more senior, umm, staff, which under some regional organizations also handle 1065s and 1120Ss for certain classes of S corporation.'

The lady extended her hand in a way that signified acquiescence.

Cusk noted that pretty much all the information the training team was offering was also in the orientation packet, although the team was presenting it in a different way. His seat was in the third row from the back and all the way to the right. His fear of an attack was considerably lessened by the fact that no one was around him or in a position to look at him closely. One or two of the new examiners toward the front were actually sitting in the planar column of sun from the damaged window shade. Cusk tried hard not to imagine how much warmer and more exposed these new hires or promotions must have felt, since he was aware that other people did not suffer from *phobic anxiety* about attacks, which combined with the other terms *ruminative obsession, hyperhydrosis,* and *parasympathetic nervous system arousal loop* in a self-diagnosis he had arrived at through scores of hours of covert research—he had even enrolled in psychology courses he had no interest in, in order to create a plausible cover for the research—in the Elkhorn-Brodhead Community College library, and an awareness of his unique anxiety was one of twenty-two identified factors that could help prime him for an attack, though not one of the really super-drive factors. The sound of the door closing behind him was what first alerted David Cusk to the fact that a change in pressure he had felt was not due to the start of the pressurized room's AC, but to someone else having entered, though turning his head to see who had come in was a sure way to draw that person's attention to him, which was imprudent because there was a reasonable chance that a late-arriving person would sit behind him, near the door through which he had first entered, and Cusk did not relish the thought of a person he had made eye contact with sitting behind him and possibly looking at the back of his hair, which was still suspiciously damp. Just the thought of the prospect of being looked at was enough to send a small aftershock of heat through Cusk's body, and he could feel selected pinpricks of sweat breaking out along his hairline and just under his lower eyelid, which were the sites where sweat usually first appeared.

Cusk realized he had also missed a minute or more of the training presentation, to which he now returned his attention with an almost physical force. The CTO was referring to control cards and batches of returns being sent someplace that Cusk deduced might well still be in the Service Center.

'They're numbered by batch, then sent for keypunching.' She accentuated her stressed syllables with the pointer, which was approximately twice the length of a conductor's baton.

'Through both gang punching and specialized binary codes, GS-9 keypunch operators scan each return and generate a computer card with 512 key points of data on it, from the TP's Social Security number—'

'Which you might hear referred to as "tin." For TIN, for Taxpayer ID Number—' The man actually took time writing this on the whiteboard while the Compliance TO held up two computer cards that looked more or less identical from Cusk's vantage.

'Please note that both Service Centers and Martinsburg have gone to ninety-column cards,' the lady said, 'thereby increasing the computing power of the Service's IDS, or Integrated Data System.' The projector moved to an image of what looked more or less exactly like the cards the GS-11 was holding up, although the holes in the card of rectangle were round instead. The Fornix corporation logo on the side was almost as large as the image of the card. 'This can, in some cases, affect the layout of the printout you'll receive along with each return you'll be examining for audit.'

'For this is what you guys are doing,' the Personnel aide said, 'is examining returns for audit-potential.'

'Which we'll be getting to in exactly eight minutes,' the CTO said, giving the Personnel aide something of a look.

Cusk was first aware of an unnaturally pleasant smell originating from somewhere behind him, more pleasant than the processed air of the room and considerably better than the faint sharp-cheddar smell he imagined came off his damp shirt.

'If the Powers card specs affect your IDS-360 in a significant way, you'll be given special supplementary training on this by your Group Manager.'

'Your Group Manager is your Team Leader's supervisor,' said the Personnel aide.

'Overall, the data include TIN, occupation code, dependents, classification of income and deductions, amounts on attached W-2s, 1099s, and similar information.'

'This is pure transcription,' the man said. 'There's no exams at this phase.'

'These are transported to Martinsburg, where Card Readers transfer the information to the Central Computers, which check for arithmetic errors, crosscheck the W-2s and income statements—'

'And very basic discrepancies, which are recorded on the internal printout for each return.'

'The printouts are known as "Internal Memo 1040-M1s" or just "M1s." '

'Although appended to the 1 is the last two digits of the relevant year for the return; for instance, a 1040-M1-84 is a printout for a 1984 1040 Individual Tax Return.'

'Although these numbers refer to the return's classification in the Master Files, the printout itself has no real code designation.'

'In the Master Files, a specific return's location would be 1040-M1-79 plus the TP's TIN, so it's actually a seventeen-character designator.'

'They're not here for Systems orientation. The point is that all you'll see is a printout with the return, because the M1 printout and the return comprise the case file, and what rote examiners do is examine case files for audit potential.'

Cusk was starting to pick up on the rhythms of the dual presentation and the interrelational cues that came from the Training Officer when the presentation had veered into a digression or was covering something comparatively less important. The main one was that she looked at her wristwatch, which made the shadow of the pointer in her hand stick out to the side on the lit screen and point directly at the Personnel aide's shadow, even though the two were not equally close to the projector. Plus the relevant points were right there in the orientation packet. In the part of his mind that was aware of his own arousal-level, sweat-situation, the room's temperature, the location of all the exits, the locations and sight lines of all people in the room who might be able to see it if he had an attack—all of which, when he was in any kind of enclosed public situation, took up some part of his awareness no matter how intently he concentrated on whatever was going on in terms of the room's official business—Cusk was aware of the presence of someone behind and slightly above him, probably just inside the exit door, possibly standing there deciding where he or she would sit. And the possibility that it was a she—for the pleasant scent in the air was perfume, it was reasonable to assume, or else an unusually floral and effeminate kind of men's cologne—caused another wave of warmth to pass through Cusk's head and scalp, though not a really severe or attack-grade wave of heat.

'In essence,' the Compliance Training Officer said, 'the master files allow us to verify the arithmetic and check for discrepancies that would take several man-hours to do by hand.'

'Fact,' the Personnel aide said. 'Between six and eleven percent of average annual 1040s contain some basic arithmetical error.'

'But the Master Files also permit cross-year and cross-return checks,' the CTO said. 'Examples: 1040 Line 11 and Line 29—Alimony received and paid.'

'These are on your Rotes Protocol sheets,' the Personnel aide said. 'But they're essentially done by the time you get the file.

Martinsburg's Master Files perform the crosschecks with the spouse's return. If there's a discrepancy, it's noted on the M1. . . . Your job will be to determine whether the amounts involved constitute an auditable item.'

'And, if so, whether it's a letter-audit through the REC's AC Pod—Automated Correspondence—or whether it's in the Service's interest to direct the entire return to its home District for an office audit.'

'In essence,' the Personnel aide said, 'this is your job. You are on the front lines of deciding which returns are audited and which are not. That's boiled down to the nutshell. And the criteria for auditability have changed substantially in the past two years, so . . .'

'One more example of how Martinsburg fits in the process,' the CTO said. 'Line 10.'

The Personnel aide slapped his forehead theatrically. 'This is one that drove them crazy in the seventies.'

'Line 10 in Income, on the 1040, requires you to declare state and local tax refunds *if* the refund is for a year in which you itemized deductions—'

'—meaning Line 34A, meaning Schedule A.'

'This was an open invitation to TPs to "misremember" whether they'd itemized the previous year. The incentive was to believe they had not itemized the previous year—'

'—because then the refunds were not income.'

'—and prior to the Master Files, it was reasonable of a clever TP to assume that this was not an item that would be checked in Exams. Because the previous year's return was something you had to fill out a Form 3IR plus 12(A) on.'

'Return Request Requisition,' the Personnel aide inserted.

'And the return had to be recovered from either the Service Center's archives or the National Records Center, and it was a pain, and took a week, and it was *expensive,* mainly in man-hours and transport and administration costs, costs which tended to far exceed the fairly small amounts of a state or local refund.'

'Line 10 was something we just could never afford to check,' the Personnel aide said. 'Not to mention the hassle of keeping a return in your Tingle's in-box for a week while you waited for the 3R to come through.'

'With the Master Files, the Line 34A option of the TP's previous return could be automatically checked—you now get alerts on the printout itself whether line 10 is tax-treatable or not, based on the previous returns and the state RE reports.'

'Although some states' computer systems aren't compatible with Martinsburg.'

The room's temperature, as experienced by David Cusk, was now 84 degrees. He heard the distinctive sound of a seat being pulled down into position directly behind him and someone sitting and placing what sounded like two or more cases or personal items in the seat next to her and unzipping what sounded like a portfolio—for it was definitely a female, there was a smell not only of floral perfume but of makeup, which has a distinct complex of scents in a warm room, as well as some type of floral shampoo, and Cusk could actually feel the twin disks of her eyes' pressure on the back of his head, since he could easily calculate that his head was at least partly within the girl's sight line of the podium. By watching the presentation, she would also be looking at at least part of the rear of Cusk's head, and also his neck's rear, which his short haircut left bare, meaning any droplets that might emerge from the rear of his hair might be clearly visible.

'That's not the point. The point is efficiency and economy, and the reason why we'll be going over the specs and layout of the Martinsburg M1 in detail in the next hour. We cannot overemphasize this. You are not inspectors—your job is not to catch every last little error and discrepancy and forward the 1040 for audit.'

'That would overwhelm District offices, whose audit resources are severely limited.'

'The truth—there is capacity in the present Audit Division to audit one-seventh of a percent of all 1040s and 1120s filed this year.'

'—although this year you'll be mostly occupied with 1984 returns, since there's an average ten-month lag between filing and exams, although in the Midwest Region they've got this down to closer to nine.'

'The *point,*' the CTO said with a bit of an edge to her voice, 'is that your job is to determine which returns give evidence of maximum auditability in terms of (a) profitability, and (b) expediency. Which are interlinked, since the more involved and time-consuming the audit, the more expensive it is for the Service, and the lower the net increase to the US Treasury at audit's end. At the same time, it is true that egregiousness of misreporting is tied to profitability, since negligence penalties kick in at certain pre-set levels of misreporting—'

'—as well as interest on all moneys due—'

'—which adds, sometimes significantly, to the audit's net proceeds.'

The worse it got, the colder the air from the overhead vent should have felt, by contrast. But perversely it didn't—the hotter Cusk's internal temperature got, the warmer the downdraft felt, until at a certain point it was like a scirocco or the air from an opened oven—positively hot. Cusk was not exactly having an attack, but he was in the fluttery initial stages of an attack, which in certain ways was worse because it could go either way. He had broken a light sweat, but this was not the problem—the nearby girl was behind him, and as long as the heat and sweat didn't escalate into a full-fledged attack, his haircut's rear would disguise any droplets of sweat. Only if it escalated into a real attack where the bits of sweat on his scalp beneath his hair grew and accreted into a density where they became actual droplets and followed gravity down over his exposed neck was there any real chance of the woman behind him noticing and seeing him as repulsive or weird. There was, by way of prophylaxis, the option of looking back and determining the age and attractiveness of the female examiner whose perfume and the faint leather scent of what was probably a purse enveloped Cusk. Since the room's clock was on the room's rear wall, there was an obvious excuse for turning quickly and looking backward.

At the podium, the Personnel aide was recounting the massive decentralization of the Service following the King Commission findings of 1952, which placed far greater authority and autonomy in the hands of the fifty-eight District offices, and the current partial re-centralization of processing and automated audit functions through Martinsburg and the Regional Centers, referring both to the 'era of Region' and something called 'the Initiative' of which Cusk had never heard. Cusk had not attended either of the twelve-week introductory sessions at the IRS's National Training Centers in Indianapolis and Rotting Flesh LA, both of which were filled through 1985. Instead, he had answered a recruiting advertisement in *Today's Accountant* magazine, to which Elkhorn-Brodhead's library had subscribed. Cusk had had a part-time stacking job in this library as part of his financial aid package.

'There are two sets of Master Files, in essence one for business entities and one for individuals, in sets that are maintained for three-year periods—'

'Three years corresponding to the audit window for a given return, meaning we have until April 15 of next year to audit and recover taxes due on returns filed for 1982 taxes, some of which may cross your desk as parts of coordinated exam programs generated either through Compliance or Martinsburg.'

Cusk was now fighting desperately to attend to every last syllable enunciated at the podium. It was his one chance not to begin dwelling on his core temperature and perspiration, which were now severe enough that he felt a sort of yarmulke of heat at his head's crown, which was one of four main symptoms of a true attack. He knew his face was now starting to gleam with sweat, which was the main reason he had opted not to turn around and get a general attractiveness-level on the tardy female examiner behind him—which could either have possibly forestalled the attack or kick-started it into a full-out attack in which he would be unable to feel or pay attention to anything except his prodigious flow and feelings of uncontrollable heat and total panic at the idea of being seen sweating this way.

The Personnel aide was describing the 3,312 employees at IRS Post 047 in terms of both shift—58 percent worked the 7:10 A.M.–3:00 P.M. (I) shift, 40 percent 3:10–11:00, plus some janitorial + physical plant activity overnight—as well as percentage breakdown of Exams, Clerical, Data Processing, and Administration, most of which Cusk missed because he had entered the incipient stages of an actual attack where his attention telescoped and the state of his own body and its emission of perspiration occupied almost 90 percent of his conscious awareness. He could hear the female behind him clicking her ballpoint pen in a nervous and arrhythmic way, and once a sound that had to be her uncrossing and recrossing her legs in what sounded like sheer hose, a sound that sent a terrible wave of internal heat through Cusk, and caused the first felt drops to go running from armpits down his torso's sides beneath the dress shirt. He automatically lowered his head during an attack, as well as slumping as far down in his plastic seat as would be inconspicuous, seeking to make himself as small as possible, visually, in terms of the woman behind him, whom he imagined by now to be a heart-stoppingly pretty girl of about Cusk's own age, with extraordinary posture and composure and a round porcelain face with intimidating blue eyes and overall an almost European hauteur about her. In short, she was Cusk's fantasy woman—which was as it were the price he paid for being too petrified with fear and self-consciousness to turn around and feign a look at the clock (which read 3:10 p.m.) in order to gauge the woman's threat in reality. The Compliance Training Officer, he could hear, was alluding to a page in the Exam Orientation Booklet that the current slide on the screen was a representation of that turned out to be exact, item for item, as Cusk lowered his running head further and pretended to study the relevant page of the booklet, circumspectly wiping away each fallen drop of perspiration before it could pucker its dime-sized section of the page, in case anyone would ever need to borrow his booklet and wonder what kind of grotesque, creepy thing had happened to p. B-3's diagram.

Cusk began gauging the exact distance to the exit in terms of both seconds and number of footsteps, another part of his brain calculating angles, sight lines, and intensities of light at various posts along the path of retreat—at as it were the periphery of his attention. Instinctively, he understood that not every item on the Rote Exams checklist was going to be equally important.

'What we have here are phases or the elements of triage,' the CTO said, then stopped briefly while the Personnel aide defined *triage* for those unfamiliar with the medical term. Claude Sylvanshine, three rows up and four seats to the left of Cusk, was battling between trying to resummon the distinctions between §162 and §212(2) deductions related to rental properties and data incursions of the annual rainfall in Zambia for even-numbered years since 1974, the latter appearing as highlighted columns on the page of a WHO atlas whose editor in chief had some form of psychomotor debility.

'If you think about it, you are not going to want to file a Memo 20 on a return just because, say, its Line 11 appears to understate alimony received by $200.'

'Since the additional tax due on $200 of income is less than 5 percent of the additional cost of conducting an audit.'

'You might, however, file a 20(a) and send the return to Automated Collections for a letter audit.'

'That will depend on your group protocols as stated by your Group Manager and group protocols packet in group orientation.'

'Which, in turn, will depend on your group assignment.' Someone whose pile of luggage was in the seat next to Sylvanshine several rows up raised his hand to ask what a group was in terms of Rote Exams assignments. What was odd was that there were no data incursions for Sylvanshine on the mysterious child that Dr. Lehrl traveled with and kept near him at all times but never seemed to talk to. Sylvanshine knew that it was not Dr. Lehrl's child, but that was only because Reynolds had told him so. It was as if the child were surrounded by a sort of impermeable factual membrane, or inhabited a fact vacuum. The big data Sylvanshine got for David Cusk, whose name he did not know, were the dimensions of his home's bathroom's medicine chest's mirror and certain temperature readouts in twin columns with the left column's numbers higher and illuminated in a kind of cheesy emergency red.

Page 16 had a diagram of the Compliance Branch's Rote Exams' Chalk—Team—Group—Pod organizational structure.

'The standard triage works like this. The M1 printout from Martinsburg will already note and list certain incongruities, either in arithmetic or a cross-reference of, say, an ex-spouse's return's Line 29 with your return's Line 11—'

'That's one reason the returns are forwarded to Exams—Martinsburg catches something.'

'Others are forwarded because of criteria that may, as far as you're concerned, appear almost random.'

'Another advantage of the Master Files—now over 50 percent of the arithmetical and cross-file verification takes place automatically at Martinsburg, which vastly increases your efficiency and the number of returns this Post can process and reach audit determinations on.'

'Though volume and throughput are no longer the criteria by which a Post's performance is judged and evaluated.'

An involuntary grimace went over the Personnel aide's face as he spoke. Sylvanshine knew this aide's shoe size and total blood volume, but not his name.

'The evaluative criteria now concern return on audit,' the CTO said.

Without looking at it, the Personnel aide held aloft a Fornix twelve-column computer card and a sheet of printout.

The CTO said, 'These represent Memo PP-47 plus a subsection for one's Pod, Group, Team, Detail, and personnel margin.'

'Margin refers to the ratio of additional tax assessed through audit to costs.'

'—Including your own salary, benefits, housing allowance if any, etc.'

'—It's the new Bible,' said the Personnel aide.

Sylvanshine, his eyes rolling up slightly white, received a whole slew of facts about the CTO that he did not wish to know, including the specs of her mitochondrial DNA and the fact that it was ever so slightly nonstandard due to her mother's having taken thalidomide four days before it was abruptly yanked from the shelves. Training Officer Pam Jensen had a .22 revolver in her purse—she had promised herself a bullet in the roof of her mouth after her 1,500th training presentation, which at current rates would be July 1986.

'In the bad old days, it was throughput.'

'The average rote examiner could clear between twenty-seven and thirty files per day.'

'Now it could be four, five files a day—if your Audit-to-Cost ratios are good, you're in line for an outstanding six-month performance review.'

'Of course, the more files you throughput each day, the wider a field of possibilities for high-ratio files you're going to have, and the better your chances of filing 20s that realize substantial gains.'

'But you don't want to concentrate so hard on getting through as many files as possible that you fail to identify especially profitable returns.'

'We prefer not to use the term "profitable,"' the CTO said. 'We prefer the term "noncompliant."'

'But a flamboyantly noncompliant return could be operating off such a low Line 23 that it's actually more efficient to forbear on it but to 20 the return right next to it, which, while containing few errors or incongruities, actually realizes a far higher audit assessment.'

'These are matters best left to your group orientation.'

Now actual drops of sweat were falling off the ends of Cusk's hair, as an inaudible scream resounded inside him.

'Right,' the CTO said. 'Let's have a break and get you freshened up, and we'll proceed with general criteria for Audit/No Audit decisions.'

There was going to be a break. David Cusk had not allowed himself to consider this. The lights would come up. Everyone would get up and leave at the same time. If he stayed, the beautiful girl behind him would see his sopped collar and the V-shaped darkening of sweat on his blue dress shirt, which it had been cocky and idiotic of him to wear instead of the more prudent and undarkenable white. He would sit there hunched over, pretending to study the M1 printout schema in his orientation packet, his core temperature well into three digits, drops of visible perspiration falling from the ends of his hair on all four sides to dot the packet, the arms of his shirt, the sizzling side of his nozzle lamp—there would be no way people could miss it. If he got up, though, and joined the crowds moving up the ramped aisles to the two exit doors, there would be no way people could fail to see what was happening with him, including the beautiful haughty

French or maybe even Italian woman behind him. It was the nightmare scenario. Thinking this way was all but guaranteed to cause an attack, which was the absolute last thing in the world David Cusk wanted. He willed himself to raise his head. The hot spotlight he felt on him did not exist. The woman behind him was a person, had her own troubles, and wasn't paying close attention to him—that was an illusion. The only thing that mattered about his head was that it was in her way, that she had to cross her thighs tight and sit way over to the side to see the podium and screen, where a split-slide shot of two desks wavered while the CTO tried to focus the projector with a handheld appliance connected to the projector by a cord that had gotten tangled around one of her legs.

Sylvanshine, before the morning of travel, had forgotten to wash the shampoo from his hair. It was this that gave him the flame-shaped coiffure.

David Wallace, meanwhile, was not enjoying any general orientation with slick slide show. Instead, he had been conducted (by someone who was not Ms. Neti-Neti)—with no opportunity to eat anything—to the REC Annex and a small room in which he and four other men, all GS-13s, listened to a presentation of the Minimum Tax on Preferences, which evidently had its origin in the Democratic administration of Lyndon Johnson in the 1960s. The room was small, stuffy, and had no whiteboard or A/V facilities. It did, though, smell strongly of Dry Erase Marker. All the other men in the room were conservatively dressed and hatted and very serious, with Treasury notebooks that came in zip-up leatherette folders with the IRS seal and motto embossed on the cover, which David Wallace had not received, and was taking notes in his private notebook folded over so that the IGA price tag in the upper-right corner was not visible.

The presentation was dust-dry and appeared to be very high-level and was made by someone dressed in a black suit and black vest over what appeared to be either a white turtleneck—which would have been bizarre in such hot weather—or one of those detachable Victorian starched collars that men used to put on and fastened with studs as the very final part of the Victorian dressing process. He was very clipped and impersonal and all-business. He seemed very severe and austere, with great black hollows in his cheeks and under his eyes. He looked a little like a popular representation of death.

'We will note, however, that RA '78 revised the expansionist tendencies of the '76 provisions by removing both long-term capital gains deduction and excess itemized deductions from the index of relevant preferences.' The term *preferences* had been used several times already. It goes without saying that David Wallace didn't know what the term *preferences* meant, or that they were Congress's clever way of reducing a certain income group's tax burden without lowering its tax rate—one simply allowed special deductions or provisions that exempted certain portions of income from the taxable base, provisions collectively known in the Service as preferences. Later, thanks mainly to Chris Acquistipace, David Wallace would figure out that the MPT/AMT Group was tasked to enforce certain special provisions that the '76 and '80 acts had put in place to keep extremely wealthy individuals and S corps from paying, through the use of what are called 'tax shelters,' in effect, no tax at all. The Immersive Group to which David Wallace was assigned was part of the Immersive AT/S Pod (for Alternative Tax/Shelters). It would be embarrassing to state outright how long it took David Wallace to figure this out, even after several days of ostensibly examining files.

'We note, however, that the '78 act also added to the list of eligible preferences the excess of Intangible Drilling Cost deductions over any and all reported income from oil and gas production, effectively attacking the energy-based shelters of the mid-seventies oil shock, as in §312(n) of the revised code.' The way David Wallace was pretending to take notes was that he was simply copying down every last word or phrase the instructor uttered, much as he had for those college lecture classes in which he'd been hired to take notes for someone who was forced to miss class by a ski trip or extreme hangover. It was one reason why David Wallace's left hand was way more muscled and substantial—especially the muscle between his thumb and forefinger, which bulged when the pencil was pressed to the paper—than his right. He could transcribe like the wind.

'The provisions most relevant to your Memo 20 protocols are that '78 increased the ATP tax rate to 15 percent and established the standard ATP exemption to the larger of (a) $30,000 or (b) 50 percent of the requisite tax due for the *current year only*, a provision which the Master Files render otiose but which the '80 act's provisions failed to address.'

One of the GS-13s raised his pen—not his hand, but just his pen with a small cool move of his wrist—and asked some kind of absurdly recondite question that David Wallace didn't write down because he was flexing and unflexing his hand to ameliorate something that happened if he transcribed for more than a few minutes, which is that his left hand assumed a sort of automatic writerly claw shape and stayed that way after he finished transcribing, sometimes for more than an hour, forcing him to hide the hand in his pocket.

'As of March of 1981, and subject to refinement in the case of fiduciaries and certain specialized industries such as if memory serves timber, sugar, and select legumes, the relevant provisions this group is required to examine for ATP computation are, excluding code sections except where immediately relevant, which sections you'll find cross-indexed in your 1M specs 412, (1) Excess of accelerated depreciation on section 1250 property over straight-line depreciation. (2) Consequent to TRA '69, excess of sixty-month amortization of certain items associated with pollution-control, child-care facilities, mining safety, and national historic sites over straight-line depreciation. (3) Excess of percentage depletion over a property's adjusted basis at year's end. (4) Bargain elements in qualified stock options—TRA '76. (5) Excess IDC over fossil income as mentioned above.' (David Wallace had no time to look above in his notes. He was trying to circle words and terms he didn't know, figuring he could find a library. This list was not in his manual—they were given no manuals. It seemed expected that they'd already know this stuff. In order to deal with his feelings of confusion and fear, Wallace had opted to turn himself more or less into a transcription machine.) '(6) Being the excess of accelerated depreciation over straight-line depreciation on Section 1245 property leased to another.'

The man stood totally still as he spoke. David Wallace didn't think he had ever before seen someone who didn't fidget in at least a few idle, unconscious ways when he spoke in public. The bodily stillness would have been more thought-provoking if David Wallace had felt less panicked and overwhelmed, and besides automatizing himself by transcribing, David Wallace was doing the other main compensatory thing he did when he was in a room where everyone seemed to understand exactly what was being talked about but him—which had happened in certain social situations at Philo High, at which David Wallace had not been part of any one particular clique but had hung out on the fringes of several different groups, from second-tier athletes to student council and A/V wonks, and was often privy to gossip or references to group situations he had no direct knowledge of, but had to stand there grinning and nodding like he knew exactly what was being referred to. Not to mention once when in a burst of absurd half-drunken freshman hubris he'd accepted a massive assignment that involved auditing a Russian Existential and Absurdist Literature class and writing the papers for a wealthy and tormented son of a Rhode Island State Supreme Court justice who was actually enrolled in the class and discovering that not only all the reading and critical background but the seminar itself was actually held in Russian, which David Wallace did not know or speak one garbled syllable of, and had to sit there with an enormous rigid grin, transcribing the phonetic versions of whatever unearthly and incredibly rapid sounds were being made by everyone else in the room every Tuesday and Thursday from 9:00 to 10:30 for three weeks before he was able to think of a plausible excuse and backed out of the arrangement. Leaving the client—who was still enrolled—with his own very special sort of existential dilemma. The point is that this is what David Wallace did in these situations, which was to assume and hold by main force an enormous grin that he imagined communicated ease and confident familiarity with whatever was going on but in fact, unbeknownst to him, in its rigid distension and lack of eye-involvement, together with the skin situation, actually looked like the agonized rictus of someone having the skin of his face slowly torn off, which luckily for him all the room's GS-13 Immersive Exam transfers and CTO shelter specialists were too serious and intent and engaged with the anti-shelter protocols—for that's what the Team to which David Wallace was mis-ID'd and erroneously assigned through no fault of his own (though this orientation might have been the place to put up his hand) turned out to be, the examination and evaluation of individual and limited-partnership shelters in realty, agriculture, and leveraged leasing, which was a small but serious component of the Spackman Initiative—to notice in anything more than a peripherally uncomfortable way, as well as David Wallace's youth, corduroy suit (which was the IRS equivalent of a Speedo and floppy clown shoes), and absence of hat.

A/NA, projected on its own b/w slide, was explained as the entire thrust and raison of Rote Exams.

'Are you cops?'

The Personnel aide raised his hands and shook them and shouted out 'Nooo.' This was the same fake evangelist bit Sylvanshine had seen at the Philadelphia REC when he was twenty-two years old. The Personnel aide's coin collection was kept in a portable safe in the rear of his mother or grandmother's closet, judging by the styles of dresses and coats on the rack overhead.

'Are you judges of civic virtue?'

'Nooo.'

'Are you sadistic bureaucrats arbitrarily deciding which TPs' lives to make miserable by subjecting them to the anxiety and inconvenience of an audit, trying to squeeze every last drop of blood from the neck you've got your boot on?'

'No.'

'In essence, in today's IRS, you're businessmen.'

'And businesswomen. Businesspersons. Or rather in the employ of what you're urged to consider a business.'

'Which returns will be profitable to audit?'

'How do you determine this?'

'Different Exam groups do it different ways. Your group orientation will have the specifics.'

Aide: 'Or your Team, since some Group Managers here have different Teams tasked to different criteria.'

'You can almost think of them as filters—what gets through, what gets Memo 20'd and routed to District.'

'Or signs, flags—at least that some return deserves an exhaustive exam.'

'You won't be going over every last return with a microscope.'

'You want to work smart as well as fast.'

'And fast means some you'll know right away—this audit wouldn't produce anything.'

'That's the criterion—will an audit produce a maximal increase when the cost of the audit is subtracted?'

'So that's one thing to discard—the idea that you're guardians of civic virtue.'

'There's another common misapprehension to disregard. Does anyone have any idea what it is?'

David Cusk had a terrible, totally ghastly impulse to raise his hand. Part of his strategy for surviving the close-order mingling of the break until he could make it to a restroom had been to think hard about the final projected image on the slide projector's screen, which the Training Officer never had gotten to quite resolve into focus but had been a split-screen view of two desks or tables, one strewn with papers and forms, plus a couple of items whose bright colors indicated they might have been food wrappers, the other clean and neat with items in piles and labeled baskets. Cusk was pretty sure the CTO wanted to stress order and organization and to banish the idea that a slovenly desk was the sign of a productive worker. Meanwhile, no one else had raised their hand. The idea came again of raising his hand and having the CTO point to him over all the turning heads, volunteering for the spotlight of all those people's attention, including the exotic Belgian transfer or émigré, whom Cusk had managed to avoid during the break, from which he had returned early, and did not know that the woman's glasses were so thick that if he'd ever seen her he'd have been able to tell that she was practically blind, at least in terms of objects more than three or four feet away, her eyes shriveled and oddly puckered in the irises, filled with cracks and fissures like a dry riverbed—she was about as exotic as a fire hydrant, and roughly the same shape—and he wouldn't have been as worried about being seen by her as wet or sweating. In any event, he was correct, it emerged:

'The common misapprehension is that a messy desk is a sign of a hard worker.'

'Get over the idea that your function here is to collect and process as much information as possible.'

'The whole mess and disorder of the desk on the left is, in fact, due to its excess information.'

'A mess is information without value.'

'The whole point of cleaning off a desk is to get rid of the information you don't want and keep the information you do want.'

'Who cares which candy wrapper is on top of which paper? Who cares which half-crumpled memo is trapped between two pages of a Revenue Ruling that pertained to a file three days back?'

'Forget the idea that information is good.'

'Only certain information is good.'

'*Certain* as in some, not as in a hundred percent confirmed.'

'Each file you examine in Rotes will constitute a plethora of information,' the Personnel aide said, stressing the second syllable of *plethora* in a way that made Sylvanshine's eyelids flutter.

'Your job, in a sense, with each file is to separate the valuable, pertinent information from the pointless information.'

'And that requires criteria.'

'A procedure.'

'It's a procedure for processing information.'

'You are all, if you think about it, data processors.'

The next slide on the screen was either a foreign word or a very complex acronym, each letter in bold and also underlined.

'Different groups and teams within groups are given slightly different criteria that help inform what to look for.'

The Personnel aide was thumbing through his laminated outline.

'Actually there's another example of the information thing.'

'I think they've got it.' The CTO had a way of turning one foot out perpendicular to its normal direction and tapping it furiously to signal impatience.

'But it's right here under the desk thing.'

'You mean the deck of cards?'

'The checkout line.'

They seemed to believe their mikes were off.

'Christ.'

'Who'd like to hear another example illustrating the idea of collecting information versus *processing* data?'

Cusk was feeling solid and confident, as he often did after a series of attacks had passed and his nervous system felt depleted and difficult to arouse. He felt that if he'd raised his hand and given an answer that turned out not to be correct it wouldn't have been that big of a deal. 'Whatever,' he thought. The 'whatever' is what he often thought when he was feeling jaunty and immune from attack. He had twice actually asked women out when in this cocky, extroverted, hydrotically secure mood, then later failed to show up or call at the appointed time. He actually considered turning around and saying something jaunty and ever so slightly flirtatious to the noisome Belgian swimsuit model—on the upswing, he now *wanted* people's attention.

At age eight, Sylvanshine had data on his father's liver enzymes and rate of cortical atrophy, but he didn't know what these data meant.

'There you are at the market while your items are being tallied. There's an individual price for each item, obviously. It's often right there on the item, on an adhesive tag, sometimes with the wholesale price also coded in the corner—we can talk about that some other time. At checkout, the cashier enters the price of each grocery, adds them up, appends relevant sales taxes—not progressive, this is a current example—and arrives at a total, which you then pay. The point—which has more information, the total amount or the calculation of ten individual items, let's say you had ten items in your cart in the example. The obvious answer is that the set of all the individual prices has much more information than the single number that's the total. It's just that most of the information is irrelevant. If you paid for each item individually, that would be one thing. But you don't. The individual information of the individual price has value only in the context of the total; what the cashier is really doing is discarding information. What you arrive at the cash register with is a whole lot of information, which the cashier runs through a procedure in order to arrive at the one piece of information that's valuable—the total, plus tax.'

'Get rid of the layman's idea that information is good. That the more information the better. The phone book has lots of information, but if you're looking for a phone number, 99.9 percent of that information is just in the way.'

'Information per se is really just a measure of disorder.' Sylvanshine's head popped up at this.

'The point of a procedure is to process and reduce the information in your file to just the information that has value.'

'There's also the matter of using your time most efficiently. You're not going to spend equal time on each file. You want to spend the most time on the files that look most promising in terms of yielding the most net revenue.'

'Net revenue is our term for the amount of additional revenue generated by an audit less the cost of the audit.'

'Under the Initiative, examiners are evaluated according to both total net revenue produced and the ratio of total additional revenue produced over total cost of additional audits ordered. Whichever is the least favorable.'

'The ratio is to keep some rube from simply filling out a Memo 20 on every file that hits his Tingle in hopes of jacking up his net.' Cusk considered: An examiner who filed no Memo 20s ever would have a ratio of 0/0 which is infinity. But the net revenue total would, he reflected, also be 0.

'The point is to develop and implement procedures that let you determine as quickly as possible whether a given file merits closer examination—'

'—that closer examination itself involving some type or types of procedures blended with your own creativity and instinct for smelling a rat in the woodwork—'

'—although at the beginning of your service, as you're gaining experience and honing your skills, it will be natural to rely on certain tested procedures—'

'—a lot of these will vary by group or team.'

'Incongruities on the Master Files, for one thing. That's pretty obvious. Disagreement of W-2s plus 1099s with stated income. Disagreement of state return with 1040—'

'But by how much? Below what floor do you simply let an incongruity go?'

'These are the sorts of matters for your group orientation.'

Sylvanshine now knew that two separate pairs of new wigglers were actually, unbeknownst to them, related, one pair through a liaison five generations ago in Utrecht.

David Cusk was now feeling so relaxed and unafraid that he was almost getting drowsy. The two trainers sometimes established a rhythm and concert that was soothing and restful. Cusk's tailbone was a tiny bit numb from settling back and slumping slightly in his seat, resting his elbow casually on the foldout desk, the heat of the little lamp of no more direct concern than news of the weather somewhere else.

'Who has an unusually big dip in income or rise in deductions compared to previous years? These are just samples.'

'A major one—who has been fruitfully audited within the past five years? This appears on some, but not all, of the Martinsburg printouts.'

'—Sometimes you have to order additional specs from the Master Files.'

'But be disciplined about it. Avoid the temptation to think that you always need more information. You can drown in it.'

'Plus it's expensive.'

'Get to know your cart boy. Your cart boy is the GS-7 who liaisons with the examiners and the Technical Pod, where data processors can get you additional information from the Master Files if you fill out a DR-104 data requisition form.'

'Not all of them are boys. "Cart boy" is just a more historical term.'

'Plus cart boys are who keep the files circulating, particularly picking up files that you've cleared and keeping your Tingle's in-box filled.'

'They do not bring refreshments or do personal errands.'

Cusk was considering the possible advantages of being a cart boy if being an examiner turned out to be too dangerous in terms of subjecting him to attacks and making it difficult to leave the area. Cart boys sounded as if they were in more or less constant motion, and constant motion meant constant chances to nip into the restroom and check the sweat situation and wipe sweat off his forehead. On the other hand, it would probably mean a large pay cut. A small gurgling noise Cusk heard behind him at five-minute intervals was the sound of Toni Ware's glasses' auto-lubricant in her eyes.

'You'll meet your cart boy in your Group and Team orientations.'

'Other general examples: Who's in a largely cash business?'

'Who's got unusually high charitable deductions compared to the averages for his income level?'

'Who's getting divorced? For reasons they'll go into if relevant to your Group, divorces tend to generate unusually high net revenue from audits.'

'Partly because of liquidation of assets, partly because the proceedings often expose a great deal of the auditable situation without our having to incur the time and cost and uncovering things like hidden income.'

'Who's got unusually high depreciation write-offs that should be amortized over several years? Over 40 percent of accelerated depreciation on 1040s is illicit or at least challengeable in audit.'

'These are all just small, random examples of criteria.'

'You can't use them all—you won't be able to turn your files around fast enough.'

'Some teams examine each file in the context of the two prior years' returns. These are called interval terms. The point is to look for large dips in income or spikes in deductions.'

'Intuition plays a part. You can tell something's off. You can justify taking extra time on a file.'

'This is the great advantage of human examiners. Intuition, creativity.'

'Some people have a special talent for smelling a rat.'

'Guessing doesn't account for the nets of certain great examiners, some of whom are at this Post—'

'A rat that's worth pursuing.'

§28

10 Laws of IRS Personnel

All GS-9 Examiners want to be GS-11 Examiners. All GS-11 Examiners want to be Auditors. All Collections want to be CID. All Auditors want to be Appeals Officers or Supervisors. All Supervisors want to be Group Managers. All CIDs want to be almost anything that doesn't involve site surveillance. Some Appeals Officers want to be Group Managers. All Group Managers want to be Deputy District Directors, or else they dream of being Examiners again, alone at a desk with no one to bother you. All Deputy District Directors want to be District Directors—it's the ones who tell you they don't to watch out for. Some District Directors want to be DRECs or DRSCs or Regional Commissioners, but all these are political appointments, and the best the District Director can do is make their District's output look really good and hope someone notices. Output is the ratio of collected tax to District expenses. It's the District's net profit. The Service code is very simple as the DDDs say as they circle the DD, plotting: Output or Kaput; Supply or Die; Revenue or Au Revoir. Au Revoir almost always means backwater postings.

§29

'I only have one real story about shit. But it's a doozy.'

'Why shit?'

'What is it about shit? We're repelled but fascinated.'

'I'm not fascinated, I can tell you that.'

'It's like watching a car wreck, impossible to tear the eyes away.'

'My fourth-grade teacher had no eyelashes. Mrs. Something.'

'I mean I'm bored, too, but why shit?'

'My earliest memory of shit is dog shit. Remember as a kid how potent a presence and threat dog shit was? It seemed to be all over. Every time you played outside, somebody was stepping in it, and then everything stopped and it was like, "OK, who stepped in it?" Everybody has to check their shoes, and sure enough somebody had it on their shoe.'

'Embedded in the sole. In the pattern.'

'Impossible to scrape off.'

'New was always wet and yellow and horrible, the most horrible. But old got embedded more deeply in the sole. You had to set the shoes aside until it dried and then try to scrape out the sole's pattern with a stick or a rusty old knife out of the garage.'

'What time is it?'

'What are we supposed to see in all this? Somebody could go right by.'

'But it never got all the way out. Scrape and scrape. You'd have to try and run the sole under the faucet and wet it then and try to scrape out the rest.'

'The garage always had old butter knives, coffee cans full of screws and nails and little metal doodads that nobody ever even knew the function of.'

'And whoever had it on their shoe, it was discovered, then that person had some kind of terrible power.'

'Nobody'd have anything to do with him until he got it out.'

'Instant butt. Odd man out.'

'Like it was ever his fault if you were all playing football or at recess or whatever and somebody had the random misfortune to step in it. Suddenly it wasn't that he'd stepped in shit so much as *become* shit.'

'The way the cruelty in a group of kids swirls and shifts, at any moment you become the target, everybody constantly shifting for position all the time—now you're the one being cruel, now you're the target of someone else's cruelty.'

'And nothing like peeing or pooping your pants in a group playing baseball or kick the can or whatever out of excitement or a reluctance to leave the game even for a moment to turn you into the target of everyone's scorn and ridicule. Forever after you were the kid who shit his pants playing kick the can and it took only a few tackles for everyone to know it was you and it could be years later, it could be your junior prom, and everybody still knew you as the kid who shit his pants in 1961.'

No one said anything. The spools' turning was the only sound. The fog made the streetlights ghostly. This was the fourth hour of a third-shift CID Surveillance on Peoria Hobby 'n Coin. There was no wind; the fog just hung there.

'But a terrible power, too, as a kid, to have come into contact with shit—you were the butt, but you could repel people just by coming at them with the part that had contacted the shit; you could make them run screaming.'

The two agents who were younger had sunglasses folded and clipped to their shirts' necks by one arm.

'Kids' obsession with shit and dog shit and coming into contact with shit has to be connected to toilet training and their own infancy, which at this age isn't that far behind them.'

'It might have been third grade. We took a long time figuring it out, what made her eyes look piggy like that. No eyelashes. She had hair, head-hair, and eyebrows, but her eyes were piggy and lashless and blue.'

As much as two minutes elapsed between each remark, sometimes. It was 2:10 and even the agents' small personal movements were languid and underwater.

'Which if you think about it remember in high school when guys got together the whole thing was insulting each other's mom and saying you'd had sex with their mom and how she wasn't any good and couldn't get enough? What do you suppose that was all about? The sexuality of everyone's mom becoming an issue just as everybody hits puberty.'

'My shit story. Hide-and-seek, gang of neighborhood kids, twilight. I'm running for home base and trip over decorative logs somebody bordered his driveway with and went flying and put my hands out to like shield the impact and what do you suppose happens.'

'No.'

'Yes. Both hands first into a big new yellow steamer. Which I can still almost smell.'

'Jesus not even on the shoes but the hands. The personal skin.'

'You bet. I have maybe a dozen vivid, seared-in memories of early childhood, this is one of them. The feeling, the color, the dispersal, the rising smell. I howled, screamed, and everyone of course comes running, and as soon as they see it *they're* screaming and 180ing and running from me, and I'm both crying and roaring like some kind of horrible shit-monster and chasing after them, horrified and repulsed but also somehow underneath it all glorious in my role as monster, with the ability to make them all scream in terror and run for home where everybody's porch lights are just starting to come on and the little fake lamps by their driveways are on automatic timers; it's that time of day.'

'The hands being especially close to your idea of your identity of who you are, adding to the horror. Exceeded only by the face in terms of closeness, maybe.'

'There was no dog shit on my face. I held my arms out straight in front of me in order to like hold my hands as far out away from me as was humanly possible.'

'That only added to the monster-aspect. Monsters almost always hold their arms out straight in front of them as they chase you. I would have run like hell.'

'They did. I remember on one hand I was both screaming in horror just like they were and on the other I was roaring with monstrousness as I'd chase first one and then sort of peel off to chase somebody else. There were cicadas in the trees and they were all screaming in rhythm and somebody's radio was on through an open window. I remember the smell coming off my hands and how they didn't look like my hands anymore at all and feeling like how was I going to open the door without getting shit on it or even if I rang the bell. There'd be shit on my parents' doorbell.'

'What'd you do?'

'Jesus, what'd your *mom* do? Did she scream? Did you stand outside moaning and kicking the door and trying to ring the bell with your elbow?'

'Our house had a knocker. I would have been screwed.'

'I bet some of the other kids were in their houses cracking the curtains to look out the front window at you like staggering around moaning from house to house with your hands out straight like Frankenstein.'

'It's not like a shoe which you can just take off.'

'I've got a story about shit, but it's not pretty.'

'I don't remember. The memory ends with the shit and my hands and trying to chase everybody, which is odd, because up to then the memory is extraordinarily clear. Then it just stops and I don't know what happened.'

'I'm assuming I haven't talked before about running around with this odd gang of guys at Bradley and the strange thing we got into junior year of breaking into people's dorm rooms and holding them down while Fat Marcus the Moneylender sat on their face.'

'I think I would have remembered.'

'This was at Bradley; you know the weird shit you get into. There were five or six of us and this senseless thing got started where it was a tradition to cruise the freshman dorms at about four in the morning and find an unlocked door and all burst in and we'd all hold the guy in bed down and Fat Marcus the Moneylender would take his pants down and sit on his face.'

'...'

'There was no reason to it. We just thought it was a gas.'

'Fat Marcus the Moneylender?'

'An enormous guy from the Chicago suburbs. Morbidly enormous. Always had cash and lent it out and kept his accounts in a small special ledger. Very careful bookkeeper, could compound daily without a calculator. Never even just Fat Marcus, it was always "the Moneylender." He was a Jew but I don't think that had anything to do with it. It was how he put himself through school after his parents had cut him off—this wasn't his first school but I don't remember his background too good.'

'Why the sitting on people's face?'

'The weirdness of it was the charm. That's all I can tell you. It was just something we started doing. I get a strange feeling even just thinking about how to describe it.'

'What did the guy in bed do?'

'The guy in the bed was not a happy camper, I can tell you that much. It would all happen real fast where we'd all just burst in and be on the guy before he was even awake. We'd each grasp an extremity and quick as shit Fat Marcus the Moneylender'd have his pants down and sit on the guy's face and stay there just long enough where the kid in the bed didn't smother. Then we'd be out of there just as fast as we came in. That was part of the whole point, so the guy in the bed probably didn't even know if it was real or a nightmare or what the hell it was.'

They weren't far off the Sticky; the fog was a storm coming in off the river. The very air was at attention. Two ledge-chested older women were peering in the window of the coin shop.

They all had unconscious habits of which maybe only Hurd, as the new one, was fully aware. Agent Lumm's habit on surveillance was in a blank absent way to use his front teeth to peel a tiny fragment of dead skin from his lip and put it on the tip of his tongue and gently blow it out his mouth to land somewhere invisible. He was wholly unaware that he did this, Hurd could tell. Gaines blinked slowly in a stony mindless way that reminded Hurd of a lizard whose rock wasn't hot enough. Todd Miller wore a corduroy coat with a sheepskin collar and bunched and unbunched his left sleeve; Bondurant stared at a point between his shoes on the van's rug as if it were a chasm. It seemed staggering to Hurd that no one smoked. He himself was an endless catalogue of tics and fidgets.

One probationary agent whose sunglasses hung from his collar wore twelve-hole Doc Martens whose holes Hurd had counted several times.

'How does Marcus the Moneylender pull his pants back up while you all are running out?'

A long silence ensued while Bondurant gave Gaines a prison-yard stare. Gaines said, 'You ever try to get dressed while you're running? Can't be done.'

'The guy thinking it might have been a dream until that is he gets up to shave and sees his nose squished flat and a big ass-imprint on his face.'

'Did he scream?'

'In a muffled way they all screamed. Of course they screamed. But the thing that was making them scream was also the thing that muffled the scream.'

'Some fat man's ass coming down and covering their face.'

'Speed and quiet were the essence of the operation, and this was important because this was breaking in and assault of a sort, and Fat Marcus had already been expelled from at least one place, and none of us were what you might call on the Dean's List, and let's don't forget this was 1971 and the draft board was just about standing at the front gate waiting for you if you got kicked out.'

'This is why Bondurant was in the war. In The Nam.'

'I was a G-2 bookkeeper in Saigon, dickhead. That's not The Nam.'

'But you're saying this is what got you drafted? Assaulting freshmen with a big Jew's ass?'

'I'm saying it was just something that started happening and that we pulled off numerous operations all up and down the underclass dorms with a hundred percent operational success until the day the door we found open belongs to this kid, *Diablo,* that everybody called Diablo the Left-Handed Surrealist, this Puerto Rican mural-painter scholarship from Indianapolis that was crazy, that for example lost his student-aid job in the faculty dining hall because one day he came in on what we're pretty sure was acid and set all the place settings at everybody's place with all knives, and saw visions and painted these spiky fluorescent Catholic murals on walls on warehouses down by the river, and was crazy—Diablo the Left-Handed Surrealist.'

'Didn't anybody at your school ever have names like Joe or Bill?'

'That for the most part nobody ever messed with because he was crazy as a fucking mudbug, this little hundred-pound spic kid from some Indianapolis barrio, but by this time the operation was a finely honed mechanism built for speed, that plus nobody even placed who it was until we'd all bursted in and deployed around the bed. I had the left ankle I remember, and Fat Marcus was up on the bed undoing his belt and getting his feet distributed on either side of what was usually the guy's pillow except this kid didn't use a pillow or even sheets; it was just the bare dorm mattress with those stripes on them.'

The only truly fat person Gestine Hurd had ever known had been a Special Examination GS-9 in the Oneida Post who'd spent the entire two years Hurd knew of him back-auditing an Oneida firm so tiny and specialized that it made nothing but the corrugated dividers that went into the cardboard boxes used to ship a very particular kind of tiny lightbulb that went into tiny brass lamps that clicked onto the top of frames that display-quality paintings in historical homes and country restaurants often hang in.

'Which should have alerted us to trouble, plus the fact that Diablo the Left-Handed Surrealist seemed already awake when we boomed the door and didn't sit up or yelp or rub his eyes or thrash around or struggle when we all came booming in and each grabbed us an extremity and Fat Marcus the Moneylender got up on the bed and commenced to lowering his gargantuan white ass down to his face; he just laid there very still with his eyes glittering with Latin cunning and all-around craziness. You didn't even want to know the decor, what-all was on the walls; if the operation's total surreal speed had allowed it, if we'd paid one bit of attention to the room or the expression on the kid's face on the mattress we could of stopped and reconnoitered and saved us all a lot of trouble and got to stay in school and not have to spend a fucking year in Saigon learning requisition-write-up accounting. Which I wouldn't wish on a dog.'

The spools turned slowly with a slight triple hiss. The IRS agents' expressions were those of Cub Scouts around a Storytime fire. A quick bob in the entry's mike's tape went unremarked.

'Waited until Fat Marcus the Moneylender's ass was right down next to him, touching his face but not with the full weight of the ass on him yet, and jerked up and bit into Fat Marcus's ass. And I'm not talking a lover-nip here, I'm talking a full front Doberman-type sinking of his whole frontal set of teeth into the buttock arc of Marcus's ass, so that even down by his ankle I could see blood going down the Surrealist's chin and see Fat Marcus the Moneylender's ass flexing as he reared back and let out a scream that made the windows shiver and knocked the two guys holding Diablo the Left-Handed Surrealist's shoulders back against the row of no-eye masks the spic's got on his wall that all fell and made a racket and could see the horrible thing of this unbelievably obese guy rearing back and up and trying with all his weight to get his ass out of the teeth of Diablo the Left-Handed Surrealist, who gentlemen just let me say wasn't letting go, the kid was a Gila monster, even as Fat Marcus had both hands hooked in the kid's nose's nostrils trying to peel him off his ass and Fat Marcus's main stooge Marvin "the Stooge" Flotkoetter actually bent in and was biting Diablo the Left-Handed Surrealist's ear and cheek, trying to make him let go, and both him and Diablo were growling and Diablo was shaking his head trying to tear the mouthful of ass clear out of Fat Marcus's ass and his nose and ear were bleeding and blood was just shooting I mean *arterially* shooting in all directions out of Marcus's ass and into the mattress and his pants and Fat Marcus took a shit in fear and pain and his screams brought everybody in pajamas and underwear and pimple cream and retainers to the still-open door, looking in at what looked of course later though none of us realized it at the time like a prison-type gang-type sexual assault gone wrong.'

§30

'The Deputy DD's a man-of-the-people type. But very much Glendenning's boy. 907313433, a full CPA, Sheehan is, a GS-13, nine years in. He was auditing out of District 10 in Chicago before he got the degree. Came over with Glendenning. Kind of Glendenning's hatchet man, very hail-fellow, let's all be friends, all smiles but the eyes go right through you. Liaisons with Internal. Not well-liked. Plus a fashion-plate. Looks like the original seventies hipster almost. Very if you know what I mean mod.'

There were sounds of Reynolds doing something unrelated.

'Meaning you got the sideburns, the bell-bottoms, the pale blue workshirt. The little leather thong thing around the neck. The whole package.'

'Spare us the Mr. Blackwell, Claude.'

'Totally Glendenning's boy. But a serious 3-D in his own right. Performance Reviews all 8-plus. Nary a 7. Made GS-11 in '77 on an independent Promotion Board bid; Glendenning had nothing to do with it. But Glendenning's boy.'

'So he'll fight it?'

'He's an implementer. Admin was his choice; he applied. If things come down through channels he won't fight you. But he won't help you. He implements.'

'Glendenning's got a lot of boys in 047, from what you're saying.' The slight rise and rounding of Reynolds's voice indicated he was knotting his tie.

'Glendenning's got a high level of Group Manager support. Rosebury and Danmeyer in Exams and Quarterlies might have come with him, their periods in Syracuse overlapped, but the rest were here before Glendenning got the kick. Not yet clear how much of the support is political versus sincere, which would indicate how much of an operator Glendenning's been at 047. I haven't been able to squeeze even a private bad word on him out of anybody. Of course that could mean several things.'

'You don't have to tell us what things mean,' without heat. Reynolds's big gray Motorola had a violin's chin-cup welded on so he could hold it with his neck alone and free his hands, which whenever Sylvanshine tried this with his own he either forgot and moved his head wrong and the thing fell on the floor and broke and he had to spend time figuring out how to requisition his fourth field phone of the year or else it gave him a stabbing pain somewhere near his shoulder blade. He held a regular touch-tone phone with one hand and bit dead skin from the edge of his thumbnail while he turned sheets on the clipboard.

'Chaney has a picture of her and Glendenning up on her office wall if you can believe it.'

'Chaney.'

'Julia Drutt Chaney, forty-four, GS-10, 952678315, Administrative Supervisor for 047B across the complex. Big, big woman. Large. Stanton-sized in Philly if you recall her. As in muumuus. As in when you see her coming across the quad thing it looks like several women all cohabiting in just one garment. Big red cheeks. But nobody's fool, Performance—'

'We're only interested in 047B for Audits, and that's collateral.' Sylvanshine was trying to recall the name of his second-grade teacher, who stood at the terminus of a long chain of idle thought whose medial steps he'd already forgotten but which had started with the maneuvers by which Reynolds had arranged to stay in DC and Martinsburg for several weeks and to keep Mel Lehrl's ear by offering to analyze Sylvanshine's initial field reports and reduce them to relevant fact-patterns for Lehrl before eventually joining Claude in this horrible place after all his usual strategies were exhausted. 'Let's concentrate on the steak and not the peas here Claudie boy what do you say.' Jocularity was a tone Reynolds often used with subordinates or those of lower GS rank, and both he and Claude knew that Sylvanshine would be looking for a way to repay the insult. 'The steak is Examination.'

'ADD for Exams is Rosebury, Eugene E., forty, GS-13, 907313433, sandy hair, tall, a little stooped, glasses don't quite fit or else his ears aren't symmetrical, looks somehow scholarly but that might be the pipe, smokes a pipe, Glendenning's boy right down the spine. Don't like his hair, something about his hair. Implementer. Wind-sniffer. Neither help nor impede.'

'Second AD is Yeagle? Yagle?'

'Is Gary NMI Yeagle. Just-call-me-Gary type. Strange-looking specimen. Big heavy slabbish face, but a long jaw, but soft, the jaw, hanging with fat, which together with the lantern jaw makes you feel like somebody's hitting you with a melting fist when you look at him. Thirty-nine no, sorry, -eight, glad-hander but in a different way from Sheehan because Sheehan's glad-handing is professional and strategic whereas with Yeagle you feel it's that he's just insecure and needs everyone to like him or the world explodes or something.'

'Which'd make him a potential weak link.'

'The sort who's very shy and nervous around you but tries to be very bluff and hearty and outgoing but can't manage it and so it's excruciating for everyone. A jaw you could plow snow with.'

'So Yeagle might be one of our boys if we're going to fine-target Mel's efforts in the intial stages.'

'Plus eyebrows out to here. I kid you not. Tolkien-like eyebrows on a thirty-eight-year-old man. Very intense smile he feigns into trying to make it look like a wicked grin or grimace by drawing these incredible brows down. The sort that shakes your hand with both of his. A GS-13 but a Group Manager since second quarter '78, so he may have something on the ball but I haven't seen it. Not the sort of hard driver you'd expect from a Group Manager in an Exams Post.'

'Glendenning promoted him?'

'Yeagle's records are sketchy. You might have somebody there pull down Yeagle's whole file; his one here's sketchy that I could find.' Sylvanshine's thumb was bleeding slightly and he looked about him for something unimportant to blot it on. Both he and Reynolds knew how very very different the substance and form of Sylvanshine's report would be if he were speaking to Merrill Lehrl, and though there was no doubt that this irked Reynolds to some degree it in no way made up for the jocularity and its implication. They both knew accounts were not yet square. Sometimes Sylvanshine pictured himself and Reynolds as partners in a kind of courtly dance, very stately and prescribed, so that the tiniest variations were what communicated personality. 'He and Sheehan are mildly interesting counterpoints in glad-handing. Can't say I like either of them. Yeagle wore the same tie three days last week. Carries the pipe around with him even when it's not going. Something that might have been a condiment stain on the tie. Don't like him, that odd pendulous jaw. Saw him dab at a nostril with the back of his hand the other day.'

Throat-noise on the other end. Tiny bits of some conversation at the fringe of their bandwidth were audible in silences; they made Sylvanshine think of strands of hair in a dusty brush. The sink was piled with dishes and half-full cartons of Chinese take-out he'd sworn to himself he'd clean up two days ago; looking at the sink made it hard to inhale.

'Tell Mel the best I can do is indications. Yeagle not yet a known quantity. Seems ineffectual, but that may be part of some larger strategic presentation. Recommend an Informal soonest after Mel gets in—loosen him up, get him talking. Possible. That's as far out on the limb as I can go with Call Me Gary at this point.'

'Anything re Glendenning himself yet then?'

'Haven't gotten in to see him. Busy guy. Constant motion. Seems purposefully busy instead of ineffectually or flailingly busy, which if it's true it's worth noting for Mel.'

'Thanks.'

Not the thumb exactly, but it was true that Sylvanshine was now sucking the edge of his thumb. 'Seen him in the halls of what-was-it, whatever building his and Sheehan's offices are in. Disorienting place, the photos don't do it justice for sheer podular confusion. Looks more like a small college or community college campus than anything. You do know my father taught at a community college.'

'So when you saw Glendenning in these unrecalled halls then . . .'

'Not much thus far. Tall silvery guy. Silver hair rigidly parted. The sort of older man you'd say "distinguished" or "formerly handsome." Medium-tallish I'd say. Nose looked a bit big but that was in moving profile.'

'Hey Claude, seriously, is there some process by which you decide I want to hear aesthetic appraisals? Is there reasoning by which somewhere inside you decide this is useful data to have in Mel's head when he starts working with these people? Don't strain now, but think about it and sometime tell me the process by which you decide I have to wait through incidentals on dress and carriage before I hear material that's going to help me do my job here.'

'*Your* job, is the point. Boil it down. Reduce to fact-pattern, relevance. My job's the raw data. Do I recall right? Was I the one who asked for the field first? Am I confused?'

But the distressed sounds were only Reynolds trying to get under the knot with his fingers to do the top button, which he had always had trouble with. Sylvanshine waited the normal interval looking at his thumb and trying to see if he could taste any actual blood—which taste always made him think of touching a nine-volt to his tongue as a kid but the exact association evaded him—and listened to at least try to identify the gender of the ghostly conversation on the line, and finally said:

'Though his secretary—one of them, he seems to have two though one might be an Admin or liaison with the Group Managers—sent a memo, it's in Mel's in-box, Welcome and heard some fine things from Henzke re the skill of the turnaround at 0104—that's Philly Collections, the Auto—'

'You have to tell me that, I wasn't there?'

'—Henzke re the Collections turnaround at Philly, etc., please call Mrs. Oooley—that's the head secretary—Mrs. Oooley soonest on your arrival and processing—'

'What's that supposed to mean? He has to go through orientation like some turdnagel?'

'I don't have it, it's still in Mel's box, which by the way it's a good in-box, same size and same row as the ADDs' and over the GM's although it's got Mel's name on tape over some other fellow's name but that doesn't necessarily mean anything unless it's still like that when he comes. And I've got SS putting his name on his door in that one building; I gave them the stencil personally tell him, and told them about the elevator thing so it's on the ground floor. Tell him the door's locked and the window outside's locked and you can't see through but from the distance of the doors on either side tell him it seems spacious. Unfortunately nearest loo's third floor; have him advise if we want to risk making a fuss about that, but it's corner just as requested. No boiling down there, you know he'll want that. Tell him the doors on either side are 15 and 16.4 and change, respectively, which is almost Philly-sized.'

'You let them see you using a tape measure on the surrounding doors?'

'Don't be a maroon. I've got a front door key already and keys to two of the remaining four. At night before returning to field-quarters you and I need to have a good long talk about before you see it and get your shorts in a tangle. Angler's Cove apartment complex. Enough said? Makes the first Rome apartment look lavish, to give you an—'

'The memo was from the secretary or from Glendenning personally you're saying.'

'The bad news is it's not in the main building, where Glendenning and the DDs' officers are, whatever it's called. They've got an odd nomenclature for facilities here just like Chicago.'

'This is still Mel's office you're talking about.'

'I'm going right down my notes just as field protocol you might recall states and the way you did in Rome. I'm afraid it's in the outbuilding where they do the Corporates; it's also got the UNIVAC in there. The building's a bit of a madhouse I'm afraid. The first floor where all the offices for the keypunch people are. You just need to get Mel ready for this so he doesn't come and see where they put him and start shitting little green men about it.'

'And you may recall initial field-briefing calls are to be ten to twelve minutes, if you've memorized the protocol.' Sylvanshine knew just what Reynolds was doing physically at this minute but he couldn't think of what the right word for it was, even to himself. Nor was he talking about losing his license in the bank's drive-through yesterday, which really when you came down to it might be Merrill Errol Lehrl's concern but was not Reynolds's concern by any stretch of the imagination, though he knew what he'd say. Sometimes Sylvanshine's thumbnails had funny little white calciumoid lines in them, sometimes they didn't. He worried about it at odd moments, what the lines signified. Not adjusting, *smoothing, smoothing* his tie, which if it was Saturday would be either the light green or the light blue with the little red lozenge shapes in it, both of which were faux silk and butt-smooth at all times anyway. It was an unconscious gesture Reynolds had, and worked as a tell in cards, and Sylvanshine had sacrificed all sorts of opportunities to score off bringing it to Reynolds's attention because he didn't want Reynolds conscious of his unconscious gestures in any way, since reading them equaled power. In Martinsburg Sylvanshine had the bigger bedroom because the lease was in his name, but in field-quarters Reynolds always got the bigger room. This time, Angler's Cove's squalor aside, the bedrooms were exactly the same size, the door-distance wasn't the only thing Claude had measured, and he knew what Reynolds's face would do when he saw. Merrill Errol Lehrl always arranged his own quarters.

'Glendenning himself sent the memo, or the secretary?'

Sylvanshine held the thumb flat and got the overhead light on it and turned it this way and that. 'You would not believe how hot it is here. And muggy. The air's like somebody breathing right in your face. Philly on its worst summer day doesn't equal. 047's drinking fountains aren't refrigerated; they're low white toilet-porcelain fountains like some elementary school and the water's room temperature, which is to say hot.'

Reynolds exhaled so the phone transmitted the sound. 'I apologize for the tone, Claude.'

'What tone?'

'All right? Happy now?'

'You overestimate me, friend.'

'And yes, I am your friend. We're a team. I shouldn't have squeezed your shoes with the underling-tone like I did. It's high-pressure this week. I've had the same tension headache all week. I don't feel well at all. And none of that's an excuse, and I really am apologizing.'

If there were lines they weren't visible. 'Secretary or head secretary sent it I'm afraid. Oooley, Carolyn or Caroline maybe. File not located, it's not on the Support router. Crisp little woman, dry tight little face. Sweater over her shoulders like a cape. Main building's air-conditioned out the wazoo; that's where Exams is, so tell Mel the good news is the work environment itself is AC'd already although no halon, but the VAX room's haloned so we can assume SS has the wherewithal; if you want I'll call and—'

'So the memo was from the secretary, not Glendenning himself.'

'I'd urge Mel not to read anything into that. Glendenning's been gone two days out of three. He's been up to Region twice since last Wednesday.'

'He's running to Region a lot already? You wait till now to include this and when you do it's an aside on the secretary's sweater?'

'From the way they approach her desk she's formidable, Oooley. You know how it is in the provinces. She may dominate Glendenning; she may be the real link. Small picture of a cat on her desk, but no visible cat hair on the sweater. Odd. And glasses on a little chain around her neck, those old-fashioned little silvery chains, what's the word. Potentially a formidable part of the equation. So far I've asked after the cat and given her a flower someone was selling on the median of the big road out here. To this comatose town. Tell Mel I'm working her already.' He didn't tell Reynolds there'd been no sign of the flower on her desk the next day.

Letting Sylvanshine hear him breathe again—'And did the memo specifically say heard good things from Henzke, from Bill, or from Bill Henzke?'

'Just Henzke.'

'Damn.'

'Other secretary or liaison or whatever's been gone. Supposedly young and the District knockout, two separate Collections fellows told me it's worth cooking up fallacious business and coming when Oooley's at lunch just for the full-frontal view.'

'I already apologized, Claude.'

'Rosebury's secretary's a big sheet-white woman named Bernays. Looks the ghost of a draft horse.'

Each Motorola mobile phone cost the Service $349 as opposed to the $380 retail and looked like an enormous walkie-talkie and weighed over two pounds and was something someone as dapper and diminutive as Reynolds Jensen Jr. looked a little silly holding.

'So. Let's sketch the week then.' Reynolds would be able to tell Dr. Lehrl they'd talked and he'd tried if what came next week wasn't what he wanted. Watching Reynolds try to maneuver politically was like watching a lumberjack dance, Harold Adny'd said. 'Need cogent relevant say again cogent relevant bios, Personnel data, evals, and impressions for Examinations by the seventeenth. This is the protocol I'm reading. The crew is what? There's Rosebury in Admin, there's this Yeagle as GM—group size is what, twenty? Exam budget's 2.4 times the size of Rome's, right, so what, twenty-two?'

'Twenty-four, maybe -five. There are some kind of unorthodox split-shift arrangements I haven't gotten a fact-pattern on yet, that Glendenning apparently vetted. Glendenning's done a lot of custom-tailoring of Exams which of course we can anticipate this will intensify. Say twenty-four to twenty-six, which doubles with then another whole twenty doing punch and sort work on cards during the Storm, though word is Glendenning's fought hard for Service personnel instead of Storm part-timers, which is understandable given the town; it's not like there's a sharp talent pool out there out here.'

'That's nice data. That's cogent.'

'Say twenty-six. Contact's been tough.'

'Guarded are they?'

'More like stupefied. They're full-timers. Glazed. What's the other word. Average burn here's three years. Obtundated is the word. Oh'—Sylvanshine winced at forgetting this before—'and the big one's that Glendenning's first big move on arrival was the elimination of first-years on Exams.'

'You're kidding.' By Service custom, graduates of the three national IRS Training Centers spent their first years assigned to Examinations, which was the most brutal and unpopular assignment in the Service. A percentage then hurried to pass their certified exams, since a GS-11 revenue agent must have a CPA, and Audits was the natural promotion out of Exams. That Glendenning had eschewed first-years in his Exams branch indicated something important, though neither of them was sure quite what. It was so important Reynolds didn't even take time to squeeze Sylvanshine's shoes for waiting till now to tell him. 'Mel you know is going to want follow-up. Move that immediately to number one on next week's protocol.'

'I provisionally agree.'

'Glad you agree.'

'Glad you're glad.'

'Outstanding.'

'Though this is pending the rest of the report, as when I get to flows and outputs.'

'Outstanding. What's the flow look like then?'

'First individual Exams is one room, couple dozen desks plus Yeagle's little frosted cubicle thing. Either the room's symmetries are off or there are rough divisions—might be one section of 1040, one of 1040A, a smaller one for Fats the way Keene was. There's a Corporate branch that's a whole separate room.'

'If Corporate changes over it won't be till after, they've run the experiment with the DIF so—'

'Hence my not mentioning it.'

'If you're cozy with Glendenning's dry-skin lady then you must have a line on the specs.'

'The specs are a mess. They're not even on cards. They use old 904 forms I haven't seen since the Training Center.'

'Huge surprise.'

'They're all in horrible old dark-green cabinets in a basement complex even spiders would be hesitant to go into.'

'But you boldly went down there with a flashlight, you want Mel to know.'

'Today or tomorrow I have to get somebody in Martinsburg to input them and tabulate the mean values; the spec forms are a mess because the work's so periodic. Underline for Mel that they get returns from both Region *and* the St. Louis SC with no set procedures or even rhythms that I can see.'

'The trucks just back up and unload the returns you're saying.'

'So what I've got pending tabs—this is going to look very strange—is for the last six months a total 1,829 returns go through 047's Exams branch per month, but that figure includes everything from individual EZs to nightmare Fats with twenty schedules each to EST-reconciliations that Rosebury lets Danmeyer hit them with in nightmarish waves quarterly.'

'This is not broken down in a way that tells me anything, Claudie.'

'It's when you get here you're going to see why. It's Dickensian. There's one UNIVAC terminal in the room. The kicks from Martinsburg come round on big carts pushed by cart boys like they had, then the results get slid down slides two levels down where the keypunch girls prepare the kicks back for Region and Collections. And/or Collections. And the examiners are operating with pencils and NCR adding machines some of which still have I Like Ike and the ilk stickers on them. They've got those angled trays or drawer things coming in at their desks from all angles like those pictures of Philly Mel had in the nightmare days. Here they get standard kicks from Martinsburg, plus ESTs, plus exam requests from CID. They do Fats that St. Louis doesn't even bother to open they're so fat. They do contract work for Corporate Audits when a CA goes multiyear. The whole thing's almost Philly-grade, tell him. But this—'

'1,829 by 26 by 22 workdays is what, three a day?'

'3.198 a day by nine-hour shifts minus lunch minus Region average 45.6 minutes for breaks which I've got as seven hours 29.4 minutes so 3.2 over 7.5 is .4266 repeating 6 returns per man-hour, which for the Region is so totally average that—'

'So it's neither here nor there, as a productivity stat, which hurts our case with Glendenning maybe but also makes 047 Exams a fine test case.'

'No, Reynolds. I mean *totally* average. The average for Region 4 for '82, '83, and the part of '84 Internal's got loads for—get this—is .42 repeating 6 returns per man-hour.'

'They're *exactly* average?'

'And anticipating just that reaction please tell Mel I checked this twice. All off cards, flowthrough totals, performance reviews, utilizations specs. .42 repeating 6. As if—'

'As if Glendenning and Rosebury and/or this Yeagle character were somehow cooking the Output books to produce an output so totally average that no one would ever suspect them of cooking the Output books.'

'I'll check it again if you like if you'll let me take just one moment here to discuss the apartment's water pressure and a commode with the single laziest flush I've seen in twelve US—'

The tone now was of Reynolds Jensen Jr. 100 percent focused, intent, which meant that whether sitting or standing he was bent slightly forward at the waist and not blinking at all. 'Do. Check. He'll want you to, you—or as if somehow Glendenning's been able to structure manpower and flow and morale in just such a way that he gets precisely the average out of Exams.'

'Meaning if and when he wants it to go up he just waves his wand and presto.'

'Could he be that good?'

'It would make him and/or the team of him and Rosebury a genius, a Mozart of production, whose management methods, if quantified and taught or if the other District Directors convinced DC it could be taught—'

'Could kill the project.'

'Especially if you could see these examiners. This is not an elite force, Reynolds. Not one over a GS-11 paygrade. Tics, spasms, eccentricities. Trembling hands. They're all in the men's room brushing their teeth after lunch. Whole lot of brushing going on. One has a violin on his desk. No reason. Just a violin. Another has a

Doberman hand puppet on his hand without the rubber, which he talks to.'

'These should all be notated, Claudie.'

'These are shells of men I'm saying. If Glendenning can get any throughput he wants out of *this* crew... Some look catatonic. One might be an idiot savant. I haven't seen him yet.'

'None of which has to do with throughput.'

'And have I mentioned the wind out here? The sound it makes through cracks near the windows? Or the heat? Or the enormous mass of these tiny cruciform rural towns with exactly one intersection that appear to consist entirely of a grain silo and a gas station with names like Arrowsmith, Anthony, Shirley, Tolono, Stayne? There's a town called Big Thistle near here. Repeat: Big Thistle, Illinois. Hey, let's us go over to the Big Thistle Diner and snap Fanny's girdle. And the humidity. Towels don't dry; your windshield gets condensation like a glass of iced tea if you run the AC on the way in. The sky the color of motel ice—no color, no depth. It's like a bad dream. And the flatness. What's the horizon at sea level, eighteen miles?'

'Let's stay on task, Claudie.'

'He's posted me to the second dimension, R.J.'

'You were doing so well, Claudie.'

'And what if I said I miss you?'

'We're not going to get into this, not—'

'Because you know the way someone really old's eyes look, with cataracts? That milky spooky anybody-home quality? Imagine a whole face like that. Philly was frenzy. This is a kind of caul of boredom. Boredom past boredom. These examiners, most—'

'You realize this is good news in a way.'

'Well it's not good to look at, I can certainly—'

'Has any of the demo equipment arrived?'

'Glendenning's letting them personalize their desks. Listen to music if they—not smoke at their desks, but get this: A couple of them *chew tobacco* at their desks.'

'Where are we in terms of profiles of the actual hardware then?'

'Have you by chance ever actually *seen* an in-use spittoon, Reynolds, because I cer—'

'I miss you, too, Claude. Happy now?'

Once he'd chewed it so badly it got infected, which made it taste just awful. 'I haven't done a list per se as such yet.'

'What should I tell Mel?'

'That I've been here only a week and am under terrific duress from the primitiveness of the field-quarters, lack of contact vectors, and numbing heat. Tell Mel that.'

'Aren't we brave in absentia.'

'As you may recall the real hardware's over with Corporate in the out-site, and except for verifying Mel's facilities I've been lurking in Exams. Per specs I believe.'

'I wasn't squeezing, Claudie. Let's just get through this. I have a nasty commute ahead of me.'

'I have so far seen a Sperry UNIVAC 3- or 4000-series mainframe with terminals apparently all at Corporate. I've seen two IBM 5486 card sorters and have deduced the presence of related 5000-series keypunch and collating equipment.'

'And ninety-six-column cards for the IBMs.'

'Except UNIVACs still use the eighty-. They've apparently got something jerry-rigged to mix the two.'

'So the examiners are all hexadecimal-proficient, or is that the punch-girls? But the punch-girls are locals, no?'

'I don't have a training protocol yet. We can assume they're natural-language-translated for temps during March to May, yes?'

'Even Rome didn't mix ninety-six and eighties.'

'This is the provinces, I've been telling you. Mel's office is right down from the Central, which I deduce is a complete mutt of different systems. I've seen a Burroughs 1005 calculator-printer.'

'Does Burroughs even use cards anymore?'

'Burroughs work off tape since the 900 series. I've told you. The whole thing's a mutt. A garage sale. I've seen two IBM RPGs in a closet with an unbelievable tangle of co-ax leading up to a ragged and sub-code hole in the closet's ceiling, presumably meant to compatibilize the RPGs with the UNIVAC. It's all very ancient and scuzzy and I wouldn't be terribly surprised if there were monkeys with abacuses and string inside.'

'This is very good news. And their assembler's COBOL?'

'Unknown at this juncture.'

'We've got good news on the hardware front.'

'And if anything's arrived from DC then SS here isn't aware of it.'

'So it could just be sitting on the loading dock?'

'So I'm to be in Records with a flashlight in my teeth, on the horn to Martinsburg getting flowthrough analyses, probing Glendenning's No-First-Year implementation, inventorying the hardware, and cabbaging keys to get a firsthand at Mel's office all at once? Oh, and on the loading dock quizzing burly men on whether any of the boxes are from Martinsburg.'

'All I'm doing is lining up a protocol for next week's field-, Claudie.'

'What am I, a machine?'

§31

Shinn was long-bodied and had very light baby-fine blond hair that hung in bangs like an early Beatle's. The man seated next to him in the IRS van had exited Angler's Cove with several others as they all stood at the curb in the pastel dawn and waited for the van. The sweet wet heavy air of summer dawns. The men with Service nametags all knew each other and spoke among themselves. Some drank from mugs or smoked cigarettes they ground out against the curb as the van came into view. One had sideburns and a cowboy hat, which now in the van he'd removed two rows of bench seats up. Some read the paper. Some of the men in the van were as old as maybe fifty. The windows tilted out rather than rolling down; it was an odd vehicle, more like a small boxy truck that had bench seats welded in.

The van stopped at two other apartment complexes along Self-Storage Parkway; at one of these it idled for several minutes, apparently dilating time for a schedule. Shinn wore a powder-blue dress shirt. A conversation behind him featured someone telling someone else that if you cut a small notch in the center of your toenail's edge, it won't ingrow. Someone else yawned loudly and gave little shivers. The man next to Shinn, their hams touching with varied pressure as the van swung slightly side to side on a loose suspension, was reading an IRM supplemental pamphlet whose title Shinn could not see because the guy was one of those people who folded pamphlets back into a single square to read them. He had a small backpack in his lap. Shinn considered introducing himself; he wasn't sure what the etiquette called for.

Shinn had stood at the curb drinking his first Coke of his first day at the Post and felt his clothes unwrinkle and sag slightly in the humidity, smelling the same honeysuckle and cut grass as suburban Chicago, listening to the songs of dawn-stirred birds in the locust trees along Self-Storage, and his thoughts had drifted all over the place, and suddenly it occurred that the birds, whose twitters and repeated songs sounded so pretty and affirming of nature and the coming day, might actually, in a code known only to other birds, be the birds each saying 'Get away' or 'This branch is mine!' or 'This tree is mine! I'll kill you! Kill, kill!' Or any manner of dark, brutal, or self-protective stuff—they might be listening to war cries. The thought came from nowhere and made his spirits dip for some reason.

§32

'Don't ask me to do this.'

I switched my live-in sister Julie over to the speaker while she was still trying to get out of doing it. We were all in my part of the cubicle. I was sitting at my workstation and they were standing around it. 'I told them and they don't believe it. In the uncanny accuracy of it, that I keep trying to describe but I can't do it justice, especially this fellow here Jon whom I've been telling you about.' I was looking over at Soane as I persuaded her. Julie is my sister. Her voice sounded less like her own voice on the speaker—it had that tinny, desiccated quality. Steve Mead always wore a counter's rubber on his right pinkie. The constant ripping metallic dental sound of a printer came from the Audit Room nearest the cubicle, a sound that set all our teeth on the edge when the printer ran. Steve Mead, Steve Dalhart, Jane Brown, and Likourgos Vassiliou were all standing around the speaker in my part of the cubicle, while Soane had rolled his chair back slightly from his own workstation to be included in the circle.

'I can't do it on demand. I feel stupid; don't make me,' Julie stated.

'Who this morning bought you three scrunchies when all you

asked for was one?' I said, making a circle of affirmation with my thumb and finger and holding it up to the others.

There was silence from my younger sister's end of the phone.

'I already told them some of the effect will be lost on the phone. Without the eyes and face. Pressure's off, nobody's expecting perfection.'

' "What an excellent day for an exorcism, Father." '

Even on the speaker. Steve Mead visibly started. I had an urge to giggle and bite my knuckle in delight. Dalhart and Jane Brown were looking at each other and they let their bodies sag and lengthen a little to indicate how astounded they were.

' "Your mother sucks cocks in hell!" ' Julie said, doing it.

'Astounding, Nugent.'

'My God' and 'It's uncanny,' Steve Mead said. He is always extremely pale and ill-looking. A Phillips screw was coming partway out of one of the supports at the back of Soane's chair's back support area. The ripping sound of the printer continued to set everyone's teeth on the edge.

Dale Gastine and Alice Pihl, who always conduct audits as a team, put their heads over the top of the cubicle to see what was going on.

'You should see the face if you could. She rolls her eyes all the way up and turns pale and puffs her cheeks out and it—she doesn't look like her at all until she does, then it's uncanny.' I said this. Soane, who is extremely cool and laid-back at all times, was doing something to his cuticle with a paperclip out of the dispenser.

Julie's regular voice came through the speaker. I consider Jane Brown attractive, but I can tell that Soane does not. 'Are we done?'

'You should see. They're all standing here agog. I really appreciate this,' I said. Jane Brown always wears the same orange blazer. 'Goggle-eyed. My credibility here has soared thanks to you.'

'We're going to talk about this when you get home, buckaroo, believe you me.'

'But can she lower the room down to freezing and write *Help* with her skin like when she—'

'One more,' whispered Mead, who does farm audits and goes out to the counter when a taxpayer rings the assistance bell (whole days go by without a taxpayer coming in for assistance, however) and has a soft square face and looks like he either never has to shave or uses moisturizer.

I told Julie on the phone, 'One more and then you'll have acquitted yourself in your usual outstanding way.'

'You promise.'

Likourgos Vassiliou, who is also unusually pale, especially for an ethnic Mediterranean, said to Dale Gastine and Alice Pihl, 'This new man Nugent does not exaggerate; make a note out of this.'

'"Can you spare a quotter fran old altaboy, Fadda. Dimmy. Why you do this to me, Dimmy? Let Jesus fuck you, fuck you!"'

'I'm practically getting the shivers,' Mead stated.

'This is positively the last time,' Julie emphasized on the speaker.

§33

Lane Dean Jr. with his green rubber pinkie finger sat at his Tingle table in his Chalk's row in the Rotes Group's wiggle room and did two more returns, then another one, then flexed his buttocks and held to a count of ten and imagined a warm pretty beach with mellow surf as instructed in orientation the previous month. Then he did two more returns, checked the clock real quick, then two more, then bore down and did three in a row, then flexed and visualized and bore way down and did four without looking up once except to put the completed files and memos in the two Out trays side by side up in the top tier of trays where the cart boys could get them when they came by. After just an hour the beach was a winter beach, cold and gray and the dead kelp like the hair of the drowned, and it stayed that way despite all attempts. Then three more, including one 1040A where the deductions for AGI were added wrong and the Martinsburg printout hadn't caught it and had to be amended on one of the Form 020-Cs in the lower left tray and then a lot of the same information filled out on the regular 20 you still had to do even if it was just a correspondence audit and the file going to Joliet instead of the District, each code for which had to be looked up on the pull-out thing he had to scoot the chair awkwardly over to pull out all the way. Then another one, then a plummeting inside of him as the wall clock showed that what he'd thought was another hour had not been. Not even close. 17 May 1985. Lord Jesus Christ have mercy on me a poor sinner. Crosschecking W-2s for the return's Line 7 off the place in the Martinsburg printout where the perforation if you wanted to separate the thing's sheets went right through the data and you had to hold it up against the light and almost sometimes guess, which his Chalk Leader said was a chronic bug with Systems but the wiggler was still accountable. The joke this week was how was an IRS rote examiner like a mushroom? Both kept in the dark and fed horseshit. He didn't know how mushrooms even worked, if it was true that you scooped waste on them. Sheri's cooking wasn't what you would call at the level of adding mushrooms. Then another return. The rule was, the more you looked at the clock the slower the time went. None of the wigglers wore a watch, except he saw that some kept them in their pockets for breaks. Clocks on Tingles were not allowed, nor coffee or pop. Try as he might he could not this last week help envisioning the inward lives of the older men to either side of him, doing this day after day. Getting up on a Monday and chewing their toast and putting their hats and coats on knowing what they were going out the door to come back to for eight hours. This was boredom beyond any boredom he'd ever felt. This made the routing desk at UPS look like a day at Six Flags. It was May 17, early morning, or early mid-morning you could maybe almost call it now. He could hear the squeak of the cart boys' carts someplace off at a distance where the vinyl panels between his Chalk's Tingles and the blond oriental fellow's Chalk one row up blocked the sight of them, the kids with the carts. One of the carts had a crazy wheel that chattered when the boy pushed it. Lane Dean always knew when that cart was coming down the rows. Chalk, Team, Group, Pod, Post, Division. He did another return, again the math squared and there were no itemizations on 34A and the printout's numbers for W-2 and 1099 and Forms 2440 and 2441 appeared to square and he filled out his codes for the middle tray's 402 and signed his name and ID number that some part of him still refused to quite get memorized so he had to unclip his badge and check it each time and then stapled the 402 to the return and put the file in the top tier's rightmost tray for 402s Out and refused to let himself count the number in the trays yet, and then unbidden came the thought that *boring* also meant something that drilled in and made a hole. His buttocks already ached from flexing, and the mere thought of envisioning the desolate beach unmanned him. He shut his eyes but instead of praying for inward strength now he found he was just looking at the strange reddish dark and the little flashes and floaters in there, that got almost hypnotic when you really looked at them. Then when he opened his eyes the In tray's stack of files looked to be still mainly the height it had been at 7:14 when he'd logged in in the Chalk Leader's notebook and started and there weren't enough files in his Out trays for Form 20s and 402s that he could see any over the side of the trays and he refused once more to stand up to check how many of them there were for he knew that would make it worse. He had the sensation of a great type of hole or emptiness falling through him and continuing to fall and never hitting the floor. Never before in his life up to now had he once thought of suicide. He was doing a return at the same time he fought with his mind, with the sin and affront of even the passing thought. The room was silent except for the adding machines and the chattering sound of that one kid's cart that had a crazy wheel as the cart boy brought it down a certain row with more files, but also he kept hearing in his head the sound a piece of paper makes when you tear it in half over and over. His six-man Chalk was a quarter of a row, separated off by the gray vinyl screens. A Team is four Chalks plus the Team Leader and a cart boy, some of these from Peoria College of Business. The screens could be moved around to reconfigure the room's layout. Similar rotes groups were in the rooms to either side. Far to the left past three other Chalks' rows was the Group Manager's office with the AGM's little cubicle of screens to the side of it. The pinkie rubbers were for traction on the forms for all deliberate speed. You were supposed to save the rubber at the end of the day. The overhead lights cast no shadow, even of your hand if you held it out like you were reaching at a tray. Doug and Amber Bellman of 402 Elk Court, Edina MN, who itemized and then some, elected to have $1 go to the Presidential Election Campaign Fund. It took several minutes to crosscheck everything on Schedule A but nothing qualified for the specs of a promising audit, even though Mr. Bellman had the jaggedy handwriting of a crazy man. Lane Dean had filed far fewer 20s than protocol called for. On Friday he had the fewest 20s of anyone else in the Chalk. Nobody'd said anything. All the wastebaskets were full of the curled strips of paper from the adding machines. Everyone's faces were the color of wet lead in the fluorescent light. You could make a semiprivate cubicle out of the screens like the Team Leader had. Then he looked up despite all best prior intentions. In four minutes it would be another hour, a half hour after that was the fifteen-minute break. Lane Dean imagined himself running around on the break waving his arms and shouting gibberish and holding ten cigarettes at once in his mouth like a panpipe. Year after year, a face the same color as your desk. Lord Jesus. Coffee wasn't allowed because of spills on the files, but on the break he'd have a big cup of coffee in each hand while he imagined himself running around the outside grounds shouting. He knew what he'd really do on the break was sit facing the wall clock in the lounge and despite prayers and effort sit counting the seconds tick off until he had to come back and do this again. And again and again and again. The imagined sound made him remember different times he'd seen people rip paper in half. He thought of a circus strongman tearing a phone book; he was bald and had a handlebar mustache and wore a stripy all-body swimsuit like people wore in the distant past. Lane Dean summoned all his will and bore down and did three returns in a row, and began imagining different high places to jump off of. He felt in a position to say he knew now that hell had nothing to do with fires or frozen troops. Lock a fellow in a windowless room to perform rote tasks just tricky enough to make him have to think, but still rote, tasks involving numbers that connected to nothing he'd ever see or care about, a stack of tasks that never went down, and nail a clock to the wall where he can see it, and just leave the man there to his mind's own devices. Tell him to pucker his butt and think beach when he starts to get antsy, and that would be just the word they'd use, *antsy,* like his mother. Let him find out in time's fullness what a joke the word was, that it didn't come anyplace close. He'd already dusted the desk with his cuff, moved his infant son's photo in its rattly little frame where the front glass slid a bit if you shook it. He'd already tried switching the green rubber over and doing the adding machine with his left hand, pretending he'd had a stroke and was bravely soldiering on. The rubber made the pinkie's tip all damp and pale beneath it. Unable to sit still at home, unable to look at anything for more than a second or two. The beach now had solid cement instead of sand and the water was gray and barely moved, just quivered a little, like Jell-O that's almost set. Unbidden came ways to kill himself with Jell-O. Lane Dean tried to control the rate of his heartbeat. He wondered if with enough practice and concentration you could stop your heart at will the same way you hold your breath—like this right here. His heart rate felt dangerously slow and he became scared and tried to keep his head inclined by rolling his eyes way up and compared the rate to the clock's second hand but the second hand seemed impossibly slow. The sound of ripping paper again and again. Some cart boys brought you files with everything you needed, some did not. The buzzer to bring a cart boy was just under the iron desk's edge, with a wire trailing down one of the desk's sides and little welded-on leg, but it didn't work. Atkins said the wiggler who'd been at the station before him, who'd got transferred someplace, had pressed on it so much it burnt the circuit. Small strange indentations in rows on the blotter's front edge were, Lane Dean had realized, the prints of teeth that somebody'd bent down and pressed real carefully into the blotter's edge so that the indentations went way down and stayed there. He felt he could understand. It was hard to keep from smelling his finger; at home he'd find himself doing it, staring into space at the table. His little baby boy's face worked better than the beach; he imagined him doing all sorts of things that he and his wife could talk about later, like curling his fist around one of their fingers or smiling when Sheri made that amazed face at him. He liked to watch her with the baby; for half a file it helped to have them in mind because they were why, they were what made this worthwhile and the right thing and he had to remember it but it kept slipping away down the hole that fell through him. Neither man on either side of him seemed to ever fidget or move except to reach up and lift things onto the desk from their Tingles' trays, like machines, and they were never in the lounge at break. Atkins claimed that after a year he could examine and crosscheck two files at once, but you never saw him try and do it, though he could whistle one song and hum a different one. Nugent's sister did the exorcist on the phone. Lane Dean watched out of the corner of his eye as a parrot-faced man by the central aisle dividing Teams pulled a file out of his tray and removed the return and detached the printout and centered both documents on his blotter. With his little homemade seat cushion and gray hat on its hook screwed into the 402s tray. Lane Dean stared down without seeing his own open file and imagined being that guy with his sad little cushion and customized banker's lamp and wondered what he possibly had or did in his spare time to make up for these soul-murdering eight daily hours that weren't even a quarter through until he just couldn't stand it and did three returns in a row in a kind of frenzy where he might have missed things and so on the next file went very slowly and painstakingly and found a discrepancy between the 1040's Schedule E and the RRA annuity tables for poor old Clive R. Terry of Alton's pissant railroad pension, but a discrepancy so small that you couldn't tell if the Martinsburg printout had even made an error or had just accepted a wide roundoff for time's sake given the amount at stake, and he had to fill out both an 020-C and a Memo 402-C(1) kicking the return over to the Group Manager's office to decide how to classify the error. Both had to be filled out with duplicated data on both sides, and signed. The whole issue was almost unbelievably meaningless and small. He thought about the word *meaning* and tried to summon up his baby's face without looking at the photo but all he could get was the heft of a full diaper and the plastic mobile over his crib turning in the breeze the box fan in the doorway made. No one in either congregation ever saw *The Exorcist*; it was against Catholic dogma and an obscenity. It was not entertainment. He imagined that the clock's second hand possessed awareness and knew that it was a second hand and that its job was to go around and around inside a circle of numbers forever at the same slow unvarying machinelike rate, going no place it hadn't already been a million times before, and imagining the second hand was so awful it made his breath catch in his throat and he looked quickly around to see if any of the examiners around him had heard it or were looking at him. When he started to see the baby's photo's face melting and lengthening and growing a long cleft jaw and the face aging years in just seconds and finally caving in from old age and falling away from the grinning yellow skull underneath, he knew he was half asleep and dreaming but did not know his own face was in his hands until he heard a human voice and opened his eyes but couldn't see who it went with and then smelled the pinkie's rubber right under his nose. He might have drooled on the open file.

Getting a little taste, I see.

It was a big older fellow with a seamed face and picket teeth. He wasn't from any Tingle that Lane Dean had ever observed from his own. The man had on a headlamp with a tan cotton band like some dentists wore and a type of thick black marker in his breast pocket. He smelled of hair oil and some kind of food. He had part of his bottom on the edge of Lane's desk and was cleaning under his thumbnail with a straightened-out paperclip and speaking softly. You could see an undershirt under his shirt; he wore no tie. He kept moving his upper body around in a slight kind of shape or circle, and the movements left a little bit of a visual trail. None of the wigglers in either adjoining row was paying attention to him. Dean checked the face in the photo to make sure he wasn't still dreaming.

They don't ever say it, though. Have you noticed? They talk around it. It's too manifest. As if talking about the air you're breathing, yes? It would be as if saying, I see so-and-so *with my eye.* What would be the point?

There was something wrong with one of his eyes; the pupil of the eye was bigger and stayed that way, making the eye look fixed. His headlamp wasn't on. The slow upper-body motions brought him in closer and then back and away and around again. It was very slight and slow.

Yes but now that you're getting a taste, consider it, the word. You know the one. Dean had the uneasy sense that the fellow wasn't strictly speaking *to* him, which would mean that he was more like ranting. The one eye looked fixedly past him. Although hadn't he just been thinking about a word? Was that word *dilated?* Had he said the word out loud? Lane Dean looked circumspectly to either side. The Group Manager's frosted door was shut.

Word appears suddenly in 1766. No known etymology. The Earl of March uses it in a letter describing a French peer of the realm. He didn't cast a shadow, but that didn't mean anything. For no reason, Lane Dean flexed his buttocks. In fact the first three appearances of *bore* in English conjoin it with the adjective *French,* that French bore, that boring Frenchman, yes? The French of course had *malaise, ennui.* See Pascal's fourth *Pensée,* which Lane Dean heard as *pantsy.* He was checking for errant spit on the file before him. One ham in dark-blue work pants was inches from his elbow. The man moved slightly back and forth like his waist was hinged. He appeared to be inspecting Lane Dean's upper body and face in a systematic gridlike fashion. His eyebrows were all over the place. The tan band was either soaked or stained. See La Rochefoucauld's or the Marquise du Deffand's well-known letters to Horace Walpole, specifically I believe Letter 96. But nothing in English prior to March, Earl of. This means a good five hundred years of no word for it you see, yes? He rotated slightly away. In no way was this a vision or moment. Lane Dean had heard of the phantom but never seen it. The phantom of the hallucination of repetitive concentration held for too long a time, like saying a word over and over until it kind of melted and got foreign. Mr. Wax's high hard gray hair was just visible four Tingles down. No word for the Latin *accidia* made so much of by monks under Benedict. For the Greek ακηδία. Also the hermits of third-century Egypt, the so-called *daemon meridianus,* when their prayers were stultified by pointlessness and tedium and a longing for violent death. Now Lane Dean was looking openly around as in like who is this fellow? The one eye was fixed at a point over past the row of vinyl screens. The tearing sound had gone, as had that one cart's squeaky wheel.

The fellow cleared his throat. Donne of course called it *lethargie,* and for a time it seems conjoined somewhat with melancholy, saturninia, *otiositas, tristitia*—that is, to be confused with sloth and torpor and lassitude and eremia and vexation and distemper and attributed to spleen, for example see Winchilsea's *black jaundice,* or of course Burton. The man was still on the same thumbnail. Quaker Green in I believe 1750 called it *spleen-fog.* Hair oil made Lane Dean think of the barber's, of the stripy pole that seemed to spiral eternally upward but you could see when the shop closed and it stopped really didn't. The hair oil had a name. No one under sixty used it. Mr. Wax used a men's spray. The fellow appeared unconscious of his upper body's underwater X-shaped rotations. Two of the wigglers in a Team near the door had long beards and black derbies and bobbed at their Tingles as they examined returns but their bobbing was rapid and back and forth only; this was different. The examiners on either side didn't look up or pay attention; their fingers on the adders never slowed. Lane Dean couldn't tell if this was a sign of their professional concentration or something else. Some wore the rubber on the left pinkie, most on the right. Robert Atkins was ambidextrous; he could fill out different forms with each hand. The fellow on his left hadn't blinked once all morning that Dean had been able to see. And then suddenly up it pops. *Bore.* As if from Athena's forehead. Noun and verb, participle as adjective, whole nine yards. Origin unknown, really. We do not know. Nothing on it in Johnson. Partridge's only entry is on *bored* as a subject complement and what preposition it takes, since *bored of* as opposed to *with* is a class marker which is all that ever really concerns Partridge. Class class class. The only Partridge Lane Dean knew was the same TV Partridge everybody else knew. He had no earthly idea what this guy was talking about but at the same time it unnerved him that he'd been thinking about *bore* as a word as well, the word, many returns ago. Philologists say it was a neologism—and just at the time of industry's rise, too, yes? of the mass man, the automated turbine and drill bit and bore, yes? Hollowed out? Forget Friedkin, have you seen *Metropolis*? All right, this really creeped Lane out. His inability to say anything to this guy or ask him what he even wanted felt a little like a bad dream as well. The night after his first day he'd dreamed of a stick that kept breaking over and over but never got smaller. The Frenchman pushing that uphill stone throughout eternity. Look for instance at L. P. Smith's *English Language,* '56 I believe, yes? It was the bad eye, the frozen eye, that seemed to inspect what he leaned toward. Posits certain neologisms as *arising from their own cultural necessity*—his words, I believe. Yes, he said. When the kind of experience that you're getting a man-sized taste of becomes possible, the word invents itself. The term. Now he switched nails. It was Vitalis that had soaked the headlamp's band, which looked more and more like a bandage. The Group Manager's door had his name on it painted on the same pebbled-glass window thing that older high schools have. Personnel's doors were the same. The wiggle rooms had windowless metal fire doors on struts up top, a newer model. Consider that the Oglok of Labrador have more than a hundred separate and distinct words for snow. Smith puts it as that when anything assumes sufficient relevance it finds its name. The name springs up under cultural pressure. Really quite interesting when you consider it. Now for the first time the fellow at the Tingle to the right turned briefly to give the man a look and turned just as fast back around when the man made his hands into claws and held them out at the other wiggler like a demon or someone possessed. The whole thing happened too fast to almost be real to Lane Dean. The wiggler turned a page in the file before him. Someone else had also called it that, *soul murdering*. Which now you will, too, yes? In the nineteenth century then suddenly the word's everywhere; see for example Kierkegaard's *Strange that boredom, in itself so staid and solid, should have such power to set in motion.* When he slid his big ham off the desktop the movement made the smell stronger; it was Vitalis and Chinese food, the food in the little white bucket with the wire handle, moo goo something. The room's light on the frosted glass was different because the door was slightly open, though Lane Dean hadn't seen the door open. It occurred to Lane Dean that he might pray.

It was the same gridlike swaying motion standing. The one eye was on the Group Manager's door, open a crack. Note too that *interesting* first appears just two years after *bore.* 1768. Mark this, two years *after.* Can this be so? He was halfway down the row; now the fellow with the cushion looked up and then back down right away. Invents itself, yes? Not all it invents. Then something Lane Dean heard as *bone after tea.* The man was gone when he reached the row's end. The file and its Schedules A/B and printout were right where they'd been, but Lane's son's picture was facedown. He let himself look up and saw that no time had passed at all, again.

§34

IRM §781(d) AMT Formula for Corporations: (1) Taxable income before NOL deduction, plus or minus (2) All AMT adjustments excepting ACE adjustment, plus (3) Tax preferences, yields (4) Alternative Minimum Taxable Income before NOL deduction and/or ACE adjustment, plus or minus (5) ACE adjustment, if any, yields (6) AMTI before NOL deduction, if any, minus (7) NOL deduction, if any (Ceiling at 90%), yields (8) AMTI, minus (9) Exemptions, yields (10) AMT base, multiplied by (11) 20% AMT rate, yields (12) AMT prior to AMT Foreign Tax Credit, minus (13) AMT Foreign Tax Credit, if any (Ceiling at 90% unless Exceptions 781(d) (13-16) apply, in which case attach Memo 781-2432 and forward to Group Manager), yields (14) Tentative Alternative Minimum Tax, minus (15) Standard tax liability before credit minus standard Foreign Tax Credit, yields (16) Alternative Minimum Tax.

§35

My Audit Group's Group Manager and his wife have an infant I can only describe as—fierce. Its expression is fierce, its demeanor is fierce, its gaze over bottle or pacifier—fierce, intimidating, aggressive. I have never heard it cry. When it feeds or sleeps, its pale face reddens, which makes it look all the fiercer. On those workdays when our Group Manager brought it in with him to the District office, hanging papoose-style in a nylon device on his back, the infant appeared to be riding him as a mahout does an elephant. It hung there, radiating authority. Its back lay directly against the Group Manager's, its large head resting in the hollow of its father's neck, forcing Mr. Manshardt's head out and down into a posture of classic oppression. They made a beast with two faces, one of which was calm, bland, and adult, and the other unformed and yet emphatically fierce. The infant never wiggled or fussed in the device. Its gaze around the corridor at the rest of us gathered there waiting for the morning elevator was level and unblinking and, it seemed, somehow almost accusing.

The infant's face, as I experienced it, was mostly eyes and lower lip, its nose a mere pinch, its forehead milky and domed, its whorl of red hair wispy, no eyebrows or lashes or ever even eyelids that I could see. I never once saw it blink. Its features seemed suggestions only. It had roughly as much face as a whale does. I did not like it at all.

In the elevator, my customary spot is often in the middle, just behind Mr. Manshardt, and on the mornings when the child rides him and hangs there facing backward and I spend the time staring into the large, stern, lashless, fiery-blue eyes, I can only say that these rides are not pleasant at all, and often affect my mood and concentration for much of the subsequent work period.

On the third floor, in Mr. Manshardt's office, the infant had a crib and also a modern, ingenious, mobile supporting device which it spent much of its time in, a large ring-shaped contraption of heavy blue plastic and a type of cloth sling or saddle in the center's hole, in which the infant was placed in a position somewhere between sitting and standing—that is, the infant's legs were nearly straight, but the sling appeared to support its weight. The device or station had four short, squat supporting legs, which terminated in plastic wheels, and was designed to be movable under the infant's power, albeit slowly, rather the way our own workstations' wheeled chairs could be maneuvered this way and that by awkward motions of the auditor's legs. However, the infant declined to move the device, as far as I ever saw, or to play with any of the bright, primary-colored toys and small, amusing developmental tchotchkes built into sockets in the ring's blue surface. Nor did it ever seem to occupy itself with the books made of cloth, dump trucks and fire engines, teething rings of liquid-filled plastic, intricate mobiles, or pull-string music-and-animal-noise-emitting toys with which its play area was replete. It just sat there, motionless and mute, gazing fiercely at whichever GS-9 auditors happened to enter our Group Manager's small, frosted-glass office on the days when Mr. Manshardt—whose wife was liberated and had her own career—brought it in with him, for which he had reportedly received special permission from the District Director. At first, many a GS-9 would enter the office on some thin pretext, trying to curry favor with the Group Manager by smiling and making soft, primal sounds at the infant, or by putting a finger or pencil in its field of vision, perhaps trying to stimulate its instinct for grasping. The infant, however, would just gaze at the auditor fiercely, with a combination of intensity and disdain, its expression rather as if it were hungry and the auditor were food but not quite the right kind. There are some small children who you can just tell are going to grow up to be frightening adults—this infant was frightening now. It was eerie and discomfiting to see something with hardly any bona fide human face yet to speak of nevertheless assume a fierce, intimidating, almost accusatory expression. For my own part, I had abandoned all ideas of ingratiating myself with Mr. Manshardt through his infant quite early on. To be honest, I was concerned that Gary Manshardt might be able to pick up my fear and dislike of the infant on some type of mysterious, occult parental radar.

His office's desk's personal-item area was lined with photos of Mr. Manshardt's infant—on a rug, newborn in an obstetrics ward, in boots and a tiny hooded coat, squatting nude with a red pail and shovel at the beach, and so on and so forth—and in all of the photos the infant looked fierce. Its presence seemed not to interfere with Manshardt's office duties, the bulk of which were administrative and required much less pure concentration than the Audit Group itself's. Once the working day began, however, the Group Manager appeared for the most part to ignore the infant, and to be ignored by it in return. Whenever I went in, try as I might, I could not interact with the infant. The nylon papoose appliance hung on a coat hook next to Mr. Manshardt's hat and jacket—he preferred to work in shirtsleeves, a further perquisite of Group Managers. Sometimes the office smelled slightly of powder or pee. I did not know when the GM changed the infant, or where, and avoided visualizing what-all might be involved or the infant's expression when this occurred. I myself could not imagine touching the infant or being touched by it in any way.

Due to our District 040(c)'s Audits Pod's administrative structure, Group Managers also did rotating duty as the District's Level 1 Appeals Officer, requiring Mr. Manshardt sometimes to put his suit jacket back on and proceed downstairs to one of the second floor's audit cubicles, where aggrieved TPs or their representatives would present their objections to a given audit's findings. And since, by the Service's Statement of Procedural Rules §601's specifications for

Appeal of Findings, the GS-9 auditor himself was never present during a Level 1 Appeal, that auditor became the logical choice for Mr. Manshardt to approach at his or her desk and ask to move his or her work materials temporarily into the Group Manager's office, and to keep an eye on the infant while Mr. Manshardt handled the Level 1 Appeal.

In due course, the day eventually came when one of my audits' findings was appealed when Mr. Manshardt was 'up' as the Post's Appeals Officer. As luck would have it, the appeal was of a field audit that I had spent nearly eight full working days conducting at All Right Flowers, a small, family-owned S corporation specializing in the arrangement and delivery of bouquets for public functions, and whose Form 1120 Schedule A, E, and G deductions for everything from depreciation and spoilage to employee compensation were so grossly inflated that I'd been forced—despite terrible, long-standing hay fever—to back-audit them for the two previous years and to amend both their Schedule Js and 1120s' Line 33s heavily in the Treasury's favor. As the field audit came directly off a Form 20 directive from the Regional Examination Center, and as the combined adjustments, penalties, and interest assessed against All Right Flowers might well exceed the TP's ability to pay unless terms were made, the appeal was hardly a cause for surprise or alarm, Mr. Manshardt assured me in the bland, kindly tone that characterized his management style. But as the Level 1 would be conducted in the office of All Right Flowers' attorney on DeKalb Street downtown—as is the prerogative of certain categories of field auditees under SPR §601.105—it would require that Mr. Manshardt be off-post for several hours, which in turn entailed that I was to have an extended period in the Group Manager's office in the company of his fierce and frightening infant, who could only be brought along on an L-1 in the field if Manshardt and the appellant's rep had a long-standing history of cordial relations, which he and All Right Flowers' attorney[1] unfortunately, he said, did not.

The Group Managers' offices were the only fully enclosed work

1 (a female Jew)

spaces on the third-floor office's Audits Pod, and have doors, affording the luxury of privacy. But the offices are not large, Manshardt's own being perhaps at most eight feet by eight, with large frosted-glass windows on two sides—these being the sides which did not abut the structural, load-bearing walls of the District building—and a double brass coat hook fixture, and a US flag and Service seal and motto flag on one corner's complex pole, as well as framed portraits of both Triple-Six's Commissioner of Internal Revenue and our own Regional Commissioner across town. In contrast to the cramped, impersonal metal desks of the Audit Group, Gary Manshardt's woodgrain desk, with its Tingle array of trays and hutches, took up nearly all of the space in the office not ceded to the infant, along with there being one of the large, multi-display easels on which all Group Managers charted both their auditors' present loads and, in a DD-mandated Charleston code that fooled no one,[2] each GS-9's total cases, adjustments, and assessed deficiencies so far in the present quarter. The air-conditioning was good.

2 Production quotas are a reality in the Service. This is not difficult to understand. Given numerous and repeated public statements to the contrary by top officials at Triple-Six, however, all such internal quotas are required to be kept and recorded in code. At the same time, administrators view the knowledge of such quotas as valuable performance incentives, which is why the Compliance Branch mandates and authorizes internal codes that are laughably familiar to most auditors. The Charleston code, in which C stands for the number 0 and H stands for 1, dot, dot, dot, up to N's standing for 9, is today most commonly employed by retailers who use a perpetual inventory system which must include the nominal cost of goods sold in each transaction record. Thus, an item's retail price tag at, let us say, a rural IGA supermarket will include both the retail price in digits and the CGS or distributor's unit price in Charleston code, often at the tag's lower border. Thus, anyone familiar with the code can determine from, let us say, a $1.49 retail price and a tiny TE beneath it, that the unit markup here is nearly 100 percent, and that the IGA supermarket he is patronizing is either disposed to gouge or has extraordinary retail overhead, possibly involving poorly leveraged debt—a common problem with the management of Midwest supermarket chains. On the other hand, one advantage of the Charleston code is that inflating its Schedule A's Cost of Goods Sold is one of the most common and effective ways for a retail franchise to cook down its Line 33, especially if the retailer uses one type of code for CGS and its distributor another type of code for its receivables—and most distributors use a much more sophisticated octal PIS code. This is why so many large corporate audits are coordinated to review all different levels of the supply chain simultaneously. Such coordinated audits are handled out of Region, often also using specially selected GS-13 examiners from the Regional Exam Center; we do not conduct such audits at the District level.

And yet I'm now advised that none of this is directly to the point, the substance of which is: Imagine my surprise and discomfiture once I had moved my briefcase, Doberman hand puppet, desk nameplate, hat, personal items, Service notebook, expandable cardboard file of Hollerith cards, M1 printouts, Memo 20s, Form 520s and 1120s, blank forms, and at least two fat folders of crosschecks and receipt-request forms into the Group Manager's office, and—glancing as little as possible at Gary's forbidding infant, which was still wearing its lunch bib and standing-slash-sitting at its circular plastic play station gumming a liquid-filled ring in what I can describe only as a studious or contemplative way—was just managing to regather my concentration in order to organize a list of preliminary receipt and supporting-document requests from a vendor that made and affixed tempered handles on a line of galvanized pails for Danville's Midstate Galvanics Co. when I heard the unmistakable adult sound of a cleared throat, albeit at an extremely high pitch, as if from an adult who had recently inhaled helium out of a decorative balloon. The infant was, like Gary Manshardt's wife, a redhead, although in the infant's case its extreme pallor and the light-yellow pajamas or jumper—or whatever exactly one calls the small and fuzzy full-body snap-up chamois bodysuits which infants today tend to wear—made its fine wisps and spirals of hair appear, in the intensive light of the office, to be the color of old blood, and its fierce and concentrated blue eyes appeared now to be almost pupilless; and, to complete the incongruous horror, the infant had set aside its teething ring—rather carefully and deliberately, as a man might set aside a file on his desk once he has completed it and is ready to turn his professional attention to another—to lie moist and shiny next to an upright bottle of what appeared to be apple juice, and had placed its tiny hands folded adultly together before it on the vivid blue plastic of its play station,[3] exactly as Mr. Manshardt or Mr. Fardelle or any of the other Group Managers or District Director's senior staff would place

3 (I observed that one of the elastic wristlets of its yellow chamois jumper was soaked through with saliva and appeared, for several inches up the infant's forearm, darker than the other wristlet, which the infant appeared to ignore and I certainly did not mention or foresee doing anything about)

their clasped hands before them on the desk to signal that you and the issue that had brought you into their office now occupied their full attention, and cleared its throat again—for it had indeed been it, he, the infant, who, like any other GM, had cleared its throat in an expectant way in order to get my attention and at the same time in some subtle way to upbraid me for requiring it to do something to get my attention, as if I had been daydreaming or digressing mentally from some issue at hand—and, gazing at me fiercely, said—yes, said, in a high and *l*-deficient but unmistakable voice—

'Well?'

It now seems probable that it was at first my shock, my as it were nonplussedness at being spoken that adultly to by an infant in diapers and jammies soaked with drool, that led me so automatically to answer, to respond as I would to any expectant 'Well?' from a Service superior, functioning on, as it were, automatic pilot:

'Excuse me?' I said, as we stared at each other across our respectively wood-grain and lurid blue surfaces and the five or six fluorescent feet of air between us, both our hands now identically out and clasped, the infant's gaze fiercely expectant and a small, creamy gout of mucus appearing and receding in one nostril as it breathed, looking directly at me, the cowlick at its crown like a tag or receipt from a register's slit, its eyes lashless and without circumference or bottom, its lips pursed as if considering how to proceed, a bubble in its bottle of juice ascending slowly, leisurely towards the bottle's top, the salient nipple brown and shiny from recent use. And the moment hung there between us, borderless and distendant, my impulse to clear my own throat only blocked by a fear of appearing impertinent—and it was in that seemingly endless, expectant interval that I came to see that I deferred to the infant, respected it, granted it full authority, and therefore waited, abiding, both of us in that small and shadowless father's office, in the knowledge that I was, thenceforth, this tiny white frightening thing's to command, its instrument or tool.

§36

Every whole person has ambitions, objectives, initiatives, goals. This one particular boy's goal was to be able to press his lips to every square inch of his own body.

His arms to the shoulders and most of the legs beneath the knee were child's play. After these areas of his body, however, the difficulty increased with the abruptness of a coastal shelf. The boy came to understand that unimaginable challenges lay ahead of him. He was six.

There is little to say about the original animus or 'motive cause' of the boy's desire to press his lips to every square inch of his own body. He had been homebound one day with asthma, a rainy and distended morning, apparently looking through some of his father's promotional materials. Some of these survived the eventual fire. The boy's asthma was thought to be congenital.

The outside area of his foot beneath and around the lateral malleolus was the first to require any real contortion. (The young boy thought, at that point, of the lateral malleolus as the funny knob thing on his ankle.) The strategy, as he understood it, was to arrange himself on his bedroom's carpeted floor with the inside of his knee on the floor and his calf and foot at as close to a perfect 90-degree angle to his thigh as he could at that point manage. Then he had to lean as far over to the side as he could, bending out over the splayed ankle and the foot's outside, rotating his neck over and down and straining with his fully extended lips (the boy's idea of fully extended lips consisted at this point of the exaggerated pucker that signified kissing in children's cartoons) at a section of the foot's outside he had marked with a bull's-eye of soluble ink, struggling to breathe against the dextrorotated pressure of his ribs, stretching farther and farther to the side very early one morning until he felt a flat pop in the upper part of his back and then pain beyond naming somewhere between his shoulder blade and spine. The boy did not cry out or weep but merely sat silent in this tortured posture until his failure to appear for breakfast brought his father upstairs to the bedroom's door. The pain and resultant dyspnea kept the boy out of school for over a month. One can only wonder what a father might make of an injury like this in a six-year-old child.

The father's chiropractor, Doctor Kathy, was able to relieve the worst of the immediate symptoms. More important, it was Doctor Kathy who introduced the boy to the concepts of spine as microcosm and of spinal hygiene and postural echo and incrementalism in flexion. Doctor Kathy smelled faintly of fennel and seemed totally open and available and kind. The child lay prone on a tall padded table and placed his chin in a little cup. She manipulated his head, very gently but in a way that seemed to make things happen all the way down his back. Her hands were strong and soft and when she felt the boy's back he felt as if she were asking it questions and answering them all at the same time. She had charts on her wall with exploded views of the human spine and the muscles and fasciae and nerve bundles that surrounded the spine and were connected to it. No lollipops were anywhere in view. The specific stretching exercises Doctor Kathy gave the boy were for the splenius capitis and longissimus cervicis and the deep sheaths of nerve and muscle surrounding the boy's T2 and T3 vertebrae, which were what he had just injured. Doctor Kathy had reading glasses on a necklace and a green button-up sweater that looked as if it were made entirely of pollen. You could tell she talked to everybody the same way. She instructed the boy to perform the stretching exercises every single day and not to let boredom or a reduction in symptomology keep him from performing the rehabilitative exercises in a disciplined way. She said the long-term goal was not relief of present discomfort but neurological hygiene and health and a wholeness of body and mind he would someday appreciate very, very much. For the boy's father, Doctor Kathy prescribed an herbal relaxant.

Thus was Doctor Kathy the child's formal introduction both to incremental stretching and to the adult idea of quiet daily discipline and progress toward a long-term goal. This proved fortuitous. During his five weeks disabled with a subluxated T3 vertebra—often in such discomfort that not even his inhaler could help the asthma that struck whenever he experienced pain or distress—the heady enthusiasm of childhood had given way in the boy to a realization that the objective of pressing his lips to every square inch of himself was going to require maximum effort, discipline, and a commitment sustainable over periods of time he could not then (because of his age) imagine.

One thing Doctor Kathy had taken time out to show the boy was a freestanding 3-D model of a human spine that had not been taken proper care of in any real or significant way. It looked dark, stunted, necrotic, and sad. Its tubercles and soft tissues were inflamed, and the annulus fibrosus of its disks was the color of bad teeth. Up against the wall behind this model was a hand-lettered plaque or sign explaining about what Doctor Kathy liked to say were the two different types of payments for the spine and associated nervosa, which were *Now* and *Later*.

Most professional contortionists are, in fact, simply persons born with congenital atrophic/dystrophic conditions of major recti, or with acute lordotic flexion of the lumbar spine, or both. A majority display Chvostek's sign or other forms of ipsilateral spasticity. Very little effort or application is involved in their 'art,' therefore. In 1932, a preadolescent Ceylonese female was documented by British scholars of Tamil mysticism as capable of inserting into her mouth and down her esophagus both arms to the shoulder, one leg to the groin, and the other leg to just above the patella, and as thereupon able to spin unaided on the orally protrusive knee at rates in excess of 300 rpm. The phenomenon of suiphagia (i.e., 'self-swallowing') has subsequently been identified as a rare form of inanitive pica, in most cases caused by deficiencies in cadmium and/or zinc.

The insides of the small boy's thighs up to the medial fork of his groin took months even to prepare for, daily hours spent cross-legged and bowed, slowly and incrementally stretching the long vertical fasciae of his back and neck, the spinalis thoracis and levator scapulae, the iliocostalis lumborum all the way to the sacrum, and the interior thigh's dense and intransigent gracilis, pectineus, and adductor longus, which fuse below Scarpa's triangle and transmit sickening pain through the pubis whenever their range of flexibility is exceeded. Had anyone seen him during these two- and three-hour sessions, bringing his soles together and in to train the pectineus, bobbing slightly and then holding a deep cross-legged lean to work the great tight sheet of thoracolumbar fascia that connected his pelvis to his dorsal costae, the child would have appeared to that person either prayerful or catatonic, or both.

Once the thighs' anterior targets were achieved and touched with one or both lips, the upper portions of his genitals were simple, and were protrusively kissed and passed over even as plans for the ilium and outer buttocks were in conception. After these achievements would come the more difficult and neck-intensive contortions required to access the inner buttocks, perineum, and extreme upper groin.

The boy had turned seven.

The special place where he pursued his strange but newly mature objective was his room, which had wallpaper with a repeating jungle motif. The room's second-floor window yielded a view of the backyard's tree. Light from the sun came through the tree at different angles and intensities at different times of day and illuminated different parts of the boy as he stood, sat, inclined, or lay on the room's carpet, stretching and holding positions. His bedroom's carpet was white shag with a furry, polar aspect that the boy's father did not think went well with the walls' repeating scheme of tiger, zebra, lion, palm; but the father kept his feelings to himself.

Radical increase of the lips' protrusive range requires systematic exercise of maxillary fasciae such as the depressor septi, orbicularis oris, depressor anguli oris, depressor labii inferioris, and the buccinator, circumoral, and risorius groups. Zygomatic muscles are superficially involved. Praxis: Affix string to Wetherly button of at least 1.5" diameter borrowed from father's second-best raincoat; place button over upper and lower front teeth and enclose with lips; hold string fully extended at 90 degrees to face's plane and pull with gradually increasing tension on end, using lips to resist pull; hold for twenty seconds; repeat; repeat.

Sometimes his father sat on the floor outside the boy's bedroom with his back to the door. It's not clear whether the boy ever heard him listening for movement in the room, although the wood of the door sometimes made a creaky sound when the father sat against it or stood back up in the hallway or shifted his seated position against the door. The boy was in there stretching and holding contorted positions for extraordinary periods of time. The father was a somewhat nervous man, with a rushed, fidgety manner that always lent him an air of imminent departure. He had extensive entrepreneurial activities and was in motion much of the time. His place in most people's mental album was provisional, with something like a dotted line around it—the image of someone saying something friendly over his shoulder as he made for an exit. Most clients found the father made them uneasy. He was at his most effective on the phone.

By age eight, the child's long-term goal was beginning to affect his physical development. His teachers remarked changes in posture and gait. The boy's smile, which appeared by now constant because of the circumlabial hypertrophy's effects on the circumoral musculature, looked unusual also, rigid and overbroad and seeming, in one custodian's evaluative phrase, 'like nothing in this round world.'

Facts: Italian stigmatist Padre Pio carried wounds which penetrated the left hand and both feet medially throughout his lifetime.

The Umbrian St. Veronica Giuliani presented with wounds in one hand as well as in her side, which wounds were observed to open and close on command. The eighteenth-century holy woman Giovanna Solimani permitted pilgrims to insert special keys in her hands' wounds and to turn them, reportedly facilitating those clients' own recovery from rationalist despair.

According to both St. Bonaventura and Tomas de Celano, St. Francis of Assisi's manual stigmata included baculiform masses of what presented as hardened black flesh extrudent from both volar planes. If and when pressure was applied to a palm's so-called 'nail,' a hardened black rod of flesh would immediately protrude from the back of the hand, just exactly as if a real so-called 'nail' were passing through the hand.

And yet (fact): Hands lack the anatomical mass required to support the weight of an adult human. Both Roman legal texts and modern examinations of first-century skeletons confirm that classical crucifixion required nails to be driven through the subject's wrists, not his hands. Hence the, quote, 'necessarily simultaneous *truth* and *falsity* of the stigmata' that existential theologist E. M. Cioran explicates in his 1937 *Lacrimi si sfinti,* the same monograph in which he refers to the human heart as 'God's open wound.'

Areas of the boy's midsection from navel to xiphoid process at the cleft of his ribs alone comprised nineteen months of stretching and postural exercises, the more extreme of which must have been very painful indeed. At this stage, further advances in flexibility were now subtle to the point of being undetectable without extremely precise daily record-keeping. Certain tensile limits in the flava, capsule, and process ligaments of the neck and upper back were gently but persistently stretched, the boy's chin placed to his (solubly arrowed and dotted) chest at mid-sternum and then slid incrementally down — 1, sometimes 1.5 millimeters a day — and this catatonic and/or meditative posture held for an hour or more.

In the summer, during his early-morning routines, the tree outside the boy's window filled with grackles and became busy with grackles coming and going; and then, as the sun rose, the tree filled with the birds' harsh sounds, tearing sounds, which as the boy sat cross-legged with his chin to his chest sounded through the pane like rusty screws turning, some complexly stuck thing coming loose with a shriek. Past the southern exposure's tree were the foreshortened roofs of neighborhood homes and the fire hydrant and street sign of the cross-street and the forty-eight identical roofs of a low-income housing development beyond the cross-street, and, past the development, just at the horizon, the edges of the verdant cornfields that began at the city limits. In late summer the fields' green was more sallow, and later in the fall there was merely sad stubble, and in the winter the fields' bare earth looked like nothing so much as just what it was.

At his elementary school, where the boy's behavior was exemplary and his assignments completed and his progress charted at the medial apex of all relevant curves, he was, among his classmates, the sort of marginal social figure so marginal he was not even teased. As early as Grade 3, the boy had begun to develop along unusual physical lines as a result of his commitment to the objective; even so, something in his aspect or bearing served to place him outside the bounds of schoolyard cruelty. The boy followed classroom regulations and performed satisfactorily in group work. The written evaluations of his socialization described the boy not even as withdrawn or aloof but as 'calm,' 'unusually poised,' and 'self-containing [*sic*].' The boy gave neither trouble nor delight and was not much noticed. It is not known whether this bothered him. The vast majority of his time, energy, and attention belonged to the long-range objective and the daily disciplines thereby entailed.

Nor was it ever established precisely why this boy devoted himself to the goal of being able to press his lips to every square inch of his own body. It is not clear even that he conceived of the goal as an 'achievement' in any conventional sense. Unlike his father, he did not read Ripley and had never heard of the McWhirters—certainly it was no kind of stunt. Nor any sort of self-evection; this is verified; the boy had no conscious wish to 'transcend' anything. If someone had asked him, the boy would have said only that he'd decided he wanted to press his lips to every last micrometer of his own individual body. He would not have been able to say more than this. Insights or conceptions of his own physical 'inaccessibility' to himself (as we are all of us self-inaccessible and can, for example, touch parts of one another in ways that we could not even dream of with our own bodies) or of his complete determination, apparently, to pierce that veil of inaccessibility—to be, in some childish way, self-contained and -sufficient—these were beyond his conscious awareness. He was, after all, just a little boy.

His lips touched the upper aureoles of his left and right nipples in the autumn of his ninth year. The lips by this time were markedly large and protrusive; part of his daily disciplines were tedious button-and-string exercises designed to promote hypertrophy of the orbicularis muscles. The ability to extend his pursed lips as much as 10.4 centimeters had often been the difference between achieving part of his thorax and not. It had also been the orbicularis muscles, more than any outstanding advance in vertebral flexion, that had permitted him to access the rear areas of his scrotum and substantial portions of the papery skin around his anus before he turned nine. These areas had been touched, tagged on the four-sided chart inside his personal ledger, then washed clean of ink and forgotten. The boy's tendency was to forget each site once he had pressed his lips to it, as if the establishment of its accessibility made the site henceforth unreal for him and the site now in some sense 'existed' only on the four-faced chart.

Fully and exquisitely real for the boy in his eleventh year, however, remained those portions of his trunk he had not yet attempted: areas of his chest above the pectoralis minor and of his lower throat between clavicle and upper platysma, as well as the smooth and endless planes and tracts of his back (excluding lateral portions of the trapezius and rear deltoid, which he had achieved at eight and a half) extending upward from the buttocks.

Four separate licensed, bonded physicians apparently testified that the Bavarian mystic Therese Neumann's stigmata comprised corticate dermal structures that passed medially through both her hands. Therese Neumann's additional capacity for inedia was attested in writing by four Franciscan nuns who attended her in rotating shifts from 1927 to 1962 and confirmed that Therese lived for almost thirty-five years without food or liquid of any kind; her one recorded bowel movement (12 March 1928) was determined by laboratory analysis to comprise only mucus and empyreumatic bile.

A Bengali holy man known to followers as 'Prahansatha the Second' underwent periods of meditative chanting during which his eyes exited their sockets and ascended to float above his head, connected only by their dura mater cords, and thereupon underwent (i.e., the floating eyes did) rhythmically stylized rotary movements described by Western witnesses as evocative of dancing four-faced Shivas, of charmed snakes, of interwoven genetic helices, of the counterpointed figure-eight orbits of the Milky Way and Andromeda galaxies around each other at the perimeter of the Local Group, or of all four (supposedly) at once.

Studies of human algesia have established that the musculoskeletal structures most sensitive to painful stimulation are: the periosteum and joint capsules. Tendons, ligaments, and subchondral bone are classified as *significantly* pain-sensitive, while muscle and cortical bone's sensitivity has been established as *moderate,* and articular cartilage and fibrocartilage's as *mild.*

Pain is a wholly subjective experience and thus 'inaccessible' as a diagnostic object. Considerations of personality type also complicate the evaluation. As a general rule, however, the observed behavior of a patient in pain can provide a measure of (a) the pain's intensity and (b) the patient's ability to cope with it.

Common fallacies about pain include:

- People who are critically ill or gravely injured always experience intense pain.
- The greater the pain, the greater the extent and severity of damage.
- Severe chronic pain is symptomatic of incurable illness.

In fact, patients who are critically ill or gravely injured do not necessarily experience intense pain. Nor is the observed intensity of pain directly proportional to the extent or severity of damage; the correlation depends also on whether the 'pain pathways' of the anterolateral spinothalamic system are intact and functioning within established norms. In addition, the personality of a neurotic patient may accentuate felt pain, and a stoic or resilient personality may diminish its perceived intensity.

No one ever did ask him. His father believed only that he had an eccentric but very limber and flexible child, a child who'd taken Kathy Kessinger's homilies about spinal hygiene to heart the way some children will take things to heart and now spent a lot of time flexing and limbering his body, which as the queer heartcraft of children went was preferable to many other slack or damaging fixations the father could think of. The father, an entrepreneur who sold motivational tapes through the mail, worked out of a home office but was frequently away for seminars and mysterious evening sales calls. The family's home, which faced west, was tall and slender and contemporary; it resembled one half of a duplex town house from which the other half had been suddenly removed. It had olive-colored aluminum siding and was on a cul-de-sac at the northern end of which stood a side entrance to the county's third-largest cemetery, whose name was woven in iron above the main gate but not above that side entrance. The word that the father thought of when he thought of the boy was: *dutiful,* which surprised the man, for it was a rather old-fashioned word and he had no idea where it came from when he thought of him in there, from outside the door.

Doctor Kathy, who sometimes saw the boy for continuing prophylactic adjustments to his thoracic vertebrae, facets, and anterior rami, and was not a loon or a huckster in a shopping-center office but simply a DC who believed in the interpenetrating dance of spine, nervous system, spirit, and cosmos as totality—in the universe as an infinite system of neural connections that had evolved, at its highest point, an organism which could sustain consciousness of both itself and the universe at the same time, such that the human nervous system became the universe's way of being aware of and thus 'accessible [to]' itself—Doctor Kathy believed the patient to be a very quiet, inner-directed boy who had responded to a traumatic T3 subluxation with a commitment to spinal hygiene and neurospiritual integrity that might well signal a calling to chiropractic as an eventual career. It was she who had given the boy his first, comparatively simple stretching manuals, as well as the copies of B. R. Faucet's famous neuromuscular diagrams (©1961, Los Angeles College of Chiropractic) out of which the boy fashioned the freestanding four-sided cardboard chart that stood as if guarding his pillowless bed while he slept.

The father's belief in ATTITUDE as the overarching determinant of ALTITUDE had been unwavering since his own adolescence, during which awkward time he had discovered the works of Dale Carnegie and of the Willard and Marguerite Beecher Foundation, and had utilized these practical philosophies to bolster his own self-confidence and to improve his social standing—this standing, as well as all interpersonal exchanges and incidents which served as evidence thereof, was charted weekly and the charts and graphs displayed for ease of reference on the inside of his bedroom's closet door. Even as a provisional and secretly tortured adult, the father still worked tirelessly to maintain and improve his attitude and so influence his own altitude in personal achievement. To the medicine cabinet's mirror in the home's bathroom, for instance, where he could not help but reread and internalize them as he tended to personal grooming, were taped inspirational maxims such as:

'NO BIRD SOARS TOO HIGH, IF HE SOARS WITH HIS OWN WINGS — *BLAKE*'

'IF WE ABDICATE OUR INITIATIVE, WE BECOME PASSIVE — RECEPTIVE VICTIMS OF ON-COMING CIRCUMSTANCES — *BEECHER FOUNDATION*'

'DARE TO ACHIEVE! — *NAPOLEON HILL*'

'THE COWARD FLEES EVEN WHEN NO MAN PURSUETH — *BIBLE*'

'WHATEVER YOU CAN DO OR DREAM, YOU CAN BEGIN IT. BOLDNESS HAS GENIUS, POWER AND MAGIC IN IT. BEGIN IT NOW! — *GOETHE*'

and so forth, dozens or at times even scores of inspirational quotes and reminders, carefully printed in block capitals on small, fortune cookie–sized slips of paper and taped to the mirror as written reminders of the father's personal responsibility for whether he soared boldly, sometimes so many slips and pieces of tape that only a few slots of actual mirror were left above the bathroom's sink, and the father had to almost contort himself even to see to shave.

When the boy's father thought of himself, on the other hand, the word that came unbidden first to mind was always: *tortured.* Much of this secret torture—whose causes he perceived as impossibly complex and protean and involving both normal male sexual drives and highly abnormal personal weakness and lack of backbone—was actually quite simple to diagnose. Wedded at twenty to a woman about whom he'd known just one salient thing, this father-to-be had almost immediately found marriage's conjugal routines tedious and stifling; and the sense of monotony and sexual obligation (as opposed to sexual achievement) had caused in him a feeling that he felt must be almost like death. Even as a newlywed, he had begun to suffer from night terrors and to wake from nightmares of some terrible confinement feeling unable to move or breathe. These dreams did not exactly take any kind of psychiatric Einstein to interpret, the father knew, and after almost a year of inner struggle and complex self-analysis he had given in and begun seeing another woman, sexually. This woman, whom the father had met at a motivational seminar, was also married, and had a small child of her own, and they had agreed that this put some sensible limits and restrictions on the affair.

Within a short time, however, the father had begun to find this other woman kind of tedious and oppressive, as well. The fact that they lived separate lives and had little to talk about made the sex start to seem obligatory. It put too much weight on the physical sex, it seemed, and spoiled it. The father attempted to cool things off and to see the woman less, whereupon she in return also began to seem less interested and accessible than she had been. This was when the torture started. The father began to fear that the woman would break off the affair with him, either to resume monogamous sex with her husband or to take up with some other man. This fear, which was a completely secret and interior torture, caused him to pursue the woman all over again even as he came more and more to despise her. The father, in short, longed to detach from the woman, but he didn't want the woman to be able to detach. He began to feel numb and even nauseous when he was with the other woman, but when he was away from her he felt tortured by thoughts of her with someone else. It seemed like an impossible situation, and the dreams of contorted suffocation came back more and more often. The only possible remedy that the father (whose son had just turned four) could see was not to detach from the woman he was having an affair with but to hang dutifully in there with the affair, but also to find and begin seeing a third woman, in secret and as it were 'on the side,' in order to feel—if only for a short time—the relief and excitement of an attachment freely chosen.

Thus began the father's true cycle of torture, in which the number of women with whom he was secretly involved and to whom he had sexual obligations steadily expanded, and in which not one of the women could be let go or given cause to detach and break it off, even as each became less and less a source of anything more than a sort of dutiful tedium of energy and time and the will to forge on in the face of despair.

The boy's mid- and upper back were the first areas of radical, perhaps even impossible unavailability to his own lips, presenting challenges to flexibility and discipline that occupied a vast percentage of his inner life in Grades 4 and 5. And beyond, of course, like the falls at a long river's end, lay the unimaginable prospects of achieving the back of his neck, the eight centimeters just below the chin's point, the galeae of his scalp's back and crown, the forehead and zygomatic ridge, the ears, nose, eyes—as well as the paradoxical *ding an sich* of his lips themselves, accessing which appeared to be like asking a blade to cut itself. These sites occupied a near-mythic place in the overall project: The boy revered them in such a way as to place them almost beyond the range of conscious intent. This boy was not by nature a 'worrier' (unlike himself, his father thought), but the inaccessibility of these last sites seemed so immense that it was as if their cast shadow fell across all the slow progress up toward his clavicle in the front and lumbar curvature in the rear that occupied his eleventh year, darkening the whole endeavor, a tenebrous shadow the boy chose to see as lending the enterprise a somber dignity rather than futility or pathos.

He did not yet know how, but he believed, as he approached pubescence, that his head would be his. He would find a way to access all of himself. He possessed nothing that anyone could ever call doubt, inside.

§37

'Certainly appears to be a nice restaurant.'

'Looks pretty nice.'

'I myself have never been here before. I'd heard good things about it, though, from some of the fellows in Administration. I've been anxious to try it.'

'...'

'And here we are.'

(Removing chewing gum and wrapping it in Kleenex removed from handbag.) 'Uh-huh.'

'...'

'...'

(Makes minute adjustments to placement of silverware.) '...'

'...'

'Do you suppose it's so much easier to make conversation with someone you already know well than with someone you don't know at all primarily because of all the previously exchanged information and shared experiences between two people who know each other well, or because maybe it's only with people we already know well and know know us well that we don't go through the awkward mental process of subjecting everything we think of saying or bringing up as a topic of light conversation to a self-conscious critical analysis and evaluation that manages to make anything we think of proposing to say to the other person seem dull or stupid or banal or on the other hand maybe overly intimate or tension-producing?'

'...'

'...'

'What did you say your name was again?'

'Russell. Russell or sometimes "Russ," though to be honest I have a marked preference for Russell. Nothing against the name Russ; I just never quite cottoned to it.'

'Do you got any aspirin with you, Russell?'

§38

Until mid-1987, the IRS's attempts at achieving an integrated data system were plagued with systemic bugs and problems, many of them exacerbated by Technical Branch's attempts to economize by updating older Fornix keypunch and card-sorter equipment to handle ninety-six-column Powers cards instead of the original eighty-column Holleriths.[1]

One particular bug is relevant here. The Personnel and Training Division's COBOL-based systems had long had special trouble with

1 Because of the heavy, more or less uninterrupted volume of data the IRS processes, its computer systems had been constructed on the fly and had to be maintained and upgraded the same way. The situation was analogous to maintaining a freeway whose high volume of traffic both necessitates and hinders serious maintenance (i.e., there is no way simply to close the road in order to fix the whole thing at one time; there's no way to divert all that traffic). In hindsight, it would ultimately have been cheaper and more efficient to shut the entire Service down for a brief period and transfer everything to a modern, freshly installed disk-based system, nationwide. At the time, though, this seemed unimaginable, especially in light of the Rome NY REC's spectacular 1982 meltdown under the pressures of a cumulative backlog. So many of the fixes and upgrades were temporary and partial and, in retrospect, wildly inefficient, e.g. trying to increase processing power by altering antiquated equipment to accommodate slightly less antiquated computer cards (plus Powers cards had round holes instead of Holleriths' old square ones, requiring all kinds of violent alterations for Fornix equipment that was already old and fragile).

what were sometimes called 'ghost redundancies' in the processing of employee promotions. The problem was especially acute in Examinations staffing because of the unusually high rates of turnover and promotion among REC personnel. Suppose, for example, that Mr. John Q. Doe, a GS-9 rote examiner, was promoted in grade to GS-11. The system would then generate a whole new personnel file, and thereafter would recognize two separate files for what appeared to be two separate employees, John Q. Doe GS-9 and John Q. Doe GS-11, causing extraordinary hassle and confusion for both payroll and Systems planning protocols down the line.

As part of a multipronged debugging effort in 1984, a **GO TO** subroutine was inserted in all Personnel systems' **FILE** sections: In cases of what appeared to be two different employees with the same name and IRS Post code, the system was now directed to recognize only the 'John Q. Doe' of higher GS grade.[2] This led pretty much directly to the snafu at IRS Post 047 in May 1985. In effect, David F. Wallace, GS-9, age twenty, of Philo IL, did not exist; his file had been deleted, or absorbed into, that of David F. Wallace, GS-13, age thirty-nine, of Rome NY's Northeast REC. This absorption occurred at the instant that David F. Wallace (i.e., the GS-13)'s Regional Transfer Form 140(c)-RT and posting Form 141-PO were generated, which instant two different systems administrators in the Northeast and Midwest Regions would eventually have to go back through a combined 2,110,000 lines of recorded code in order to find in order to override the **GO TO** absorption. None of this, of course, was explained in any detail to David F. Wallace (GS-9, formerly GS-13—meaning the David F. Wallace of Philo IL) until much later, after the whole administrative swivet was over and various outlandish charges had been retracted.

2 What might appear to a layman as the obvious problem caused by this debugging—i.e., the loss of the system's ability to recognize and classify IRS demotions—was not in fact much of a problem, comparatively, for Personnel. The fact is that fewer than .002 percent of Internal Revenue Service employees are ever demoted in grade, thanks in large part to the collective-bargaining power of the National Association of Treasury Employees. In effect, the conditions and procedural hurdles required for demotion were gradually strengthened until in most cases they were no less stringent than those required for termination with cause . . . although this is all very much a side issue, mentioned only to head off certain possible confusions on the part of the reader.

The problem was not, in other words, that no one in the Midwest Regional Examination Center's Personnel and Training office noticed that two separate David F. Wallaces were scheduled for intake and processing at the Midwest REC over two successive days. The problem was that the office's computer system recognized, and generated a Powers card and Intake Protocol Form for, only one such David F. Wallace, whom the system further conflated into both (a) the higher-ranked employee transferring from Philadelphia and (b) the employee whose physical arrival was scheduled first in the system, this latter viz. the twenty-year-old ephebe from Philo, whom the system also listed, in a further conflation, as arriving on CT Flight 4130 from Midway (due to the ticketing and travel information generated as part of the Form 140(c)-RT's arrival specs) rather than by Trailways bus, which was why no one was waiting to meet and transport the supposedly elite and valuable David F. Wallace at the Peoria bus terminal on 15 May, and why the second (i.e., the 'real') David F. Wallace, who arrived at the REC by ordinary commercial taxi the following day—which taxi this other, older David Wallace was evidently so meek and passive that it didn't even register on his consciousness that there'd been some foul-up in REC transport, that his rank and value merited a special pickup with his name on a cardboard sign, or even that he should at least get a receipt from the taxi driver so that he could apply for reimbursement, and who furthermore arrived for permanent transfer and a complete change in residence with (rather incredibly) his entire life contained in only one carry-on bag—why that older, elite, highly valued David F. Wallace spent almost two full working days with his Xerox copies of the Forms 141 and chintzy brown suitcase in first the lines for the GS-13 Intake Station and then Problem Resolution desks in the REC's main building's lobby, then sitting in a corner of the lobby itself, then in the Security offices off Level 2's[3] southeast corridor, sitting there with his neotenous face blank and his hat in his lap, unable to proceed, since of course the bureaucracy's computer system had him listed as already having gone through Intake and received his Post 047 ID and badge—in

3 (which, again, was actually the main building's ground floor)

which case where were his badge and ID, a Security part-timer kept asking him, over again each time he checked the system, and if he hadn't lost them then why couldn't he produce them? and so on and so forth.[4]

At the IRS's National Computer Center in Martinsburg WV,[5] the

4 It's probably worth noting two additional bugs or systemic weaknesses or whatever that contributed to the fuck-up and my initial misassignment at Post 047. The first problem was that, due to limitations imposed by the reconfiguration of certain core programs to accommodate round-holed ninety-column Powers cards, the Personnel computer system's file labels could accommodate only an employee's middle initial, which in the case of David Francis Wallace, incoming high-value transfer from Philadelphia, was not enough to distinguish him in the system from David Foster Wallace, incoming low-value contract hire. The second, much more serious problem was that IRS Personnel's original Social Security numbers (i.e., the civilian SSs issued to them in childhood) are always deleted and replaced systemwide by the new, IRS-issued SSs that serve also as Service IDs. An employee's original SS is 'stored' only on his original employment application—which applications are always copied to microfiche and stored in the National Records Center, which NRC by 1981 was dispersed throughout a dozen different regional annexes and warehouse complexes and was notoriously ill-managed and disorganized and difficult to extract specific records from in any kind of timely way. Plus the Personnel systems' file labels can accommodate only one SS # anyway, and that's obviously going to be the new '9'-based SS that functions as one's Service ID number. And since the 975-04-2012 that the new, low-value David F. Wallace was issued upon Expedited Intake was also the 975-04-2012 Service ID # of the older, high-value GS-13 David F. Wallace, the two employees became, so far as the Service's computer system was concerned, the same person.

5 In retrospect, it's now clear that there was actually a third, even more severe systemic problem, which was that, prior to 1987, the Service's computer systems were organized around what's now known as a 'Bad Wheel' model of network integration. Again, there's a great deal of arcana and explanation—most of it involving not only the trying-to-maintain-a-freeway-while-still-letting-people-use-it maintenance situation detailed above but also the piecemeal and jerry-rigged quality of systems whose maintenance depended on annual budget allocations to the Technical Branch, which for a variety of bureaucratic/political reasons fluctuated wildly from year to year—but the point of the Bad Wheel thing was that Technical Branch's networking setup through the mid-1980s resembled a wheel with a hub but no rim. In terms of computer interface, everything had to go through Martinsburg's NCC. A transfer of data from Peoria's Midwest Regional Exam Center to Midwest Region HQ up in Joliet, for example, actually entailed two separate data transfers, the first from Peoria to Martinsburg and the second from Martinsburg to Joliet. Martinsburg's modems and dedicated lines were (for that era) high-baud and efficient, but there was still often a delay in 'routing time,' which bland term actually referred to incoming data's sitting there in Martinsburg's Fornix mainframes' magnetic cores until that data's turn came up in the routing queue. Meaning there was always a lag. And, for understandable reasons, the queue was always longest and the lag worst in the weeks following April 15's tidal influx of individual tax returns. Had there been anything like lateral networking in the IRS system—i.e., had the Midwest REC's Systems/Personnel computers been able to interface directly with their Systems/Personnel counterparts at the

'ghost conflation' problem for employees with identical names had been recognized as early as December 1984—thanks mainly to a hideous mess involving two separate Mary A. Taylors at the Southeast Regional Service Center in Atlanta—and Technical Branch programmers were already in the process of inserting a **BLOCK** and **RESET** sub-subroutine that overrode the **GO TO** subroutine for the thirty-two most common surnames in the United States: viz., Smith, Johnson, Williams, Brown, & c. But Wallace was, according to 1980 US Census figures,[6] only the 104th most common American surname, way down the list between Sullivan and Cole; and any override of **GO TO** that countenanced more than thirty-two surnames ran a statistically significant risk of reintroducing the original 'ghost redundancy' problem. In short, the name David F. Wallace fell in that statistical middle area where the original debugging's consequent 'ghost conflation' bug could still cause significant problems and woe, especially for any employee too new to understand why or whence these accusations of everything from contractual fraud to 'impersonation of an immersive' (that latter an unprecedented charge that may well have been simply made up out of whole cloth by Dick Tate's hatchet men as a way of deflecting what at one point they feared might be construed as negligence or administrative error on the part of REC Personnel, a fear that even Mr. Stecyk, the DDP, conceded was simply bureaucratic paranoia, once the 'unreal' David Wallace [i.e., the author][7] had gotten in to see him and more or less thrown himself on his mercy).

Northeast REC in Philadelphia, the whole David F. Wallace swivet could have been resolved (and unjust blame averted) much more quickly. (Not to mention that the whole rimless-wheel model was at odds with the much-touted decentralization of the Service following the 1952 King Commission report, not much of which is relevant here except in that it just adds to the overall Rube Goldberg idiocy of the whole setup.)

6 (This was the latest published data available, and the Service had to rely exclusively on published data because the US Dept. of Commerce's new UNIVAC system was incompatible with the more antiquated Fornix hardware that Martinsburg was still using.)

7 (Now you can probably see why this occasional 'author' appositive thing is sometimes necessary; it turned out that there were two separate David Wallaces posted at the Midwest REC, of whom the one who ended up accused of impersonation was guess who.)

§39

GS-9 Claude Sylvanshine, back in the Martinsburg Systems compound as part of the April run-up to his advance work at the Midwest REC, went twice into the directed-input tank and tried, under Reynolds's audio supervision, running RFA[1] on Post 047's top brass, the first of which RFA sessions yielded some fruit. Sylvanshine got interpretable fact-sets on DeWitt Glendenning Jr.'s pathological hatred of mosquitoes born of his Tidewater childhood, his failed attempt to become a US Army Ranger in 1943, his violent allergy to shellfish, his evident belief that his genitals were somehow malformed, his run-in with the dreaded Internal Inspections Division while a District Audit Director in Cabin John MD, parts of the home and/or office address of his psychiatrist in suburban Joliet, his memorization of the birthday of every last member of the Midwest Regional Commissioner's family, and a great deal of esoterica about home furniture-construction and -refinishing and power tools that led to an abrupt SDI[2] into certain specs surrounding a male adult's severed thumb. This leading some in Systems to conclude that current Midwest REC

1 Remote Fact Acquisition

2 Spontaneous Data Intrusion

Director and Regional toady DeWitt 'Dwitt' Glendenning had lost or would shortly lose a thumb in some type of home woodworking accident, and to tailor certain plans and expectations around this fact.

The truth—which Claude Sylvanshine will and can never know despite the repeated column of figures on both the aerodynamics of arterial blood and the rates at which a 1420-rpm standing band-saw blade can cut through the various conic sections of a human hand of certain mass and angle—is that an adult severed thumb's factual relevance was actually to the life and psyche of Leonard Stecyk, Post 047's DDP, who as a practical matter undertook to do not only his own work but much of his superior's. The severed-thumb incident figures in the psychic development that transformed L. M. Stecyk into one of the most brilliant and able Service administrators in the Region, though the thumb incident is by now buried deep in Mr. Stecyk's unconscious, his conscious life dominated by the REC's Personnel office and by issues surrounding the gathering storms in both Systems and Compliance.

The incident itself is not immediately relevant and so can be recounted quite fast. For reasons now lost in the administrative mists, Industrial Arts was then required of male tenth-graders across the upper Midwest, giving the Vocational Ed pupils a last chance to savage and torment the College Prep boys from whom they'd been (in Michigan) split off the previous year. And Leonard Stecyk had an especially hard time of it in Mr. Ingle's third-hour Industrial Arts class at Charles E. Potter High School in the autumn of 1969. It was not just that at almost sixteen Stecyk was 5' 1" and 105 pounds soaking wet, which he was (soaking wet) when the boys in his PE class's shower all urinated on him after knocking him to the tile floor, which ritual they called a Stecyk Special—he ending up the only boy in the history of Grand Rapids to carry an umbrella into a school's showers. Nor was it a matter just of the special OSHA-approved safety goggles and special homemade carpenter's apron inscribed in Palmer cursive with LEN'S THE NAME; WOOD'S THE GAME that he wore to class. Nor that third-hour IA featured two separate future convicted felons, one of whom had already served a week's suspension for heating an ingot of cast iron red-hot with an acetylene torch, waiting just until the last color had vanished from it, and then casually asking Stecyk to go bring him that one ingot over by the scroll saw real quick. The real problem was practical: Leonard turned out to have no talent or affinity whatsoever for Industrial Arts, whether it came to basic dynamics or welding, rudimentary construction or custom carpentry. True, the kid's drafting and measurement specs were, Mr. Ingle admitted, exceptionally (almost effeminately, he felt) neat and precise. It was with actual projects and operations of the machinery that Stecyk was terrible, whether it was cutting to an angle, following a pre-drawn jig, or even sanding smooth the base of the special pinewood cigar box that Mr. Ingle (who liked cigars) forced all the pupils to make for their fathers, but on which Stecyk's apparently loose or insufficiently masculine grip caused the belt-sander to shoot the box like a piece of ordnance across the Industrial Arts classroom, where it exploded against the cement wall not ten feet from the head of Mr. Ingle, who told Stecyk (whom he despised without guilt or reservation) that the only reason he didn't force him and his little apron over to Home Economics with the girls was that he'd probably burn the whole everloving school down! at which some of the larger and crueler tenth-grade boys (one of whom would be expelled the following autumn for not only bringing a USFWS bear trap onto school property but going so far as to open and set it—the dagger-sharp spring-loaded trap—outside the door to the vice principal's office, where it had to be deactivated with the pole of a custodian's push broom, which it snapped with a sound that caused students in classrooms all up and down the hall to duck and cover) actually pointed directly at Stecyk as they laughed.

On the other hand, it's possible that the severed-thumb incident did not so much actually change or shape Leonard Stecyk's character as alter his own perspectives on it (if any), as well as others' perceptions of him. As most adults know, the distinctions between one's essential character and value and people's perceptions of that character/value are fuzzy and hard to delineate, especially in adolescence. There is also the fact that a certain amount of situational setup and context to the incident Leonard Stecyk no longer recalls, not even in dreams or peripheral flashes. It had to do with cutting a sheet of drywall into lathes or strips for some kind of reinforcement involving the framing and hanging of a door in an interior wall. The band saw was set in a broad metal table with gauges and calibrated clamps to hold what you were cutting just so while you pushed the piece carefully along the smooth surface so that the band saw's high-speed blade cut along the pencil line you'd drawn after measuring at least twice. There were, of course, detailed safety procedures as codified by Mr. Ingle in both the mimeographed Shop Rules and several stenciled all-cap signs on and around the band saw's rear housing, which procedures Leonard Stecyk had not only memorized but tried helpfully to point out some instances of typos or ambiguous phrasing in the terse imperatives of, which had caused one side of Mr. Ingle's big face to start jumping and crinkling involuntarily, a notorious sign that the man was just barely keeping his temper under control. The reality behind the surfeit of signs and yellow caution lines painted on the shop room floor was that Mr. Ingle operated under great felt pressure and constant borderline frustration and rage, since it was his responsibility if anybody got hurt, and yet at the same time many of the kids in the classes were either inept effeminate 'mathlete' pansies like Stecyk and Moss here or else long-haired delinquents in army coats that sometimes came to class smelling of marijuana and peppermint schnapps, and screwed around with rules and equipment they didn't have the sense to respect the dangerousness of, including standing around watching within the clearly marked yellow line to the side of the band saw and its unshielded blade despite the clearly painted instructions on both machine and floor to STAY BEHIND LINE WHEN IN OPERATION, where all it would then take is a careless shove or even gesture where you waved one of your arms around when standing in the unauthorized side area; and in illustrating this at the top of his lungs for maybe the fifth time this quarter as the sad excuse for kids stood at the yellow line and watched him exaggerate a childish gesture, his right hand inadvertently made contact with the blade of the band saw, which just as quickly as Mr. Ingle had promised it could, took off his thumb and the surrounding material from the interdigital webbing down to the abductor pollicis longus tendon, also opening the radial artery, which caused a tremendous fan of blood-spatter as Mr. Ingle brought the red thing to his chest and toppled sideways, gray with shock and the paralytic reflexes of trauma. As was more or less everyone else in the class—gray-faced, openmouthed—watching from the yellow line as blood from the radial and also first volar metacarpal arteries shot rhythmically up and out and spattered even some of the taller boys' khaki coats and the control panel of the drill press against which they bumped as they stepped reflexively back. This was not the slow welling of a skinned knuckle or the trickle of a punched nose. This was arterial blood under great systolic pressure, which shot up and fanned out from where the teacher knelt cradling the hand against his chest with the other hand and staring at the phalanx of boys, mouthing something that could not be heard over the band saw's A# scream, some of the College Prep boys' faces also distended in screams which could be seen but not heard, a few others at the extreme back peeling off around the drill press's clamps and running for the classroom door with their arms up and hands waving in the universal movement of blind panic, the rest splayed against the nearest peer or machine with their eyes wide and minds in deep neutral.

...All but little Leonard Stecyk, who after only the briefest neural pause moved forward, quickly and decisively, came out around the group's flank, punching at the band saw's double-marked Power button with the heel of his bandaged hand as he swept around the back of the machine, looking neither right nor left in his apron and pressed white shirt, elbowing aside a large boy in a paisley headband who stood with his Keds' soles in human blood—a boy who only days before had menaced Stecyk with a pair of blacksmith's tongs behind the lathe's peg-board tool display—and seemed instantly to be at the side of Mr. Ingle, implementing the first rule of on-site treatment for hemorrhagic trauma, which was simultaneously to elevate the wound and to identify the severity of the trauma using the five-point Ames Scale from Cherry Ames RN's 1962 *First Aid for Industrial Injury*, which Stecyk had checked out of the public library as part of his standard preparation for the Autumn '69 class schedule. Stecyk simply lifted the hand as high as he could, to about eye level, while Mr. Ingle knelt hunched and slumped beneath it. It cannot be overstressed how fast this all was happening. The thumb and surrounding base tissues were not completely detached but hung by a flap of dermis such that Mr. Ingle's thumb itself pointed straight down in a parody of imperial judgment as Stecyk, ignoring both the blood and the high-pitched diminutives for 'Mother' that began to be audible as the band saw cycled down, removed with one hand first his slacks' belt and then the metric-conversion ruler he carried in a special narrow pocket of the carpenter's apron Mr. Ingle had ridiculed and—after running mentally through the protocols and determining à la Cherry Ames RN that digital pressure around the wrist did not alone control the bleeding—fashioned a deft two-knot tourniquet (w/ just a hint of Edwardian flourish to the top's four-loop bow, which was even more amazing given that Stecyk constructed the special knot with slippery scarlet hands that also supported a man's half-fainting weight) that stanched the flow with only one and a half turns of the ruler, such was the memorized precision with which Stecyk had placed the tourniquet just at the crucial branch between the forearm's ulnar and radial arteries. In the belling stillness after the saw's blade stopped you could now hear the sounds of the pneumatic jack from the Intro Auto Mechanics classroom next door. It was also now, with the spray's cessation, that Mr. Ingle lost consciousness, so that the last sight some of the taller boys at the flanks had was Stecyk cupping Mr. Ingle's skull at the back like a child's and gently lowering him—it, the big man's head—to the floor with one hand while the other held the tourniquet in place at the upraised wrist, there being something both dancerly and maternal and yet not one bit girlish about the sight that reverberated within the souls of a few in strange ways for days and even weeks after they were shouldered aside and told to break it up and give the man some air by the Auto Mechanics and Appliance Repair teachers, who also were brisk and adultly unfrozen but did not try to move Len aside or ask the Home Ec aide to shoo him outside with all the others and their red footprints but rather stood like subalterns at either side of the man's upraised arm with pendent thumb, awaiting instructions from the boy on whether they should wait for the ambulance or maybe try and put Mr. Ingle in one of their cheap but faultlessly tuned cars and rush him right to Calvin, speaking to Stecyk as more of a peer and being spoken to in return without deference or hesitation.

Voc Ed students tend not to be very sensitive or emotionally agile, and it would be too much to say that 'everything changed' after that day in Industrial Arts. It was not that Leonard Stecyk became popular, or that the hard boys started inviting him to come out with them on school nights to perpetrate vandalism or abuse gateway drugs. A few of them, though, were surprised—not ashamed so much as shaken—by their paralysis in the face of trauma and the noxious little faggot's actions. It was strange. These were tough boys: They fought freely, took beatings from stepdads and older brothers. For the brightest among them, their idea of what toughness was, of the relations between coolness and actual value, had now been somewhat fucked with. Their accounts of the incident were confused and varied from boy to boy. More than one alluded to *Lost in Space,* which was a popular show at the time. The main change in the quality of the future DDP's life was that most of the Stecyk Specials and sudden hallway punches in the upper arm's radial nerve and other daily bits of cruelty ceased, mostly because a strange unease came over the hard boys when they saw or even thought of Stecyk, and real cruelty—as every adolescent knows—requires a close attention to the object of that cruelty. Stecyk's actions that day did not make him more but less special; the hard boys ceased to see him or single him out. It was strange, and stranger still was how fast Stecyk himself forgot the whole thing, even after Mr. Ingle returned to C. E. Potter after Thanksgiving for his new duties as a Driver Ed instructor with his maimed right hand encased in some kind of protective black polyurethane glove or sheath, resulting in the student sobriquet 'Dr. No' throughout the early 1970s. Everyone seemed to have incentive to forget the whole thing. A Voc Ed hard boy who would serve in the Plaine des Joncs region of Indochina twenty months later was the only one with a clear conscious memory of Stecyk and Ingle's thumb that one day, and this when a fat-body draftee who'd almost flunked Basic and been the object of a savage blanket party had taken a squad that had lost its corporal and regrouped them and brought them around between two separate NVA platoons to reform with Able Company; he had just stood up and told them to strip ordnance off the dead and form a defilade against the opposite side of the creek-bed, and everyone had obeyed—unthinkingly, for reasons they could not later explain or admit—and the hard boy had thought of Stecyk in his little apron and paisley bow tie (the latter a distortion of memory) and of the fact, again, that what they'd then thought was the wide round world was a little boy's preening dream.

§40

Cusk had been ushered into the psychiatrist's office and was counting the boxes of Kleenex in a little room lined with big books and diplomas. The sixth was on the little desk in the corner the psychiatrist used for filling out prescriptions. The office was minus the little sink some physicians had—he'd spent whole days girding himself for the sink. When his name had been called, Cusk had shaken the psychiatrist's hand and taken a padded chair the psychiatrist's other hand had indicated. The psychiatrist hitched her trousers up slightly at the knee and had sat down opposite Cusk across a glass coffee table on which were two boxes of Kleenex. Her hand had been large, warm, and soft. Her chair was the same model as Cusk's chair—one, maybe two levels of comfort below an easy chair—but seemed, unless it was his imagination, to be slightly taller than his chair.

...'of spiders, of dogs, of mail,' Cusk was listing—the psychiatrist listened intently, nodding, but did not take notes, which relieved Cusk—'Fear of spiral notebooks, the kind with the spiral or wire down the spine; fear of fountain pens—though not felt-tip or ballpoint pens, unless the ballpoint is one of those expensive ones with an aspect of permanence—Cross, Montblanc, the kind that look gold—but not plastic or disposable ballpoints.' Having exhausted Kleenex boxes to count, Cusk was mentally repeating *'large, soft, and warm, large, soft and warm,'* over and over, a ruminative chant just below the level of thought.

'Fear of disks. Fear of drains. Fear of pretty much all spiral movements in liquid, across the board.'

The psychiatrist's eyebrows were extraordinarily thin and sparse, and when she raised them it meant she didn't quite follow—

'Whirlpools, maelstroms, bathtubs draining,' Cusk illustrated. He had a fine sheen of sweat on his upper lip, but could tell by feel that the forehead was staying dry, hanging in there. 'Briskly stirred beverages. Flushing toilets.'

§41

'You sent Cardwell to get him?'

'What's the problem?'

'He's demented, Charlie, that's what's the problem.'

'He's a good driver. He's dependable.'

'He'll rant at the guy the whole way here; the guy'll think it's a post of evangelist goons. This is Lehrl's aide, Charlie. Jesus.'

§42

There were long silences between periods of attention.

'Shit I got one for you. This was a while ago, though, when I was in school in St. Louis, when we were the Reserve Rangers.'

'I'll bite.'

'You won't get some of it. You had to be alive in the late sixties.'

'We weren't alive?'

'I don't mean playing-with-your-toes alive or squeezing-the-pores-of-your-nose alive. I mean of age, aware. I mean culturally.'

'Counterculturally you mean.'

'I could say to eat shit off a thick wooden stick, Gaines. But I don't. Instead I say if there's something cool with this unmistakable quality and I say the thing's quality is just so Beatles, you don't get it.'

'You had to be there.'

'It's not the same thing as just owning Beatles records, you're saying. You had to be *there,* in it.'

'Grooving. Being groovy.'

'That's just it. Nobody really said groovy. People that said groovy or called you man were just playing out some fantasy they'd seen on CBS reports. I'm saying if I say Baxter-Bathing or Owsley or mention Janis's one dress she wore you think in terms of data. There's none of the feeling attached to it—this was a feeling. It's impossible to describe.'

'Except as saying it's so very Beatles.'

'And some of it not even data. What if I say Lord Buckley? What if I say the Texas tower or Sin Killer Griffin on tape from jail or Jackson going on *Today* and sitting across from that J. Fred chimp in a shirt that's still got Martin's blood and brain matter on it and nobody says anything even though *Today*'s in New York which means fucking Jackson flew all the way in from Memphis in that shirt so he could wear blood on TV—do you feel anything if I say that? Or *Bonanza* or *I Am Curious* parenthesis *Yellow*? J. Fred Muggs? Jesus, *The Fugitive*—if I say the one-armed man, what interior state does it provoke?'

'You mean nostalgia.'

'I mean methamphetamine hydrochloride. Say *December's Children* or *Dharma Bums* or Big Daddy Cole at the House of Blues in Dearborn or crew cuts and horn-rims or even let me think of rolled-up Levi's showing three inches of white cotton over penny loafers and I taste the hydrochloride from the days at Wash U when we were the Reserve Rangers. How odd I can have all this inside me and to you it's just words.'

'We have our own little cultural signposts and cathexes and things that make us feel nostalgia.'

'It's not nostalgia. It's a whole set of references you don't even know you don't have. Suppose I say Sweater Puppies—you feel nothing. Christ, Sweater Puppies.'

'Not acid?'

'Pardon?'

'Why methamphetamine and not acid? LSD? Weren't grass and LSD the era's like defining drugs?'

'That's what I mean. None of the nuance or complexity introduces into your field. Acid was the West Coast and a small cell around Boston. Acid wasn't even in Greenwich Village until Kesey and Leary's thing upstate in '67. By '67 the sixties were over. The Midwest was meth and designer hallucinogens. We had a small sort of inner set at Wash U who were in with the Dogtown crowd; one reason I'm here instead of private is I don't think one of us cracked a book in two years, then I had to move because of the Rescue Rangers and this older guy named, perversely, McCool, who wanted in with us, hung around, but desperately uncool, from hunger we'd say but to you this means nothing. McCool was a district rep for Welch Lambeth. I presume Welch Lambeth is part of your cultural index.'

'Chemicals. Now part of Lilly. University City, Miz, heavily diversified, chemical and largely industrial solvents, medical supplies, adhesive, polymers, chassis molds.'

'Medical supplies at this time including for instance sometimes he'd bring stuff in, we'd be at the usual table at Jaegerschnitzel, a rathskeller for WU's most countercultural and antiestablishment but not mod or groovy crowd, and one night in the midst of some bull session in comes McCool, who had a larcenous heart, with a half-pound insulated box he'd got from some sample room and said, "I know some of you fellows like this, so when I saw it I said, Holy Smokes I gotta liberate this for the fellows" and like that. From hunger, but plucky in that Eisenhower way. He's in his thirties and already bald with a blinky hunger for acceptance; you can only imagine what must have happened to him as a kid. The sort of guy who comes to your party and you get him drunk enough to pass out by nine and put him in the Rescue Rangers minibus and strip off everything but his shoes and socks and leave him propped up on a bus stop bench in East St. Louis and he'll not only survive somehow but the next night he'll be back at the Jaegerschnitzel punching you in the shoulder and saying Good One like you'd just given him a hotfoot, desperate to be one of the guys.'

'My brothers taught me that desperation is the chief, like, bar to being accepted as one of the guys. I learned this the hard way I can tell you. One time because as a kid I was scared of the water and they let me come with them on a camping trip and my oldest brother said this was my one big chance to be one of the guys and instead of camping it turned out it was a fishing trip and when I tried to climb in the boat it turned out they—'

'And we're like right, great, but then Eddie Boyce opens it up and inside are these long insulated corrugated-cardboard tubes, and inside each tube is a little three-inch double-stoppered test tube with... pharmaceutical-grade methamphetamine hydrochloride, three-point-something grams each. We're all sitting there looking at each other and Boyce's eyebrows are about on top of his head. McCool trying to play it casual but saying "See? What do you think?" Do you know what this means? There were 224 grams of pure pharmaceutical meth in that box. Do you know what even crummy adulterated garage-lab meth can do to a twenty-year-old nervous system?'

'I would have sold it off and used the net to establish a position in silver and then gone to my professors and pulled their beards, tell them I could buy and sell them now and they could put that in their pipes and smoke it.'

'We didn't sell enough of it, I'll tell you. But what we did wreaked havoc. Classes were a zoo. Carbuncular kids who'd sat in the back row and never made a peep were grabbing their profs by the lapels and citing the surplus theory of value in the voice of SS interrogators. Newman Club mainstays were copulating with abandon on the library steps. The infirmary was besieged by philosophy grad students begging someone to shut their heads off. Dining halls were empty. The entire Wash U defensive backfield was jailed for assault on the Kansas State water boy. Coeds whose hymens could be used for a vault door were giving it up in the bushes outside Lambda Pi. Most of the next two months we spent as the Reserve Rangers, in the van, answering distress calls from boys who had gotten hold of a tenth of a gram of this stuff and now found their girlfriends hanging off the ceiling by their nails grinding their perfect little white teeth into nubbins. Reserve Rangers!

'Awake for a week at a time, all of us flying on meth and never coming down because coming down off meth is like having terrible flu while in hell, Boyce's palms with permanent indentations from gripping the bus's wheel so hard, and all our eyeballs looking like novelty-shop eyeballs. The closest we're coming to eating is shuddering in distaste when we see a restaurant sign on our way to the literally dozens of Rescue Ranger calls we're getting every night, booming the doors and scanning the elevators and taking stairs five at a time singing our Rescue Rangers on the Job fight song.'

'What's this Rescue Rangers angle, Todd, if—?'

'Because in very short order as the power and purity of this stuff starts to ramify throughout Dogtown we impress upon McCool the need for some kind of remedial help from the good offices of Welch Lambeth.'

'What possible medical use does methamphetamine have? Obesity? Sleep deprivation research? Controlled-psychosis experiments?'

'And two or three days later—just as all of us are reaching just about the limits of endurance and our ribs are showing and the skin around our eyes is starting to look like hamburger—there was one terrible accident where I was alone and I decided all right this time we take the emergency brake off and shoot almost an eighth of a gram uncut and was in a very very strange state of mind indeed one step short of clinical paranoia and the doorbell rings and I open it on the chain and all I see is a hat with plastic flowers on the brim and it's this tiny old little blameless Welcome Wagon lady, welcoming us in our caved-in rental house to the neighborhood with a little basket of cookies and hygienic products looking up at me but with those weird little hypnotic spirals of red in one eye and green in another and her little peanut of a face convexly bulging out horribly like a crocodile's face and then receding and then coming out up at me again, and I'll spare you the details of how I reacted except to tell you that this incident led directly to my having to drop out and move to Colorado less than two months later, which is how I got the Service Moniker Colorado Todd.'

§43

Tuesday morning I had an ENT appointment and clocked in at 10:05. The complex was even more subdued than usual. People spoke quietly and had a slight shoulder-first quality to their walk. A few of the women who were known to react to any sort of upset by becoming pale were pale. There was a quality of slow-motion milling to everybody's activities, as if they were all reacting to something but were aware of themselves reacting and that everybody else was reacting. I was out of aspirin. For some reason I was reluctant to ask anybody what had happened. I hate being the person who always doesn't know what's going on and has to ask somebody; it always seems like everybody else knows what's going on. This is a clear low-status marker, and I resisted it. It wasn't until after eleven that I overheard Trudi Keener, Jane-Ann Heape, and Homer Campbell in the UNIVAC room collating stacks of backdated EST vouchers.

There had been an explosion in another Region. In either Muskegon or Holland, both tenth annexes. Either a car or a light truck had parked directly in front of the District office and then at some later time blown up. Trudi Keener had quoted George Molesworthy as saying that the Posse Comitatus was known to be both extreme and active in Michigan. This meant that it was a terrorist attack on a

Service Post, which in any depressed agricultural region is going to send chills. I stood in the room pretending to check something in the file catalogue for as long as I figured I could without Jane-Ann Heape being able to discern that I was eavesdropping and deduce that I was the sort of person who didn't know what was going on and recalibrate her idea of me accordingly. Her hair today was up and done in a complex set of curls and waves that appeared darker in the blue-end fluorescence of the UNIVAC room. She had on a pale blue acetate blouse and skirt whose plaid was so dark and low-contrast it was hard to identify it as true plaid. No casualty information emerged, but I did learn that two or three of 047's Audit-Coordination Support Systems staff had been posted in Michigan early in their careers; I had no connection to Audit-Coordination Support Systems and didn't recognize the names.

When my break came the coffee room smelled sour, which meant that Mrs. Oooley hadn't cleaned out the pots and filters before clocking out last night. It was a personnel gold mine in there, however. Mr. Glendenning and Gene Rosebury were drinking coffee out of their complimentary Service mugs (for GS-13s and up) and Meredith Rand was eating a cup of yogurt out of the GS-9 refrigerator with a plastic fork (which meant Ellen Bactrim was hoarding spoons again). They were having the conversation, and Gary Yeagle and James Rumps and several others were standing just off to the side, listening. I came in in the middle and pretended to study the vending machines and then to count the coins in my hand.

'This isn't terrorism. This is people not wanting to pay their taxes,' Gene Rosebury said. There were faint remains of his customary Mylanta mustache. The 'this' indicated that there was a great deal of conversational context and information that had gone on heretofore.

'If I'm terrified, that doesn't make it terrorism?' Meredith Rand said. She removed a tiny bit of yogurt from the corner of her mouth with her little finger. It seemed significant that no one laughed, not even the GS-9s. Rand's was the sort of low-cal sally that was meant not so much to be funny as to give the room the opportunity to laugh and so dispel tension. No one took this opportunity. This seemed telling. Mr. Glendenning had on a tan suit and a string tie with a medallion of turquoise at the crux. The REC Director was a man who was accustomed to being the center of attention in any room he was in, although with him this manifested as an air of quiet self-possession instead of exhibitionism. I didn't know a person at the Post who didn't like and admire DeWitt Glendenning. I had been with the Service long enough by this time to understand that this was one quality of a successful administrator, to be liked. And not to *act* in such a way as to be liked, but to *be* that way. Nobody ever felt that Mr. Glendenning was putting on any kind of act, the way less gifted administrators do, even an act for themselves, for instance acting like a martinet because someplace inside they have a picture of a good administrator as a hard-ass and are trying to contort their own personalities to fit the picture. Or that glad-handing, my-door-is-always-open type who believes a good administrator needs to be everyone's friend and so acts very open and friendly even though the responsibilities of his office require him to discipline people or cut budgets and deny requests or reassign people to Examination or any number of things that aren't friendly at all. This type puts himself in a terrible position, because each time he has to do something for the good of the Service that is going to hurt some employee or piss her off, the action now carries the additional emotional freight of a friend dicking over a friend, and frequently the administrator feels so uncomfortable over this and his divided loyalties that he has to get personally angry—or act angry—at the employee to do it, which makes the thing personal in an inappropriate way and adds greatly to the dicked-over employee's hurt and resentment, and over time this totally undermines the administrator's authority, and in very short order everybody sees him as a fake and a backstabber, pretending to be your friend and colleague but ready to dick you over whenever he feels like it. It's interesting that these two false administrative styles—the tyrant and the fake friend—are also the two main stereotypes that books and television shows and comic strips present administrators as. One suspects, in fact, that the mental picture the insecure administrator erects inside himself is based partly on these pop-culture stereotypes.

Mr. Glendenning seemed not so much to subvert the stereotypes as to transcend them. His self-possession allowed him to be and act precisely as he was. What he was was a taciturn, slightly unapproachable man who took his job very seriously and required his subordinates to do the same, but he took them seriously as well, and listened to them, and thought about them both as human beings and as parts of a larger mechanism whose efficient function was his responsibility. That is, if you had a suggestion or a concern, and you decided that it merited his attention, his door *was* open (that is, you could make an appointment through Caroline Oooley), and he would pay attention to what you said, but whether and how he would *act* on what you said would depend on reflection, input from other sources, and larger considerations he was required to balance. In other words, Mr. Glendenning *could* listen to you because he did not suffer from the insecure belief that listening to you and taking you seriously obligated him to you in any way—whereas someone in thrall to the martinet-picture would have to treat you as unworthy of attention, and someone in thrall to the peer-picture would feel that he needed either to take your suggestion to avoid offending you, or give an exhausting explanation about why your suggestion wasn't implementable or maybe even enter into some kind of debate about it—to avoid offending you or violating his picture of himself as the sort of administrator who would never treat a subordinate's suggestion as unworthy of serious consideration—or get angry as a way of anesthetizing his discomfort at not welcoming the suggestion of someone he feels obligated to see as a friend and equal in every way.

Mr. Glendenning was also a man of style, the sort of man whose clothes hang on him just right even after he's ridden in cars and sat at desks in them. All his clothes had a sort of loose but symmetrical hang to them that I associated with European clothes. He always put one hand in his hip pocket and leaned back against the lip of the counter when he drank coffee. It was, in my opinion, his most approachable posture. His face was tan and ruddy even under the fluorescents. I knew one of his daughters was a gymnast of some national repute, and sometimes he wore a tiepin or brooch or something that seemed to consist of two horizontal bars and a platinum figure bent complexly over both. Sometimes I imagined coming into the coffee room and finding Mr. Glendenning alone, leaning back against the counter, staring down into the coffee in his mug and thinking deep administrative thoughts. In my fantasy he looks tired, not haggard but careworn, weighed down by the responsibilities of his position. I come in and get some coffee and approach him, he calling me Dave and I calling him DeWitt or even D.G., which was rumored to be his nickname around other District Directors and Assistant Regional Commissioners—Mr. G is up for Regional Commissioner, is the rumor—and I ask him what's up and he confides to me about some administrative dilemma he's on the horns of, like how the Systems guy Lehrl's constant reconfiguration of people's spaces and the passages between them was a ridiculous pain in the ass and waste of time and if it were up to him he'd personally pick the officious little prick up by the scruff of the neck and put him in a box with only one or two air-holes in it and FedEx him back to Martinsburg but that Merrill Lehrl was a protégé and favorite of the Assistant Commissioner for Taxpayer Service and Returns at Triple-Six, whose other big protégé was the Midwest Region's Regional Commissioner for Examination, who was essentially if not formally Mr. Glendenning's immediate superior in terms of Post 047's Corporate Examination Function and was the sort of disastrous administrator who believed in alliances and patrons and politics, and who could deny 047's application for an additional half-shift of GS-9 examiners on a number of pretexts that would appear reasonable on paper, and only D.G. and the RCE would know it was over Merrill Lehrl, and DeWitt felt beholden to the beleaguered examiners to get them some relief and to take some time off the Return Turnaround Schedule, which two different studies indicated could be accomplished better through relief and expansion than through motivation and reconfiguration (an analysis with which Merrill Lehrl disagreed, D.G. noted wearily). In the fantasy, D.G.'s head and mine are lowered somewhat, and we speak quietly, even though no one else is in the coffee room, which smells good and has cans of fine-ground Melitta instead of the Jewel-brand white cans with the khaki lettering, and it's then, perfectly in the context of the exact beleaguered-and-distracted-examiners problem he's confiding to me about, that I hit D.G. with the idea of these new Hewlett-Packard document scanners and the way the software could be reconfigured to scan both returns and schedules and to apply the TCMP code to red-flag selected items, so that examiners would have only to check and verify the important red-flag items instead of wading through line after line of unimportant OK stuff in order to reach the important items. D.G. listens to me intently, respectfully, and it's only his judiciousness and administrative professionalism that keep him from expressing on the spot the enormous acuity and potential of my suggestion, and his gratitude and care that here a GS-9 examiner has come out of nowhere and given a lateral, outside-the-box solution that will both relieve the examiners and free up D.G. to send the odious Merrill Lehrl packing.

§44

I learned it at just twenty-one or twenty-two, at the IRS's Regional Examination Center in Peoria, where I spent two summers as a cart boy. This, according to the fellows who saw me as fit for a Service career, put me ahead of the curve, to understand this truth at an age when most guys are starting only to suspect the basics of adulthood—that life owes you nothing; that suffering takes many forms; that no one will ever care for you as your mother did; that the human heart is a chump.

I learned that the world of men as it exists today is a bureaucracy. This is an obvious truth, of course, though it is also one the ignorance of which causes great suffering.

But moreover, I discovered, in the only way that a man ever really learns anything important, the real skill that is required to succeed in a bureaucracy. I mean really succeed: do good, make a difference, serve. I discovered the key. This key is not efficiency, or probity, or insight, or wisdom. It is not political cunning, interpersonal skills, raw IQ, loyalty, vision, or any of the qualities that the bureaucratic world calls virtues, and tests for. The key is a certain capacity that underlies all these qualities, rather the way that an ability to breathe and pump blood underlies all thought and action.

The underlying bureaucratic key is the ability to deal with boredom. To function effectively in an environment that precludes everything vital and human. To breathe, so to speak, without air.

The key is the ability, whether innate or conditioned, to find the other side of the rote, the picayune, the meaningless, the repetitive, the pointlessly complex. To be, in a word, unborable. I met, in the years 1984 and '85, two such men.

It is the key to modern life. If you are immune to boredom, there is literally nothing you cannot accomplish.

§45

Toni's mom was a bit nuts, as was her own mom, who was a notorious recluse and eccentric who lived in the Hubcap House in Peoria. Toni's mom took up with a succession of bad-news men in the US Southwest. The last one was giving them a ride back to Peoria, where Toni's mom had decided to return after the relationship before that one had gone bad. Blah blah. On this ride, the mom had more or less gone crazy (stopped taking her meds) and stolen the guy's truck at a rest stop, leaving the guy behind.

Both the mom and the grandmother had been given to catatonic/cataleptic states, which as far as I can tell is a symptom of a certain kind of schizophrenia. The girl, ever since young, had amused herself by trying to imitate this state, which involved sitting or lying extremely still, slowing your pulse, breathing in such a way that your chest doesn't even rise, and holding your eyes open for long periods, such that you're blinking only every couple minutes. It's the last that's hardest—the eyes start to burn as they dry out. Very, very hard to push through this discomfort... but if you do, if you can resist the almost involuntary urge to blink that comes when the burning and drying is the very worst, then the eyes will start lubricating themselves without blinking. They will manufacture a kind of false or ersatz tears, just to save themselves. Almost no one knows this, because the incredible discomfort of having your eyes open without blinking stops most people before they hit that critical point. And there's usually damage, anyway. The girl had called it 'playing dead,' since that's the way her mother had tried to describe and discount the states to the girl when she was very tiny, saying that she was only playing and that the game was called 'play dead.'

The abandoned man had caught up with them somewhere in eastern Missouri. They'd been on a little blacktop highway, and the first sign that he was behind was a pair of headlights that showed just when they were on a downslope that extended a mile or more—they'd see the headlights appear when the trailing vehicle hit the crest, then they'd lose them when they started to climb the slow grade again.

As Toni Ware remembers it and recounted it just one time to X on a night that turned out to be the anniversary of the occurrence, the vehicle that the man had commandeered or hired came up fast behind them—it turned out to be going quite a bit faster than the truck, which had a camper shell—and the man was not driving the vehicle. He was standing on the front hood of what emerged to be the trailerless cab of an enormous semi truck, swollen by rage and malice to at least twice his normal size, holding his arms up and out in a terrible gesture of almost Old Testament retribution, and hollering (in the rural sense of 'holler,' which is almost a special kind of art form; it used to be the way that people who lived way out in hill country out of sight of each other would communicate—it was the way of letting other people know that they were around, because otherwise it could seem, in the rural hills, like you were the only person anywhere within thousands of miles) with an ecstatic black evil rage and glee that caused Toni's mother—who, let's recall, was not a paragon of stability—to become hysterical and floor the accelerator and try to outrun the vehicle while at the same time trying to extract from her purse a bottle of prescription pills and to open the childproof cap, which the mother was terrible at and usually needed Toni to open for her—causing the vehicle, which was top-heavy because of the LEER camper shell, to swerve off the road and go over on its side in some kind of field or area of weeds, injuring the mom terribly such that she was half-stunned and moaning and blood covering her face and Toni was lying against the passenger-side window, and in fact still has the window's crank imprinted into her side if you can get her to raise her top and show you the eerie reproduction. The vehicle came to rest on its right side, and the mom wasn't wearing a seat belt, which people like that never do, and she was lying partly on top of Toni Ware, pinning her against the window so that she couldn't move or even tell whether she was injured. There was nothing but that terrible silence and hissing and ticking of a vehicle that's just had an accident, plus the sound of spurs or maybe just a great deal of pocket change jingling as the man negotiated the downslope down to them. Her own window was driven into the ground and the driver's-side window was now pointing up at the sky, but the windshield, though buckled and hanging halfway off, had turned into a four-foot vertical slot through which Toni Ware got a full-length view of the man standing there, cracking his knuckles and looking at the occupants of the car. Toni lay there with her eyes opened and slowed her breathing and played dead. The mom's eyes were closed, but she was alive because you could hear her breathing and occasionally giving little unconscious exclamations in her coma or whatever it was. The man looked at Toni, locked eyes with her, for a long time—later, she understood that he was trying to ascertain if she was alive. It is unimaginably hard to be staring straight ahead and have someone lock eyes with you and yet to appear like you're not looking back at them. (This is what had started the story; David Wallace or someone else had remarked that Toni Ware was creepy because, even though she wasn't shy or evasive and would maintain eye contact, she seemed to be staring *at* your eyes rather than *into* them; it was a bit the way a fish in a tank swimming past as you watched through the glass and looked into its eyes looked back at you—you knew that it was aware of you in some way, but it was unsettling because it wasn't anything like the way a human being seems aware of you when he meets your gaze.)

Toni's eyes were open. It was too late to shut them. If she suddenly did, the man would know she was alive. Her only chance was to appear so dead that the man didn't check her pulse or hold a piece of glass to her mouth to check. What would keep him from checking was if her eyes were open and stayed open—no living human being could hold its eyes open for long periods of time. There was no one around; the man had plenty of time to look through the windshield and see if they were alive. Her mother's face was right up against her face, but luckily the blood was dripping into some hollow of Toni's throat; if it had been dripping into her eyes it would have made her blink involuntarily. She stayed rigid like that with her eyes open. The man climbed up and tried the driver's-side door but it was locked from the inside. The man went back and got some kind of tool or crowbar and pried the windshield off, shaking the truck violently. He got on his side and edged through the slot of the windshield, looking first at the unconscious mom and then at the girl. The mom moaned and stirred slightly, and the man killed her by reaching in and pinching her nostrils shut with one hand and covering her mouth with a greasy rag with the other and pressing hard, so hard that the mom's head strained against the side of Toni's as she unconsciously resisted being suffocated. Toni stayed there, shell-breathing, with her eyes still open and only inches from the man's eyes as he suffocated her mother, which took over four minutes of pressure for the man to be totally sure. Toni staring sightlessly and not blinking even though the dryness and discomfort must have been terrific. And somehow succeeded in convincing the man she was dead, because he did not pinch her nostrils shut and use the greasy rag on her, even though it would only have taken an extra four or five minutes . . . but no regular living human can sit there with their eyes open that long without blinking, so he knew. And so he got one or two valuables out of the glove compartment and she heard him jingling his way back up the upslope and the tremendously powerful sound of the truck's motor starting up and the truck leaving, and then the girl lay there trapped between the door and her dead mom for what must have been several hours before someone happened by and saw the wreck and called the police, and then probably an additional long time for them to extract her from the truck, uninjured in any real physical sense, and put her in some kind of charity ambulance...

Sheesh.

So do not mess with this girl; this girl is damaged goods.

§46

What usually happens is that on Friday afternoons a percentage of Pod C's revenue officers meet for Happy Hour cocktails at Meibeyer's. As is the case with most of the north side's taverns that serve as Service hangouts, Happy Hour at Meibeyer's lasts exactly sixty minutes and features drink specials that are indexed to the approximate cost of gasoline and vehicle depreciation involved in the 2.3-mile drive from the REC to the Southport-474 interchange. Different levels and Pods tend to congregate at different places, some of which are downtown and ape in various ways the more stylized venues of Chicago and St. Louis. The Bell Shaped Men can be found nearly every evening at Father's, which is right there on Self-Storage Parkway and owned outright by the area's Budweiser distributor; its function is less social than intubatory. Many of the wigglers, on the other hand, frequent the steroidal college bars around PCB and Bradley. Homosexuals have the Wet Spot in the downtown arts district. Most of the examiners with children, of course, go home to spend time with their family, although Steve and Tina Geach are often at Meibeyer's together for Friday's 2-H. Nearly everyone finds it necessary to blow off some of the unvented steam that's accreted during a week of extreme tedium and concentration, or extreme volume and stress, or both.

Meibeyer's has ash-gray laminate paneling, electric tiki torches whose origins are unknown but may date from a past incarnation, a Wurlitzer 412-C jukebox, two pinball machines, a foosball table and an air hockey game, and a small darts area prudently set off apart near the little hallway for the pay phone and restrooms. Meibeyer's broad windows overlook Southport's highway-side franchises and the complicated exits of the I-474 overpass. There's been the same Friday bartender for at least the past three years, according to Chuck Ten Eyck. Drinks are somewhat expensive because Service employees do not, as a rule, drink very much or fast, even at Happy Hour, which affects what the tavern has to charge for drinks in order to stay solvent. In winter weather Meibeyer's plows its own lot with a bladed pickup. In the summer, the bar's neon sign, which features the semion of a disembodied trilby whose angle changes twice a second, is reflected off something unapparent before it and appears faintly, reflected at least twice, in the tavern's front windows. Meibeyer's brim goes up and down against the malarial light of a gathering dusk in which shelving clouds and a spike in humidity only sometimes mean real rain that hits the ground.

Being mainly single, heterosexual transfers and replacements fall right into this groove. Robby van Noght comes a lot, though not this Friday. Gerry Moeller has been here all five weeks he's been posted at the REC. Harriet Candelaria comes but nearly always leaves after one round whenever Beth Rath happens to bring Meredith Rand, with whom Candelaria has problems that none of the transfers has the slightest inkling of the origins of. Steve and Tina Geach, who work in different groups and have different break rotations, and who are very devoted to each other and by general consensus have the sort of marriage that increases the attraction and credibility of marriage a great deal for people who are wired to be in such a close, enduring relation, always arrive together in their rust-ruddled VW microbus, and sit close together, always consuming the very same type and brand of beverage, and usually leaving the moment the bell rings for Happy Hour's end, often showing an odd ability to embrace and walk at the same time without looking clumsy. Chris Acquistipace and Russell Nugent, Dave Witkiewicz, Joe Biron-Maint, Nancy

Johnson, Chahla ('the Iranian Crisis') Neti-Neti, Howard Shearwater, Frank Brown, Frank Friedwald, and Frank De Chellis haven't missed a Meibeyer's Happy Hour night since their posting. Dale Gastine sometimes brings a date. Keith Sabusawa now always brings Shane ('Mr. X') Drinion, the UTEX transfer with whom Sabusawa now rooms at Angler's Cove in a suite with two other transfers who never seem to come to Meibeyer's. Schedule F specialists like Chris Fogle and Herb Dritz bat about .500 in terms of attendance. Chuck Ten Eyck and 'Second-Knuckle' Bob McKenzie (both at Peoria REC the longest) are reliable as iron and always seem to want to somehow preside. R. L. Keck and Thomas Bondurant usually come. Toni Ware and Beth Rath nearly always drop by, and, as mentioned, some of the time Beth Rath brings the legendarily attractive but not universally popular Meredith Rand. Rath and Rand work adjoining Tingle tables in Sabusawa's group, which is tasked to utility/overflow, and the two are confidantes. Drinion, who has no vehicle, must remain as long as Sabusawa stays and no longer. According to Sabusawa, the UTEX from La Junta CA has no problem with this, and his response to Sabusawa's invitations to come along to Meibeyer's after shift change is always either 'All right' or 'Why not.' Meredith Rand's deal is that she tends to come only if her husband is somehow stuck at work or out of town on business. Like Drinion, she doesn't seem to have her own vehicle or even a driver's license. Sometimes she catches a ride home from Meibeyer's with Beth Rath but more often gets picked up by her husband, whom she apparently calls from the Pod in advance to say where she'll be, and whom no one in Meibeyer's has ever met but always simply pulls up into the lot and toots the horn for Meredith Rand, who in turn often starts gathering her things a minute or two before the car horn sounds, rather (according to Nancy Johnson) like a dog that can hear the pitch of its master's approaching engine and assumes its position at the home's window long before the master's car heaves into view. She has been at Meibeyer's for the last five weeks running, which implies that her husband has been working late or on the road a great deal. According to Sabusawa, no one knows what he does.

It is not difficult to see the way the energy and dynamics of the

Pod C table change when Meredith Rand is present for Happy Hour at Meibeyer's. In many respects, it's a phenomenon that happens at bars, taverns, and grills everywhere when a woman of sufficient prettiness appears. Meredith Rand is one of only a handful of females at the REC that every male with an opinion on such matters agrees is totally, wrist-bitingly attractive. Beth Rath is far from homely, but Meredith Rand is a whole different order. Meredith Rand has bottomless green eyes and exquisite facial bone structure and a creamy poreless complexion with almost no lines or signs of wear, and a great cataract of curly dark-blond hair that, according Sabusawa, when worn down and allowed to frame her face and shoulders has been known to produce facial tics even in gay or otherwise asexual men. She is a cut of pure choice prime, is the consensus, not always unspoken. Her entry into any sort of Service social setting produces palpable changes, especially in males. The specifics of these sorts of changes are familiar enough to everyone not to spend time enumerating. Suffice it that Meredith Rand makes the Pod's males self-conscious. They thus tend to become either nervous and uncomfortably quiet, as though they were involved in a game whose stakes have suddenly become terribly high, or else they become more voluble and conversationally dominant and begin to tell a great many jokes, and in general appear deliberately unself-conscious, whereas before Meredith Rand had arrived and pulled up a chair and joined the group there was no real sense of deliberateness or even self-consciousness among them. Female examiners, in turn, react to these changes in a variety of ways, some receding and becoming visually smaller (like Enid Welch and Rachel Robbie Towne), others regarding Meredith Rand's effect on men with a sort of dark amusement, still others becoming narrow-eyed and prone to hostile sighs or even pointed departures (q.v. Harriet Candelaria). Some of the male examiners are, by the second round of pitchers, performing for Meredith Rand, even if the performance's core consists of making a complex show of the fact that they are not performing for Meredith Rand or even especially aware that she's at the table. Bob McKenzie, in particular, becomes almost manic, addressing nearly every comment or quip to the person on either the right or left side of Meredith Rand, but never once addressing her or appearing even to look at her. Since Beth Rath is usually one of the people on either the right or left side of Meredith Rand, McKenzie's habit of doing this tends visibly to either annoy or depress Rath, depending on her mood.

For the past four weeks, really only Shane Drinion has seemed unaffected by the presence of a terribly attractive woman. Granted, it's not clear to anyone just what Drinion is affected by. The other transfers from La Junta CA (Sandy Krody, Gil Haight) describe him as a very solid Fats and S corp examiner but a total lump in terms of personality, possibly the dullest human being currently alive. Drinion tends to sit very quiet and self-contained at his place with his hand around a glass of Michelob (which is what's on tap at Meibeyer's), his face expressionless unless someone tells a joke that's somehow directed at everyone around the table, at which time Drinion will smile briefly and then his face will go back to being expressionless. But not expressionless in a glazed or catatonic way. He watches whoever is speaking very intently. Actually, intently isn't even the right word. There is no particular kind of study in his gaze; he just gives whoever's speaking his complete attention. His bodily movements, which are minimal, give the suggestion of being clipped and precise without being fussy or prissy. He will respond to a question or comment directed explicity to him, but other than these rare times he is not one of the people who speaks. But he's not one of these people who shrinks or recedes in groups until he's barely there. There's no sense that he's shy or inhibited. He's there but in an unusual way; he becomes part of the table's environment, like the air or ambient light. It's 'Second-Knuckle' Bob McKenzie and Chuck Ten Eyck who've conferred on Drinion the name 'Mr. X,' short for 'Mr. Excitement.'

At one Happy Hour in June things eventuate such that Drinion and Meredith Rand are left alone together at the table, more or less right across from each other, at the part of the evening when a lot of the other examiners have left for home or other venues. But they're both still there. Meredith Rand is evidently waiting for a pickup from her husband, who is said to possibly be some kind of medical student. Keith Sabusawa and Herb Dritz are once again playing foosball while

Beth Rath (who rather likes Sabusawa; they go all the way back to the IRS Training Center in Columbus) watches with her arms crossed and a More-brand cigarette going in one hand.

So they're sitting alone at the table. Shane Drinion seems to be neither nervous nor not to be sitting alone opposite the galvanic Meredith Rand, with whom he's exchanged not one direct word since his posting in late April. Drinion looks directly at her, but not in the challenging or smoldering way of a Keck or Nugent. Meredith Rand has had two gin and tonics and is on her third, slightly more to drink than normal but has not yet smoked. Like most married examiners, she wears both an engagement ring and a wedding band. She looks back at him, though it's not as if they're staring into each other's eyes or anything. Drinion's expression could be called pleasant in the way that certain kinds of weather are called pleasant. He is on either his first or second glass of Michelob from one of the pitchers that's still on the table, some not wholly empty. Rand has asked Drinion one or two innocuous questions about his origins. The thing about the Kansas Youth Authority orphanage seems to interest her, or else it's just the flat candor with which Drinion says he spent much of his childhood in an orphanage. Rand tells Drinion a brief childhood vignette about her going to a girlfriend's house and their using their hands and feet to climb up inside doorjambs and remain there high up in the jambs splayed and as if framed, though later on she will not be able to remember the reason for telling this anecdote or any of the context behind it. She does notice, almost right away, the same thing that Sabusawa and many of the other examiners have noticed—which is that although Drinion seems only partly socially present in a large gathering, there is a very different quality to any kind of tête-à-tête with him; he has the quality of being easy or good to talk to, which is an attribute for which there is no good single word in English, which is slightly odd, although so is whatever is good about talking to Drinion, since he possesses nothing that could be called charm or social grace or even evident compassion. He is, as Rand will say later to Beth Rath (though not to her husband), a very odd bird indeed. There is a brief exchange that Meredith Rand won't remember so well, involving Drinion's being an itinerant examiner and the

REC and Examinations and the Service in general, i.e., Rand: 'You like the work?' which it seems to take Drinion a moment or two to process. D: 'I think I don't like it or dislike it either.' R: 'Well, is there something else you'd rather be doing?' D: 'I don't know. I don't have any experience doing anything else. Wait. That's not true. I worked in a supermarket three evenings a week between the ages of sixteen and eighteen. I would not prefer working in a supermarket to what I'm doing now.' R: 'It sure doesn't pay as well.' D: 'I put things on shelves and affixed small adhesive price tags to them. There wasn't much to it.' R: 'Sounds boring.' D: '...'

'We look like we're having a tête-à-tête' is the first thing that Meredith Rand will later be able to remember clearly having said to Shane Drinion.

'That's a foreign term for a private conversation,' Drinion responds.

'Well, I don't know how private it is.'

Drinion looks at her, but not in the way of someone who's not sure what to say in reply. One thing about him is that he's completely the same, affectwise and demeanorwise, by himself as he is in a large group. If he gave off a sound it would be like a single long tone from a tuning fork or EKG flatline instead of anything that varies.

'You know,' Meredith Rand says, 'if you want to know the truth, you kind of interest me.'

Drinion looks at her.

'I'm guessing you don't hear that a lot,' Meredith Rand says. She gives a little bit of a dry smile.

'It's a compliment, that you find me of interest.'

'I guess it is, isn't it,' Rand says, smiling again. 'For one thing, it's that I could say something like that, that there's something sort of interesting about you, without you thinking I'm coming on to you.'

Drinion nods, one hand around the base of his glass. He is very still, Meredith Rand notices. He doesn't fidget or change positions in his chair. He's a bit of a mouth-breather; his mouth hangs slightly open. With some people the mouth hanging open thing makes them look not too bright.

'For instance,' she says, 'imagine if I said something like that to "2K" Bob, how he'd react.'

'All right.'

Something goes slightly opaque for a moment in Shane Drinion's eyes, and Meredith can tell he is literally doing it, imagining her saying 'I find you interesting' to Second-Knuckle Bob McKenzie. 'What would his reaction be, do you think?'

'Do you mean his outer, visible reaction or his inner reaction?'

'The visible one I kind of don't even want to imagine,' Meredith Rand says.

Drinion nods. He is, it is true, not all that interesting to look at, in terms of looks. His head is somewhat smaller than average, and very round. No one's seen him in any sort of hat or coat yet; it's always a white dress shirt and sweater vest. His hairline is receding in a way that makes his forehead seem elaborate. There are some pimple scars around his temple areas. His face isn't very defined or structured; his nostrils are two different sizes or shapes, she can see, which is usually bad news for how good-looking someone is. His mouth is slightly too small for the width of his face. His hair is that dull or waxy kind of dark blond that sometimes goes with a reddish complexion and not the greatest skin. He's the sort of person you'd have to look at very intently even to be able to describe. Meredith Rand has been looking expectantly at him.

'You're asking me to describe what I believe his inner reaction might be?' Drinion says. His face at least isn't quite the same abraded-looking red when they're not in the fluorescence of the Pod, a reddishness in people that for some reason always depresses Meredith Rand first thing in the morning.

'Let's say I'm curious.'

'Well, I don't know for certain. When I was imagining it, my impression was that he'd be frightened.'

There's a slight change in Meredith Rand's posture, but she keeps her facial expression very neutral. 'How come?'

'My impression is that he's frightened of you. This is just my impression. It's hard to explain out loud.' He stops for a moment.

'Your attractiveness presents McKenzie with some kind of test that he is afraid he won't pass. He's anxious about this. When others are around and he can act out a role, he can go into an adrenalized state that makes him forget he's afraid. No, that's not right.' Drinion pauses again for a moment. He doesn't look frustrated, though. 'My sense is that the adrenaline of performing makes the fear feel like excitement. In this type of setting, he can feel as though you excite him. That's why he acts so excited and pays so much attention to you, but he knows that others are watching,' Drinion concludes and takes a sip of Michelob; the motion of his arm is very nearly right-angled without being stiff or robotic. There is a precision and economy of movement about him. Meredith Rand has noticed this also during work hours, when she stretches and looks around as a kind of break and looks over and sees Drinion sitting and removing staples and moving different forms into different piles at his Tingle table. His posture is very good without being stiff or rigid. He looks like a man whose back and neck never hurt. He appears confused, or speculative. 'Fear and excitement seem to be closely related.'

'Ten Eyck and Nugent do the same thing, though, when the whole table's going at it like that,' Rand says.

Drinion nods in a slightly off way that indicates that's not quite what she has asked to talk about. It's not the same as his registering impatience, though. 'In a private, tête-à-tête conversation with you, though, my impression is that he would feel the fear more as real fear. He wouldn't like being directly conscious of this. Of feeling it. He wouldn't be sure what it was even fear of. He would be on edge, confused, in a way that could not be made to feel like excitement. If you told him that you found him interesting, I believe he would not know what to say. He would not know how he was supposed to act. I think not knowing this would make Bob very uncomfortable.'

Drinion looks at her steadily for a moment. His face, which is a bit oily, tends to shine in the fluorescence of the Examination areas, though less so in the windows' indirect light, the shade of which indicates that clouds have piled up overhead, though this is just Meredith Rand's impression, and one not wholly conscious.

'You're pretty observant,' Meredith Rand says.

Drinion replies: 'I don't know that that's true. I don't think I have any direct observation or fact-pattern to base this on. It's a guess. But my guess, for some reason, is that he might actually burst into tears.'

Meredith Rand looks suddenly pleased, which almost literally lights up her face. She reaches out and pats the table smartly with the fingers of one hand. 'I think you're right.'

'Somehow it's awful to contemplate.'

'I think he might fall out of his chair and run away crying and flapping his hands hysterically in the air.'

Drinion says, 'That I couldn't guess at one way or the other. I do know that you dislike him. I know he makes you feel uncomfortable.'

Drinion is facing Meibeyer's front windows, Meredith Rand the tavern's rear section, where there is the hallway and darts area and a decorative display of different types of formal or business-type hats glued by the rims to a varnished board. Meredith Rand leans forward and makes as if to rest her chin on the knuckles of one hand, though it's easy to see that the actual weight of her chin and skull is not really resting on these knuckles; it's more a stance than a way of making herself comfortable. 'And then if I say you're interesting, though, what's your inward reaction?'

'That it's a compliment. It's a pleasantry, but also an invitation to continue the tête-à-tête. To make it more personal or revealing.'

Rand waved that hand in a small gesture of impatience or acknowledgment. 'But how does it make you feel, as they say in Evaluation?'

'Well,' Shane Drinion says, 'I think an expression of interest like that makes a person feel good. Provided the person saying it isn't trying to propose a level of intimacy that makes you feel uncomfortable.'

'Did it make you uncomfortable?'

Drinion pauses for another brief moment, though he doesn't move and his expression does not change. There's again maybe the smallest instant of blankness or withdrawal. Rand has the sense of an optical reader scanning a stack of cards very fast and efficiently; there is a kind of ambient unsonic hum about him. 'No. I suppose if you meant it sarcastically it would be uncomfortable—I would think you were angry at me or found me unpleasant. But you gave no sign that you meant it sarcastically. So no, I'm not sure what you meant by interesting, but people naturally like to be found interesting to other people, so the curiosity about just what you mean is not uncomfortable. In fact, if I understand it, it is this curiosity that the remark "You know, if you want to know the truth, you kind of interest me" is meant to arouse. The conversation then becomes about just what the person who said it meant. Then the other person gets to find out just what about him interests another person, which is enjoyable.'

'Ex—'

'At the same time,' Drinion continues, showing no sign that he's noticed Rand starting to say something even though he's been looking right at her, 'someone who finds you interesting seems then suddenly, almost by virtue of their interest in you, more interesting to you. That is a very interesting dimension to it also.' He stops. Meredith Rand pauses a little extra bit of time to make sure he's now stopped for good. Like her own left pinkie, Drinion's left pinkie finger is noticeably puckered and pale from wearing the rubber all day in Exams. There's no way she even wants to notice Drinion's clothing enough to even catalogue or characterize it to herself. Just the sweater vest alone is a tremendous downer. She has her white vinyl cigarette case out and unsnaps it and withdraws a cigarette, since it's just the two of them at the table.

'So, and do you think you're interesting?' Meredith Rand asks him. 'Do you see how someone could think you're interesting?'

Drinion takes another sip from his glass and puts it back down. Meredith Rand notices that he places it perfectly centered on the napkin without trying to or without having to adjust the glass's base in small fussy ways to get it perfectly centered on the napkin. That Drinion in not graceful the way dancers or athletes are, but there is something graceful. His movements are very precise and economical without being prissy. The glasses on the table that are not on napkins have large and variously shaped pools of condensation around them. Someone has selected the same popular song to play twice in a row on Meibeyer's big jukebox, which has concentric rings of red and white lights on an integrated circuit that allows them to go on and off in such a way that they accompany the chosen song's bass line.

Shane Drinion says: 'I don't think I've ever really considered it.'

'Do you know why they call you Mr. X?'

'I think so.'

'Do you know why they call Chahla the Iranian Crisis?'

'I don't think so.'

'Do you know why they call McKenzie Second-Knuckle Bob?'

'No.'

Meredith Rand sees Drinion looking at the cigarette. Her lighter is in a special loop attached to the cigarette case, which is cheap pebbled vinyl—Meredith Rand ends up losing her cigarettes in different places so often that it makes no sense to have an expensive cigarette case. She knows, from the Pod's workday breaks, that it would be pointless to offer Drinion a cigarette.

'What about you? Do you think I'm interesting?' Rand asks Shane Drinion. 'I mean, apart from me saying you were interesting.'

Drinion's eyes are on hers—he makes a lot of eye contact without being in any way challenging or flirty—while he seems to do the same internal card-sorting thing he's done before. Drinion wears an argyle sweater vest, strange, pebbly-textured polyester slacks, and brown Wallabee knockoffs that might literally be from JC Penney. The cold stream from the vent overhead tears the smoke ring to shreds the minute she shapes and exhales it. Beth Rath is now playing foosball with Herb Dritz while Keith Sabusawa watches the pregame warmup to a Cardinals baseball game on the television above the bar. You can tell that Beth would rather be sitting with Sabusawa but isn't sure how forward to be about her feelings for Sabusawa, who has always struck Meredith Rand as awfully tall for an oriental. Drinion also has a way of nodding where the nod has nothing to do with etiquette or affirmation. He says: 'You're pleasant, and so far I'm enjoying the tête-à-tête. It's a chance to pay direct attention to you, which is otherwise hard to do, because it seems to make you uncomfortable.' He waits for a moment to see if she wants to say anything. Drinion's facial expression isn't blank, but it's bland and neutral in a way that might as well be blank for all it tells you. Meredith Rand has, without being quite aware of it, quit trying with the rings.

'Is liking paying attention the same thing as being interested in somebody?'

'Well, I would say almost anything you pay close, direct attention to becomes interesting.'

'Is that true?'

'I think so, yes.' Drinion says: 'Of course you're especially interesting to pay attention to because you're attractive. It's almost always pleasant to pay attention to beauty. It requires no effort.'

Rand's eyes have narrowed, though part of this may have been the bits of cigarette smoke being blown back into her face by the AC vent.

Shane Drinion says: 'Beauty is almost by definition interesting, if by interesting you mean something that compels attention and makes attention feel pleasant. Although the word you just used was *interested* rather than *interesting*.'

'You do know I'm married,' says Meredith Rand.

'Yes. Everyone knows you're married. You wear a wedding ring. Your spouse picks you up at the south entrance several days a week. His car has a small hole in the exhaust that gives the engine a powerful sound. A sound that makes the car sound more powerful than normal, I mean.'

Meredith Rand does not look pleased at all. 'Maybe I'm confused. If you just said that it makes me uncomfortable, why even bring up the attractiveness thing?'

'Well, you asked me a question,' Drinion says. 'I told you what I decided is the truth. It took a second to decide what the true answer is and what is and isn't part of it. Then I said it. It isn't intended to make you uncomfortable. But it isn't intended to keep you from being uncomfortable, either—you didn't ask about that.'

'Oh, and you're the authority on what the truth is because...?'

Drinion waits a moment. In just the same tiny interval as the pause, it occurs to Meredith Rand that Drinion's pausing to see whether there's more or whether the truncated question is meant to invite him to supply the answer. Meaning is it sarcastic. Meaning he has no natural sense of whether something was sarcastic or not. 'No. I'm not an authority on the truth. You asked me a question about me being interested, and I tried to determine the truth of what I felt, and to say that truth to you, because my assumption was that's what was wanted.'

'I notice you weren't nearly as, like, blunt and forthcoming about how me saying I found you interesting made you feel.'

Drinion's expression and tone haven't changed even a little bit. 'I'm sorry. I'm having a hard time understanding what you just said.'

'I'm saying when I asked you how me finding you interesting made you feel, you weren't as blunt about answering. You skittered and skipped all over. Now with me all of a sudden there's a sudden concern for the blunt truth.'

'Now I understand.' Again a slight pause. The light-brand's smoke does taste thin against the aftertaste of tonic and lime. 'I don't recall any part of me trying to be evasive or false in that answer. Maybe I'm able to express some things better than others. I think that's a common finding for people. Also, I don't usually speak very much. I'm hardly ever in a tête-à-tête, actually. It may be that I'm not as skilled as other people at speaking in a consistent way about how something makes me feel.'

'Can I ask you a question?'

'Yes.'

Rand is now having no problem looking directly at Drinion. 'It doesn't occur to you that all that might strike somebody as a little condescending?'

Drinion's brow moves ever so slightly upward as he thinks. The baseball game has now started on the television, which may explain why Keith Sabusawa, who's usually keen to leave after Happy Hour has ended, hasn't left yet, and so neither has Shane Drinion. Sabusawa is tall enough that he has his loafers partly on the floor instead of hooked into the little support near the barstool's base. Ron, the bartender, has a small towel and a glass in his hand and is making cleaning motions but is also looking up at the game, and he's saying something to Keith Sabusawa, who in fact sometimes keeps whole long lists of baseball statistics in his head, which according to Beth

Rath he finds soothing and restful to think about. Two great flashing, twittering pinball machines stand against the wall just south of the air hockey game, which no Meibeyer's patron ever plays because there's some chronic malfunction that makes air blow too hard through the table's pinholes and the puck rides several inches off the surface and is next to impossible to keep from flying off the table altogether. On the nearer of the pinball machines, a beautiful Amazon in a Lycra bodysuit is lifting by the hair a man whose limbs appear to gyrate in time with the syncopated lights of the obstacles and gateways and flippers.

Drinion says: 'That doesn't occur to me. But I do notice that you've become angry or upset in response to something I've said. This I can tell,' he says. 'It occurs to me that you might want to end this tête-à-tête conversation even though your spouse hasn't arrived yet to pick you up, but that possibly you're not sure how to do it, and so you feel somewhat trapped, and this is part of what's angering you.'

'And you, you don't have to be someplace?'

'No.'

An interesting bit of trivia is that Meredith Rand actually outranks Drinion, technically, since she's a GS-10 and Drinion a GS-9. This even though Drinion is several orders of magnitude more effective than Rand as an examiner. Both his daily average of returns and his ratio of total returns examined to total additional revenue produced through audit are much higher than Meredith Rand's. The truth is that utility examiners have a harder time getting promoted, since promotions usually result from Group Managers' recommendations, and UTEXs are rarely at one Post or Pod long enough to develop the sort of rapport with superiors that makes the superior willing to go through the paperwork hassle of recommending someone for a promotion. Also, since utility examiners are often the best at what they do, there is a disincentive in the Service against promoting them, since at GS-15 a Service employee moves into administration and can no longer travel from Post to Post. One of the things that regular posted wigglers find mysterious about UTEXs is what motivations induce them to serve as UTEXs when the position is something of a career-killer in terms of advancement and pay raises. As of 1 July 1983, the difference between a GS-9's and a GS-10's annual salary is $3,220 gross, which is not pocket change. Like many wigglers, Meredith Rand assumes that there's a certain type of basic personality that's maybe drawn to the constant movement and lack of attachment of being a utility examiner, plus the variety of challenges, and that Personnel has ways to test for these personality traits and so to ID certain examiners as likely UTEX candidates. There is a certain prestige or romance to the UTEX lifestyle, but part of this is married or elsewise dug-in employees' romanticization of the unattached lifestyle of somebody who goes from Post to Post at the institutional whim of the Service, like a cowboy or mercenary. Lots of UTEXs have come to Peoria since late winter / spring '84—there are a variety of theories about why.

'Do you usually keep hanging out here after the hour and the whole Second-Knuckle crowd leaves?'

Drinion shakes his head. He doesn't mention the fact that he cannot leave Meibeyer's until Keith Sabusawa does. Meredith Rand doesn't know whether he fails to mention this obvious fact because he knows that Meredith already knows it, or whether this guy is so totally literal that what he does is just answer whatever question she asks, literally, like a machine, like with only a yes or a no if it's a yes-or-no question. She puts out her cigarette in the little yellow foil disposable-type ashtray that you have to request directly from Ron if you want to smoke, because Meibeyer's has had problems with ashtrays disappearing, hard as that is to really believe given their chintziness. She extinguishes the cigarette a bit more thoroughly and emphatically than she usually does, in order to reinforce a certain tonal impatience in what she says as she puts the cigarette out: 'All right then.'

Drinion rotates his upper body slightly in his chair to see just where Keith Sabusawa is at the bar. Rand is 90 percent sure that the movement isn't any sort of performance or anything that is meant to communicate something nonverbally to her. Outside in the sky to the northwest are great sheer walls of rim-lit sunset clouds in whose interior there is sometimes muttering and light. None of the people in Meibeyer's can see these clouds, although you can always tell physically that rain's on the way if you pay attention to certain subliminal physical signals like sinuses, bunions, a particular kind of incipient headache, a slight felt change in the quality of the cold of the air-conditioning.

'So tell me why you think the prettiness thing makes me uncomfortable.'

'I don't know for certain. All I could give you is a guess.'

'You know, you're not really quite as direct as you seem at first, it turns out.'

Drinion continues to look directly at Meredith Rand but without any sort of challenge or evident agenda. Rand, who is certainly in a position to know that guilelessness can be a form of guile, will tell Beth Rath that it was a little like having a cow or horse look at you: Not only did you not know what they were thinking as they looked at you, or if they were thinking at all—you had no sense of what they were even really seeing as they looked, and yet at the same time you felt yourself truly seen.

'All right, I'll play the little game here,' Meredith Rand says. 'Do you think I'm pretty?'

'Yes.'

'Do you find me attractive?'

'...'

'Well, do you?'

'I find that question confusing. I've heard it in movies and read it in books. It's strangely phrased. There's something confusing about it. It seems to ask for an objective opinion as to whether the person you're talking to would describe you as attractive. From the context it usually appears in, though, it seems almost always to be a way of asking whether the person you're talking to is sexually attracted to you.'

Meredith Rand says: 'Well, sometimes you have to let a roundabout way of saying things pass, don't you? Some things can't be said straight out or it's just too gross. Can you imagine somebody saying "Are you sexually attracted to me?" '

'Actually yes, I can.'

'But it'd be awfully uncomfortable to ask it that way, wouldn't it?'

'I can understand how it could be uncomfortable or even unpleasant, especially if the other person wasn't sexually attracted. I'm fairly sure that packed into the straightforward question is the suggestion that the asker is sexually attracted to the other person and wants to know whether the feeling is reciprocated. So—yes, this means I was wrong. There are questions or assumptions also packed into the underlying question, too. You're correct—the business of sexual attraction seems to be a subject that it's not possible to be wholly straightforward in talking about.'

Rand's expression is now patronizing enough to be irksome or annoying to the vast majority of people she might be speaking with. 'And why do you think that is?'

Drinion pauses a moment. 'I think it's probably because direct sexual rejection is intensely unpleasant for people, and the less directly you express information about your sexual attraction to someone, the less directly you feel rejected if there's no corresponding expression of attraction.'

'There's something kind of tiring about you,' Rand observes. 'Talking to you.'

Drinion nods.

'It's like you're both interesting and really boring at the same time.'

'I've certainly been told that people feel I'm boring.'

'The Mr. Excitement thing.'

'The nickname is obviously sarcastic.'

'Have you ever been on a date?'

'No.'

'Have you ever asked someone out, or expressed being attracted to somebody?'

'No.'

'Don't you get kind of lonely?'

A small pause for this. 'I don't think so.'

'Do you think you'd know if you did?'

'I think I would.'

'Do you know what's on the jukebox right now?'

'Yes.'

'Are you by any chance a homo?'

'I don't think so.'

'You don't think so?' Rand says.

'I don't think I'm really anything. I don't think I've ever had what you mean by sexual attraction.'

Rand is very good at reading affect on people's faces, and as far as she can tell there's nothing here on Drinion's face to read. 'Not even when you were a teenager?'

That little pause for scanning again. 'Not really.'

'Did you worry you might be a homo?'

'No.'

'Did you worry that something was maybe wrong with you?'

'No.'

'Did other people worry that something was wrong?'

Another pause, both blank and not. 'I don't think so.'

'Really?'

'You mean as an adolescent?'

'Yes.'

'I think the truth is that no one paid enough attention to me to even wonder what was going on inside me, much less to worry about it.' He hasn't moved a bit.

'Not even your family?'

'No.'

'Did that kind of bum you out?'

'No.'

'Were you lonely?'

'No.'

'Do you ever get lonely?'

Rand has come almost to be able to expect the pause after some questions, or to absorb it as a normal part of Drinion's conversational rhythm. Drinion doesn't acknowledge that she has already asked this before.

'I don't think so.'

'Not ever?'

'I don't think so.'

'Why not?'

Drinion takes another sip from his glass of warm beer. There is something about the economy of his movements that Rand enjoys watching without even being quite aware that she enjoys it. 'I don't think I know how to answer that,' the utility examiner says.

'Well, like when you notice other people having romances or sex lives, and you don't, or you can tell they feel lonely and you don't, what do you think about the difference between you and them?'

There is a pause. Drinion says: 'I think there's a doubleness about what it is you're asking. It's really about comparing. I think it's more like if I'm watching someone and paying attention to them and thinking about what they're like, I'm not paying so much attention to myself and what I'm like. So there's no way to compare.'

'You don't ever compare anything to anything?'

Drinion looks at his hand and the glass. 'I have a hard time paying attention to more than one thing at a time. I think it's one reason I don't drive, for instance.'

'But you know what's playing on the jukebox.'

'Yes.'

'But if you're paying attention to our little conversation here, how do you know what's on the jukebox?'

There is now a longer pause. Drinion's face looks slightly different when he comes to the end of his two-second-scan thing.

Drinion says: 'Well, it's very loud, and also I've heard this song several times on the radio, either four or five times, and when it plays on the radio when it's over they often give the song's title and artist. I believe this is how radio stations are able to play copyrighted songs without being required to pay any sort of per-use fee. The radio play is part of the advertising of the record album that the song is part of. It's a bit confusing, though. The idea that hearing the song several times for free on the radio makes the customer more likely to go to the store and buy the song seems somewhat confusing to me. Granted, often what is being sold is the entire record album that the song is only one part of, so it may be that the song on the radio functions a little bit like a preview of a movie that they show as an inducement to buy a ticket for that later movie, of which the preview is obviously only one small part. There's also the matter of how the record companies' accounting personnel treat the expenses involved in free radio play. It seems to be not a matter of corporate and ICE but rather *inter*-corporate, if you think about it. Surely there are significant shipping and distribution costs involved in placing the recording of the song in the hands of the radio stations that will play it. Can the record company or its parent write off these costs if the radio stations are not paying any fee for the rights to air the song and so there is no income against which to write off the expenses? Or can they be deducted as marketing and advertising expenses if in fact no moneys are being paid to the ostensible advertiser, here the radio stations or their parent companies, but rather only to the postal service or some private carrier? How would the Service examiner be able to distinguish such expenses from illicit or padded deductions if no larger compensation could be referenced against which to add or subtract these distribution costs?'

Meredith Rand says: 'Can I say that one of the reasons you come off as a little boring is that you don't seem like you have any sense of what the real topic of a conversation is? This stuff doesn't have anything to do with what we were just talking about, does it?'

Drinion looks slightly puzzled for a moment, but not hurt or embarrassed. Rand says: 'What makes you imagine anybody possibly even wants to hear some long job-related noodle you don't even know about if the whole point of being here is that it's Friday and we don't have to think about shit like this for two days?'

Drinion says: 'You don't normally choose to devote time to matters like this unless you're clocked in, you're saying.'

'I'm talking about loneliness and people paying attention to you or not and you launch into this whole long like thing about radio expense protocols and it turns out the point of the whole thing is only that there's procedural stuff you don't know?'

Drinion nods in a thoughtful way. 'I understand what you're saying.'

'What do you imagine is going through the other person's mind when you're ranting like that? Do you just automatically assume they're interested? Who cares about radio accounting if you're not tasked to it?'

Beth Rath is now seated between Keith Sabusawa and somebody else at the bar, all on stools in identical stool-postures that to Meredith Rand always look vulturelike. Howard Shearwater is playing pinball, at which he's said to excel—his pinball machine is the more distant one from their table, and the angle of incidence doesn't allow Rand to see the design or motif of the machine. The sun is not yet all the way down but the bar's low lights in the artificial tiki torches on the wall have come up, and the air-conditioner vents' rate seems at least to have been cranked back a bit. As baseball fans, real Peorians tend to be equally divided between the Cubs and the Cardinals, though in this era the Cubs fans tend to keep their partisanship more to themselves. Baseball on television is just about the most tedious type of sport there is, in Meredith Rand's husband's opinion. It may or may not rain, as usual. There are different-shaped puddles of condensation on all the places that do or did have a glass, and none of these ever evaporate. Drinion still hasn't spoken or fidgeted or changed his facial expression much at all. This now right here is cigarette number three since 5:10. There are no attempted rings.

Meredith Rand says: 'What are you thinking now?'

'I'm thinking that you raise a number of points that seem valid, and that I'm going to maybe have to give the whole matter of what someone is thinking when I'm speaking to them about something more thought.'

Rand does the thing she can do where she smiles broadly with everything except the muscles around her eyes. 'Are you patronizing me?'

'No.'

'Are you being sarcastic?'

'No. I can tell you've become angry, though.'

She exhales two brief tusks of smoke. Because of less backdraft from the air-conditioner vent, some of the smoke is going into Shane Drinion's face. 'Did you know that my husband is dying?'

'No. I didn't,' Drinion says.

They both sit for a moment, doing the respective sorts of facial things they are inclined to do.

'Aren't you going to say you're sorry?'

'What?' Drinion says.

'It's what you say. It's the standard etiquette thing to say.'

'Well, I was considering this fact in the light of your asking me about sexual feelings and loneliness. Receipt of this fact changes the context for that conversation, it seems.'

'Should I ask how so?' Meredith Rand says.

Drinion inclines his head. 'I don't know that.'

'Did you think finding out he was dying might mean you've got some kind of sexual chance with me?'

'I had not thought that, no.'

'Good. That's good.'

Beth Rath has started back over to the table with her mouth partly open to maybe say something or try to join the conversation, but Meredith Rand gives her a look that makes Rath turn around and return to her place on the red leather stool at the bar, where Ron is changing out the club soda cartridge. Meredith Rand puts her purse on the table and rises to recharge her glass.

'Do you want another Heineken or whatever?'

'I still haven't finished this one.'

'You don't exactly party down, do you?'

'I get full quickly. My stomach doesn't seem to hold very much.'

'Lucky you.'

Rand, Rath, and Sabusawa have some kind of quick conversation while Ron is making Meredith Rand's gin and tonic, which Drinion doesn't hear, though he can see slight reflections of the people at the bar in Meibeyer's front window. Nobody knows what he looks like or what his face is doing as he sits at the table alone, or even what he's looking at.

'Do you know what cardiomyopathy is?' Rand asks when she sits back down. She looks at her purse, which is almost more of a bag in terms of shape. Half the gin and tonic is already gone.

'Yes.'

'Yes what?'

'I think it's a disease of the heart.'

Meredith Rand taps her cigarette lighter experimentally against her front teeth. 'You seem like a good listener. Are you? You want to hear a sad story?'

After a moment, Drinion says: 'I'm not certain how to answer that.'

'I mean my sad story. Part of mine. Everybody's got their sad story. You want to hear part of mine?'

'. . .'

'It's actually a disease of the muscle of the heart. Cardiomyopathy.'

'I thought that the heart was itself a muscle,' Shane Drinion says.

'It means as opposed to the vasculature of the heart. Trust me, I'm kind of an expert on this. What they call heart disease is the major vessels. As in a heart attack. Cardiomyopathy is the muscle of the heart, the stuff of it, the thing that squeezes and relaxes. Especially when it's of unknown cause. Which it is. They aren't sure what caused it. The theory was that he'd had a terrible flu or some virus when he was in college that seemed to get better but nobody knew it had settled in his myocardium somehow, the muscle tissue of his heart, and gradually infected it and compromised it.'

'I think I understand.'

'You're thinking how sad, maybe, to fall in love and get married and then have your husband get a fatal disease—because it is, it's fatal. Like the rich kid in that movie, what's it called, except there it's the wife, who's kind of a lump if you want my opinion, but the rich kid gets disinherited and everything and marries her and then she gets fatally ill. It's a tear-jerker.' Rand's eyes, too, change slightly when she's scanning some kind of memory. 'It's a little like congestive heart failure. Actually, in many cases of cardiomyopathy the actual cause of death when the person finally dies is listed as congestive heart failure.'

Shane Drinion has his hand around his glass with a little beer but does not raise the glass. 'Is this because the muscle of the heart becomes compromised and can't squeeze well enough to circulate the blood?'

'Yes, and he had it before we got married, he had it even before I met him, and I met him when I was super young, I wasn't even eighteen yet. And he was thirty-two, and a ward attendant in Zeller.' She is extracting a cigarette. 'Do you happen to know what Zeller is?'

'I think you mean the mental health center building near the Exposition Gardens on Northmoor.' Drinion's bottom is hovering very slightly—perhaps one or two millimeters at most—above the seat of his wooden chair.

'It's actually on University, the main entrance is.'

'...'

'It's a psych hospital. Do you know what a psych hospital is?'

'In a general sense, yes.'

'Are you just being polite?'

'No.'

'The bin. The mental Marriott. A nut ward. Do you want to know why I was there?'

'Were you visiting someone important to you?'

'Negative. I was a patient there for three and a half weeks. Do you want to know how come?'

'I can't tell whether you're really asking me, or whether this question is simply an overture to telling me.'

Meredith Rand makes her mouth into a sardonic sideways shape and clicks her tongue a couple times. 'All right. That's kind of annoying, but I can't say you don't have a point. I was a *cutter.* Do you know what a *cutter* is?'

There is no difference—Drinion's face remains composed and neutral without seeming in any way to be trying to stay neutral. Meredith Rand has a very good subliminal antenna for this sort of thing—she's allergic to performance. 'My assumption is that it's someone who cuts.'

'Was that like a witticism?'

'No.'

'I didn't know why I did it. I'm still not sure, except he taught me that trying to analyze it or understand all the whys was bullshit—the only important thing was knocking it off, because if I didn't it would land me right back in the psych ward, that the idea I could hide it with bandages or sleeves and keep it a totally private thing that didn't affect anybody else was arrogant bullshit. And he's right. No matter where you do it or how carefully you do it, there's always a time when somebody sees something and says something, or when somebody is funking around in the hall and pretending to beg you to cut algebra and go to the park and get stoned and climb on the statue of Lincoln and grabs your arm too hard and some of the cuts open up and you bleed through your long sleeves, even if you've got two shirts on, and somebody sends for the nurse even if you tell them to fuck off and it was an accident and you'll just go home and get it seen to at home. There always comes a day when somebody sees something in your face that tells them you're lying and then the next thing you know there you are, in a lit room with your arms and legs uncovered, trying to explain yourself to somebody with zero sense of humor, actually a little bit like talking to you right now.' With a quick tight smile.

Drinion nods slowly.

'That was kind of nasty. I need to apologize for that.'

'I don't have a very good sense of humor, it's true.'

'This is different. It's like they do this initial intake interview, with a legal form on a white clipboard they ask you questions from as required by law, and if they ask you if you ever hear voices and you say sure, I hear yours right now asking me a question, they don't think it's funny or even acknowledge you're even trying to be funny but just sit there looking at you. Like they're a computer and you can't proceed until you give the properly formatted answer.'

'The question itself seems ambiguous. For instance, what voices are they referring to?'

'So they have, like, three different kinds of wards at Zeller, and two of them are locked, and the one they put me on as a mental patient is the one that he also worked on, on the third floor, with mostly rich girls from the Heights who wouldn't eat or took a bottle of Tylenol when their boyfriend dumped them, et cetera, or stuck their finger down their throat every time they ate something. There were a lot of barfers there.'

Drinion keeps looking at her. Now no part of his bottom or back is touching the chair, although the separation is so slight that no one else could see this unless somehow a very bright light were shined from the side, illuminating the slight gap between Drinion and the chair.

'You might be asking how I got in there, since we definitely were not rich or from the Heights.'

'. . .'

'The answer is good insurance through my dad's union. He ran the baling wire line at American Twine and Wire from 1956 until it closed down. The only days of work he ever missed were some of the days I was in Zeller.' Rand makes a very brief distended horror-face whose exact meaning is unclear and lights the cigarette she has been holding and looking at. 'To give you an idea.'

Drinion finishes the last bit of the Michelob and wipes his mouth a little on the napkin the glass has rested on. He then replaces the napkin and the glass. His beer's been at room temperature for much too long to produce any new condensation.

'And it's true that he already looked sick when I met him. Not gross or anything, it's not like he oozed or went around coughing or anything, but pale, even for winter. He looked delicate, like somebody old. He was totally skinny, too, although compared to the anorexic girls it was hard to see right off how skinny he was—it was more like he was so pale and got tired easily; he couldn't move very fast. With the terrible dark circles under his eyes. Some of the time he looked tired or sleepy, although it was also late at night, because he was the second-shift ward attendant on the ward, from five to the middle of the night when the night guy came on, who we never even really saw except for breakfast or if somebody had a crisis in the middle of the night.'

'He wasn't a doctor, then,' Drinion says.

'The doctors were a joke. At Zeller. The psychiatrists. They came in in the afternoon for like an hour, in suits—they always wore nice suits; they were professionals—and talked more to the RNs and the parents when they came in, mostly. And then they'd finally come in and you'd have a weird, stiff conversation, like they were your dad or something. And they had zero sense of humor, and looked at their watch the whole time. Even the ones who you could halfway see might be human beings were more interested in your case, not in you. Like in what your case might mean, how it was like or different than other cases in the textbooks. Don't get me started on the medical establishment at psych wards. They were bizarre to deal with; it could really mess with your head. If you said you hated it there and it wasn't helping and you wanted to leave, they saw it as a symptom of your case, not as you wanting to leave. It was like you weren't a human being, you were a piece of machinery they could take apart and figure out how it worked.' She snaps and unsnaps her cigarette case. 'It was really scary, actually, because they could sign papers to keep you in there or move you to a worse ward, the other locked ward was a lot worse and people talked about it, you don't want to hear about it. Or they could decide to give you meds that turned some of the girls into zombies; it's like one day they were there and the next there was nobody home. Like zomboids in really nice bathrobes from home. It was just very creepy.'

'. . .'

'They couldn't do horror-movie stuff, though, they couldn't give you electroshock treatments like in that one movie, because everybody's parents were right there practically every day and knew what was going on. If you were on that ward you weren't *committed* to Zeller, you were *admitted,* and after seven days they actually had to let you go if your parents said so. Which some of them did, of the zombie girls. But they could legally sign forms that changed you to *committed.* The doctors in the suits could, so they were the scariest ones.'

'. . .'

'Plus the food was beyond gross.'

'You had been giving yourself small, hidden cuts as some sort of psychological compensation,' Shane Drinion says.

Meredith Rand gives him a level look. She does notice that he seems to be sitting up slightly straighter or something, because the very lowest part of the display of different kinds of hats is obscured, and she knows she isn't slumped down. 'It felt good. It was creepy, and I knew it couldn't be good if I was so secret and creepy about it, but it felt good. I don't know that else to say.' Every time she taps ash, it's three taps of the same speed and angle with a red-nailed finger. 'But I had fantasies about cutting on my neck, my face, which was creepy, and I'd been moving further up my arms all year without being able to help it, which scared me in hindsight. It was good I was in there; it was crazy—so maybe they were right after all.'

Drinion simply watches her. There is no way to tell whether it is building up to really rain or if the mass will miss them. The light outside is the approximate color of a spent flashbulb. It's too loud in here to know if there is thunder. Sometimes the air-conditioning seems to get colder or more insistent when it is about to storm, but that is not what it feels like is happening now.

Meredith Rand says: 'You have to say little things occasionally, like it's a real conversation, to show you're at least interested. Otherwise the person just feels like they're yammering and the other person could be thinking about God only knows what.'

'But putting cuts on your face would have externalized the situation too much,' Drinion says.

'There you go. Plus I didn't want to cut my face. As he ended up showing me, my surface face was all I really thought I had. My face and my body, that I was supposedly a *fox*. I was one of the *foxes* at Central Catholic. That's a high school here. They called us that—the *foxes*. Most of them were cheerleaders, too.'

Drinion says: 'So you were raised in the Catholic faith.'

Rand shakes her head as she taps the cigarette. 'That's not relevant. That's not the kind of little occasional response I meant.'

'...'

'The connection is the stuff about prettiness and loneliness you were talking about. Or we were, which is hard to understand, probably, given how supposedly being considered as good-looking in high school is the female ticket to popularity and being accepted and all the things that are supposed to be the opposite of loneliness.' She sometimes uses direct questions as an excuse to meet his gaze directly: 'Were you lonely in high school?'

'Not really.'

'Right. Oh, right. Plus beauty is a form of power. People pay attention to you. It can be very seductive.'

'Yes.'

Only in close retrospect does Meredith Rand consider the strange intensity of talking to the utility examiner. Ordinarily very conscious of her surroundings and what other people around her were doing, Rand later realized that large blocks of the tête-à-tête at Meibeyer's seemed removed from any kind of environment at all. That within these blocks of intense engagement she had been unconscious of the jukebox's intrusive music or the thud of its excessive bass in her breastbone, the insistent burbles and dings of the pinball machines and video raceway game, the televised baseball above the bar, the normally distracting roar of surrounding conversations in which different audible snatches sometimes rose out and commanded attention and then receded into the ambient distracting noise of mixed-together voices all raised to overcome the room's own noise. The only way she is able to explain it to Beth Rath is that it was as if a sort of insulated container had formed around their table and sometimes hardly anything else had penetrated through it. Even though it wasn't like she just sat there looking right at the utility man all the time; it wasn't like a hypnotic thing. She also hadn't been aware of how much time had passed or was passing, which for Meredith Rand was a very unusual thing.* The best theory Meredith Rand could come up with was that it was that 'Mr. X' paid such close, intense attention to what she was saying—an intensity that had nothing to do with flirting or anything romantic; this was a whole different type of intensity—although it was also true to say that Meredith Rand had experienced absolutely zero romantic or sexual attraction to Shane Drinion at that table in Meibeyer's. It was something else entirely.

'It was him who told me this. Who laid it out that way. At night, after dinner, after all the groups and OT were over and the doctors in their nice suits went home and there was just one nurse on the meds desk and him. He had the white staff coat with a sweater and these plastic sneakers and a big ring of keys. You could hear him down the hall without looking, just from the ring of keys. We used to

* Meredith Rand becomes no less comely or beautiful when she speaks to someone else about ritualistically cutting herself and being pink-paper'd into the Zeller Center. But she does look abruptly older or more drawn. You can see, not just imagine but see the way her face will look at forty—which after all, as is well known, will be only a different form of beauty, a less received and more severe or 'earned' beauty, in which the emergent flaws and lines do not mar her beautiful features but rather frame them, show seams in a face that is made and not just stamped out at random. Meredith Rand's nose and chin's slight cleft shine slightly in the red light of the walls' fake flames.

tell him it looked like the ring of keys weighed more than he did. Some of the girls gave him a lot of grief, because it wasn't like he could really do anything to them.'

'. . .'

'There wasn't anything to do after visits at night except watch TV in the community room, or play Ping-Pong on a table that had a really low net so even the girls on heavy meds could feel like they could play, too, and all he had to do was do med checks and give people passes for the phone, and at the end of his shift he had to fill out evals on everybody, which was totally routine unless there was some kind of psych crisis.'

'So you observed him closely, it seems,' Shane Drinion says.

'It wasn't like he was much to look at if you were going to call somebody good-looking or not. Some of the girls called him the corpse. They had to have their mean little names for everybody. Or they called him the grim reaper. It was all just physical. But it was like no part of him touched his clothes on the inside; they just hung on him. He moved like he was about sixty. But he was funny, and he really talked to you. If anybody wanted to talk about something, meaning really talk, he'd go in the conference room off the kitchen with them and talk.' Meredith Rand has a set of routines for putting the cigarette out, all of which, whether fast and stabbing or slow and more grinding from the side, are quite thorough. 'He didn't make anybody do it. It wasn't like he was tugging on your sleeve to go do tête-à-tête or let him practice on you. Most people just vegged out in front of the TV, or the ones in for drugs had to go to their drug meeting in the van. He had to put his feet up on the table, usually, when you had a one-on-one with him. The table in the conference room that the doctors spread out their files to talk to the parents at. He'd lean way back and put his sneakers up on the table, which he said it was because he had a bad back, but really it was because of the cardiomyopathy, which he'd gotten mysteriously in college and was why he didn't finish college, which was why he was working this shitty nut ward attendant job, even though he was about seven thousand times smarter and more perceptive about what was really going on with people than the doctors and so-called counselors were. They saw everybody through this professional lens that was about half an inch across—whatever didn't fit in the lens they either didn't see or twisted it or squished it in so it fit. And having his feet in those chintzy Kmart shoes up on the table like that made him seem more like at least a person, like somebody you were really talking to instead of somebody trying to just diagnose you or trace your etiology so they'd have something to say that fit their little lens. They were a total joke, those shoes.'

'May I ask a question?'

'Why not just ask the question instead of taking the time to make me say yes you can ask a question?'

'I see what you're saying.'

'So?'

'Elevating his feet was to help him circulate blood more efficiently?'

'That's what you wanted to ask?'

'Is that not the sort of small, reinforcing question you were talking about?'

'For Christ's sake,' Rand says. 'Yes, it's for circulation. Although at the time who knew why it was. It was believable he had a bad back. He sure didn't look comfortable. All you could really tell was that this was somebody who was not in great shape.'

'He appeared frail, especially for his age.'

Sometimes now Rand will every so often toss her head back and to the side a tiny bit, very rapidly, as if rearranging her hair's feathering without touching it, which certain types of adolescent girls do a great deal without necessarily being aware of it. 'By the way, he taught me the word *etiology*. And he explained why the doctors had to be so distant and stiff; it was just part of their job. He didn't force anybody, but at times it seemed like he picked certain people to talk to, and he made it hard to resist. The nights could be hard, and it wasn't like watching *Maude* with suicidal people or people on heavy meds was going to help very much.'

'. . .'

'Do you remember *Maude*?'

'No I don't.'

'My mom loved that show. It was about the last thing in the world I wanted to see in there. If her husband got mad and told her "Maude, *sit,*" she'd sit, like a dog, and it got a big laugh on the canned laughter. Some feminism. Or *Charlie's Angels,* which was just totally insulting, if you were a feminist.'

'. . .'

'The way he started talking to me was in the pink room, which was the isolation room, which is where they put you if you were on suicide watch and the law said you had to be legally observed twenty-four hours a day, or if you acted out in a disciplinary way where they said you presented a danger or disruptive influence—they could put you in there.'

'Called the pink room because that was the room's color?' Drinion asks.

Meredith Rand smiles coolly. 'Baker-Miller pink, to be exact, because there had been experiments showing that seeing pink soothed mental agitation, and soon every nut ward everywhere started painting their isolation room pink. He told me that, too. He explained the color of the room they put me in; it had a sloped floor and a drain in the middle like something out of the Middle Ages. I was never on suicide watch, if you're wondering. I have no idea how tripped out you are by any of this, like uh-oh here's this crazy person, she was in Zeller when she was seventeen.'

'I wasn't thinking that.'

'What I did was tell a doctor who wasn't even my doctor, I mean the one my dad's insurance was paying for, but this was a different doctor who'd come in and *cover* for the doctor's cases when he couldn't come in, they all covered for each other all the time this way, so in like five days you'd talk to three different doctors, and they had to spread your file and case notes or whatever out on the table to even remember who you were—and this doctor, who never even blinked, kept trying to get me to talk about being *abused and neglected* as a child, which I never was, and I ended up telling him he was a freaking idiot and that he could either believe me when I told him the truth or just stick it up his stupid fat butt. And then that night I'm in the pink room, he'd ordered it, which was bullshit. Not like they dragged me in there and threw me in and slammed the door—everybody was pretty nice about it. But you know, one of the weird things about being in a psych hospital is you gradually start to feel like you have permission to say whatever you're thinking. You feel like it's OK or maybe even in some way expected to act crazy or uninhibited, which at first feels kind of liberating and good; there's this feeling like no more smiley masks, no more pretending, which feels good, except it gets kind of seductive and dangerous, and actually it can make people worse in there—some inhibitions are good, they're normal, he said, and part of the syndrome they call some people eventually getting *institutionalized* is that they get put in a nut ward at a young age or a fragile time when their sense of themselves is not really very fixed or resilient, and they start acting the way they think people in nut wards are expected to act, and after a while they really *are* that way, and they get caught in the system, the mental-health system, and they never really get out.'

'And he told you that. He warned you about using uninhibited insults with the psychiatrist.'

Her eyes have changed; she puts her chin in her hand, which makes her seem even younger. 'He told me a lot of things. A lot. We talked for like two hours the night I was in the pink room. We both laugh about it now—he talked way more than I did, which is not how it's supposed to be done. After a while every night we were in there like clockwork, ta—'

'You went to the isolation room?'

'No, I was just in there that one night, and the regular case doctor, I have to admit it, he got the substitute one in some kind of disciplinary trouble for signing me in there; he said it was reactive.' Rand stops and taps her fingers against the side of her cheek. 'Shit, I forget what I was saying.'

Drinion looks slightly upward for an instant. ' "Every night we were in there like clockwork." '

'In the conference room, after visits and whoever was freaking out because of something in visits got calmed down or medicated.

We'd sit in there and talk, except he had to get up every so often to do checks on where everybody was and make sure nobody was in anybody else's room, and make whoever was due for meds go to the meds desk. Every night on weekday nights we'd go in, and he'd do this thing he always did of filling up a Coke can with water at the fountain, he'd use a Coke can instead of a cup, and we'd sit down at the table and he'd go, "So shall we go intense tonight, Meredith, or just do some laid-back chitchat?" and I'd almost act like somebody looking at a menu and go, "Well, hmm, tonight I think I'd like to go intense, please." '

'Can I ask a question?'

'Grr. Go ahead.'

'Should I infer that *intense* refers to the cutting behavior and your reasons for doing it?' Drinion asks. His hands are now on the table with the fingers laced together, which for most people causes the back to bow and slump, but with Drinion does not—his posture stays the same.

'Negative. He was too smart for that. We didn't talk about cutting often. That wouldn't do any good. It wasn't the kind of thing you could come at directly that way. What he—it's more like he mostly just told me all these things about myself.'

One of Drinion's interlaced fingers moves very slightly. 'Not asked you things?'

'Negative.'

'And that didn't make you angry? Presuming to tell you about yourself?'

'The big difference is the way he was right. Just about everything he said was right.'

'In what he told you about yourself.'

'Look, and he did this mostly in the beginning, when he needed to establish credibility. That's what he told me later—he knew I wouldn't be there long, at Zeller, and he knew I needed to talk to somebody, and he needed to let me know very fast that he understood me, knew me, he wasn't just dealing with me as a case or a problem to be figured out for his own career, which he knew was how the doctors and counselors seemed to me, which he said it didn't matter if I was right about them or not, the point is that I believed it, it was part of my defenses. He said I was one of the most strongly defended people he'd ever seen come in there. In Zeller. Short of the outright psychotics, I mean, who were just about impregnable, but they got transferred out almost right away; he rarely had any one-on-ones with real psychotics. The psychotic thing is just defensive structures and beliefs so strong that the person can't get out, they become the real world, and then it's usually too late, because the structure of the brain gets changed. That person's only hope is medication and a whole lot of pink around him at all times.'

'He understood you as a person, you're saying.'

'What he did, right in the pink room, while I'm sitting there on the bunk and going oh my God there's a *drain* in the floor, he right away told me two separate things about myself that I knew but nobody else knew. Nobody. I'm serious,' Meredith Rand says. 'It's like, I couldn't believe it. He was dead-on.'

'...'

'Now you're wondering what the things are,' she says.

Drinion does that very small thing with the angle of his head. 'Are you saying you'd like me to ask you what they are?'

'No way.'

'Almost by definition, I doubt that you'd tell them to someone.'

'Bingo. Right. No way. Not that they're all that interesting,' she says. 'But he did. He knew them, and you can bet that got my attention. That made me sit up and take notice. How could it not?'

Drinion says: 'I can understand that.'

'Exactly. That he knew me, understood me, was interested in understanding. People always say that, *understand, I understand you, please help us understand you.*'

'I've said it several times, too, while we've been talking,' Drinion says.

'Do you know how many times?'

'Nine, though I believe only four in quite the sense that you appear to be referring to, if I understand what you mean.'

'Is that a joke?'

'My using the word *understand* again just now?'

Rand makes an exasperated expression and directs it off to one side and then the other as if there were still more people at the table with them.

Drinion says: 'Not if I follow the sense of *understand* you mean, which doesn't refer to understanding a statement or somebody's implication but more a person, which seems to me less cognitive than a matter of empathy or I think even *compassion* would be the word you mean by this kind of understanding.'

'The thing,' she says, 'is he really did. Use whatever word you want. Nobody knew these things he told me—one of them I don't even think I knew, really, until he just put it out there in blunt words.'

'This made an impression,' Drinion says helpfully.

Rand ignores him. 'He was a natural therapist. He said it was his calling, his art. The way painting or being able to dance really well or to sit there reading the same thing for hours on end without moving or getting distracted is other people's calling.'

'. . .'

'Would you say you have a calling?' the POTEX asks Shane Drinion.

'I doubt it.'

'He wasn't a doctor, but when he saw somebody in there he thought he could maybe help, he'd try to help them. Otherwise he was more like a security guard, he said.'

'. . .'

'One time he said he was more just like a mirror. In the intense conversations. If he seemed mean or stupid, what it really meant was that you saw yourself as mean and stupid. If one time he struck you as smart and sensitive, it meant you were smart and sensitive that day—he just showed you what was there.

'He looked terrible, but that was also part of the power of sitting in there with him and doing these intense bits of work. He looked so sick and washed out and delicate that you never got the idea that here was this smug, normal, healthy, rich doctor judging you and being glad he wasn't you or just seeing you as a case to resolve. It was like really talking to somebody, with him.'

'Anyone could tell that he made a great impression on you in this difficult time, your future husband,' Shane Drinion says.

'Are you being ironic?'

'No.'

'Are you thinking, like, here's this messed-up seventeen-year-old falling in love with the therapist-type adult figure that she thinks is the only one that *understands?*'

Shane Drinion shakes his head exactly twice. 'That's not what I'm thinking.' It occurs to Rand that he could conceivably be bored out of his skull and she'd have no way of telling.

'Because that's pathetic,' Meredith Rand says. 'That's like the oldest story in the book, and however messed up you might think this is, it sure wasn't that.' She's sitting up very straight now for a moment. 'Do you know what monopsony is?'

'I think so.'

'What is it then?'

Shane Drinion clears his throat slightly. 'It's the reverse of monopoly. There's a single buyer and multiple sellers.'

'All right.'

'I think bids for government contracts, such as when the Service upgraded its card readers at the La Junta center last year, are an example of a monopsonistic market.'

'All right. Well, he taught me that one, too, although in a more of a personal context.'

'As in a metaphor,' Drinion says.

'Do you see what it could have to do with loneliness?'

Another very brief moment of inward scanning. 'I can see how it might lead to distrust, since contract-bidding situations are susceptible to rigging, dishonest cost-projections, and things like that.'

'You're a very literal person, did you know that?'

'...'

'Here's the literal thing, then,' Meredith Rand says. 'Say you're pretty, and there's things about being pretty that you like—you get treated special, and people pay attention to you and talk about you, and if you walk in someplace you can almost feel the room change, and you like it.'

'It's a form of power,' Drinion says.

'But at the same time you also have less power,' Meredith Rand says, 'because the power you have is all totally connected to prettiness, and at some point you realize that the prettiness is like a kind of box you're always in, or prison, that nobody's ever going to see you or think about you apart from the prettiness.'

'...'

'It's not like I even thought I was all that pretty,' Meredith Rand says. 'Especially in high school.' She's rolling a cigarette back and forth between her fingers but not lighting it. 'But I sure knew everybody else thought I was pretty. Ever since like twelve, people were saying how lovely and beautiful I was, and in high school I was one of the foxes, and everybody knew who they were, and it became sort of official, socially: I was pretty, I was desirable, I had the power. Do you get this?'

'I think so,' Shane Drinion says.

'Because this is what intense meant—he and I really talked about it, the prettiness. It was the first time I ever really talked about it with anybody. Especially a guy. I mean except for "You're so beautiful, I love you" and trying to put their tongue in your ear. Like that was all you needed to hear, that you were beautiful, and you were supposed to fall over and let them boff you.'

'...'

'If you're pretty,' Meredith Rand says, 'it can be hard to respect guys.'

'I can understand that,' Drinion says.

'Because you never even get to see what they might really be like. Because the minute you're around, they change; if they've decided you're beautiful, they change. It's like the thing in physics—if you're there to look at the experiment, it supposedly messes up the results.'

'There's a paradox involved in it,' Drinion says.

'And except for a while you like it. You like the attention. Even if they change, you know it's you making them change. You're attractive, they're attracted to you.'

'Hence the tongues in the ear.'

'Although with a lot of them it turns out it's got the opposite effect. They almost avoid you. They get scared or nervous—it makes them want something, and they're embarrassed or scared of wanting it—they can't talk to you or even look at you, or else they start putting on a little show like Second-Knuckle Bob, this flirty sexist thing where they think they're doing it to impress you but really it's to impress other boys, to show they're not afraid. And you haven't even done or said anything to start it; all you have to do is just be there, and everybody changes. Presto change-o.'

'It sounds taxing,' Drinion says.

Meredith Rand lights the cigarette she's been holding. 'Plus other girls hate you; they don't even know you or talk to you and they decide they hate you, just because of how the boys all react—like you're a threat to them, or they assume you're a stuck-up bitch without even trying to get to know you.' She has a definite style of averting her head to exhale and then bringing it back. Most people think she's very direct.

'I wasn't a ditz,' she says. 'I was good with figures. I won the algebra prize in tenth-grade algebra. But of course nobody cared about me being smart or good at math. Even the men teachers got all googly and nervous or pervy and flirty when I came up after or something to ask about something. Like I was a fox and there was no way anybody could ever even think to see anything more than that.

'Listen,' Meredith Rand says. 'Don't misunderstand me. It's not like I think I'm all that pretty. I'm not saying I'm beautiful. Actually I've never thought I was all that beautiful. My eyebrows are too heavy, for one thing. I'm not going to go around plucking them, but they're too heavy. And my neck is, like, twice as long as a normal person's, when I look in the mirror.'

'...'

'Not that it even matters.'

'No.'

'No what?'

'No, I understand it doesn't really matter,' Drinion says.

'Except it does. You don't get it. The prettiness thing—at least when you're that age, it's like a kind of trap. There's a greedy part of you that really likes the attention. You're special, you're desirable. It's easy to start thinking of the prettiness as you, like it's all you've got, it's what makes you special. In your designer jeans and little sweaters you can put in the dryer so they're even tighter. Walking around like that.' Although it's not as if what Meredith Rand wears at the Post is effacing or dowdy. They're professional ensembles, well within code, but many of the Post's examiners still bite their knuckles when she goes by, especially in cold months, when the extremely dry air produces static cling.

She says: 'The flip side being how you also start understanding that you're really just a piece of meat. Is what you are. Really desirable meat, but also that you'll never get taken seriously and never, like, be the president of a bank or something because no one will ever be able to see past the prettiness, the prettiness is what affects them and what makes them feel anything, and that's all that matters to them, and it's hard not to get sucked into that, to start, like, arranging yourself and seeing yourself the same way.'

'You mean seeing and reacting to people through whether or not they're attractive?'

'No, *no*.' You can see that Meredith Rand would have a hard time quitting cigarettes, since she uses the way she smokes and exhales and moves her head to convey a lot of affect. 'I mean starting to see yourself as a piece of meat, that the only thing you've got is your looks and the way you affect boys, guys. You start doing it without even knowing you're doing it. And it's scary, because at the same time it also feels like a box; you know there's more to you inside you because you can feel it, but nobody else will ever know—not even other girls, who either hate you or are scared of you, because you're a monopsony, or else if they're also the foxes or the cheerleaders they're competing with you and feel like they have to do this whole competitive catty thing that guys don't have any idea of, but trust me, it can be really cruel.'

The fact that one of Drinion's nostrils is slightly larger than the other sometimes makes it look as though he's cocking his head a little bit, even when he is not. It's somewhat parallel to the mouth-breathing thing. Meredith Rand usually interprets expressionlessness as inattention, the way someone's face blanks out when you're talking and they're pretending to listen but not really listening, but this is not the way Drinion's expressionlessness seems. Also, it's either her imagination or Drinion is sitting up steadily straighter and taller, because he seems to be slightly taller than when the tête-à-tête started. A collection of different kinds of old-fashioned fedoras and homburgs and various business hats glued or pinned somehow to a varnished rosewood board that had been visible on the opposite wall of Meibeyer's over Drinion's head is now partly obscured by the crown of his head and the slight cowlick that sticks up at his round head's apex. Drinion is actually levitating slightly, which is what happens when he is completely immersed; it's very slight, and no one can see that his bottom is floating slightly above the seat of the chair. One night someone comes into the office and sees Drinion floating upside down over his desk with his eyes glued to a complex return, Drinion himself unaware of the levitating thing by definition, since it is only when his attention is completely on something else that the levitation happens.

'Which is part of the feeling of the box,' Meredith Rand is continuing. 'There's the feeling, which in teenagers is really bad anyway, of feeling like nobody can really ever know you or love you for who you are because they can't really see you and for some reason you won't let them even though you feel like you want them to. But it's also at the same time a feeling that you know it's boring and immature and like a bad type of movie problem, "Boo hoo, no one can love me for who I am," so you're also aware that your loneliness is stupid and banal even while you're feeling it, the loneliness, so you don't even have any sympathy for yourself. And this is what we talked about, this is what he told me about, that he knew without me telling him: how lonely I was, and how the cutting had something to do with the prettiness and feeling like I had no right to complain but still being really unhappy at the same time believing that not being pretty seemed like it would be the end of the world, I'd just be a piece of meat nobody wanted instead of a piece of meat they did happen to want. Like I was trapped inside it, and I still really had no right to complain about it because look at all the girls who were jealous and thought no one who's pretty could be lonely or have any problems, and even if I did complain, then all the complaining was banal, he taught me *banal,* and *tête-à-tête,* and how this can become part of the whole loneliness—the truth of saying "I'm just meat, people only care about me as beautiful, no one cares what I really am inside, I'm lonely" is totally boring and banal, like something corny in *Redbook,* not beautiful or unique, or special. Which was the first time I thought of the scars and the cutting as letting the unbeautiful inside truth come out, be on the outside, even if I was also hiding it under long sleeves—although your blood is really actually quite pretty if you really look at it, I mean when it first comes out, although the cut has to be very careful and fine and not too deep so the blood just more appears as a line that kind of slowly wells up, so it's thirty seconds or more before you have to wipe because it's starting to run.'

'Does it hurt?' Shane Drinion asks.

Meredith Rand exhales sharply and looks right at him. 'What do you mean does it? I don't do it anymore. I never have, since I met him. Because he more or less told me all this and told me the truth, that it doesn't ultimately matter why I do it or what it, like, represents or what it's about.' Her gaze is very level and matter-of-fact. 'All that matters is that I was doing it and to stop doing it. That was it. Unlike the doctors and small groups that were all about your feelings and why, as though if you knew why you did it you'd magically be able to stop. Which he said was the big lie they all bought that made doctors and standard therapy such a waste of time for people like us—they thought that diagnosis was the same as cure. That if you knew why, it would stop. Which is bullshit,' Meredith Rand says. 'You only stop if you stop. Not if you wait for somebody to explain it in some magic way that will presto change-o make you stop.' She makes a sardonic flourish with her cigarette hand as she says presto change-o.

Drinion: 'It sounds as though he really helped you.'

'He was very blunt,' she says. 'It turned out being blunt is something he's proud of—it's part of his act that there is no act. Only I only found that out later.'

'. . .'

'You can see, of course, how having somebody have this kind of compassion and understanding of what's really going on inside you, how this would affect somebody that thought her big problem was the impossibility of anybody seeing past the prettiness to what was inside. Would you like to know his name?'

Drinion blinks once. He doesn't blink very often. 'Yes.'

'Edward. "Ed Rand, partial BS," he'd say. So you can see why I was pretty much primed to fall in love with him.'

'I think so.'

'So I don't need to spell it out,' Meredith Rand says. 'In a way, if he was a perv or a creep that played things that way, it would be a perfect setup for getting pretty young girls to fall for him. Work in a place that everybody comes in all mucked up and lonely and in crisis, and find the young girls, whose basic problem is probably always going to be their looks. So all he had to do, if he was smart, and he'd seen hundreds of messed-up girls come through, who starved themselves, or stole clothes from shopping malls, or ate and couldn't stop eating, or cut on themselves, or got into drugs, or kept running away with older black guys and getting dragged back over and over again by the parents, whatever, you get the idea, but that all had the same really essential problem, each time one of them came in, no matter what they were officially in for, which was not feeling like they were really known and understood and that was the cause of their loneliness, of the constant pain they were in that made them cut, or eat, or not eat, or give blowjobs to the whole basketball team in a row out back behind the cafeteria dumpster, which is what one cheerleader I know for a total fact did all the time junior year, although she was never really quite one of the foxes because she was known as such a total slut; a lot of the foxes just hated her.' Rand looks briefly right at Drinion to see whether there is any visible reaction to the word *blowjob,* which he does not appear to provide. 'And it'd be easy to get them in the conference room, and to tell them some stuff about themselves that totally shocked and amazed them because they hadn't ever told *anybody* about it and yet it was totally easy to spot and know about because at the core it was all the same.'

Drinion asks: 'Did you tell him this, during the therapy sessions that were designated as intense?'

Rand shakes her head as she extinguishes the Benson & Hedges cigarette. 'They weren't therapy sessions. He hated that term, all that terminology. They were just tête-à-têtes, talking.' Again she uses the same number of stabs and partial rolls to extinguish it, although with less force than when she's appeared impatient or angry with Shane Drinion. She says: 'That was all he said it seemed like I needed, just to talk to somebody with no bullshit, which was what the Zeller Center doctors didn't realize, or like they couldn't realize it because then the whole structure would come down, that here the doctors had spent four million years in medical school and residency and the insurance companies were paying all this money for diagnosis and OT and therapy protocols, it was all an institutional structure, and once things became institutionalized then it all became this artificial, like, organism and started trying to survive and serve its own needs just like a person, only it wasn't a person, it was the opposite of a person, because there was nothing inside it except the will to survive and grow as an institution—he said just look at Christianity and the whole Christian Church.'

'But my question was whether you talked to him about your possible suspicion, the possibility that he didn't really understand you, and care, but was a creep?'

Sometimes throughout the conversation Meredith Rand looks down critically at her fingernails, which are almond-shaped and neither too short nor too long, and painted a lustrous red. Shane Drinion looks at her hands only when Rand does, as a rule.

'I didn't have to,' Rand says. 'He brought it up. Edward did. He said given my problem it was only a matter of time before it occurred to me that maybe he didn't understand and care but only understood me the way a mechanic understands a machine—this was a time in the second week in the nut ward that I was having all these dreams about different kinds of machinery, with gears and dials, which the doctors and so-called therapists wanted to talk about and get me to see the symbolism of, which he and I both laughed about because it was so obvious an idiot could have seen it, which he said wasn't the doctors' fault or that they were stupid, that was just the way the machine of the institution of in-patient therapy worked, and the doctors had no more choice about how much importance they put on the dreams than a little piece of machinery does about doing the little task or movement it's been put there to do over and over again as part of the larger operation of the larger machine.' Rand's rep at the REC is that she's sexy but crazy and a serious bore, just won't shut up if you get her started; they argue about whether they ultimately envy her husband or pity him. 'But he brought it up before I had a chance to even start thinking about it.' She unsnaps her white vinyl case but does not extract a cigarette from it. 'Which I have got to say was kind of surprising, because by this time I was eighteen, and I'd had such bad experiences with creeps and pervs and jocks and college boys' "I love you" on the first date that I was very suspicious and cynical about guys' double motives, and normally the minute this sickly little orderly started paying attention to me I'd have my defensive shields way up and be considering all kinds of creepy, depressing possibilities.'

Drinion's red forehead crinkles for just a moment. 'Were you eighteen, or seventeen?'

'Oh,' Meredith Rand says. 'Right.' As she acts younger, she begins to laugh sometimes in a fast and toneless way, like a reflex. 'I was just eighteen. I had my eighteenth birthday on my third day in Zeller. My dad and mother even came out and brought a cake and noisemakers during visiting hours and tried to have this celebration, like whoopee, which was so embarrassing and depressing I didn't know what to do, like, a week ago you're hysterical about some cuts and put me in the bin and now you want to pretend it's happy birthday, let's ignore the girl screaming in the pink room while I blow out the candles and you fix the elastic of the hat under your chin, so I just played along because I didn't know what to say about how totally weird it was for them to be acting like, happy birthday, Meredith, whoopee.' She is kneading the flesh of one arm with the other arm's hand as she recounts this. Sometimes, as Drinion sits with his hands laced on the tabletop before him, he changes having one thumb or the other be the thumb on top. His former glass of beer sits empty except for a semicircle of foamy material along the bottom's edge. Meredith Rand now has three different narrow straws she can choose to chew on; one of them is already quite thoroughly chewed and flattened at one end. She says:

'So he brought it up. He said it was probably going to occur to me on some level soon, so if I wanted it really intense we might as well talk about it. He'd always drop little bombs like this, and then while I sat there like':—she forms an exaggerated taken-aback expression—'he'd groan and swing his feet around off the table and go out with his clipboard to do checks—he had to officially check on everybody every quarter hour and note down where they were and make sure nobody was making themselves barf or looping pillowcases together to hang themselves with—and he'd go out and leave me there in the conference room with nothing to look at or do, waiting for him to come back, which tended to take him a long time because he never felt well, and if there was no nursing supervisor or anybody around to watch him he walked very slow and used to lean against the wall every so often to catch his breath. He was white as a ghost. Plus he took all these diuretics, which made him have to pee all the time. Except when I asked him about it all he'd say is that it was his own private business and we weren't in here talking about him, it didn't matter about him because all he really was was a kind of mirror for me.'

'So you didn't know that he had cardiomyopathy.'

'All he'd say was that his health was a mess but that the advantage of being a physical mess was that he looked like exactly as much of a mess as he really was, there was no way to hide it or pretend he was less of a mess than he felt like. Which was very different than people like me; he said the only way for most people to show the mess was to fall apart and get put someplace like this, like Zeller, where it was undeniably obvious to you and your family and everybody else that you were a mess, so there was at least a certain relief to being put in the nut ward, but he said given the realities here, meaning insurance and money and the way institutions like Zeller worked, given the realities it was almost sure that I wouldn't be in here that long, and what was I going to do when I got back out there in the real world where there were all these razor blades and X-Acto knives and long-slaved shirts. Long-sleeved shirts.'

'Can I ask a question?'

'You bet.'

'Did you react? When he brought up the idea that his helping you and intense conversations with you were connected to your attractiveness?'

Rand snaps and unsnaps her white cigarette case. 'I said something like, so you're saying you'd be in here with me all concerned and interested if I was fat with zits and a, like, big old jaw? And he said he couldn't say one way or the other, he'd worked with all kinds of people that came through, and some were plain girls and some were pretty, he said it had more to do with how defended people were. If they were too defended in terms of their real problems—or if they were just outright psycho, and when they looked at him they saw some shiny terrifying four-faced statue or something—then he couldn't do anything. It was only if he felt a kind of vibe off the person where he felt like he could maybe understand them and maybe offer real interpersonal talking and help with them instead of just the inevitable doctor-and-institution thing.'

'Did you accept that as an answer to your question?' Drinion says, without any kind of incredulous or judging expression that Meredith Rand can see.

'No, I said something sarcastic like blah blah blah whatever, but he said that wasn't his real answer, he wanted to answer the question because he knew how important it was, he could totally understand the anxiety and suspicion of would he really even care and pay attention if I wasn't pretty, because he said in actuality this was my whole core problem, the one that would follow me when I got out of Zeller, and that I had to find out how to deal with or I'd be back in here or worse. Then he said it was close to lights-out and we had to quit for today, and I was, like, you're telling me there's this major core problem I have to deal with or else and then that's it, time for noddy blinkums? I was so ticked off. And then the next two or three nights he wasn't even there, and I was totally spasming out, and there was only this other guy there from the weekends, and the day staff won't ever tell you *anything*, all they see is that you're agitated and they report that you're agitated but nobody actually cares about what you're agitated about, no one wants to even know what your question is, if you're an in-patient you're not a human being and they don't have to tell you anything.' Rand makes her face assume a look of frustrated distance. 'It turned out he'd been in the hospital—the real hospital; when the inflammation gets bad then the heart doesn't pump the blood out all the way, and it's a little like what they call congestive heart failure; they have to put you on oxygen and heavy-duty anti-inflammatories.'

'So you were concerned,' Drinion says.

'But at the time I didn't even know that, all I knew was he wasn't there, and then it was the weekend, so it was a long time before he got back, and at first when he did I was totally ticked and wouldn't even talk to him in the hall.'

'You'd been left hanging.'

'Well,' Rand says, 'I took it personally that he'd gotten me all involved and said all these heavy therapeutic things and then disappeared, like it was all just a sadistic game, and when he got back the next week and asked me in the TV room, I just pretended I was into the TV show and pretended he wasn't even there.'

'You didn't know that he'd been in the hospital,' Drinion says.

'After I found out how sick he was, I felt pretty bad about it; I felt like I acted like a spoiled child or some girl that was jilted for the prom. But I also realized I cared about him, I felt like I almost sort of needed him, and except for my dad and a couple friends when I was little I couldn't even remember how long it had been since I felt like I really cared and needed somebody. Because of the prettiness thing.'

Meredith Rand says: 'Have you ever only found out you cared about somebody when they're not around and you're like Oh my God, they're not around, now what am I going to do?'

'Not really.'

'Well anyway, but it made an impression. What came out when I finally said oh all right whatever and started talking to him in the conference room again is that maybe I'd felt like I'd ticked him off and sort of drove him away when I asked him if he'd be in here doing the intense tête-à-tête thing with me if I was fat and cross-eyed. Like that it ticked him off, or that he'd finally decided I was so cynical and suspicious of men only being interested in me because of the prettiness thing that he'd finally figured out that he wasn't going to be able to con me into thinking he actually cared enough that he'd get to boff me or even just feed his ego that here was this so-called beautiful girl that got into him and cared and wrote his name over and over in big loopy cursive in her diary or whatever his trip was. I think all this ugly stuff came out because I was mad because he'd disappeared like that, I thought, and just ditched me and left me here. But he was pretty good about it; he said he could see how I'd feel that way, considering what my real problem was, which then for a while after that I think he let me think he hadn't come in for work for those days just so I could start to see the problem for myself, to figure out what it was and start to see it for what it was.'

'Did you demand any sort of explanation?' Drinion asks.

'A bunch of times. The weird thing is that now, so much later on, I can't remember for sure if he eventually spat it out or if he got me to figure it out for myself,' Meredith Rand says, now looking ever so slightly up in order to meet Drinion's eyes, which if she'd think about it is rather strange, given their respective heights and places at the table, 'the so-called core problem.' Drinion's forehead crinkles slightly as he looks at her. She rotates the fingers of one hand in a procedural or summarizing way: 'Subject, who is seen as very pretty, wants to be liked for more than her prettiness, and is angry that she isn't liked or cared about for reasons that don't have anything to do with her prettiness. But in fact, everything about her is filtered through her prettiness *for her*—she is so angry and suspicious that she couldn't even accept real, true, no-agenda caring even if it's offered to her, because deep down inside *she,* the subject *herself,* can't believe that anything except prettiness or sex appeal is the motive for anybody's caring. Except her parents,' she inserts, 'who are nice but not too bright, and anyway they're her parents—we're talking about people out in the world.' She makes a summing-up gesture that may or may not be ironic. 'Subject is really her own core problem, and only she can solve it, and only if she quits wanting to be lonely and feeling sorry for myself and going "Poor me, I'm so lonely, nobody understands how bad I hurt, boo hoo." '

'To be honest, I was asking about a different explanation.' By now, Drinion appears considerably taller than he had when the tête-à-tête started. The rows of hats on the wall behind him are almost completely obscured. It is also odd to have someone stare into your eyes this continuously without feeling challenged or nervous, or even excited. It will occur to Rand later, as she's driven home, that during the tête-à-tête with Drinion she'd felt sensuously aroused in a way that had little to do with being excited or nervous, that she'd felt the surface of the chair against her bottom and back and the backs of her legs, and the material of her skirt, and the sides of her shoes against the sides of her feet in hose whose microtextured weave she could also feel, and the feel of her tongue against her teeth's rear and palate, the vent's air against her hairline and the room's other air against her face and arms and the taste of cigarette smoke's residue. At one or two points she'd even felt she could feel the exact shape of her eyeballs against her lids' insides when she blinked—she was aware when she blinked. The only kind of experience she could associate with it involved their cat that she'd had when she was a girl before it got hit by a car and the way she could sit with the cat in her lap and stroke the cat and feel the rumble of the cat's purring and feel every bit of the texture of the cat's warm fur and the muscle and bone beneath that, and that she could sit for long periods of time stroking the cat and feeling it with her eyes half-shut as if she was spaced out or stuporous-looking but had felt, in fact, like she was the opposite of stuporous—she felt totally aware and alive, and at the same time when she sat slowly stroking the cat with the same motion over and over it was like she forgot her name and address and almost everything else about her life for ten or twenty minutes, even though it wasn't like spacing out at all, and she loved that cat. She missed the feel of its weight, which was like nothing else, neither heavy nor light, and at times for almost the next two or three days she felt like she feels now, like the cat.

'You mean of the wanting to boff me thing?'

Drinion: 'I think so.'

Meredith Rand: 'He said he was basically a dead man, he used the words *dead man* and *walking dead,* so the point is he couldn't be into me in that way, he said. He wouldn't have the physical energy to try to get in my pants even if he'd wanted to.'

Shane Drinion: 'He told you about his condition, then.'

Meredith Rand: 'Not in so many words; he said it was really none of my business except in how it bore down on my problem. And I said my suspicion was starting to be that he was dropping all these hints about "my problem, my problem" but not just spitting out what it was supposed to be, to sort of string me along for some reason, and that I wasn't going to pretend I knew exactly what the reason was or what he wanted but it was hard not to think on some level it was creepy or pervy, which I simply flat-out told him. I'd quit being polite by then.'

'I'm a little confused,' Drinion says. 'This was all before he'd simply stated what he believed your main problem was?'

Meredith Rand shakes her head, though in response to what is now doubly unclear. One of the examiners' complaints is that she goes off on these long stories but at some point loses the thread and it's nearly impossible not to drift off or zone out when you can't understand what the hell she's getting at anymore. Several of the single posted examiners have decided she's simply crazy, great to look at from a distance but definitely a wide-berth-type girl, especially on breaks, when every moment of diversion is precious, and she can be worse than the work itself. She is saying: 'By this time I was either getting hit on or rapped to by every guy in Zeller, from the day attendant to the men on the second floor when we came down for OT, which was a major drag in all kinds of ways. Although he did point out that if it bummed me out so much, why did I put mascara on even if I was in a mental hospital. Which you have to admit was a valid thing to point out.'

'Yes.'

She is grinding the heel of her hand into one eye, to signify either fatigue or an attempt to stay on track in the story, although Drinion gives no sign of being bored or impatient. 'Plus also by around this time he said the Zeller doctors started saying that my so-called attachment to this one attendant—they also saw all the rapping and sniffing around everybody was doing—all the intense solo tête-à-têtes were starting to look dependent or unhealthy, and not saying anything to me about it but asking him all kinds of questions and basically starting to give him a really hard time, so we started having to wait for everybody to get all engrossed at TV time and then go talk in the stairwell just outside the ward, where it wasn't so public, where he'd usually lie down on the cement of the landing with his feet up on the second or third stair up, which by this time he admitted wasn't for his back but he needed the elevation to keep his circulation going. So we ended up spending a lot of the first couple days out in the stairwell talking about the whole business of my suspicions about what he wanted from me and why he was doing this, around and around, and he did tell me a little more about himself and getting cardiomyopathy in college, but he also kept saying OK, he'd talk about all this as long as I wanted to, but that it was kind of a vicious circle because anything he said I could be suspicious of and attribute some kind of secondary agenda to if I wanted to, and I might think it was all honest and open but it wasn't really intense or efficacious, in his opinion, it was more like going around and around inside the problem instead of really looking at the problem, which he said because he was a walking dead man and not really part of the institution of the nut ward he felt like maybe he was the only person there who'd really tell me the truth about my problem, which he said was basically that I needed to grow up.'

Meredith Rand pauses here and looks at Shane Drinion in anticipation of his asking what that diagnosis was supposed to mean, exactly; but he does not ask. He appears to have become reconciled to something, or to have decided to accept the way Meredith Rand remembers the story on her own terms, or to have concluded that trying to impose a certain kind of order on her side of the tête-à-tête was going to have the opposite effect.

She is saying, 'And naturally the "grow up" thing ticked me off, and I told him to go sit on something sharp, but I didn't really mean it, because by around this time he'd said also that the word was starting to come down that I was going to get discharged soon, the treatment team was starting to talk about it, even though of course nobody ever thought to tell me anything about what was going on, and that my mother had been trying to set up outpatient counseling and trying to get one of the doctors to keep seeing me in his private practice, which was very full and also not totally covered by my dad's insurance, so the whole thing was a bureaucratic nightmare, and it would take some time, but it was starting to sink into me that this wasn't forever, that by as early as maybe next week or the week after I wouldn't be seeing him or having intense conversations with him anymore, or even maybe ever see him again—I realized I didn't know where he lived or even his last name, for Christ's sake. This all sort of hit me, and I start freaking out when I think about it, because I'd already got a taste of what a couple days of suddenly not getting to talk to him or know where he was was like, and I'm freaking out, and in my mind I'm toying with the idea of sharpening something and doing some cutting that I didn't even really feel like doing, just so I'd get kept in the nut ward a little longer, which I knew was completely nuts.' She looks up very quickly at Drinion to see whether he's reacting to this information. 'Which was crazy, and actually I think he knew this was going on, he knew how important he'd gotten to be to me by then, I think, so he had extra leverage or ammo to use to tell me to just cut the shit—I'd be sitting on the stairway up to Four and he'd be lying on his back at the bottom of the stairway with his feet up right below me, so I spent all this time looking at his shoe soles, which were like Kmart shoes and the soles were plastic—and that "grow up" meant *now,* right this second, and quit being childish, because it would kill me. He said the girls that came through Zeller were all the same, and none of us had any idea of what being a grown-up was. Which was totally condescending, and normally the totally wrong thing to say to an eighteen-year-old. So there was this little argument about that. His point was that being childish wasn't the same thing as being like a child, he said, because watch a real child play or stroke a cat or listen to a story and you'll see it's like the opposite of what we were all doing there in Zeller.' Shane Drinion is leaning slightly forward. His bottom is now almost 1.75 inches off the chair seat; his work shoes' gumlike soles, darkened at the perimeter by the same process that darkens pencils' erasers, swing slightly just above the tile floor. Were it not for the sport coat hanging off the back of his chair, Beth Rath and others would be able to see light through the substantial gap between the seat of his chair and his slacks. 'It's more like he was explaining than arguing,' Rand says. 'He said there is a particular kind of stage of life where you get cut off from the, like, unself-conscious happiness and magic of childhood—he said only seriously disturbed or autistic children are without this childhood joy—but later in life and puberty it's possible to leave that childhood freedom and completeness behind but still remain totally immature. Immature in the sense of waiting or wanting some magical daddy or rescuer to see you and really know and understand you and care as much about you as a child's parents do, and save you. Save you from yourself. He also kept yawning a lot and hitting his shoes together, and I'd watch the soles go back and forth. He said this is how immaturity shows up in young women and girls; in men it's somewhat different in how it looks but really it's all the same, which is wanting to be distracted from what you've lost and fixed and saved by somebody. Which is pretty banal, it's like something out of a doctor's textbook, and I go so this is my core problem? This is what I've been stringing along waiting for? And he goes no, that's everybody's core problem, and it's why girls are so obsessed with prettiness and whether they can attract somebody and arouse enough love in that person to save them. *My* core problem, he said, and this connects to the core problem I told you about just now, was the neat little trap I'd made for myself to ensure that I never really had to grow up and so I could stay immature and waiting forever for somebody to save me because I'd never be able to find out that nobody else can save me because I'd made it impossible for me to get what I was so convinced I needed and deserved, so I could always be angry and I could always get to go around thinking that my real problem was that no one could see or love the real me the way I needed so I'd always have my problem to sit and hold and stroke on and make believe was the real problem.' Rand looks up sharply at Shane Drinion. 'Does that seem banal?'

'I don't know.'

'It kind of did to me,' Meredith Rand says. 'I told him that was incredibly helpful and now I knew just what to do when I got discharged from Zeller, which was click my heels together and transform diagnosis into cure, and how could I ever repay him.'

Drinion says, 'You were being deeply sarcastic.'

'I was pissed!' Meredith Rand says, a bit loudly. 'I told him lo and behold it looked like it turned out he was just like the diagnosis-is-cure doctors in their nice suits, except of course his diagnosis was also insulting, which he could call honesty and get extra jollies hurting people's feelings. I was just so pissed! And he laughed and said he wished I could see myself right now—he could see me because he was lying down and I was standing right over him, because every like fifteen minutes or so I had to help him up so he could sneak back in out of the hallway and go around with his clipboard and do checks. He said I looked like a little child that just had its toy taken away.'

'Which probably made you even angrier,' Drinion says.

'He said something like all right then, OK, he'd explain it like he was talking to a child, to somebody so locked into the problem that she can't even see that it's her problem and not just the way the world is. I wanted to be liked and known for more than just the prettiness. That I wanted people to look past the prettiness thing and the sexual thing and see who I was, like as a person, and I felt really mad and sorry for myself that people didn't.'

Meredith Rand, in the tavern, looks briefly up at Drinion. 'Didn't look past the surface,' he says, to signify that he understands what she's saying.

She cocks her head. 'But in reality everything was the surface.'

'Your surface?'

'Yes, because under the surface were just all these feelings and conflicts about the surface, and anger, about how I looked and the effect on people I had, and really all there was inside was this constant tantrum about how I wasn't getting saved and it was because of my prettiness, which he said if you think about it is really unattractive—nobody wants to get close to somebody who's in the middle of this constant tantrum. Who'd want that?' Rand makes a sort of ironic ta-da gesture in the air. 'So, he said, I'd actually set it up so that the only reason anybody *would* be attracted to me as a person was that I was pretty, which was exactly the thing that made me so angry and lonely and sad.'

'That sounds like a psychological trap.'

'His comparison was he compared it to making a kind of machine that gave you an electric shock every time you said "Ow!" Of course, he knew I'd been having the machine dreams. I know I kept just looking at him, giving him this death-ray look that all the foxes in school get good at giving people, like they're just supposed to melt away and die if you look at them like that. He was lying down with his feet up on the stairs as he's saying all this. His lips were a little bit blue, the cardiomyopathy was getting worse all the time, and the Zeller stairways had those horrid fluorescent tube light things in the stairwell that made him look worse; he wasn't even pale as much as gray, with this kind of frothy paste on his lips, because he couldn't sip his little can of water when he was lying down on his back.' Her eyes look like she's really seeing him again *in situ* in the stairwell at Zeller. To tell the truth, he looked gross to me, scary, repulsive, like a corpse, or somebody in one of those pictures of people in stripes in concentration camps. The weird thing is that I cared about him at the same time I found him gross. He grossed me out,' she says. 'And that I was so deep in my problem that I couldn't accept real, genuine, nonsexual or nonromantic or non-prettiness-type interest in me even if it was offered to me—he was talking about himself, which I knew, even though he didn't spell it out; we'd gone over that ground for days and days before, and time was running out, we both knew. I'd be getting discharged and I'd never see him again. But I said some pretty horrible things.'

'You're referring to the stairwell,' Shane Drinion says.

'Because deep down inside, he said, I only saw myself in terms of the prettiness. I saw myself as so mediocre and banal inside that I couldn't imagine anybody except my parents being interested in me for anything except what I looked like, as a fox. I was so angry, he said, that all anybody cared about or paid any attention to was the prettiness, but he said that was a smoke screen, theater of the human mind, that what really bothered me so much was I felt the same way, boys and men were treating me the same sort of way I really treated myself, and in reality it was really myself I was angry at except I couldn't see it—I projected it onto the pervs whistling on the street or the sweaty boys trying to boff me or the other girls deciding I'm a bitch because I'm stuck up about the prettiness.'

There is a brief moment of silence, meaning nothing but the noise of pinball and the baseball game and the sounds of people unwinding.

'Is this boring?' she asks Drinion abruptly. She's unaware of how she's looking at Drinion as she asks this. For just a moment she appears to be almost a different person. It has suddenly occurred to Meredith Rand that Shane Drinion might be one of those ingratiating but ultimately shallow people who could *seem* to be paying attention while in fact allowing their attention to wander hill and dale all over the place, including possibly to considering how he wouldn't be sitting here nodding politely and listening to this incredibly boring dribble, narcissistic dribble, if it didn't afford him a chance to look directly at Meredith's bottomless green eyes and exquisite bone structure, plus a bit of visible cleavage, since she'd taken off her flounce and unbuttoned her top button the minute the 5:00 buzzer had sounded.

'Is it? Is this boring?'

Drinion responds: 'The major part of it isn't, no.'

'What part of it is boring?'

'Boring isn't a very good term. Certain parts you tend to repeat, or say over again only in a slightly different way. These parts add no new information, so these parts require more work to pay attention to, alth—'

'Like what parts? What is it that you think I keep telling over and over?'

'I wouldn't call it boring, though. It's more that attending to these parts requires work, although it wouldn't be fair to call that effort unpleasant. It's that listening to the parts that do add new information or insights, these parts compel attention in a way that doesn't require effort.'

'What, is it that I keep going on and on about how supposedly beautiful I am?'

'No,' Drinion says. He cocks his head slightly. 'In fact, to be honest, in those parts where you do repeat the same essential point or information in a slightly different way, the underlying motive, which I get the feeling is a concern that what you're imparting might be unclear or uninteresting and must get recast and resaid in many different ways to assure yourself that the listener really understands you—this is interesting, and somewhat emotional, and it coheres in an interesting way with the surface subject of what Ed, in the story you're telling, is teaching you, and so in that respect even the repetitive or redundant elements compel interest and require little conscious effort to pay attention to, at least so far as I'm concerned.'

Meredith Rand extracts another cigarette. 'You sound like you're reading off a card or something.'

'I'm sorry it seems that way. I was trying to explain my answer to your question, because I got the sense you were hurt by my answer, and I felt that a fuller explanation would prevent the hurt. Or obviate it if you were angry. In my view, there was just a misunderstanding based on a miscommunication around the word *boring*.'

Her smile is both mocking and not. 'So I'm not the only one who's worried about misunderstanding and keeps trying to head off misunderstanding for emotional reasons.' But she can tell he is sincere; he is neither yanking her around nor kissing butt. Meredith can feel it. There is a feeling that comes with sitting across from Shane Drinion and having his eyes and attention on you. It isn't excitement, but it is intense, a little bit like standing near the high-voltage transformer park south of Joliet Street.

'Can I ask,' Drinion says, 'is it projection when you project emotions about yourself onto other people? Or is that displacement?'

She makes another face. 'He hated those kinds of words, actually. He said they were part of the self-nourishing institution of the mental-health system. He said even the word was contradictory—mental-health *system*. This was the next night, in the service elevator now, because somebody on the stairs on some other floor heard our voices the night before because the stairwell was all cement and metal and echoey, and Ed got ragged on somehow by the nursing supervisor for encouraging my unhealthy attachment to him that they'd gotten the idea of from how upset I was the time when he was out for two days—it turned out he was right on the edge of getting fired, mainly because he'd started missing the fifteen-minute checks sometimes and one girl was putting her finger down her throat and throwing up dinner and somebody found some of the throw-up and Ed had missed it because he'd been lying in the stairwell and it was harder to get up from lying all the way down with his feet on the stairs, even if I helped him up, and he'd blown off getting up to do checks. Some of the girls had also gotten all bitchy about us having conversations, like I was the favorite or something, and started a whole rumor with the treatment teams that I was always pretending I had to talk secretly to him and dragging him off and trying to make out with him or whatever. A couple of those girls were just beyond horrible, they were such bitches I'd never seen anything like it.'

'...'

'And it was also the day I got discharged, or got told that I was getting discharged the next day; my parents had worked it out and there were about seven million papers to sign the next day and then I was going home. There'd been this whole thing with my mom getting some doctor to sign off on outpatient counseling, blah blah. Nobody used the service elevator at night after the supper trays, so he opened it up and we went in there and he sat on the floor, the floor had a metal pattern thing and you couldn't lie down. It stunk, it was worse than the stairwell.

'He said it was the last night, the last conversation, and when I said I wanted intense he said it was showtime, we probably wouldn't ever meet or see each other after this. I said what did he mean. I was totally freaking out, though. I was the one with double motives. It was showtime. I knew I couldn't pull some kind of scam so I could stay, I knew he'd see through that, he'd just laugh at me. But I was ready to say I had romantic feelings—that I was attracted to him, even though I felt like I really wasn't, sexually, even though later on it turned out I was. I just couldn't admit it to myself, how I felt about him, because of my problem. Although I have to say now I'm not so sure,' Meredith Rand says. 'Being married is totally different than being seventeen and in total identity crisis and idealizing somebody that seems to really see you and care.' She looks far more like herself now. 'But he was the first guy that it felt like told me the truth, that didn't just start having double motives and start performing or being all sweaty and intimidated and was willing to really see me and know me and just tell the truth about what he saw. And he really did know me—remember, he told me all those things about my mom and the neighbor that nobody knew.' Her face hardens again, somewhat, or tightens, as she looks directly at Drinion, holding the cigarette but not lighting it. 'Is this one of the parts that you said I repeat over and over?'

Drinion shakes his head a little bit and then waits for Meredith Rand to continue. The hyperattractive POTEX continues looking at him.

Drinion says: 'No. I think the original subject of the story was you getting married. Getting married obviously assumes a mutual attraction and romantic emotions, so your first mention of a willingness to acknowledge romantic attraction is new information, and very relevant.' His expression hasn't changed at all.

'So it's not boring.'

'No.'

'And you've never had romantic attraction feelings yourself.'

'Not that I'm aware of, no.'

'And if you ever had them, wouldn't you be aware of them?'

Drinion: 'I think so, yes.'

'So your answer was a little bit slippery, wasn't it?'

'I suppose it was,' Drinion says. Later she'd consider that he didn't seem taken aback at all. It seemed like he was merely absorbing information and adding it to himself. And that (Rand wouldn't consider this so much as just remember it as part of the sensuous memory of her making a bit of fun of Drinion and the odd way he responded whenever she did this, which she could more or less at will, make fun of him, because in certain ways he was a total nerd and dweeb) the display of different kinds of hats on the rear wall was now completely obscured except for the very tip of the bill of a fisherman's cap in the upper row.

'Well, but anyway,' Meredith Rand says. She has had her chin in the same hand that holds the unlit Benson & Hedges, which looks like the opposite of comfortable. 'So I do know that that last night, in the elevator, I wasn't fully listening to him and, like, engaging with him on what he was telling me, because I was wrestling with all these inner feelings and conflicts about attraction to him and also totally freaking out about hearing that I'd never see him again, because the deal was that I was set up for outpatient counseling but that was on the second floor where all the doctors had their real offices, and he was only on on nights on the third floor, which was a locked ward. Just the idea that I didn't know where he lived freaked me out. Plus I knew he might get fired soon, because he could barely even do checks anymore, and there'd been trouble with one of the vomiters that had been vomiting and he hadn't checked her, plus I knew he hadn't told the Zeller people about his health thing, the cardiomyopathy, which had been more or less under control when they first hired him, it sounded like, but had gotten worse and worse—'

'He still hadn't told you about the cardiomyopathy, though.'

'Right, but whatever it was, the Zeller people didn't know about it, and they just thought that he didn't take care of himself very well, or he was hungover or lazy, something terrible. So I kept spacing out and thinking about what if I took my shirt off and, like, made out with him right here, would he let me or would he be grossed out or laugh at me, and how could I get him to see me again and still have intense conversations after I got out and had to go back to Mom and Central Catholic, and what if I told him I loved him, and what if he died after I got out and I didn't even know he died because I didn't know who he was or where he lived. It occurred to me I didn't even know how he really felt about me as me and not some girl he was helping, like did he think I was interesting, or smart, or pretty. It was so hard to think that somebody that seemed to understand me so well and tell me the truth didn't care for me in that special way.'

'You mean having romantic feelings.'

Rand shrugs a little with her eyebrows. 'He was a guy, after all.

So...and then it occurred to me that I was sort of doing just what he said my core problem was—thinking about him and not losing him and that he could save me and that the way to keep him was through sexual feelings because that's all I had.

'So then I know at some point he gave me a quiz about the overall topics we'd covered. It was both a joke and not.' She lights the cigarette, finally. 'Later on, he confessed it was because he thought he was really dying from this spell of cardiomyopathy—it turned out there were whole days at a time that he couldn't catch his breath, like he was running even when he was just lying there; his lips were blue for a reason—and he said he'd been pretty sure he wouldn't ever see me again and be able to tell if he'd been any help, he wanted to reassure himself that he'd helped somebody a little before he died. And of course on my end I was freaking out, I couldn't figure out whether it would be better to ace the quiz or flunk it, in terms of getting to see him again. Even though he pretended the whole quiz was a joke, like I was a kindergartner getting quizzed by a kindergarten teacher. He was really good at being serious and making fun of himself at the same time—it's one reason I loved him.'

Drinion: 'Loved?'

'Like, question one: What have we learned about cutting ourself? And I said, like, we learned that it doesn't matter why I cut or what the psychological machinery is behind the cutting, like if it's projecting self-hatred or whatever. Exteriorizing the interior. We've learned all that matters is to not do it. To cut it out. Nobody else can make me cut it out; only I can decide to stop it. Because whatever the institutional reason, it's hurting myself, it's me being mean to myself, which was childish. It was not treating yourself with any respect. The only way you can be mean to yourself is if you deep down expect somebody else is going to gallop up and save you, which is a child's fantasy. Reality meant nobody else was for sure going to be nice to me or treat me with any respect—that was the point of his thing about growing up, realizing that—and nobody else was for sure going to see me or treat me the way I wanted to be seen, so it was my job to make sure to see myself and treat myself like I was really worthwhile. It's called being responsible instead of childish. The real responsibilities are to myself. And if liking my looks was part of that and part of what I thought was deep-down worthwhile, that was OK. I could like being pretty without making prettiness the only thing I had going for me, or feeling sorry for myself if people spazzed out about the prettiness. That was my answer to the quiz.'

Shane Drinion: 'As I understand it, though, your actual experience is that someone else *was* being nice to you and treating you as worthwhile.'

Rand smiles in a way that makes it seem as though she's smiling in spite of herself. She's also smoking her cigarette in a more thorough, sensuous way. 'Well, yes, that's what I was actually thinking about, standing there in the elevator and looking down at him and answering his quiz, which I did sincerely, but secretly I was totally freaking out. The truth is I felt like in reality he was just what he was saying was impossible and childish, he was exactly the other person he was saying I'd never really find. I felt like he loved me.'

'So there is a very intense emotional conflict going on,' Shane Drinion says.

Rand holds her hands to the sides of her head and makes a quick face that mimics someone having some kind of nervous breakdown. 'I was telling him about forgetting about other people and why they were or weren't attracted and if they really cared and just being decent to myself, treating myself like I was worthwhile, loving myself in a grown-up way—and it was all true, I really had learned it, but I was also saying it all for him, because it's what he wanted me to say, so he could feel like he'd really helped me. But if I said what he wanted me to say, would it mean he could leave and I'd never see him again, and he'd never miss me, because he'd think I was OK and going to be OK? But I still said it. I knew if I said I loved him or stripped down and kissed him right there, he'd think I was still in the childish problem, he'd think I still mixed up being treated like a valuable worthwhile person with sex and romantic feelings, and he'd think he wasted his time and it was hopeless, he'd think it was hopeless and he hadn't reached me, and I couldn't do that to him—if he was going to die or get fired then at least I could let him have this, the knowledge that he'd helped me, even though I really did feel like I was maybe in love with him, or needed him.' She puts out her cigarette without any of the previous stabbing aspect, almost sort of tenderly, as if thinking tenderly of something else. 'I all of a sudden felt like: Oh my God, this is what people mean when they go "I'll die without you, you're my whole life," you know, "Can't live, if living is without you," ' Meredith Rand accompanying this last bit to the tune of Harry Nilsson's 'Can't Live (If Living Is Without You).' 'All the terrible country songs my dad used to listen to in his shop in the garage, it seemed like every one of them was about somebody talking to some lover they'd lost and why and how they couldn't live without them, how terrible their life was now, and drinking all the time because it hurt so terribly to be without them, that I could never stand because I thought they were so banal and I never said anything but I couldn't believe he could listen to it all without almost barfing. . . . Actually he said if you listen to these songs and change the *you* to *me,* like, you understand that what they're really singing about is losing some part of themself or betraying themself over and over for what they think other people want until they're just dead inside and don't even know what *me* means, which is why the only way they can think of it and why they're feeling so dead and sad is to think of it as needing somebody else and not being able to live without them, this other person—which by some coincidence is the exact situation of a teeny baby, that without somebody to hold it and feed it and take care of it, it'll die, literally, which he said is not such a coincidence at all, really.'

Drinion's forehead is ever so slightly wrinkled with thought. 'I'm confused. Ed explained the true meaning of country-and-western songs in the elevator? So you told him about the lyrics and now understanding the lyrics' sentiments?'

Rand is looking around, possibly for Beth Rath. 'What? No, that was later on.'

'So you did see each other again, after the elevator.'

Rand raises the back of her hand to display the wedding ring. 'Oh, yes.'

Drinion says, 'Is there some extra information I need to understand this?'

Rand looks both distracted and annoyed. 'Well, he didn't die, obviously, Mr. Einstein.'

Drinion rotates his empty glass. His forehead has a definite wrinkle. 'But you've spent time describing the conflict between confessing love and your real motives, and how upset and uncomfortable you were at the prospect of not seeing him again.'

'I was seventeen, for Christ's sake. I was a drama queen. They take me home, I look in the phone book, and he's right there in the phone book. His apartment building was like ten minutes from my house.'

Drinion's mouth is in the distended position of someone who wants to ask something but isn't sure where to even start, and is signifying that facially instead of out loud.

Rand's arm is up in some kind of signal to Beth Rath.

'Anyway, that's how I met him.'

§47

Toni Ware stood at the pay phone on the lot's fringes. Instead of a booth it was just on a post. She leaned slightly against the front bumper of her car, which shone. One of the dogs' faces appeared over the backseat; when she looked hard at it a moment it dropped back out of sight. In the front passenger seat were a dozen standard six-pound bricks, each with a Return-Postage-Paid card from a different marketer. She was a standard-sized woman, just on the pale side of fair in slacks and a beige spring coat that flapped and popped in the wind. The man at the phone's other end was repeating her order, which was complex and involved several feet of #6 copper tubing angle-cut into four-inch lengths; the angle on the cuts was to be 60 degrees. This woman had twenty different voices; all but two were warm and pleasant. She didn't cup the phone's speaker to cut the wind but let it roar in the phone. Everyone has unconscious mannerisms they fall into on a telephone; hers was to look at the cuticles of the hand that didn't hold the phone and to use that hand's thumb to feel at each cuticle in turn. There were four women in the convenience store's lot, and a bust of the store's cashier through a gap between signs on the window for bulk-purchase beer. Two women were at the pumps; another was in a tan Gremlin waiting for a pump to free. They wore plastic wraps over their hair against the wind. There was a period when Toni had to wait for the hardware wholesaler to verify her credit card, which meant that the place was on a tight margin and couldn't afford even a four-hour float on the order, which meant they could be affected. Everyone conducts a rapid unconscious scan of each social sense object they encounter. Some scans' big concern involved fear and the threat-potential of each new datum; others' involved sexual potential, revenue potential, aesthetic grade, status indicators, power, and/or susceptibility to domination. Toni Ware's scans, which were detailed and thorough, were concerned entirely with whether the object could be affected. Her hair appeared grayish-blond, or the sort of dry blond that in certain kinds of light appears almost gray. The wind hit the door hard as people came out; she watched its force affect their faces and the small unconscious ingathering gestures they made as they attempted to huddle and walk quickly at the same time. It wasn't especially cold but the wind made it *seem* cold. The color of her eyes depended on what lenses she wore. The credit card number she gave the man was her own, but neither the name nor the federal ID# she gave belonged to her as such. Both dogs had the same name but knew without fail which one she was calling. Her love for the dogs transcended all other experience and informed her life. The voice she used with the Butts Hardware clerk was younger than she, conspicuously jejune, causing merchants whose emotional tastes were more refined than simple exploitation to feel paternal—superior and tender at the same time. What she said when he confirmed her order was: 'Great. Very great. Yay,' with 'Yay' stated instead of shouted. It was a voice that caused the listener to imagine someone with long blond hair and bell-bottoms who cocked her head and gave even statements an interrogative lilt. She played on this knife-edge most of the time—giving a false impression that was nevertheless concrete and tightly controlled. It felt like art. The issue was not destruction. Just as total order is dull, so is chaos dull: There's nothing informing about a mess. The store's cashier gave each customer a cool smile and engaged in a brief exchange. Toni Ware had twice in three years been part of an investigation of the store, whose name was QWIK 'N'

EZ—its sign's icon was suspiciously like Bob's Big Boy—and was one of the first of the off-interstate stations to eliminate the full-serve pumps and attach a tiny grocery with cigarettes and soda pop and junk for Qwik Stop shopping. They did a phenomenal cash business and had been tagged by the local DIF function every year; but they were whistle-clean, field-audit was judged a waste of salary, their receipts jibed perfectly and their books were just messy enough to be uncooked, the owner a Pentecostal Christian who'd already started construction on another of what Bondurant called Ramp Tumors on the second 74 exit and had bids in for lots on two more.

She had two home lines and a bulky mobile phone and two office patch codes but used pay phones for personal business. She was neither attractive nor ugly. Except for a certain anemic intensity to her face there was nothing to attract or repel or cause any more notice than a thousand other Peoria women who'd been described as 'cute' in their bloom and were now invisible. She liked to come in under people's radar. The only person who might have noticed her hanging up the phone was someone who'd wanted to use it himself. Two women and a reddish man in flannel were filling their tanks. A child in one of the cars was crying, its face a knot. The cars' windows rendered its weeping a dumbshow. Its mother had a caved-in face and stared stolidly by the tank, smoothing her hair's plastic as the hose dispensed gas on auto. The station's flagpole's flag's rope's pulleys and joists clinked dully in the wind. Her own car's slight idled throb behind her, the two dogs hunkered down in identical postures. She slowed just enough to lock eyes with the child as she passed the rear right window, its face clenched and red, her own face empty of intent as for a moment the whole lot and street blazed with intensity, a non-connotative tone in her head like a rung bell. Interesting the way some people will stand still by the tank and let it fill and others like the pudgy woman up ahead cannot, must busy themselves with small tasks like squeegeeing the windshield or using blue towels to wipe at the brake lights, unable to stand still and wait. The man dispensed by hand, rounding off to an even sum. Half the child's face was cut off by the window's reflection of the sky and flag that popped high above her. And she liked the sound of her own footfalls, the solid sound and feeling the impact in her teeth. #6 tube was hard enough to go in all the way and soft enough that driving it made little sound; three at the base would do for any tree.

The Tumor's inside had a grocery's bleached light and was laid out with glass doors of pop at the back and two aisles of corporate gauge retail coffee and pet food and snacks E-W with your sundries and tobacco behind the orange counter where the young woman in denim workshirt and red bandanna done up slave-style with tiny rabbit ears at the back asked about fuel and totaled beer and snuff and sent change down an anodized chute into a steel cup. Behind the door at the rear of the second aisle was the stockroom and manager's office. The larger chain models had introduced video cameras, but these Ramp Tumors were blind. There were five other US citizens in the store and then a sixth when the woman sans child came in to pay, and while Toni selected enough items to fill a bag she observed them interact or not and felt again the acquaintance she always assumed all strangers in rooms she entered enjoyed, the conviction that everyone in the room all knew each other well and felt the connection and sameness they shared by virtue of what they had in common, the quality of not being her. None of them was affected by her in any way. One can of Mighty Dog Gourmet Beef was 69¢, which given wholesale and overhead was still a 20 percent margin of pure cream. The counter woman, who was in her early thirties and had incorporated her weight into a country mother presentation that involved pink cheeks and a laugh like a roar and a worldly good-humored sexuality, asked if she had any fuel today.

'Full up,' Toni said. 'Stopped to use the phone and come in to get out of the damn wind!'

'Still tootin' out there I see.' The counter woman smiled, totaling pet food Toni would throw away on a cut-rate NCR 1280 that totaled receipts on a one-day roll they stored in canisters and had to be taken out and unfurled to run a Field, the office filled with eighty-foot strips like a liner's bunting at sail.

'Like to blow me right off the road comin' in,' Toni said. The counter woman seemed unaware that Toni Ware was affecting the exact accent and cadence of her own speech. The assumption that everyone else is like you. That you are the world. The disease of consumer capitalism. The complacent solipsism.

'Got you some dogs that can do some eating.'

'Don't tell me. Don't I know.'

'That was $11.80.' The smile long-practiced to seem so sincere. As if Toni would be remembered one moment after she forced the door and staggered off under the flag like the rest of them. And why the conventional *was?* The stunted creature behind her smelled of hair oil and ambient breakfast; she imagined particles of meat and eggs in his facial hair and under his nails as she produced a Treasury note.

'The big Two-O,' the counter woman said, as if to herself, punching the keys with the slight extra force a 1280 takes.

A moment later Toni was out around the side of the store, sheltered from the lot's view by the Kluckman Ice dispenser, with the plastic bag's top whipping and popping between her shoes as she removed a traveler's Kleenex from her handbag, tore it in two and again, and wrapped a quarter of the tissue tightly around her little finger, whose nail was perfect and almond-shaped and done in arterial red. Up into the right nasal cavity and around in a comprehensive spiral, and what came out included a standard-colored clot, both viscous and hard, with even a tiny thread of capillary inside the right border. The only thing someone in a store or line might remark about her was a faint affective abstraction, a quality of detachment that was not the detachment of peace or a personal relation with Our Lord Jesus Christ. Which she carefully wiped onto the left lapel of her cream-colored coat, with enough pressure to give it some length but not enough to compromise its adhesion or distort the nougat at its heart. A plasticized flatness about her reminiscent of processed air, airline food, transistorized sound. This was merely to pass the time until her order at Butts Hardware was assembled. The stockroom as she entered it had only paper goods and large cardboard boxes and borax in the floor-wall seam for roaches, and the manager's little office door with its snap-on pinups and Peace with Honor poster of an eagle with a ski-jump nose and 5:00 shadow was ajar and emitted

Dutch Masters and the mollified twang of country on a pocket radio. The day manager, who had no nametag (the counter woman was 'Cheryl') and had his feet up reading just what she'd have imagined, and who had a high convex forehead and one of those rapid and overhard blink rates like someone almost wincing when they blinked that signified something just a little neurally amiss, just a bit, swung his feet around and rose with complex squeaks of the chair as her timid knock and the force with which she all but staggered through the door spelled out all the innocent shock anyone'd need to read in her character. She'd drained her face of color and kept her eyes open in the wind on the way back from side to storefront, which wetted her eyes, and had her shoulders up and arms out in an attitude of speechless defilement. She appeared both smaller and larger than she really was, and the manager with the ticcy blink did not move or come around or find within himself the power to respond even during her setup, which was halting and hypoxic and sketched a scenario in which she was a frequent nay even habitual customer at this QWIK 'N' EZ Ramp Tumor and had always received not only good value for the hard-earned money she earned taking in mending at home which as the single mother of two was all she could do, even though she'd been trained as a legal secretary over five years of night school during the time she was nursing her blind mother through her lengthy terminal illness, not just value and gas but always cheerful and courteous service from the gals at the counter, until—here a shudder that brought the manager, still holding the remains of a Little Debbie product in his left hand, halfway around the desk to comfort her until he saw the two-inch mess on her left lapel, which was the result of several Q-Tipless days and near-sneeze feeling and was indeed a mucal clot of sheer clock-stopping horror—until today just now, just, she didn't know how to say this—her strongest impulse had just been to drive half-blind with tears home to throw the coat that had cost months of going without to buy so she could take her two babies to church in something they didn't have to feel ashamed to be with into the low-income housing development's dumpster and spend the rest of the day praying God to help her make some sense out of the senseless violation she'd just had happen and to avoid forever thereafter this QWIK 'N' EZ out of degradation and horror but no, she'd always had such good value and service at this establishment that she felt it almost her duty, however embarrassing and degrading to account, to tell him what the employee behind the cash register had done, even though it made no sense, to her least of all, who certainly looked normal and even friendly and to whom she'd tried to be pleasant and had done nothing more than try to pay for the items she'd elected to buy here, who had, while she'd reached for her change and while looking her steadily in the eye had, had, with the other hand put her finger up her nose and then reached out and . . . and . . . here giving way completely to sobs and a kind of high-pitched keening sound and looking down at the lapel of a coat she gave the impression of somehow trying to back away from in horror as if the only reason she hadn't already taken off the green-dolloped coat was that she couldn't bear to take it off, feeling the clonic blinks upon the wad to note even the thread of red blood that made it more ghastly, then turning to stagger out as if too upset to continue or press for redress, lurching out until the transistor's song of whiskey and loss had receded and she was back in the bleached light of the store itself, the sound of her heels in the aisle and lot rapid and satisfying as the counter woman's wave and farewell-till-next-time receded unacknowledged and the manager stood there working his way from the shock to outrage and the boys silent and docile as gargoyles in the back even as she leapt into the car and all but peeled out, in case the manager had made it out front yet which she doubted, fishtailing onto the Frontage Road with such hysteric force that one dog was thrown into another, steadying herself with a right arm against the bag of bricks, half-humming the country tune's refrain, coat defiled and already half off one shoulder, mailbox-bound.

§48

'It's all a little hazy.'

'That's certainly understandable, Sir.'

'I think I should tell you I'm very upset.'

'We can certainly appreciate that.'

'No. No. I mean inside. Upset inside.'

'I think they've anticipated that, Sir, and that every possible—'

'Down low I mean.'

'Perhaps if you could just relay it to us as if you were relating data, Sir.'

'You know: *down low?* You take my meaning?'

'That's just the effects, Sir, lingering. Take your time.'

'It was the annual picnic. Is that what you want?'

'That we know already, Sir.'

'Every year, summer. In Coffield Park, bond-financed. Examinations annual picnic. Mummified fried chicken, potato salad. Deviled eggs I believe with flecked paprika like dots of dried blood—horrid. Great arrayed fans of luncheon meat. All this protein. Examiners eat like wild beasts, I'm sure you know. Audits more sparingly. You must know this. The variance in—'

'We've certainly had reports, Sir.'

'And grilled things. Those odd bolted park grills, also bond-financed to be sure. Wieners, patties in tiers on shiny white paper. Great swarms and shrouds of insects on the food on the table. Flies rubbing their little legs together. Do you know what that means when a fly does that? Hornets at the waste cans, hovering. Watermelon with ants on it. When it rubs its legs together like that?'

'. . .'

'A raw hamburger patty's like blood in the water to an insect, men.'

'You were just inventorying the picnic's provisions, Sir.'

'Iced tea, Kool-Aid. There was pop in a chest the GM brought. Some primary-colored Jell-O. Red or green or red-and-green. It's for morale, the annual picnic, change the interactive context.'

'Nothing wrong with a picnic, Sir.'

'See everyone's families, children. The children. One doesn't think of GS-9s having children, playing with children, little Line 40s. And yet every year there they are. The mothers arranged games. And bottles of beer in a chest Marge van Hool's husband brought.'

'We've spoken to Mr. van Hool, Sir.'

'And mosquitoes everywhere. The terrible kind, that cast a shadow and have hairy legs. You can hear them but you can't see them. Not until. Blood draws every—and Audits, Audits were playing some type of children's game with that flying disk from Hasbro. Aerodynamic disk, bright color, Hasbro, where did—?'

'A Frisbee, perhaps, Sir?'

'Hasbro now a division of I believe one United Amusements, supposedly based in St. Paul but with substantial offshore accounts.'

'. . .'

'And you know as well as I what that so often means.'

'And you noticed nothing out of the ordinary regarding the iced tea, the Jell-O.'

'They think it was the Jell-O then.'

'That wouldn't be our department, Sir.'

'The Jell-O had very small marshmallows in it as I recall. One of those exceedingly bright primary colors, the Jell-O. The flies left it alone, although those bloody mosquitoes my God if you—'

'Yes, Sir.'

'I should tell you I'm extremely agitated and upset.'

'We're making a second note of that, Mr. Director, Sir, for emphasis.'

'I don't believe the effects have entirely worn off yet.'

'Just proceed on the assumption that we're the ones in the middle, please, Sir.'

'I spoke with law enforcement agents, I believe, unless that was the effects.'

'That was several hours ago, Sir. We're with the Service. I am Agent Clothier, this is Special Agent Aylortay.'

'Pleased to meet you, Sir, although it's damn unfortunate it has to be under these circumstances.'

'You're CID?'

'No, Sir, we're Inspections, out of Chicago, Post 1516.'

'They brought you down.'

'Everyone's very concerned, Sir, understandably.'

'Mosquitoes are just needles with wings.'

'Not entirely sure how to respond to that, Sir.'

'There were no CID at the picnic.'

'No, Sir, as you might recall CID had a forensic accounting in-service this weekend at Region, Sir.'

'They don't mix well, as a rule, CID.'

'No, Sir.'

'Hold themselves a bit aloof if you know what I mean. Vomiting.'

'Vomiting, Sir?'

'When they rub their legs together. It looks innocuous, but the flies are in fact vomiting digestive juices onto their legs and applying it to the food. They're one of the animals which pre-digest. Mosquitoes do the same thing.'

'Sir, I—'

'Vomit inside you. That's what raises the lump. They're pre-digesting the blood before they suck it out of you. Great hairy-legged things. They breed in the fields, you know. Needles with wings. Disease-vector. None finer. Whole civilizations down. Read your history.'

'We can appreciate the bug situation down here, Sir.'

'I was grilling. Brats and patties. At least for a time. They gave me an apron. Something witty on the front. A certain impertinence permissible at picnics, the Christmas party. Let everyone's hair down a bit if you get me.'

'You estimate you were grilling throughout the early intervals of the picnic, then, Sir, which would square with Mr. van Hool's account.'

'The iced tea was brewed, not that horrible mix iced tea with the slight scum on top.'

'The iced tea was consumed by you'd say how many at the picnic, Sir?'

'Copious. Terribly hot you understand. No one wants pop when it's hot, except of course children, which then they have sticky mouths, which then the sugar in the pop excites the bugs.'

'Jesus, Clothier, now with the bugs again.'

'Utitshay.'

'Nothing against CID, you understand. Indispensable part of the mechanism. Fine hardworking fellows. Notwithstanding all the junk cases, deplorable waste of resources, Region had figures on—'

'So if there was a common denominator, Sir, you might point at the iced tea, you're telling us.'

'We all drank it. Ungodly hot. Who wants beer under a sun like that? Do either of you hear a—a sound?'

'And yet you yourself you're saying did not see anyone bringing the iced tea into the picnic area or making the iced tea.'

'An urn. Dispenser. Orange pebbled plastic, nozzle like a barrel's bung, yes?'

'The iced tea, you're saying.'

'I don't know that I've ever felt this agitated. It's as if.'

'They tell us it will come and go for a time, Sir, as the blood level stabilizes.'

'You'll be up and around in no time they tell us, Sir.'

'Trying to be glad to be of help. Our boys in uniform.'

'Clothier, what say—'

'You were helping us identify the urn, Sir, with the iced tea.'

'Orange dispenser that said Gatorade on the side. Some of the older children were excited; they thought it was Gatorade.'

'No children drank the tea.'

'The examiners call their children their little Line 40s. That's of course where you enter your CCDC from Form 2441 on the 1040. Some of the children were playing Collections. Near the horseshoe courts. Some of the older children. Liens on the toys, a jeopardy assessment and seizure of some of the smaller childrens' plates; there was some of the usual crying.'

'And you'd say you might first have noticed any unusual effects or anything out of the ordinary when, then, Sir, if you had to say?'

'Terrible activity to teach children. Collections is Ghent's problem. Was Ghent's. I avoid Collections.'

'Understandable from our vantage, Sir.'

'Are those sunglasses, then?'

'Sir, we're not wearing eye protection of any kind.'

'My nose itches something awful.'

'I'm afraid we aren't permitted to touch any part of your person, Sir.'

'My thoughts are normally so much more organized than this.'

'Please take all the time you need.'

'They seemed just awful. Whole clouds of them. Shrouds, clouds, crowds of them. They're a disease-vector you know. Read your history. Breed in the trees. When I looked in one of their shades two of the smaller children were covered. A shroud of them around both, in their eyes, nose, smothering them—I saw one of them fall; it couldn't cry out. Pendleton's little Line 40.'

'So then you'd say that was the first observable sign of any effect, then, Sir.'

'I had a very long fork, you know.'

'For the grilling you mean, Sir.'

'Let's didi, Norm, man. This guy's still gone. Scratch his nose and let's go.'

'Aitway, Aylortay.'

'The *Culex* and malaria. The *Aedes aegypti* and dengue. Read it. It's written. Fork or no.'

'For your duties at the grill at the picnic area's southeast quadrant according to this schematic, Sir.'

'A *very* long fork. I don't think you can appreciate. Jagged tines. It cast a shadow.'

'And were—were you able to observe at this time any of the other agents or families behaving in any way out of the ordinary or engaged with the iced tea in any way, Sir?'

'Though I did notice the settings. At the tables. With checked cloths. The settings were all knives. No spoons, no forks. *I* had the fork. Knife, plate, knife, knife. Three wicked knives at each place. Some years the breeze blows the plates away. Not this year, I can tell you.'

'So this was an effect, or you were observing an effect, Sir, can you say which?

'Fechner has a glass eye.'

'That would be Revenue Agent Fechner, Sir. You observed him setting knives at the tables?'

'Lost an eye in the war. How he put it: "Lost an eye." The idea. Say there, fellows, anyone seen my *eye* by any chance?'

'So you hadn't observed any person or persons actually setting the table with all knives, then, Sir.'

'Norm, man, what knives? Let's didi.'

'That's a war term if I'm not mistaken. Agent Taylor. You think I don't know what this is?'

'It's Aylortay, Sir. Pleased to meet you, Sir, although it's damn unfortunate it has to be under these circumstances.'

'They were coming out of the *trees*.'

'They were rappelling, Sir. The incursion may or may not have been tactical, that much we know.'

'There was an egg-toss and gunny—the egg wouldn't move; it stayed there in midair. The three-legged race under way when they came from the trees and they were trying to run away, to get to their children but their legs were tied together. It was a feeding frenzy, the mosquitoes—I was waving the long fork around.'

'And you said you observed Revenue Agent Fechner suffering effects from the adulterated tea.'

'So it was the tea.'

'That's not our area, Sir, I'm afraid. We're collecting data.'

'On the knives.'

'A handsome set of knives indeed, Sir, would you care to see them?'

'Who is this really? Who are you men?'

'You were saying Revenue Agent Fechner and his glass eye.'

'That he was at van Hool's beer chest; he had his glass eye out so there was just the socket.'

'And did the knives oh by some chance look like... *this,* Sir?'

'Atiencepay, Aylortay. Onay uttingcay etyay.'

'You think I don't speak Latin?'

'Sir, I'm pleased you speak Latin.'

'Who is this man to your right and left?'

'Try to focus, Sir. I know it's difficult.'

'Fechner was at the chest, had the eye out and was... was opening bottles of beer with the socket. Socket as bottle opener. In goes the bottle, downward yank. The little Line 40s were watching—it was awful!'

'Revenue Agent Fechner's going to be fine, Sir. They found the eye and he's going to be right as rain.'

'Was it raining, Sir?'

'Placing the cap in the socket and then yanking down on the bottle, then the children would scream and clap because the cap was in the socket. A little gray sun in the eye. Eye eye!'

'I say we just cut it out of him right now. It's right there, Clothier, see it?'

'Scopolamine you say. Loco weed. Parentis. Mens sano in corpus. And not plastic knives, either. And may I say what handsome skulls you have beneath that skin, boys.'

'And you last saw Revenue Agent Drinion before the tactical incursion, Sir, or after?'

'Drinion was at the table. Holding down the table as they say. Almost asleep he seemed. Drinion never takes part. They weren't touching him—the mosquitoes. His chin in his hand.'

'You don't mean that literally, Sir.'

'Note the honed edge. Note the seven-inch length, you old drone.

Note the five stars on the blade and where it says No Stain and Ice Hardened and Zwilling and J.A. Henckels, Solingen FRG. You know what this is?'

'I just don't feel well at all, still. The examiners—a whole writhing boiling mass of them on the ground.'

'From the three-legged race you mean, Sir, you don't mean what Miriam calls your "third leg," back in the days when she wanted that leg, Sir, didn't she, Sir, before it repelled her.'

'They were rappelling. Ropes in the trees. Victor Charles. A writhing mass of GS-9 examiners—mass copulation among the examiners which I personally observed—it's all there in my report on a Form 923(a) for personal observations of impropriety; you Inspections men know all about 923(a)s, do you not.'

'You observed this from the grill, then, Sir.'

'I observed the effect of the tea in opened sockets and mass frenzied orgylike copulation and humping under the trees, on the table, under the tossed egg, on both ends of the horseshoe grotto. There were actual buttocks thrusting under my grill.'

'And I believe you said you were wearing an apron, Sir.'

'Cut him. Take it right off, Clothier.'

'So by this point in time everyone with the possible exception of the children was suffering definite effects, Sir, you're saying.'

'The wieners themselves were writhing, thrusting. Plump, thrusting, shiny, moist, there on the grill, on Mrs. Kagle's aluminum platter, in the air. I with the fork and observing it all until out of the *trees* where they breed! Breeding, ever breeding!'

'I think we've got a decent picture of the situation from your particular vantage, Sir.'

'You know it doesn't go, Sir. Not really. You'll stay like this. Look at me. You'll look like this, Sir. Always. We came to tell you. We'll cut it off right now if you like. Say the word.'

'Needles with wings. Knives with wings, all dancing on their sharp tips, shrouds of mosquitoes making it dark. The sky is no longer the sky.'

'He doesn't want it, Clothier.'

'The air no longer white with it.'

'Get used to it, you impotent old fag. That's right: *fag*.'

'Ixnay, Taylor.'

'I have seen my wife take her skin off, you know. Since you came all the way down, eh? Peel the white skin of her arm clean off like an opera glove. Take off her face from the top down.'

'Like: *this*, Sir?'

'I think I'm going to be moving over to the next subject of the debriefing now, Sir. With much gratitude for taking the time.'

'As if it's even yours, eh, Dwitt? Eh?'

'I'm simply unprecedentedly upset. I don't think it's getting better.'

'You know what doctors do, don't you? When you're asleep. From the top down, like you're a soft old grape in the back of the fridge that someone's forgot to throw out. DeWitt, if I've told you once I've told you a thousand times.'

'I'm noting that, Sir, as well as Inspections' appreciation for your cooperation under the circumstances.'

'Well don't just lie there say something. Tell them what they want or they'll cut it off. They've as much as said so. Are you a fool?'

'And I know they'll be back in, and doing everything possible for your comfort until it comes off, Sir. I mean wears off. The blood level.'

'I'm naked, you know. Under all this.'

'We may or may not be needing to interview you again, Sir. When the effects are less noticeable if you understand.'

'As a jaybird. Buck-naked. Birthday suit.'

'Tell them, hurry. It's *German*.'

'Yes and I do, I have a penis. Penis.'

'Hate that word, Clothier.'

'Dreadful word, eh? Penis? Like something you'd touch with a thick rubber glove if at all.'

'Why DeWitt you old scalawiggle! I'm still a woman, you know!'

'Say it with me, boys. Penis penis penis penis penis.'

'You didn't forget, oh DeWitt, *it's* lovely.'

'You just get some rest, Sir.'

'Its name is—I won't tell you. How do you like that? I won't!'

'I remember when you looked at *me* that way.'

'It's got a name. Its name is—I won't tell you. It's mine. It's my third leg, Miriam calls it. But never from the forehead. It's not a mask. They start with the chin. Upsy daisy. In comes the needle on wings!'

'Allweshay, Aylortay?'

'My proboscis itches so I sink it *deep* before vomiting.'

'Not in me, DeWitt. It's like you're vomiting inside me. Even your expression is as if you're taken ill. If you could ever see it you'd—'

'Miriam's frigid you know.'

'I'll be locking this behind me, Sir, but it's just procedural.'

'Since our third. A terrible labor. Stillborn. Blue and cold. You know what we named it?'

'Taylor?'

'That's right. Taylor. Fine little Clothier just like his gumpappy.'

'I just don't want it. Don't torture me for not, I beg you.'

'Shall we... there you are, Sir.'

'No interest since. Frigid. Dry as a fine martini, Bernie Cheadle'd say.'

'So then toodleoo, Sir.'

'Thank God we have our work, boys, eh? And our hobbies. Our home workshops, yes? Fashioning needles and wings for the commonweal? Yes, Aylor?'

'I'll be back with more of these if you don't lie still like a good boy though, Sir, and wait for them to come for it, Sir, so you can look like: *THIS!* Just one firm tug and off she comes.'

'She'll say *Give it a tug yourself, you old degenerate.*'

'Barely feel a thing. This'll get 'em cracking at their desks, Sir, eh what?'

'I can inhale, but I can't seem to exhale.'

[Voices in hall.]

'My workshop *is* organized, it *is,* you should *see* it.'

[Voices in hall.]

'I can find anything in there.'

[Voices in hall.]

'You'll see.'

[Voices in hall.]

§49

Fogle sat waiting in the small reception area of the Director's office. No one knew what it meant that Merrill Errol Lehrl was using Mr. Glendenning's office. Mr. Glendenning and his senior staff were up at Region; it might just be a cordial professional-courtesy thing that Lehrl was using Mr. Glendenning's office. Mrs. Oooley wasn't at her desk in the reception area; instead at the desk was one of Lehrl's aides, whose either first or last name was Reynolds. He'd moved a certain amount of Caroline's stuff around, you could see. The area had a large rug whose geometric patterns, which were intricate, made the carpet look Turkish or Byzantine. The overheads were off; someone had placed several lamps around the little room, creating attractive oases in a general atmosphere of gloom. Fogle found low light gloomy. Dr. Lehrl's other aide, Sylvanshine, was in a chair just off to Fogle's right, so that the two aides were just outside the peripheries of Fogle's vision and could not both be seen at the same time, and he had to turn his head slightly to look at either directly. Which he was forced to do, rather a lot, because they appeared to be prebriefing him for some reason. Doing so in tandem. But also, in a way, to be talking across Fogle to each other. When they addressed Chris Fogle directly, they tended to wax a bit didactic, but at the same time it was not totally uninteresting. Both Reynolds and Sylvanshine were knowledgeable about various powerful administrators' career trajectories and résumés. It was the sort of thing that aides at National could be expected to know a lot about; they were a little like royal courtiers. Most of the names of the people they spoke of were people at Nation; only a few were known to Fogle. As was customary in the Service, the aides spoke in a rapid, excited way without either's face showing any excitement or even interest in the subject at hand, which started out with a small lecture on the two basic different ways that a person could rise to prominence and large responsibility within the bureaucracy of the IRS. Bureaucratic aerodynamics and modes of advancement were very common topics of interest among examiners; it was unclear whether Reynolds and Sylvanshine didn't know that much of this was familiar ground to Fogle or didn't care. Fogle imagined that at whatever Post these two were normally at, they were legendary dickheads.

According to the two aides, one way to advance to managerial levels beyond GS-17 was through slow, steady demonstrations of competence, loyalty, reasonable initiative, interhuman skills with the people above and below you, etc., moving slowly up through the promotional ranks.

'The other, lesser known, is the éclat.'

'The éclat means the sudden, extraordinary idea or innovation that brings you to the notice of those at high levels. Even national levels.' One got the sense they were parroting others.

'Dr. Lehrl is the latter kind. The éclat kind.'

'Allow us to give you some background.'

'It's some time ago. Should I specify the year?'

The rhythms of Reynolds and Sylvanshine's back and forth were quite precise. There was no wasted time. Questions had a vaguely staged quality. If Dr. Lehrl himself was back behind that frosted door, it wasn't clear whether Reynolds and Sylvanshine thought that he could hear what they were saying.

'The details are unimportant. He was just one of a low-level audit group in a backwater district somewhere, and he got an idea.'

'He's not even on 1040s within the group, mind you. He's small business and S.'

'The idea, however, concerns 1040s.'

'Specifically exemptions.'

'An area not unfamiliar to you, I assume.' Neither had any accent at all.

'You may, for example, know or not know that up until 1979, filers could declare dependents just by name.'

'On the 1040 of the time.'

'Dependents. Children, elderly in the filer's care.'

'I think we can assume he knows what dependents are, Claude.'

'But do you know the 1040 of that period? What the filer had to do was put the dependent children's first names on Line 5c, others' names and relations on 5d.'

'Now, of course, it's all 6c and 6d. We're talking about 1977.'

'But the point is just the name and relation. Which you can see the problem.'

'There's no way to check,' Sylvanshine said.

'In retrospect, it appears absurd,' Reynolds said.

'But that's after the éclat that it looks so naive. Since there was no way to check.'

'Not really. Just a name and relation.'

'It was the honor system. There was no real way to ensure that dependents were real.'

'No efficient way, that is.'

'Oh sure, sure, they figured that the filer figured we *could* check, but as a practical matter we couldn't check. Not really. Not in any definitive way.'

'Especially since data processing was in such a primitive state. You could track consistency of dependents listed over successive years, but it was time-consuming and inconclusive.'

'A kid could have turned eighteen. An elderly dependent could have died. A new kid could have been born. Who was going to chase all this down? It wasn't worth the man-hours for anybody.'

'True, if there was an audit and some of the dependents were made up the filer was in huge trouble and there were criminal penalties plus interest and penalties. But that was just random chance. The dependents themselves couldn't trigger an audit.'

'Each dependent was I think two hundred dollars added to the standard deduction.'

'Which you guys now know as the zero bracket amount.' Both aides were in their late twenties, but they spoke to Fogle as if they were much, much older than he. 'But before '78 everyone knew it as the standard deduction.'

'But this was '77.'

Sylvanshine gave Reynolds a look whose impatience was conveyed through duration instead of expression. Then he said: 'In case this sounds picayune or inconsequential, let's stress right here that we're talking $1.2 billion.'

'That's b-b-*billion,* from this one tiny change.'

Fogle wondered if he was supposed to ask what change, whether they were including him in the choreography here as a kind of prompter, whether the sophistication of their routine was that advanced.

Sylvanshine said: 'What Dr. Lehrl saw, as some no-account GS-9 auditor, was insufficient incentive for the filer to report dependents accurately. Institutional incentive. In retrospect, it seems obvious.'

'That's the way of genius, of éclat.'

'And his solution looks simple. He simply suggested requiring taxpayers to include the SS number of each dependent.'

'Requiring an SSN right next to each name.'

'Since everything in the Martinsburg database at the time was keyed to SSNs.'

'Which actually didn't make it all that much easier to really check.'

'But the filer didn't know that. The requirement would greatly increase the filer's fear of a phantom dependent being detected.'

'Such was the power of the SSN.'

'It created, in other words, an added incentive for compliance on dependents.'

'And it was very easy and inexpensive. Just add "and Social Security Number" in the directions for 5c and 5d.'

'His District Director had the sense to recognize an éclat and kicked the idea up to the Region, who routed it to the DC-Compliance's office at 666 Independence.'

'No one could believe it hadn't been thought of before.'

'The first tax year it's actually implemented is '78, as Section 151(e) of the Code. So '79 is the first year the new instructions are on 1040s. Six-point-nine million dependents disappear.'

'From the nation's 1040s.'

'Vanish, poof.'

'As compared to the '77 returns.'

'There are no sanctions. Everybody decides simply to pretend the fake dependents never happened.'

'Netting $1.2 billion the first year.'

'It's a textbook éclat.'

'It's also politically brilliant. There's more than one kind of éclat.'

'This was both.'

'Because although it costs next to nothing to implement, it requires a written change in Section 151 of the US Tax Code, which requires one of the Three-Personed God's senior staff to shepherd it through the Ways and Means process, to get codified as law.'

'Which means the idea gets bruited about at the very highest levels of Triple-Six.'

'And from out of nowhere Dr. Lehrl jumps four grades and even jumps Region after only two quarters and becomes in short order the DC-Systems' most valuable—'

'Well, one of the most valuable, to be fair, since there's also —— in ——.'

'Who is a whole other story involving your more slow, conventional rise through the pipeline.'

'But certainly one of Systems' most valuable utility men.'

'Like an in-house consultant.'

'Especially since the Initiative.'

'Especially in Personnel Systems.'

'Which is where you come in, Mr. Fogle.'

'Essentially, he comes in and reconfigures Posts to maximize revenue.'

'Essentially, he's a reorganizer.'

'An idea man.'

'More bang for the buck.'

'True, largely at the District level.'

'But this is hardly his first Regional Center.'

'There's a certain amount of this we can't talk about.'

'We're enjoined.'

'You can think of him as a Personnel guy, or a Systems guy.'

'Personnel Systems, essentially.'

'But he answers to Systems. He serves at the pleasure of the Deputy Commissioner–Systems. He's the DCS's instrument, you could say.'

'But he's not a slave to any one system.'

'He's a reader of people.'

'He's an administrator, ultimately.'

'Or more like an administrator of administrators.'

'The Systems Division, you may or may not know, used to be called Administration.'

'It's a vague term, admittedly.'

'He'd describe himself more as a cyberneticist.'

'The Service is, after all, a system composed of many systems.'

'His job is to come in and redesign Posts to get the most out of them. To find ways to streamline and enhance productivity, remove bottlenecks, debug. This blends an expertise in automation, personnel, support logistics, and overall systems.'

'He goes where he's sent. His assignment is simply a certain Post. The assignment memos are always about one line long.'

'Phase One is fact-finding. Feeling out the situation.'

'His real genius is incentive. Creating incentive. Finding out what makes people tick.'

'He'll take you apart like a little machine.'

'It's not as if Line 5 was his only éclat. We're just giving you an example. What he really is is a genius of human motivations and incentives and designing systems to achieve them.'

'He'll test you.'

'When you go in.'

'He reads people. It can be a little scary.'

'Be ready is all we mean.'

'But don't look nervous or like you're braced for some battery of tests.' Fogle knew of eastern cultures where any small piece of business had to be worked up to through involved systems of small talk and ritual indirection. Only an idiot would not have wondered whether this was what was going on, or whether Reynolds and Sylvanshine were just extremely boring and took a very long time to come to the point, assuming there was any point. Fogle had been away from his table for over half an hour already. Sylvanshine was continuing. 'Because it doesn't work like that. It's not that kind of testing.'

'Give him an example, maybe,' Reynolds said to Sylvanshine, indicating Fogle with a movement of his head as if there were anyone else he could possibly be referring to.

'OK.' Sylvanshine made a show of looking right at Chris Fogle. 'Where'd you go to school?'

'Umm, what kind of school?'

'Your college. Your alma mater.'

'I went to several, actually.'

If Sylvanshine was impatient, it was impossible to discern this. He had no poker tell whatsoever that Fogle could see. 'Pick one.'

'UIC. DuPage. DePaul.'

'Perfect. DePaul. So he'll ask, you'll say DePaul, he'll say "Ah, the Blue Demons." Well, it's not the Blue Demons, it's the Blue Devils. But do you correct him?'

'Actually, it is the Blue Demons. The Blue Devils is Duke.'

A one-beat pause. 'Whatever. Whatever the team name is, he says the wrong team name. Now, though: Do you correct him?'

Fogle looked from Sylvanshine to Reynolds. Their suit coats were not identical, but their shirts and slacks were, he could see. Reynolds said, 'Do you?'

'Do I correct him?' Fogle said.

'That's the question.'

'I'm not sure exactly what you're asking.'

'You do. The correct answer is you do correct him,' Sylvanshine said. 'Because it's a test. He's testing as to are you a toady, are you intimidated, are you a yes-man.'

'A sycophant,' Reynolds said.

'It was a test?'

'If he says Blue Devils and you just nod and smile, he won't say anything, but you'll have failed a test.'

Fogle looked quickly up at the clock. 'Is there more than one?'

'Well, yes and no,' Sylvanshine said. 'It's extremely subtle. You'd have no idea anything was going on. But the whole time you're interfacing he'll be testing you, probing you. The whole time.'

'One other thing,' Reynolds said, forcing Fogle to turn his head again. 'There'll be a kid in there with him. A seven-, eight-year-old kid.'

There was a moment of silence. An unparsable look passed between Reynolds and Sylvanshine. Sylvanshine had a very small, thin, neatly groomed mustache.

'Is it Dr. Lehrl's kid?' Fogle asked finally.

'Don't ask him that. That's the thing. The kid will be in a corner, reading, playing with something. Don't acknowledge the kid. Nor do you ask him or refer to the kid. The kid won't acknowledge you, you don't acknowledge him.'

'There may also be a hand puppet. It's an old thing from Audits that he's hung on to. Call it an eccentricity. If I were you, I wouldn't mention the hand puppet, either.'

'For the record,' Sylvanshine said, 'it's not his kid.'

Fogle was looking straight ahead in a ruminative way.

'The kid's the kid of one of Dr. Lehrl's senior staff back at Danville,' Reynolds said. 'Dr. Lehrl just likes having the kid around.'

'Even if the dad isn't there.'

'It's all a long, tedious story. The point, as far as you're concerned, is don't acknowledge the kid, and it's up to you but our advice is don't acknowledge the Doberman hand puppet either.'

Fogle's eyelid was doing the maddening fluttery thing again, which neither aide could see. He said: 'The thing is, can I ask a question?'

'Shoot.'

'The college sports team thing—how come you're telling me?'

Reynolds, at the desk, made a minute adjustment to one of his cuffs. 'What do you mean?'

'Well, if it's going to be a test when he asks me, why tell me in advance what I should say? Doesn't that defeat the purpose of the test?'

Sylvanshine opened the file on top of the stack beside him and made a small show of marking something inside. Reynolds leaned back in Caroline Oooley's chair and lifted his arms, smiling: 'Nice. You got us.'

'Pardon?'

'You got us. You passed. The test was: Are you just a toady, so anxious to please the hotshot from National that you'd suck up inside dope and go in there and say what we told you to?'

'Which you didn't,' Sylvanshine said.

'But I'm not even in there yet,' Fogle said.

'Instead, you challenged us on a point of logic.'

'Granted, a fairly obvious point.'

'But you'd be amazed how many don't. How many GS-9s will scuttle in there and correct Dr. Lehrl's so-called mistake, trying to be a sycophant.'

'A brown-nose toaderooski.'

What his eyelid felt like was the eyelid equivalent of somebody shuddering. 'So then *this* was the test?'

'Consider yourself slapped five.'

Raising his arms in a gesture of surrender and congratulation had caused Reynolds's cuffs to protrude unevenly again from the sleeves of his jacket, and he was adjusting them again.

'So but can I ask another question?'

'The kid's on a roll,' Sylvanshine said.

'When I go in there, is Dr. Lehrl going to ask me about schools? Did you just make that up?'

'Let's turn that around,' Sylvanshine said.

So now he had to look back over at Sylvanshine again, who hadn't changed position in his chair over by the magazine and bulletin table even once the whole time, Fogle saw.

Sylvanshine said: 'Say you were to go in there and interface and at some point he misidentifies your football team—what do you do?'

'Because,' Reynolds said, 'if you don't correct his mistake, you're being a toady, and if you do correct him, you're maybe also being a toady in that you're acting on inside information we just gave you.'

'And he despises toadies,' Sylvanshine said, opening the file again.

'But is he even in there?' Fogle said. 'With some mysterious child I'm supposed to pretend isn't there? And is that another test—do I acknowledge the kid or not, given what you've said?'

'One item at a time,' Reynolds said. He and Sylvanshine were looking at Fogle very intently; Fogle thought, for the first time, that maybe they could see the eyelid thing. 'He calls it the Blue Devils—what do you do?'

§50

The office could be any office. Cove fluorescents on a dimmer, modular shelving, the desk practically an abstraction. The whisper of sourceless ventilation. You are a trained observer and there is nothing to observe. An open can of Tab whose color seems lurid against the beige and white. The stainless steel hook for your jacket. No photos or diplomas or personal touches—the facilitator is either newly posted or on outside contract. A woman with a pleasant, pop-eyed face, hair beginning to gray, in a padded chair identical to your own. Some protrusive eyes give the faces a creepy, staring aspect; the facilitator's do not. You have declined to remove your shoes. The knob beside the dimmer is your chair's control; it reclines and the feet go up. It is important that you be comfortable.

'You do have a body, you know.'

She has no notebook, it occurs. And given its position in the building's northwest leg, the office should by all rights have a window.

The setting at which you do not feel your own weight in the chair is two-thirds reclined. There is a disposable piece of paper attached to the headrest. Your sight line is the seam of the wall and drop ceiling; the toes of your shoes are visible at the lower periphery. The facilitator is not visible. The seam appears to thicken as the overheads are lowered to the level of a false dawn.

'The way we start is to relax and become aware of the body.

'It is at the level of body that we proceed.

'Do not try to relax.' Her voice is amused. It is gentle without being soft.

Since we all breathe, all the time, it is amazing what happens when someone else directs you how and when to breathe. And how vividly someone with no imagination whatsoever can see what he's told is right there, complete with banister and rubber runners, curving down and rightward into a darkness that recedes before you.

It is nothing like sleeping. Nor does her voice alter or seem to recede. She's right there, speaking calmly, and so are you.

Notes and Asides

Throughout the manuscript of *The Pale King,* David Foster Wallace wrote hundreds of notes, observations, and larger ideas. Some of these asides suggest where the plot of the novel might have headed. Others provide additional information about characters' backgrounds or their future development. Contradictions and complications abound among them. For instance, some notes say it's DeWitt Glendenning who is bringing examiners with unique abilities to Peoria; others that it's Merrill Errol Lehrl. A note from chapter 22 suggests that Chris Fogle knows a string of numbers that, when recited, give him the power of total concentration, but nowhere in the chapters we have does Fogle display this power. (Perhaps this ability is the reason Fogle has been summoned to meet Merrill Lehrl in chapter 49.) The hope in including this selection of notes is that they allow a fuller understanding of the ideas David was exploring in *The Pale King* and illuminate how much a work in progress the novel still was.

Notes that were attached to specific chapters in *The Pale King* appear first, followed by notes from other parts of the manuscript.

—Ed.

§7 Sylvanshine wants desperately to be CID—that's why he wants to pass the CPA exam. CID must be CPAs, just as FBI must be lawyers. Sylvanshine plays in front of mirror—"Freeze! Treasury!"

3 high end players—Glendenning, Special HR guy Glendenning needs to find gifted examiners, Lehrl. But we never see them, only their aides and advance men.

§12 Stecyk flown in via Lehrl's design to help drive examiners crazy.

§13 *Primed* is one of the IRS words for putting Examiners in a state where they pay maximum attention to returns.

footnote 34 The dragon-image always guards some priceless thing. This other boy never, in all his endless introspection and analysis, conceived the attacks as forms of all-body weeping or sadness itself—for childhood's end, for the split self required by society, for any number of possible traumas and estrangements. The disgust of others was a rank projection of his innermost secret, which the dragon both guarded and embodied—he was ignorant of mercy.

§15 It's Sylvanshine who's the fact psychic, and Lehrl, who believes in the occult, has sent him to find and place the very finest GS-7 wigglers he can in a given group, so that when the A/NADA outperforms them on revenue, it'll be convincing to Triple 6. This would require rewriting the Sylvanshine arrival sequence...S wants to become CPA because everyone else in Internal Control Systems is CPA? Or so that he can get out of the Service?

§19 It's the HR guys who ultimately get replaced by computers—they're too distractible, too into side-issues.

Glendenning's kid in navy on ship off Iranian coast? Terrified he's risking his life for an America that's no longer worth fighting for.

§22 'Irrelevant Chris' is irrelevant only on the subject of himself? On all other topics/subjects, he's focused & cogent and interesting?

Dictum on him around REC is that he's OK as long as you keep him off the topic of himself—then you're in for it?

Fogle ends up in IRS as the insufferable do-gooder that Stecyk was, as child?

'Film interview' a sham? Point is to extract from Chris Fogle the formula of numbers that permits total concentration? Point is he can't remember—he wasn't paying attention when he happened to read the series of documents that added up to the string of numbers that, when held in serial in his head, allows him to maintain interest and concentration at will? Has to be sort of tricked into it? Numbers have downside of incredible headache.

§24 Richard 'Dick' Tate is Director of Personnel. Ned Stecyk is his Deputy Director. Tate opposes Lehrl and ICS because he wants power, control—no power if fewer living personnel.

Glendenning ineffectual—lost in a mist of civic idealism—the actual REC is run mostly by Tate and Stecyk, and by the Information Systems person.

When DW and Stecyk lock eyes as Stecyk is soothing guy in his inner office, a look of tremendous compassion and sympathy spreads over Stecyk's face, mainly because of DW's hideous skin. Stecyk thus searches out DW and tries to be nice to him, figuring that he's been shunned and traumatized his whole life. DW resents this—his position is that if people are shallow enough to regard someone's skin as the be-all and end-all of his value and character, then fuck them; he doesn't need them—but is ready to exploit Stecyk's kindness in order to win various advantages for himself.

David Wallace, once settled, has thing where he'll look out the window and see, in the other, more elite building, someone at a window in the computer center looking back. Wearing thick glasses. Their eyes meet but they never meet or say anything.

Light-blue Pacer with fish bumper sticker. This car is Lane Dean's—who has to hurry like crazy in the AM because he goes to church services (or Sheri, his wife, does) at dawn, and is always on the edge of being late (Dean has become less fervently Christian since starting at REC, while Sheri has gotten more so)—that made this maneuver almost every morning.

§26 Stecyk knows about Blumquist. He was at the REC when Blumquist died. He was just out of the IRS academy in Columbus and working as a chalk leader in rotes. He was the one who had to interview the wigglers (in 1978?) who had continued coming to work and working for something like three days while Blumquist sat rigidly at his desk, deceased. Some of them had felt bad about this. A few put in for transfers. Stecyk will discover that Examiners' total down-the-line audit revenue every month increases when Blumquist sits with them, not talking to them or distracting them but simply sitting there, being *with* them. Theorizes that double teams of Examiners might be worth the cost—the doubled salary might be exceeded by the overall realized audit-revenue. But how to get this idea sold? Region Personnel Director would want to know how this originally came to light... how can Stecyk refer to a ghost? Or perhaps this was the idea of a previous Personnel Deputy, who got in trouble, because Region figured that he'd tried the experiment with two actual examiners, meaning double salary. It this a plausible plotline?

What is Stecyk like now, as an adult? Still incredibly nice, but no longer a total dweeb? A bit sadder? A dispenser of pop-psych bromides? What happened to make him realize that the Niceness of his childhood was actually sadistic, pathological, selfish? That other people, too, want to feel nice and do favors, that he'd been massively selfish about generosity? In a college sport, did he keep letting other team score out of 'niceness,' and got a visit from a referee— someone dressed all in black and white, like Irrelevant Chris Fogle's Jesuit in college—who very bluntly told him he was full of shit and that true decency was very different from pathological generosity, because pathological generosity did not take into account the feelings of the people who were the object of the generosity? Stecyk had caused traffic jams at 4-way stops by always letting everyone else go first? Or referee magically gives Stecyk insight into how his mother had felt when Stecyk got up very early every morning to do her housekeeping for her—like she was useless, like the family felt she was incompetent, etc. Stecyk tells David Wallace the story of the butterfly—if you let it out of the cocoon when it seems to be struggling and dying, then its wings don't get strengthened and it can't survive.

The pathologically nice is one of the basic types who gravitate to the IRS, because it's such a grim, unpopular job—no gratitude, which only increases the sense of sacrifice.

Sylvanshine has a different take on Blumquist. Sylvanshine has educed that some of the very best Examiners—most attentive, most thorough—are those with some kind of trauma or abandonment in their past. He's there to intuit which are the best so that they can be auditioned for the test against A/NADA. Blumquist, it turns out, had had brutal Fundamentalist parents—the kind for whom fans and mattresses were luxuries. They had a special punishment: they made him face the wall in the parlor—blank wall—stand there facing it for hours at a time. This was the trauma. There had been a mirror on the other wall behind him; it showed only his back. This is the image Sylvanshine gets for Blumquist: a view of his childhood back, very still, with a scrolled wooden frame around it. Blumquist had had productivity numbers that were much, much higher than anyone else's, though he had declined offers to be promoted to higher civil service grade and managerial job. Sylvanshine looking for similarly great rote examiner, to do the series of tests against the A/NADA program and digital computer. Several of the recently transferred Examiners are among the very best tested rote examiners left at national RECs. Lehrl's Systems boys want a fair test, the computer and A/NADA against the very finest rote examiners they can get...so that when the A/NADA crushes them, the test'll be all that much more definitive.

§30 LEHRL & PRO-TECH VS. GLENDENNING & DISTRICT DIRECTORS: Project is replacing human Examiners with computers the way Lehrl invented Automated Collection Systems—the District Directors don't want it, because they're Old School IRS-as-Civics believers, whereas the new school has a corporate philosophy: maximize revenue while minimizing costs. Big Q is whether IRS is to be essentially a corporate entity or a *moral* one.

Charles Lehrl preparing to computerize Exams the way he computerized Automated Collection System in Collections—the experiments there were in Rome and Philadelphia. Invented the IRP that compares W2s and 1099s to Returns—made Examiners' jobs otiose.

Reynolds & Sylvanshine (lovers? roomies?) vie for Lehrl's attention & favor like courtiers or children—it's how they pass the time in the dullness of IRS intrigue.

Reynolds & Sylvanshine live together—sort of like Rosencrantz & Guildenstern in *Hamlet.* They have an incredibly nice reproduction of Gerard ter Borch's *Parental Admonition* (28 x 29 in., Rijksmuseum, Amsterdam) that they hang wherever they live—or else an incredibly good forgery, done by one of the great painter-imitators of the modern US.

§38 DW, because of snafu, favors upgrading IRS computer systems—Stecyk wants to preserve human examiners?

§43 There is no bomb. It turned out that an actual load of nitrate fertilizer had been blown up. Again, something big *threatens* to happen but doesn't actually happen.

This becomes disaster—the scanners are viewed as able to *replace* examiners—their jobs are threatened: contest between Drinion + scanner set up.

§46 Rand works in Problem Resolution, not Exams? Because her prettiness helps defuse appellants and keep them from making as much trouble as they would otherwise? Another Personnel coup from X, the talent-arrangement genius?

Drinion came home as child to find whole family gone—at least that's the rumor. A lot of stuff about Drinion, his manner of paying attention, should be implicit, or should unfold over a much longer time.

IRS rap on Meredith Rand: She's pretty but a yammerer of the most dire kind, on and on, excruciating to be around—they speculate that her husband must have some kind of hearing aid that he can turn off at will.

At Rand and Drinion's last meeting, in book, Drinion asks: "Would you prefer it intense, or casual?" Rand breaks into tears.

Rand gets obsessed with Drinion (as type of "savior"?) in the same way she'd been obsessed with Ed Rand in hospital?

REC Center in outlying Peoria district called "Anthony, Illinois"? Who is Saint Anthony? The tornado continues...

End pt. 1. In pt. 2 (forthcoming?) Rand describes, quickly, how they got romantically involved (or Rath or someone else does, or it gets out through summary mediated by several different tellers): M.R. felt she needed Rand, or rather she felt sorry for him because he was sick and unattractive (additional repulsive symptoms in private) and going to die soon. Always expecting him to die in the near future. And she saw how lonely and sad his life was, his apartment was. So she married him, at just age 19...But he didn't die, hasn't died; and now M.R. is trapped, miserable, especially because Ed isn't grateful to her, and would laugh spitefully at her if she ever tried to say to him that he should be grateful, that she'd taken pity—Rand would say that the real person she'd pitied was herself, and that marrying someone always on the edge of possible death was a great way to let herself feel both safe and heroic.

Every day at day's end they have the same exchange:

"How was your day?"

"I work in a mental hospital. How do you think my day was?"

It's not funny or intimate, no shared joke—they've been in the same basic relationship for 6 years, w/o growth or change, and Rand is looking for someone to save her, extract her from it.

* * *

Big issue is human examiners or machines. Sylvanshine is after the best human examiners he can find.

Embryonic outline:

2 Broad arcs:

1. Paying attention, boredom, ADD, Machines vs. people at performing mindless jobs.
2. Being individual vs. being part of larger things—paying taxes, being "lone gun" in IRS vs. team player.

David Wallace disappears 100 pp in.
Central Deal: Realism, monotony. Plot a series of set-ups for stuff happening, but nothing actually happens.

David Wallace disappears—becomes creature of the system.

Overall movement: Old IRS guard are driven by self-righteousness, tax cheats as deadbeats, tax payment as virtue, or to work out their own psych stuff like anger, resentment, subservience to authority, etc. Or else they're drab civil servants in it for security, standard government workers. New IRS guard are not only good accountants but good strategic and business planners: whole point is to maximize revenue—disregard civic virtue, disregard moral warrior aspect of being in tax collection. New Peoria REC Personnel guy is new guard: his whole deal is finding employees and organizing stuff so that examiners maximize the revenue that auditors/collections can yield. His willingness to experiment/think in fresh new ways leads, paradoxically, to deep mysticism: a certain set of numbers that lets examiners concentrate better, etc. The ultimate point is the question whether humans or machines can do exams better, can maximize efficiency in spotting which returns might need auditing and will produce revenue.

Drinion is *happy*. Ability to pay attention. It turns out that bliss—a second-by-second joy + gratitude at the gift of being alive, conscious—lies on the other side of crushing, crushing boredom. Pay close attention to the most tedious thing you can find (tax returns, televised golf), and, in waves, a boredom like you've never known will wash over you and just about kill you. Ride these out, and it's like stepping from black and white into color. Like water after days in the desert. Constant bliss in every atom.

STECYK?

There is a counterpart to Sylvanshine. This is a high-end Personnel person for the REC (for the side that advocates human examiners over computers and the DIF). He searches for immersives. Ringers who can be brought in and examine complex returns without the sort of boredom that numbs you. (Or it's Stecyk, an examiner totally devoted to his job—hated, an abstract application of probity and virtue—constantly on the lookout for ways to help. It's he who goes to Meckstroth's office with the idea of how to send receipts directly to bank, save money and time.) Stecyk now in Personnel and Personnel Training?

They're rare, but they're among us. People able to achieve and sustain a certain steady state of concentration, attention, despite what they're doing. The first one Stecyk spotted was in the library of Peoria College of Business, in the reading room, an Asian kid in one of the reading chairs that looks a great deal more comfortable than it really is, slumped back and legs crossed ankle on knee, reading a statistics textbook. Stecyk goes by twenty minutes later, kid is still in exactly the same position, reading. Stecyk crosses the room just behind him to verify that the kid's several pages along. His notes are precise and flush-left in a tiny neat script. An hour later, the kid is <u>still</u> in same position, reading same book, now 14 pages later.

A guard working security outside a credit union. Standing at parade rest all day. Can't read or chat. Simply watching people come in and out, nodding when nodded at. In Midstate Security faux-police uniform. There in case of any trouble. Stecyk walks in and out several times, as occasion to watch guard. What's impressive is that the guard pays closer attention to him each time, meaning the guard registers the fact that Stecyk is coming in and out more than is normal. He's able to <u>pay attention</u> even in what has to be a staggeringly dull job.

Midwest meditation semifinals. Contestants hooked up to EEG—it's who can achieve and maintain theta waves for the longest period of time.

Woman on assembly line counting number of visible loops of twine on outside of bale of twine. Counting, over and over. When the whistle blows, every other worker practically runs for the door. She stays briefly, immersed in her work. It's the ability to be <u>immersed</u>.